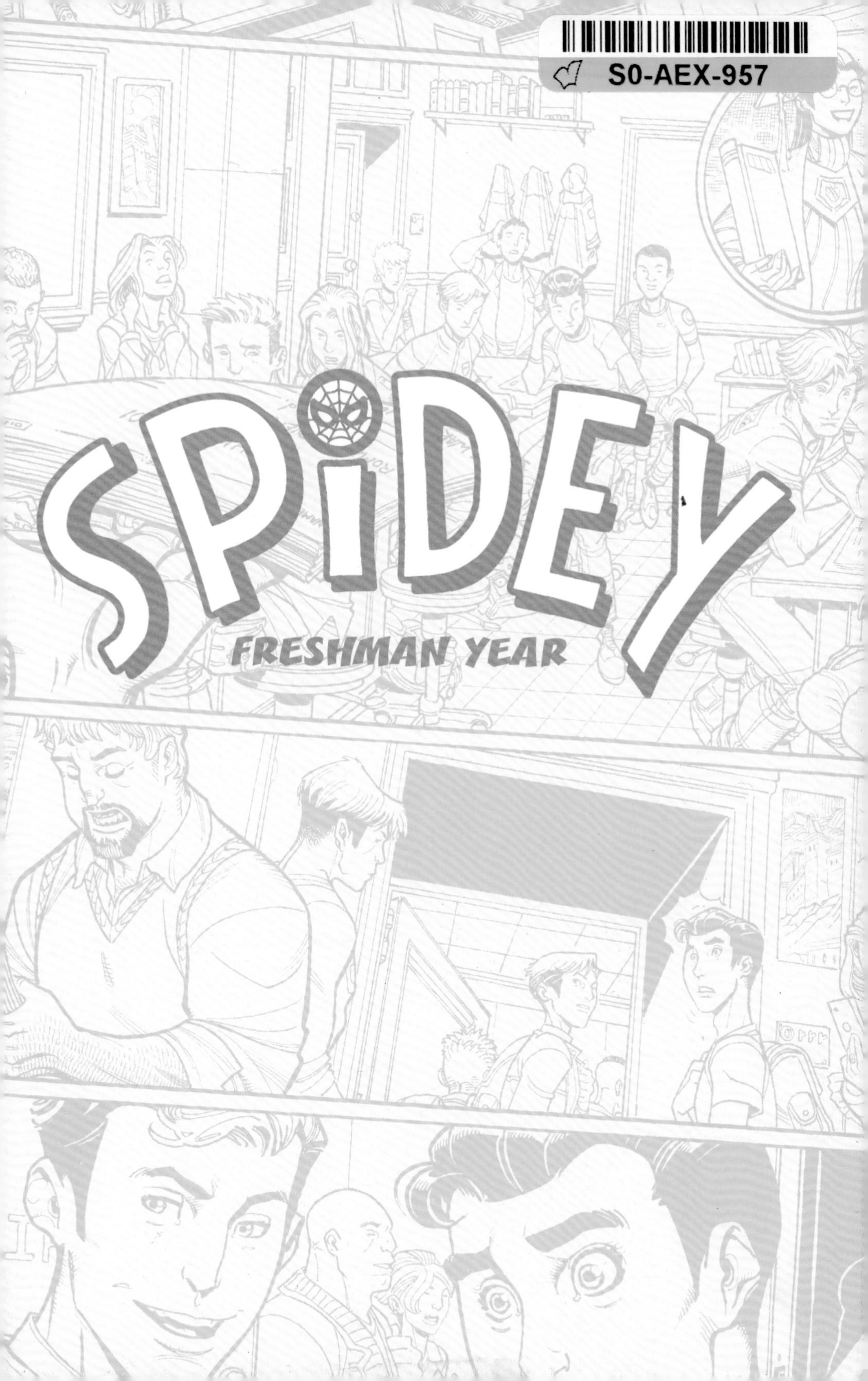
SPIDEY
FRESHMAN YEAR

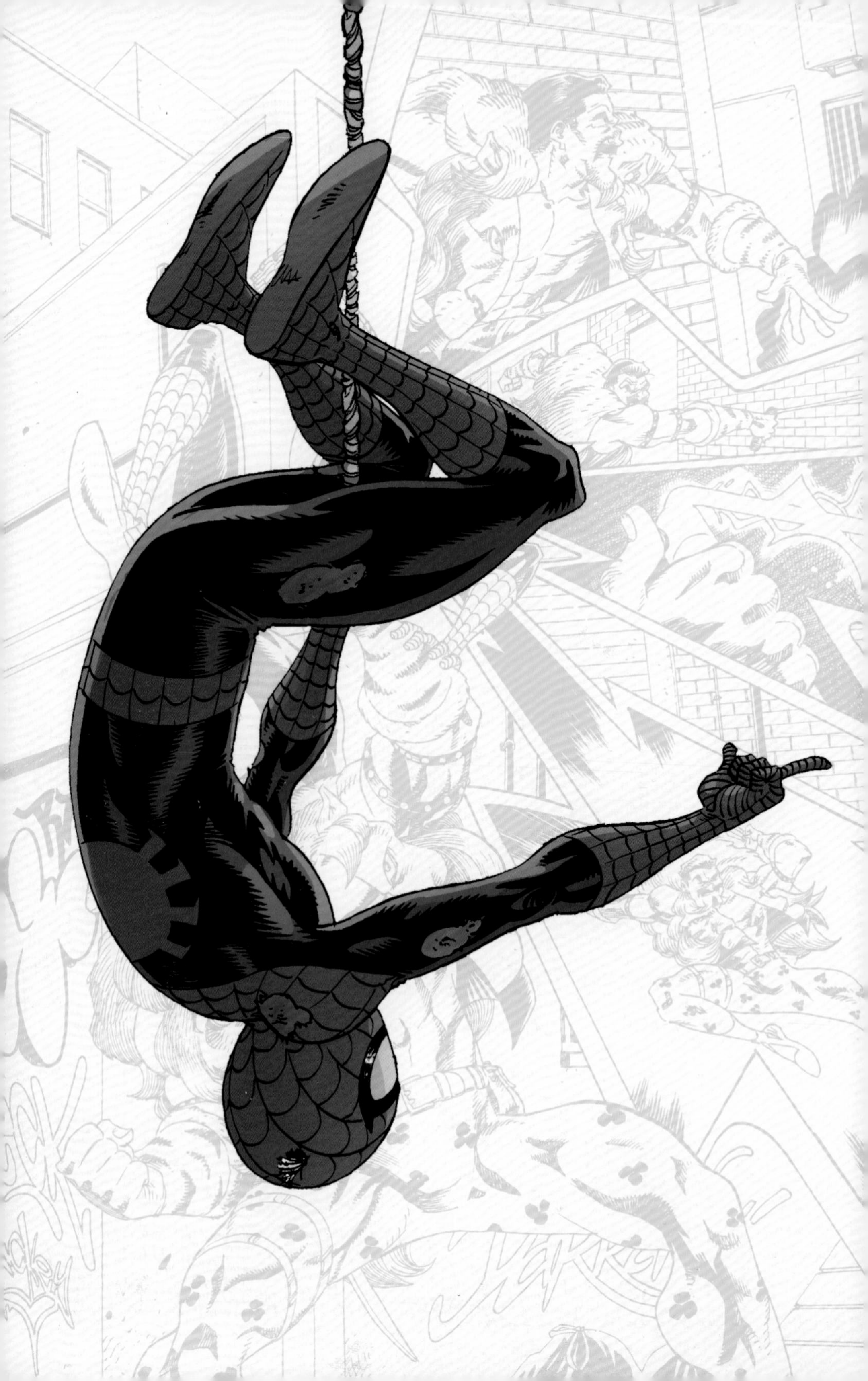

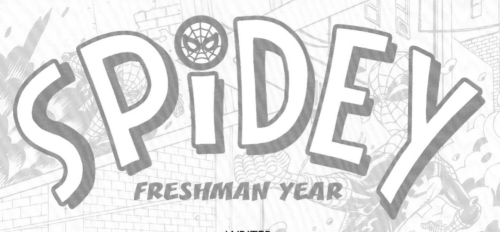

SPIDEY

FRESHMAN YEAR

WRITER
ROBBIE THOMPSON

ARTISTS
NICK BRADSHAW (#1-3), **ANDRÉ LIMA ARAÚJO** (#4-7)
& NATHAN STOCKMAN (#8-12)

COLOR ARTISTS
JIM CAMPBELL (#1-3, #5-12) **& RACHELLE ROSENBERG** (#3-4)
WITH JAVA TARTAGLIA (#5)

LETTERER
VC's TRAVIS LANHAM

COVER ART
NICK BRADSHAW & JIM CAMPBELL (#1-4, #6);
ANDRÉ LIMA ARAÚJO & JIM CAMPBELL (#5)
AND KHARY RANDOLPH & EMILIO LOPEZ (#7-12)

ASSOCIATE EDITOR
DEVIN LEWIS

EDITOR
DARREN SHAN

EXECUTIVE EDITOR
TOM BREVOORT

COLLECTION COVER
NATHAN STOCKMAN & JIM CAMPBELL

Spider-Man created by STAN LEE & STEVE DITKO

collection editor JENNIFER GRÜNWALD
assistant editor CAITLIN O'CONNELL • associate managing editor KATERI WOODY
editor, special projects MARK D. BEAZLEY • vp production & special projects JEFF YOUNGQUIST
svp print, sales & marketing DAVID GABRIEL

editor in chief C.B. CEBULSKI • chief creative officer JOE QUESADA
president DAN BUCKLEY • executive producer ALAN FINE

SPIDEY: FRESHMAN YEAR. Contains material originally published in magazine form as SPIDEY #1-12. First printing 2019. ISBN 978-1-302-91655-8. Published by MARVEL WORLDWIDE, INC., a subsidiary of MARVEL ENTERTAINMENT, LLC. OFFICE OF PUBLICATION: 135 West 50th Street, New York, NY 10020. **Printed in Canada.** DAN BUCKLEY, President, Marvel Entertainment; JOHN NEE, Publisher; JOE QUESADA, Chief Creative Officer; TOM BREVOORT, SVP of Publishing; DAVID BOGART, SVP of Business Affairs & Operations, Publishing & Partnership; DAVID GABRIEL, SVP of Sales & Marketing, Publishing; JEFF YOUNGQUIST, VP of Production & Special Projects; DAN CARR, Executive Director of Publishing Technology; ALEX MORALES, Director of Publishing Operations; DAN EDINGTON, Managing Editor; SUSAN CRESPI, Production Manager; STAN LEE, Chairman Emeritus. For information regarding advertising in Marvel Comics or on Marvel.com, please contact Vit DeBellis, Custom Solutions & Integrated Advertising Manager, at vdebellis@marvel.com. For Marvel subscription inquiries, please call 888-511-5480. **Manufactured between 1/25/2019 and 2/26/2019 by SOLISCO PRINTERS, SCOTT, QC, CANADA.**

10 9 8 7 6 5 4 3 2 1

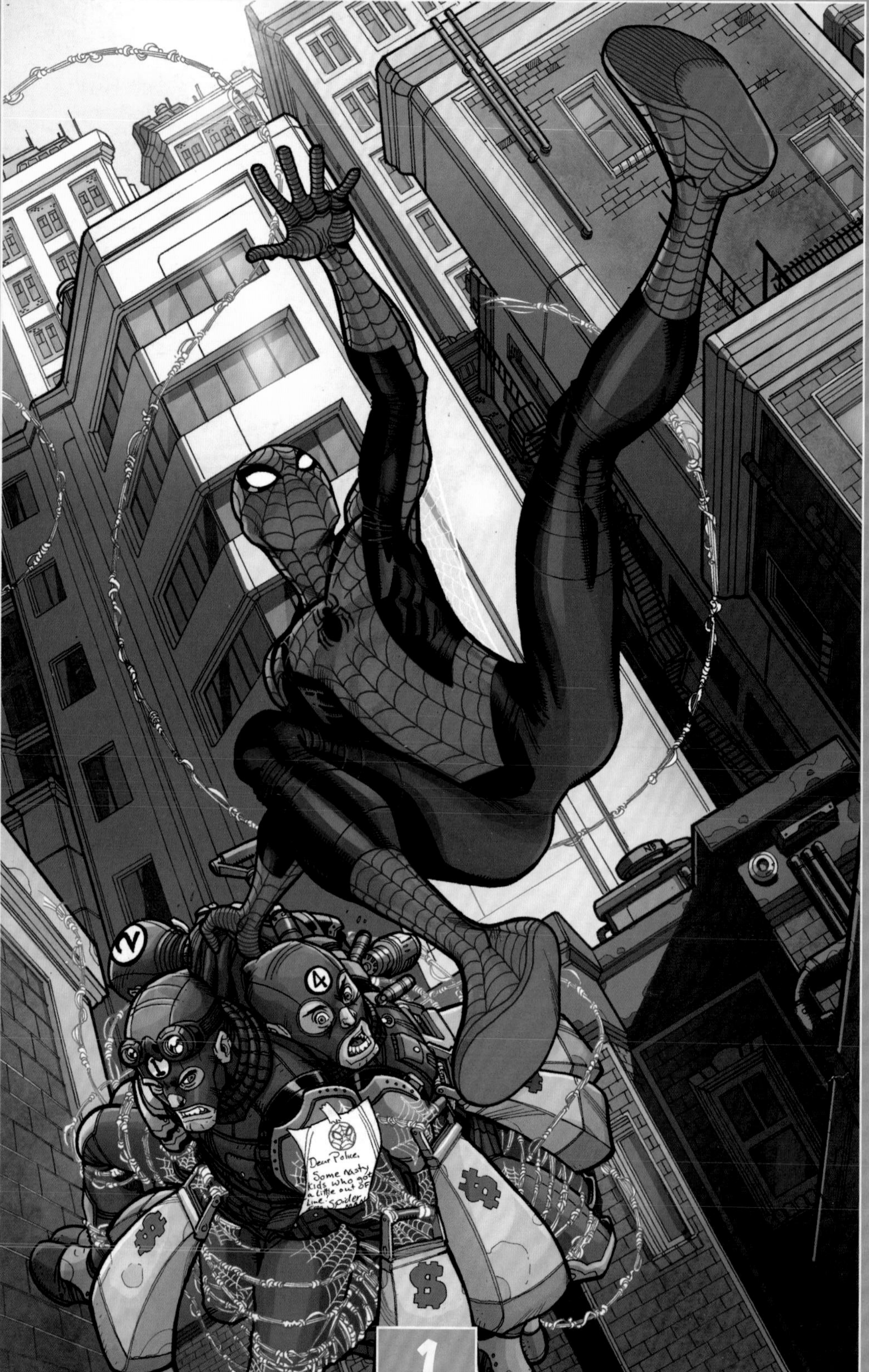
Dear Police,
Some nasty kids who got a little out of line. -Spider

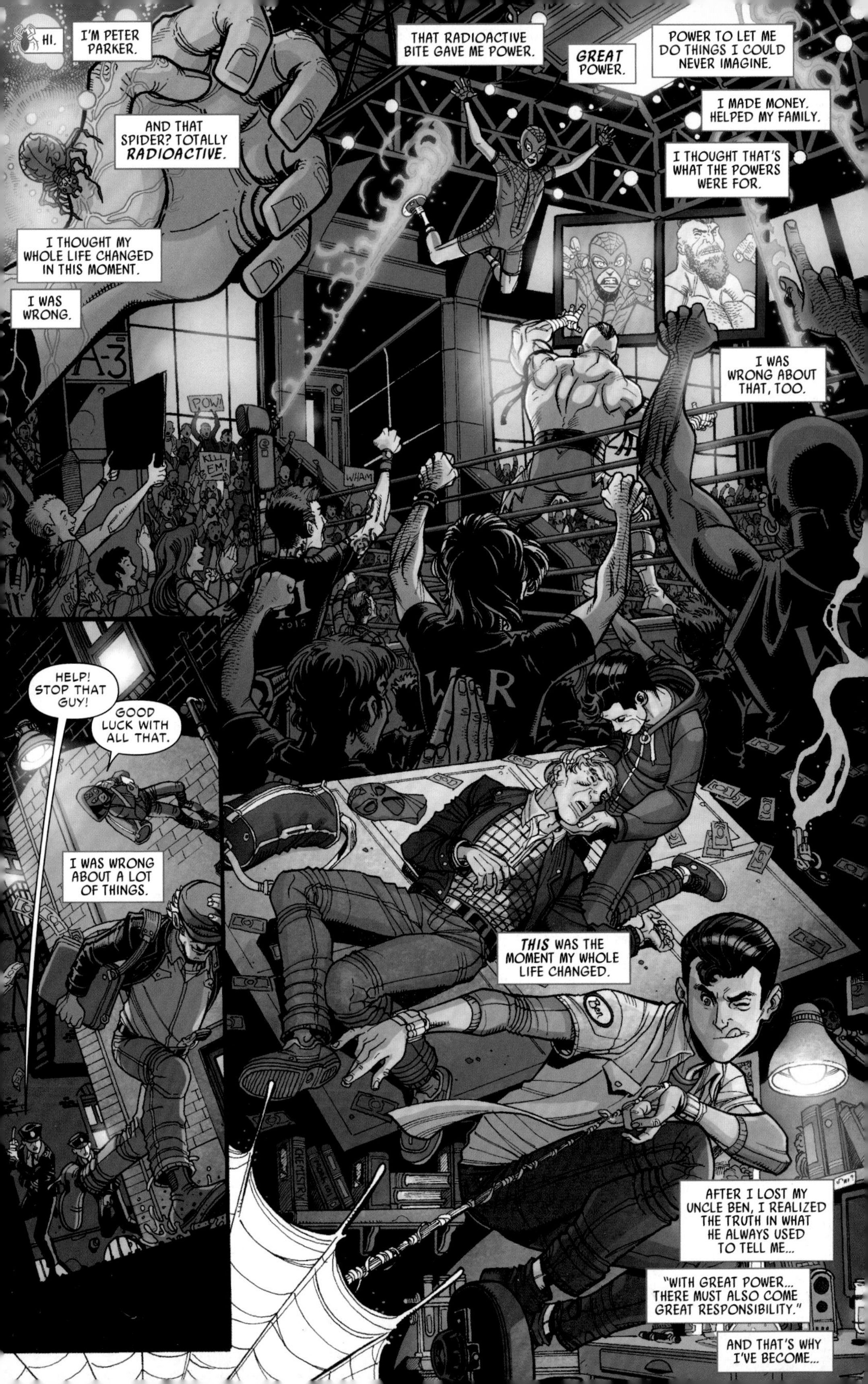
HI.
I'M PETER PARKER.
AND THAT SPIDER? TOTALLY RADIOACTIVE.
I THOUGHT MY WHOLE LIFE CHANGED IN THIS MOMENT.
I WAS WRONG.
THAT RADIOACTIVE BITE GAVE ME POWER.
GREAT POWER.
POWER TO LET ME DO THINGS I COULD NEVER IMAGINE.
I MADE MONEY. HELPED MY FAMILY.
I THOUGHT THAT'S WHAT THE POWERS WERE FOR.
I WAS WRONG ABOUT THAT, TOO.
A-3
POW!
KILL 'EM!
WHAM
HELP! STOP THAT GUY!
GOOD LUCK WITH ALL THAT.
I WAS WRONG ABOUT A LOT OF THINGS.
THIS WAS THE MOMENT MY WHOLE LIFE CHANGED.
AFTER I LOST MY UNCLE BEN, I REALIZED THE TRUTH IN WHAT HE ALWAYS USED TO TELL ME...
"WITH GREAT POWER... THERE MUST ALSO COME GREAT RESPONSIBILITY."
AND THAT'S WHY I'VE BECOME...

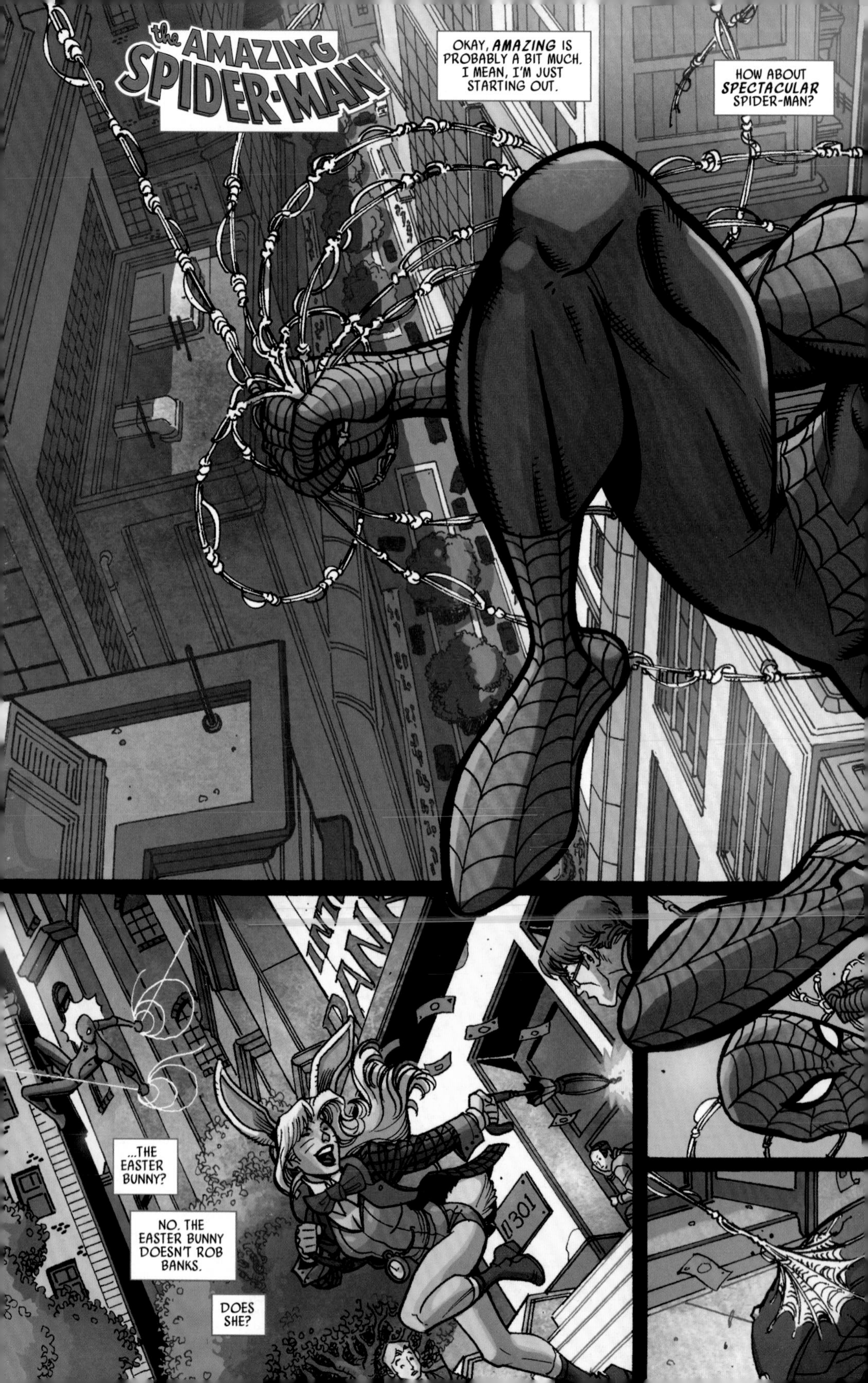
the AMAZING SPIDER-MAN
OKAY, AMAZING IS PROBABLY A BIT MUCH. I MEAN, I'M JUST STARTING OUT.
HOW ABOUT SPECTACULAR SPIDER-MAN?
...THE EASTER BUNNY?
NO. THE EASTER BUNNY DOESN'T ROB BANKS.
DOES SHE?
1301

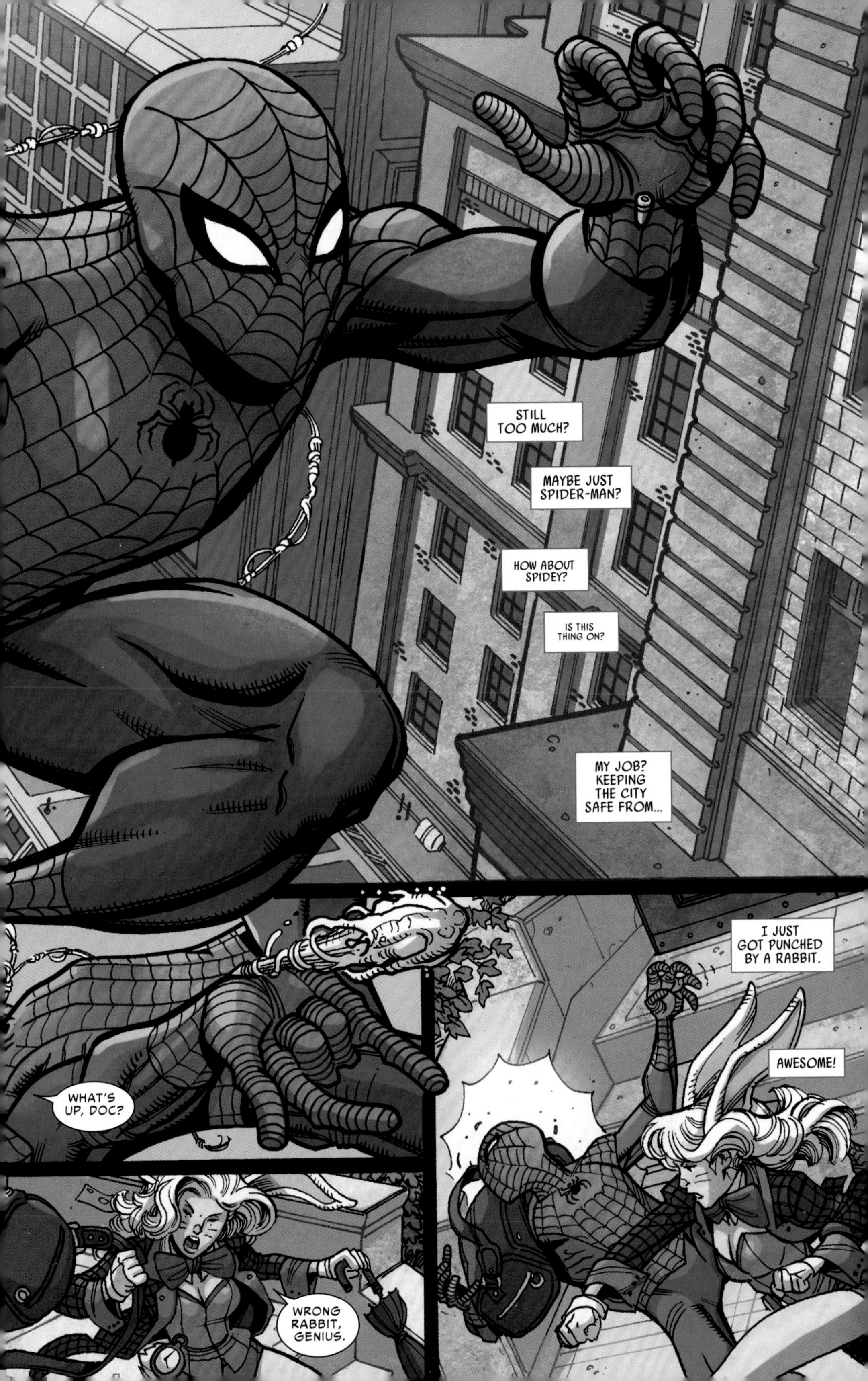
STILL TOO MUCH?
MAYBE JUST SPIDER-MAN?
HOW ABOUT SPIDEY?
IS THIS THING ON?
MY JOB? KEEPING THE CITY SAFE FROM...
WHAT'S UP, DOC?
WRONG RABBIT, GENIUS.
I JUST GOT PUNCHED BY A RABBIT.
AWESOME!

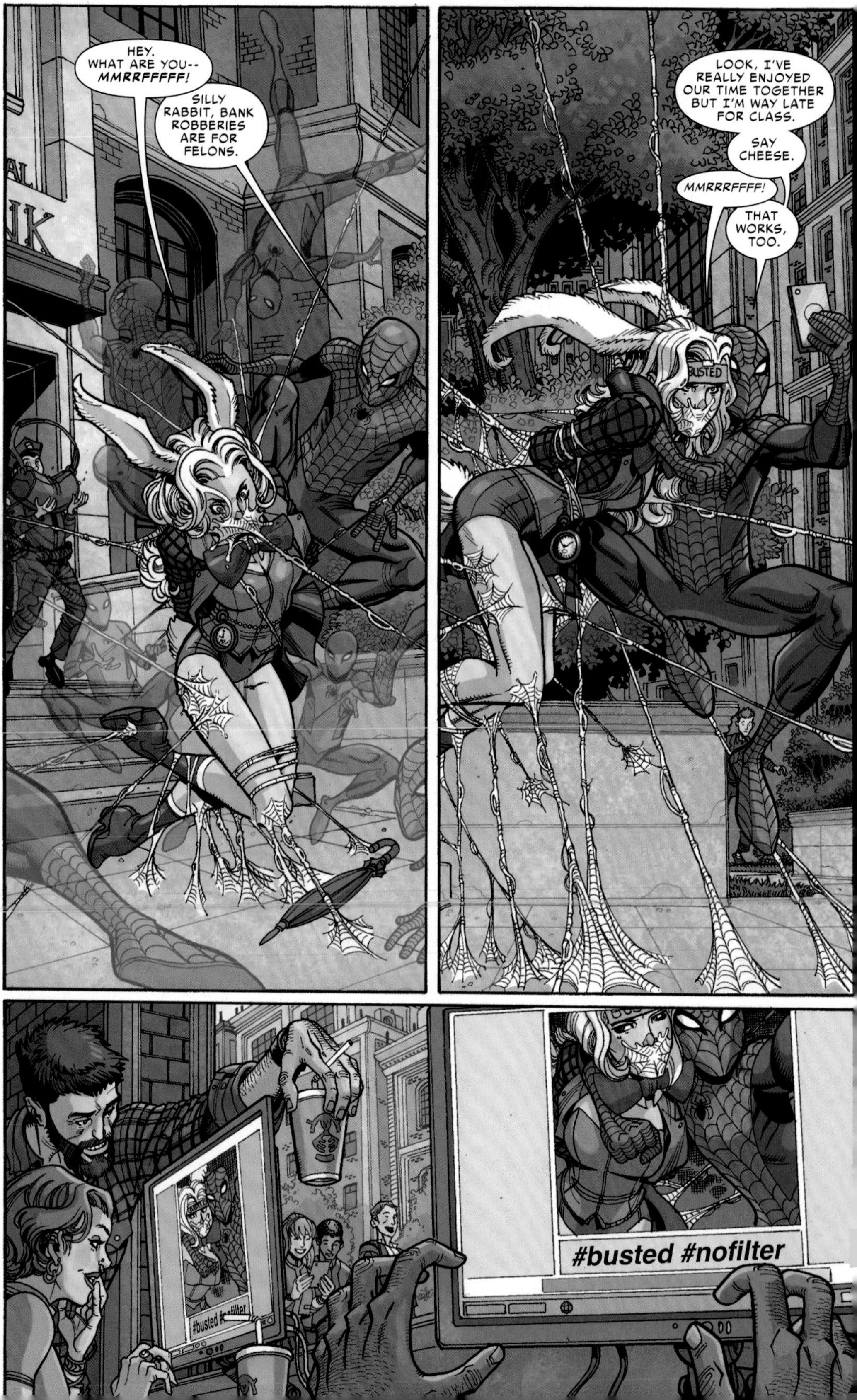
HEY. WHAT ARE YOU-- MMRRFFFFF!
SILLY RABBIT, BANK ROBBERIES ARE FOR FELONS.
LOOK, I'VE REALLY ENJOYED OUR TIME TOGETHER BUT I'M WAY LATE FOR CLASS.
SAY CHEESE.
MMRRRFFFF!
THAT WORKS, TOO.
BUSTED
#busted #nofilter

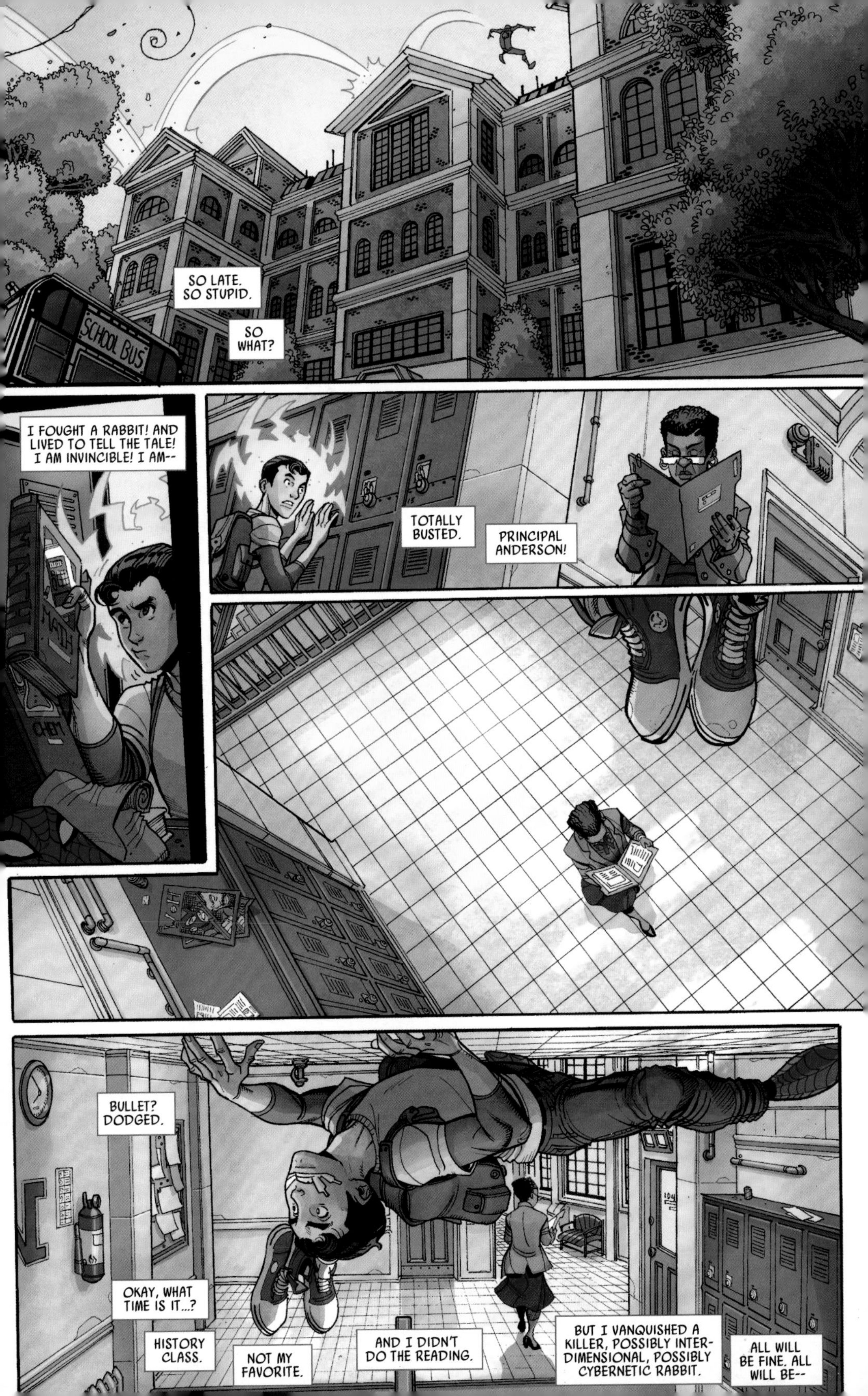
SO LATE. SO STUPID.
SO WHAT?
SCHOOL BUS
I FOUGHT A RABBIT! AND LIVED TO TELL THE TALE! I AM INVINCIBLE! I AM--
MATH
CHEM
TOTALLY BUSTED.
PRINCIPAL ANDERSON!
BULLET? DODGED.
OKAY, WHAT TIME IS IT...?
HISTORY CLASS.
NOT MY FAVORITE.
AND I DIDN'T DO THE READING.
BUT I VANQUISHED A KILLER, POSSIBLY INTER-DIMENSIONAL, POSSIBLY CYBERNETIC RABBIT.
ALL WILL BE FINE. ALL WILL BE--

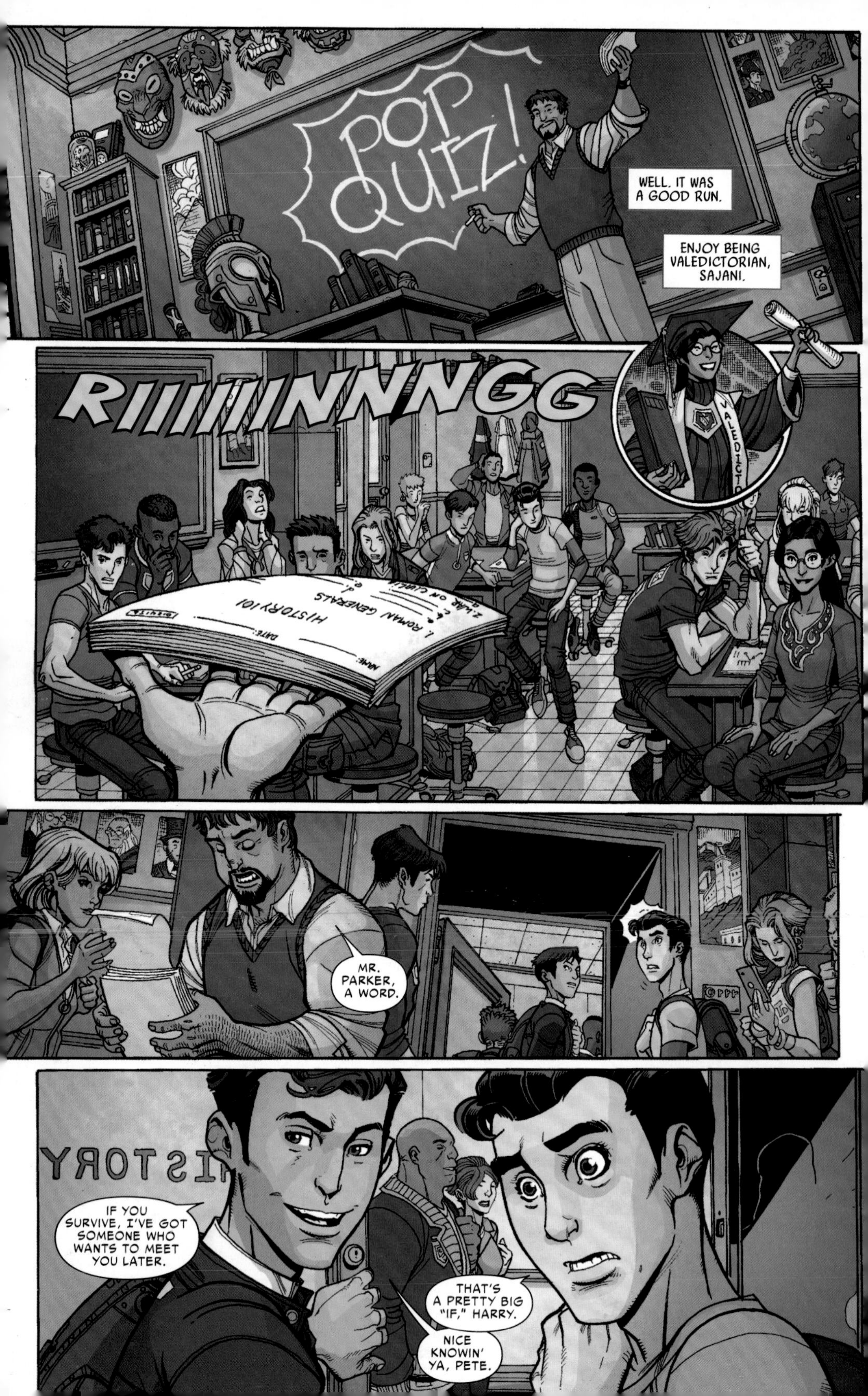
POP QUIZ!
WELL. IT WAS A GOOD RUN.
ENJOY BEING VALEDICTORIAN, SAJANI.
RIIIIIINNNNGG
VALEDICTO
HISTORY 101
NAME:
DATE:
1. ROMAN GENERALS
MR. PARKER, A WORD.
HISTORY
IF YOU SURVIVE, I'VE GOT SOMEONE WHO WANTS TO MEET YOU LATER.
THAT'S A PRETTY BIG "IF," HARRY.
NICE KNOWIN' YA, PETE.

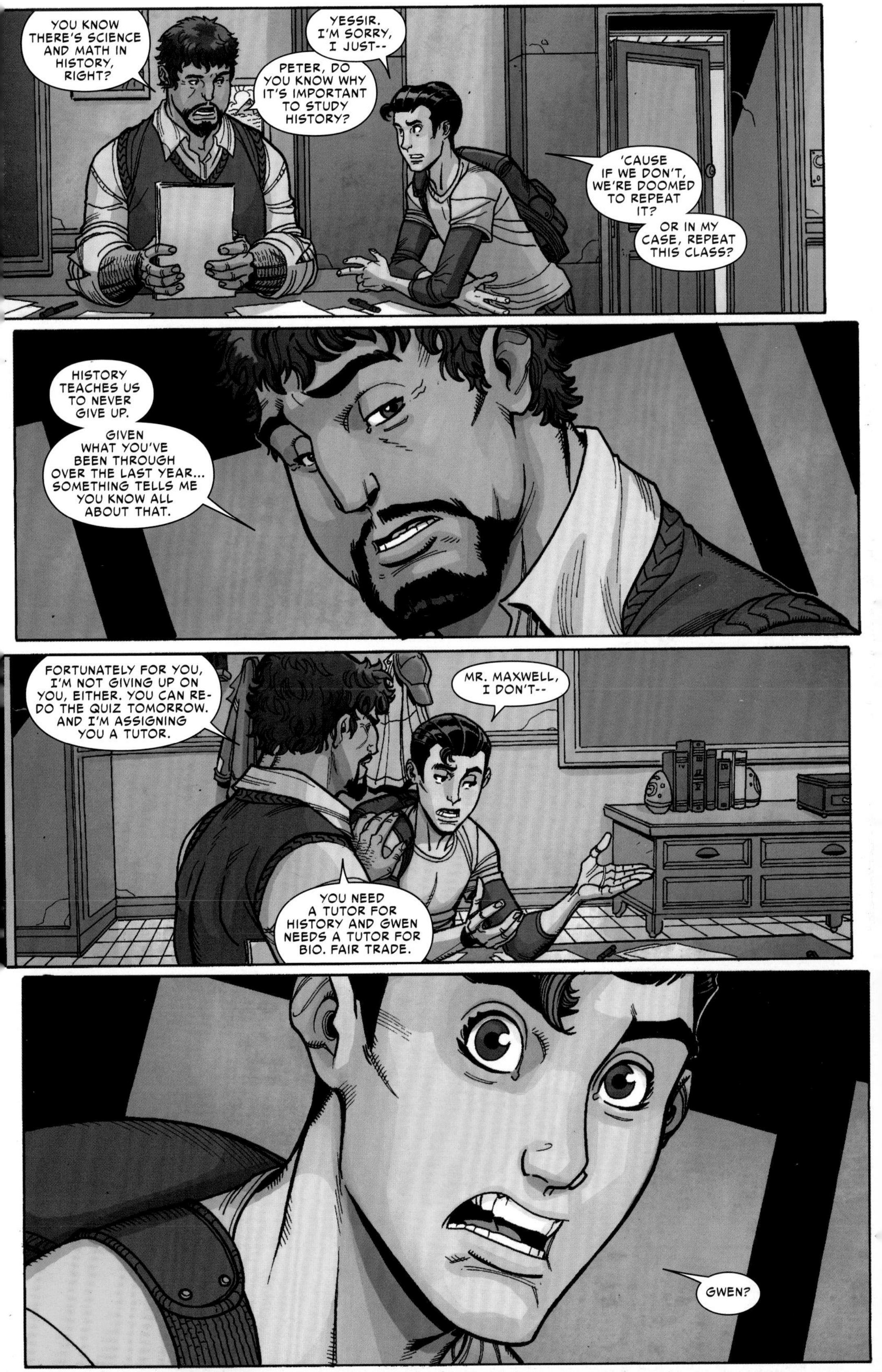
YOU KNOW THERE'S SCIENCE AND MATH IN HISTORY, RIGHT?
YESSIR. I'M SORRY, I JUST--
PETER, DO YOU KNOW WHY IT'S IMPORTANT TO STUDY HISTORY?
'CAUSE IF WE DON'T, WE'RE DOOMED TO REPEAT IT?
OR IN MY CASE, REPEAT THIS CLASS?
HISTORY TEACHES US TO NEVER GIVE UP.
GIVEN WHAT YOU'VE BEEN THROUGH OVER THE LAST YEAR... SOMETHING TELLS ME YOU KNOW ALL ABOUT THAT.
FORTUNATELY FOR YOU, I'M NOT GIVING UP ON YOU, EITHER. YOU CAN RE-DO THE QUIZ TOMORROW. AND I'M ASSIGNING YOU A TUTOR.
MR. MAXWELL, I DON'T--
YOU NEED A TUTOR FOR HISTORY AND GWEN NEEDS A TUTOR FOR BIO. FAIR TRADE.
GWEN?

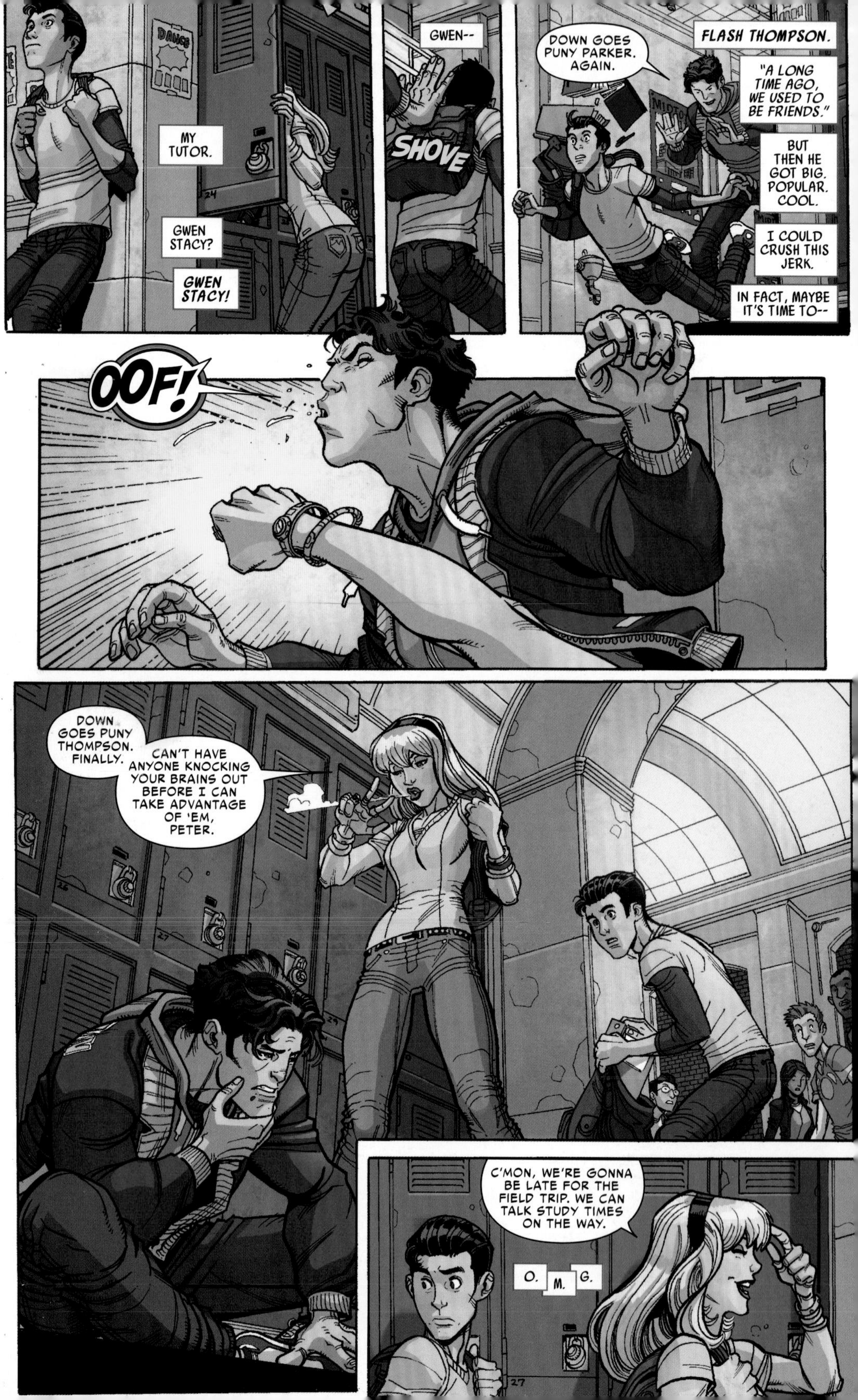
DANCE
MY TUTOR.
GWEN STACY?
GWEN STACY!
GWEN--
SHOVE
DOWN GOES PUNY PARKER. AGAIN.
FLASH THOMPSON.
"A LONG TIME AGO, WE USED TO BE FRIENDS."
BUT THEN HE GOT BIG. POPULAR. COOL.
I COULD CRUSH THIS JERK.
IN FACT, MAYBE IT'S TIME TO--
OOF!
DOWN GOES PUNY THOMPSON. FINALLY.
CAN'T HAVE ANYONE KNOCKING YOUR BRAINS OUT BEFORE I CAN TAKE ADVANTAGE OF 'EM, PETER.
C'MON, WE'RE GONNA BE LATE FOR THE FIELD TRIP. WE CAN TALK STUDY TIMES ON THE WAY.
O.
M.
G.

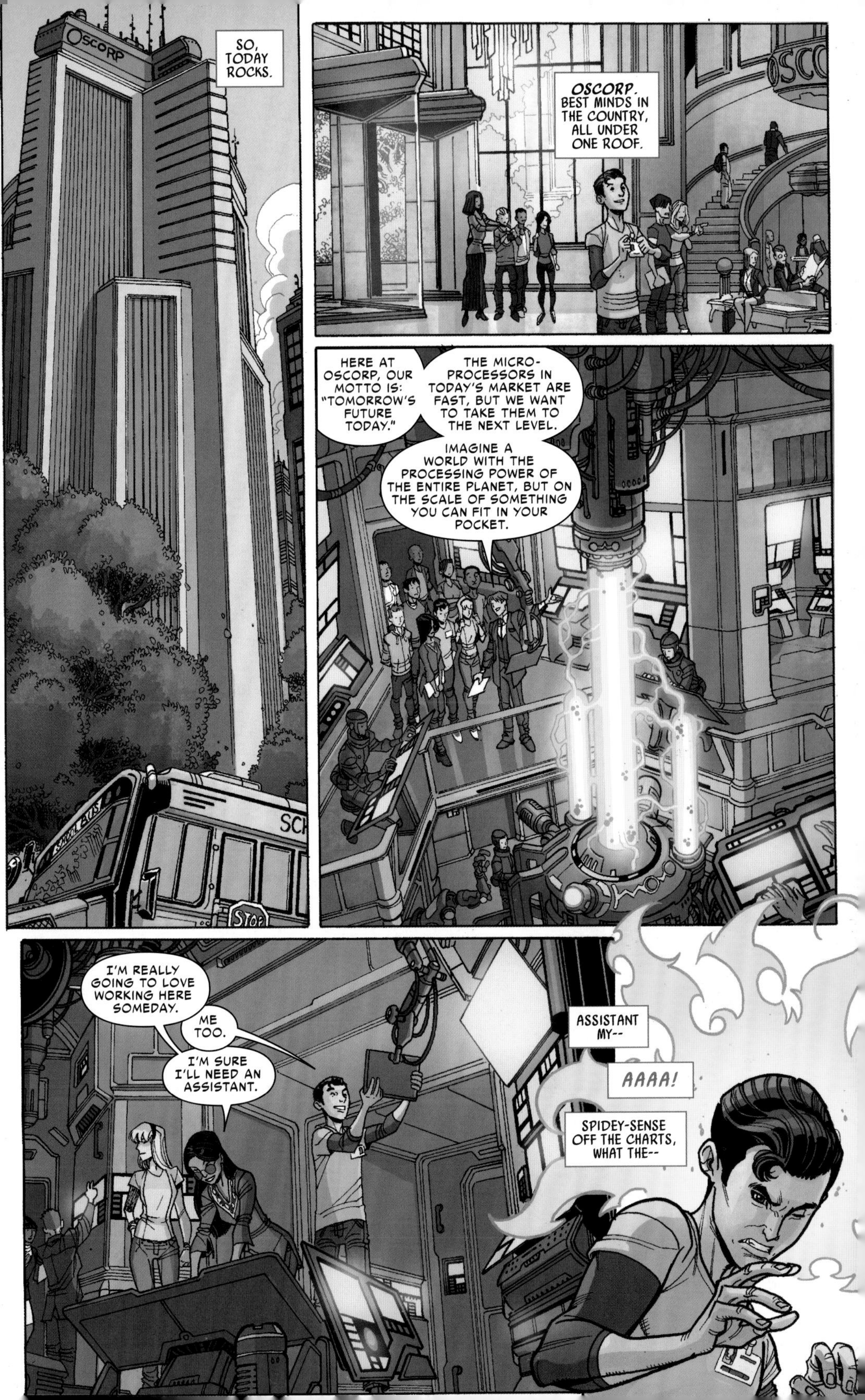

OSCORP
SO, TODAY ROCKS.
SCHOOL BUS
STOP
OSCORP. BEST MINDS IN THE COUNTRY, ALL UNDER ONE ROOF.
HERE AT OSCORP, OUR MOTTO IS: "TOMORROW'S FUTURE TODAY."
THE MICRO-PROCESSORS IN TODAY'S MARKET ARE FAST, BUT WE WANT TO TAKE THEM TO THE NEXT LEVEL.
IMAGINE A WORLD WITH THE PROCESSING POWER OF THE ENTIRE PLANET, BUT ON THE SCALE OF SOMETHING YOU CAN FIT IN YOUR POCKET.
I'M REALLY GOING TO LOVE WORKING HERE SOMEDAY.
ME TOO.
I'M SURE I'LL NEED AN ASSISTANT.
ASSISTANT MY--
AAAA!
SPIDEY-SENSE OFF THE CHARTS, WHAT THE--

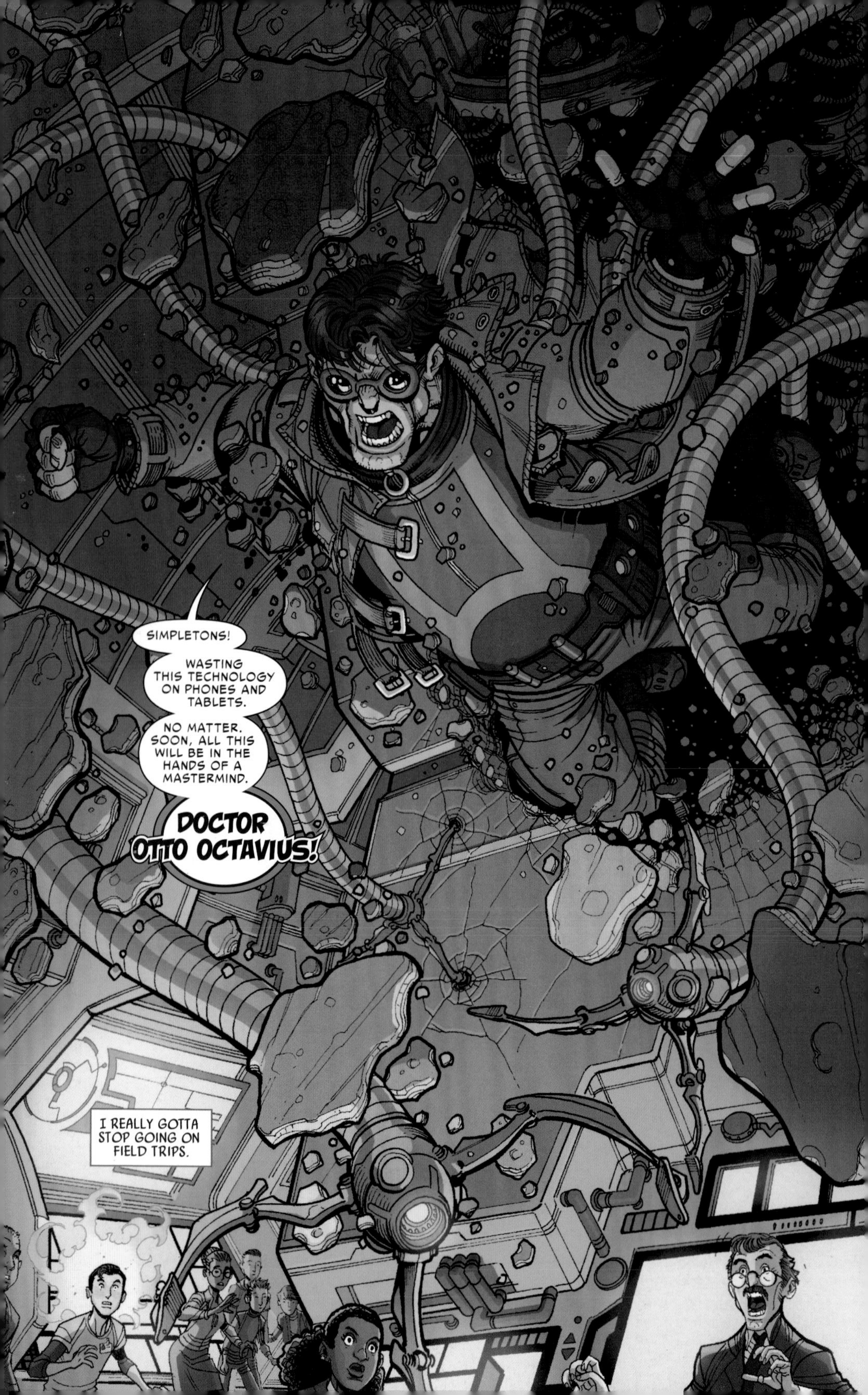
SIMPLETONS!
WASTING THIS TECHNOLOGY ON PHONES AND TABLETS.
NO MATTER. SOON, ALL THIS WILL BE IN THE HANDS OF A MASTERMIND.
DOCTOR OTTO OCTAVIUS!
I REALLY GOTTA STOP GOING ON FIELD TRIPS.

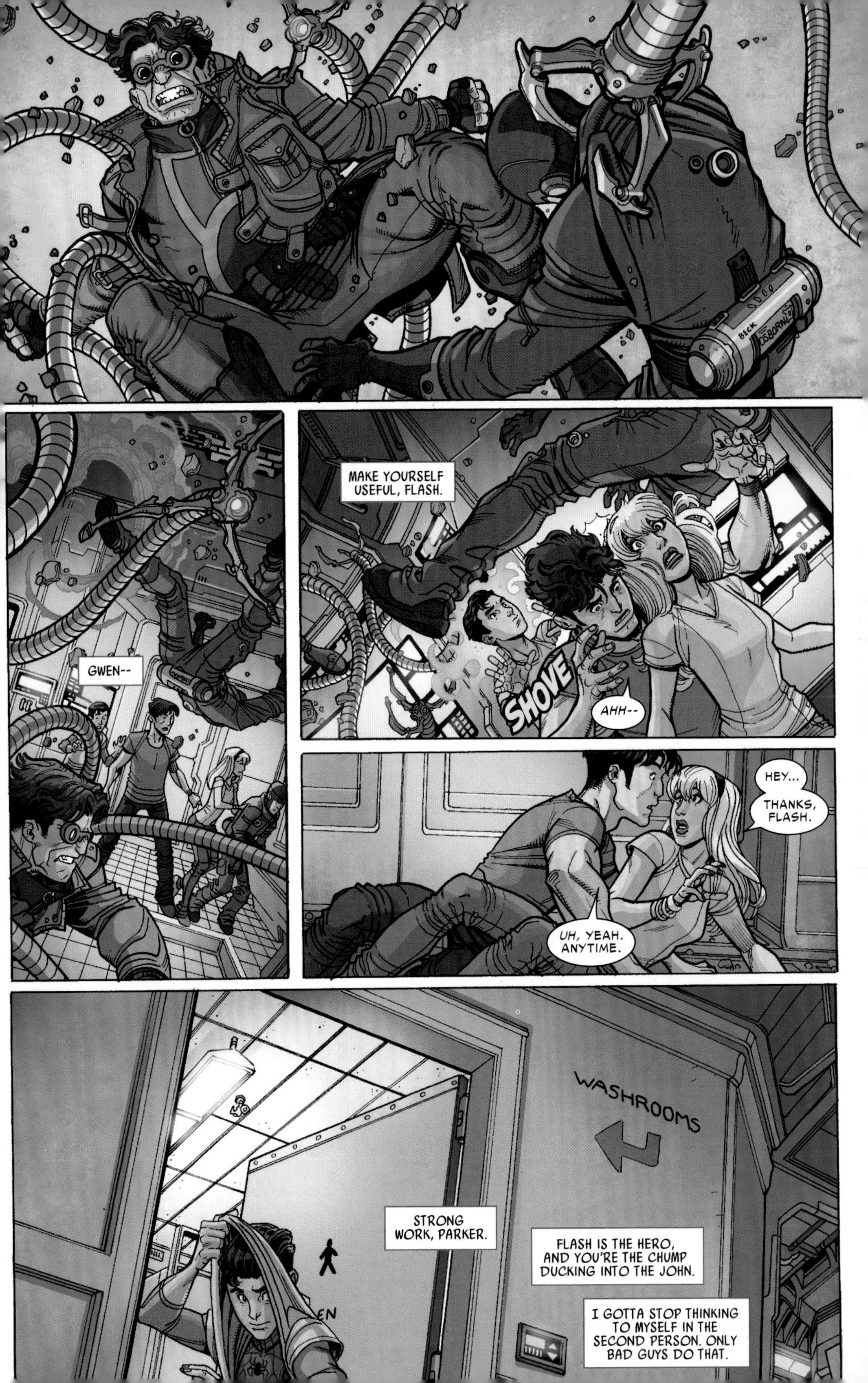
BECK
OSBORN
GWEN--
MAKE YOURSELF USEFUL, FLASH.
SHOVE
AHH--
HEY...
THANKS, FLASH.
UH, YEAH. ANYTIME.
WASHROOMS
STRONG WORK, PARKER.
FLASH IS THE HERO, AND YOU'RE THE CHUMP DUCKING INTO THE JOHN.
I GOTTA STOP THINKING TO MYSELF IN THE SECOND PERSON. ONLY BAD GUYS DO THAT.

I HAVE TO GET BACK OUT THERE. DOC OCK IS NOTHING BUT TROUBLE.

DOORS ARE LOCKED. BUT THE VENTS LEAD BACK INTO THE LAB.

SORRY FOR THE DAMAGE, FUTURE EMPLOYER!

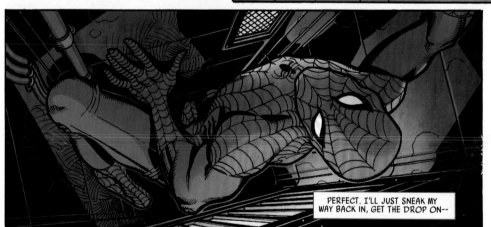

PERFECT. I'LL JUST SNEAK MY WAY BACK IN, GET THE DROP ON--

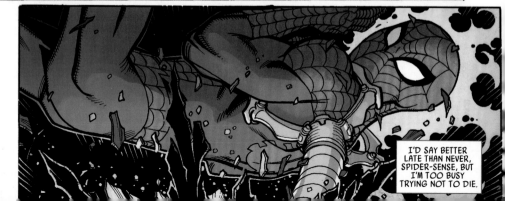

I'D SAY BETTER LATE THAN NEVER, SPIDER-SENSE, BUT I'M TOO BUSY TRYING NOT TO DIE.

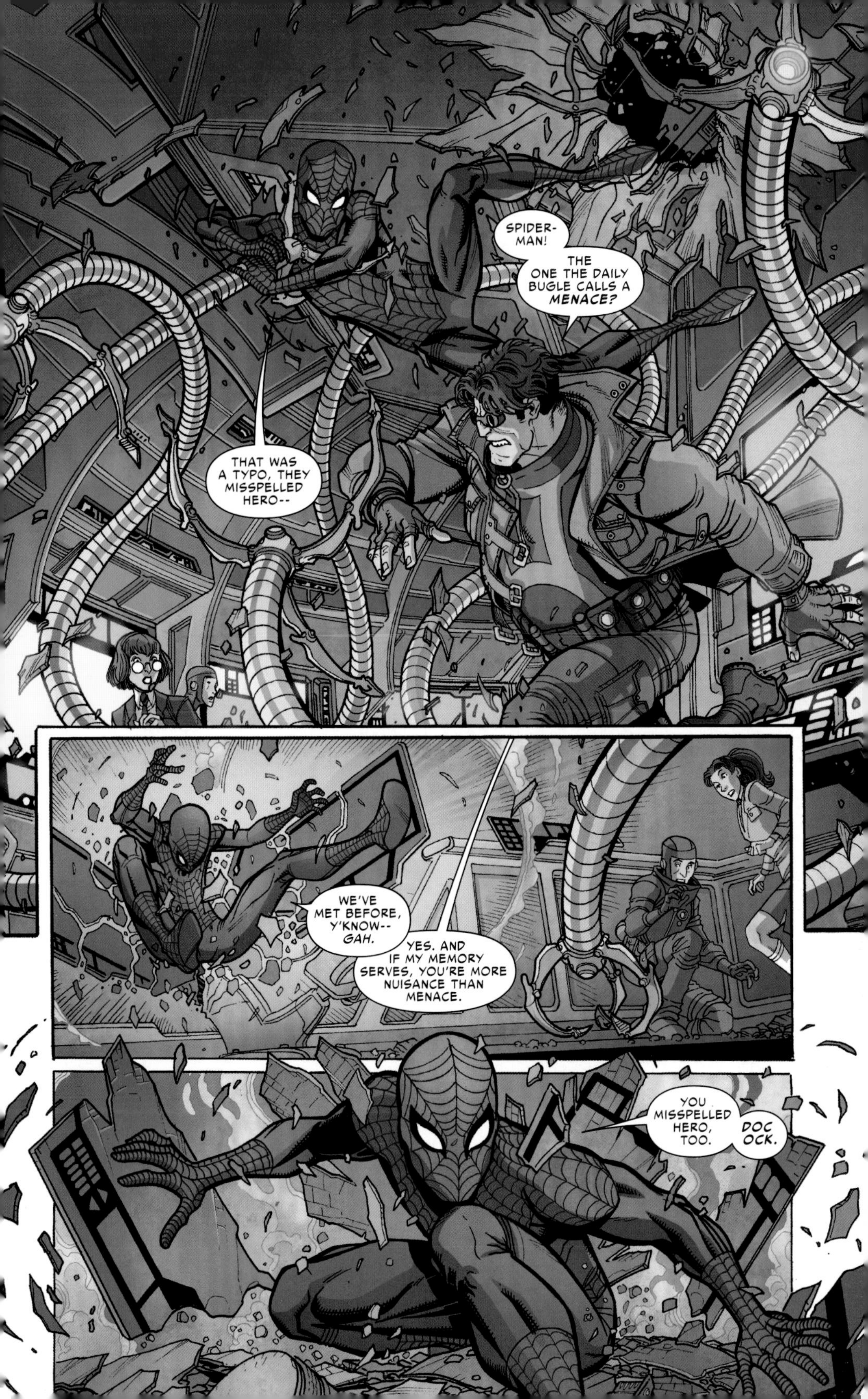
SPIDER-MAN!
THE ONE THE DAILY BUGLE CALLS A *MENACE?*
THAT WAS A TYPO, THEY MISSPELLED HERO--
WE'VE MET BEFORE, Y'KNOW-- *GAH.*
YES. AND IF MY MEMORY SERVES, YOU'RE MORE NUISANCE THAN MENACE.
YOU MISSPELLED HERO, TOO.
DOC OCK.

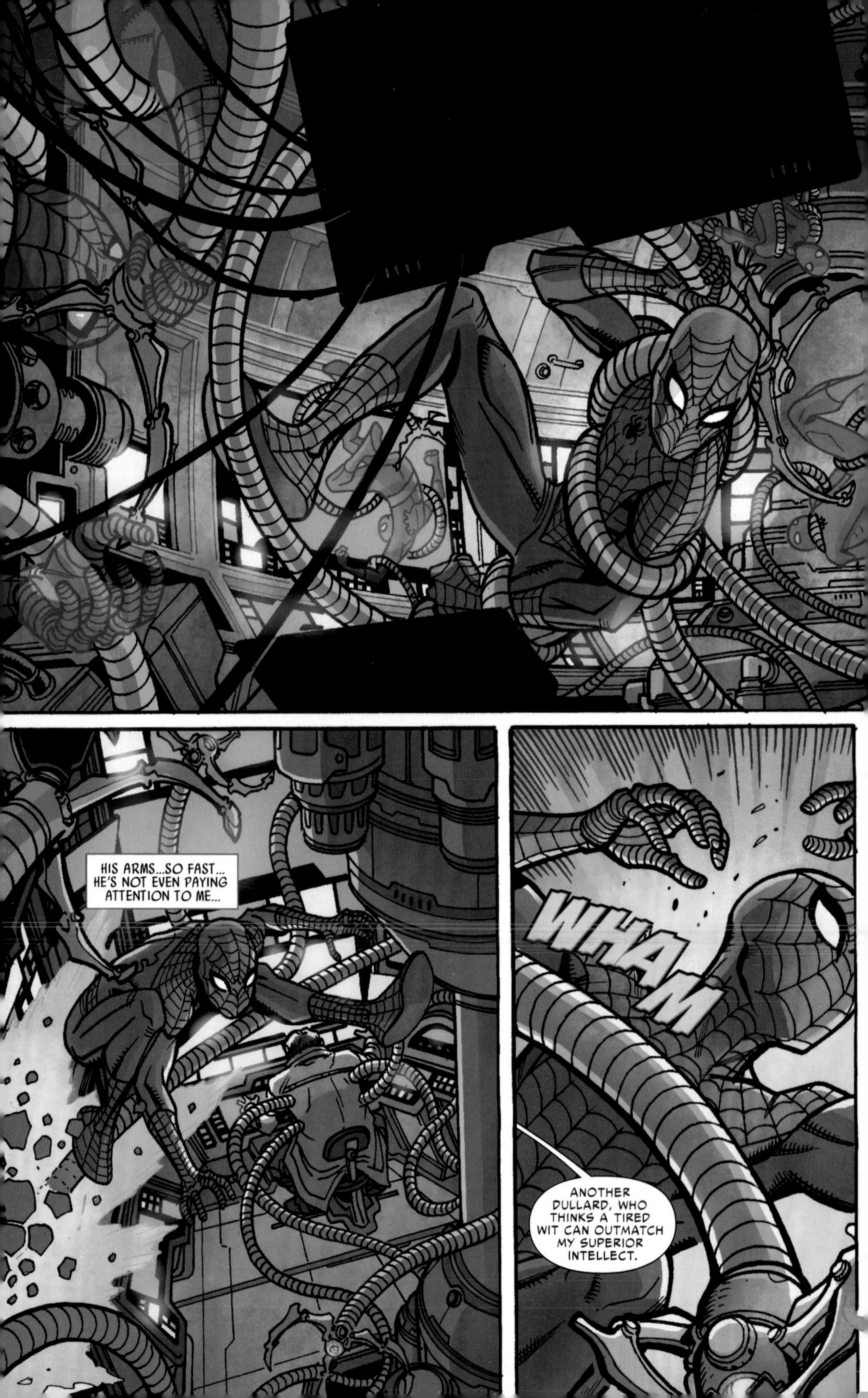
HIS ARMS...SO FAST... HE'S NOT EVEN PAYING ATTENTION TO ME...
WHAM
ANOTHER DULLARD, WHO THINKS A TIRED WIT CAN OUTMATCH MY SUPERIOR INTELLECT.

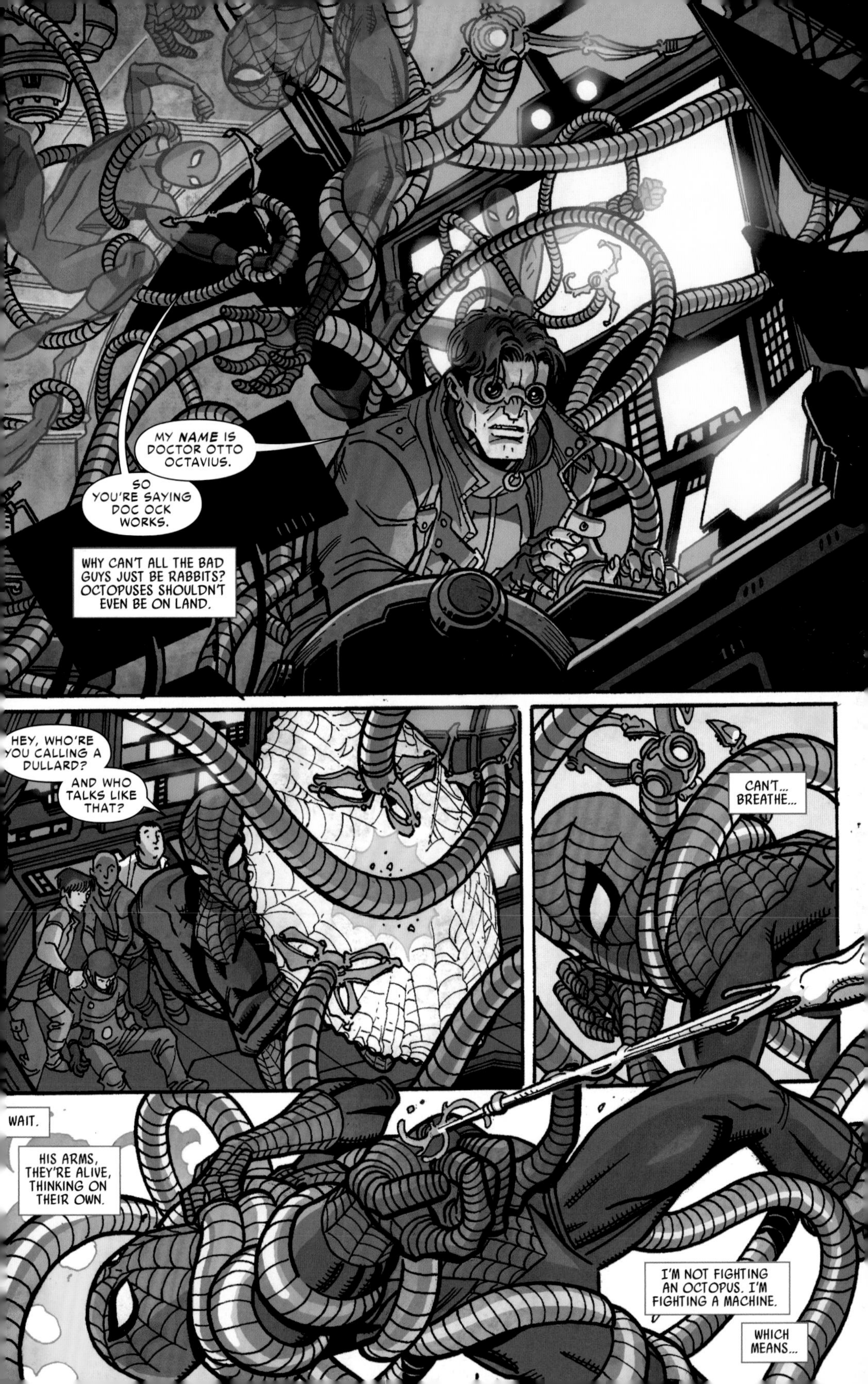
MY NAME IS DOCTOR OTTO OCTAVIUS.
SO YOU'RE SAYING DOC OCK WORKS.
WHY CAN'T ALL THE BAD GUYS JUST BE RABBITS? OCTOPUSES SHOULDN'T EVEN BE ON LAND.
HEY, WHO'RE YOU CALLING A DULLARD?
AND WHO TALKS LIKE THAT?
CAN'T... BREATHE...
WAIT.
HIS ARMS, THEY'RE ALIVE, THINKING ON THEIR OWN.
I'M NOT FIGHTING AN OCTOPUS. I'M FIGHTING A MACHINE.
WHICH MEANS...

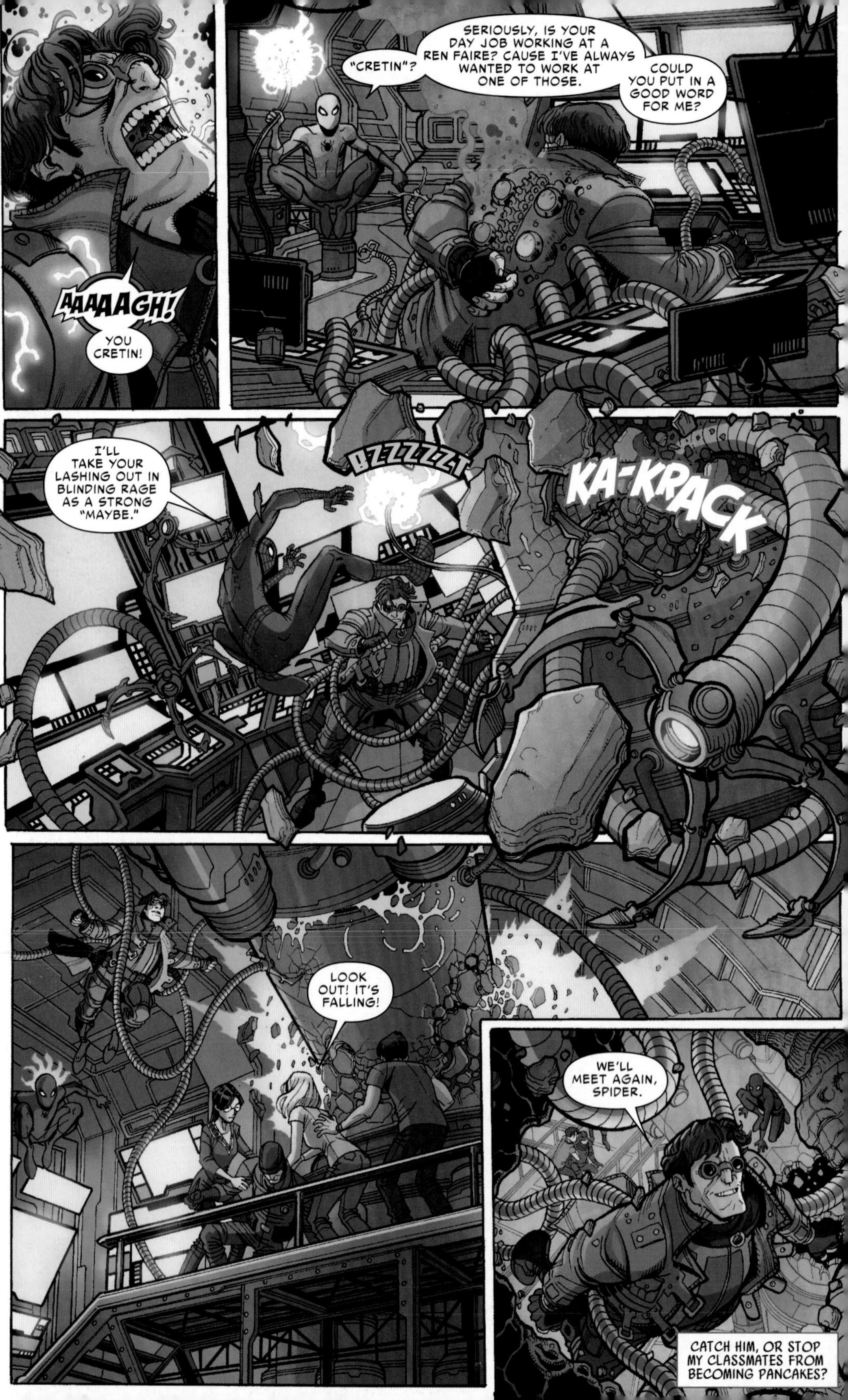
AAAAAGH!
YOU CRETIN!
"CRETIN"?
SERIOUSLY, IS YOUR DAY JOB WORKING AT A REN FAIRE? CAUSE I'VE ALWAYS WANTED TO WORK AT ONE OF THOSE.
COULD YOU PUT IN A GOOD WORD FOR ME?
I'LL TAKE YOUR LASHING OUT IN BLINDING RAGE AS A STRONG "MAYBE."
BZZZZZZT
KA-KRACK
LOOK OUT! IT'S FALLING!
WE'LL MEET AGAIN, SPIDER.
CATCH HIM, OR STOP MY CLASSMATES FROM BECOMING PANCAKES?

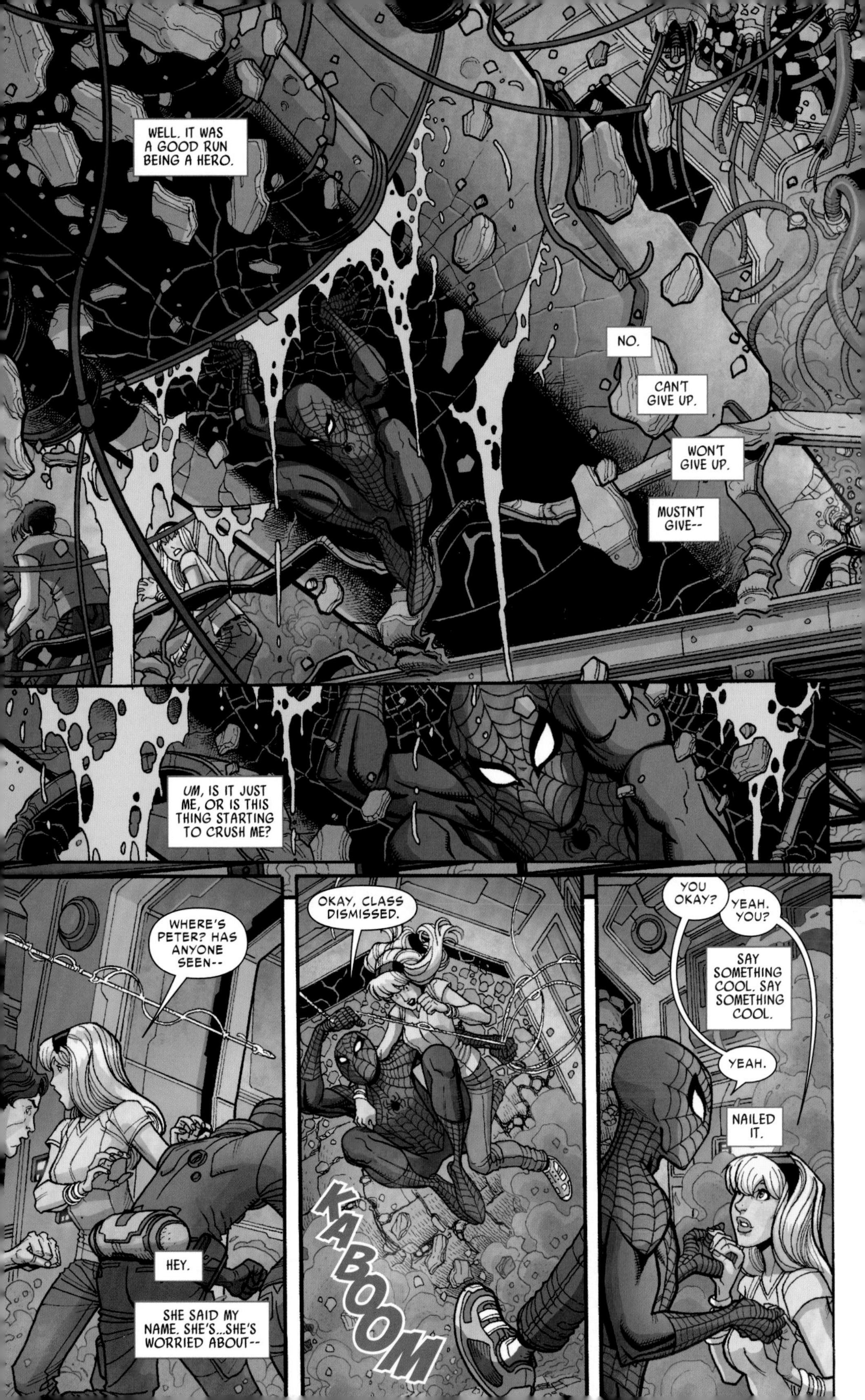
WELL, IT WAS A GOOD RUN BEING A HERO.
NO.
CAN'T GIVE UP.
WON'T GIVE UP.
MUSTN'T GIVE--
UM, IS IT JUST ME, OR IS THIS THING STARTING TO CRUSH ME?
WHERE'S PETER? HAS ANYONE SEEN--
HEY.
SHE SAID MY NAME. SHE'S...SHE'S WORRIED ABOUT--
OKAY, CLASS DISMISSED.
KABOOM
YOU OKAY?
YEAH. YOU?
SAY SOMETHING COOL. SAY SOMETHING COOL.
YEAH.
NAILED IT.

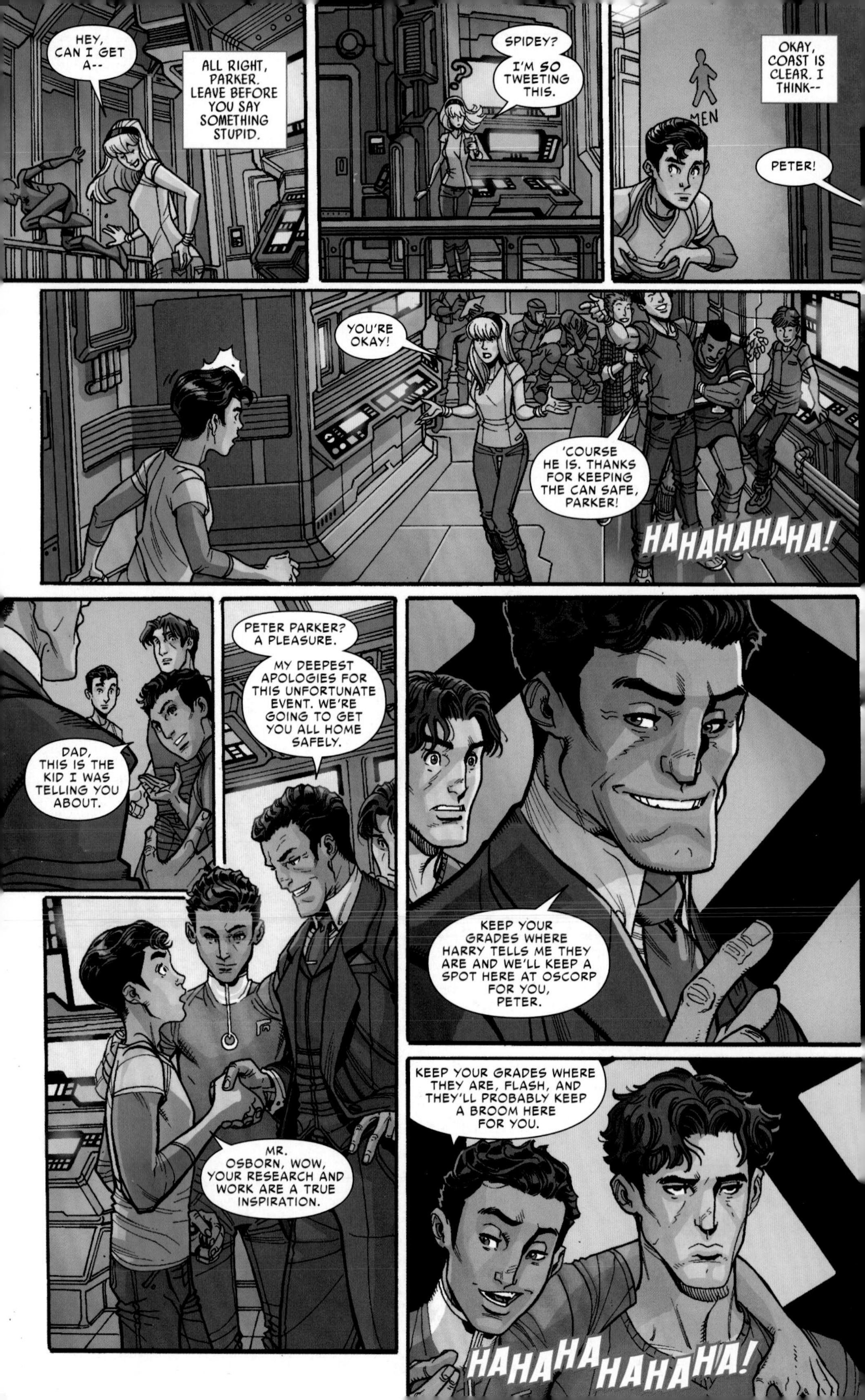
HEY, CAN I GET A--
ALL RIGHT, PARKER. LEAVE BEFORE YOU SAY SOMETHING STUPID.
SPIDEY?
I'M SO TWEETING THIS.
MEN
OKAY, COAST IS CLEAR. I THINK--
PETER!
YOU'RE OKAY!
'COURSE HE IS. THANKS FOR KEEPING THE CAN SAFE, PARKER!
HAHAHAHAHA!
DAD, THIS IS THE KID I WAS TELLING YOU ABOUT.
PETER PARKER? A PLEASURE.
MY DEEPEST APOLOGIES FOR THIS UNFORTUNATE EVENT. WE'RE GOING TO GET YOU ALL HOME SAFELY.
MR. OSBORN, WOW, YOUR RESEARCH AND WORK ARE A TRUE INSPIRATION.
KEEP YOUR GRADES WHERE HARRY TELLS ME THEY ARE AND WE'LL KEEP A SPOT HERE AT OSCORP FOR YOU, PETER.
KEEP YOUR GRADES WHERE THEY ARE, FLASH, AND THEY'LL PROBABLY KEEP A BROOM HERE FOR YOU.
HAHAHA HAHAHA!

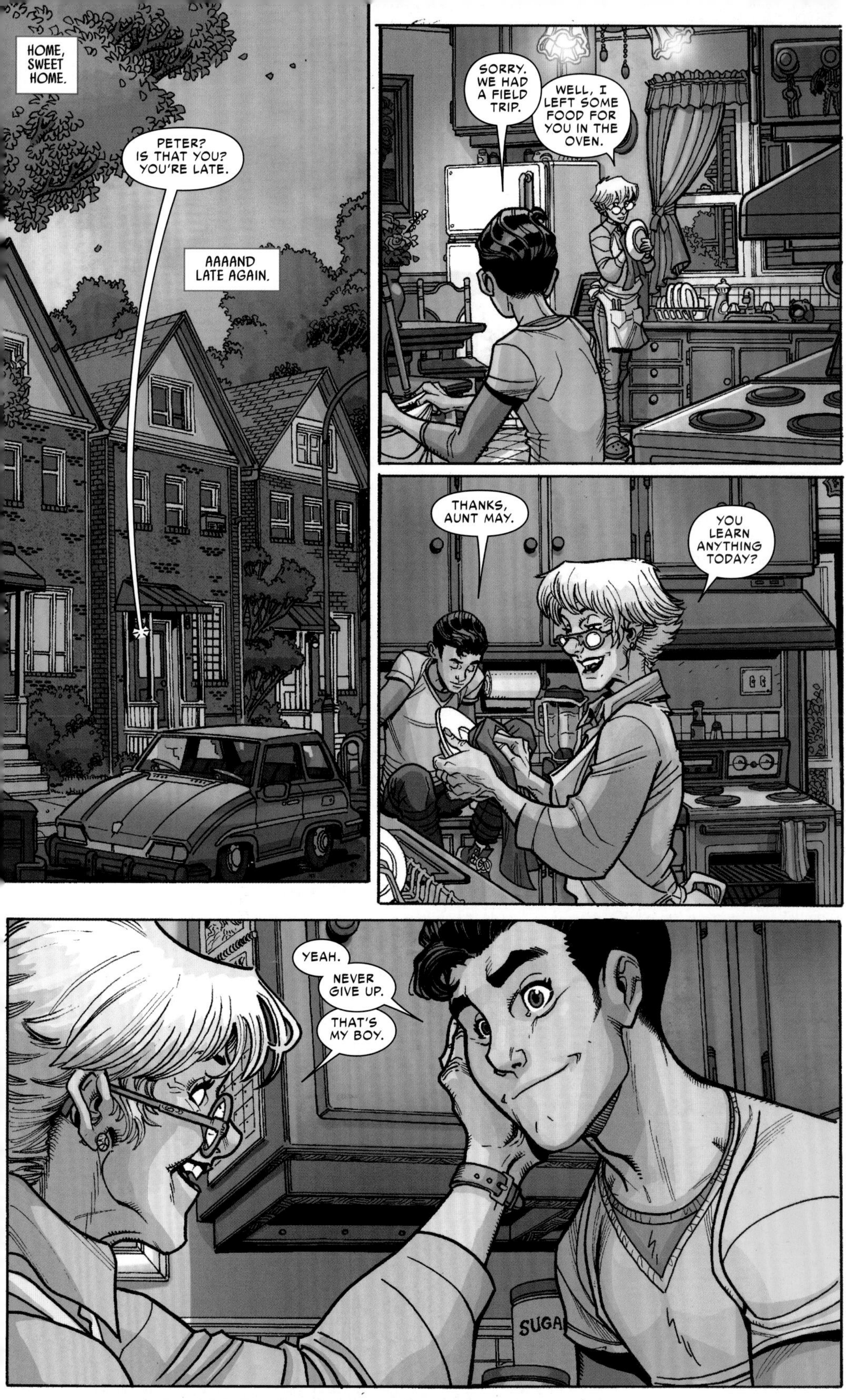

HOME, SWEET HOME.
PETER? IS THAT YOU? YOU'RE LATE.
AAAAND LATE AGAIN.
SORRY. WE HAD A FIELD TRIP.
WELL, I LEFT SOME FOOD FOR YOU IN THE OVEN.
THANKS, AUNT MAY.
YOU LEARN ANYTHING TODAY?
YEAH.
NEVER GIVE UP.
THAT'S MY BOY.
SUGA

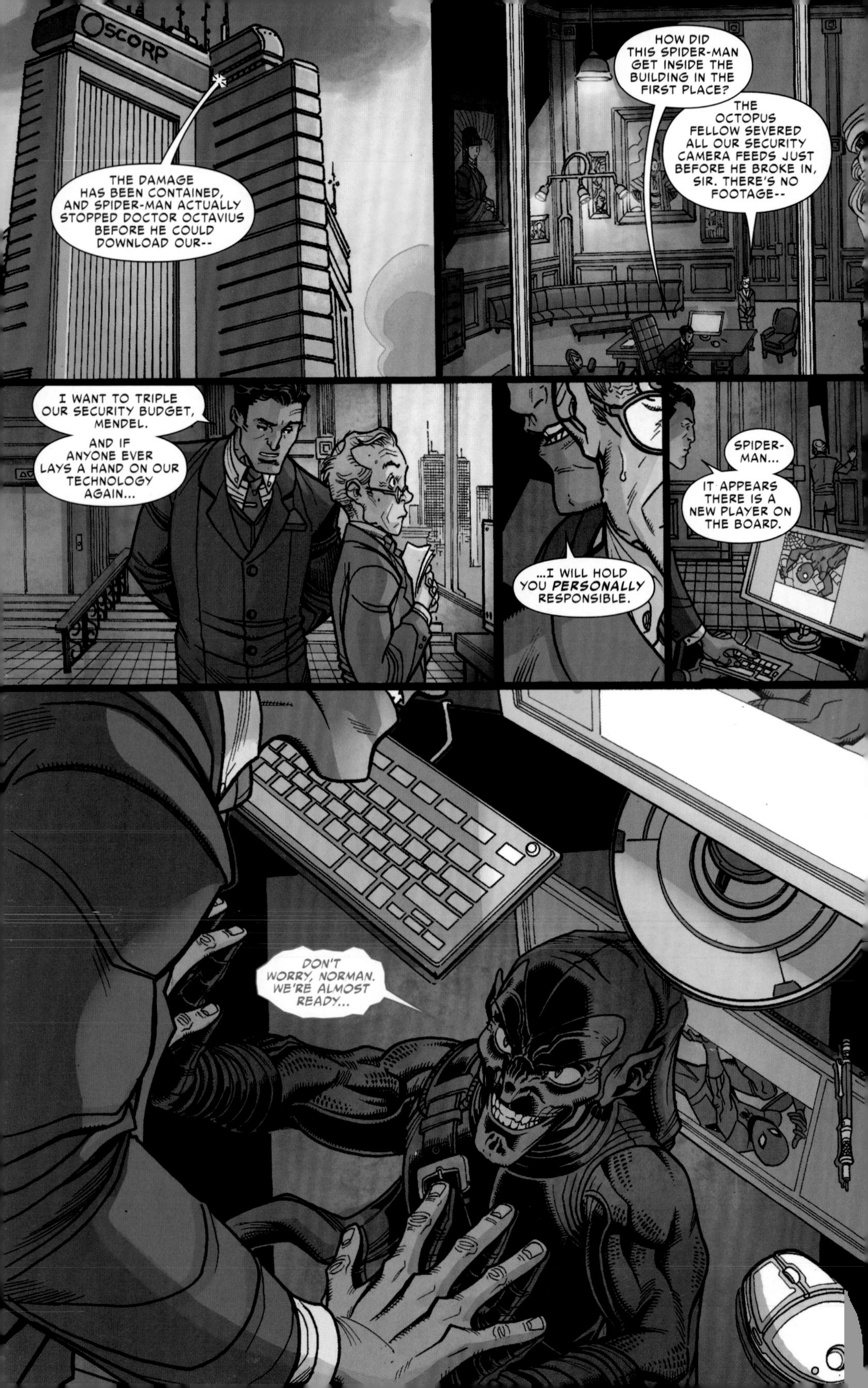
OSCORP
THE DAMAGE HAS BEEN CONTAINED, AND SPIDER-MAN ACTUALLY STOPPED DOCTOR OCTAVIUS BEFORE HE COULD DOWNLOAD OUR--
HOW DID THIS SPIDER-MAN GET INSIDE THE BUILDING IN THE FIRST PLACE?
THE OCTOPUS FELLOW SEVERED ALL OUR SECURITY CAMERA FEEDS JUST BEFORE HE BROKE IN, SIR. THERE'S NO FOOTAGE--
I WANT TO TRIPLE OUR SECURITY BUDGET, MENDEL.
AND IF ANYONE EVER LAYS A HAND ON OUR TECHNOLOGY AGAIN...
...I WILL HOLD YOU PERSONALLY RESPONSIBLE.
SPIDER-MAN...
IT APPEARS THERE IS A NEW PLAYER ON THE BOARD.
DON'T WORRY, NORMAN. WE'RE ALMOST READY...

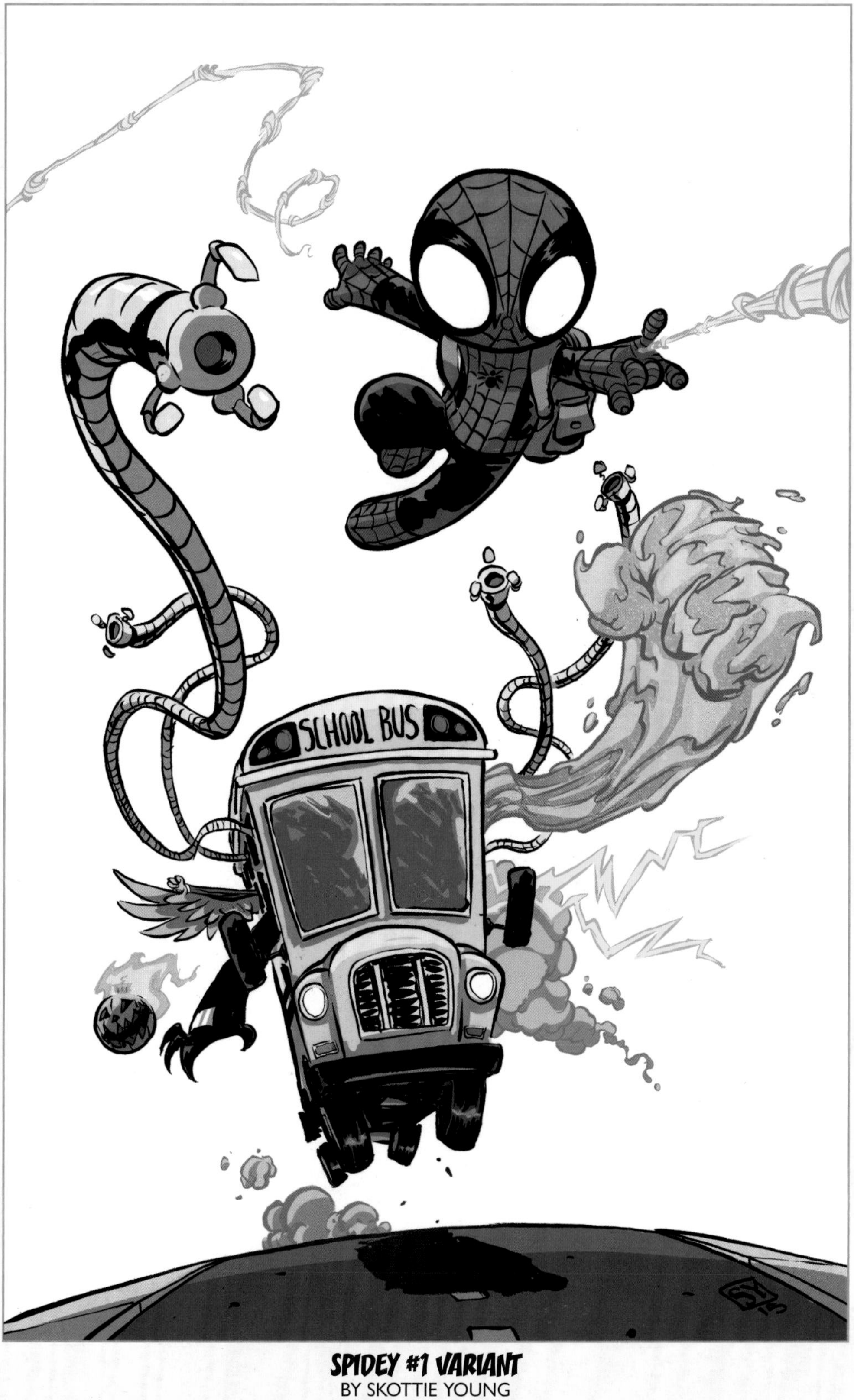
SCHOOL BUS

SPIDEY #1 VARIANT
BY SKOTTIE YOUNG

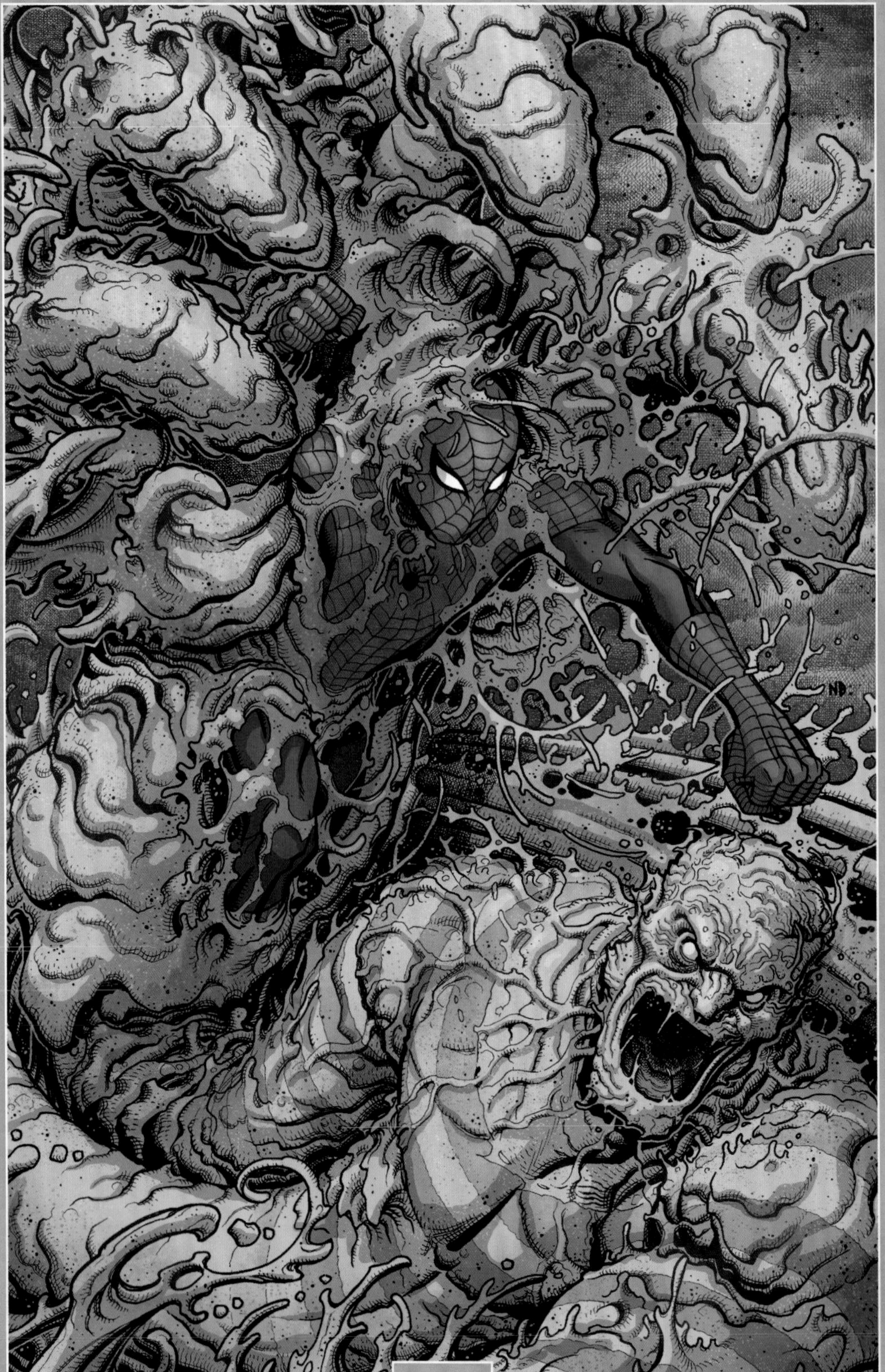

2

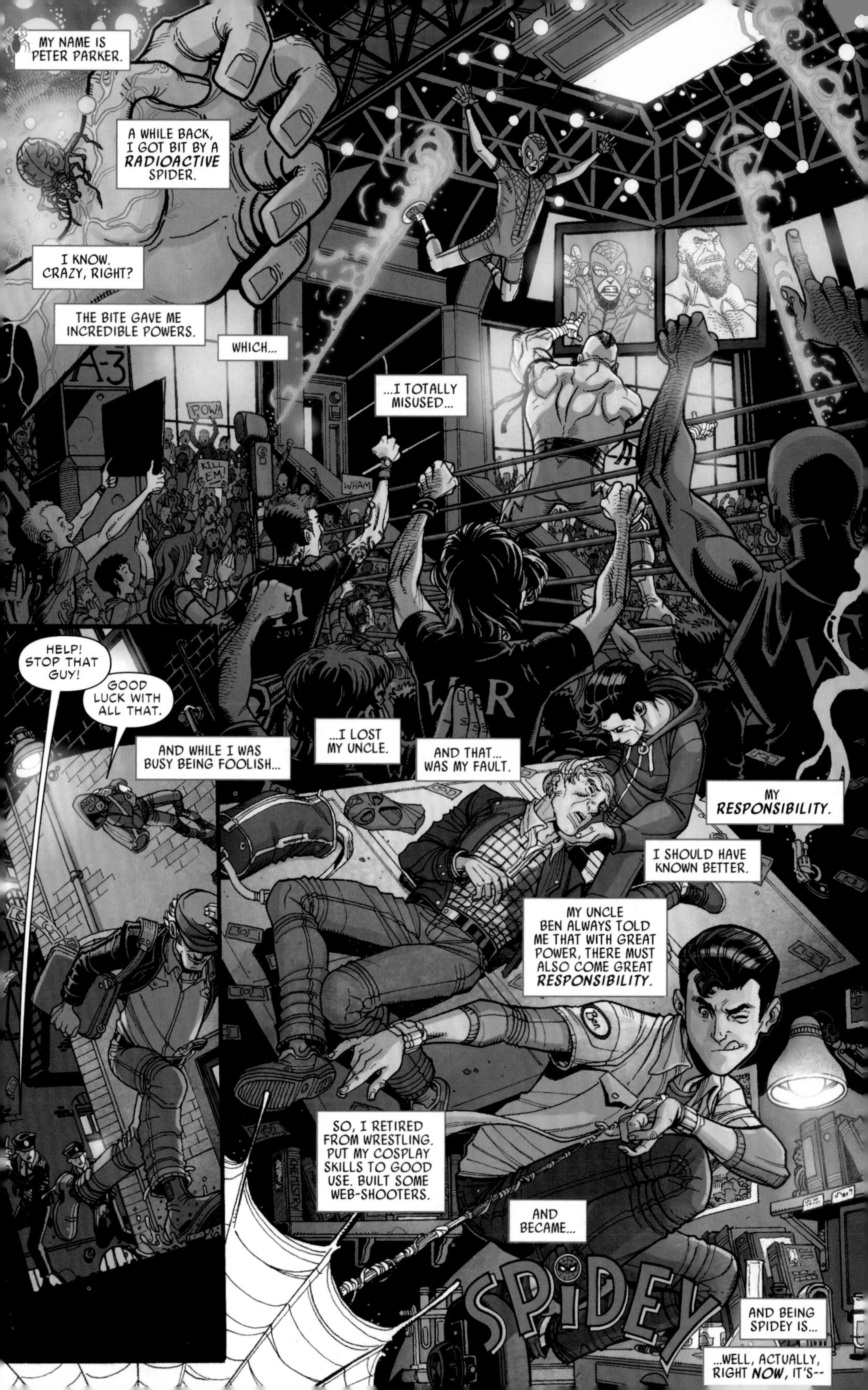
MY NAME IS PETER PARKER.
A WHILE BACK, I GOT BIT BY A RADIOACTIVE SPIDER.
I KNOW. CRAZY, RIGHT?
THE BITE GAVE ME INCREDIBLE POWERS.
WHICH...
...I TOTALLY MISUSED...
POW
KILL 'EM!
WHAM
HELP! STOP THAT GUY!
GOOD LUCK WITH ALL THAT.
AND WHILE I WAS BUSY BEING FOOLISH...
...I LOST MY UNCLE.
AND THAT... WAS MY FAULT.
MY RESPONSIBILITY.
I SHOULD HAVE KNOWN BETTER.
MY UNCLE BEN ALWAYS TOLD ME THAT WITH GREAT POWER, THERE MUST ALSO COME GREAT RESPONSIBILITY.
Ben
SO, I RETIRED FROM WRESTLING. PUT MY COSPLAY SKILLS TO GOOD USE. BUILT SOME WEB-SHOOTERS.
AND BECAME...
SPIDEY
AND BEING SPIDEY IS...
...WELL, ACTUALLY, RIGHT NOW, IT'S--

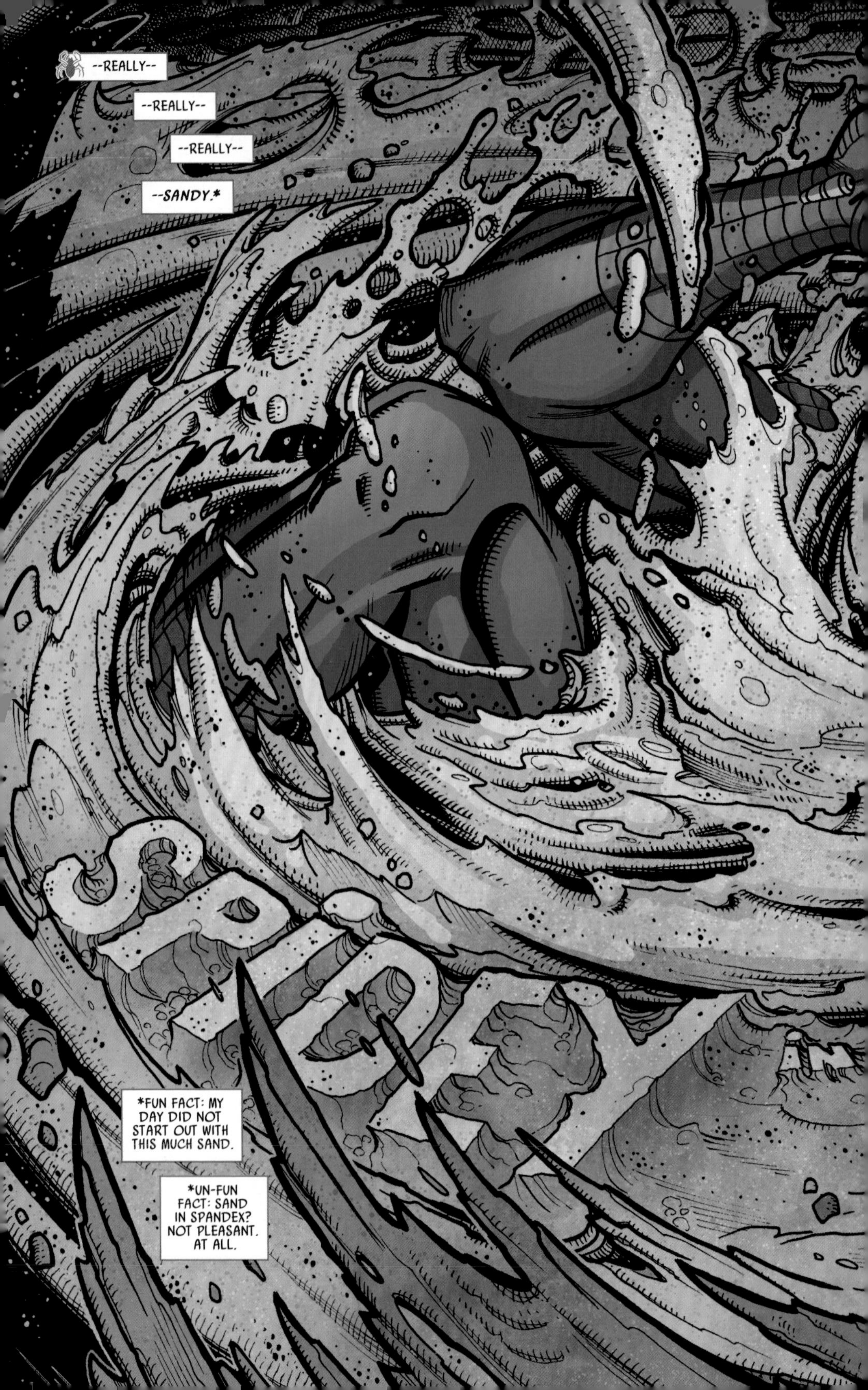
--REALLY--
--REALLY--
--REALLY--
--SANDY.*
*FUN FACT: MY DAY DID NOT START OUT WITH THIS MUCH SAND.
*UN-FUN FACT: SAND IN SPANDEX? NOT PLEASANT. AT ALL.

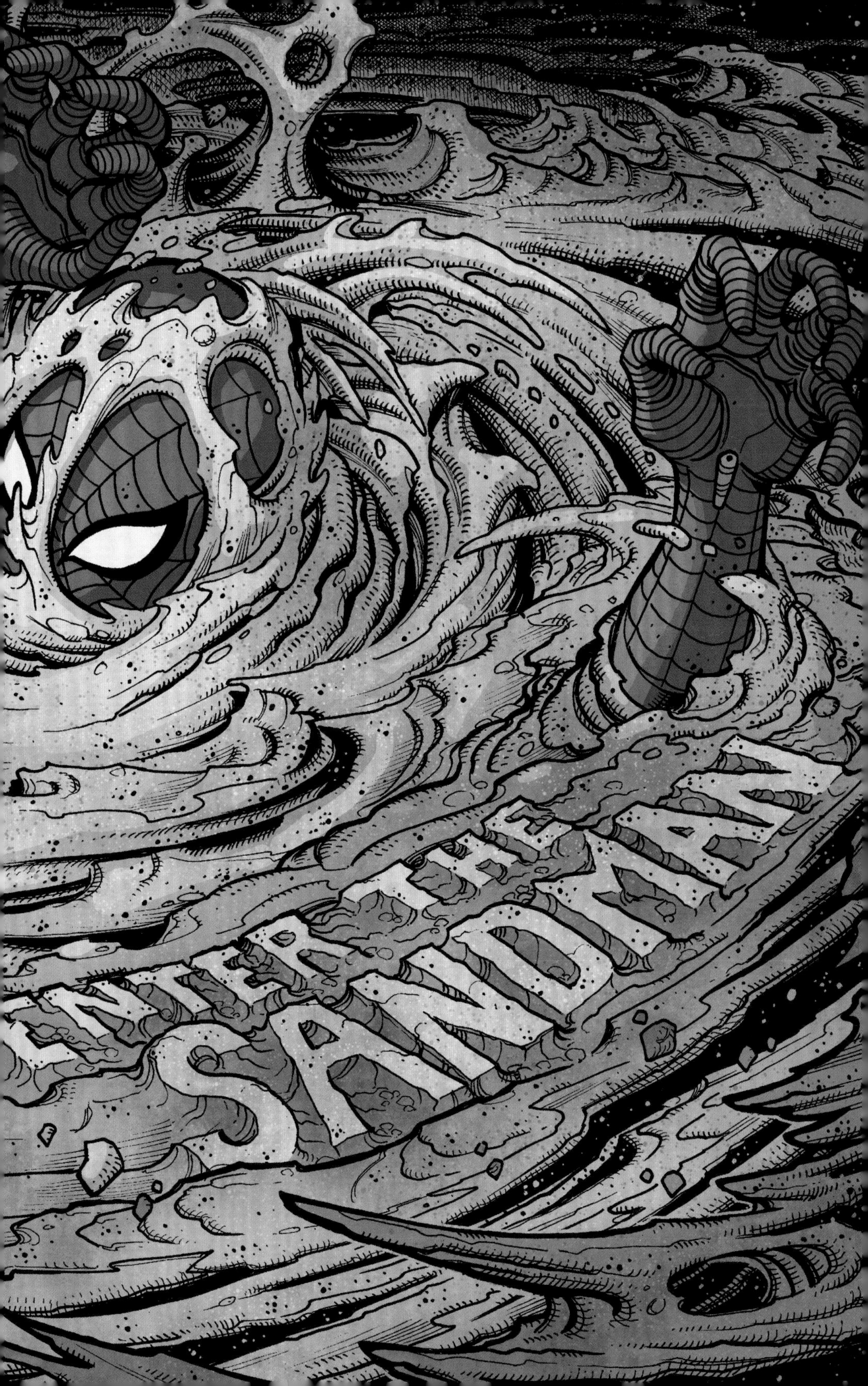

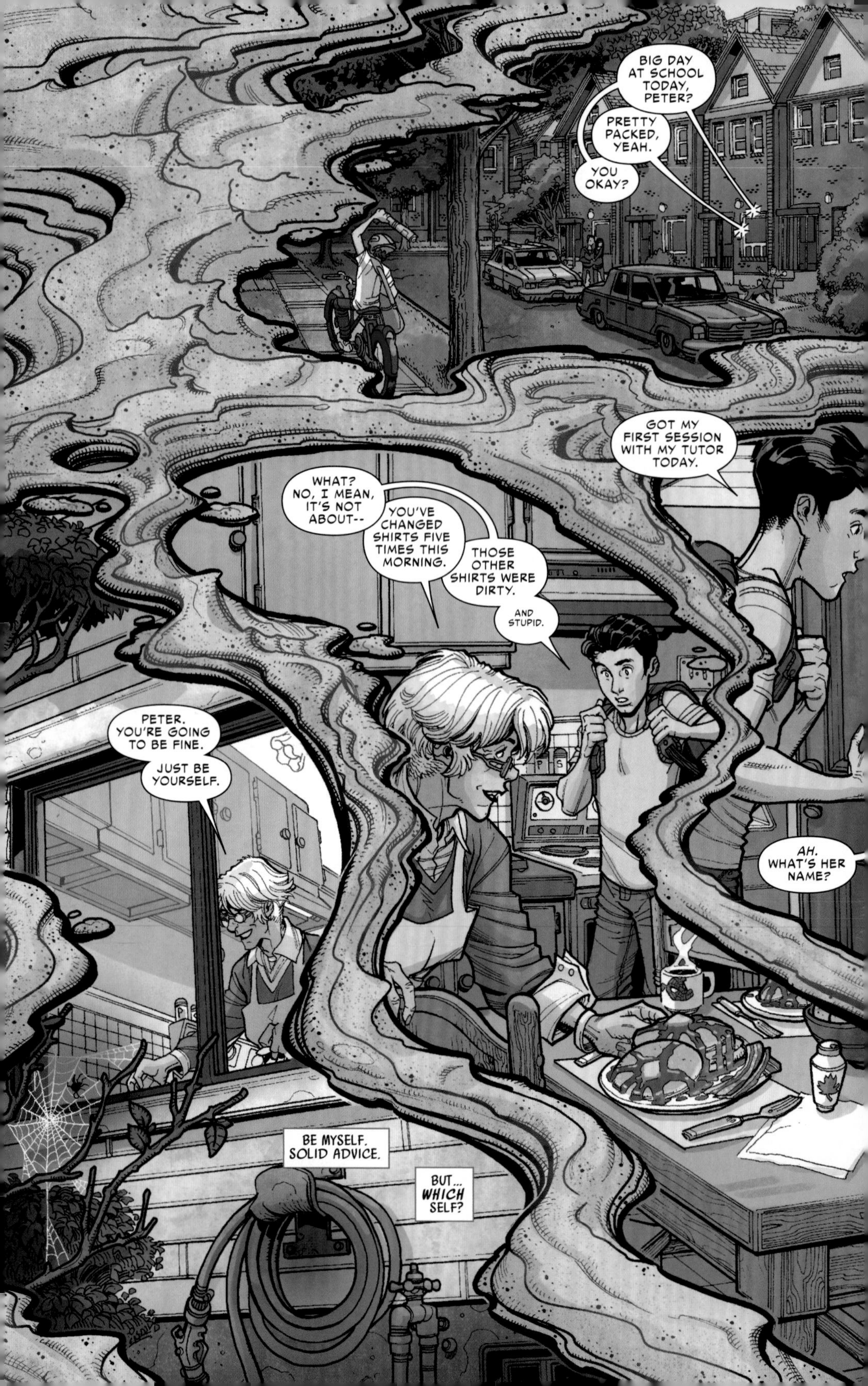
BIG DAY AT SCHOOL TODAY, PETER?
PRETTY PACKED, YEAH.
YOU OKAY?
GOT MY FIRST SESSION WITH MY TUTOR TODAY.
AH. WHAT'S HER NAME?
WHAT? NO, I MEAN, IT'S NOT ABOUT--
YOU'VE CHANGED SHIRTS FIVE TIMES THIS MORNING.
THOSE OTHER SHIRTS WERE DIRTY.
AND STUPID.
PETER. YOU'RE GOING TO BE FINE.
JUST BE YOURSELF.
BE MYSELF. SOLID ADVICE.
BUT... *WHICH* SELF?

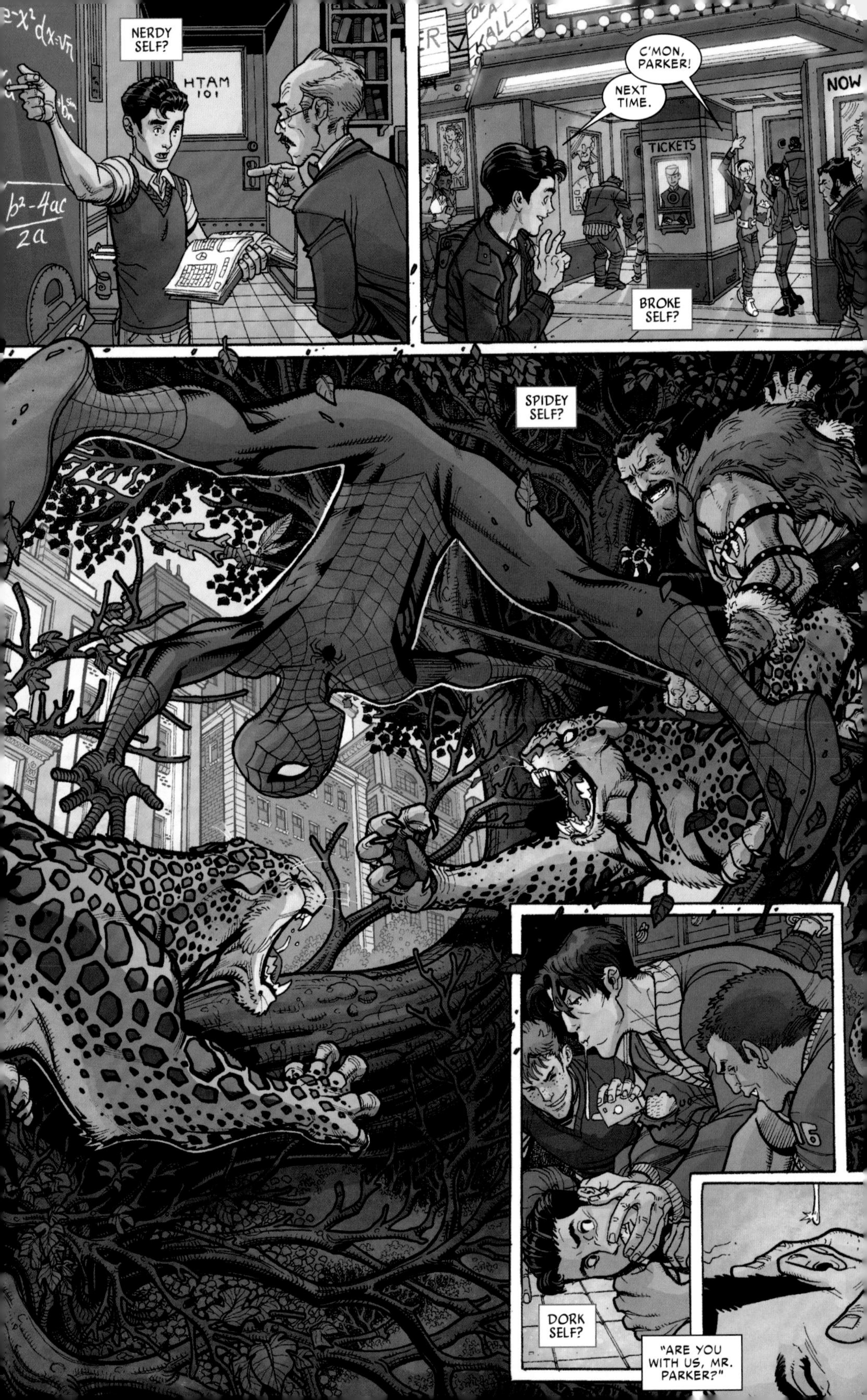
NERDY SELF?
HTAM 101
C'MON, PARKER!
NEXT TIME.
TICKETS
BROKE SELF?
SPIDEY SELF?
DORK SELF?
"ARE YOU WITH US, MR. PARKER?"

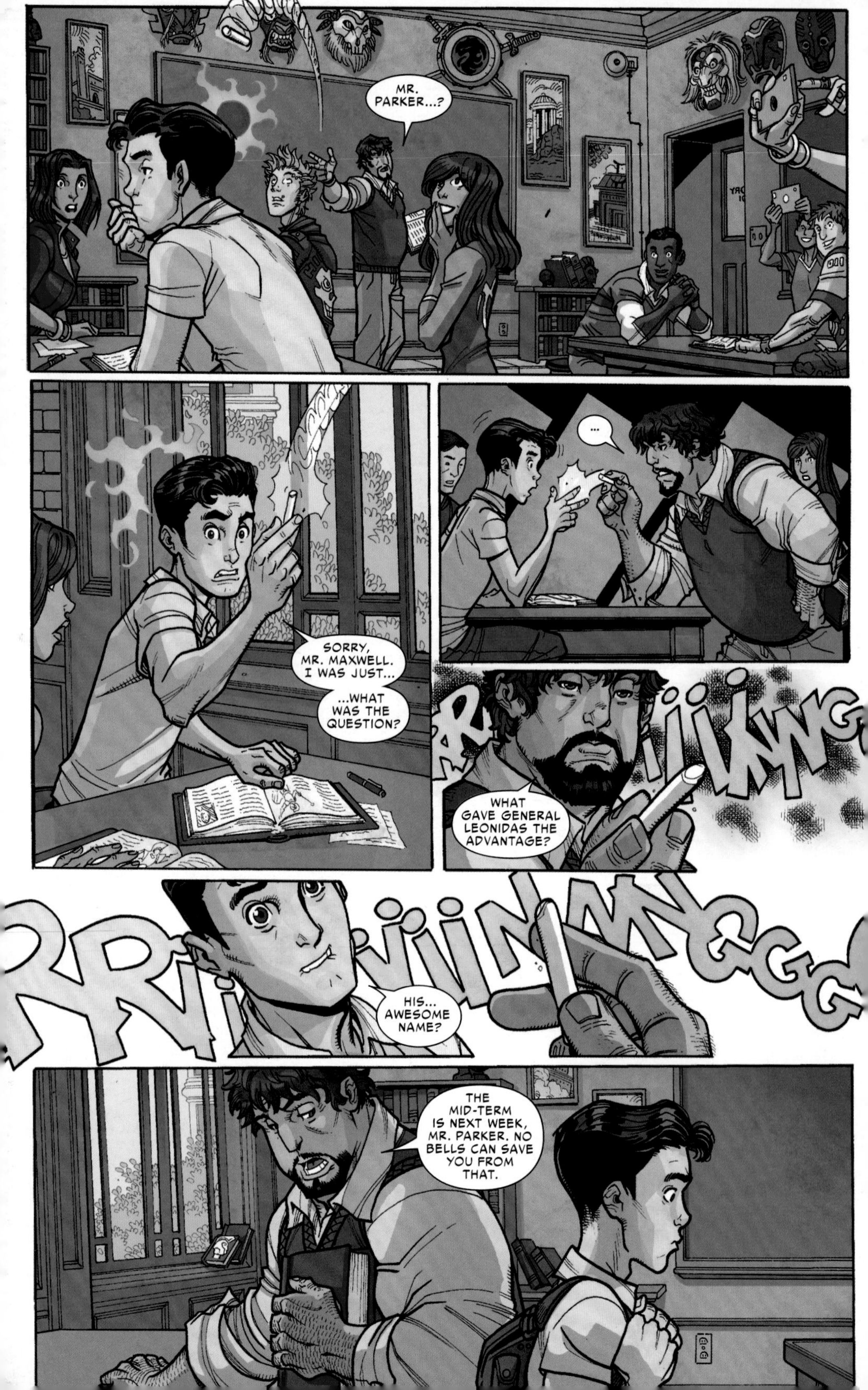
MR. PARKER...?
SORRY, MR. MAXWELL. I WAS JUST...
...WHAT WAS THE QUESTION?
...
WHAT GAVE GENERAL LEONIDAS THE ADVANTAGE?
HIS... AWESOME NAME?
THE MID-TERM IS NEXT WEEK, MR. PARKER. NO BELLS CAN SAVE YOU FROM THAT.

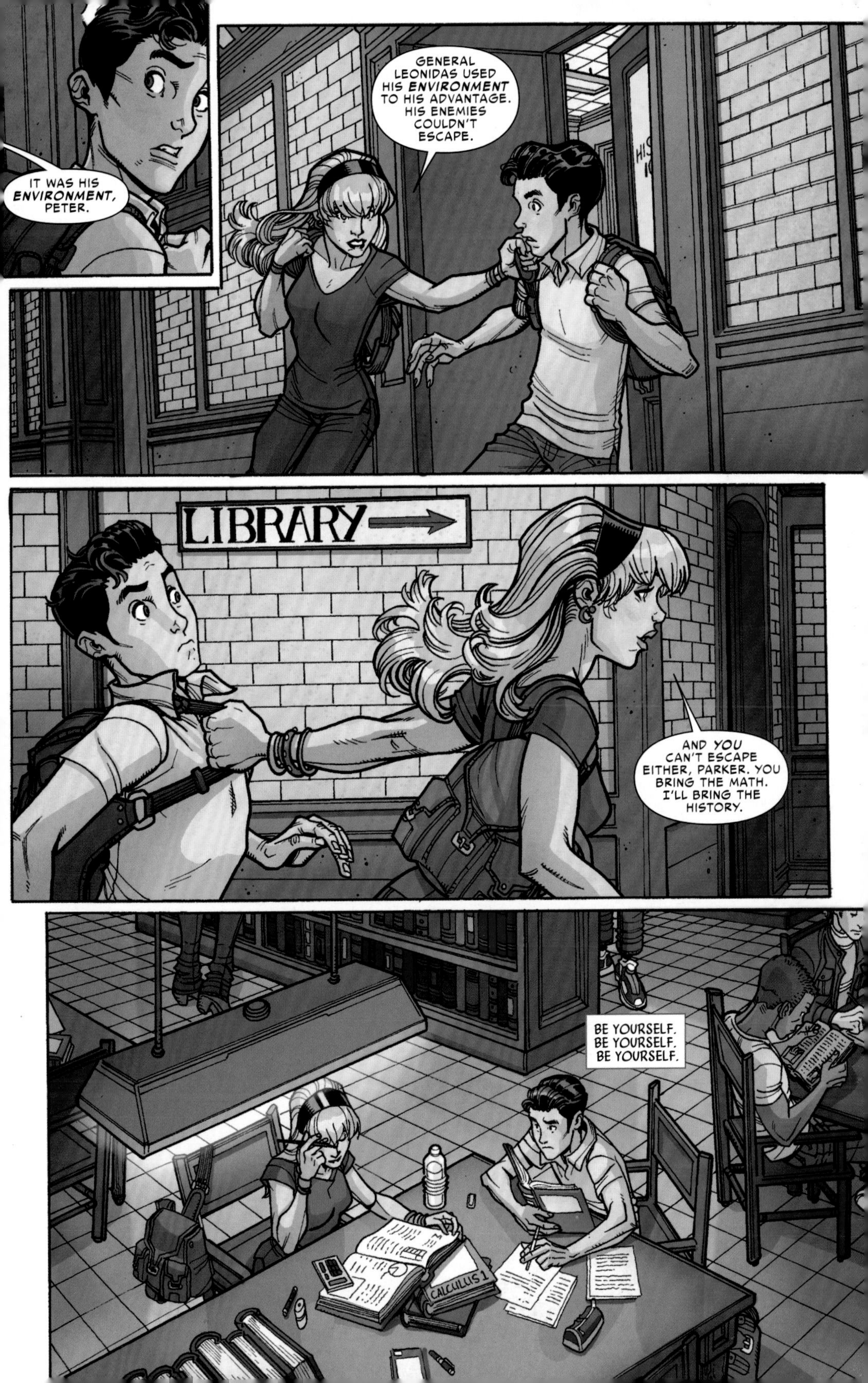
IT WAS HIS *ENVIRONMENT*, PETER.
GENERAL LEONIDAS USED HIS *ENVIRONMENT* TO HIS ADVANTAGE. HIS ENEMIES COULDN'T ESCAPE.
LIBRARY
AND *YOU* CAN'T ESCAPE EITHER, PARKER. YOU BRING THE MATH. I'LL BRING THE HISTORY.
BE YOURSELF. BE YOURSELF. BE YOURSELF.
CALCULUS 1

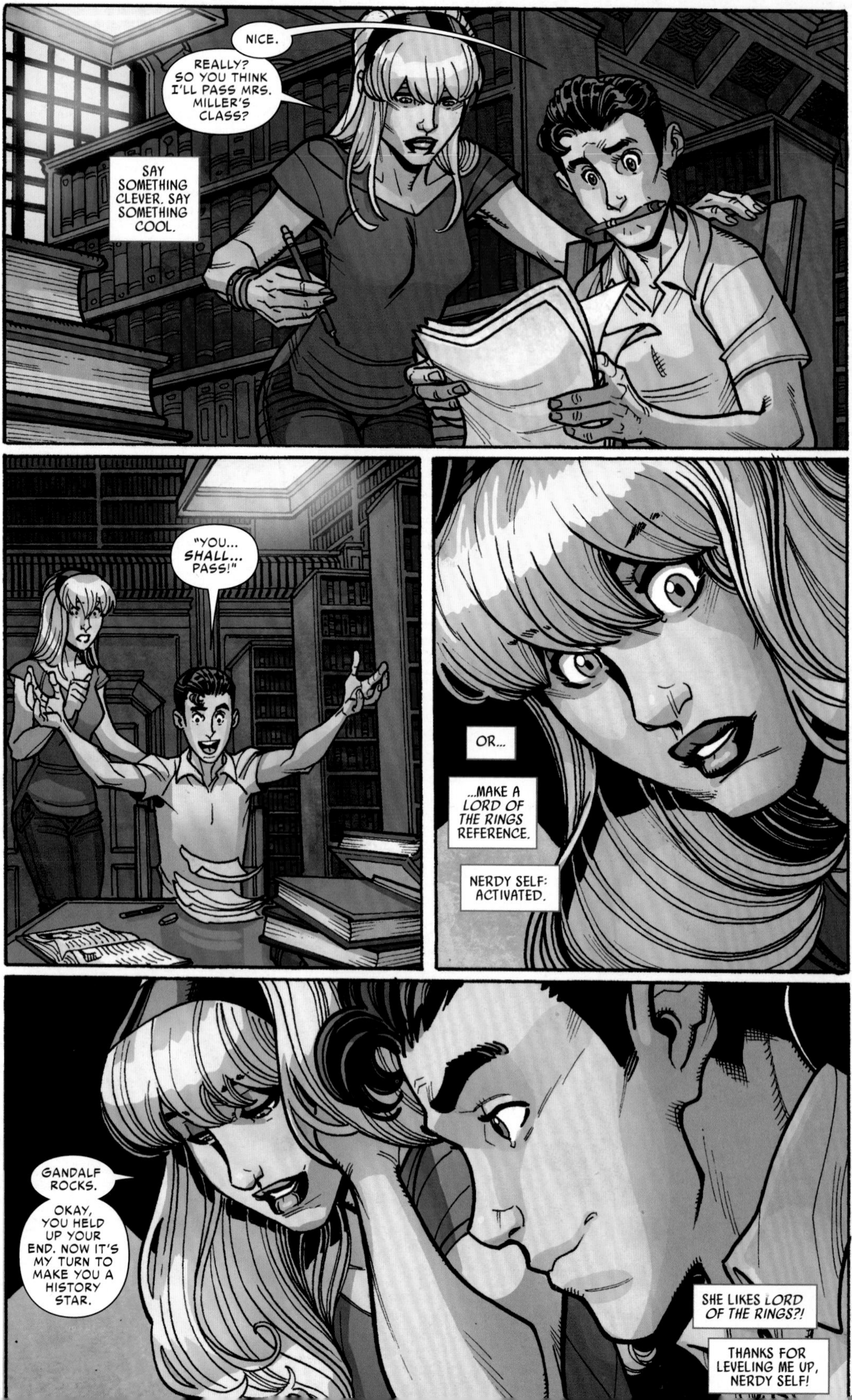
NICE.
REALLY? SO YOU THINK I'LL PASS MRS. MILLER'S CLASS?
SAY SOMETHING CLEVER. SAY SOMETHING COOL.
"YOU... SHALL... PASS!"
OR...
...MAKE A LORD OF THE RINGS REFERENCE.
NERDY SELF: ACTIVATED.
GANDALF ROCKS.
OKAY, YOU HELD UP YOUR END. NOW IT'S MY TURN TO MAKE YOU A HISTORY STAR.
SHE LIKES LORD OF THE RINGS?!
THANKS FOR LEVELING ME UP, NERDY SELF!

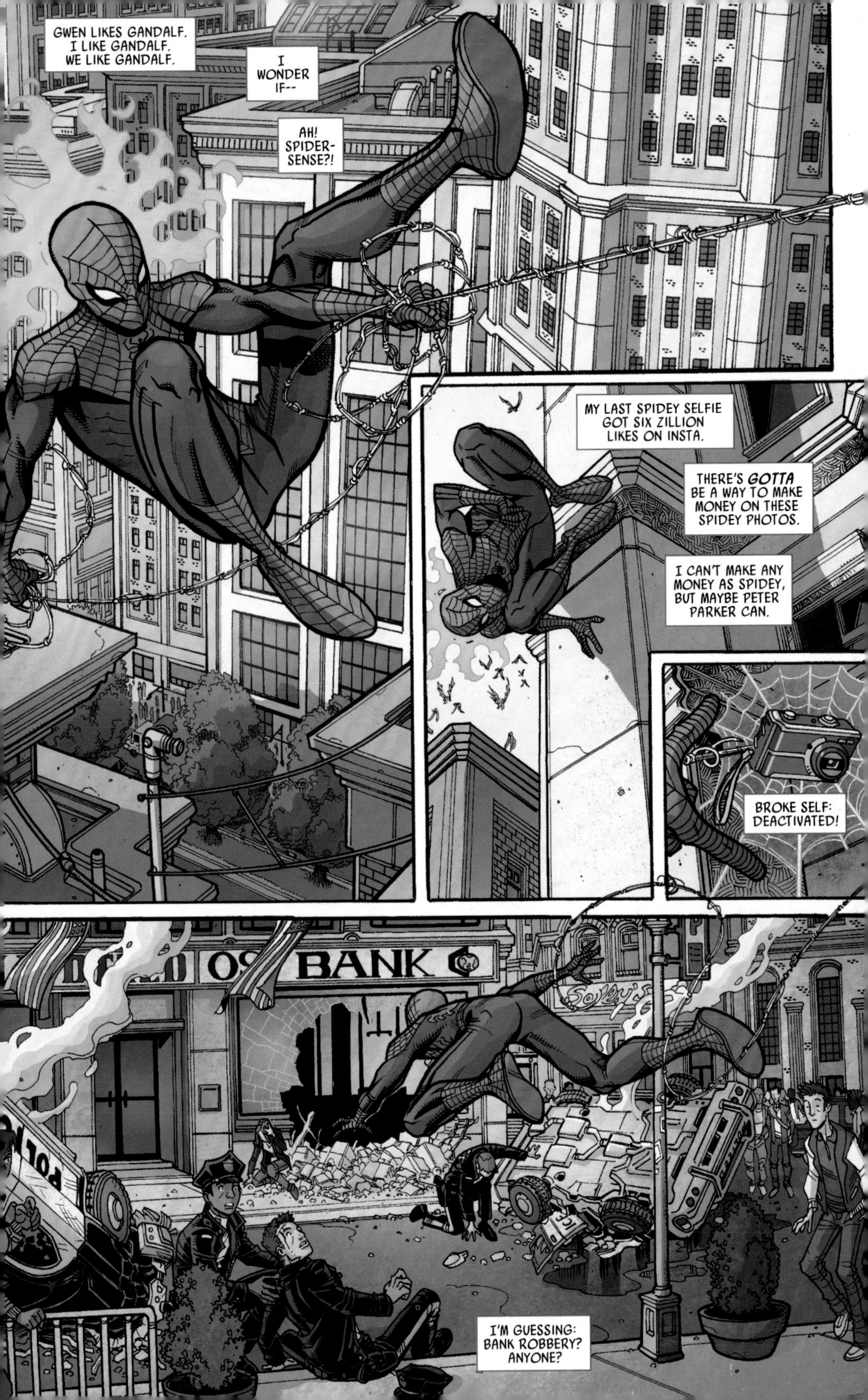

GWEN LIKES GANDALF. I LIKE GANDALF. WE LIKE GANDALF.
I WONDER IF--
AH! SPIDER-SENSE?!
MY LAST SPIDEY SELFIE GOT SIX ZILLION LIKES ON INSTA.
THERE'S *GOTTA* BE A WAY TO MAKE MONEY ON THESE SPIDEY PHOTOS.
I CAN'T MAKE ANY MONEY AS SPIDEY, BUT MAYBE PETER PARKER CAN.
BROKE SELF: DEACTIVATED!
OS BANK
I'M GUESSING: BANK ROBBERY? ANYONE?

LIGHTS OUT.

THAT'S NOT GOOD.

LOOKS LIKE I MISSED THE PARTY.

WAIT...

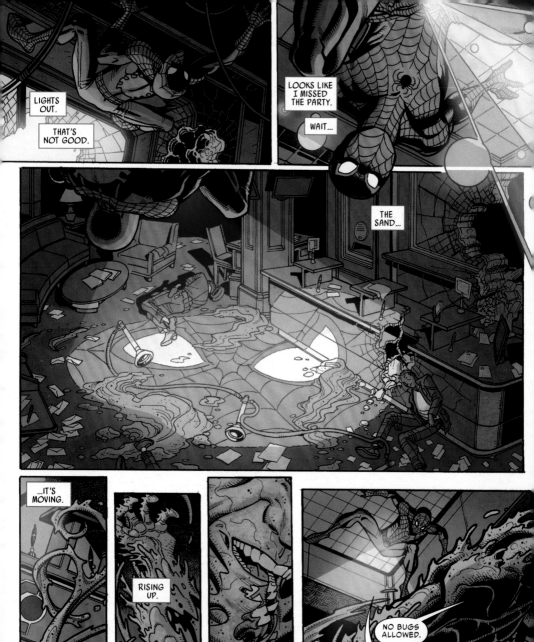

THE SAND...

...IT'S MOVING.

RISING UP.

WHICH MEANS--

NO BUGS ALLOWED.

THAT WORKS FOR ME: I'M NOT A BUG.

I'M A--

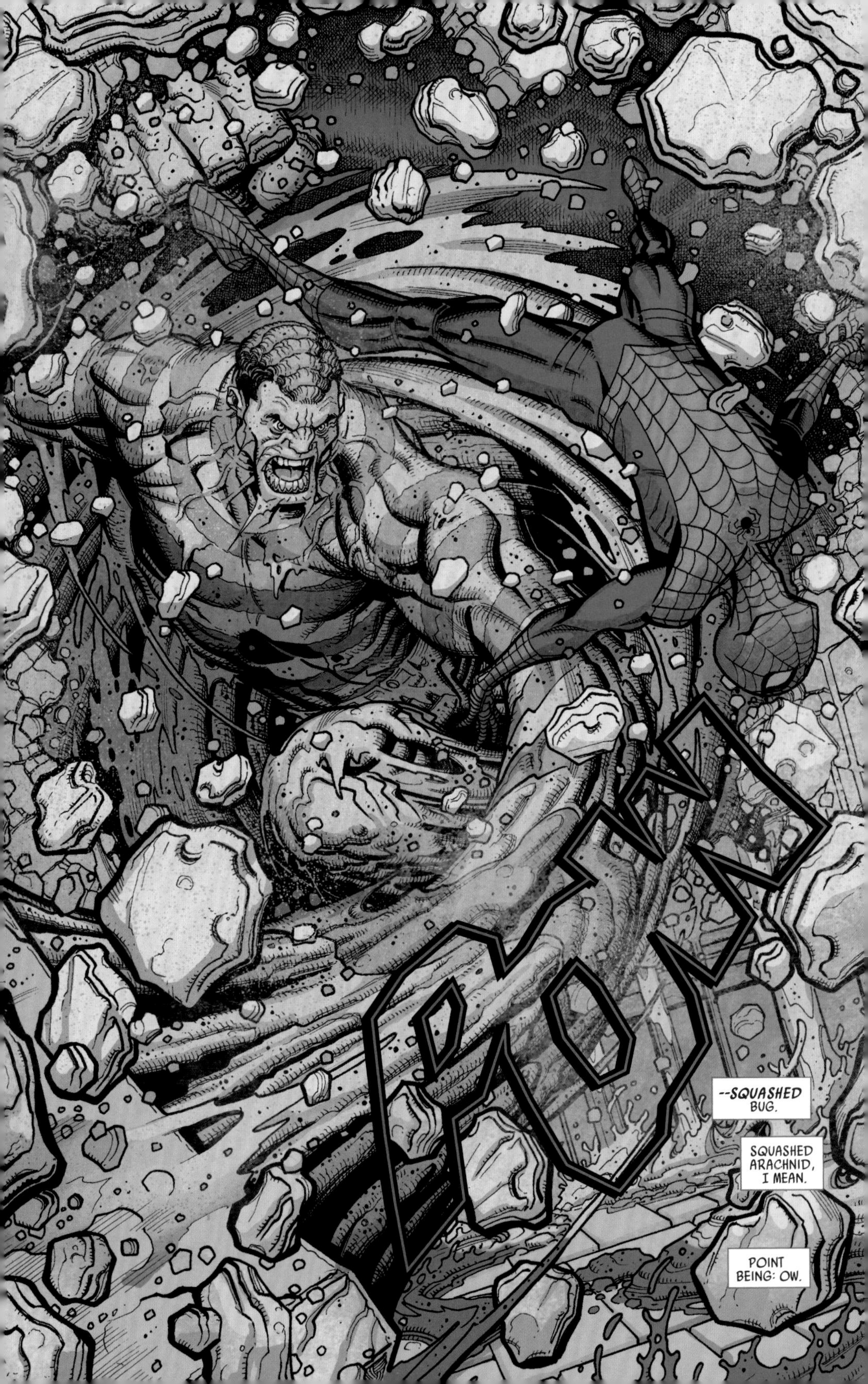
--SQUASHED BUG.
SQUASHED ARACHNID, I MEAN.
POINT BEING: OW.

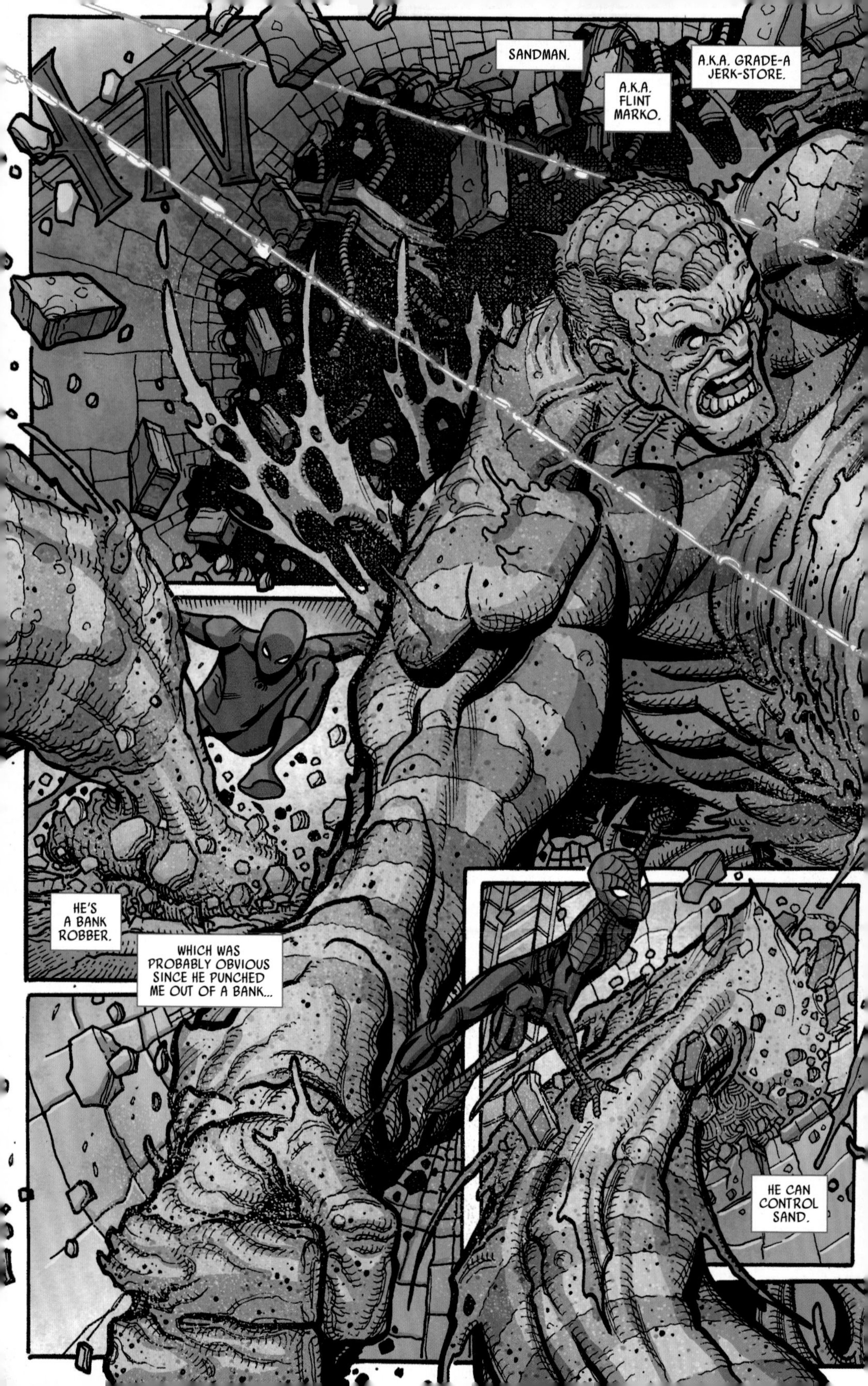
SANDMAN.
A.K.A. FLINT MARKO.
A.K.A. GRADE-A JERK-STORE.
HE'S A BANK ROBBER.
WHICH WAS PROBABLY OBVIOUS SINCE HE PUNCHED ME OUT OF A BANK...
HE CAN CONTROL SAND.

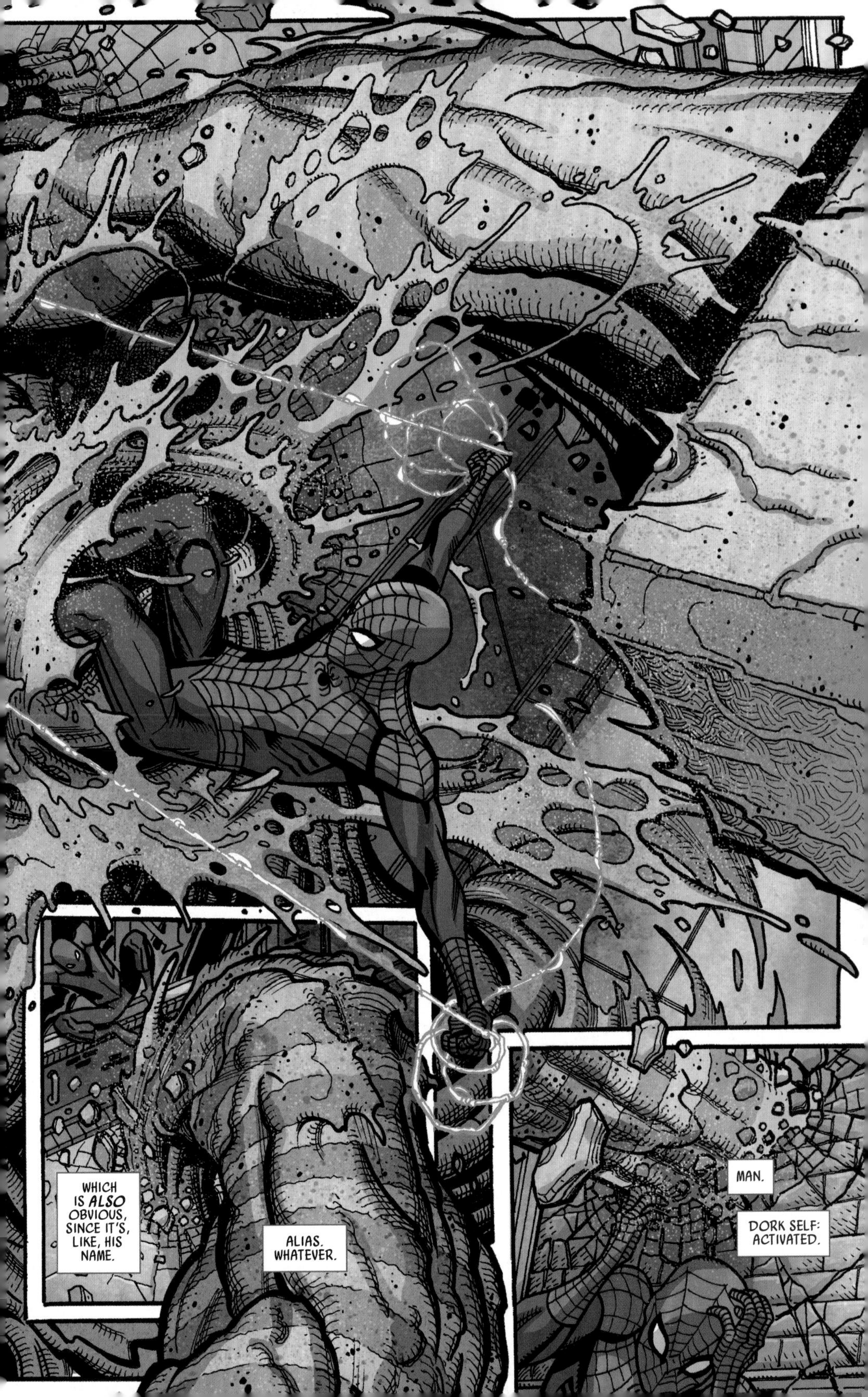
WHICH IS *ALSO* OBVIOUS, SINCE IT'S, LIKE, HIS NAME.
ALIAS. WHATEVER.
MAN.
DORK SELF: ACTIVATED.

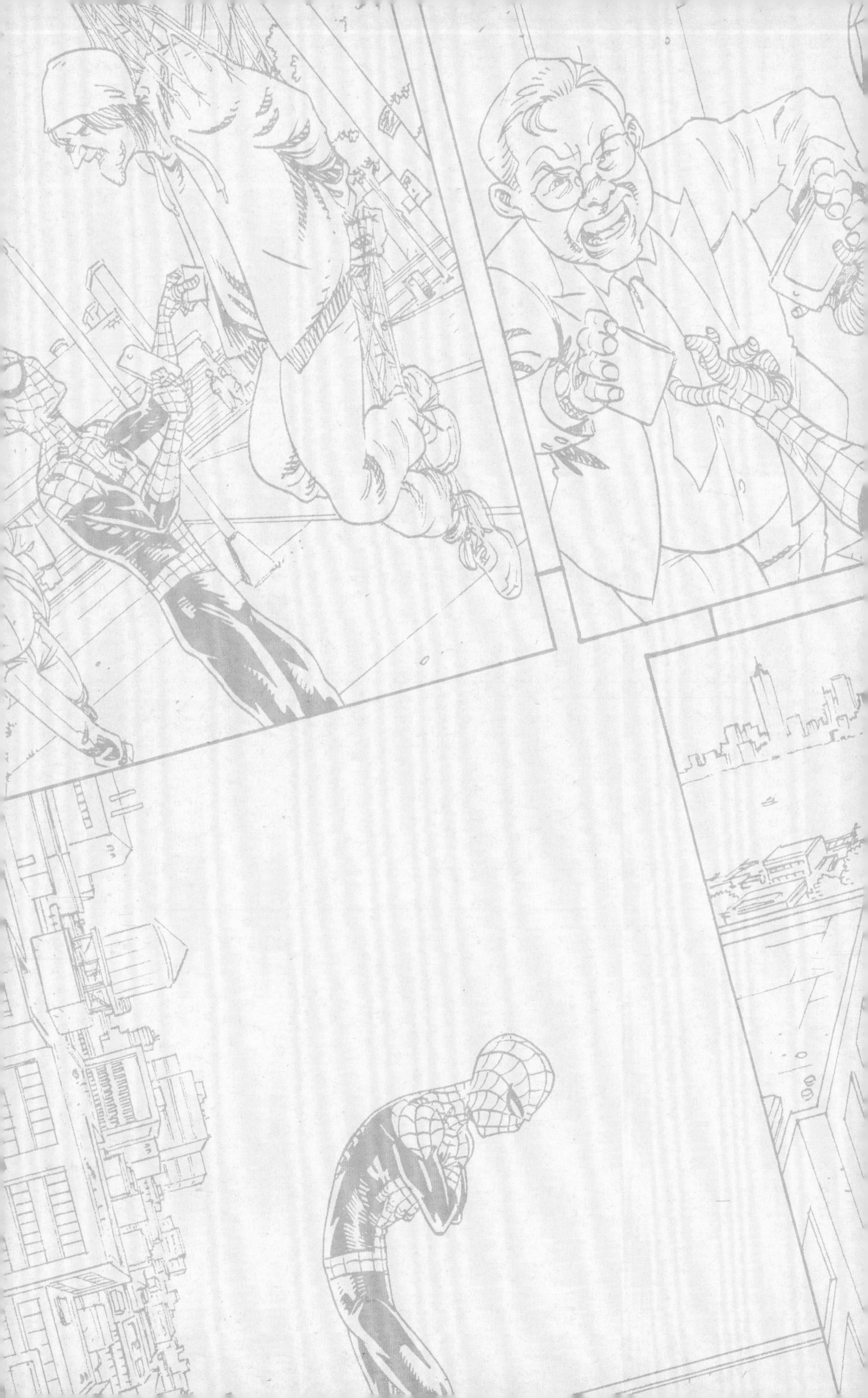

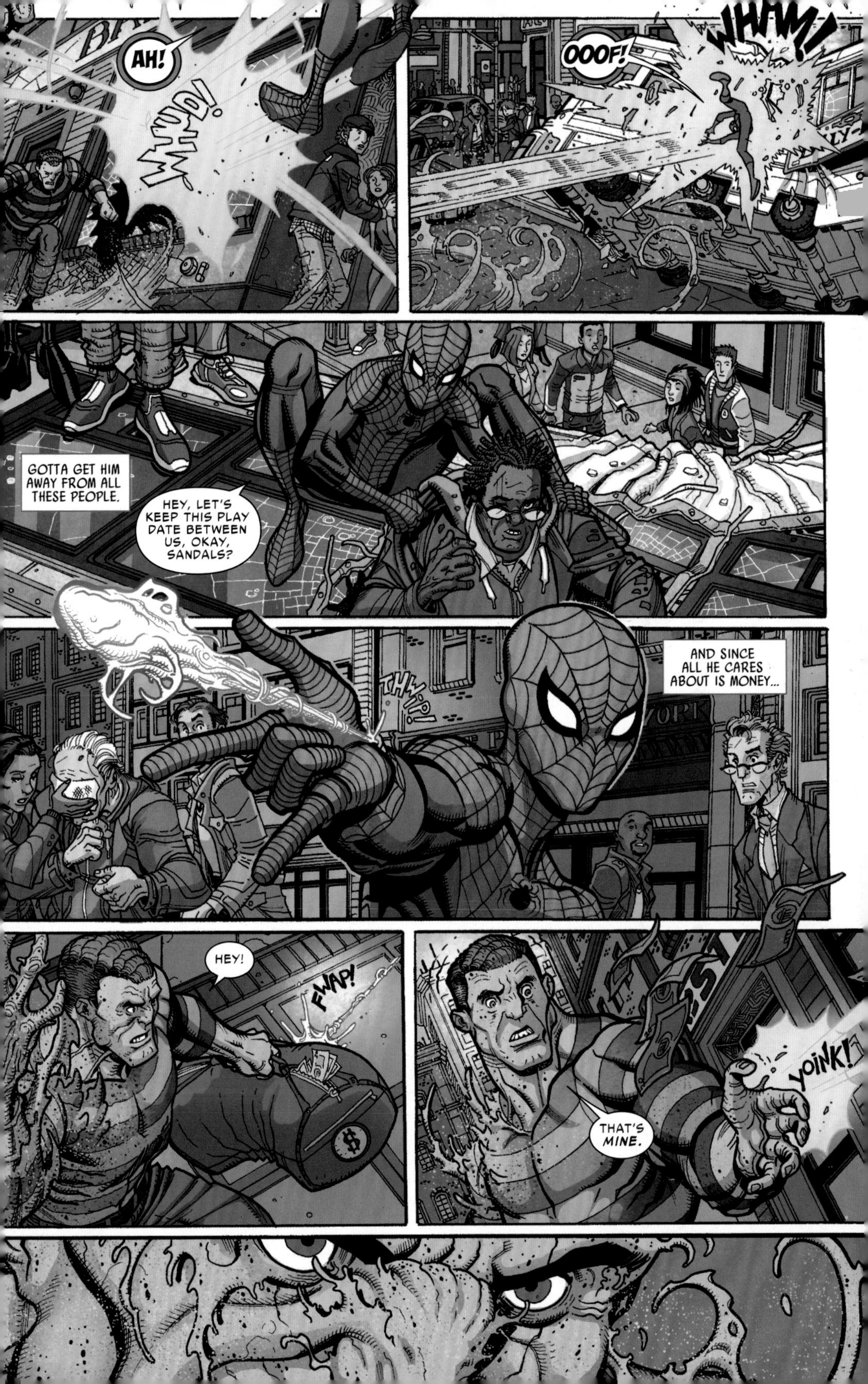

AH!
WHUD!
OOOF!
WHAM!
GOTTA GET HIM AWAY FROM ALL THESE PEOPLE.
HEY, LET'S KEEP THIS PLAY DATE BETWEEN US, OKAY, SANDALS?
AND SINCE ALL HE CARES ABOUT IS MONEY...
THWIP!
HEY!
FWAP!
THAT'S MINE.
YOINK!

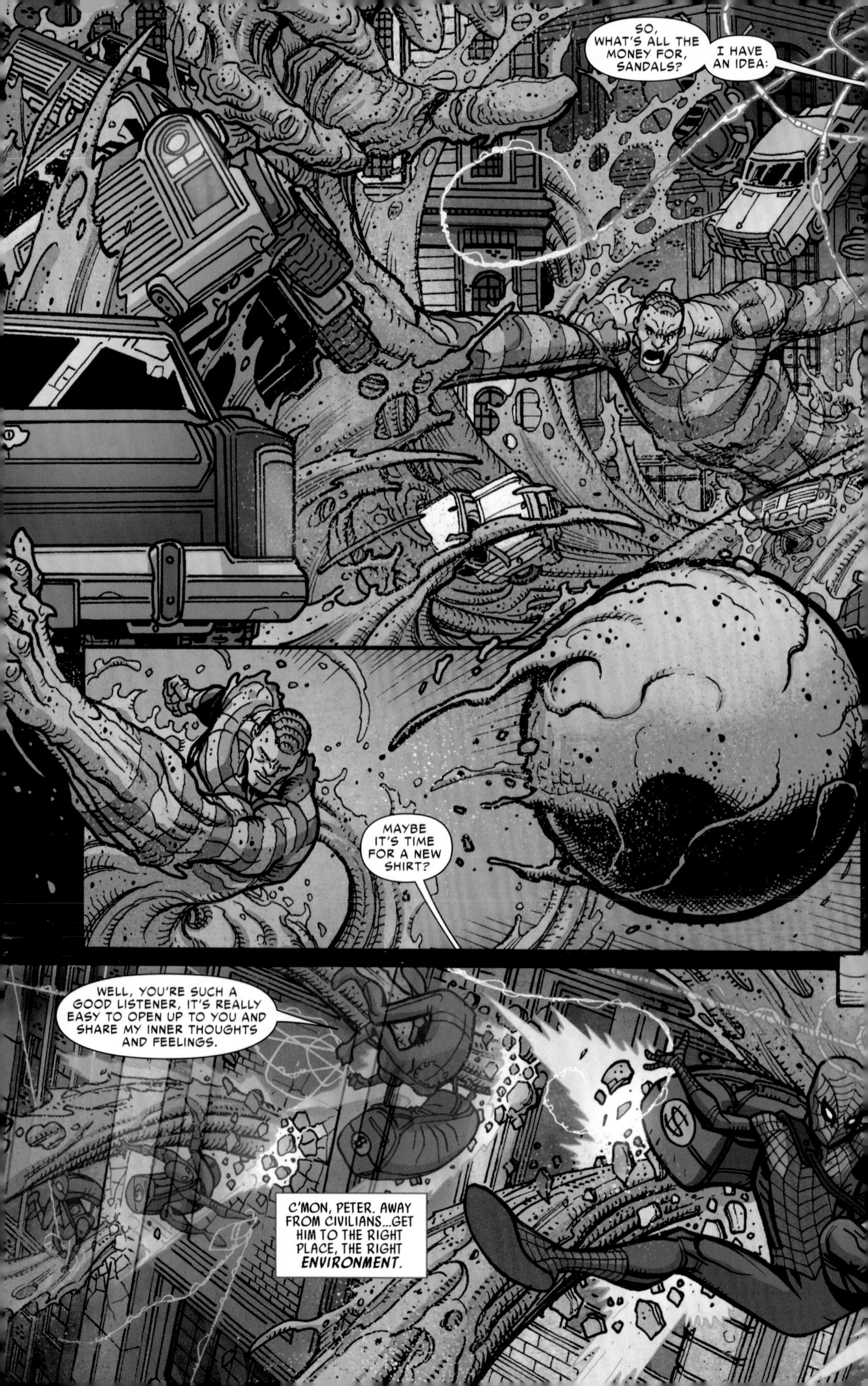
SO, WHAT'S ALL THE MONEY FOR, SANDALS?
I HAVE AN IDEA:
MAYBE IT'S TIME FOR A NEW SHIRT?
WELL, YOU'RE SUCH A GOOD LISTENER, IT'S REALLY EASY TO OPEN UP TO YOU AND SHARE MY INNER THOUGHTS AND FEELINGS.
C'MON, PETER. AWAY FROM CIVILIANS...GET HIM TO THE RIGHT PLACE, THE RIGHT ENVIRONMENT.

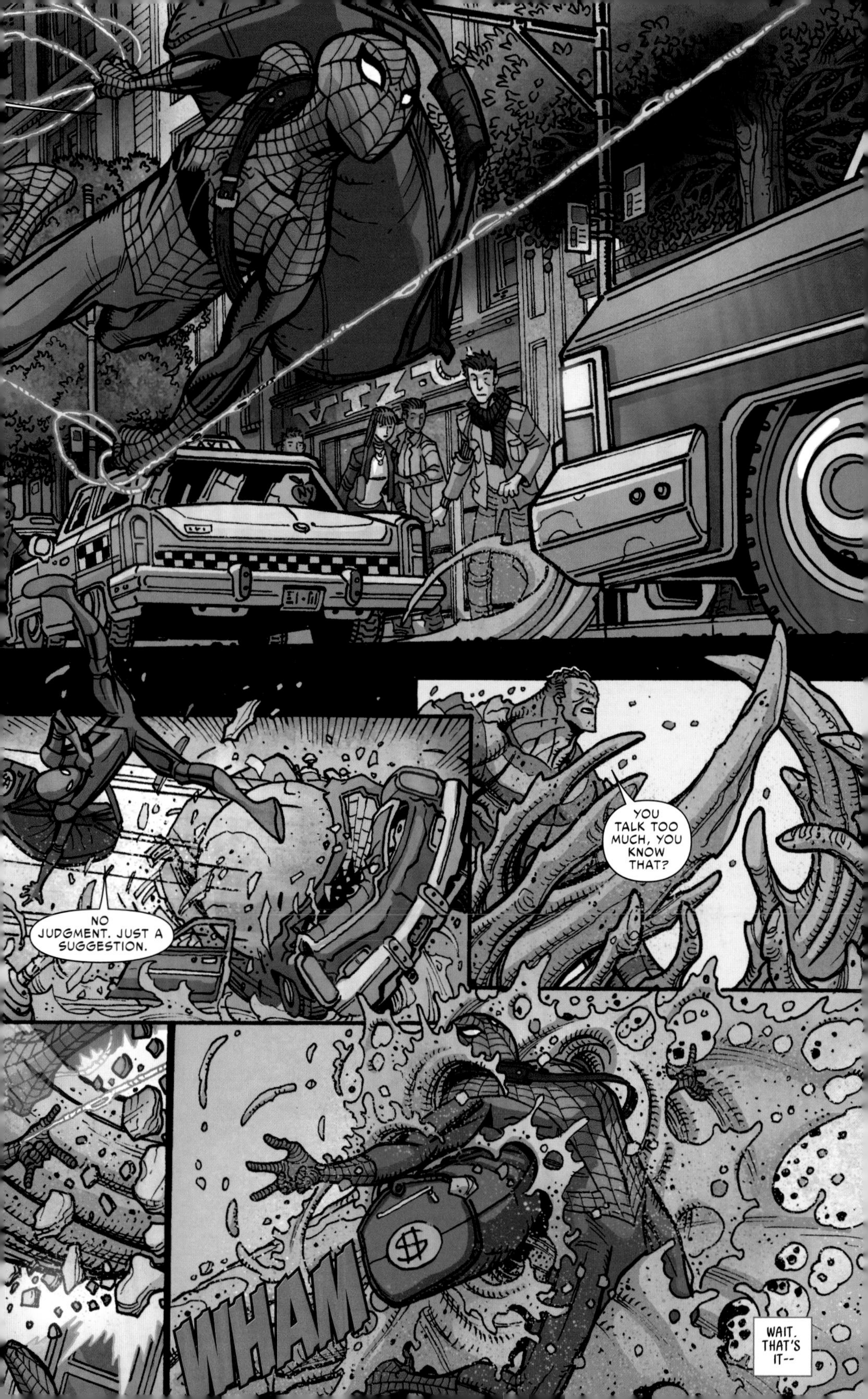
NO JUDGMENT. JUST A SUGGESTION.
YOU TALK TOO MUCH, YOU KNOW THAT?
WHAM
WAIT. THAT'S IT--

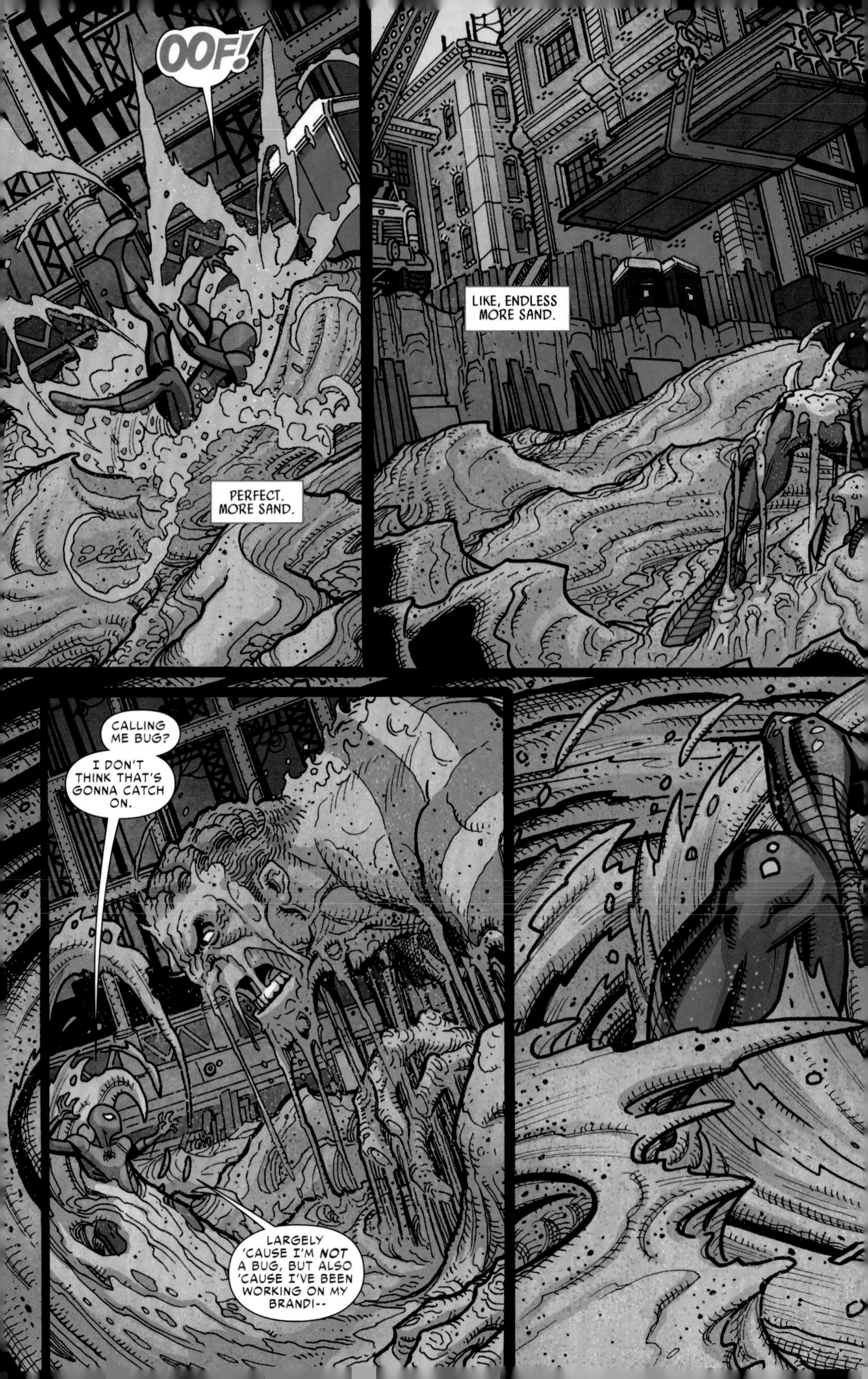
OOF!
PERFECT. MORE SAND.
LIKE, ENDLESS MORE SAND.
CALLING ME BUG?
I DON'T THINK THAT'S GONNA CATCH ON.
LARGELY 'CAUSE I'M NOT A BUG, BUT ALSO 'CAUSE I'VE BEEN WORKING ON MY BRANDI--

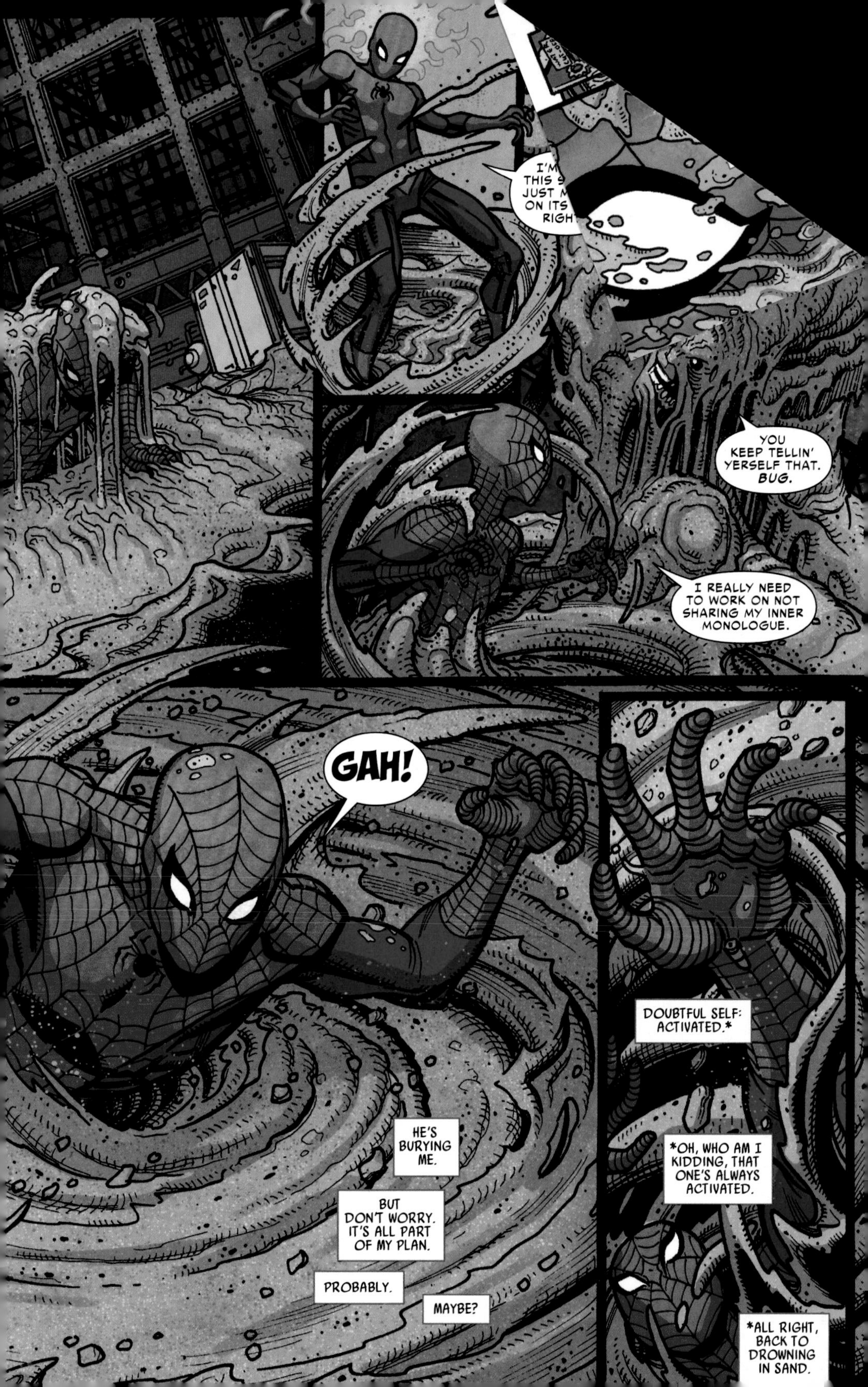
YOU KEEP TELLIN' YERSELF THAT. BUG.
I REALLY NEED TO WORK ON NOT SHARING MY INNER MONOLOGUE.
GAH!
HE'S BURYING ME.
BUT DON'T WORRY. IT'S ALL PART OF MY PLAN.
PROBABLY.
MAYBE?
DOUBTFUL SELF: ACTIVATED.*
*OH, WHO AM I KIDDING, THAT ONE'S ALWAYS ACTIVATED.
*ALL RIGHT, BACK TO DROWNING IN SAND.

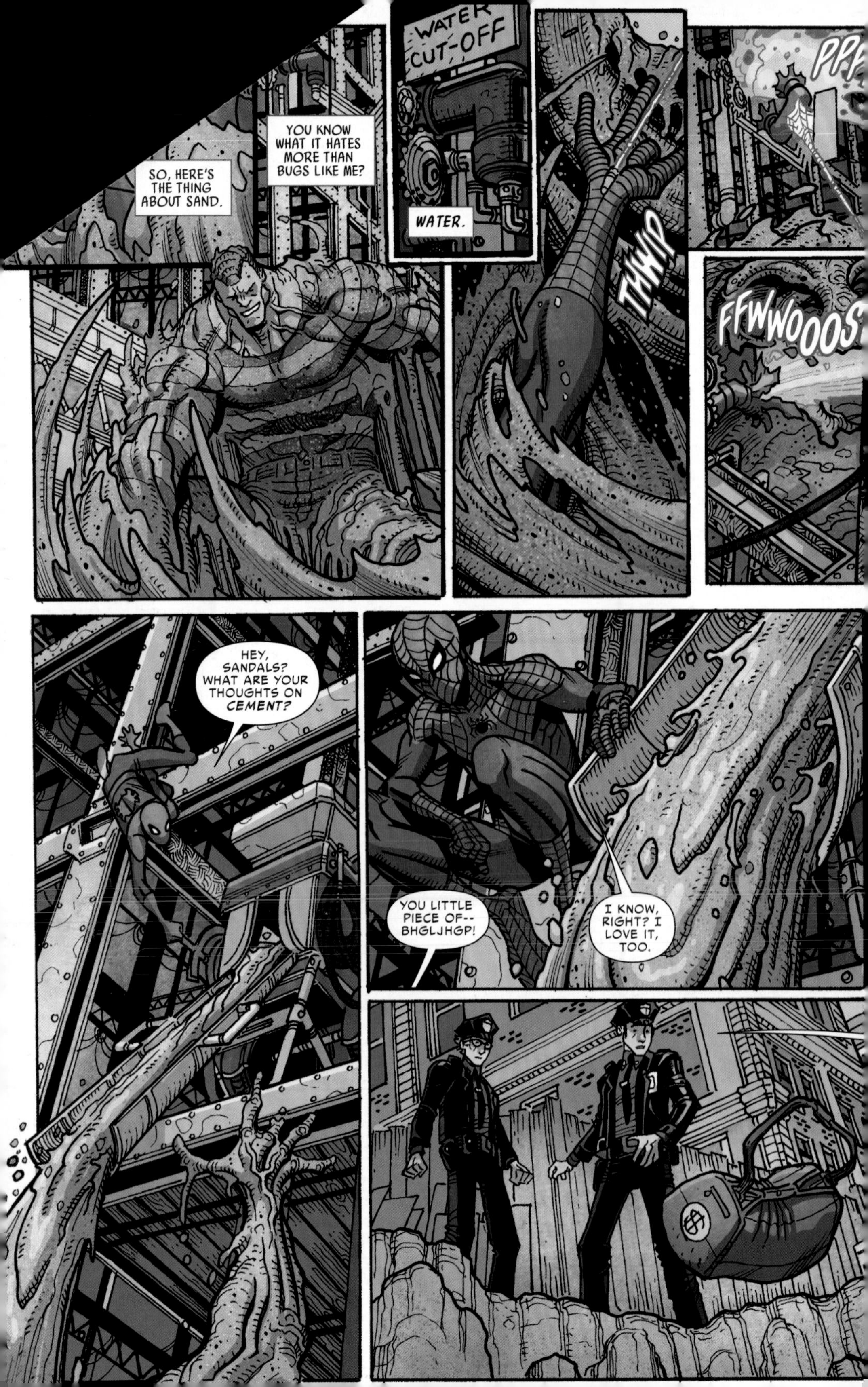
SO, HERE'S THE THING ABOUT SAND.
YOU KNOW WHAT IT HATES MORE THAN BUGS LIKE ME?
WATER CUT-OFF
WATER.
THWIP
FFWWOOOS
HEY, SANDALS? WHAT ARE YOUR THOUGHTS ON CEMENT?
YOU LITTLE PIECE OF-- BHGLJHGP!
I KNOW, RIGHT? I LOVE IT, TOO.

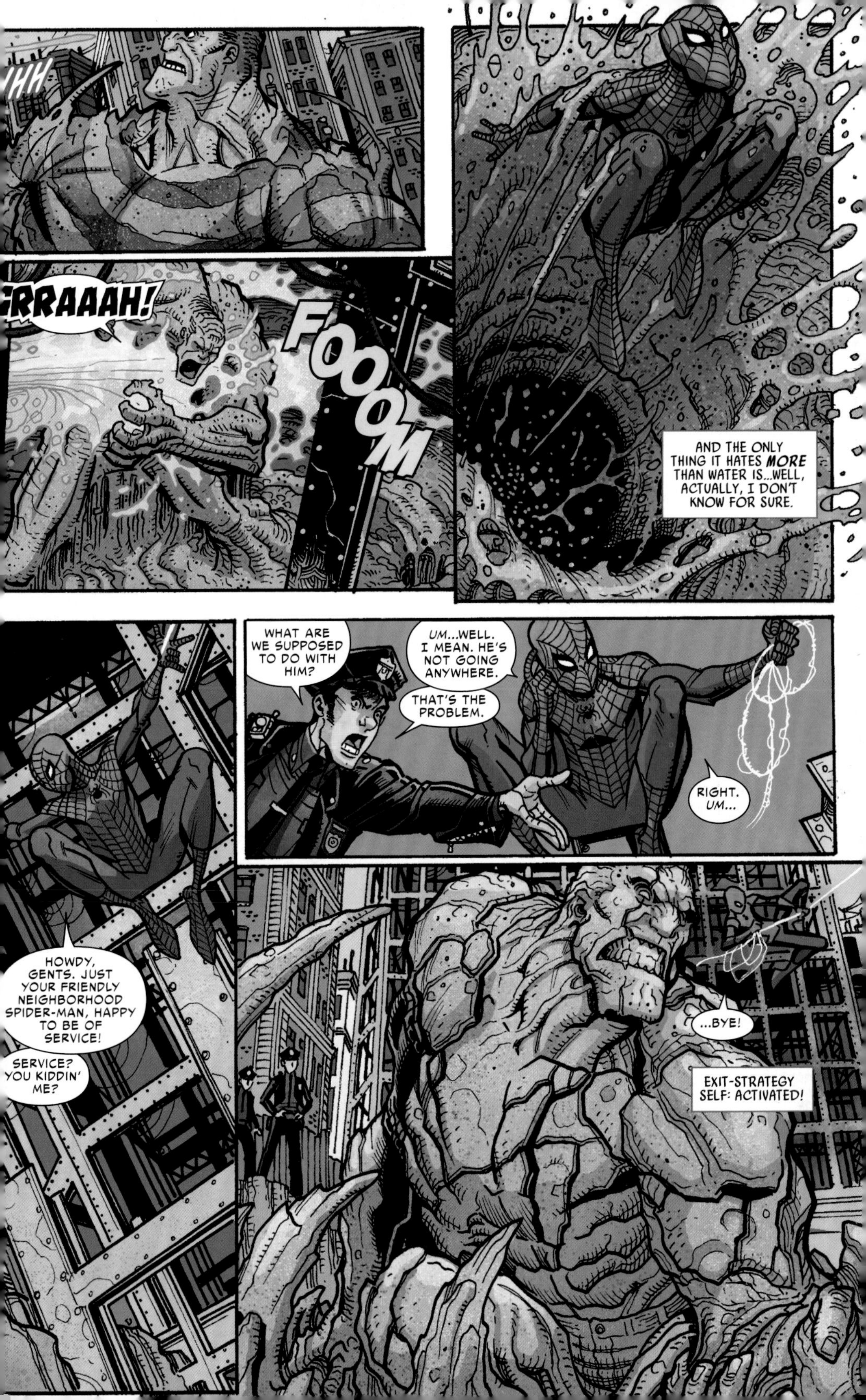

HHH
RRAAAH!
FOOOOM
AND THE ONLY THING IT HATES *MORE* THAN WATER IS...WELL, ACTUALLY, I DON'T KNOW FOR SURE.
HOWDY, GENTS. JUST YOUR FRIENDLY NEIGHBORHOOD SPIDER-MAN, HAPPY TO BE OF SERVICE!
SERVICE? YOU KIDDIN' ME?
WHAT ARE WE SUPPOSED TO DO WITH HIM?
UM...WELL. I MEAN. HE'S NOT GOING ANYWHERE.
THAT'S THE PROBLEM.
RIGHT. UM...
...BYE!
EXIT-STRATEGY SELF: ACTIVATED!

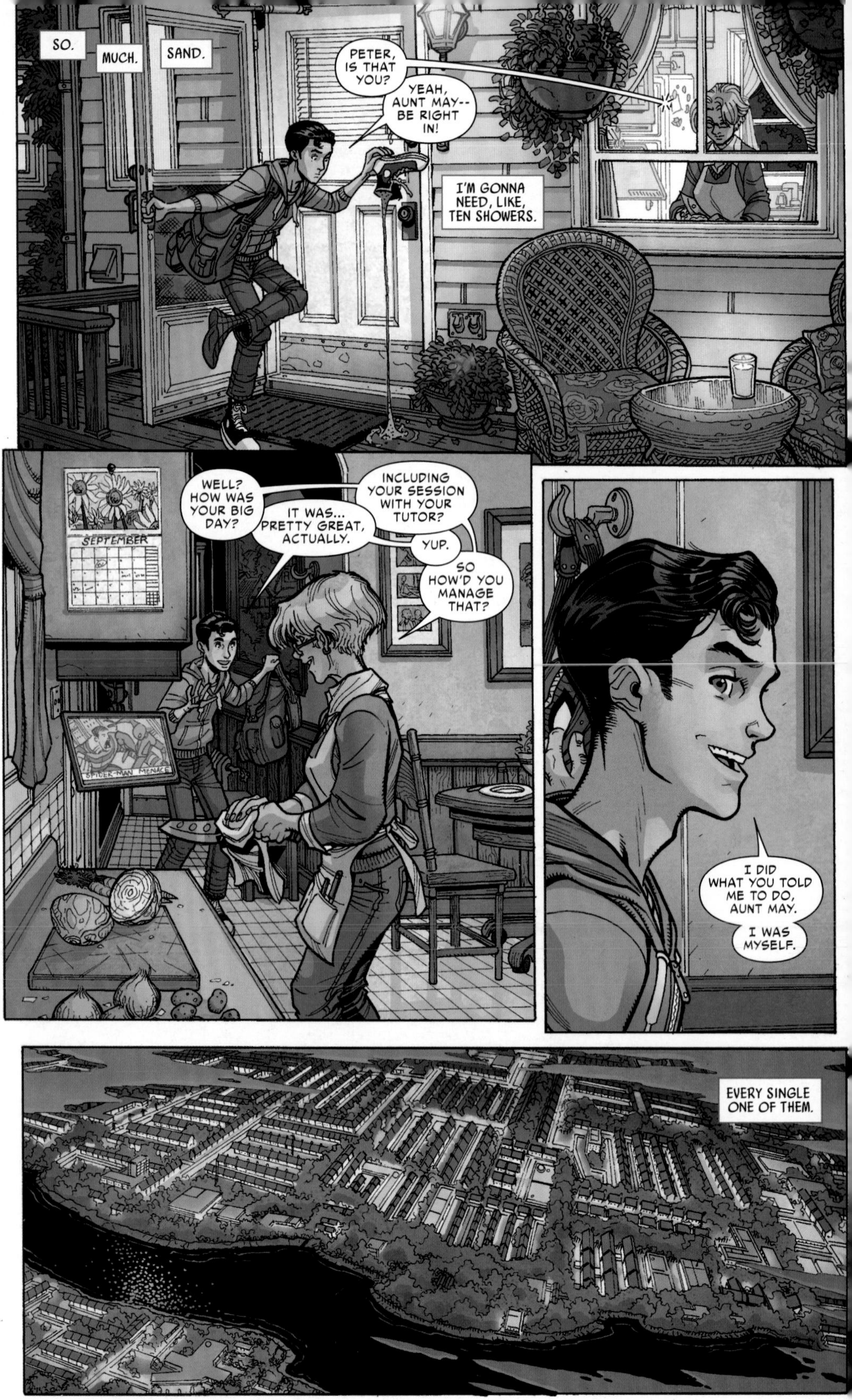
SO.
MUCH.
SAND.
PETER, IS THAT YOU?
YEAH, AUNT MAY-- BE RIGHT IN!
I'M GONNA NEED, LIKE, TEN SHOWERS.
WELL? HOW WAS YOUR BIG DAY?
IT WAS... PRETTY GREAT, ACTUALLY.
INCLUDING YOUR SESSION WITH YOUR TUTOR?
YUP.
SO HOW'D YOU MANAGE THAT?
SEPTEMBER
SPIDER-MAN MENACE
I DID WHAT YOU TOLD ME TO DO, AUNT MAY.
I WAS MYSELF.
EVERY SINGLE ONE OF THEM.

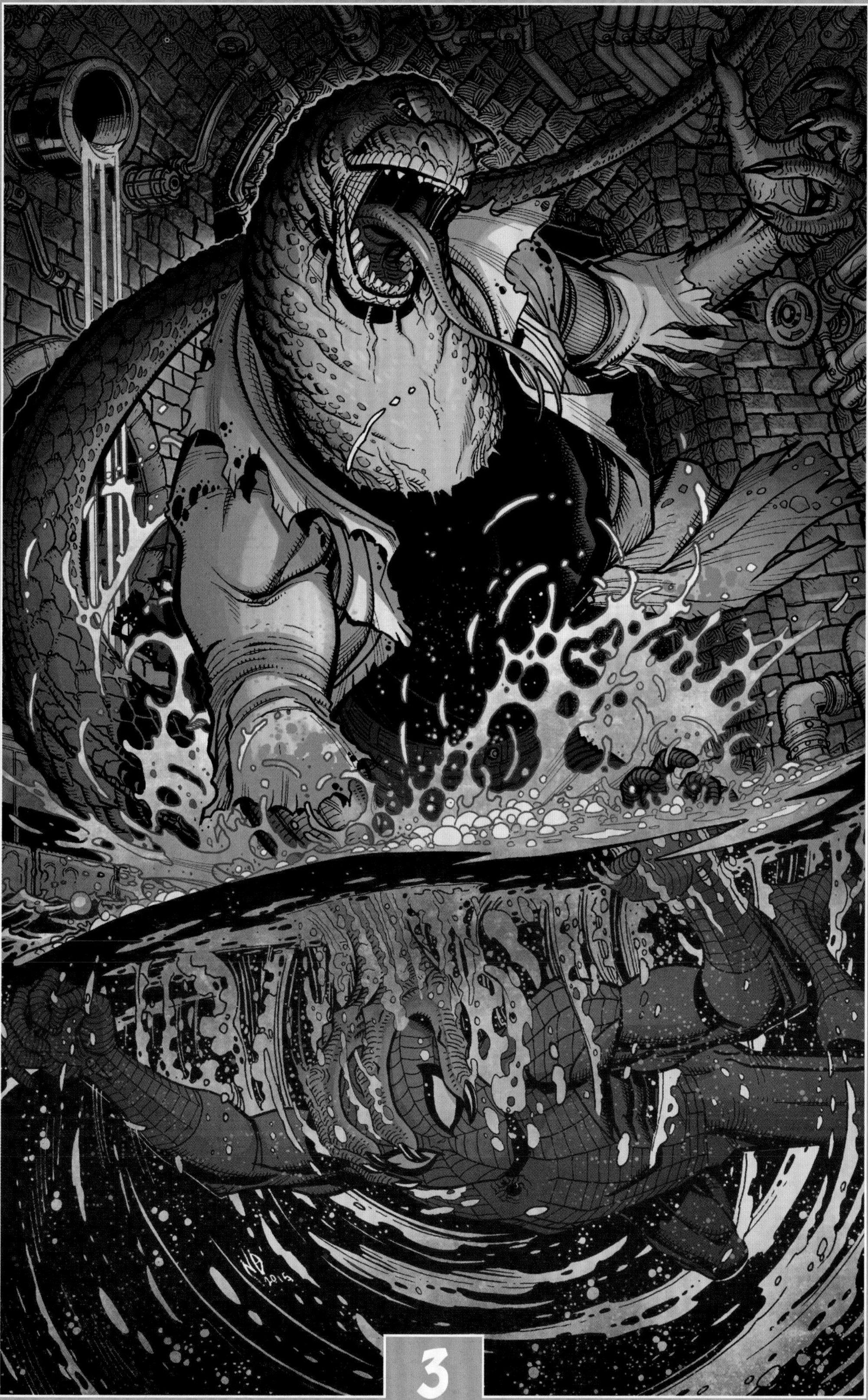

3

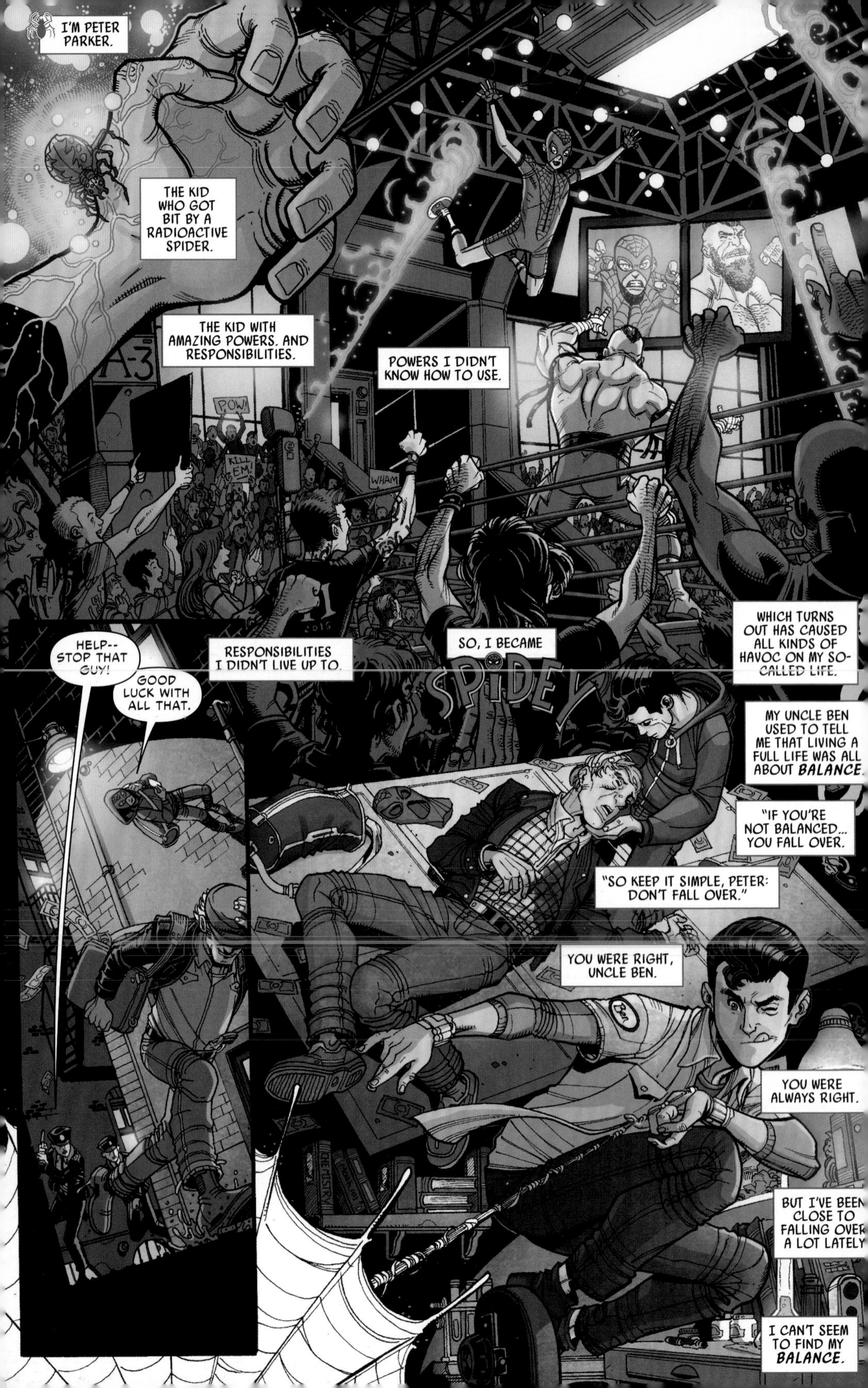
I'M PETER PARKER.
THE KID WHO GOT BIT BY A RADIOACTIVE SPIDER.
THE KID WITH AMAZING POWERS. AND RESPONSIBILITIES.
POWERS I DIDN'T KNOW HOW TO USE.
POW!
KILL 'EM!
WHAM
RESPONSIBILITIES I DIDN'T LIVE UP TO.
SO, I BECAME
SPIDEY
WHICH TURNS OUT HAS CAUSED ALL KINDS OF HAVOC ON MY SO-CALLED LIFE.
HELP--STOP THAT GUY!
GOOD LUCK WITH ALL THAT.
MY UNCLE BEN USED TO TELL ME THAT LIVING A FULL LIFE WAS ALL ABOUT *BALANCE*.
"IF YOU'RE NOT BALANCED... YOU FALL OVER.
"SO KEEP IT SIMPLE, PETER: DON'T FALL OVER."
YOU WERE RIGHT, UNCLE BEN.
YOU WERE ALWAYS RIGHT.
BUT I'VE BEEN CLOSE TO FALLING OVER A LOT LATELY
I CAN'T SEEM TO FIND MY *BALANCE*.

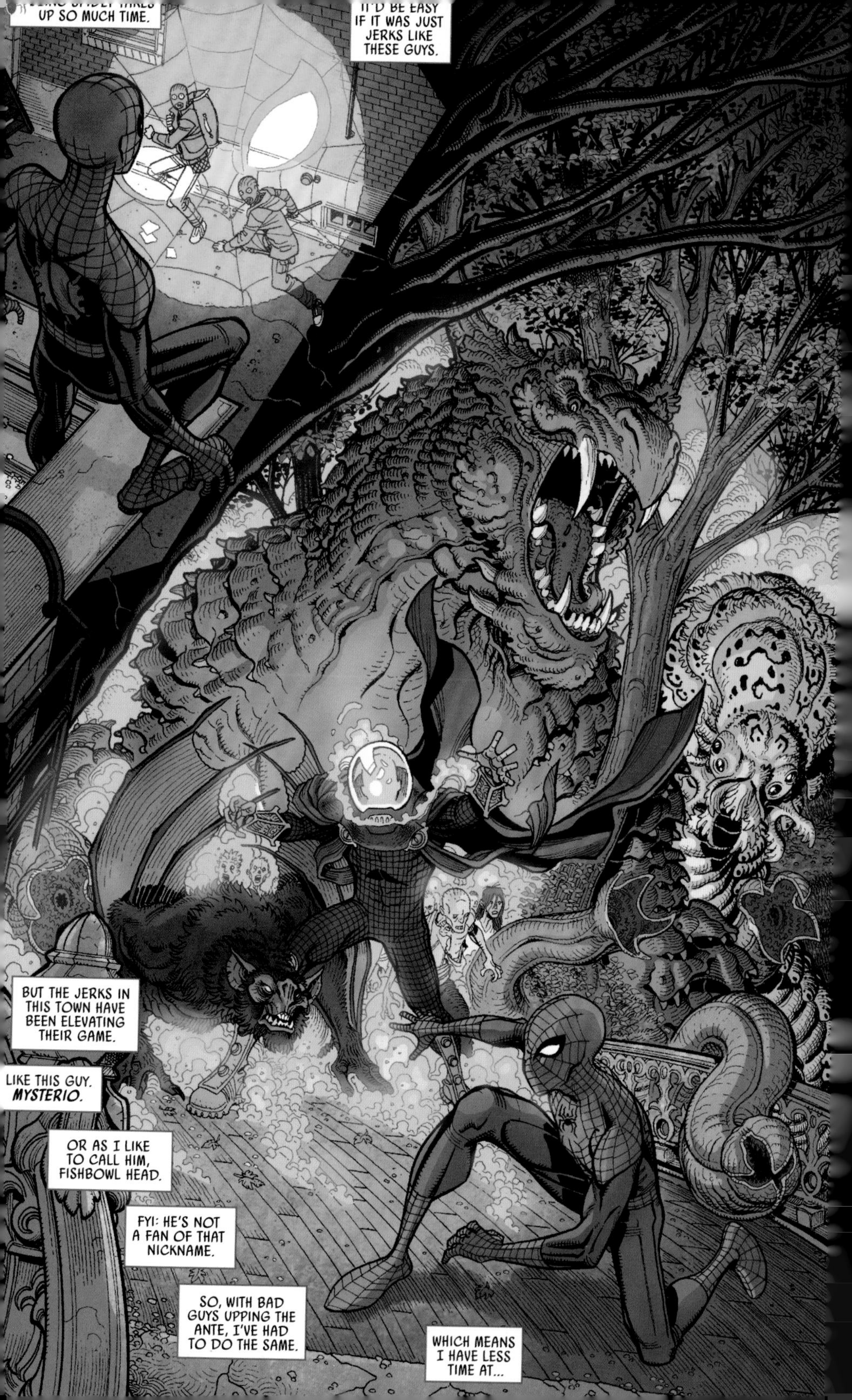
UP SO MUCH TIME.
IT'D BE EASY IF IT WAS JUST JERKS LIKE THESE GUYS.
BUT THE JERKS IN THIS TOWN HAVE BEEN ELEVATING THEIR GAME.
LIKE THIS GUY. *MYSTERIO.*
OR AS I LIKE TO CALL HIM, FISHBOWL HEAD.
FYI: HE'S NOT A FAN OF THAT NICKNAME.
SO, WITH BAD GUYS UPPING THE ANTE, I'VE HAD TO DO THE SAME.
WHICH MEANS I HAVE LESS TIME AT...

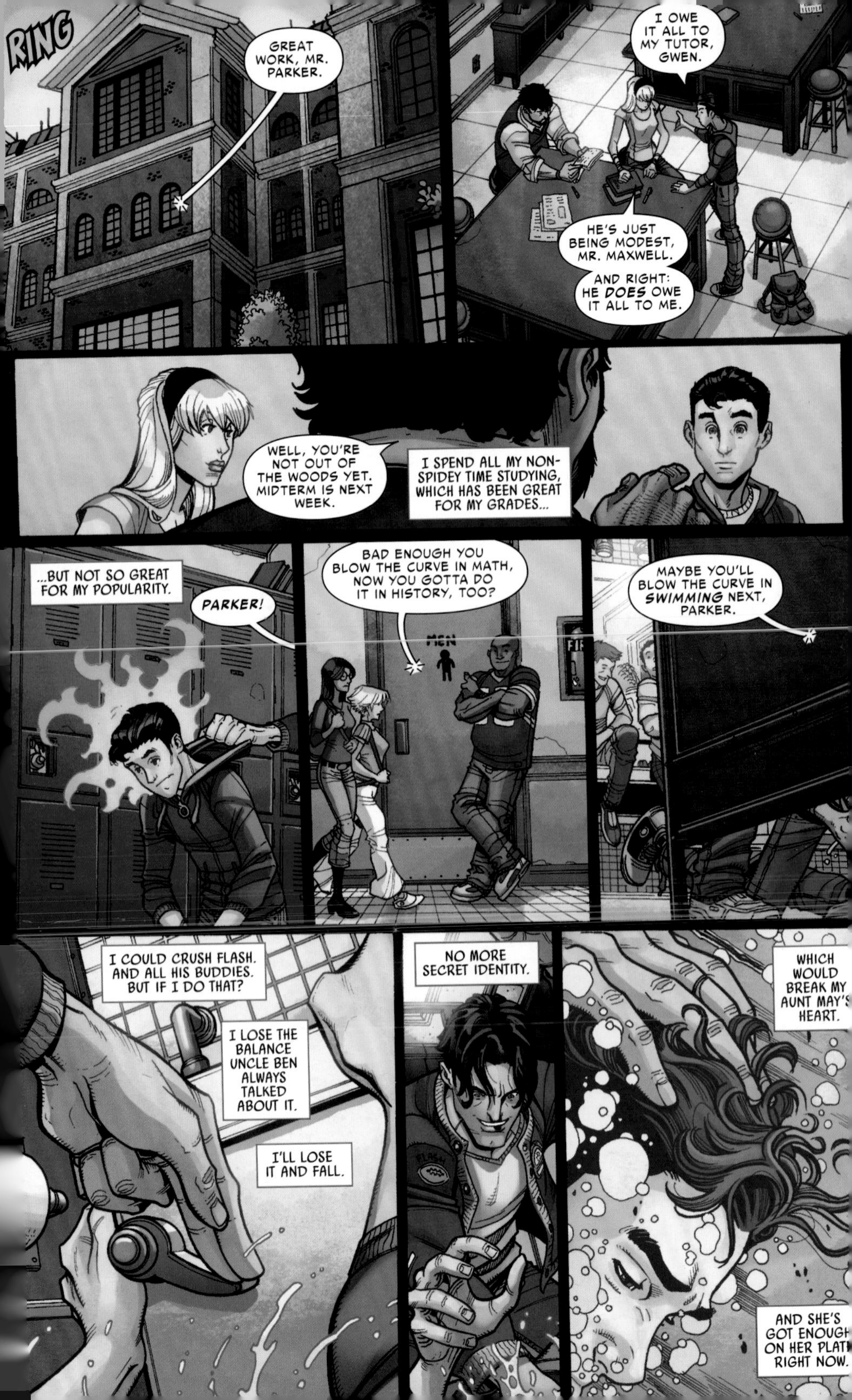
RING
GREAT WORK, MR. PARKER.
I OWE IT ALL TO MY TUTOR, GWEN.
HE'S JUST BEING MODEST, MR. MAXWELL.
AND RIGHT: HE DOES OWE IT ALL TO ME.
WELL, YOU'RE NOT OUT OF THE WOODS YET. MIDTERM IS NEXT WEEK.
I SPEND ALL MY NON-SPIDEY TIME STUDYING, WHICH HAS BEEN GREAT FOR MY GRADES...
...BUT NOT SO GREAT FOR MY POPULARITY.
PARKER!
BAD ENOUGH YOU BLOW THE CURVE IN MATH, NOW YOU GOTTA DO IT IN HISTORY, TOO?
MEN
MAYBE YOU'LL BLOW THE CURVE IN SWIMMING NEXT, PARKER.
I COULD CRUSH FLASH. AND ALL HIS BUDDIES. BUT IF I DO THAT?
I LOSE THE BALANCE UNCLE BEN ALWAYS TALKED ABOUT IT.
I'LL LOSE IT AND FALL.
NO MORE SECRET IDENTITY.
FLASH
WHICH WOULD BREAK MY AUNT MAY'S HEART.
AND SHE'S GOT ENOUGH ON HER PLAT RIGHT NOW.

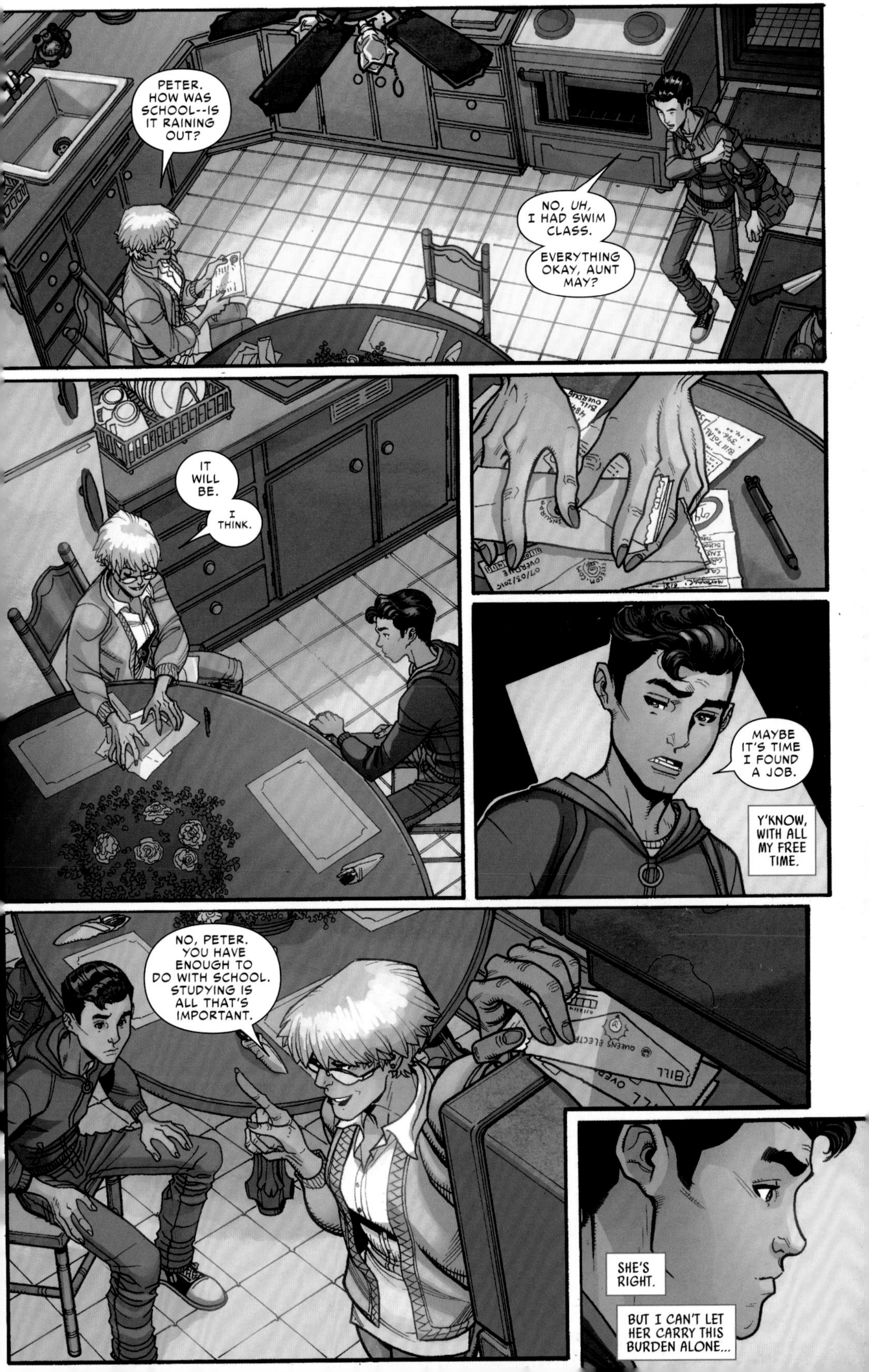
PETER. HOW WAS SCHOOL--IS IT RAINING OUT?
NO, *UH,* I HAD SWIM CLASS.
EVERYTHING OKAY, AUNT MAY?
IT WILL BE.
I THINK.
MAYBE IT'S TIME I FOUND A JOB.
Y'KNOW, WITH ALL MY FREE TIME.
NO, PETER. YOU HAVE ENOUGH TO DO WITH SCHOOL. STUDYING IS ALL THAT'S IMPORTANT.
SHE'S RIGHT.
BUT I CAN'T LET HER CARRY THIS BURDEN ALONE...

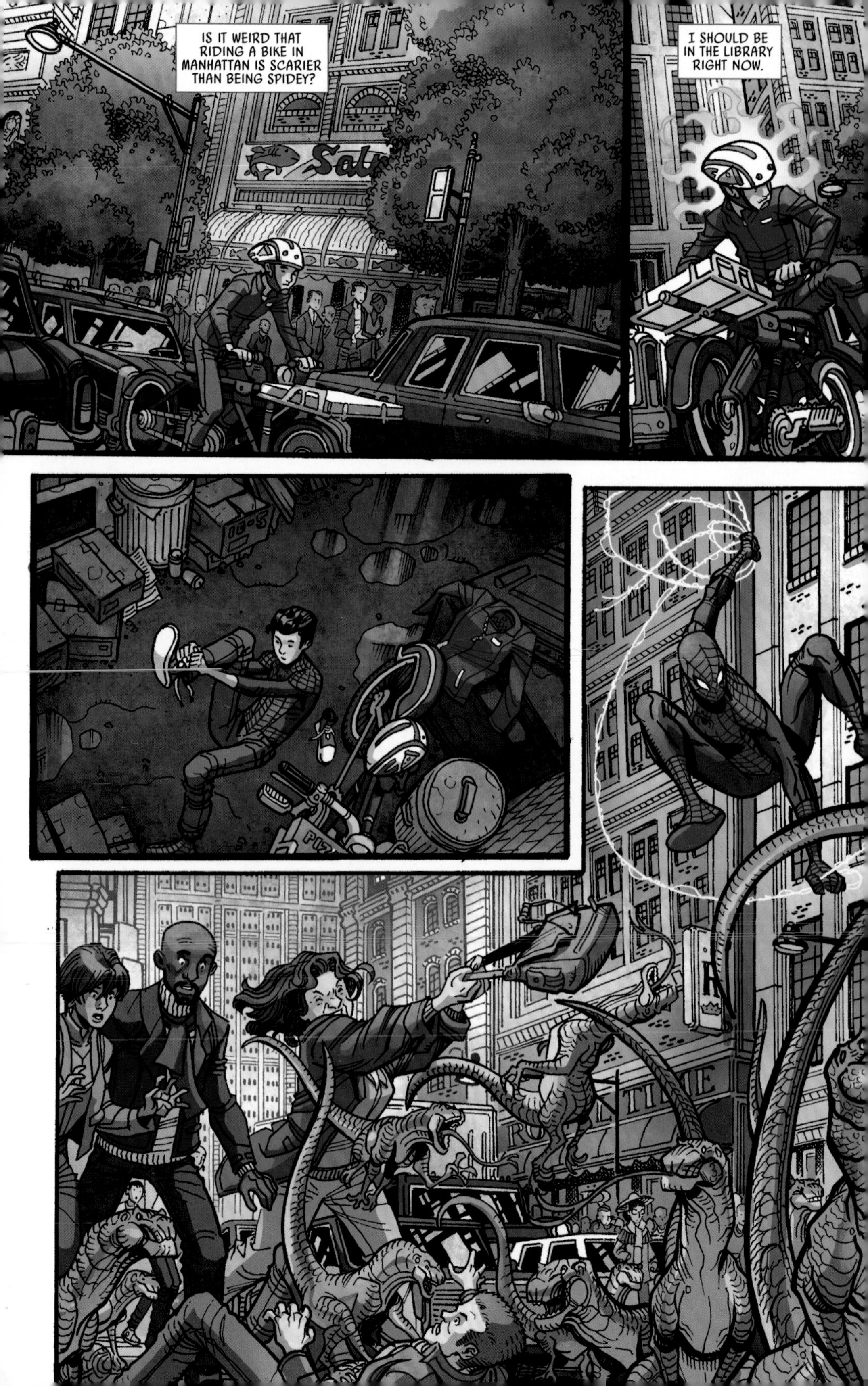
IS IT WEIRD THAT RIDING A BIKE IN MANHATTAN IS SCARIER THAN BEING SPIDEY?
I SHOULD BE IN THE LIBRARY RIGHT NOW.

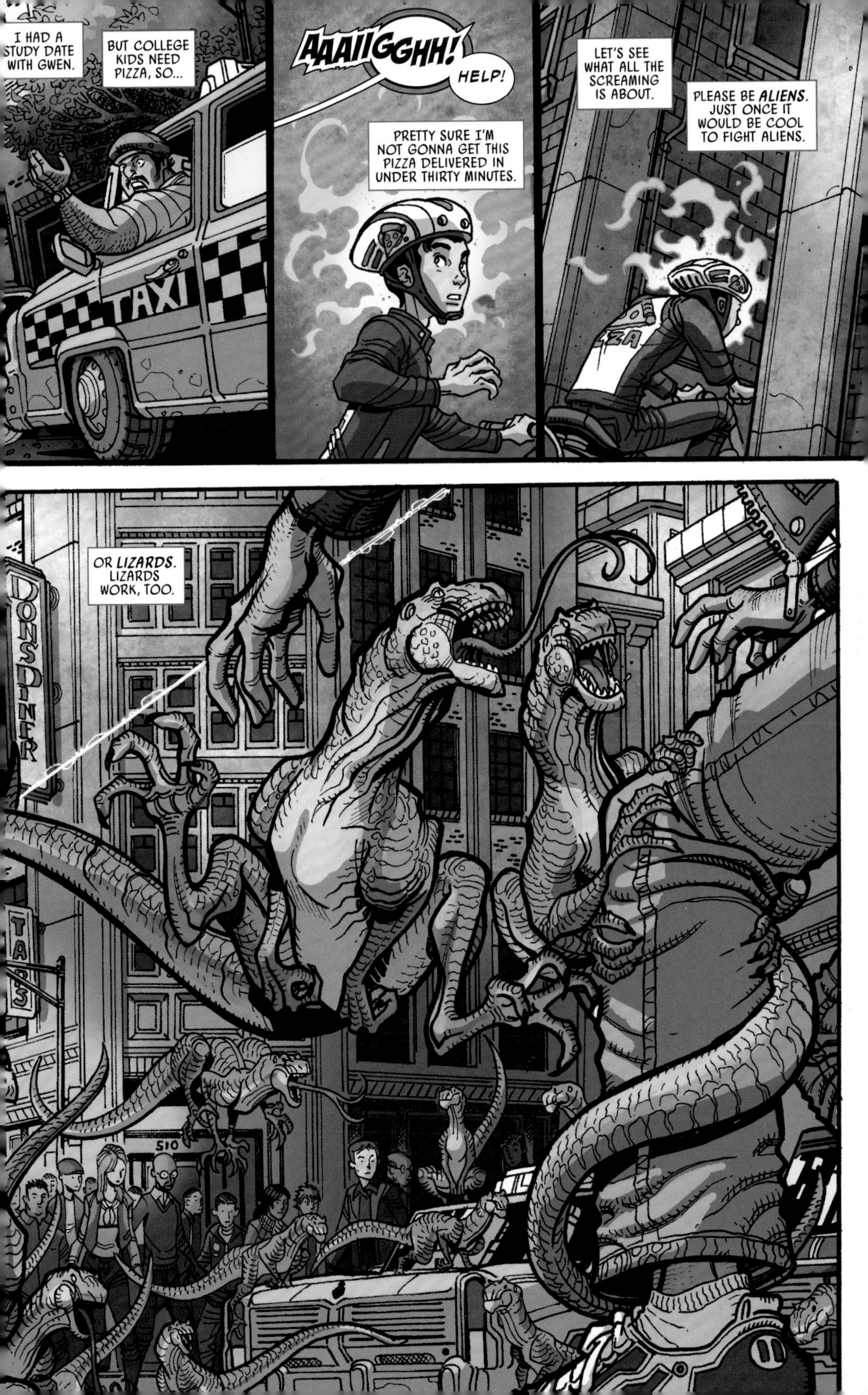
I HAD A STUDY DATE WITH GWEN.
BUT COLLEGE KIDS NEED PIZZA, SO...
TAXI
AAAIIGGHH!
HELP!
PRETTY SURE I'M NOT GONNA GET THIS PIZZA DELIVERED IN UNDER THIRTY MINUTES.
LET'S SEE WHAT ALL THE SCREAMING IS ABOUT.
PLEASE BE ALIENS. JUST ONCE IT WOULD BE COOL TO FIGHT ALIENS.
OR LIZARDS. LIZARDS WORK, TOO.
DONS DINER
510

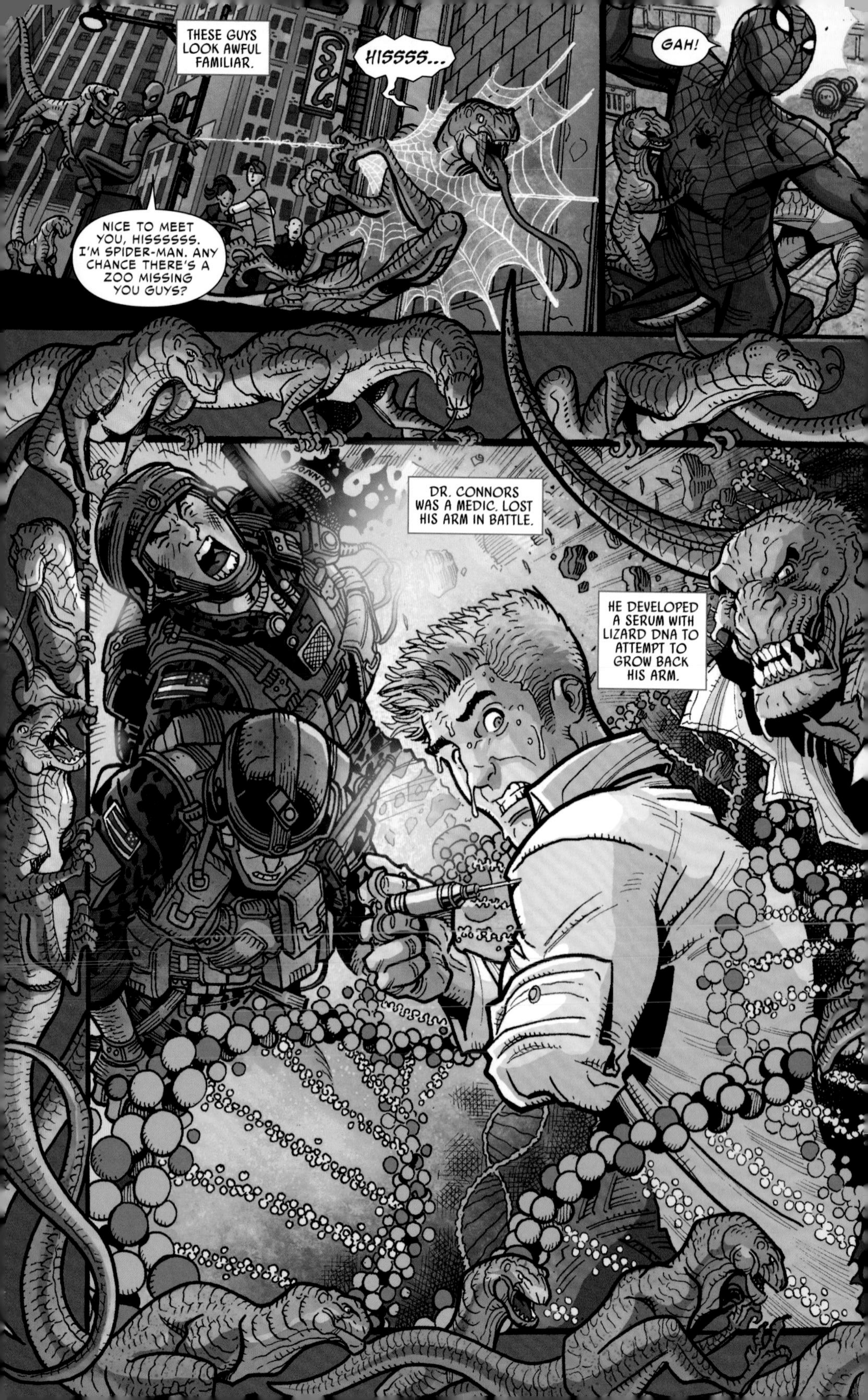
THESE GUYS LOOK AWFUL FAMILIAR.
HISSSS...
NICE TO MEET YOU, HISSSSSS. I'M SPIDER-MAN. ANY CHANCE THERE'S A ZOO MISSING YOU GUYS?
GAH!
DR. CONNORS WAS A MEDIC. LOST HIS ARM IN BATTLE.
HE DEVELOPED A SERUM WITH LIZARD DNA TO ATTEMPT TO GROW BACK HIS ARM.

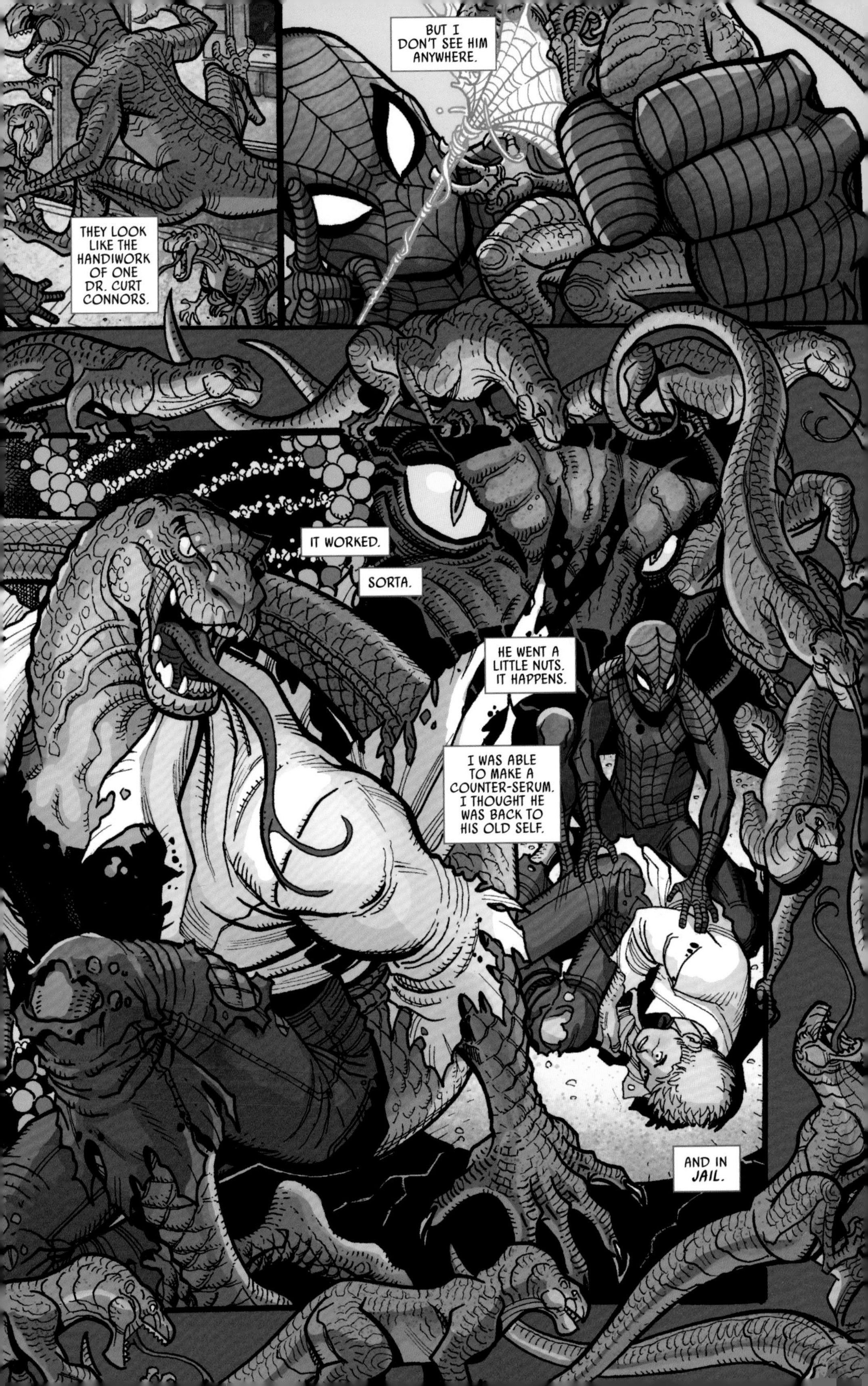
THEY LOOK LIKE THE HANDIWORK OF ONE DR. CURT CONNORS.
BUT I DON'T SEE HIM ANYWHERE.
IT WORKED.
SORTA.
HE WENT A LITTLE NUTS. IT HAPPENS.
I WAS ABLE TO MAKE A COUNTER-SERUM. I THOUGHT HE WAS BACK TO HIS OLD SELF.
AND IN JAIL.

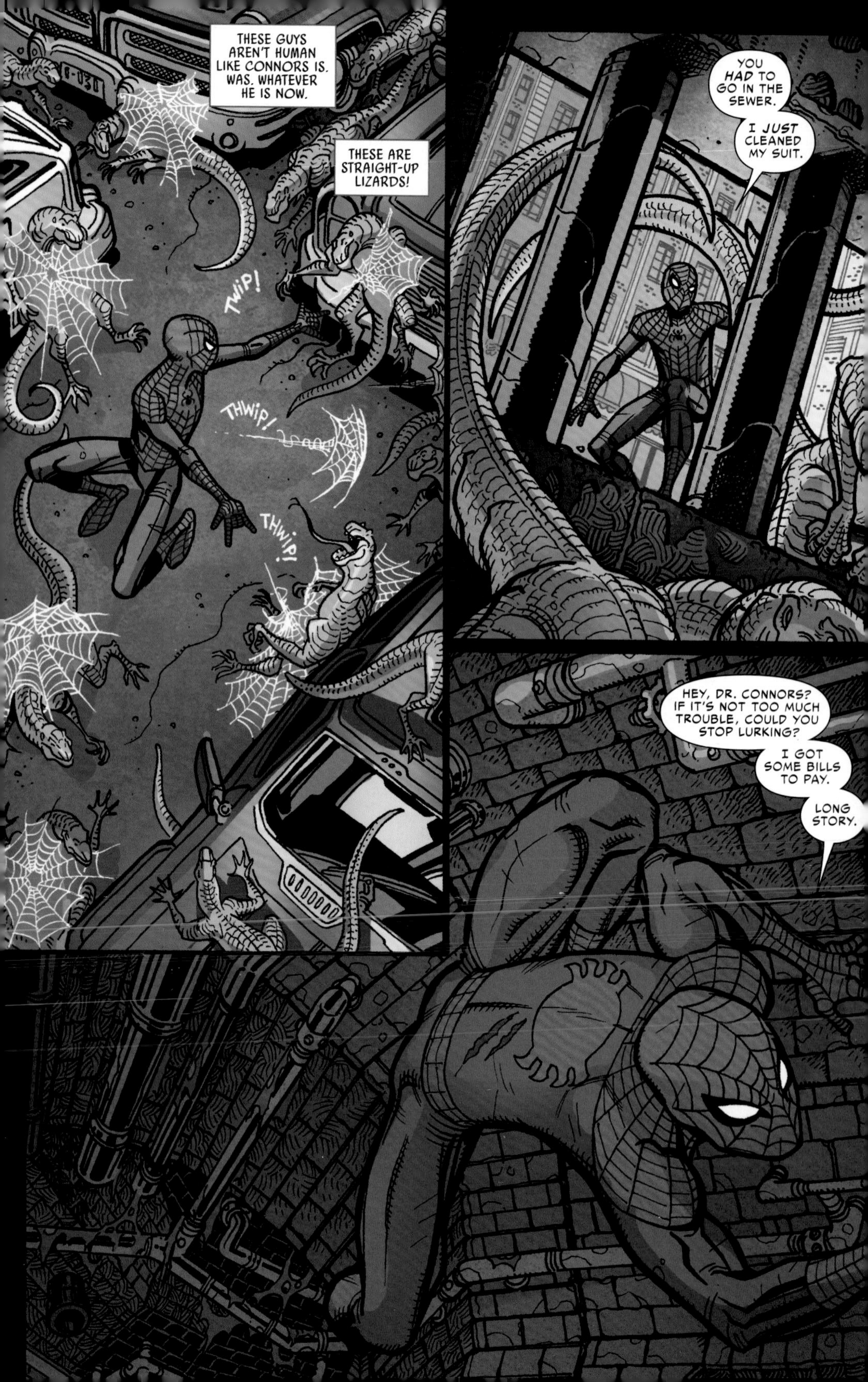
THESE GUYS AREN'T HUMAN LIKE CONNORS IS. WAS. WHATEVER HE IS NOW.
THESE ARE STRAIGHT-UP LIZARDS!
TWIP!
THWIP!
THWIP!
YOU HAD TO GO IN THE SEWER.
I JUST CLEANED MY SUIT.
HEY, DR. CONNORS? IF IT'S NOT TOO MUCH TROUBLE, COULD YOU STOP LURKING?
I GOT SOME BILLS TO PAY.
LONG STORY.

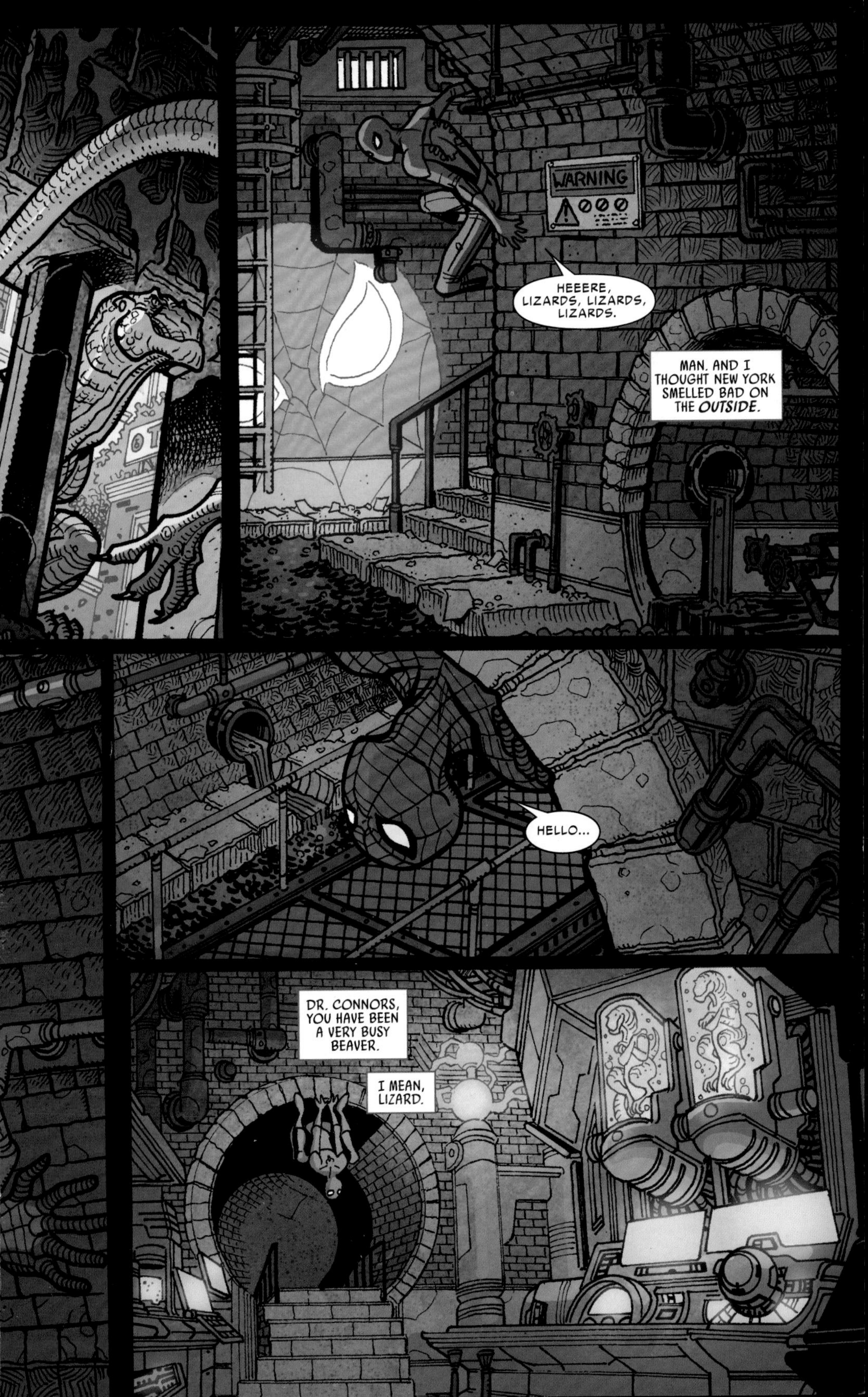
WARNING
HEEERE, LIZARDS, LIZARDS, LIZARDS.
MAN. AND I THOUGHT NEW YORK SMELLED BAD ON THE *OUTSIDE.*
HELLO...
DR. CONNORS, YOU HAVE BEEN A VERY BUSY BEAVER.
I MEAN, LIZARD.

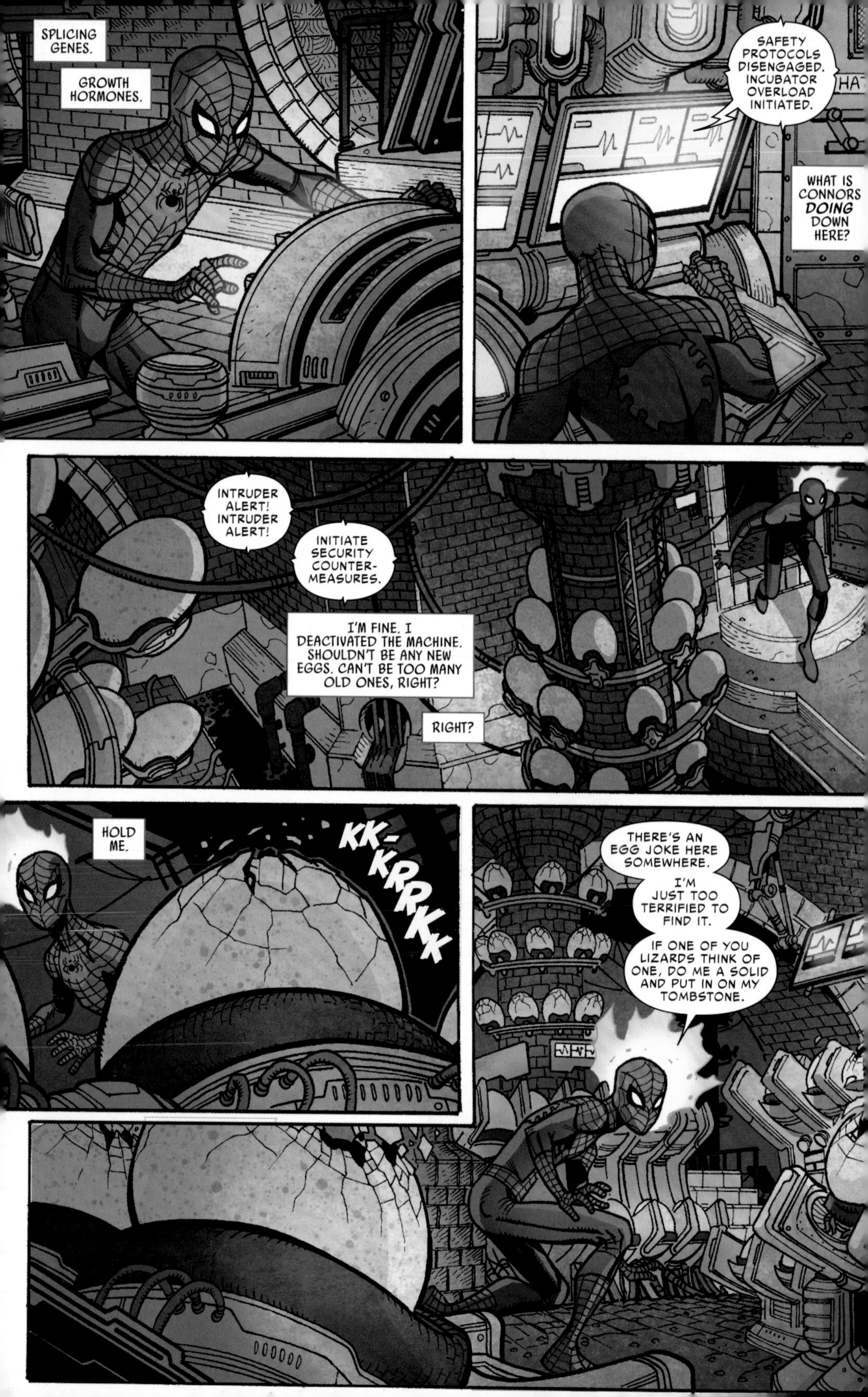
SPLICING GENES.
GROWTH HORMONES.
SAFETY PROTOCOLS DISENGAGED. INCUBATOR OVERLOAD INITIATED.
WHAT IS CONNORS DOING DOWN HERE?
INTRUDER ALERT! INTRUDER ALERT!
INITIATE SECURITY COUNTER-MEASURES.
I'M FINE. I DEACTIVATED THE MACHINE. SHOULDN'T BE ANY NEW EGGS. CAN'T BE TOO MANY OLD ONES, RIGHT?
RIGHT?
HOLD ME.
KK-KRRKK
THERE'S AN EGG JOKE HERE SOMEWHERE.
I'M JUST TOO TERRIFIED TO FIND IT.
IF ONE OF YOU LIZARDS THINK OF ONE, DO ME A SOLID AND PUT IN ON MY TOMBSTONE.

WHATEVER IT IS, IT'S ALL KINDS OF BAD.

SO, LET'S JUST POWER THIS DOWN AND GET RID OF THESE BAD EGGS (SORRY) BEFORE THEY LEAVE THE NEST.

THERE'S NOT TOO MANY OF THEM.

BUT BETTER TO BE SAFE THAN...

...SORRY.

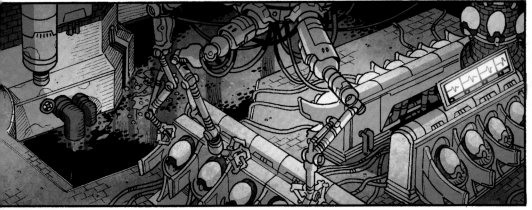

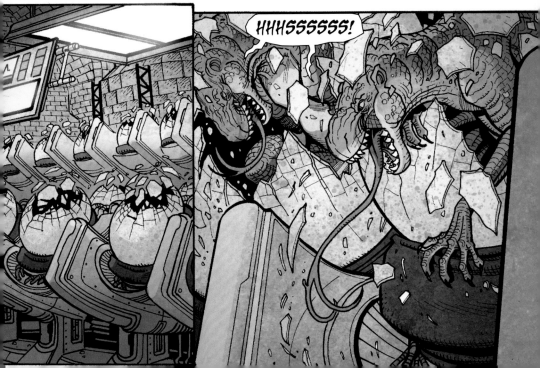

HHHSSSSSS!

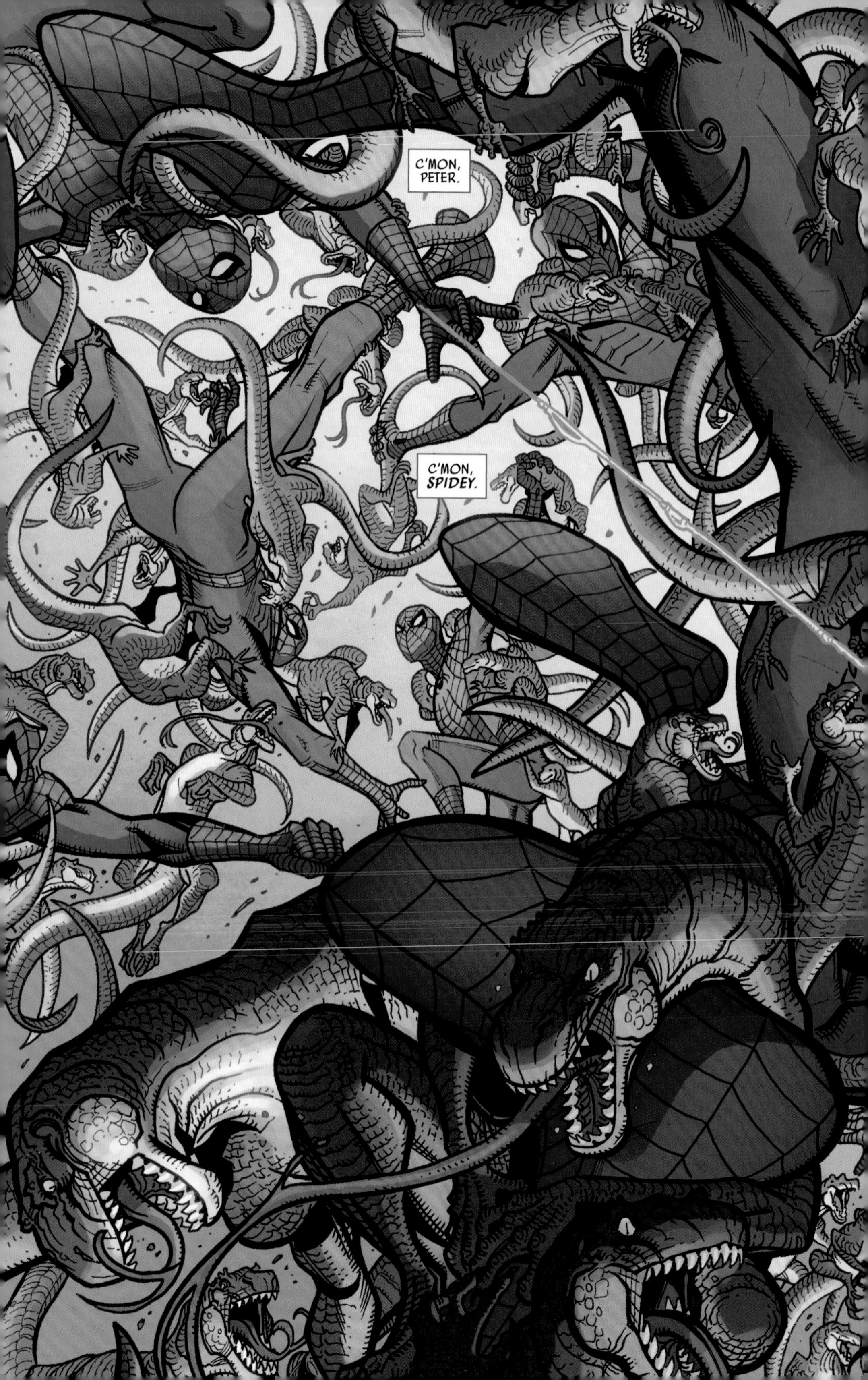
C'MON, PETER.
C'MON, *SPIDEY.*

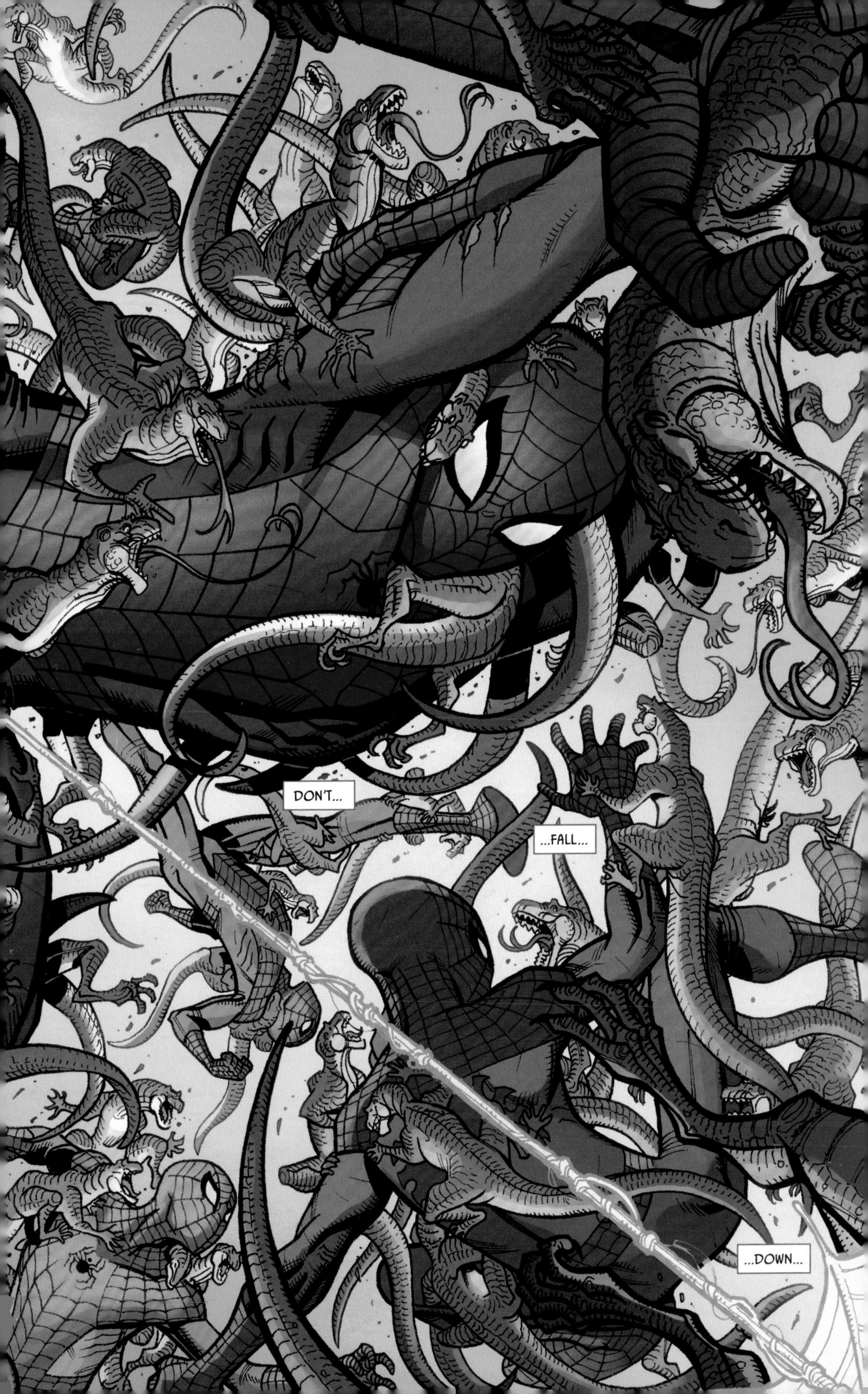
DON'T...
...FALL...
...DOWN...

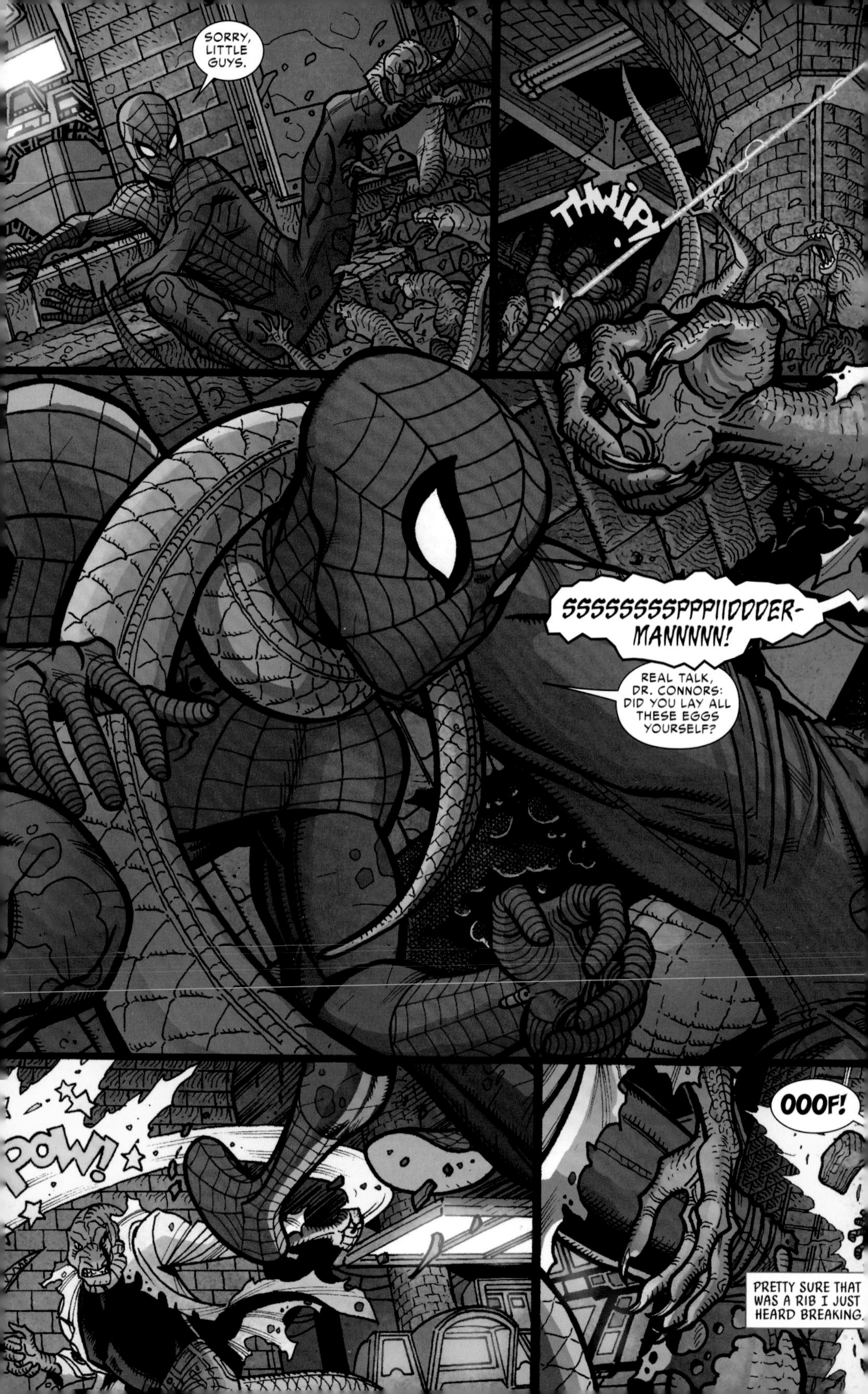
SORRY, LITTLE GUYS.
THWIP!
SSSSSSSSPPPIIDDDER-MANNNNN!
REAL TALK, DR. CONNORS: DID YOU LAY ALL THESE EGGS YOURSELF?
POW!
OOOF!
PRETTY SURE THAT WAS A RIB I JUST HEARD BREAKING.

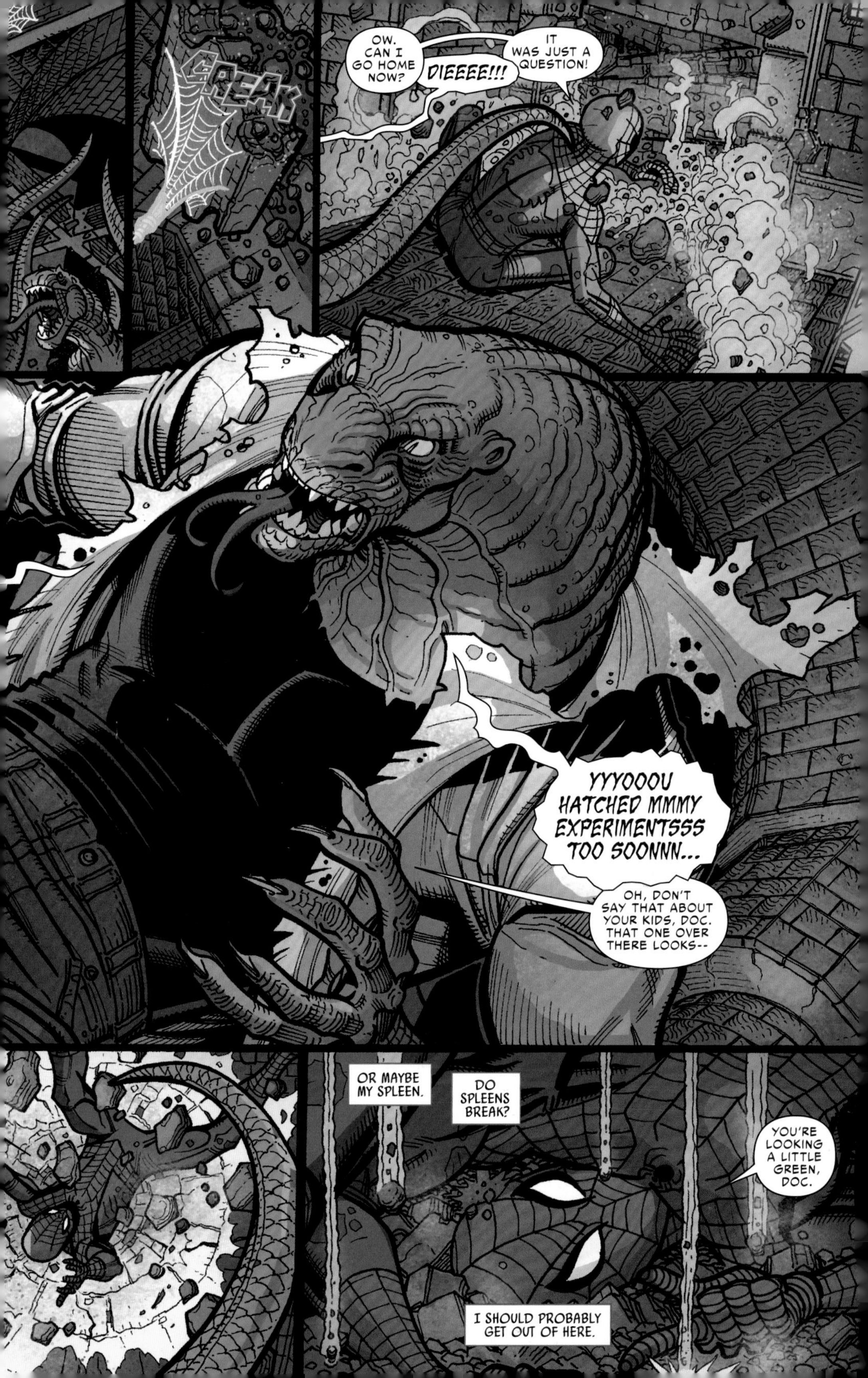
CREAK
OW. CAN I GO HOME NOW?
DIEEEE!!!
IT WAS JUST A QUESTION!
YYYOOOU HATCHED MMMY EXPERIMENTSSS TOO SOONNN...
OH, DON'T SAY THAT ABOUT YOUR KIDS, DOC. THAT ONE OVER THERE LOOKS--
OR MAYBE MY SPLEEN.
DO SPLEENS BREAK?
YOU'RE LOOKING A LITTLE GREEN, DOC.
I SHOULD PROBABLY GET OUT OF HERE.

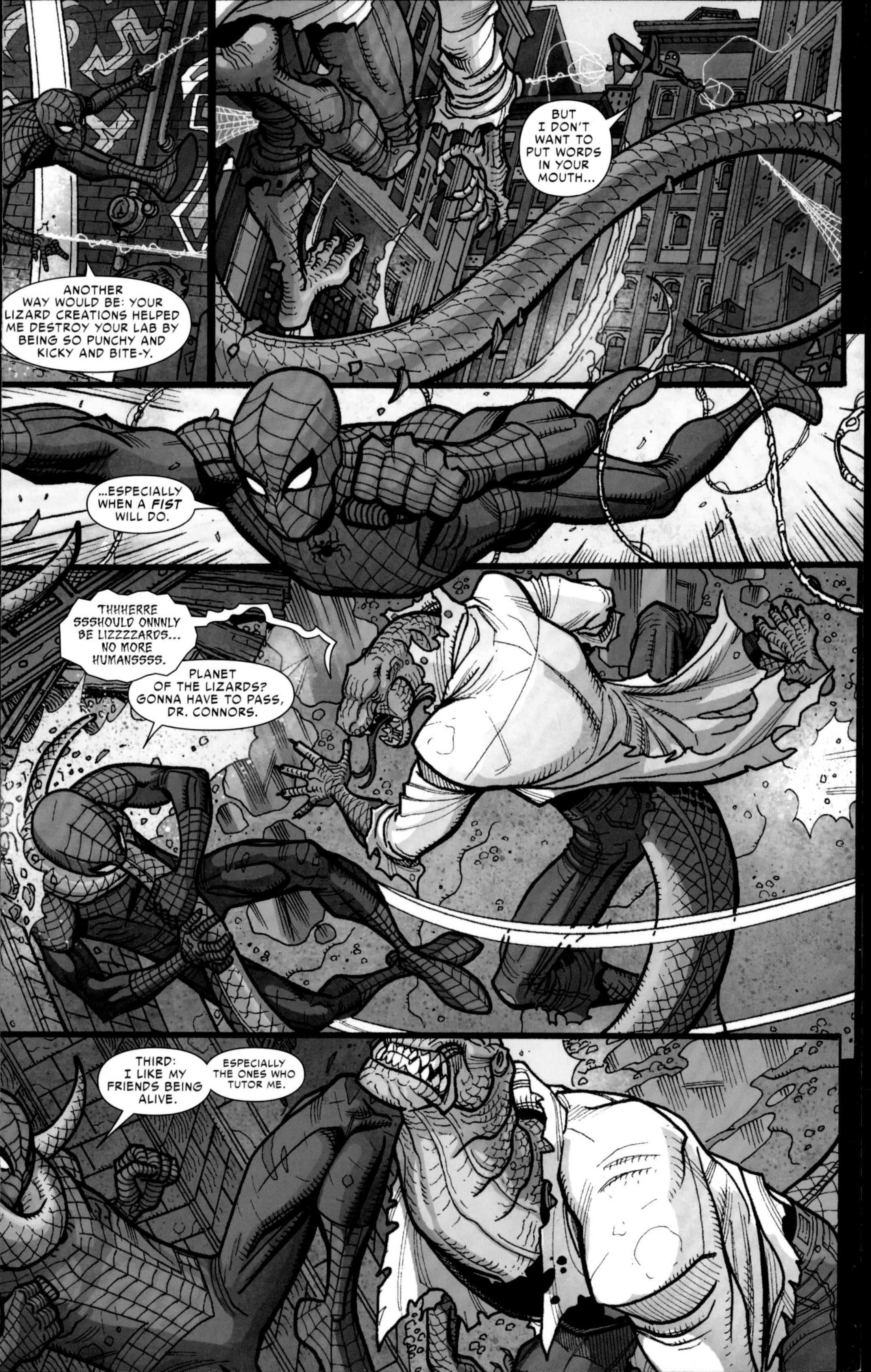
BUT I DON'T WANT TO PUT WORDS IN YOUR MOUTH...
ANOTHER WAY WOULD BE: YOUR LIZARD CREATIONS HELPED ME DESTROY YOUR LAB BY BEING SO PUNCHY AND KICKY AND BITE-Y.
...ESPECIALLY WHEN A FIST WILL DO.
THHHERRE SSSHOULD ONNNLY BE LIZZZZARDS... NO MORE HUMANSSSS.
PLANET OF THE LIZARDS? GONNA HAVE TO PASS, DR. CONNORS.
THIRD: I LIKE MY FRIENDS BEING ALIVE.
ESPECIALLY THE ONES WHO TUTOR ME.

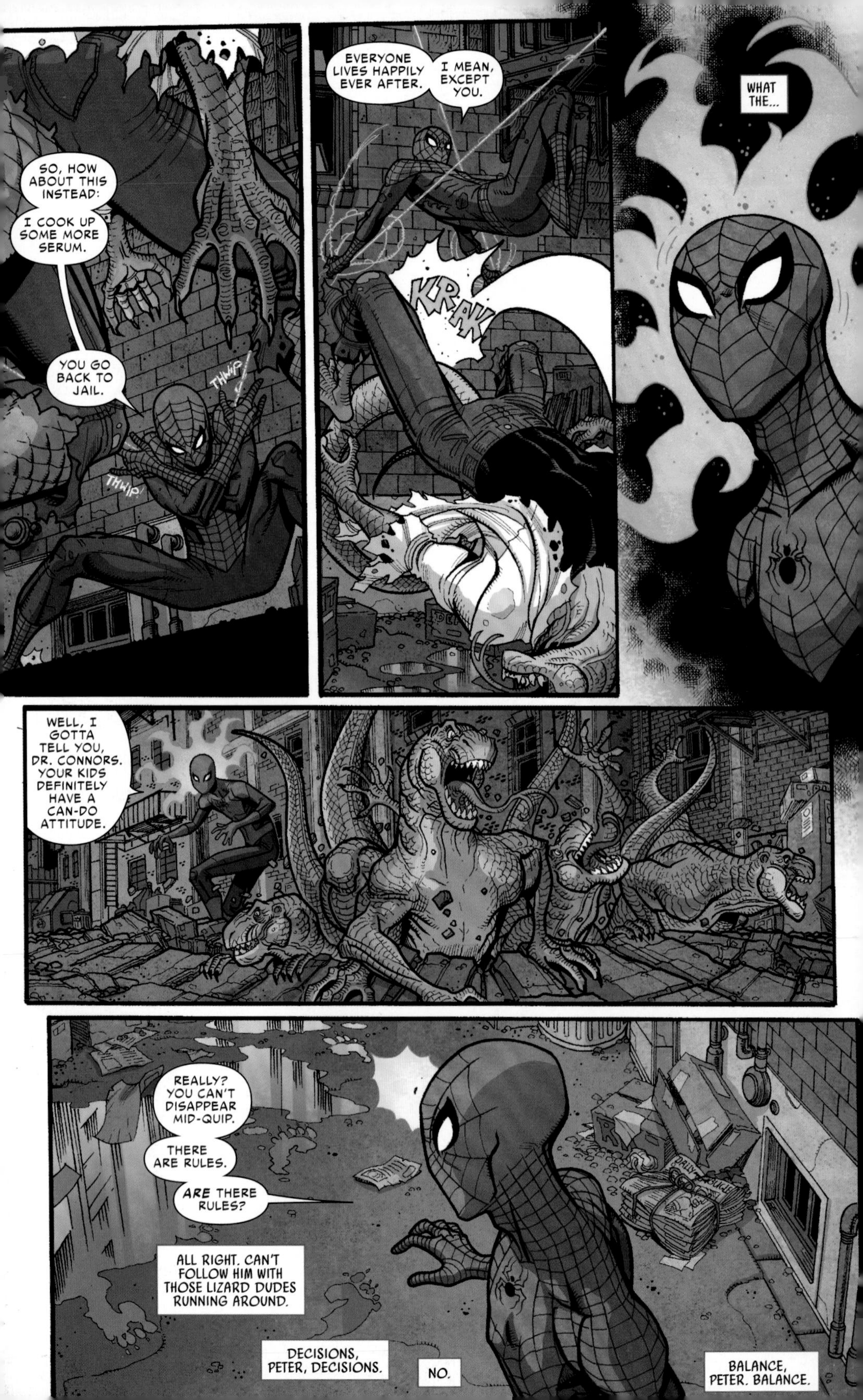
SO, HOW ABOUT THIS INSTEAD:
I COOK UP SOME MORE SERUM.
YOU GO BACK TO JAIL.
THWIP
THWIP!
EVERYONE LIVES HAPPILY EVER AFTER.
I MEAN, EXCEPT YOU.
KRAK
WHAT THE...
WELL, I GOTTA TELL YOU, DR. CONNORS. YOUR KIDS DEFINITELY HAVE A CAN-DO ATTITUDE.
REALLY? YOU CAN'T DISAPPEAR MID-QUIP.
THERE ARE RULES.
ARE THERE RULES?
ALL RIGHT. CAN'T FOLLOW HIM WITH THOSE LIZARD DUDES RUNNING AROUND.
DECISIONS, PETER, DECISIONS.
NO.
BALANCE, PETER. BALANCE.

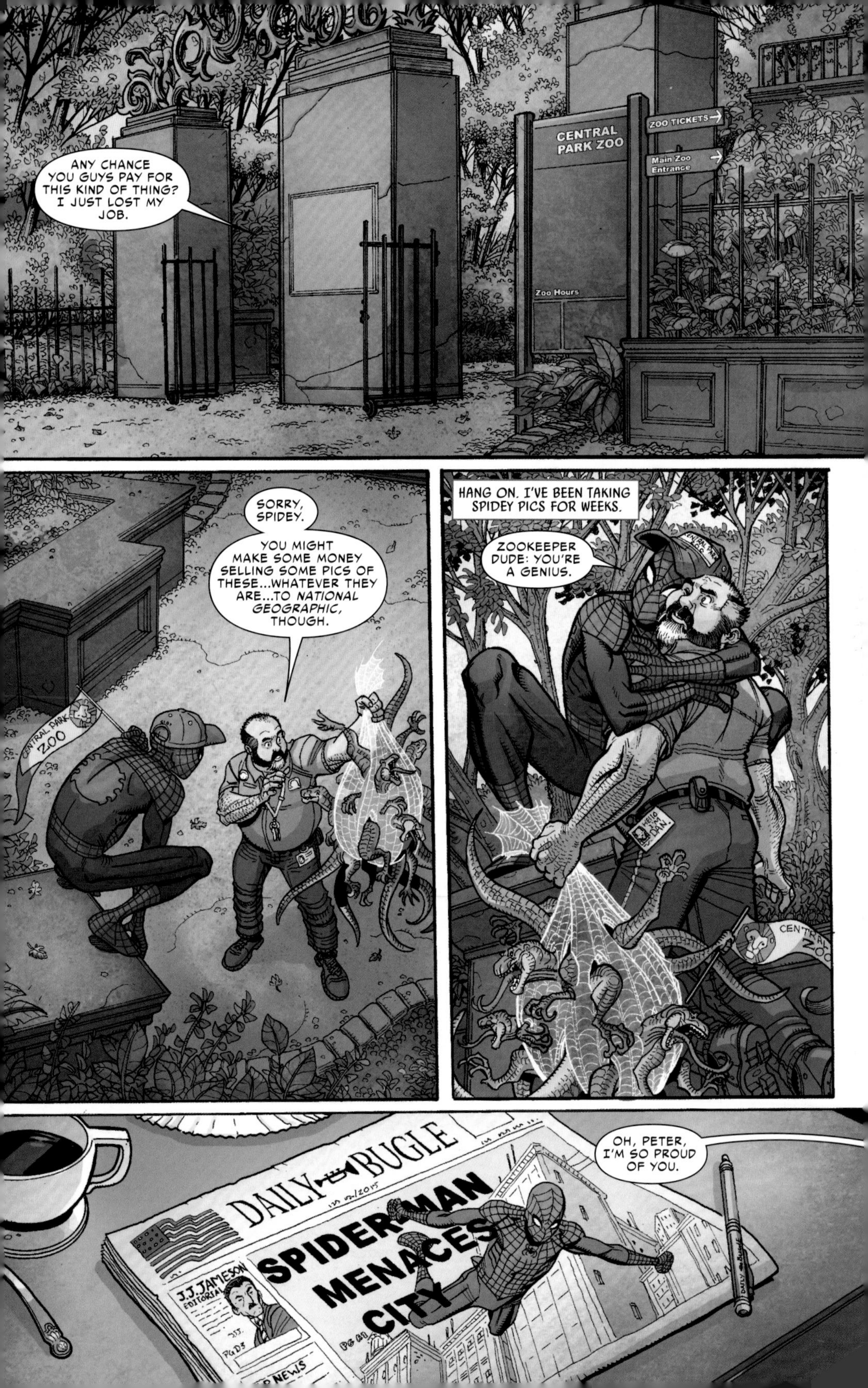

ANY CHANCE YOU GUYS PAY FOR THIS KIND OF THING? I JUST LOST MY JOB.
CENTRAL PARK ZOO
ZOO TICKETS
Main Zoo Entrance
Zoo Hours
SORRY, SPIDEY.
YOU MIGHT MAKE SOME MONEY SELLING SOME PICS OF THESE...WHATEVER THEY ARE...TO *NATIONAL GEOGRAPHIC,* THOUGH.
CENTRAL PARK ZOO
HANG ON. I'VE BEEN TAKING SPIDEY PICS FOR WEEKS.
ZOOKEEPER DUDE: YOU'RE A GENIUS.
OH, PETER, I'M SO PROUD OF YOU.
DAILY BUGLE
SPIDER-MAN MENACES CITY
J.J. JAMESON EDITORIAL

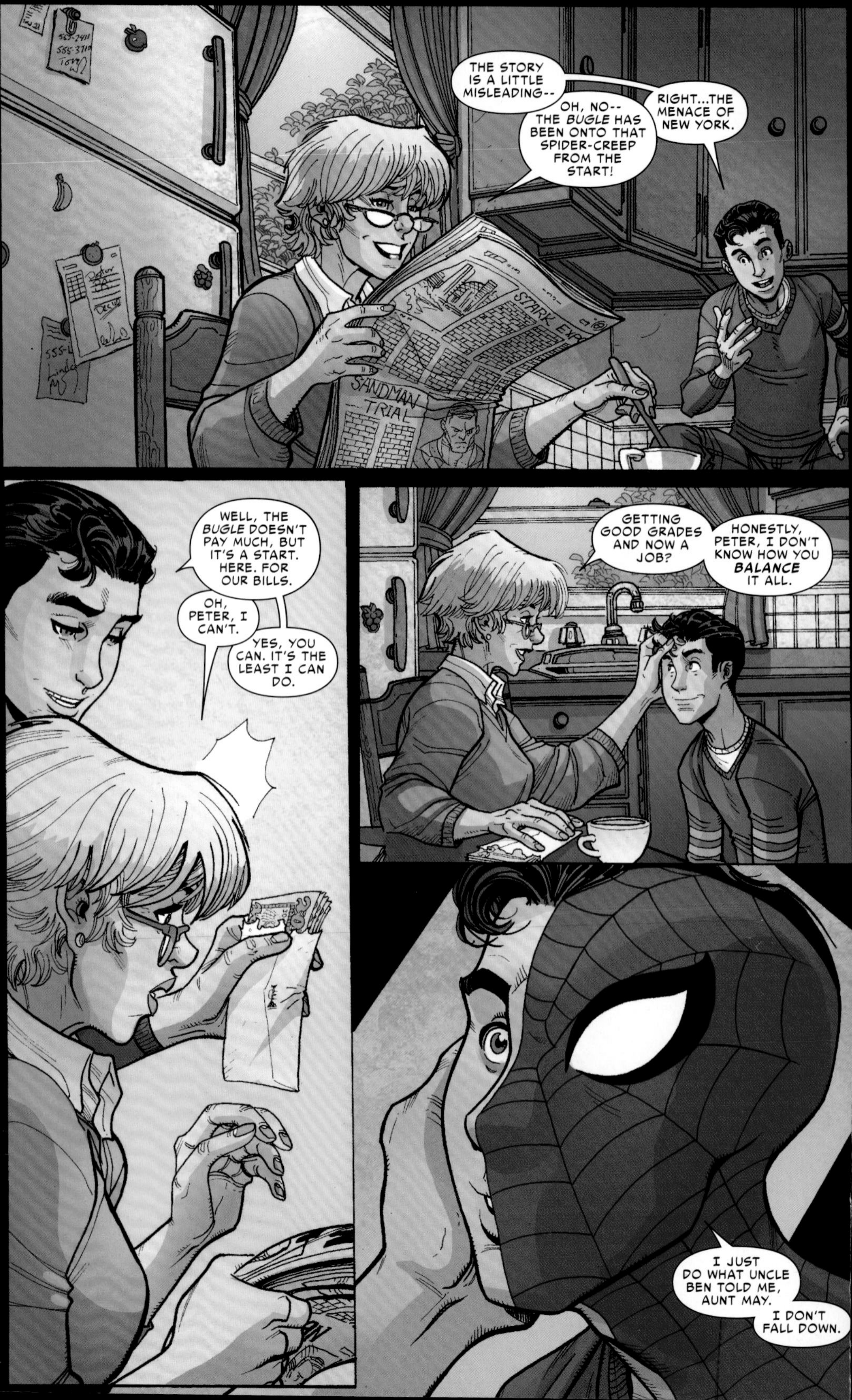

THE STORY IS A LITTLE MISLEADING--
RIGHT...THE MENACE OF NEW YORK.
OH, NO-- THE *BUGLE* HAS BEEN ONTO THAT SPIDER-CREEP FROM THE START!
SANDMAN TRIAL
WELL, THE *BUGLE* DOESN'T PAY MUCH, BUT IT'S A START. HERE. FOR OUR BILLS.
OH, PETER, I CAN'T.
YES, YOU CAN. IT'S THE LEAST I CAN DO.
GETTING GOOD GRADES AND NOW A JOB?
HONESTLY, PETER, I DON'T KNOW HOW YOU ***BALANCE*** IT ALL.
I JUST DO WHAT UNCLE BEN TOLD ME, AUNT MAY.
I DON'T FALL DOWN.

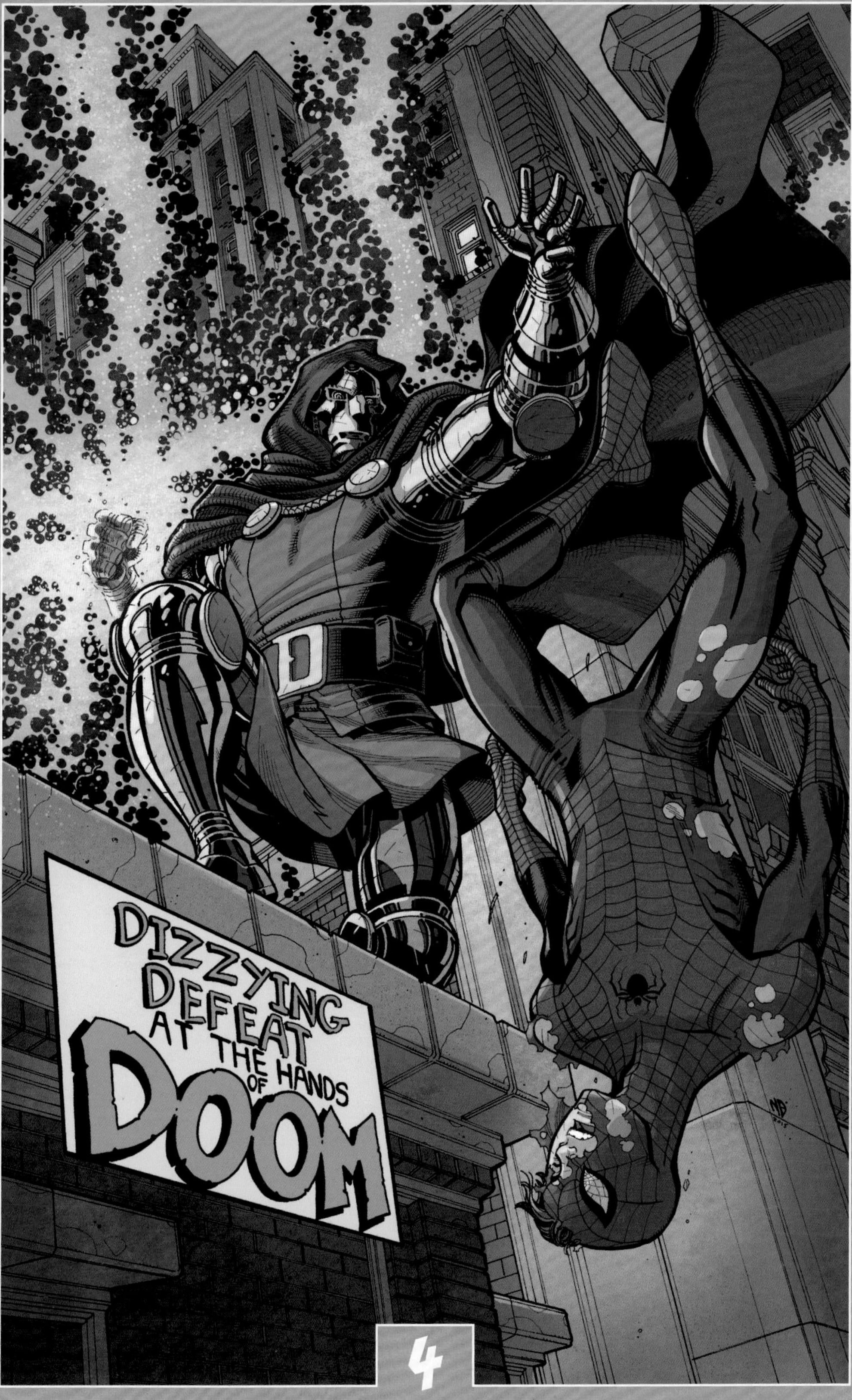
DIZZYING DEFEAT AT THE HANDS OF DOOM

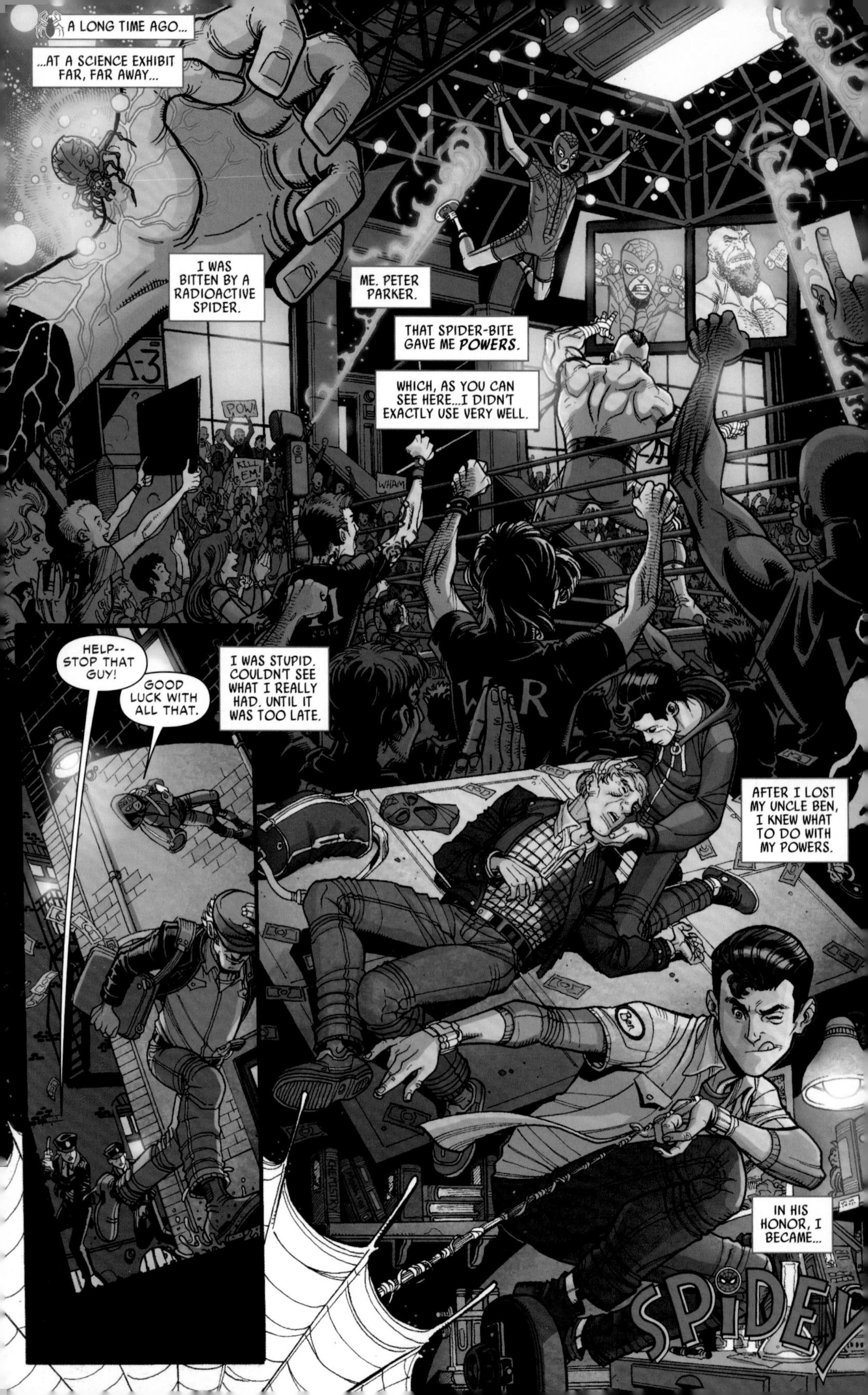

A LONG TIME AGO...
...AT A SCIENCE EXHIBIT FAR, FAR AWAY...
I WAS BITTEN BY A RADIOACTIVE SPIDER.
ME. PETER PARKER.
THAT SPIDER-BITE GAVE ME POWERS.
WHICH, AS YOU CAN SEE HERE...I DIDN'T EXACTLY USE VERY WELL.
POW!
KILL 'EM!
WHAM
HELP-- STOP THAT GUY!
GOOD LUCK WITH ALL THAT.
I WAS STUPID. COULDN'T SEE WHAT I REALLY HAD. UNTIL IT WAS TOO LATE.
AFTER I LOST MY UNCLE BEN, I KNEW WHAT TO DO WITH MY POWERS.
IN HIS HONOR, I BECAME...
SPIDEY

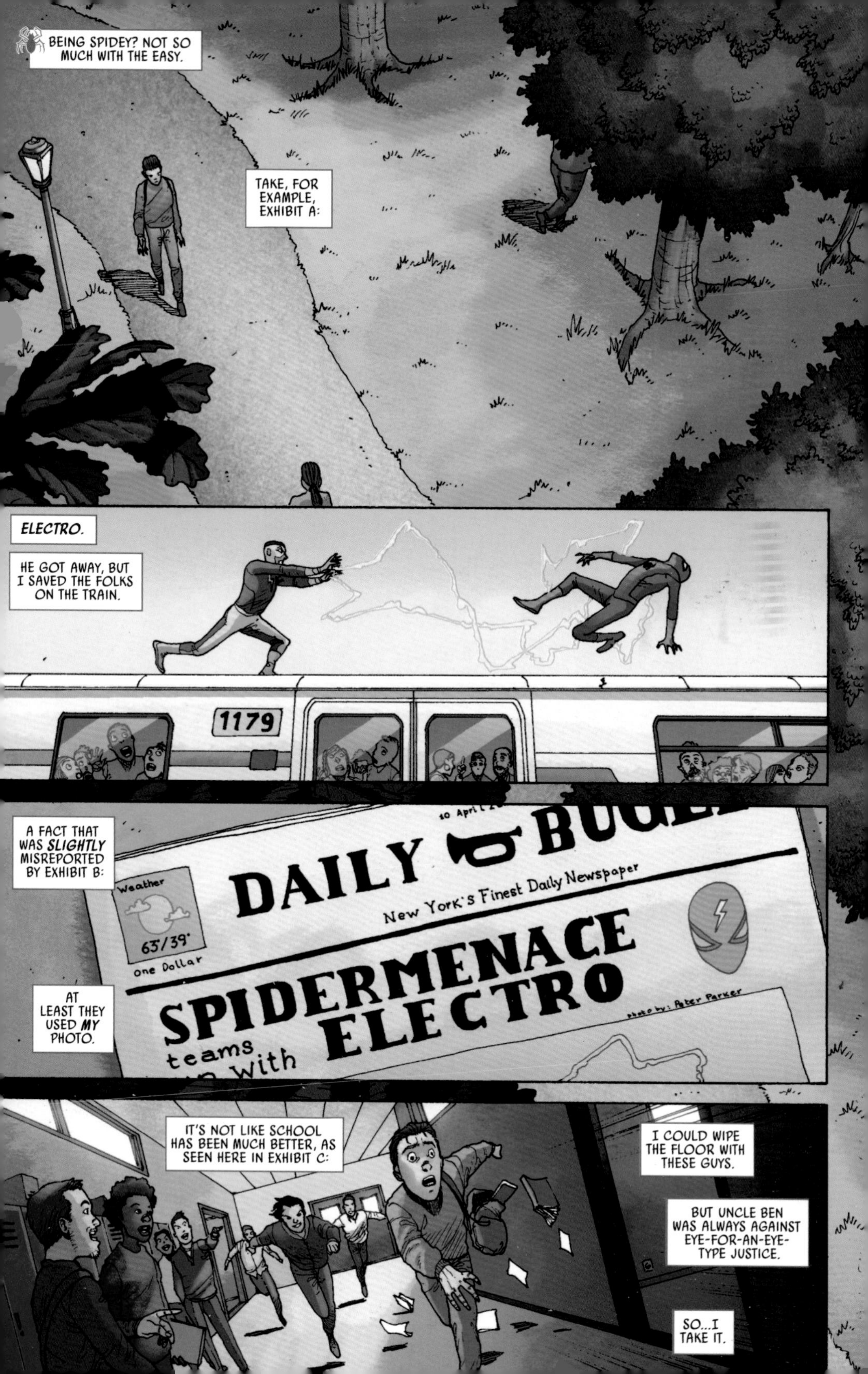
BEING SPIDEY? NOT SO MUCH WITH THE EASY.
TAKE, FOR EXAMPLE, EXHIBIT A:
ELECTRO.
HE GOT AWAY, BUT I SAVED THE FOLKS ON THE TRAIN.
1179
A FACT THAT WAS SLIGHTLY MISREPORTED BY EXHIBIT B:
DAILY BUGLE
New York's Finest Daily Newspaper
Weather
63°/39°
One Dollar
SPIDERMENACE teams up with ELECTRO
photo by: Peter Parker
AT LEAST THEY USED MY PHOTO.
IT'S NOT LIKE SCHOOL HAS BEEN MUCH BETTER, AS SEEN HERE IN EXHIBIT C:
I COULD WIPE THE FLOOR WITH THESE GUYS.
BUT UNCLE BEN WAS ALWAYS AGAINST EYE-FOR-AN-EYE-TYPE JUSTICE.
SO...I TAKE IT.

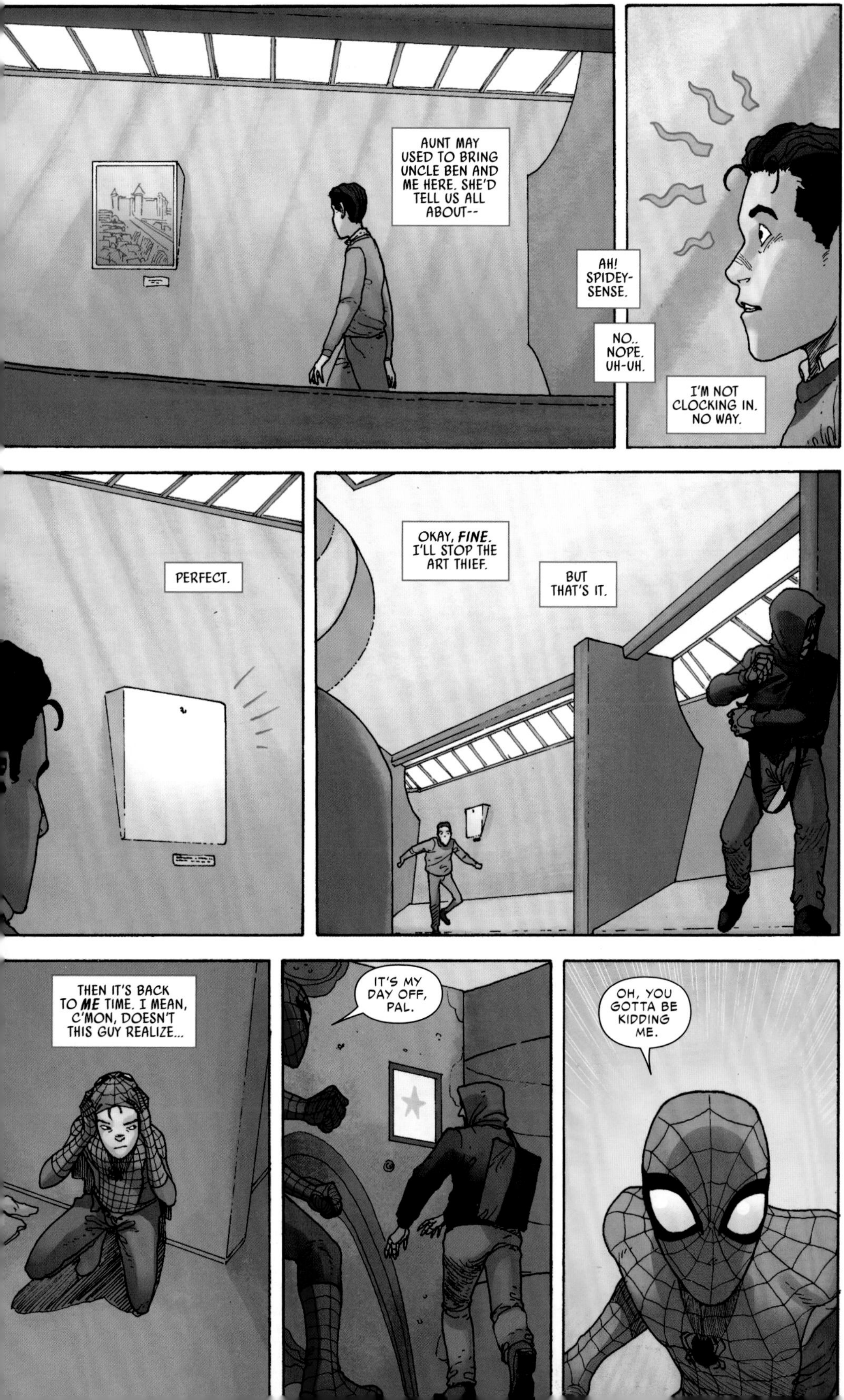
AUNT MAY USED TO BRING UNCLE BEN AND ME HERE. SHE'D TELL US ALL ABOUT--
AH! SPIDEY-SENSE.
NO.. NOPE. UH-UH.
I'M NOT CLOCKING IN. NO WAY.
PERFECT.
OKAY, FINE. I'LL STOP THE ART THIEF.
BUT THAT'S IT.
THEN IT'S BACK TO ME TIME. I MEAN, C'MON, DOESN'T THIS GUY REALIZE...
IT'S MY DAY OFF, PAL.
OH, YOU GOTTA BE KIDDING ME.

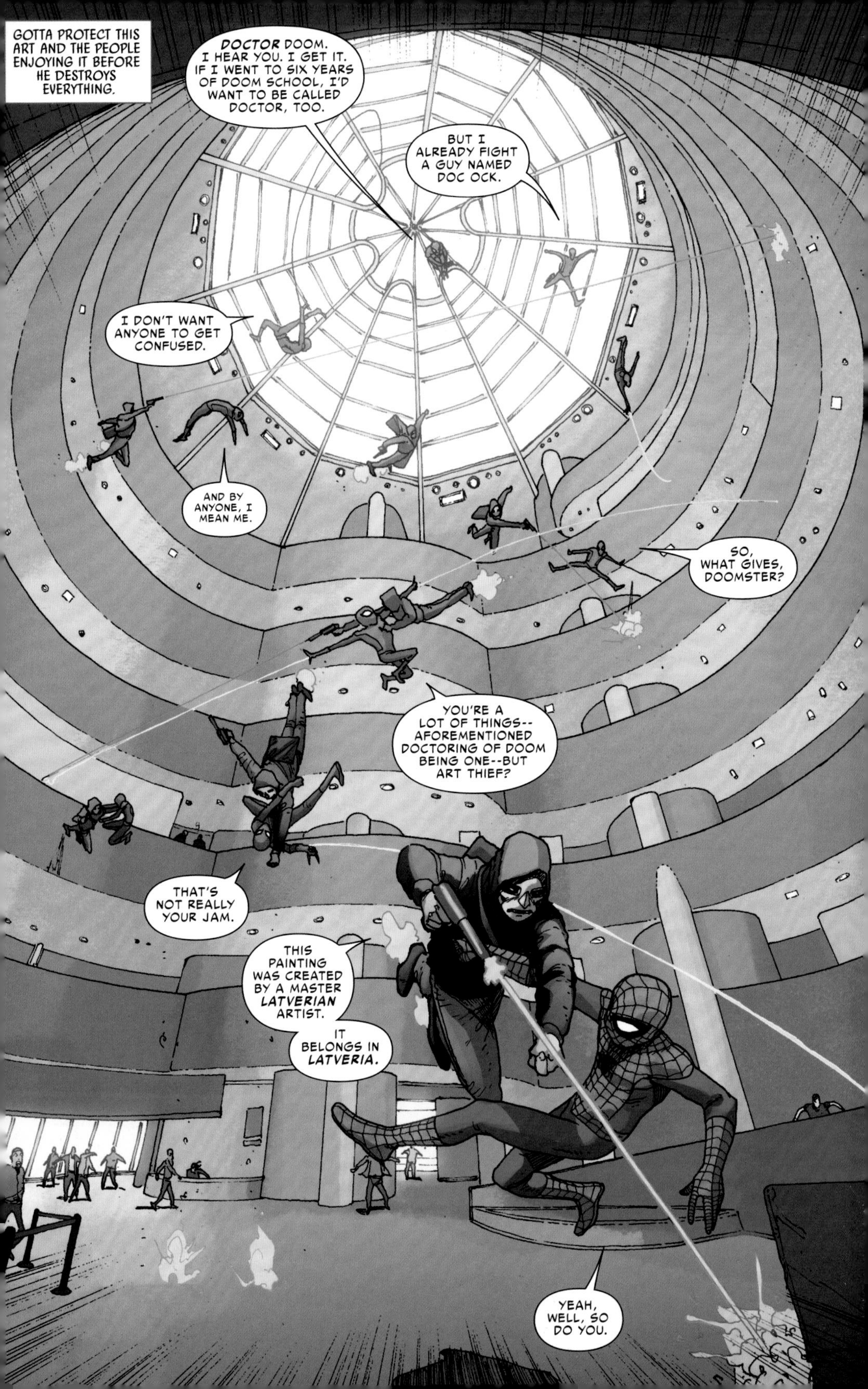
GOTTA PROTECT THIS ART AND THE PEOPLE ENJOYING IT BEFORE HE DESTROYS EVERYTHING.
DOCTOR DOOM. I HEAR YOU. I GET IT. IF I WENT TO SIX YEARS OF DOOM SCHOOL, I'D WANT TO BE CALLED DOCTOR, TOO.
BUT I ALREADY FIGHT A GUY NAMED DOC OCK.
I DON'T WANT ANYONE TO GET CONFUSED.
AND BY ANYONE, I MEAN ME.
SO, WHAT GIVES, DOOMSTER?
YOU'RE A LOT OF THINGS-- AFOREMENTIONED DOCTORING OF DOOM BEING ONE--BUT ART THIEF?
THAT'S NOT REALLY YOUR JAM.
THIS PAINTING WAS CREATED BY A MASTER LATVERIAN ARTIST.
IT BELONGS IN LATVERIA.
YEAH, WELL, SO DO YOU.

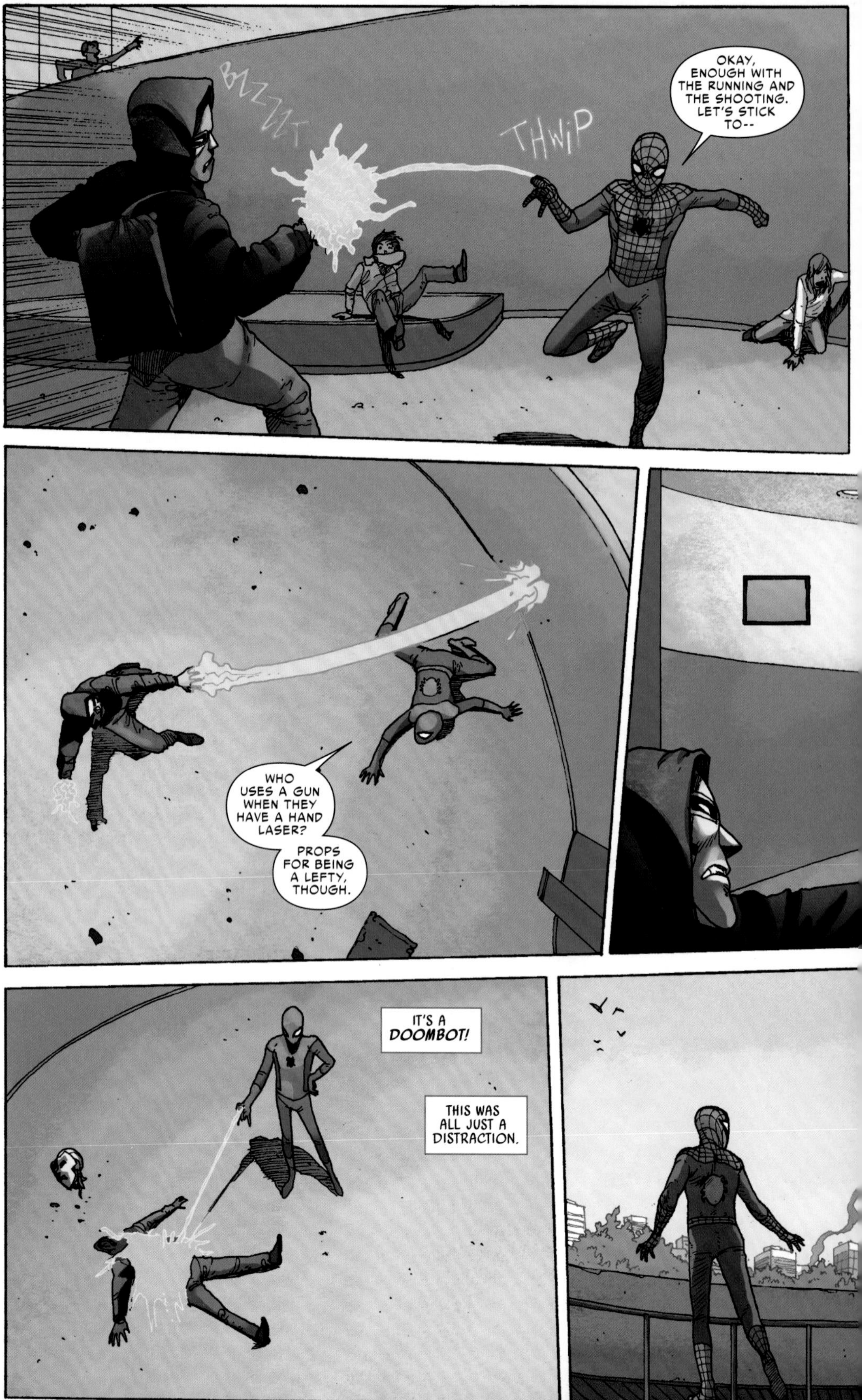
BZZZZT
THWIP
OKAY, ENOUGH WITH THE RUNNING AND THE SHOOTING. LET'S STICK TO--
WHO USES A GUN WHEN THEY HAVE A HAND LASER?
PROPS FOR BEING A LEFTY, THOUGH.
IT'S A *DOOMBOT!*
THIS WAS ALL JUST A DISTRACTION.

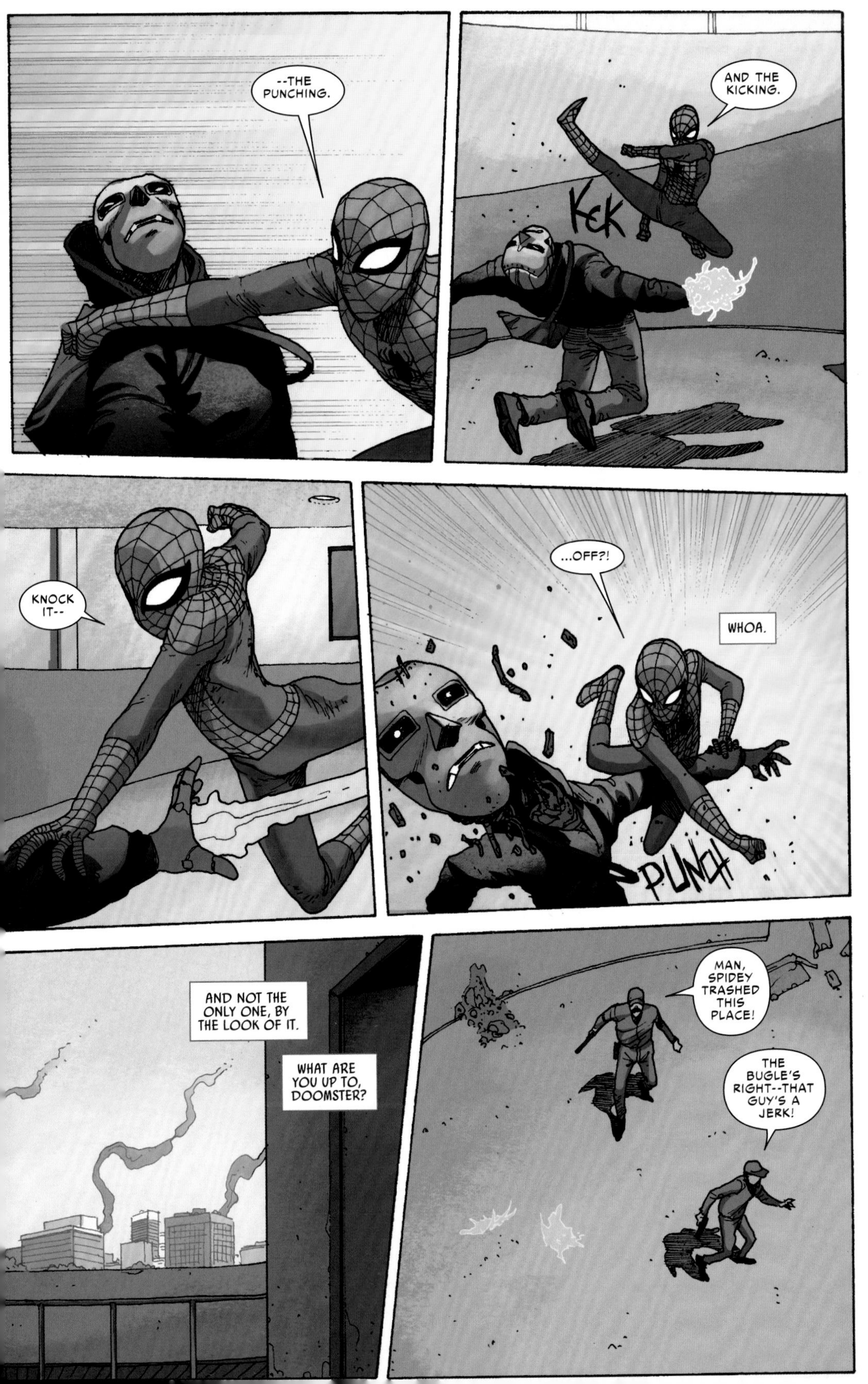
--THE PUNCHING.
AND THE KICKING.
KICK
KNOCK IT--
...OFF?!
WHOA.
PUNCH
AND NOT THE ONLY ONE, BY THE LOOK OF IT.
WHAT ARE YOU UP TO, DOOMSTER?
MAN, SPIDEY TRASHED THIS PLACE!
THE BUGLE'S RIGHT--THAT GUY'S A JERK!

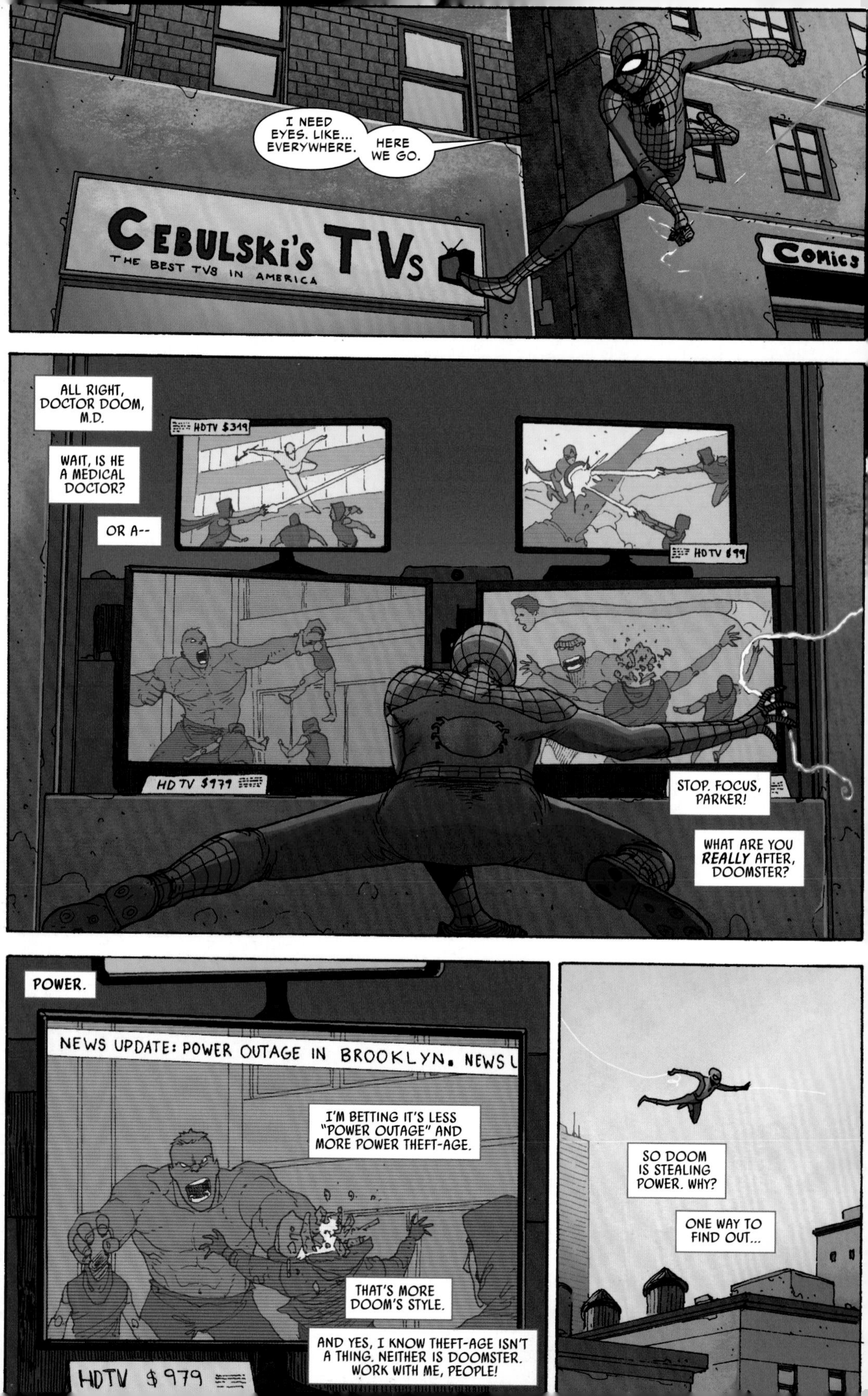
I NEED EYES. LIKE... EVERYWHERE.
HERE WE GO.
CEBULSKI'S TVS
THE BEST TVS IN AMERICA
COMICS
ALL RIGHT, DOCTOR DOOM, M.D.
WAIT, IS HE A MEDICAL DOCTOR?
OR A--
HDTV $319
HDTV $99
HDTV $979
STOP. FOCUS, PARKER!
WHAT ARE YOU REALLY AFTER, DOOMSTER?
POWER.
NEWS UPDATE: POWER OUTAGE IN BROOKLYN. NEWS U
I'M BETTING IT'S LESS "POWER OUTAGE" AND MORE POWER THEFT-AGE.
THAT'S MORE DOOM'S STYLE.
AND YES, I KNOW THEFT-AGE ISN'T A THING. NEITHER IS DOOMSTER. WORK WITH ME, PEOPLE!
HDTV $979
SO DOOM IS STEALING POWER. WHY?
ONE WAY TO FIND OUT...

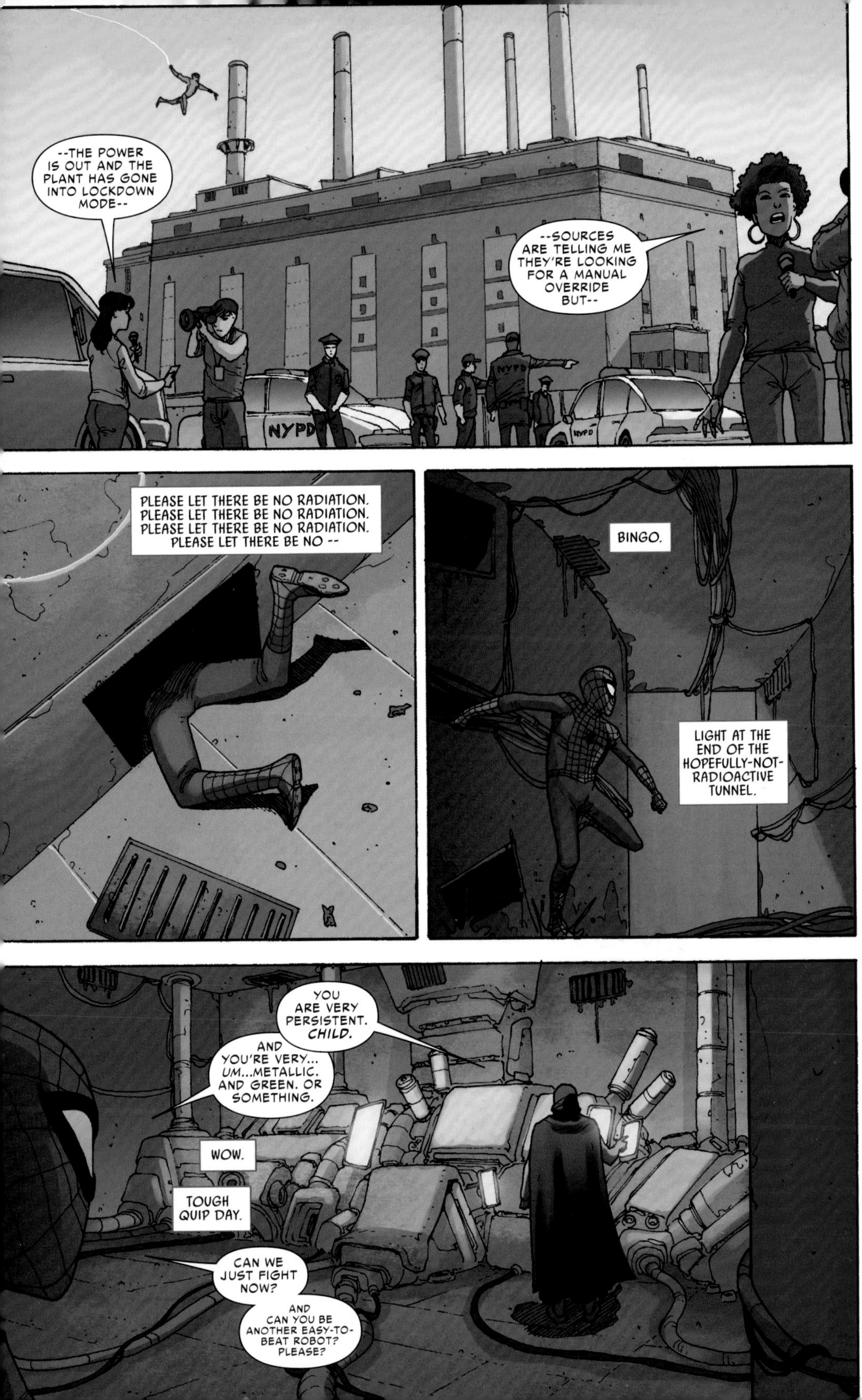
--THE POWER IS OUT AND THE PLANT HAS GONE INTO LOCKDOWN MODE--
--SOURCES ARE TELLING ME THEY'RE LOOKING FOR A MANUAL OVERRIDE BUT--
NYPD
NYPD
PLEASE LET THERE BE NO RADIATION. PLEASE LET THERE BE NO RADIATION. PLEASE LET THERE BE NO RADIATION. PLEASE LET THERE BE NO --
BINGO.
LIGHT AT THE END OF THE HOPEFULLY-NOT-RADIOACTIVE TUNNEL.
YOU ARE VERY PERSISTENT. *CHILD.*
AND YOU'RE VERY... UM...METALLIC. AND GREEN. OR SOMETHING.
WOW.
TOUGH QUIP DAY.
CAN WE JUST FIGHT NOW?
AND CAN YOU BE ANOTHER EASY-TO-BEAT ROBOT? PLEASE?

I'M GUESSING YOUR WISH TO "NOT FIGHT ME" HAS BEEN REVOKED?
I WOULD NOT DEIGN TO FIGHT YOU, CHILD.
LOOK, I DON'T WANT TO TELL YOU HOW TO BE AN EVIL SOCIOPATH, BUT YOUR "ROCK 'EM, SOCK 'EM" BOTS NEED WORK. THEY ARE WAY TOO EASY TO--
PUNCH
GAH!
SCRATCH THAT. THESE ARE GREAT. THAT DEGREE IN DOOMOLOGY IS TOTALLY WORKING FOR YOU, DOOMSTER.
TOO MANY...
...GOTTA GET OUTTA HERE.
GOTTA--
KRATHOOM

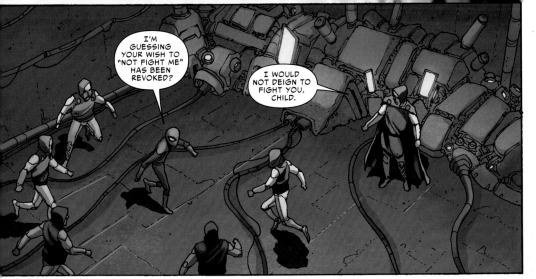

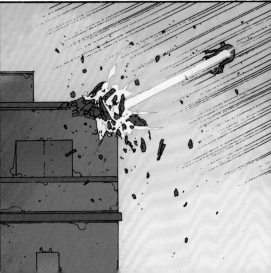

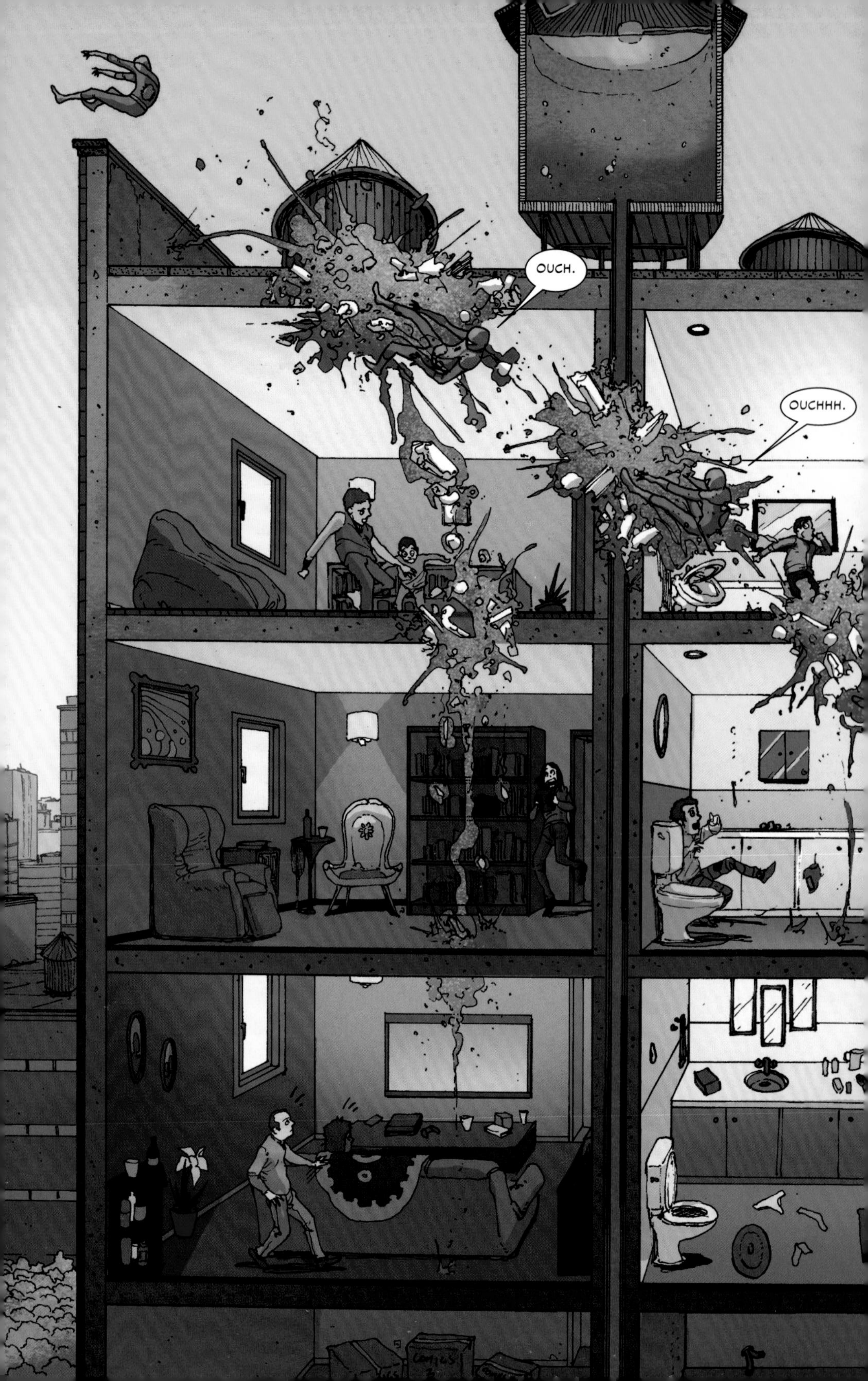
OUCH.
OUCHHH.

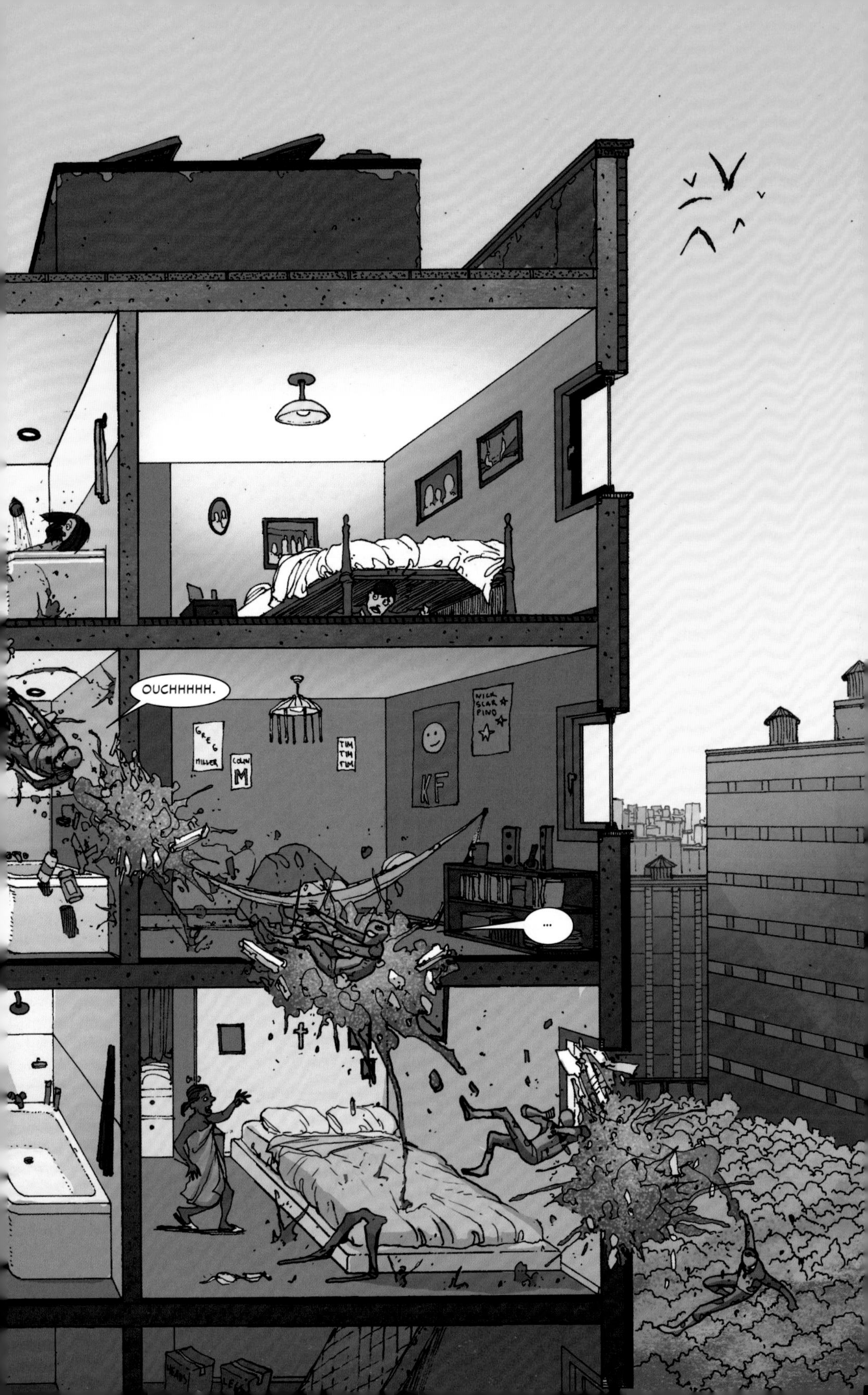
OUCHHHHH.
...
TIM TIM TIM
KF

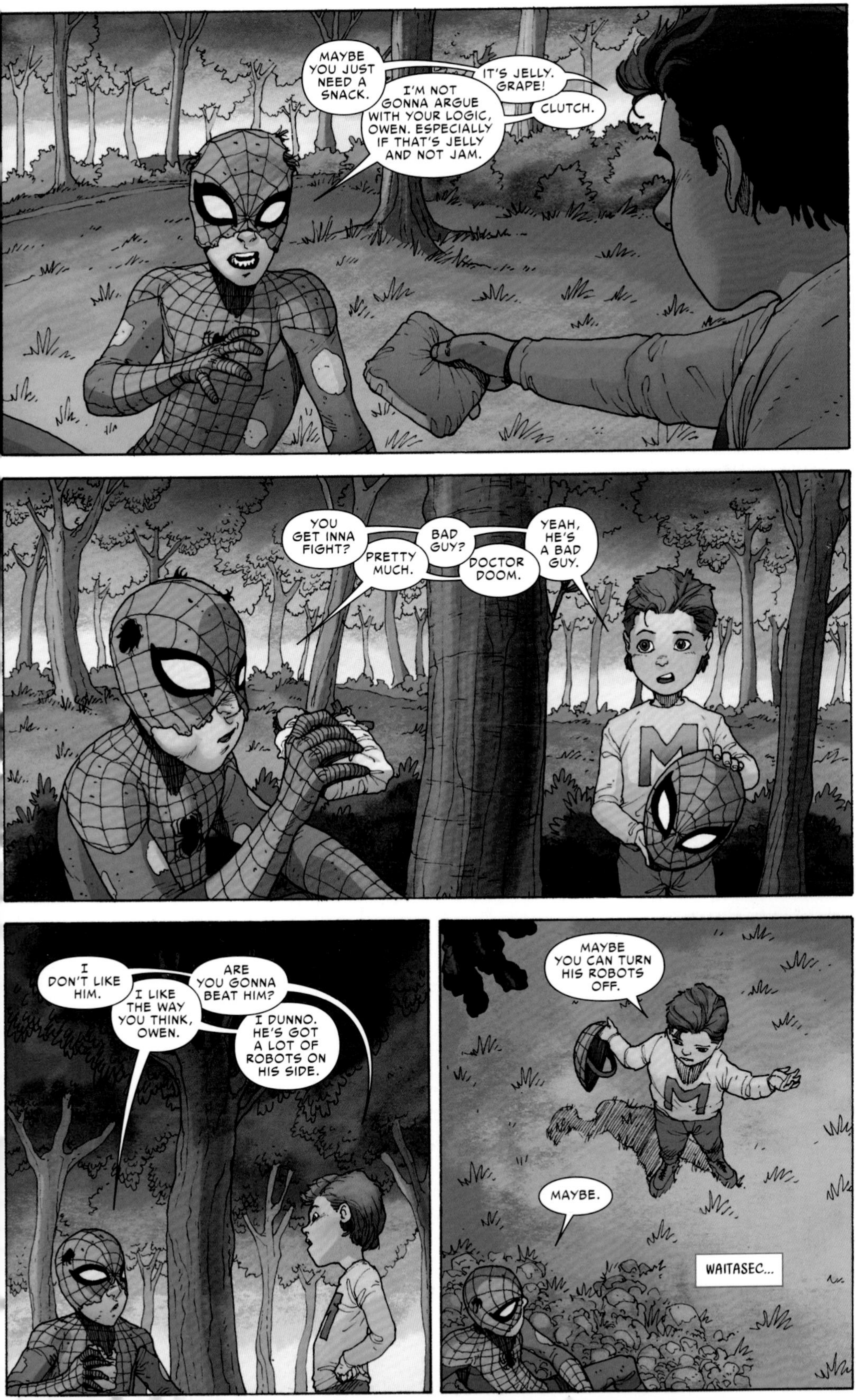

MAYBE YOU JUST NEED A SNACK.
IT'S JELLY. GRAPE!
I'M NOT GONNA ARGUE WITH YOUR LOGIC, OWEN. ESPECIALLY IF THAT'S JELLY AND NOT JAM.
CLUTCH.
YOU GET INNA FIGHT?
PRETTY MUCH.
BAD GUY?
DOCTOR DOOM.
YEAH, HE'S A BAD GUY.
I DON'T LIKE HIM.
I LIKE THE WAY YOU THINK, OWEN.
ARE YOU GONNA BEAT HIM?
I DUNNO. HE'S GOT A LOT OF ROBOTS ON HIS SIDE.
MAYBE YOU CAN TURN HIS ROBOTS OFF.
MAYBE.
WAITASEC...

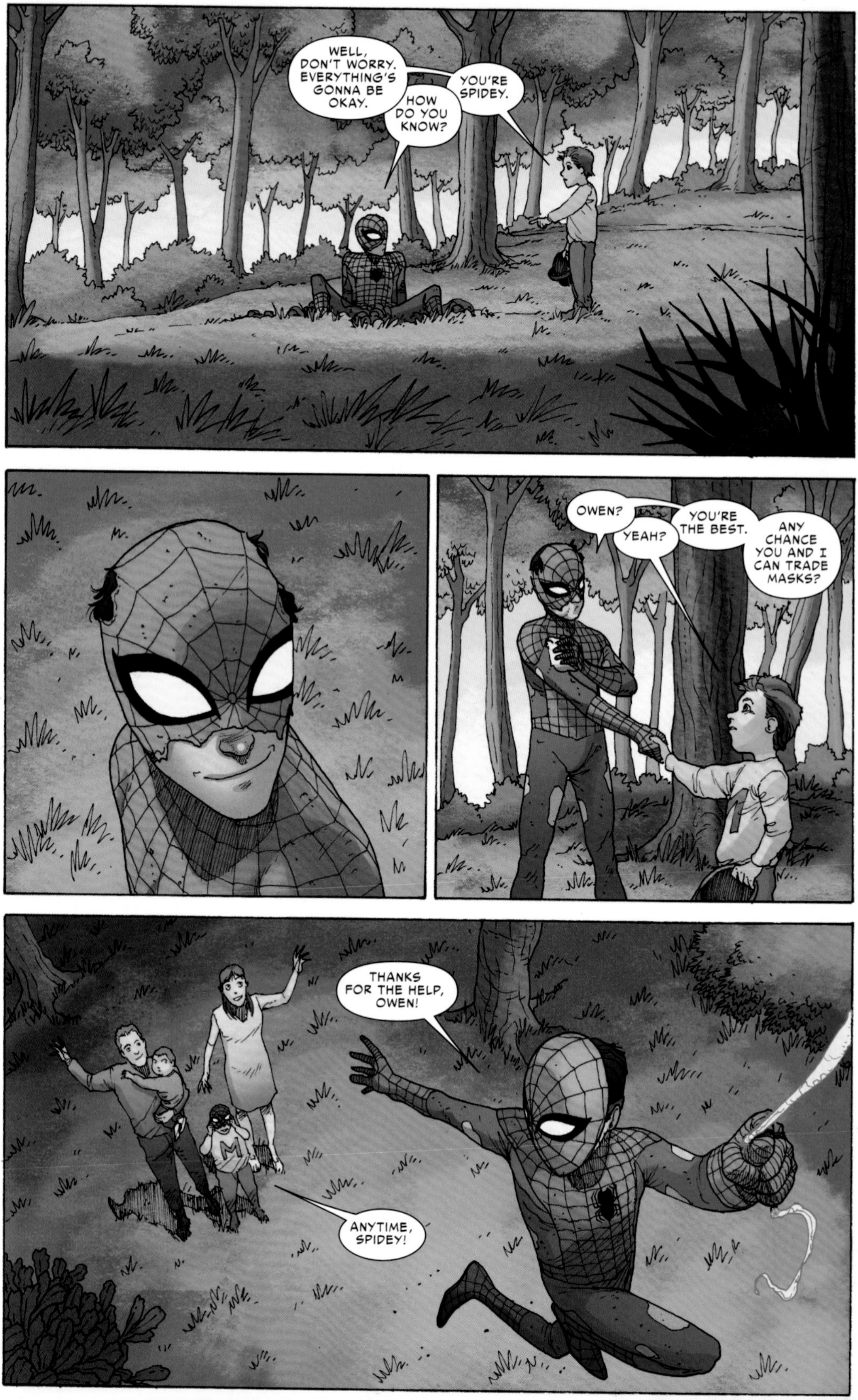
WELL, DON'T WORRY. EVERYTHING'S GONNA BE OKAY.
YOU'RE SPIDEY.
HOW DO YOU KNOW?
OWEN?
YEAH?
YOU'RE THE BEST.
ANY CHANCE YOU AND I CAN TRADE MASKS?
THANKS FOR THE HELP, OWEN!
ANYTIME, SPIDEY!

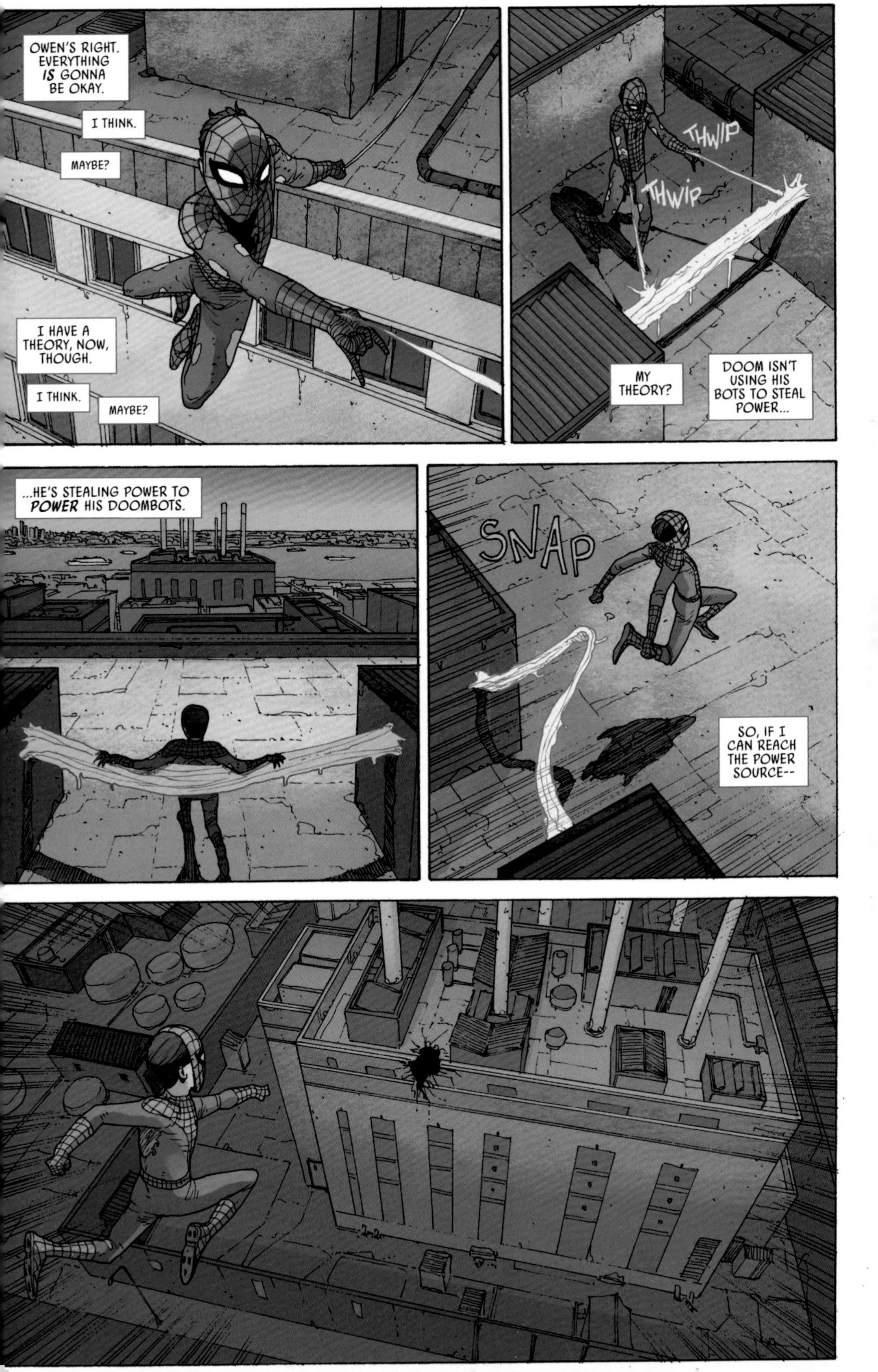
OWEN'S RIGHT. EVERYTHING IS GONNA BE OKAY.
I THINK.
MAYBE?
I HAVE A THEORY, NOW, THOUGH.
I THINK.
MAYBE?
THWIP
THWIP
MY THEORY?
DOOM ISN'T USING HIS BOTS TO STEAL POWER...
...HE'S STEALING POWER TO POWER HIS DOOMBOTS.
SNAP
SO, IF I CAN REACH THE POWER SOURCE--

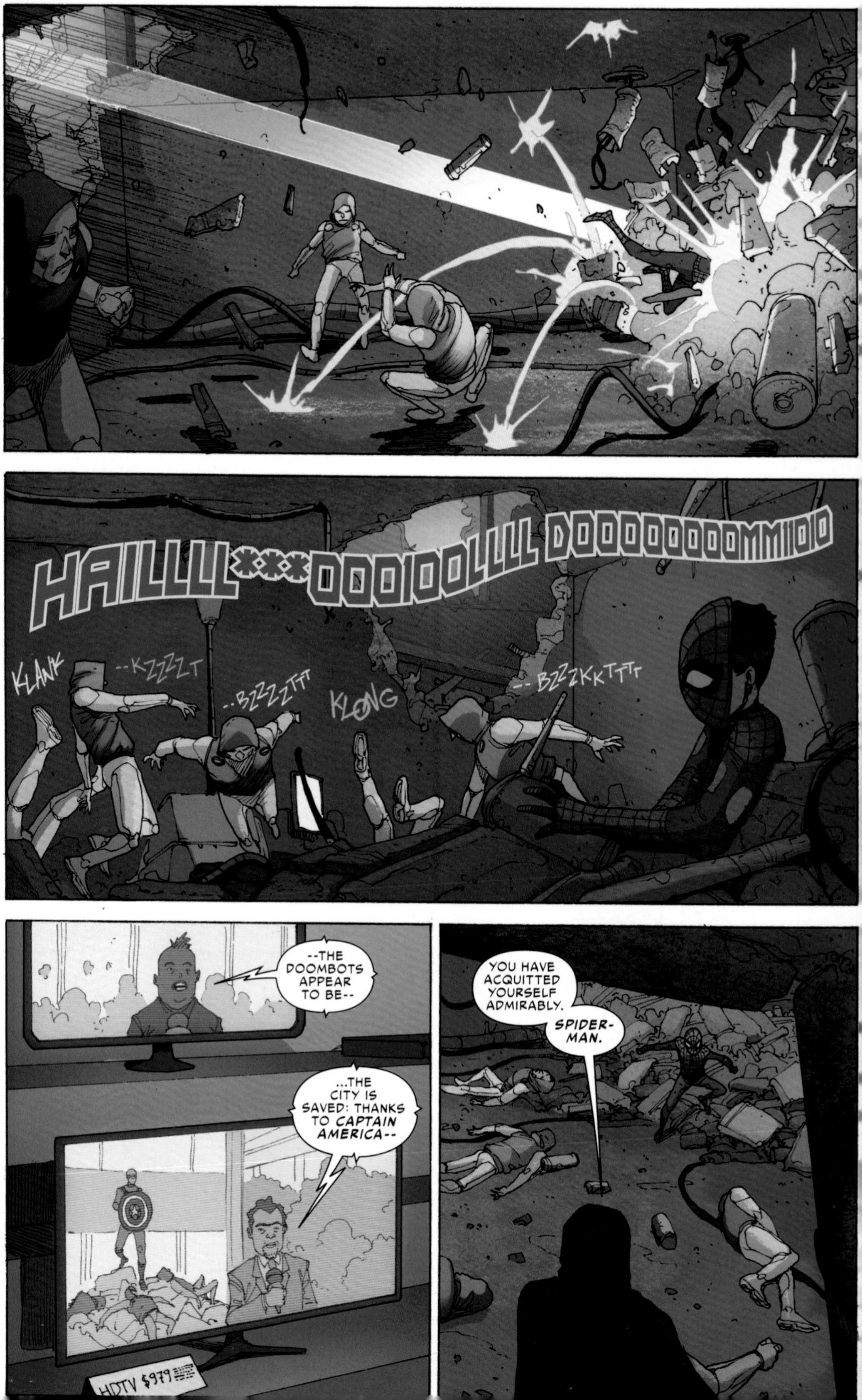
HAILLLL***OOOIOOLLLL DOOOOOOOOMMIIOIO
KLANK
--KZZZZT
--BZZZZTTT
KLONG
--BZZZKKTTTT
--THE DOOMBOTS APPEAR TO BE--
...THE CITY IS SAVED: THANKS TO CAPTAIN AMERICA--
HDTV $979
YOU HAVE ACQUITTED YOURSELF ADMIRABLY.
SPIDER-MAN.

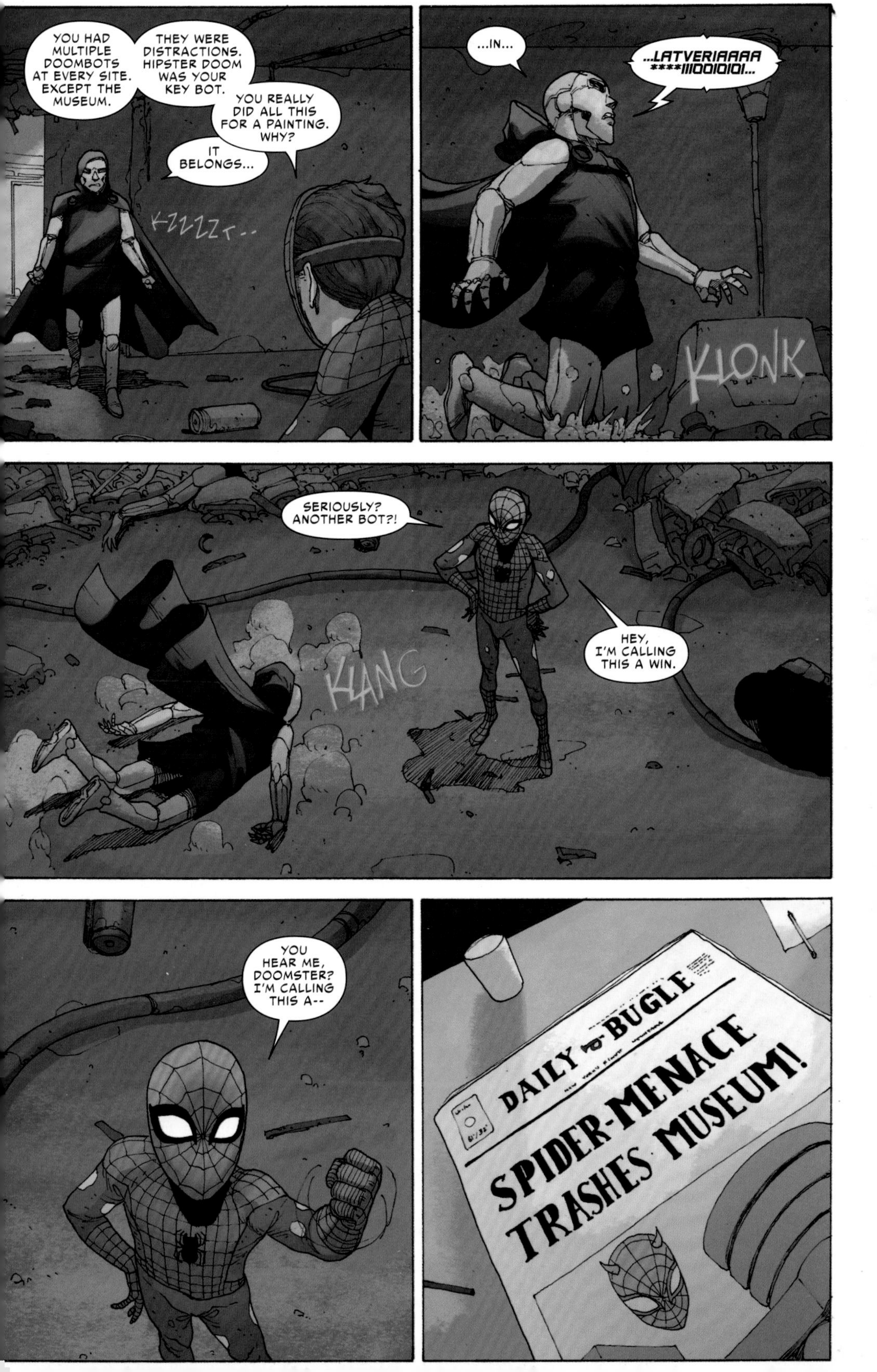
YOU HAD MULTIPLE DOOMBOTS AT EVERY SITE. EXCEPT THE MUSEUM.
THEY WERE DISTRACTIONS. HIPSTER DOOM WAS YOUR KEY BOT.
YOU REALLY DID ALL THIS FOR A PAINTING. WHY?
IT BELONGS...
KZZZZT...
...IN...
...LATVERIAAAA ****1110010101...
KLONK
SERIOUSLY? ANOTHER BOT?!
KLANG
HEY, I'M CALLING THIS A WIN.
YOU HEAR ME, DOOMSTER? I'M CALLING THIS A--
DAILY BUGLE
SPIDER-MENACE TRASHES MUSEUM!

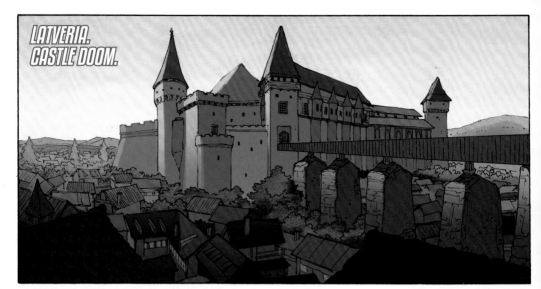

LATVERIA.
CASTLE DOOM.

THE DOOMBOT WAS ABLE TO COMPLETE ITS MISSION BEFORE LOSING POWER, SIR.

YOUR PRIZE IS SECURE.

HANG IT IN THE MUSEUM FOR ALL OF LATVERIA TO VIEW AND BASK IN ITS GLORY.

AS YOU WISH.

SIR...DID YOU MEAN THOSE THINGS THAT YOU SAID TO THE CHILD? ABOUT BEING--

OF COURSE NOT.

DOOM IS NEVER ALONE...

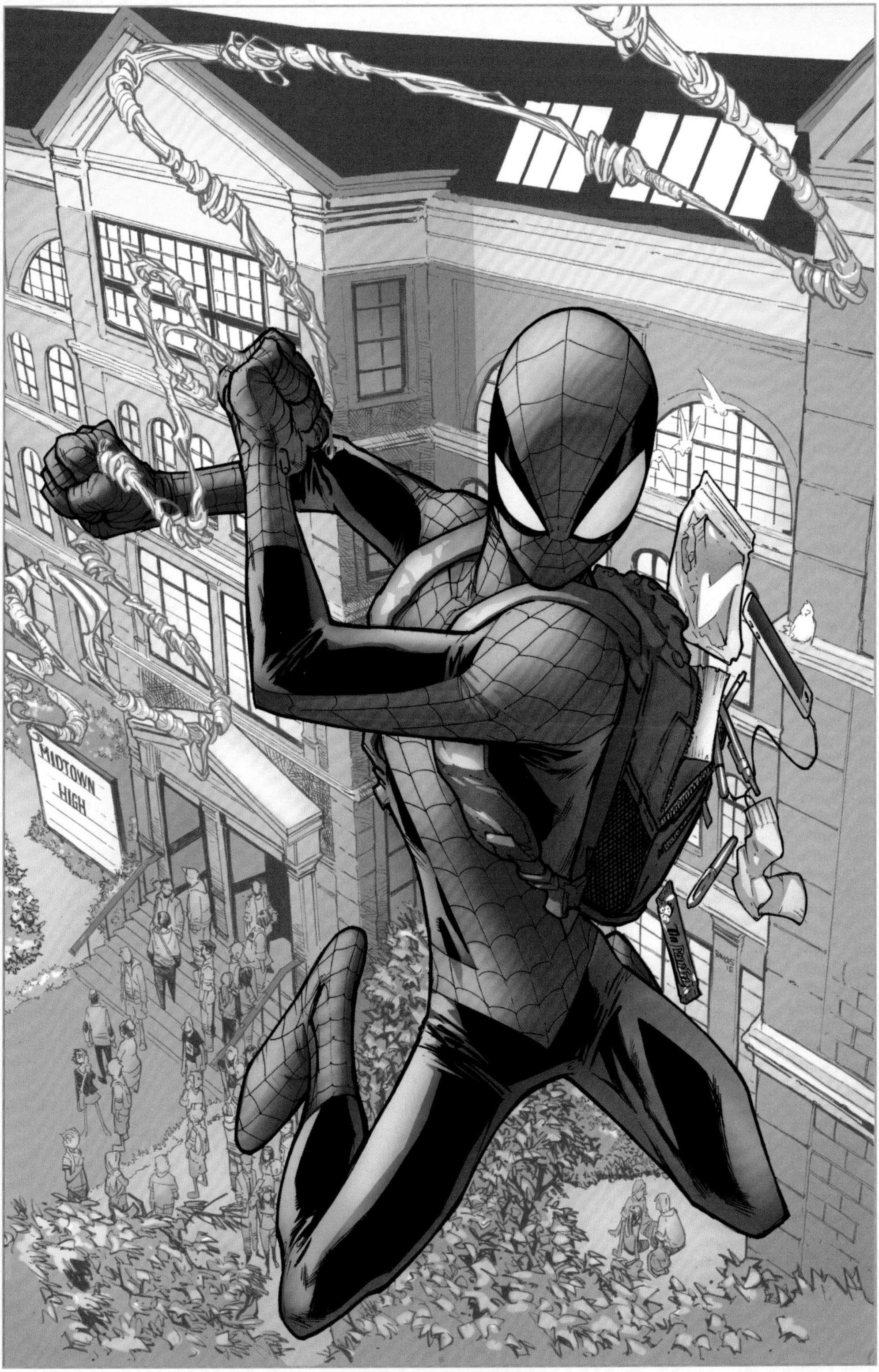
MIDTOWN
HIGH

SPIDEY #1 VARIANT
BY HUMBERTO RAMOS & EDGAR DELGADO

IS THIS THE END OF THE WALL-CRAWLER?!
FIND OUT IN THE PAGES OF...
SPIDEY
AIA 16

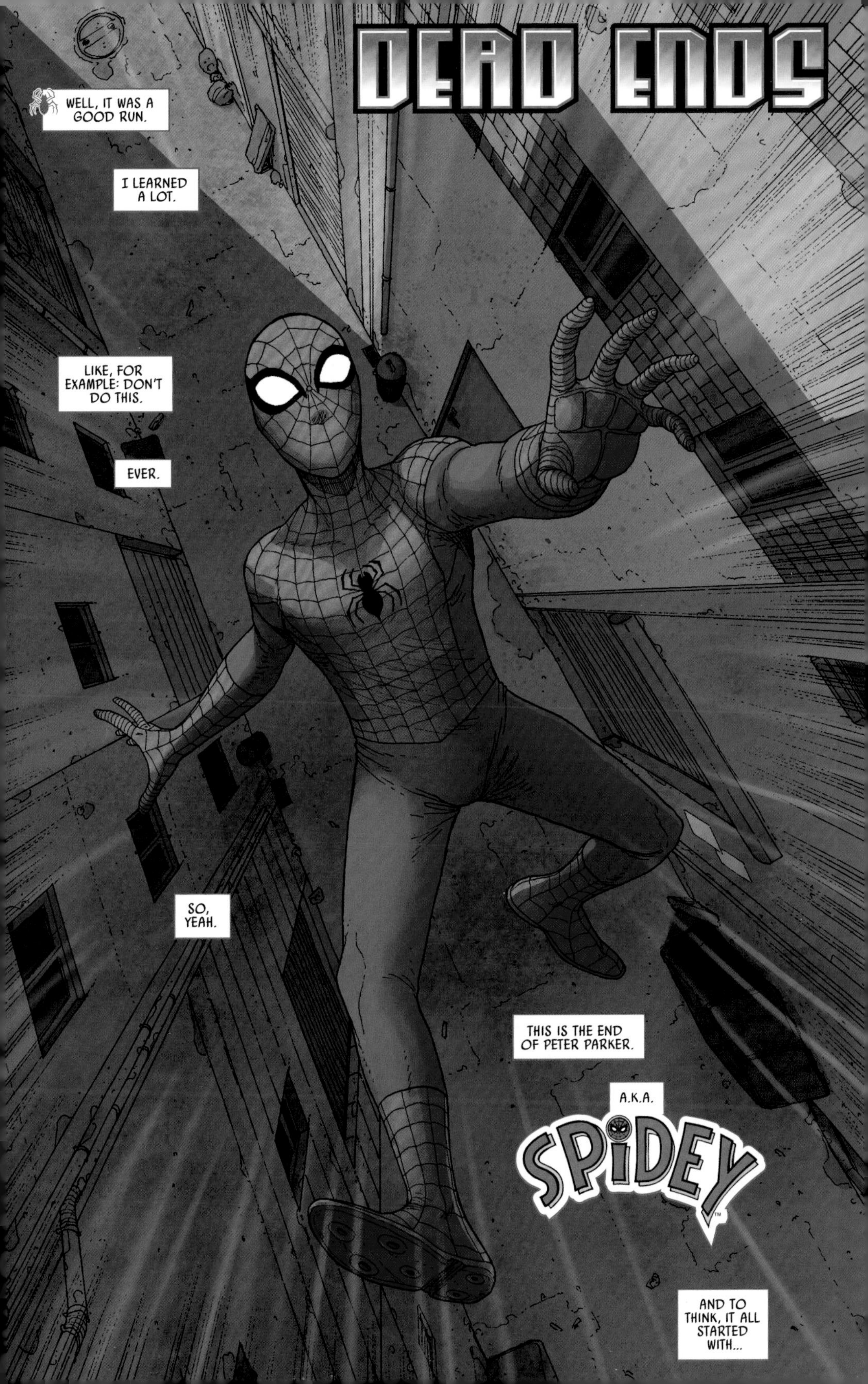
DEAD ENDS
WELL, IT WAS A GOOD RUN.
I LEARNED A LOT.
LIKE, FOR EXAMPLE: DON'T DO THIS.
EVER.
SO, YEAH.
THIS IS THE END OF PETER PARKER.
A.K.A.
SPIDEY
AND TO THINK, IT ALL STARTED WITH...

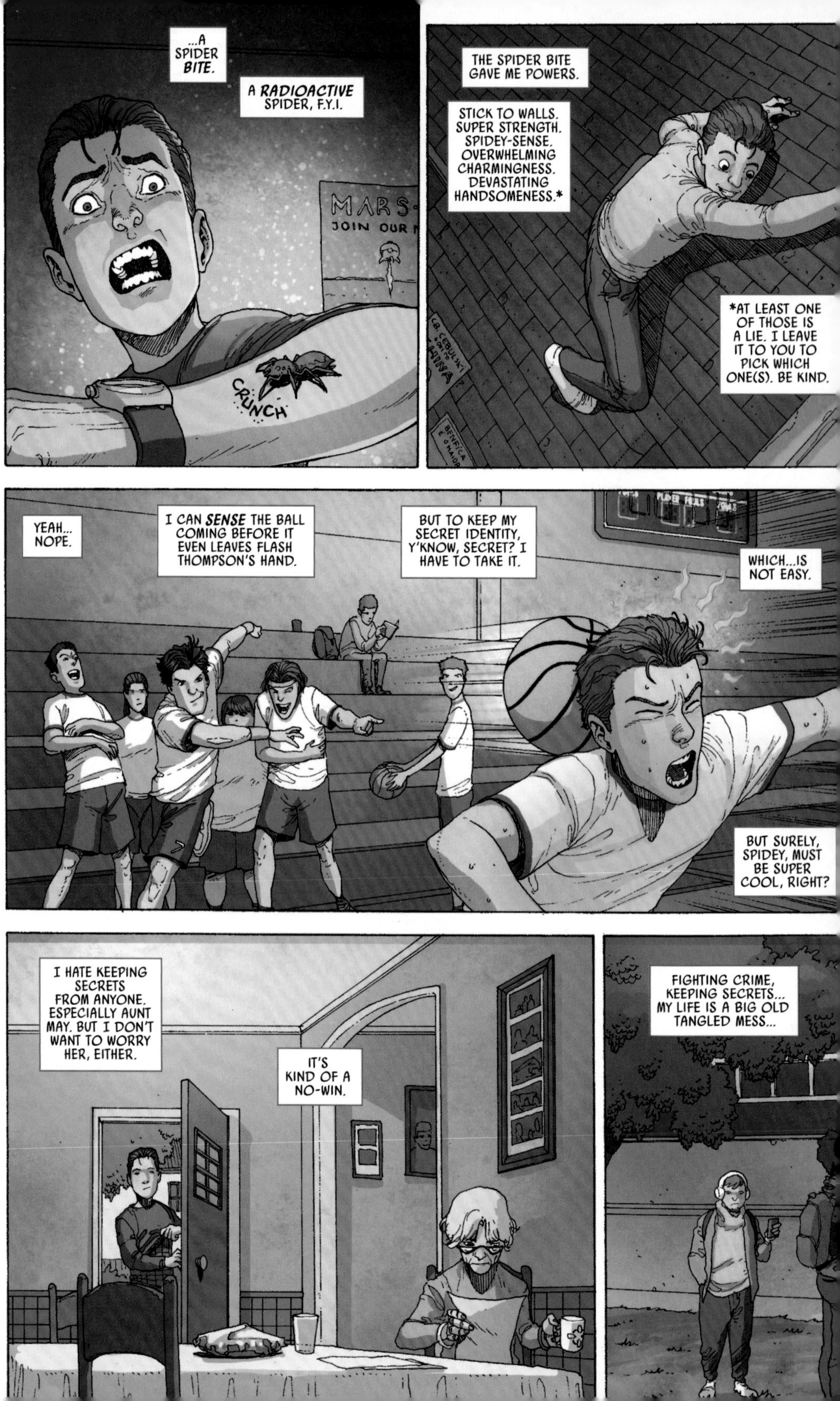
...A SPIDER *BITE*.
A *RADIOACTIVE* SPIDER, F.Y.I.
MARS-
JOIN OUR
CRUNCH
THE SPIDER BITE GAVE ME POWERS.
STICK TO WALLS. SUPER STRENGTH. SPIDEY-SENSE. OVERWHELMING CHARMINGNESS. DEVASTATING HANDSOMENESS.*
*AT LEAST ONE OF THOSE IS A LIE. I LEAVE IT TO YOU TO PICK WHICH ONE(S). BE KIND.
BUT SURELY, SPIDEY, MUST BE SUPER COOL, RIGHT?
YEAH... NOPE.
I CAN *SENSE* THE BALL COMING BEFORE IT EVEN LEAVES FLASH THOMPSON'S HAND.
BUT TO KEEP MY SECRET IDENTITY, Y'KNOW, SECRET? I HAVE TO TAKE IT.
WHICH...IS NOT EASY.
I HATE KEEPING SECRETS FROM ANYONE. ESPECIALLY AUNT MAY. BUT I DON'T WANT TO WORRY HER, EITHER.
IT'S KIND OF A NO-WIN.
FIGHTING CRIME, KEEPING SECRETS... MY LIFE IS A BIG OLD TANGLED MESS...

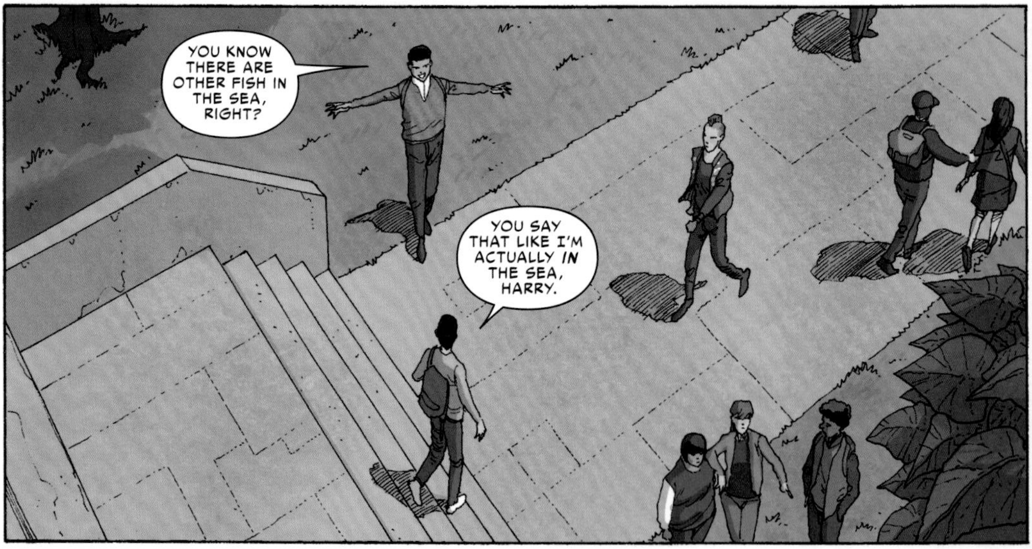
YOU KNOW THERE ARE OTHER FISH IN THE SEA, RIGHT?
YOU SAY THAT LIKE I'M ACTUALLY *IN* THE SEA, HARRY.

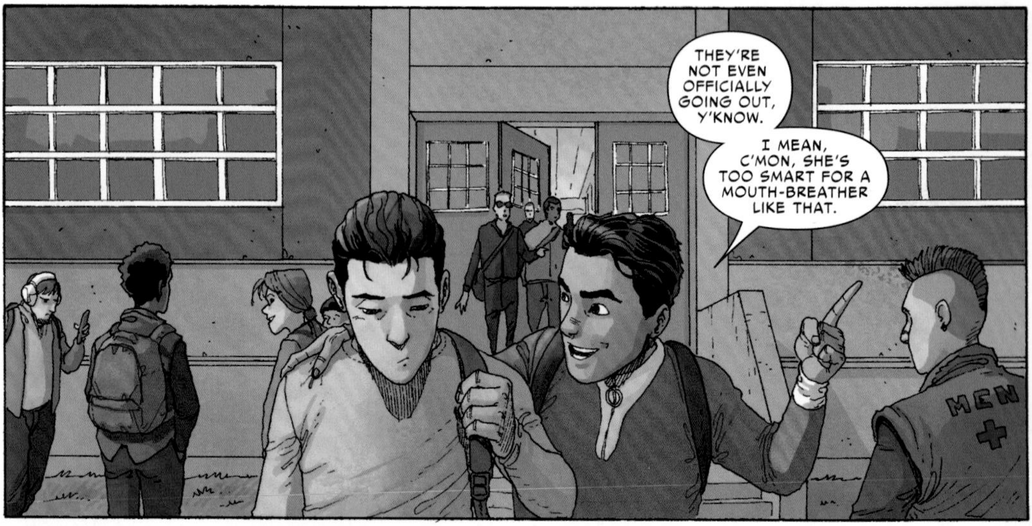
THEY'RE NOT EVEN OFFICIALLY GOING OUT, Y'KNOW.
I MEAN, C'MON, SHE'S TOO SMART FOR A MOUTH-BREATHER LIKE THAT.

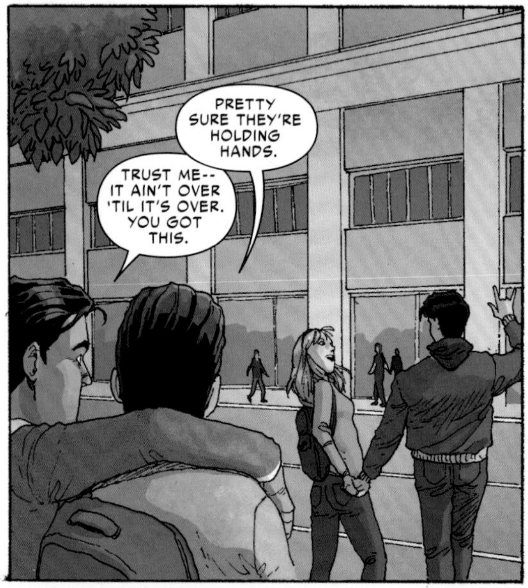
PRETTY SURE THEY'RE HOLDING HANDS.
TRUST ME-- IT AIN'T OVER 'TIL IT'S OVER. YOU GOT THIS.

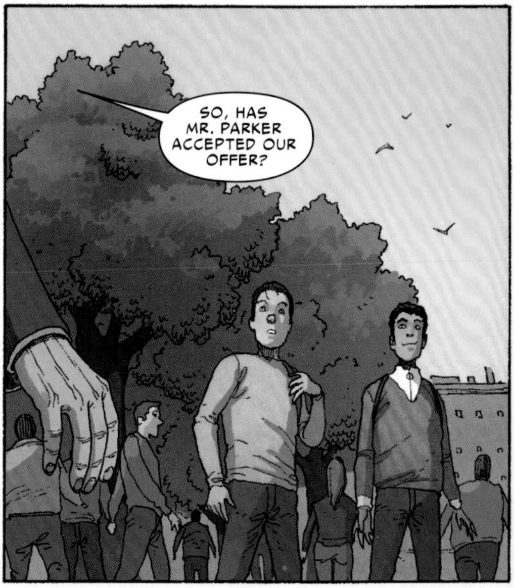
SO, HAS MR. PARKER ACCEPTED OUR OFFER?

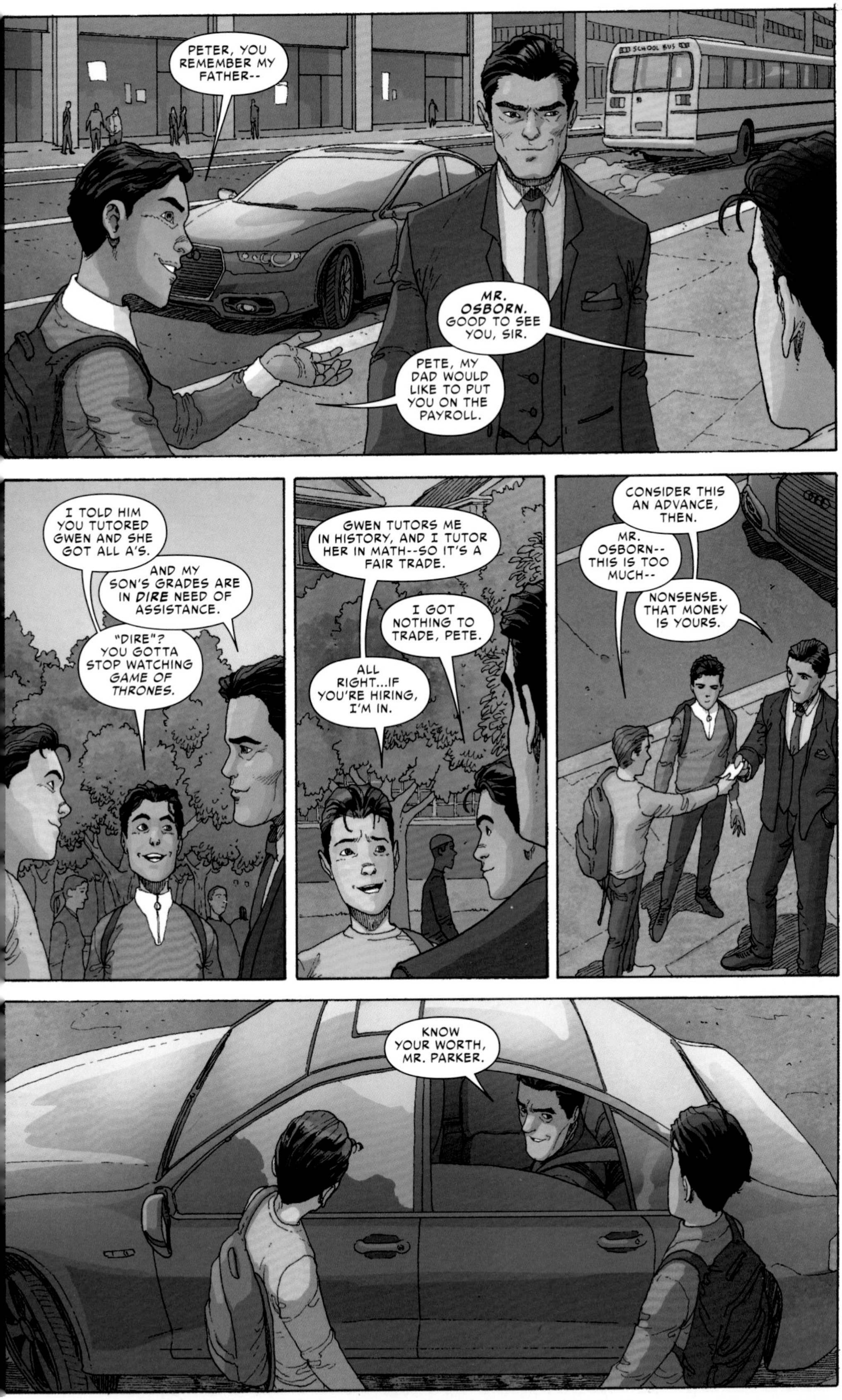
PETER, YOU REMEMBER MY FATHER--
MR. OSBORN. GOOD TO SEE YOU, SIR.
PETE, MY DAD WOULD LIKE TO PUT YOU ON THE PAYROLL.
I TOLD HIM YOU TUTORED GWEN AND SHE GOT ALL A'S.
AND MY SON'S GRADES ARE IN DIRE NEED OF ASSISTANCE.
"DIRE"? YOU GOTTA STOP WATCHING GAME OF THRONES.
GWEN TUTORS ME IN HISTORY, AND I TUTOR HER IN MATH--SO IT'S A FAIR TRADE.
I GOT NOTHING TO TRADE, PETE.
ALL RIGHT...IF YOU'RE HIRING, I'M IN.
CONSIDER THIS AN ADVANCE, THEN.
MR. OSBORN-- THIS IS TOO MUCH--
NONSENSE. THAT MONEY IS YOURS.
KNOW YOUR WORTH, MR. PARKER.

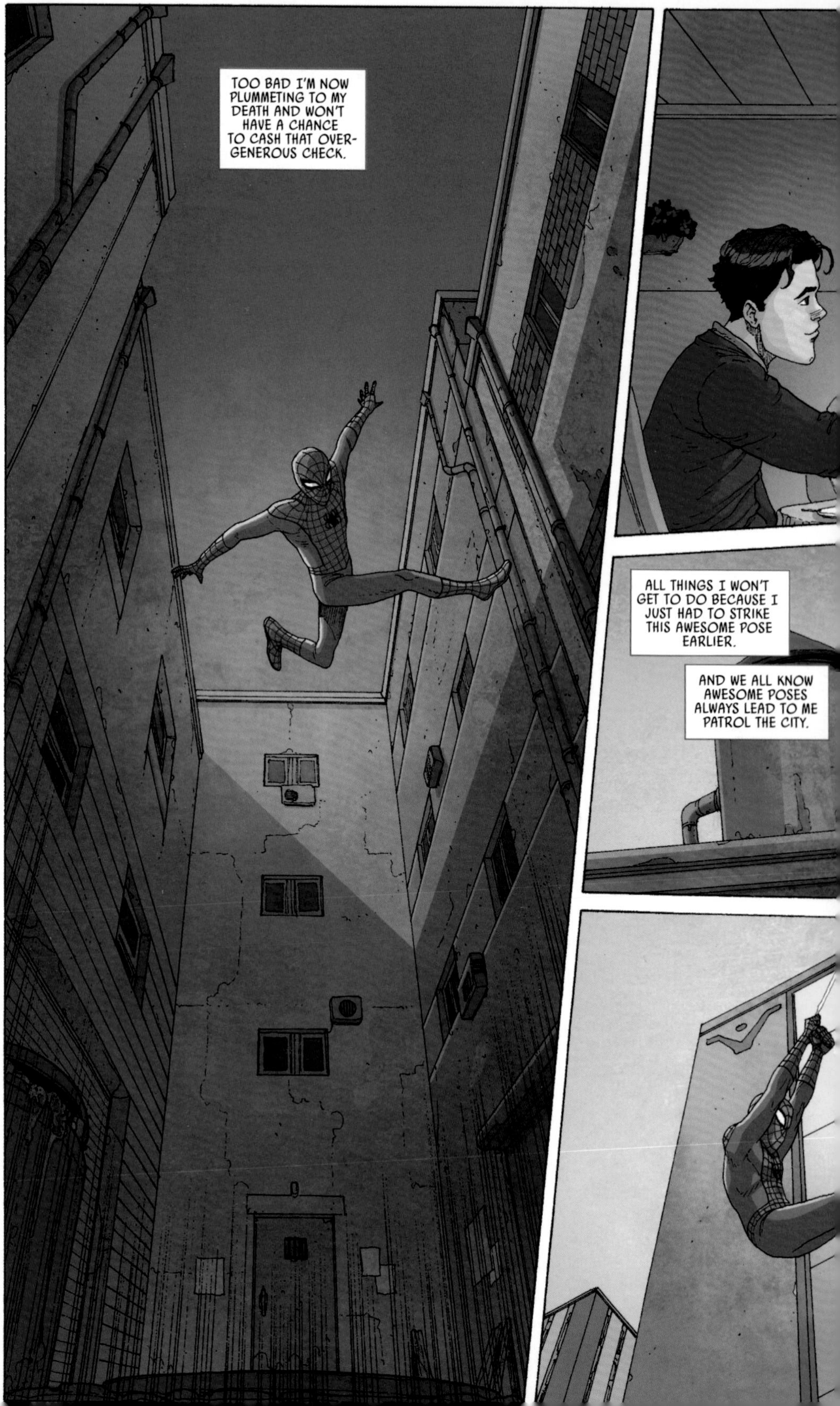
TOO BAD I'M NOW PLUMMETING TO MY DEATH AND WON'T HAVE A CHANCE TO CASH THAT OVER-GENEROUS CHECK.
ALL THINGS I WON'T GET TO DO BECAUSE I JUST HAD TO STRIKE THIS AWESOME POSE EARLIER.
AND WE ALL KNOW AWESOME POSES ALWAYS LEAD TO ME PATROL THE CITY.

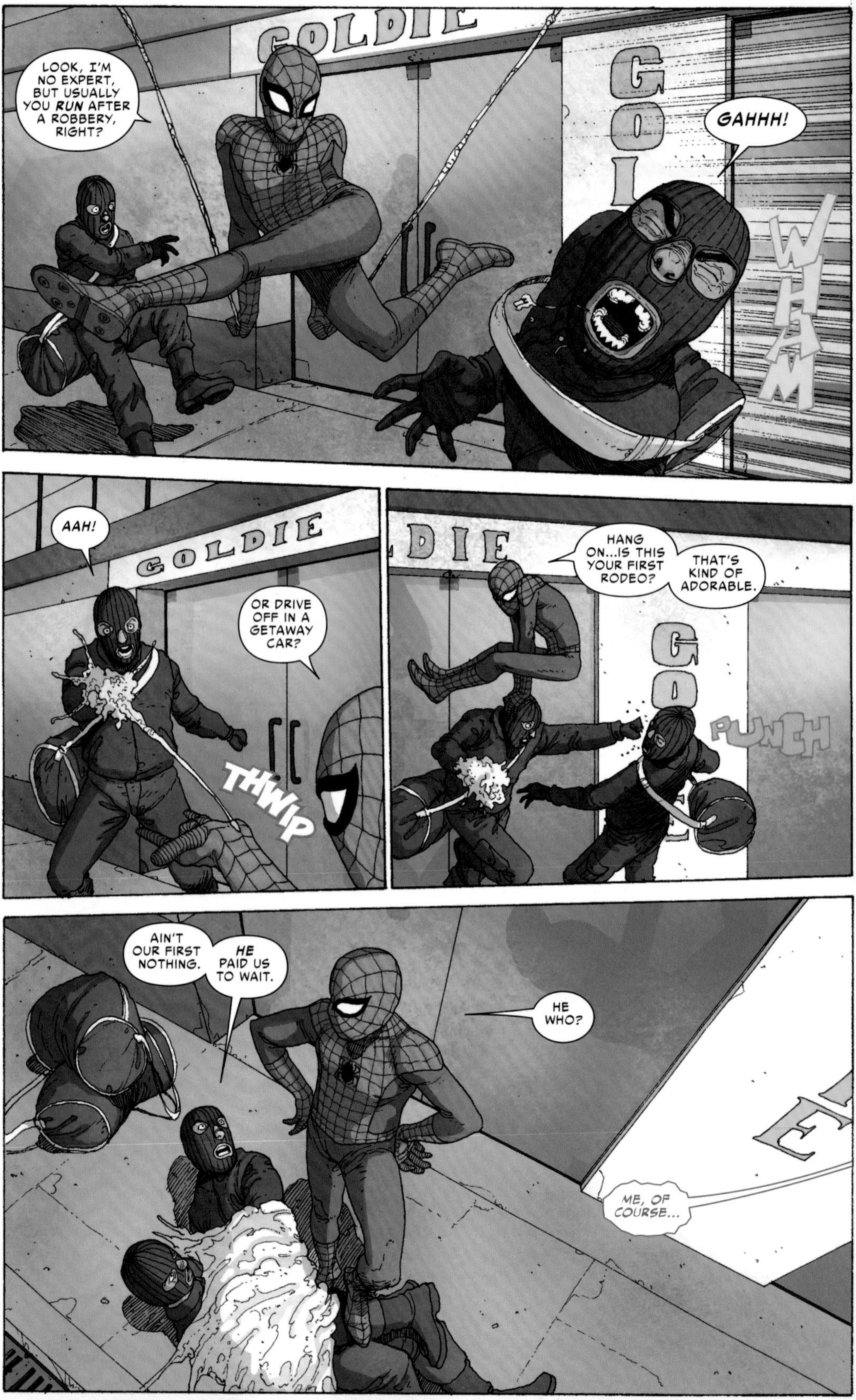
GOLDIE
LOOK, I'M NO EXPERT, BUT USUALLY YOU RUN AFTER A ROBBERY, RIGHT?
GAHHH!
WHAM
AAH!
GOLDIE
OR DRIVE OFF IN A GETAWAY CAR?
THWIP
HANG ON...IS THIS YOUR FIRST RODEO?
THAT'S KIND OF ADORABLE.
PUNCH
AIN'T OUR FIRST NOTHING.
HE PAID US TO WAIT.
HE WHO?
ME, OF COURSE...

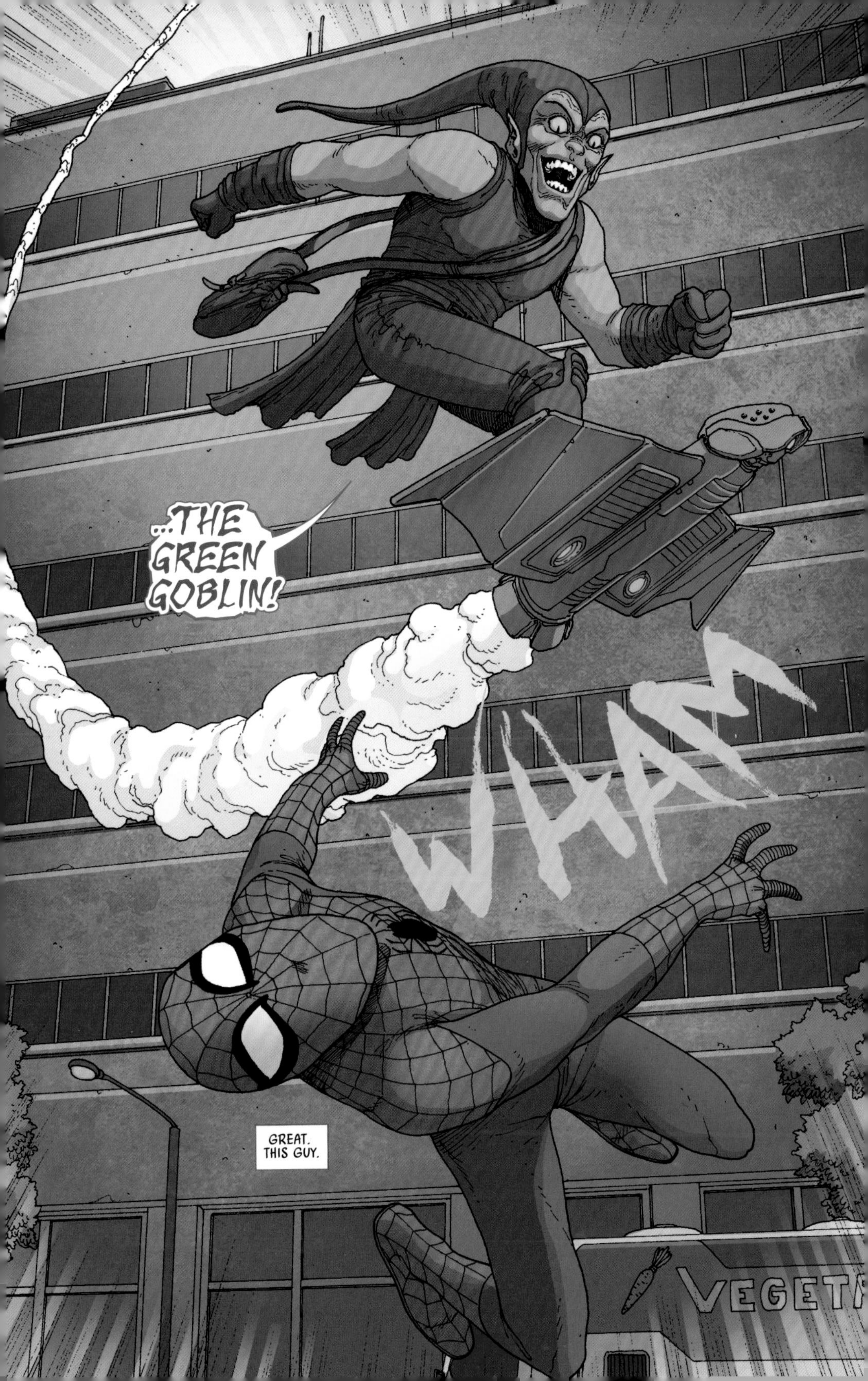
...THE GREEN GOBLIN!
WHAM
GREAT. THIS GUY.
VEGET

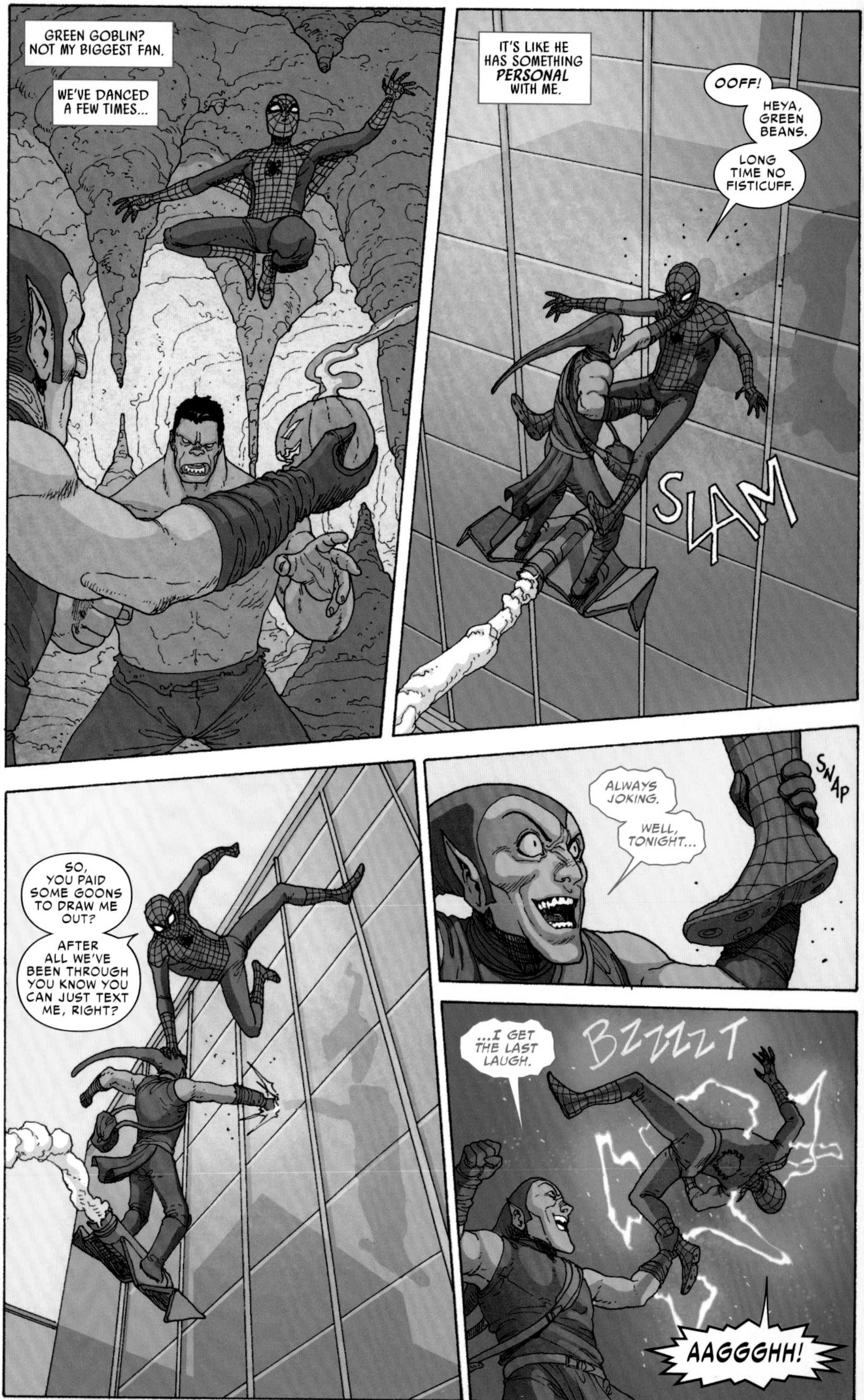
GREEN GOBLIN? NOT MY BIGGEST FAN.
WE'VE DANCED A FEW TIMES...
IT'S LIKE HE HAS SOMETHING PERSONAL WITH ME.
OOFF!
HEYA, GREEN BEANS.
LONG TIME NO FISTICUFF.
SLAM
SO, YOU PAID SOME GOONS TO DRAW ME OUT?
AFTER ALL WE'VE BEEN THROUGH YOU KNOW YOU CAN JUST TEXT ME, RIGHT?
SNAP
ALWAYS JOKING.
WELL, TONIGHT...
...I GET THE LAST LAUGH.
BZZZZZT
AAGGGHH!

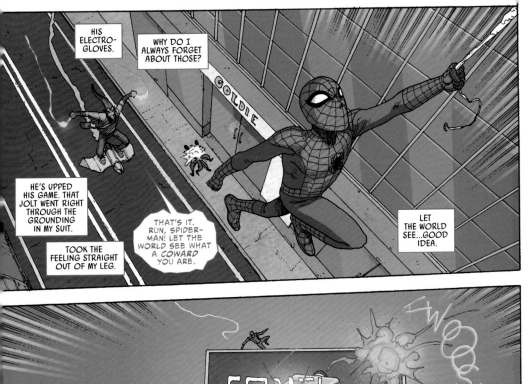

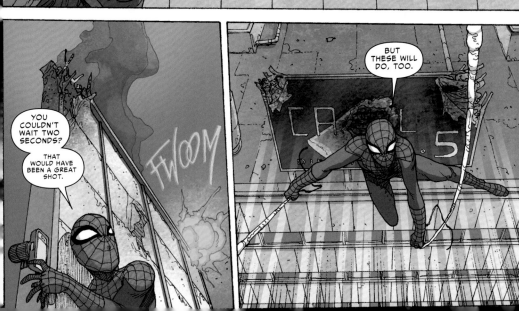

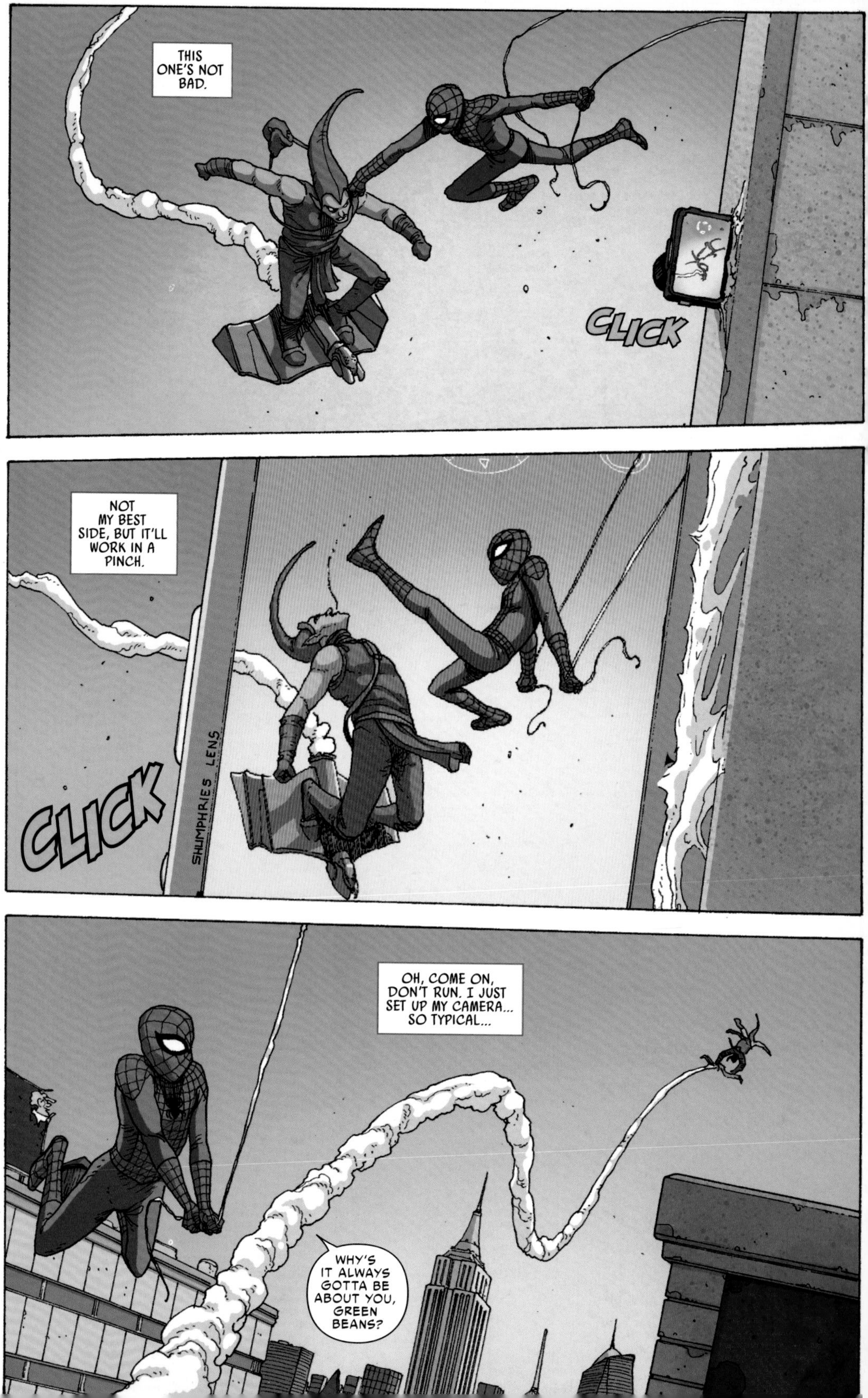

THIS ONE'S NOT BAD.
CLICK
NOT MY BEST SIDE, BUT IT'LL WORK IN A PINCH.
SHUMPHRIES LENS
CLICK
OH, COME ON, DON'T RUN. I JUST SET UP MY CAMERA... SO TYPICAL...
WHY'S IT ALWAYS GOTTA BE ABOUT YOU, GREEN BEANS?

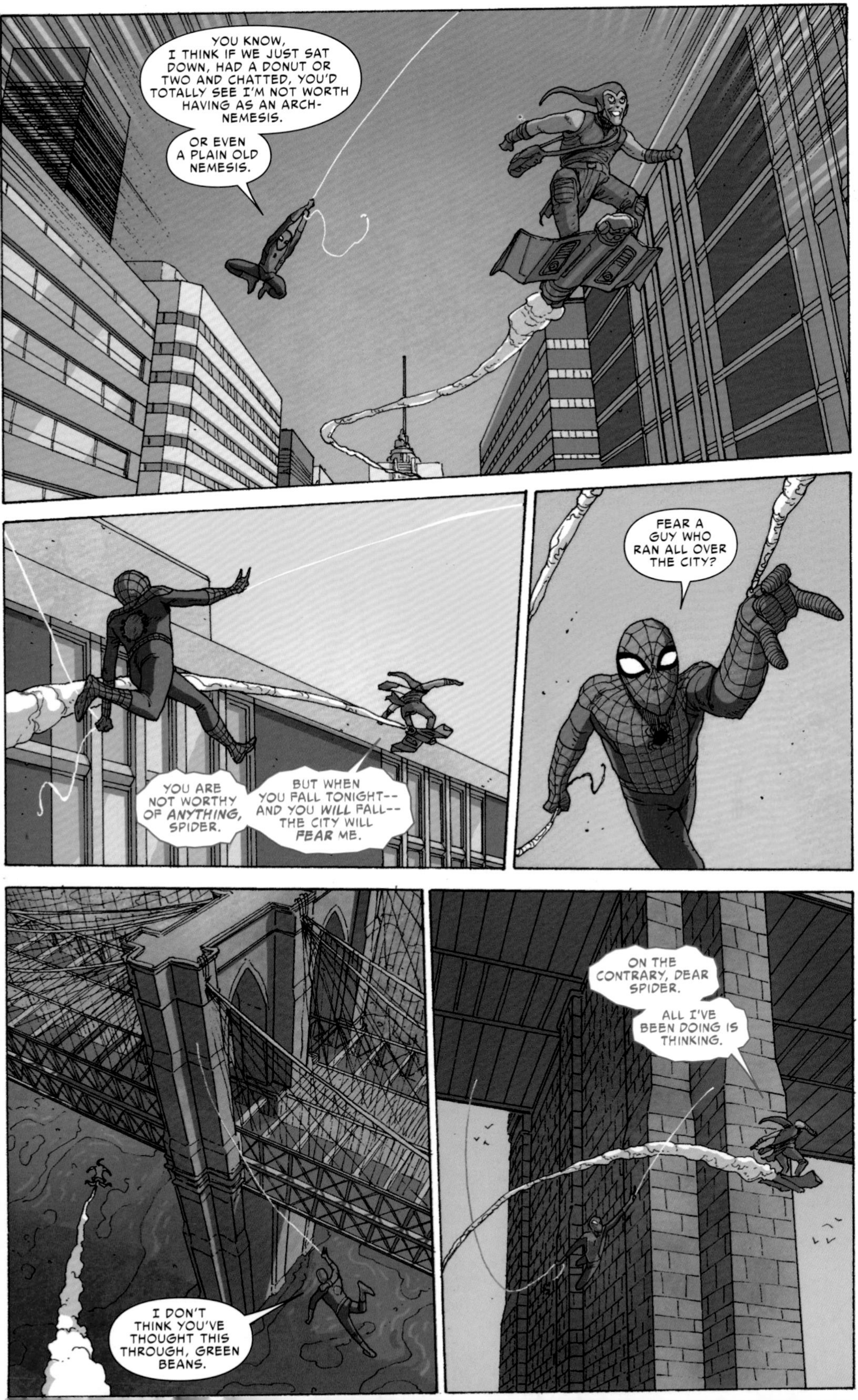
YOU KNOW, I THINK IF WE JUST SAT DOWN, HAD A DONUT OR TWO AND CHATTED, YOU'D TOTALLY SEE I'M NOT WORTH HAVING AS AN ARCH-NEMESIS.
OR EVEN A PLAIN OLD NEMESIS.
YOU ARE NOT WORTHY OF ANYTHING, SPIDER.
BUT WHEN YOU FALL TONIGHT-- AND YOU WILL FALL-- THE CITY WILL FEAR ME.
FEAR A GUY WHO RAN ALL OVER THE CITY?
I DON'T THINK YOU'VE THOUGHT THIS THROUGH, GREEN BEANS.
ON THE CONTRARY, DEAR SPIDER.
ALL I'VE BEEN DOING IS THINKING.

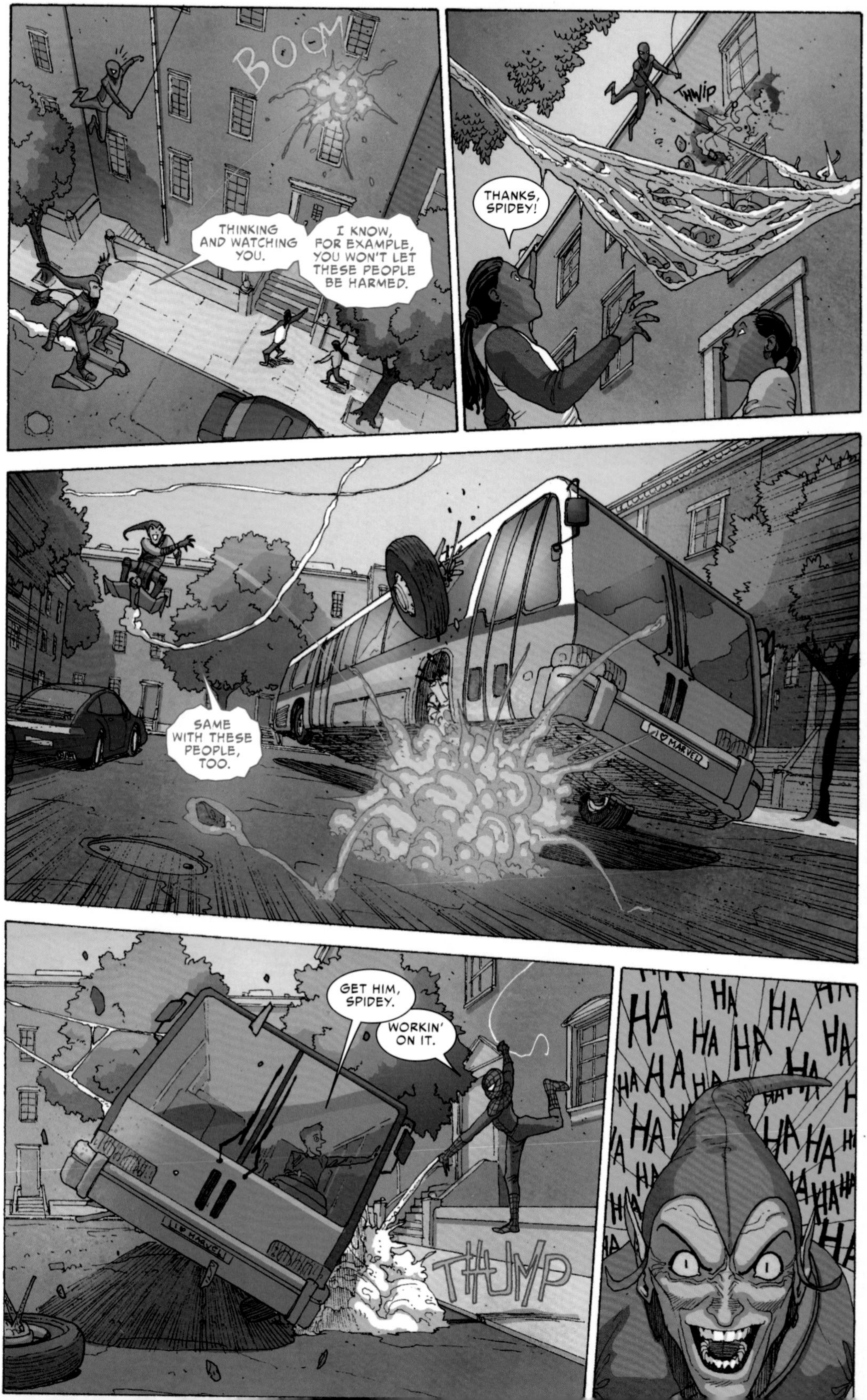
BOOM
THINKING AND WATCHING YOU.
I KNOW, FOR EXAMPLE, YOU WON'T LET THESE PEOPLE BE HARMED.
THWIP
THANKS, SPIDEY!
SAME WITH THESE PEOPLE, TOO.
I ♥ MARVEL
GET HIM, SPIDEY.
WORKIN' ON IT.
THUMP
HA HA HA HA HA HA HA HA HA HA HA HA HA HA HA HA HA HA HA HA HA HA

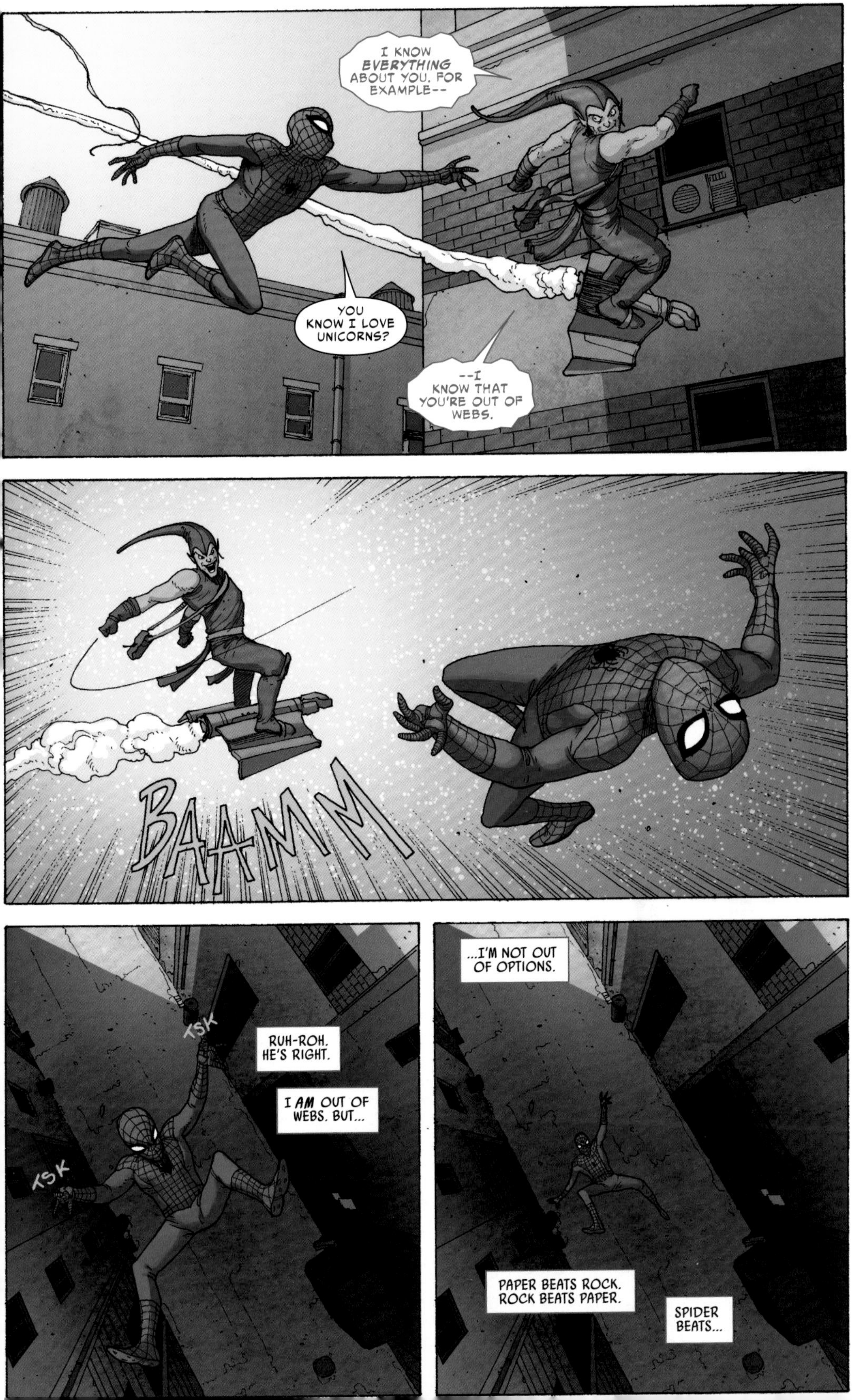
I KNOW EVERYTHING ABOUT YOU. FOR EXAMPLE--
YOU KNOW I LOVE UNICORNS?
--I KNOW THAT YOU'RE OUT OF WEBS.
BAAMM
TSK
RUH-ROH. HE'S RIGHT.
I AM OUT OF WEBS. BUT...
TSK
...I'M NOT OUT OF OPTIONS.
PAPER BEATS ROCK. ROCK BEATS PAPER.
SPIDER BEATS...

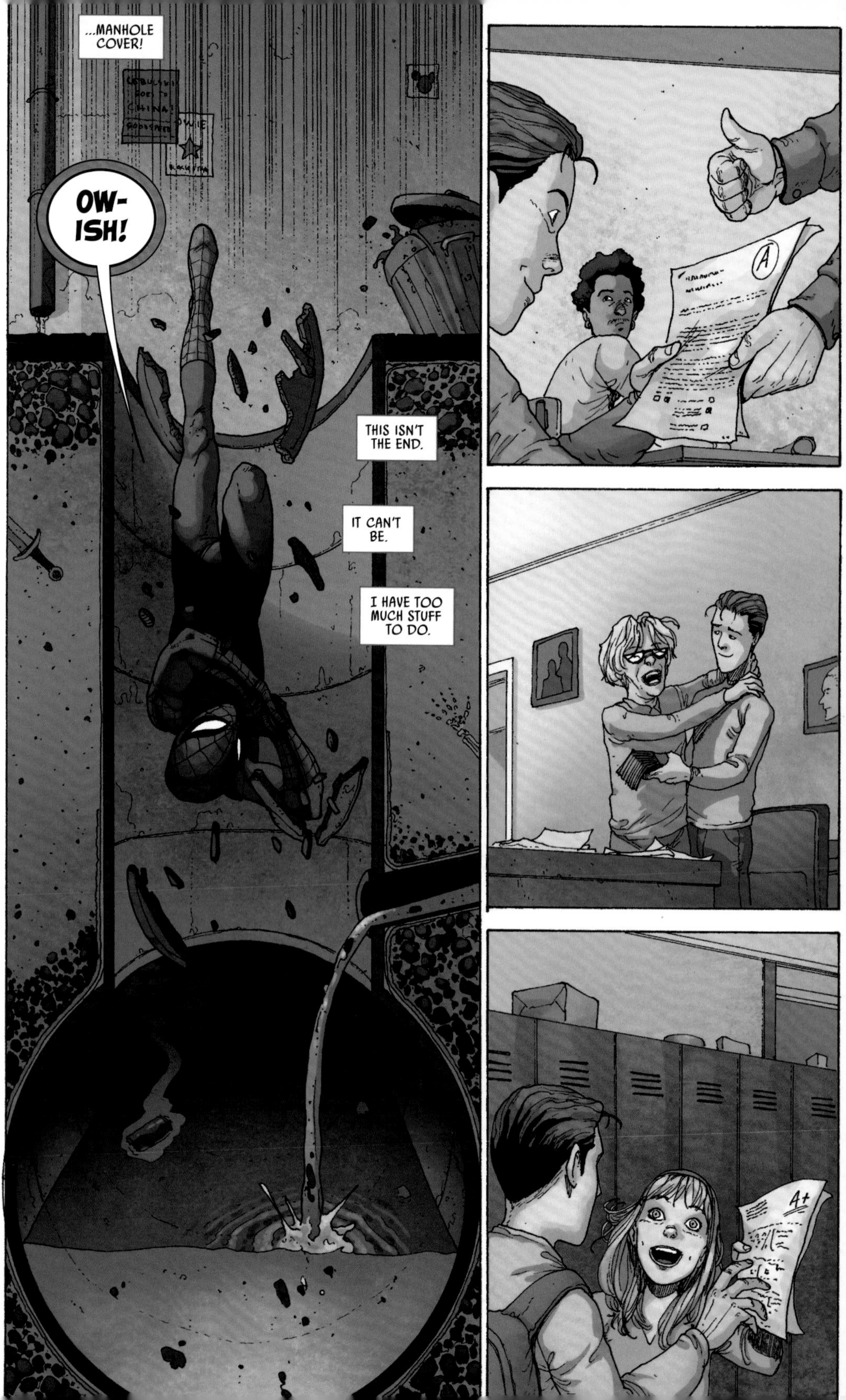

...MANHOLE COVER!
OW-ISH!
THIS ISN'T THE END.
IT CAN'T BE.
I HAVE TOO MUCH STUFF TO DO.
A+

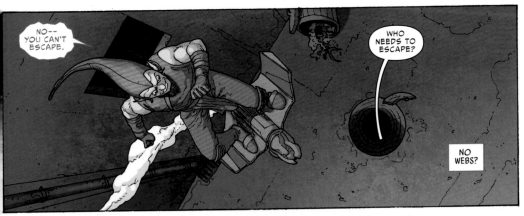

NO—
YOU CAN'T
ESCAPE.

WHO
NEEDS TO
ESCAPE?

NO
WEBS?

NOTHING A
LITTLE *WATER*
CAN'T FIX.

GAH!

BzZZZZT

GAHHH!

SLAM

I
WAS RIGHT
ABOUT YOU,
SPIDER.

YOU KNEW
I DIG WATER
RIDES, IN ADDITION
TO UNICORNS? HAVE
YOU BEEN STALKING
MY FACEBOOK
PAGE?

YOU ARE
FOOLISH. AND
LUCKY. BUT YOU
ARE ALSO...

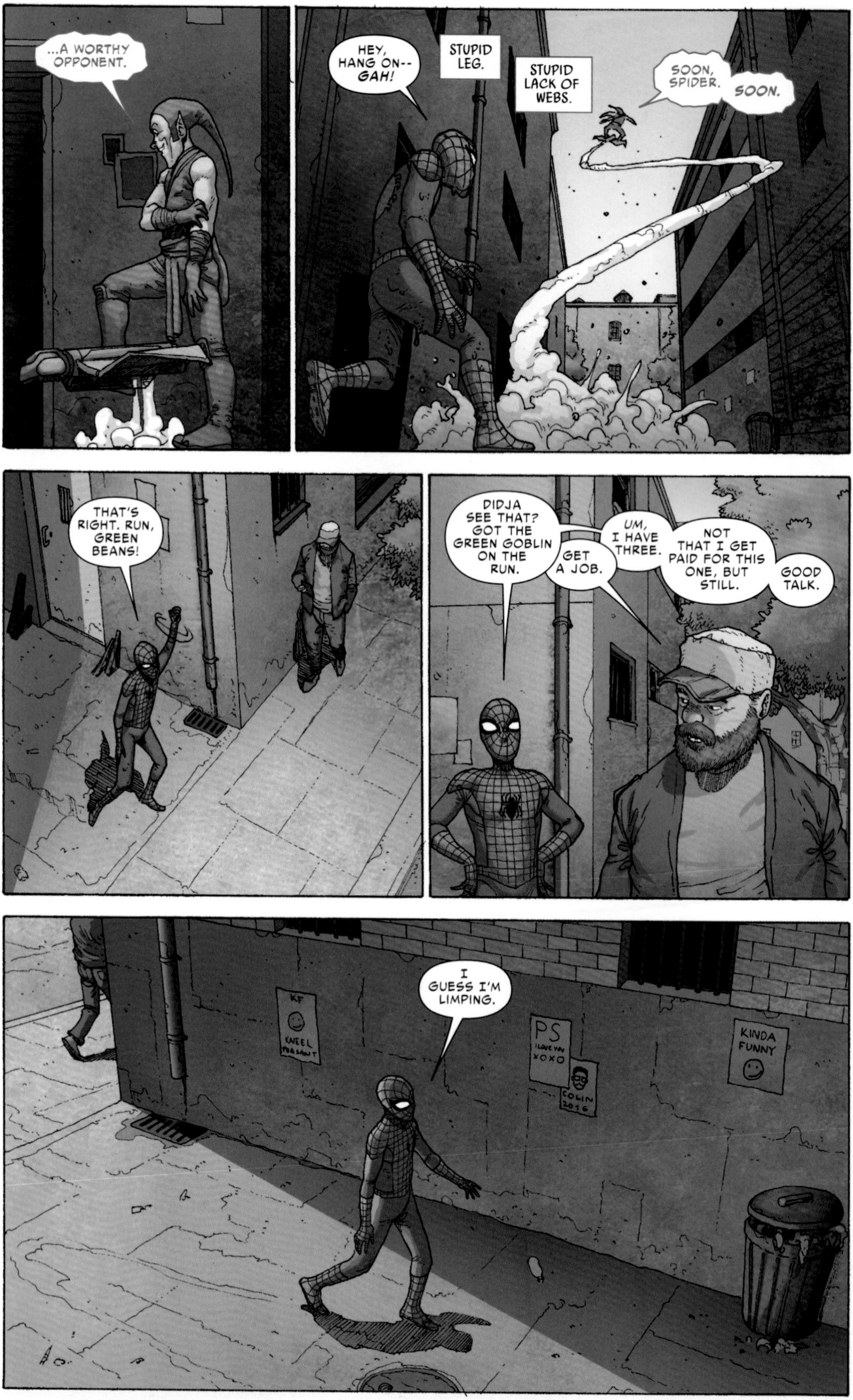
...A WORTHY OPPONENT.
HEY, HANG ON-- GAH!
STUPID LEG.
STUPID LACK OF WEBS.
SOON, SPIDER.
SOON.
THAT'S RIGHT. RUN, GREEN BEANS!
DIDJA SEE THAT? GOT THE GREEN GOBLIN ON THE RUN.
GET A JOB.
UM, I HAVE THREE.
NOT THAT I GET PAID FOR THIS ONE, BUT STILL.
GOOD TALK.
I GUESS I'M LIMPING.
KF
KNEEL PEASANT
PS
XOXO
COLIN 2016
KINDA FUNNY

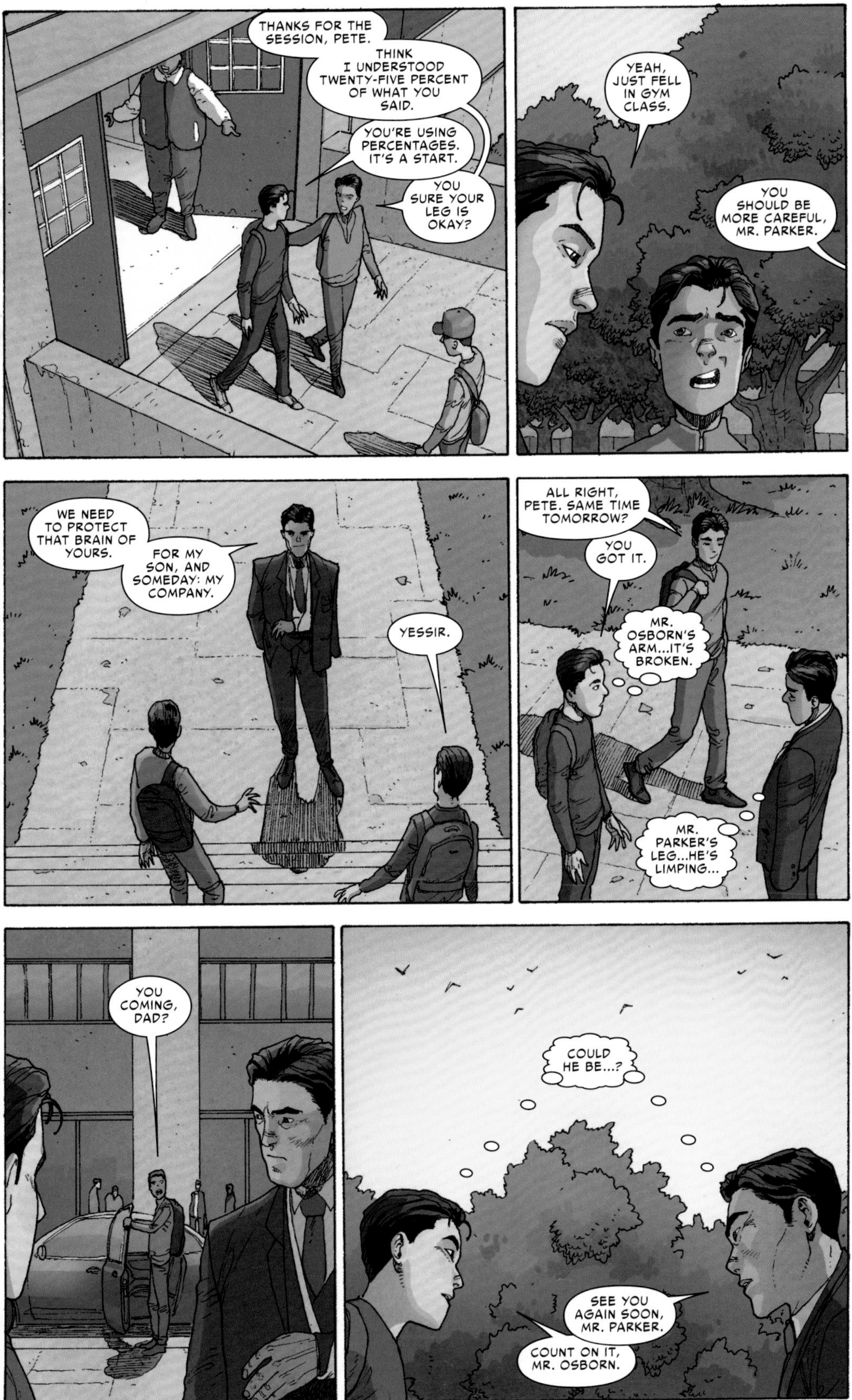
THANKS FOR THE SESSION, PETE.
THINK I UNDERSTOOD TWENTY-FIVE PERCENT OF WHAT YOU SAID.
YOU'RE USING PERCENTAGES. IT'S A START.
YOU SURE YOUR LEG IS OKAY?
YEAH, JUST FELL IN GYM CLASS.
YOU SHOULD BE MORE CAREFUL, MR. PARKER.
WE NEED TO PROTECT THAT BRAIN OF YOURS.
FOR MY SON, AND SOMEDAY: MY COMPANY.
YESSIR.
ALL RIGHT, PETE. SAME TIME TOMORROW?
YOU GOT IT.
MR. OSBORN'S ARM...IT'S BROKEN.
MR. PARKER'S LEG...HE'S LIMPING...
YOU COMING, DAD?
COULD HE BE...?
SEE YOU AGAIN SOON, MR. PARKER.
COUNT ON IT, MR. OSBORN.

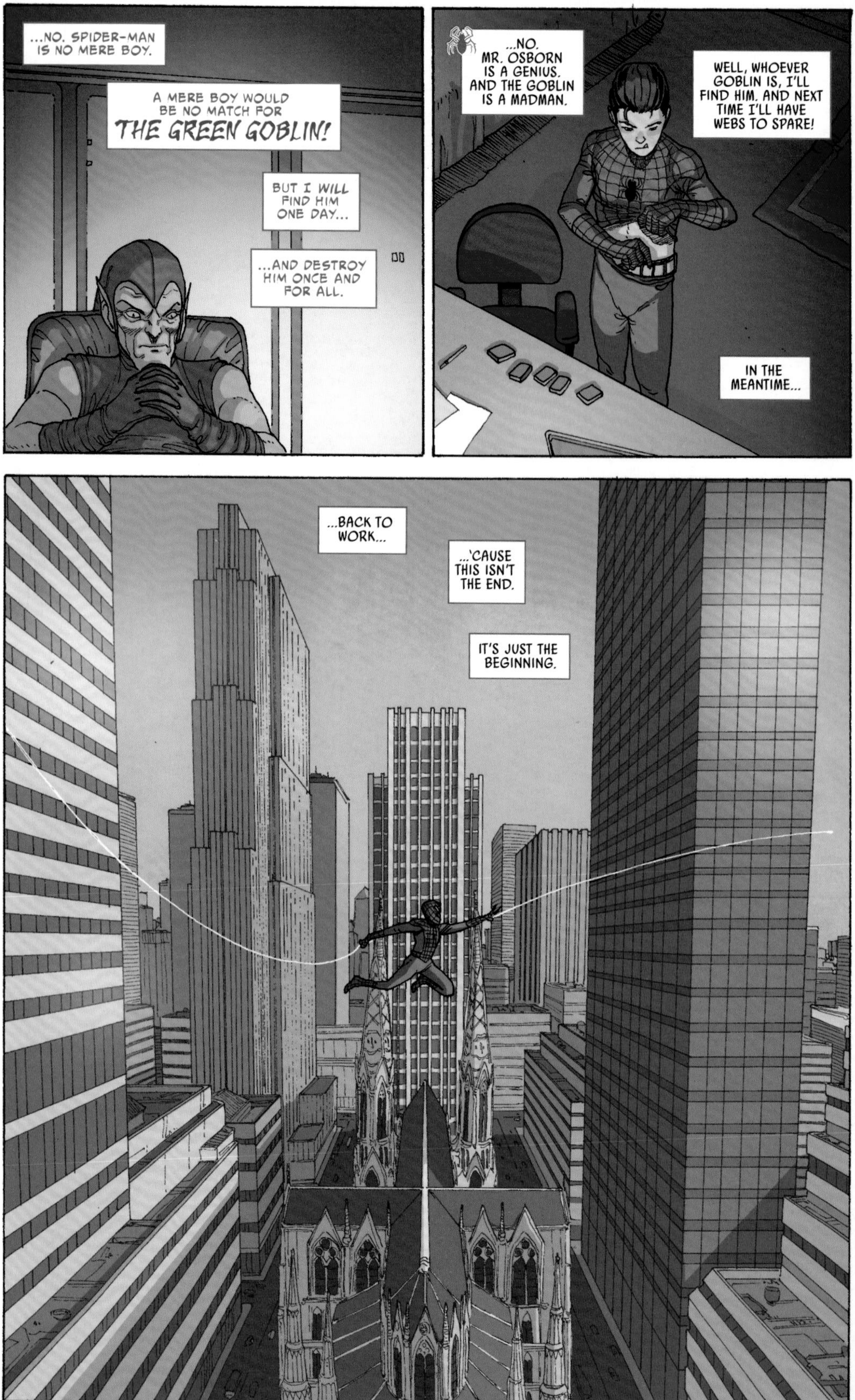
...NO. SPIDER-MAN IS NO MERE BOY.
A MERE BOY WOULD BE NO MATCH FOR THE GREEN GOBLIN!
BUT I WILL FIND HIM ONE DAY...
...AND DESTROY HIM ONCE AND FOR ALL.
...NO. MR. OSBORN IS A GENIUS. AND THE GOBLIN IS A MADMAN.
WELL, WHOEVER GOBLIN IS, I'LL FIND HIM. AND NEXT TIME I'LL HAVE WEBS TO SPARE!
IN THE MEANTIME...
...BACK TO WORK...
...'CAUSE THIS ISN'T THE END.
IT'S JUST THE BEGINNING.

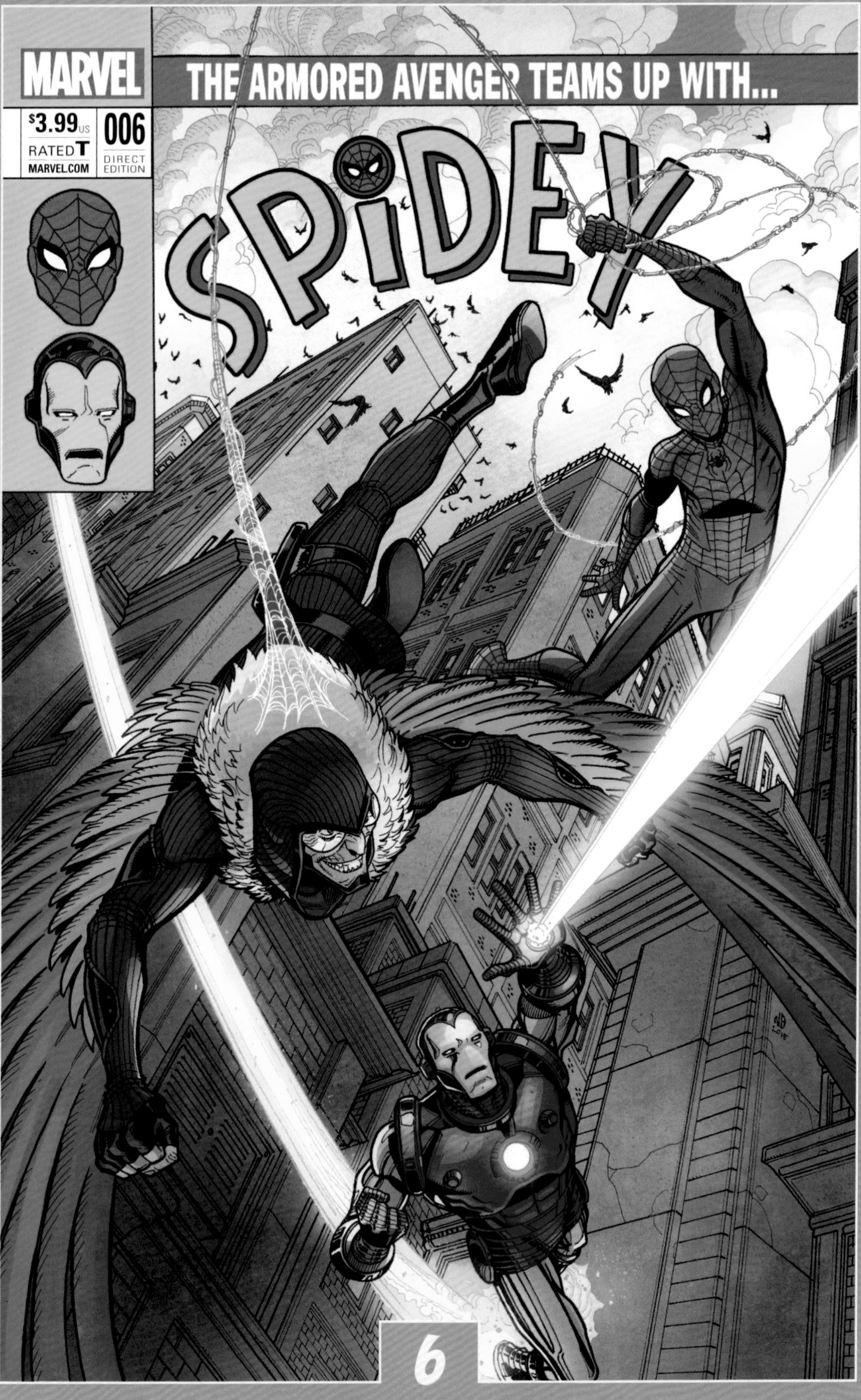
MARVEL
THE ARMORED AVENGER TEAMS UP WITH...
SPIDEY
$3.99 US
006
RATED T
MARVEL.COM
DIRECT EDITION

6

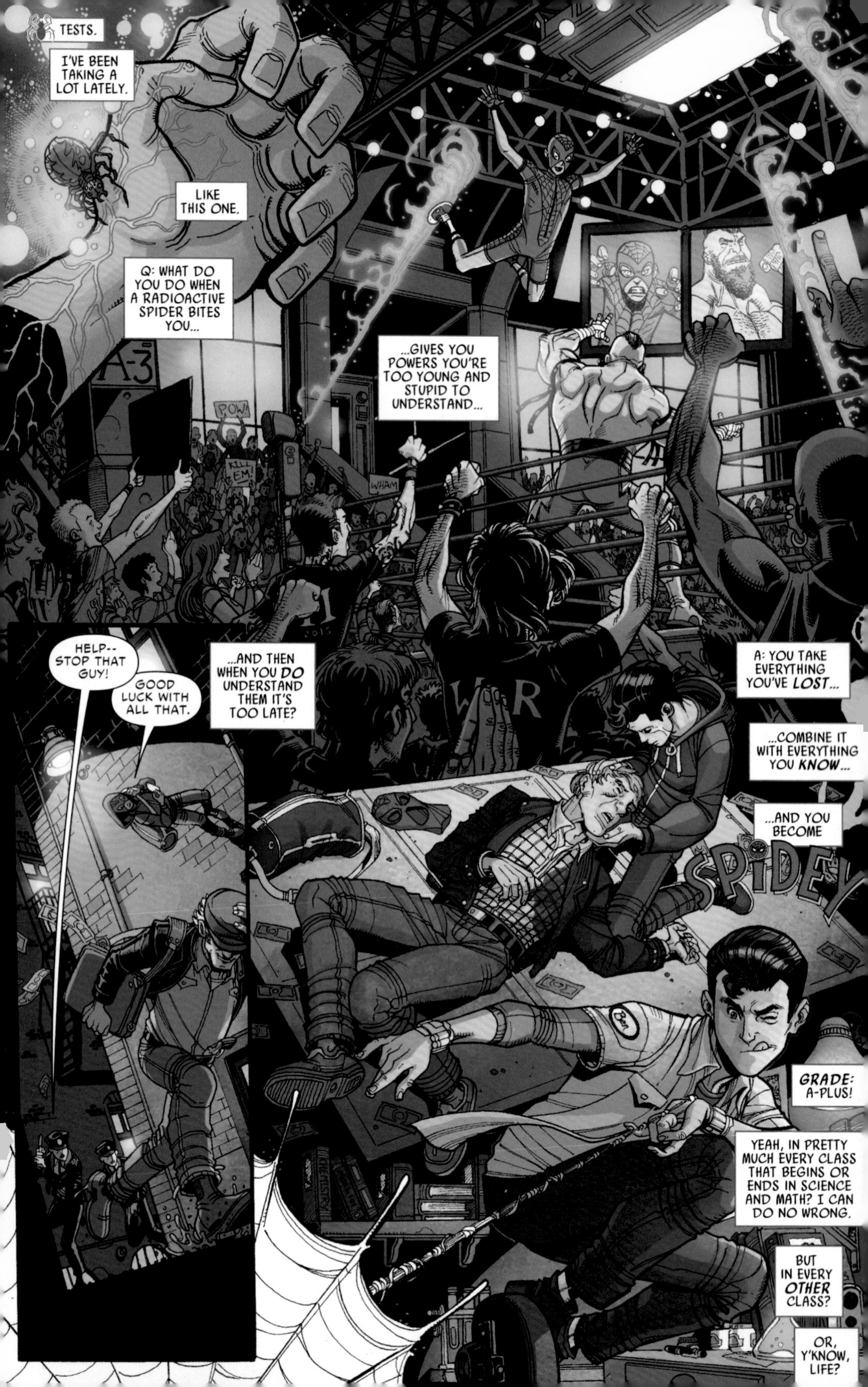

TESTS.
I'VE BEEN TAKING A LOT LATELY.
LIKE THIS ONE.
Q: WHAT DO YOU DO WHEN A RADIOACTIVE SPIDER BITES YOU...
...GIVES YOU POWERS YOU'RE TOO YOUNG AND STUPID TO UNDERSTAND...
POW
KILL 'EM!
WHAM
HELP-- STOP THAT GUY!
GOOD LUCK WITH ALL THAT.
...AND THEN WHEN YOU DO UNDERSTAND THEM IT'S TOO LATE?
A: YOU TAKE EVERYTHING YOU'VE LOST...
...COMBINE IT WITH EVERYTHING YOU KNOW...
...AND YOU BECOME
SPIDEY
GRADE: A-PLUS!
YEAH, IN PRETTY MUCH EVERY CLASS THAT BEGINS OR ENDS IN SCIENCE AND MATH? I CAN DO NO WRONG.
BUT IN EVERY OTHER CLASS?
OR, Y'KNOW, LIFE?

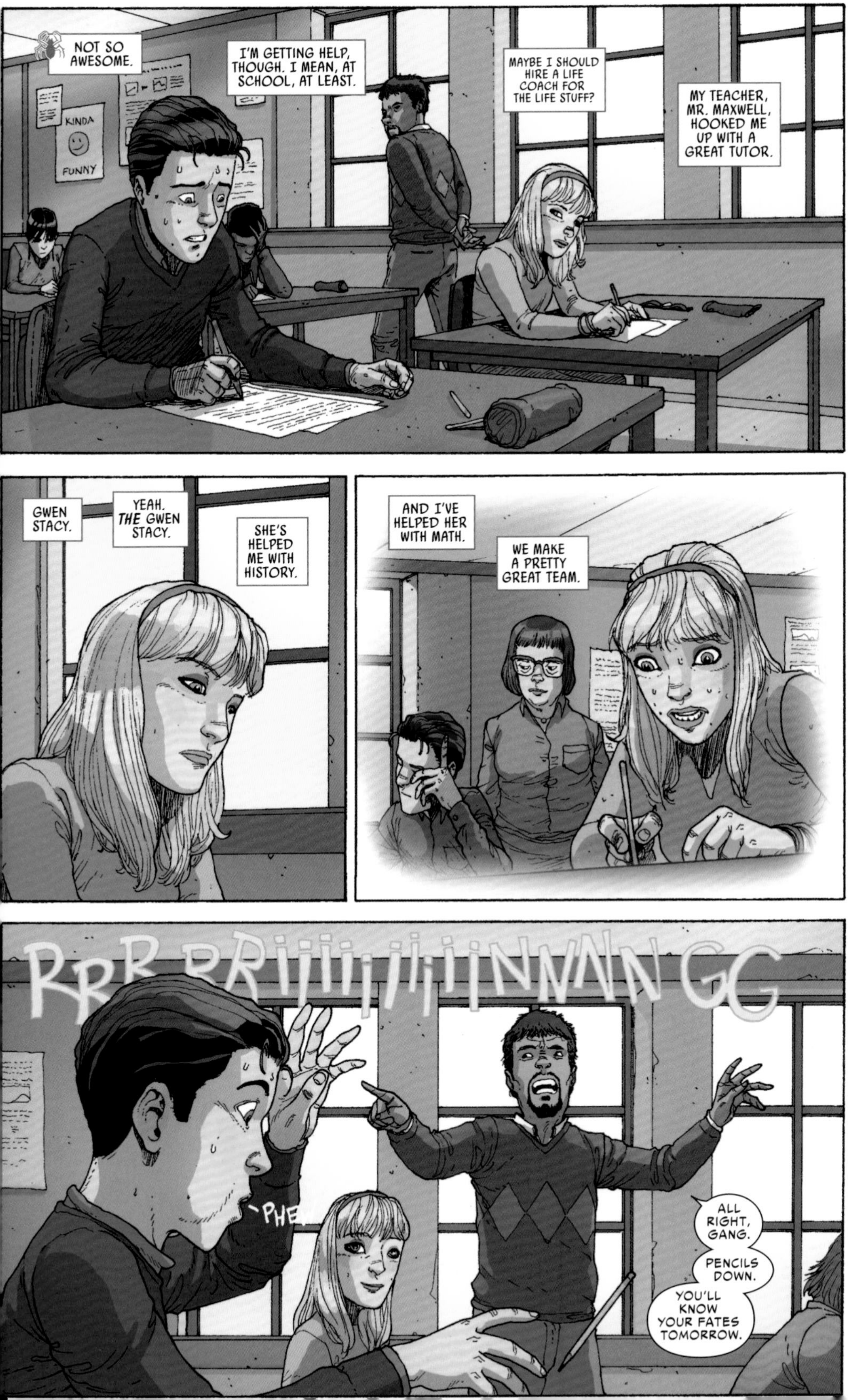
NOT SO AWESOME.
I'M GETTING HELP, THOUGH. I MEAN, AT SCHOOL, AT LEAST.
MAYBE I SHOULD HIRE A LIFE COACH FOR THE LIFE STUFF?
MY TEACHER, MR. MAXWELL, HOOKED ME UP WITH A GREAT TUTOR.
KINDA
FUNNY
GWEN STACY.
YEAH. *THE* GWEN STACY.
SHE'S HELPED ME WITH HISTORY.
AND I'VE HELPED HER WITH MATH.
WE MAKE A PRETTY GREAT TEAM.
RRRRRIIIIIIIIIINNNNNGG
PHEW
ALL RIGHT, GANG.
PENCILS DOWN.
YOU'LL KNOW YOUR FATES TOMORROW.

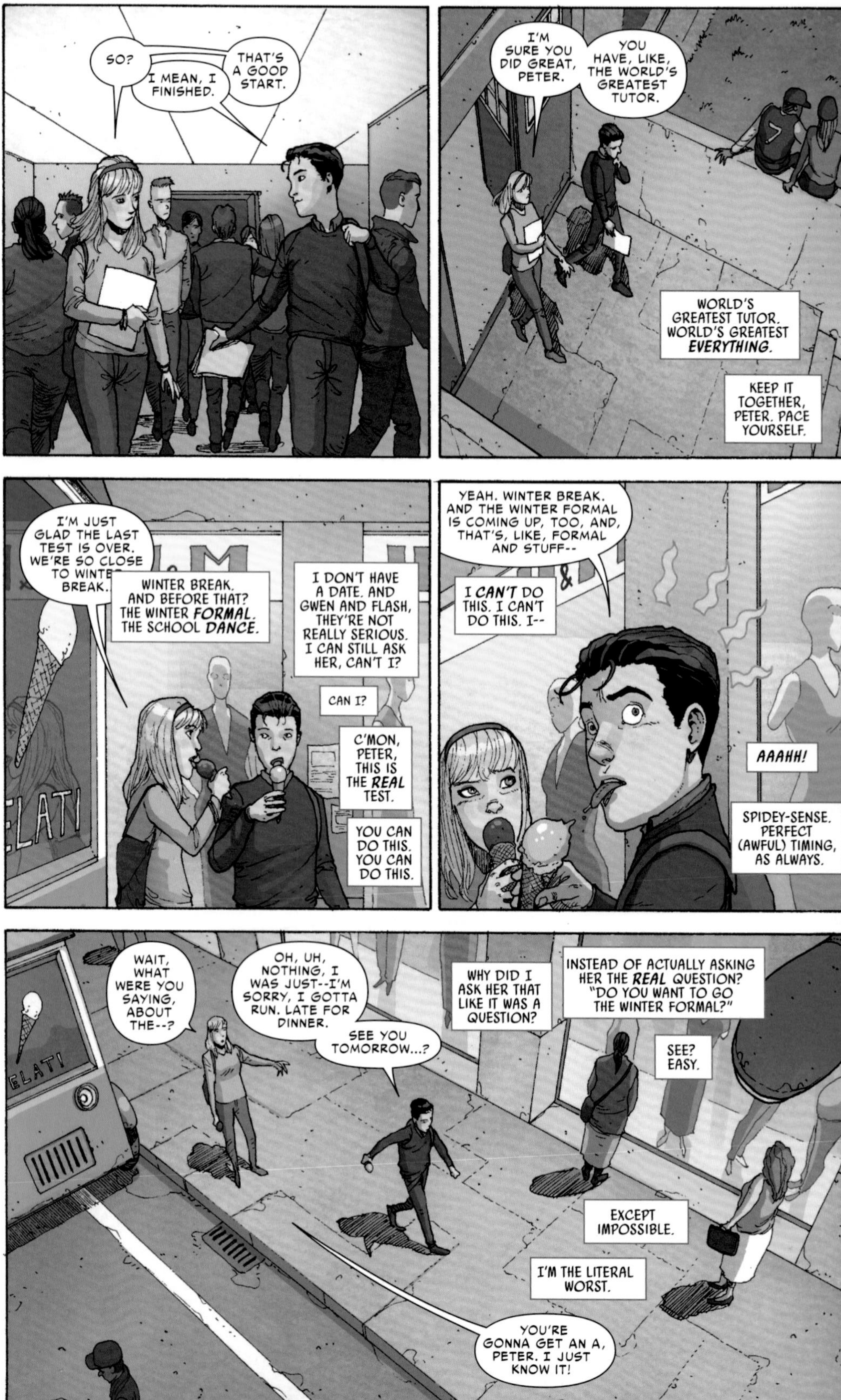
SO?
I MEAN, I FINISHED.
THAT'S A GOOD START.
I'M SURE YOU DID GREAT, PETER.
YOU HAVE, LIKE, THE WORLD'S GREATEST TUTOR.
WORLD'S GREATEST TUTOR. WORLD'S GREATEST *EVERYTHING.*
KEEP IT TOGETHER, PETER. PACE YOURSELF.
I'M JUST GLAD THE LAST TEST IS OVER. WE'RE SO CLOSE TO WINTER BREAK.
WINTER BREAK. AND BEFORE THAT? THE WINTER *FORMAL*. THE SCHOOL *DANCE.*
I DON'T HAVE A DATE. AND GWEN AND FLASH, THEY'RE NOT REALLY SERIOUS. I CAN STILL ASK HER, CAN'T I?
CAN I?
C'MON, PETER, THIS IS THE *REAL* TEST.
YOU CAN DO THIS. YOU CAN DO THIS.
YEAH. WINTER BREAK. AND THE WINTER FORMAL IS COMING UP, TOO, AND, THAT'S, LIKE, FORMAL AND STUFF--
I *CAN'T* DO THIS. I CAN'T DO THIS. I--
AAAHH!
SPIDEY-SENSE. PERFECT (AWFUL) TIMING, AS ALWAYS.
WAIT, WHAT WERE YOU SAYING, ABOUT THE--?
OH, UH, NOTHING, I WAS JUST--I'M SORRY, I GOTTA RUN. LATE FOR DINNER.
SEE YOU TOMORROW...?
WHY DID I ASK HER THAT LIKE IT WAS A QUESTION?
INSTEAD OF ACTUALLY ASKING HER THE *REAL* QUESTION? "DO YOU WANT TO GO THE WINTER FORMAL?"
SEE? EASY.
EXCEPT IMPOSSIBLE.
I'M THE LITERAL WORST.
YOU'RE GONNA GET AN A, PETER. I JUST KNOW IT!

Q: HOW DO YOU ASK A GIRL OUT?

A:...

GRADE:
EPIC FAIL.

ZOMBIES
THE MOVIE

WHY IS THIS SO HARD?

"DO YOU WANT TO GO TO THE WINTER FORMAL?"

IT *SOUNDS* EASY. IN MY HEAD ANYWAY.

MAYBE I SHOULD TRY IT OUT LOUD.

DO YOU WANT TO GO TO THE WINTER FORMAL?

(TERRIBLE)

DO *YOU* WANT TO GO TO THE WINTER FORMAL?

(WORSE)

BREAK-IN. WHAT BUILDING IS THIS?

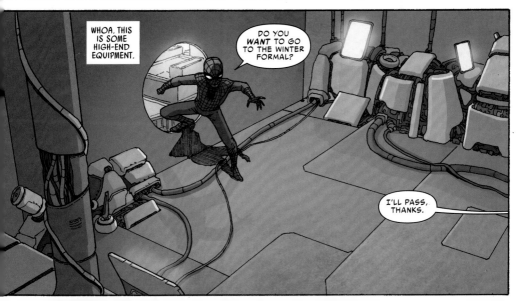

WHOA. THIS IS SOME HIGH-END EQUIPMENT.

DO YOU *WANT* TO GO TO THE WINTER FORMAL?

I'LL PASS, THANKS.

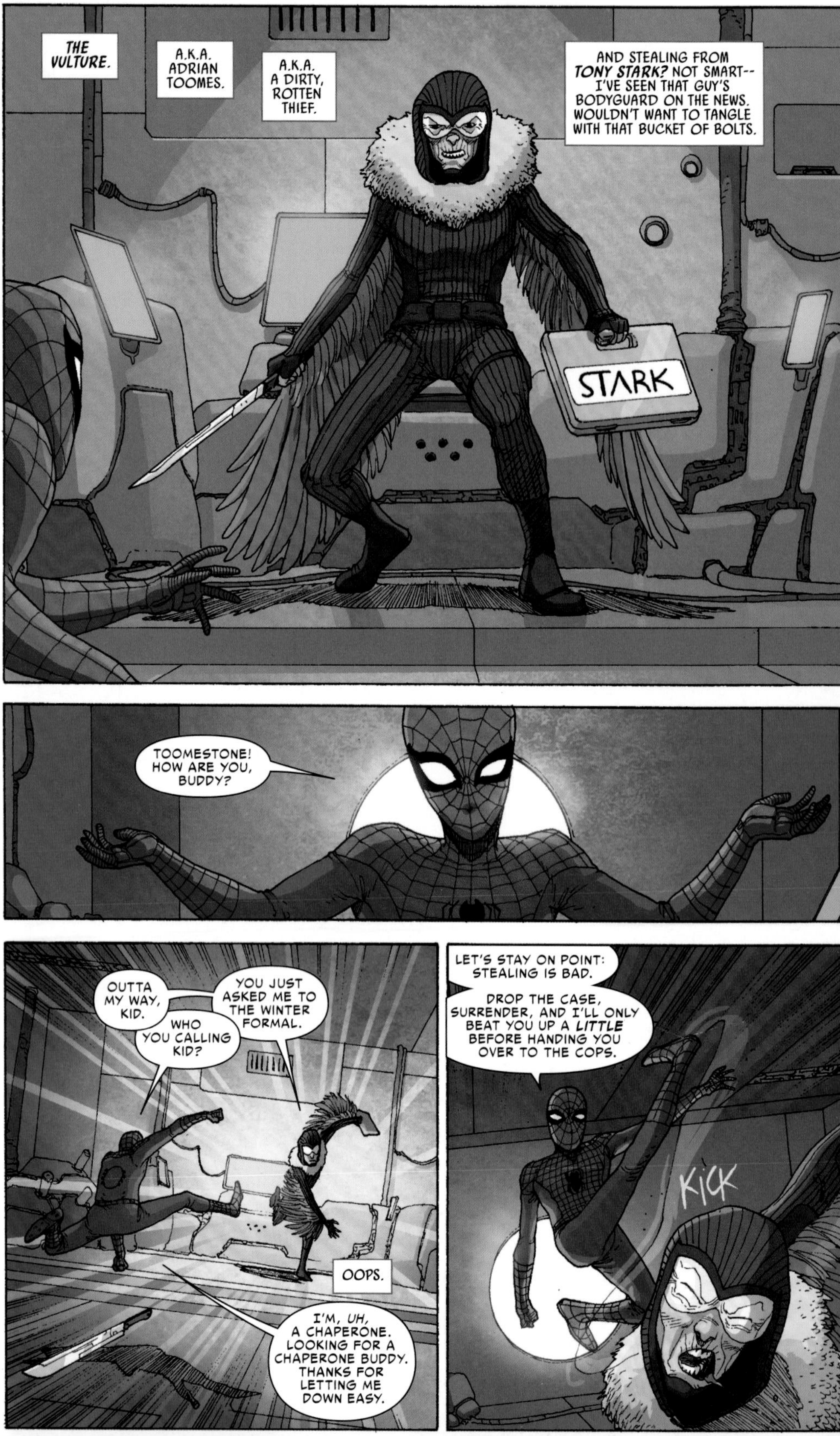

THE VULTURE.
A.K.A. ADRIAN TOOMES.
A.K.A. A DIRTY, ROTTEN THIEF.
AND STEALING FROM TONY STARK? NOT SMART-- I'VE SEEN THAT GUY'S BODYGUARD ON THE NEWS. WOULDN'T WANT TO TANGLE WITH THAT BUCKET OF BOLTS.
STARK
TOOMESTONE! HOW ARE YOU, BUDDY?
OUTTA MY WAY, KID.
WHO YOU CALLING KID?
YOU JUST ASKED ME TO THE WINTER FORMAL.
OOPS.
I'M, UH, A CHAPERONE. LOOKING FOR A CHAPERONE BUDDY. THANKS FOR LETTING ME DOWN EASY.
LET'S STAY ON POINT: STEALING IS BAD.
DROP THE CASE, SURRENDER, AND I'LL ONLY BEAT YOU UP A LITTLE BEFORE HANDING YOU OVER TO THE COPS.
KICK

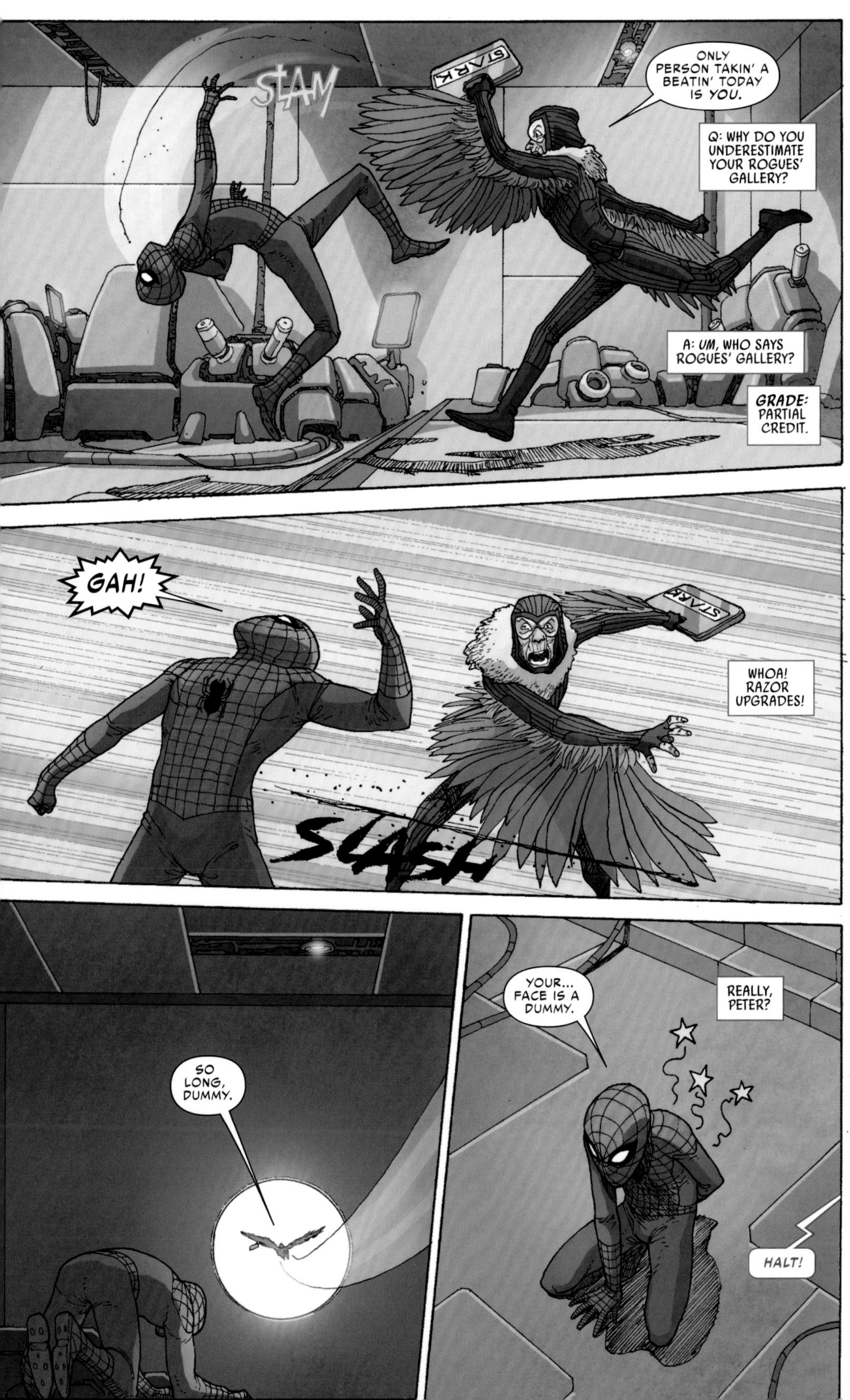
SLAM
STARK
ONLY PERSON TAKIN' A BEATIN' TODAY IS YOU.
Q: WHY DO YOU UNDERESTIMATE YOUR ROGUES' GALLERY?
A: UM, WHO SAYS ROGUES' GALLERY?
GRADE: PARTIAL CREDIT.
GAH!
STARK
WHOA! RAZOR UPGRADES!
SLASH
SO LONG, DUMMY.
YOUR... FACE IS A DUMMY.
REALLY, PETER?
HALT!

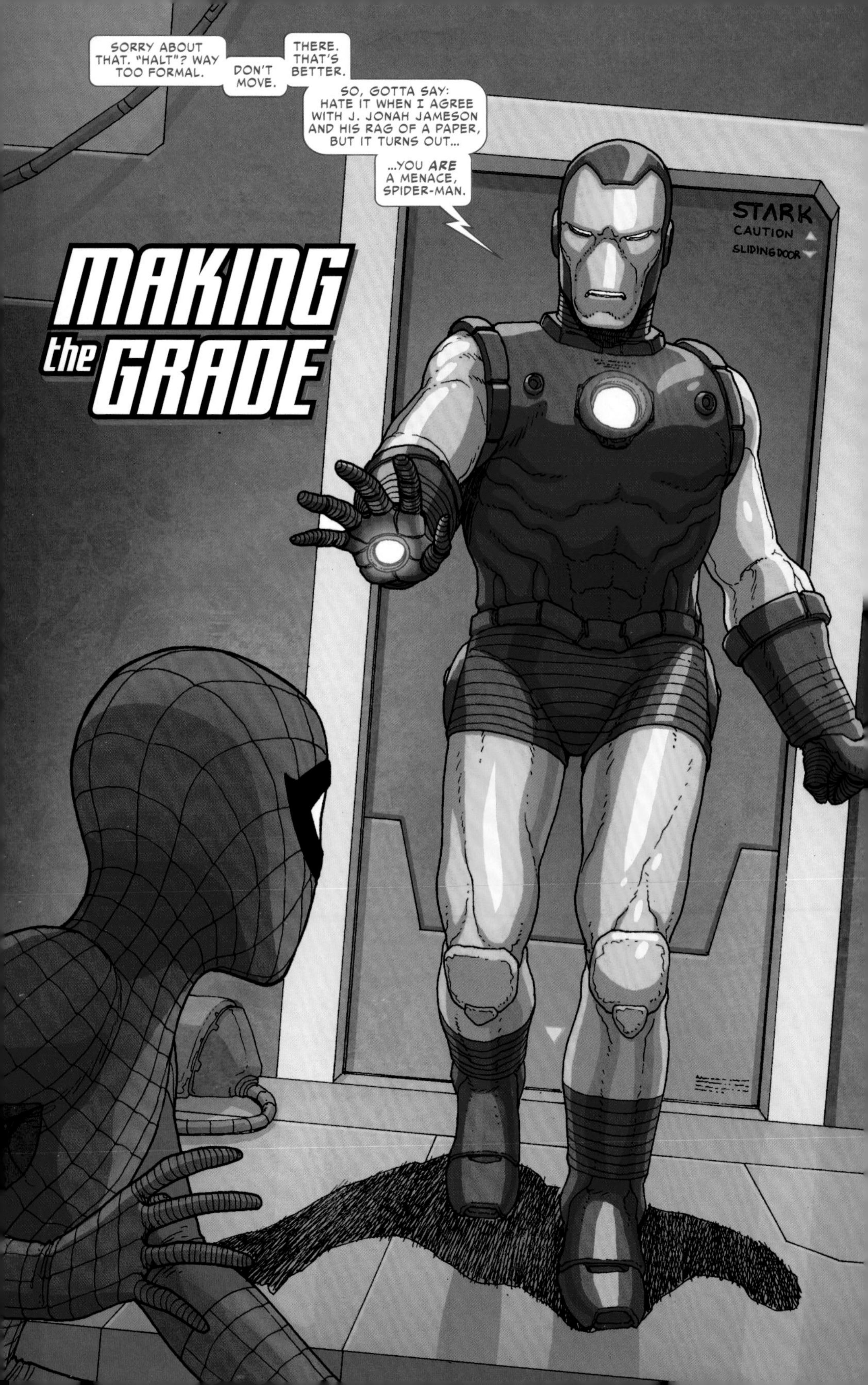
SORRY ABOUT THAT. "HALT"? WAY TOO FORMAL.
DON'T MOVE.
THERE. THAT'S BETTER.
SO, GOTTA SAY: HATE IT WHEN I AGREE WITH J. JONAH JAMESON AND HIS RAG OF A PAPER, BUT IT TURNS OUT...
...YOU **ARE** A MENACE, SPIDER-MAN.
MAKING the GRADE
STARK
CAUTION
SLIDING DOOR

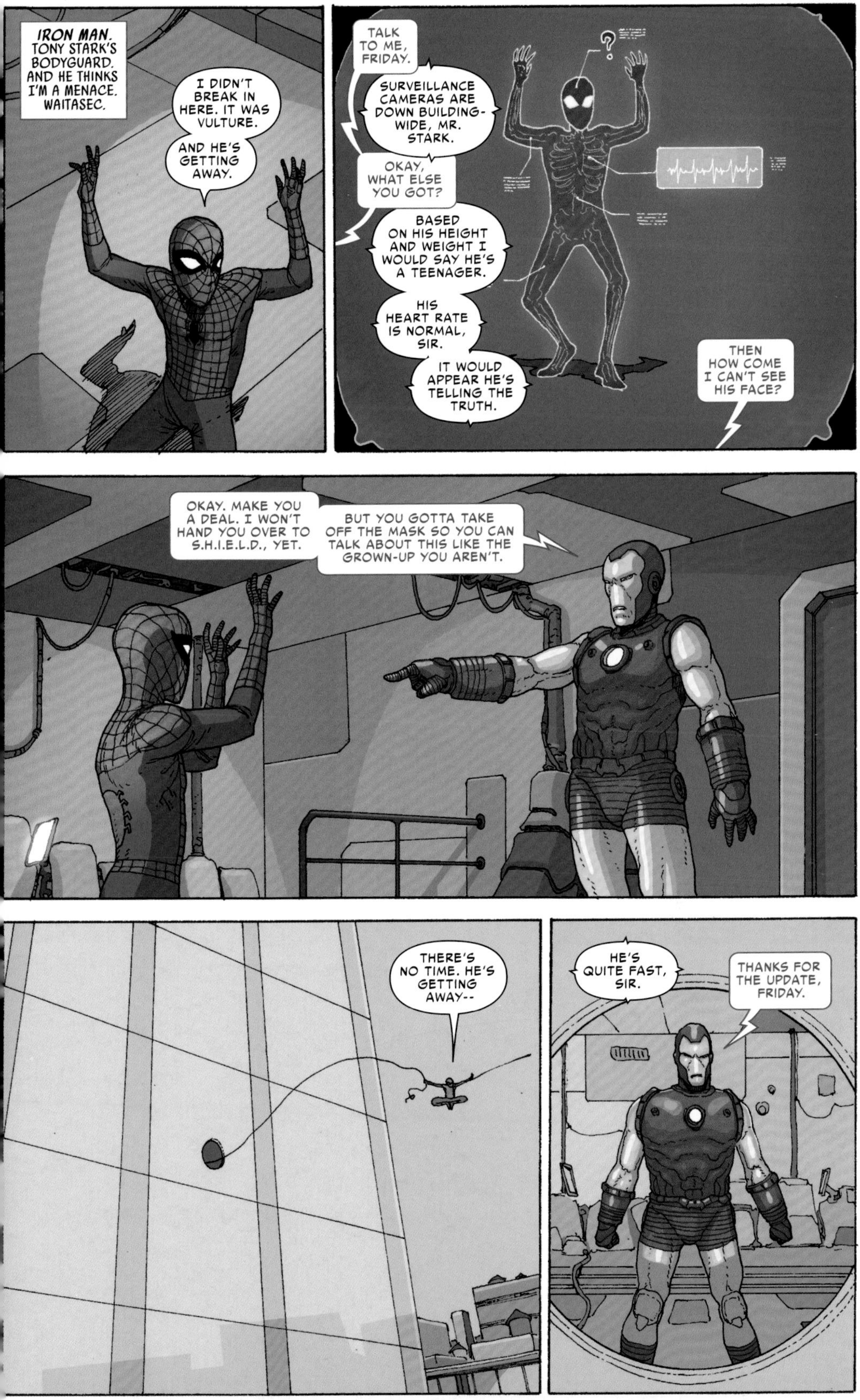
IRON MAN. TONY STARK'S BODYGUARD. AND HE THINKS I'M A MENACE. WAITASEC.
I DIDN'T BREAK IN HERE. IT WAS VULTURE.
AND HE'S GETTING AWAY.
TALK TO ME, FRIDAY.
SURVEILLANCE CAMERAS ARE DOWN BUILDING-WIDE, MR. STARK.
OKAY, WHAT ELSE YOU GOT?
BASED ON HIS HEIGHT AND WEIGHT I WOULD SAY HE'S A TEENAGER.
HIS HEART RATE IS NORMAL, SIR.
IT WOULD APPEAR HE'S TELLING THE TRUTH.
THEN HOW COME I CAN'T SEE HIS FACE?
OKAY. MAKE YOU A DEAL. I WON'T HAND YOU OVER TO S.H.I.E.L.D., YET.
BUT YOU GOTTA TAKE OFF THE MASK SO YOU CAN TALK ABOUT THIS LIKE THE GROWN-UP YOU AREN'T.
THERE'S NO TIME. HE'S GETTING AWAY--
HE'S QUITE FAST, SIR.
THANKS FOR THE UPDATE, FRIDAY.

LOOK, IT'S BEEN A LONG DAY, AVENGER BUSINESS AND WHATNOT--AND I'D *REALLY* RATHER NOT HAVE TO BLAST YOU OUT OF THE SKY, SO--

YOU'RE JUST GONNA KEEP RUNNING AREN'T YOU?

I'M NOT RUNNING. I'M CHASING.

[STUN MISSILES LOCKED]

OKAY, BUDDY BOY. TIME FOR A LITTLE NAP.

AND ON TOP OF THAT: I'M A HUGE FAN OF YOUR BOSS, TONY STARK.

I WOULDN'T BREAK INTO STARK INDUSTRIES.

FOR STARTERS: I'M NOT A THIEF.

DUDE'S A GENIUS.

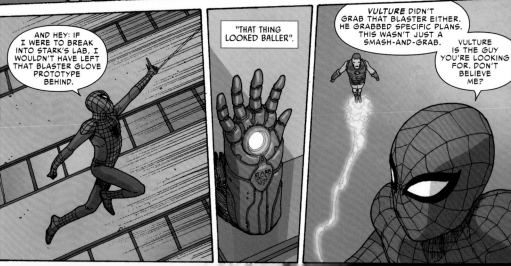

AND HEY: IF I WERE TO BREAK INTO STARK'S LAB, I WOULDN'T HAVE LEFT THAT BLASTER GLOVE PROTOTYPE BEHIND.

"THAT THING LOOKED BALLER".

VULTURE DIDN'T GRAB THAT BLASTER EITHER. HE GRABBED SPECIFIC PLANS. THIS WASN'T JUST A SMASH-AND-GRAB.

VULTURE IS THE GUY YOU'RE LOOKING FOR. DON'T BELIEVE ME?

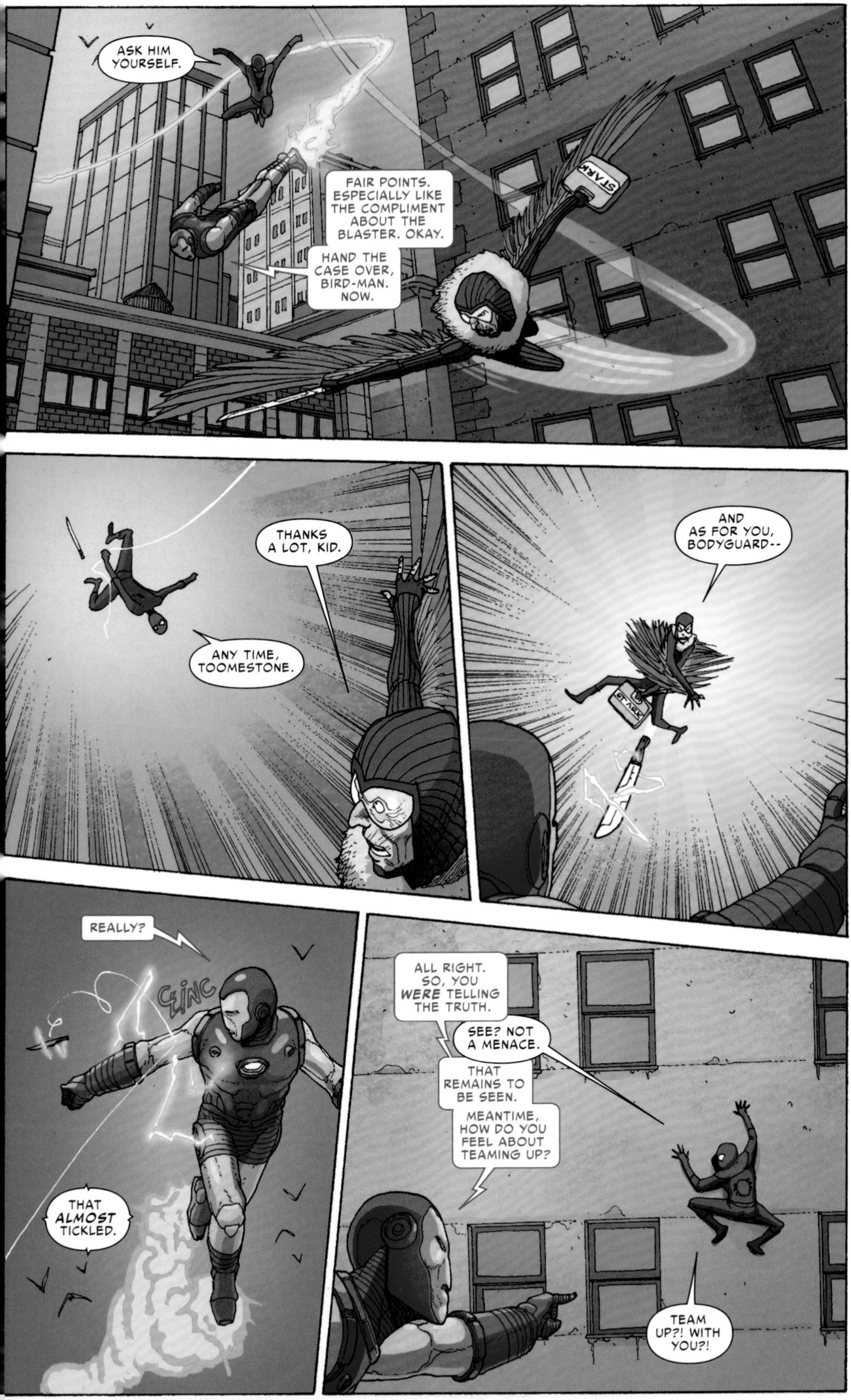
ASK HIM YOURSELF.
FAIR POINTS. ESPECIALLY LIKE THE COMPLIMENT ABOUT THE BLASTER. OKAY.
HAND THE CASE OVER, BIRD-MAN. NOW.
STARK
THANKS A LOT, KID.
ANY TIME, TOOMESTONE.
AND AS FOR YOU, BODYGUARD--
REALLY?
CLINC
THAT ALMOST TICKLED.
ALL RIGHT. SO, YOU WERE TELLING THE TRUTH.
SEE? NOT A MENACE.
THAT REMAINS TO BE SEEN.
MEANTIME, HOW DO YOU FEEL ABOUT TEAMING UP?
TEAM UP?! WITH YOU?!

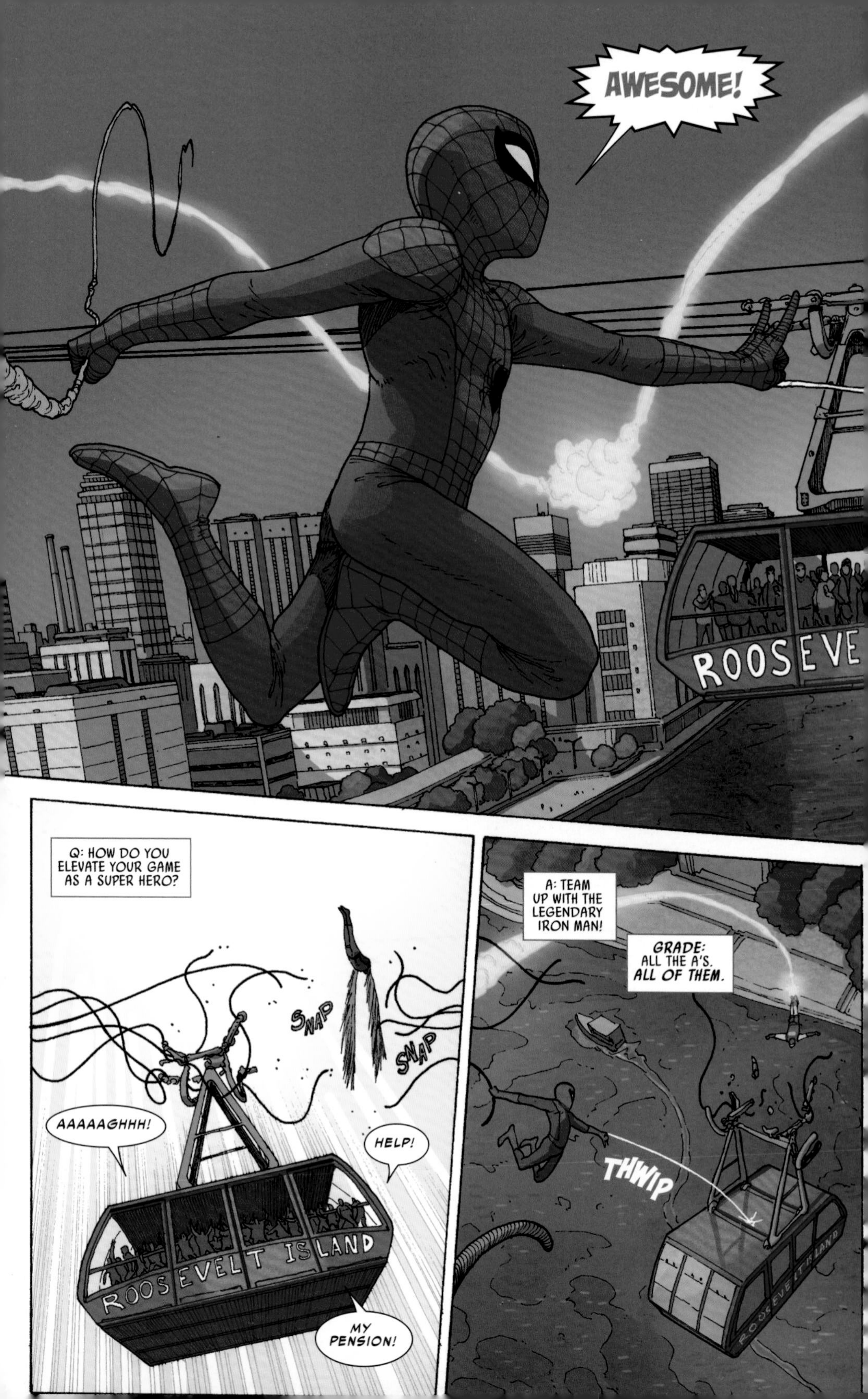
AWESOME!
ROOSEVE
Q: HOW DO YOU ELEVATE YOUR GAME AS A SUPER HERO?
SNAP
SNAP
AAAAAGHHH!
HELP!
ROOSEVELT ISLAND
MY PENSION!
A: TEAM UP WITH THE LEGENDARY IRON MAN!
GRADE: ALL THE A'S. ALL OF THEM.
THWIP
ROOSEVELT ISLAND

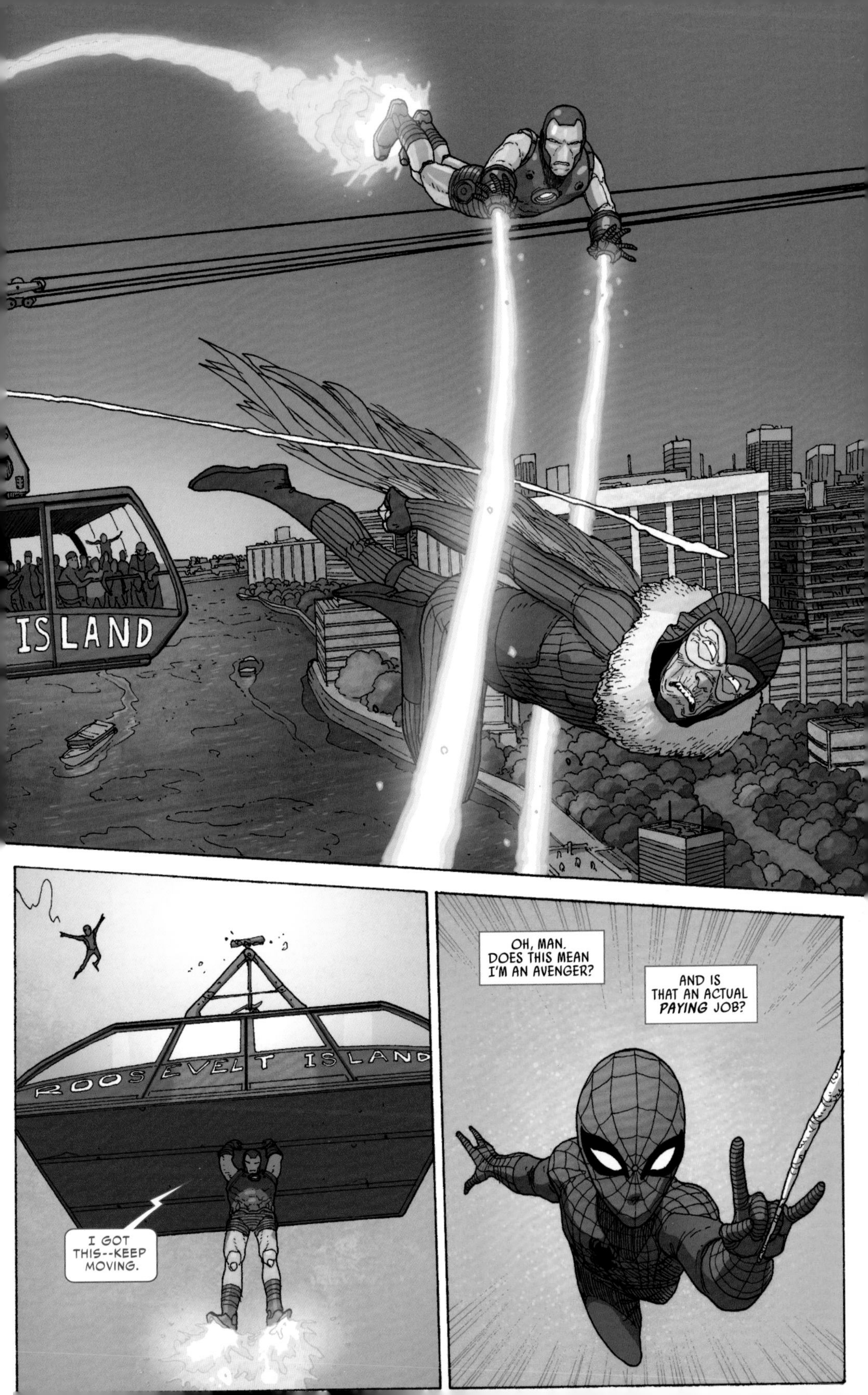
ISLAND
ROOSEVELT ISLAND
I GOT THIS--KEEP MOVING.
OH, MAN. DOES THIS MEAN I'M AN AVENGER?
AND IS THAT AN ACTUAL PAYING JOB?

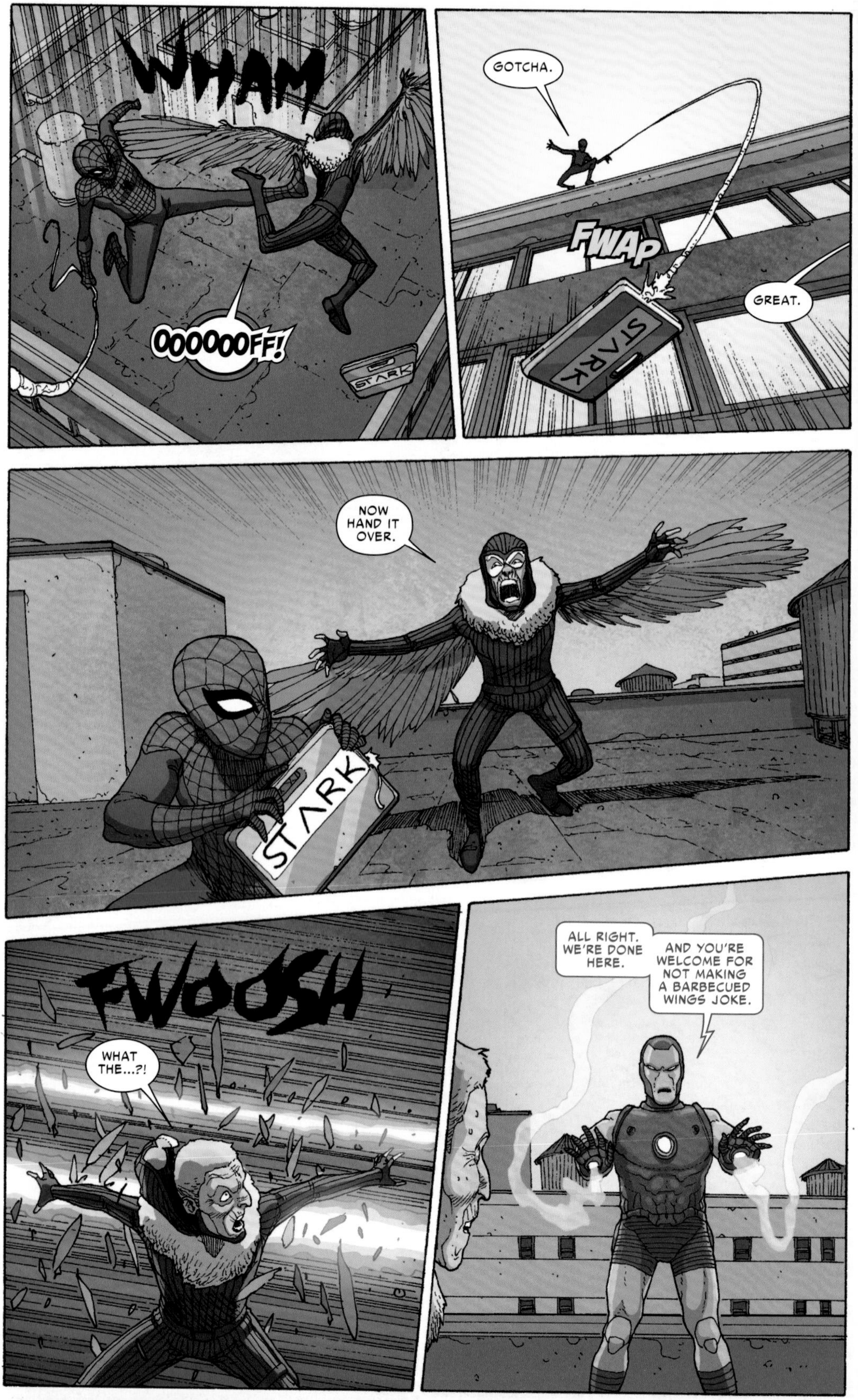
WHAM
OOOOOOFF!
GOTCHA.
FWAP
GREAT.
NOW HAND IT OVER.
FWOOSH
WHAT THE...?!
ALL RIGHT. WE'RE DONE HERE.
AND YOU'RE WELCOME FOR NOT MAKING A BARBECUED WINGS JOKE.

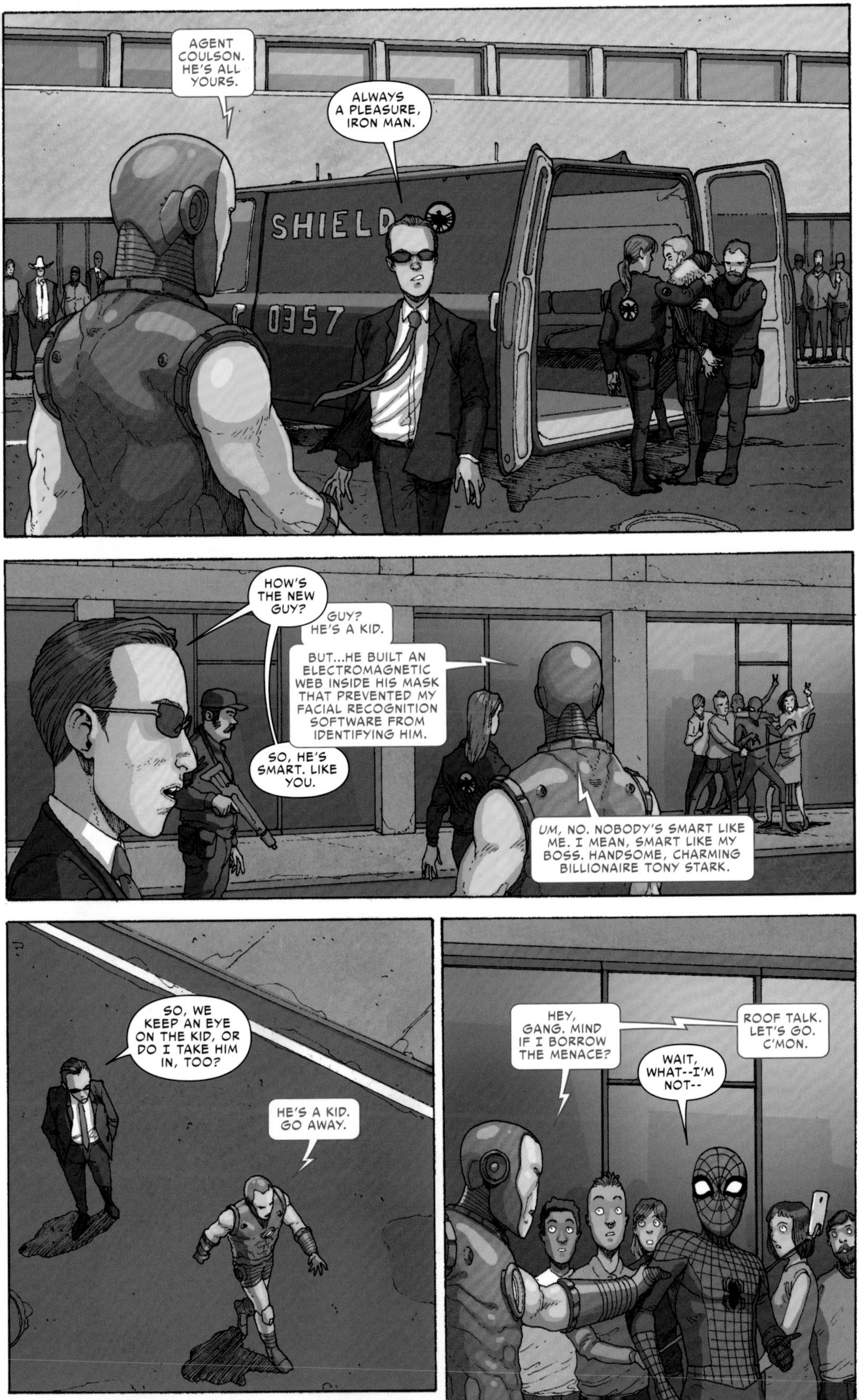
AGENT COULSON. HE'S ALL YOURS.
ALWAYS A PLEASURE, IRON MAN.
SHIELD
0357
HOW'S THE NEW GUY?
GUY? HE'S A KID.
BUT...HE BUILT AN ELECTROMAGNETIC WEB INSIDE HIS MASK THAT PREVENTED MY FACIAL RECOGNITION SOFTWARE FROM IDENTIFYING HIM.
SO, HE'S SMART. LIKE YOU.
UM, NO. NOBODY'S SMART LIKE ME. I MEAN, SMART LIKE MY BOSS. HANDSOME, CHARMING BILLIONAIRE TONY STARK.
SO, WE KEEP AN EYE ON THE KID, OR DO I TAKE HIM IN, TOO?
HE'S A KID. GO AWAY.
HEY, GANG. MIND IF I BORROW THE MENACE?
ROOF TALK. LET'S GO. C'MON.
WAIT, WHAT--I'M NOT--

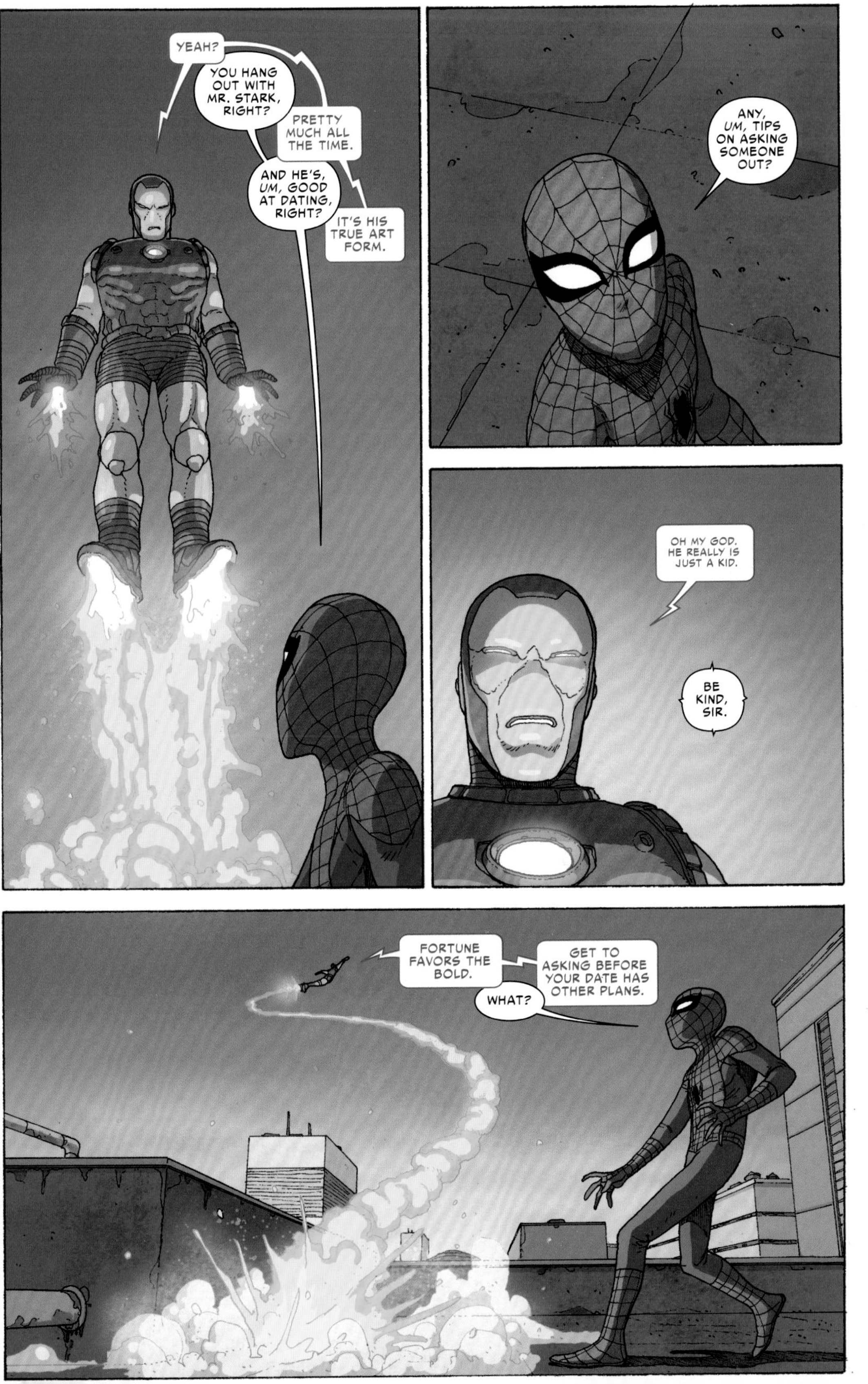
YEAH?
YOU HANG OUT WITH MR. STARK, RIGHT?
PRETTY MUCH ALL THE TIME.
AND HE'S, *UM*, GOOD AT DATING, RIGHT?
IT'S HIS TRUE ART FORM.
ANY, *UM*, TIPS ON ASKING SOMEONE OUT?
OH MY GOD. HE REALLY IS JUST A KID.
BE KIND, SIR.
FORTUNE FAVORS THE BOLD.
GET TO ASKING BEFORE YOUR DATE HAS OTHER PLANS.
WHAT?

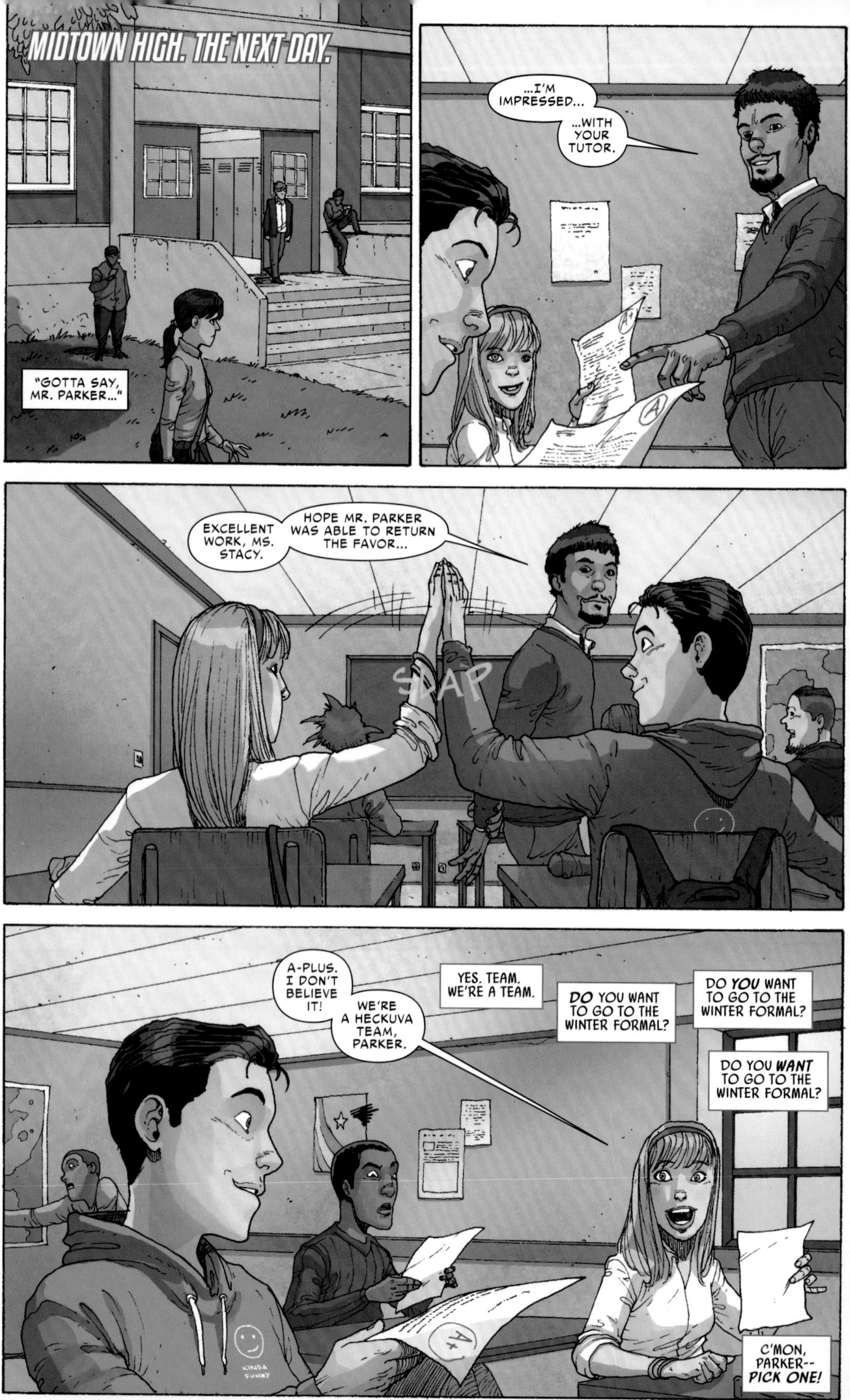
MIDTOWN HIGH. THE NEXT DAY.
"GOTTA SAY, MR. PARKER..."
...I'M IMPRESSED...
...WITH YOUR TUTOR.
EXCELLENT WORK, MS. STACY.
HOPE MR. PARKER WAS ABLE TO RETURN THE FAVOR...
SLAP
A-PLUS. I DON'T BELIEVE IT!
WE'RE A HECKUVA TEAM, PARKER.
YES. TEAM. WE'RE A TEAM.
DO YOU WANT TO GO TO THE WINTER FORMAL?
DO YOU WANT TO GO TO THE WINTER FORMAL?
DO YOU WANT TO GO TO THE WINTER FORMAL?
C'MON, PARKER-- PICK ONE!
KINDA FUNNY

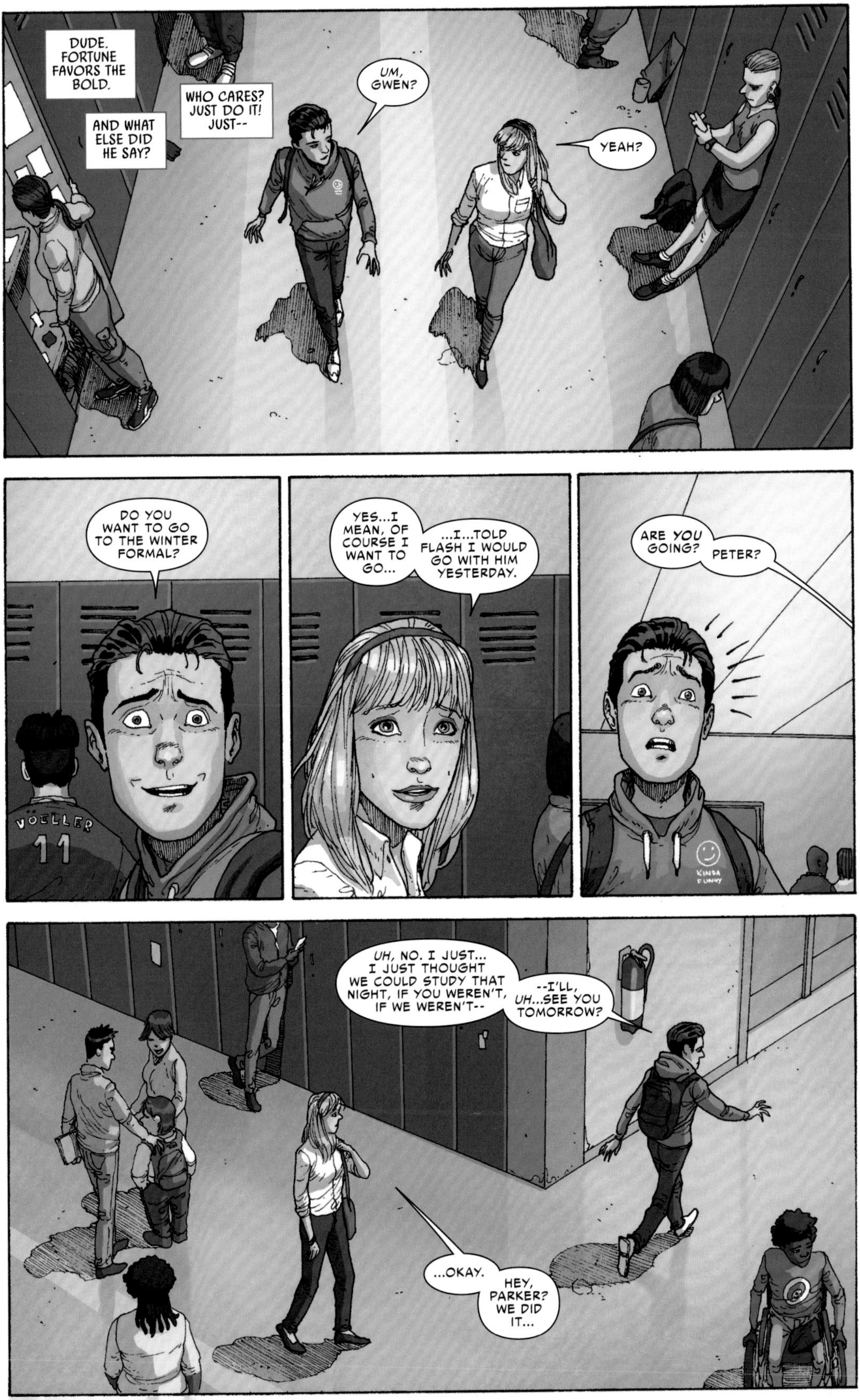
DUDE. FORTUNE FAVORS THE BOLD.
AND WHAT ELSE DID HE SAY?
WHO CARES? JUST DO IT! JUST--
UM, GWEN?
YEAH?
DO YOU WANT TO GO TO THE WINTER FORMAL?
YES...I MEAN, OF COURSE I WANT TO GO...
...I...TOLD FLASH I WOULD GO WITH HIM YESTERDAY.
ARE YOU GOING?
PETER?
KINDA FUNNY
VOELLER 11
UH, NO. I JUST... I JUST THOUGHT WE COULD STUDY THAT NIGHT, IF YOU WEREN'T, IF WE WEREN'T--
--I'LL, UH...SEE YOU TOMORROW?
...OKAY.
HEY, PARKER? WE DID IT...

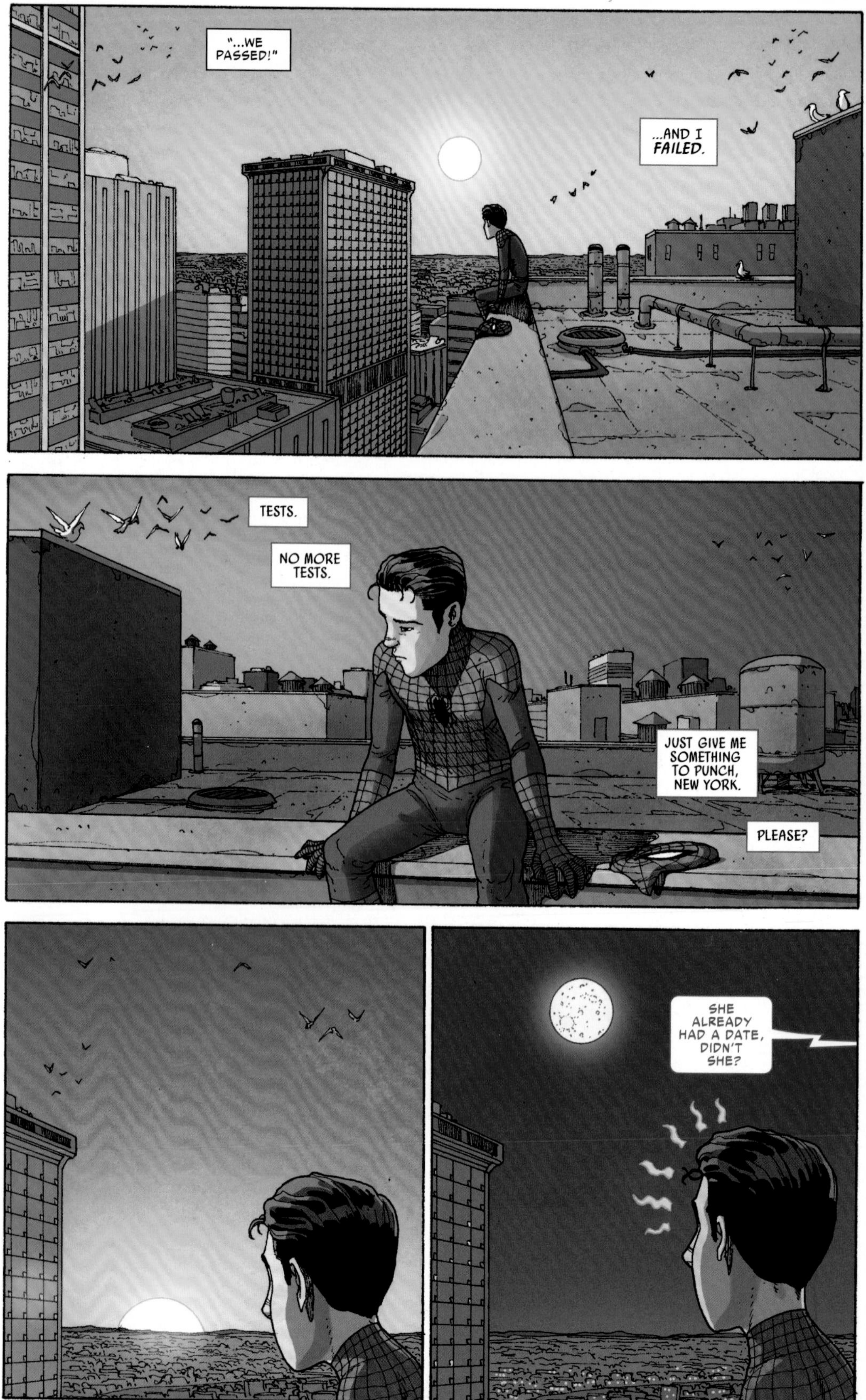
"...WE PASSED!"
...AND I *FAILED.*
TESTS.
NO MORE TESTS.
JUST GIVE ME SOMETHING TO PUNCH, NEW YORK.
PLEASE?
SHE ALREADY HAD A DATE, DIDN'T SHE?

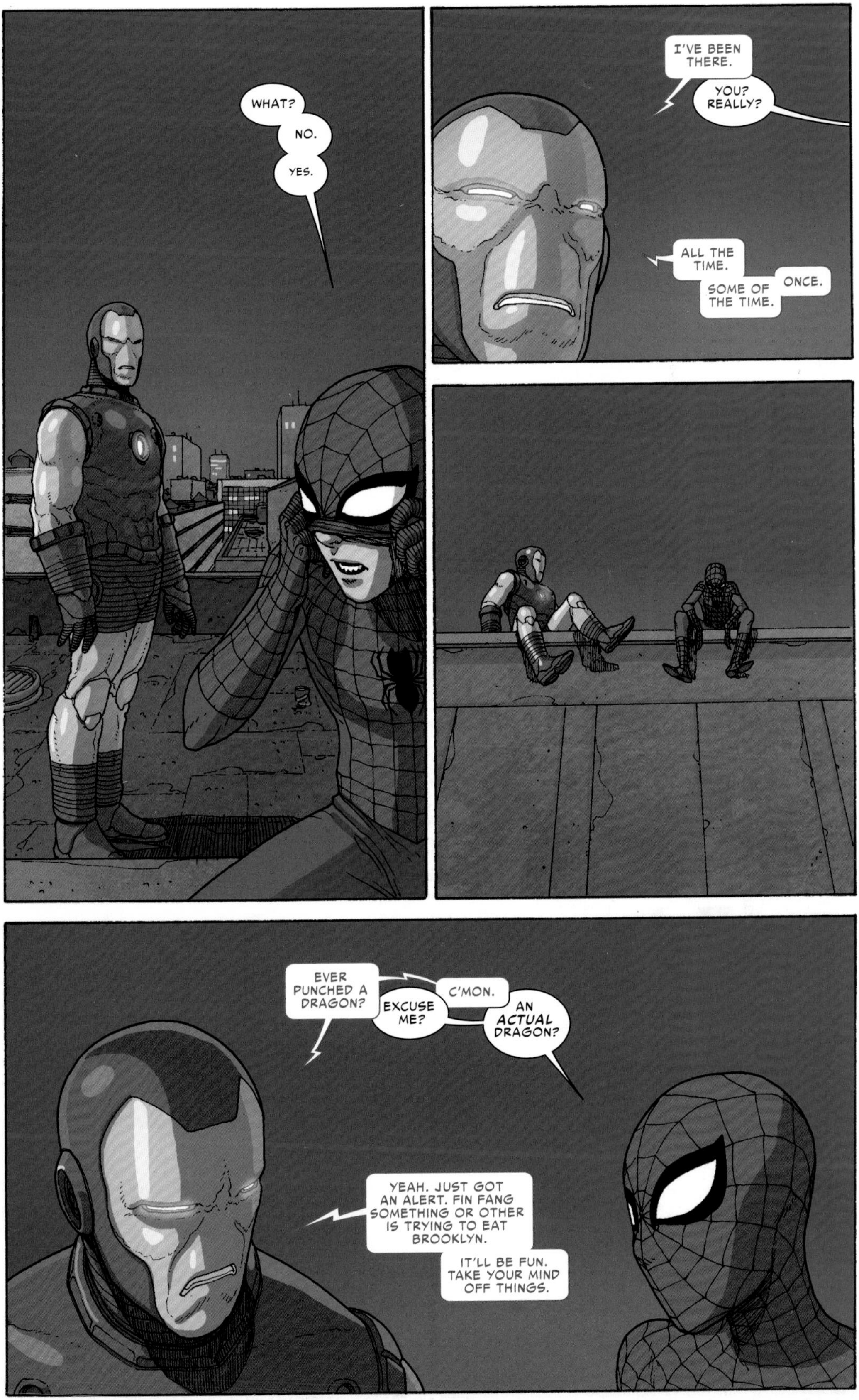
WHAT?
NO.
YES.
I'VE BEEN THERE.
YOU? REALLY?
ALL THE TIME.
SOME OF THE TIME.
ONCE.
EVER PUNCHED A DRAGON?
C'MON.
EXCUSE ME?
AN *ACTUAL* DRAGON?
YEAH. JUST GOT AN ALERT. FIN FANG SOMETHING OR OTHER IS TRYING TO EAT BROOKLYN.
IT'LL BE FUN. TAKE YOUR MIND OFF THINGS.

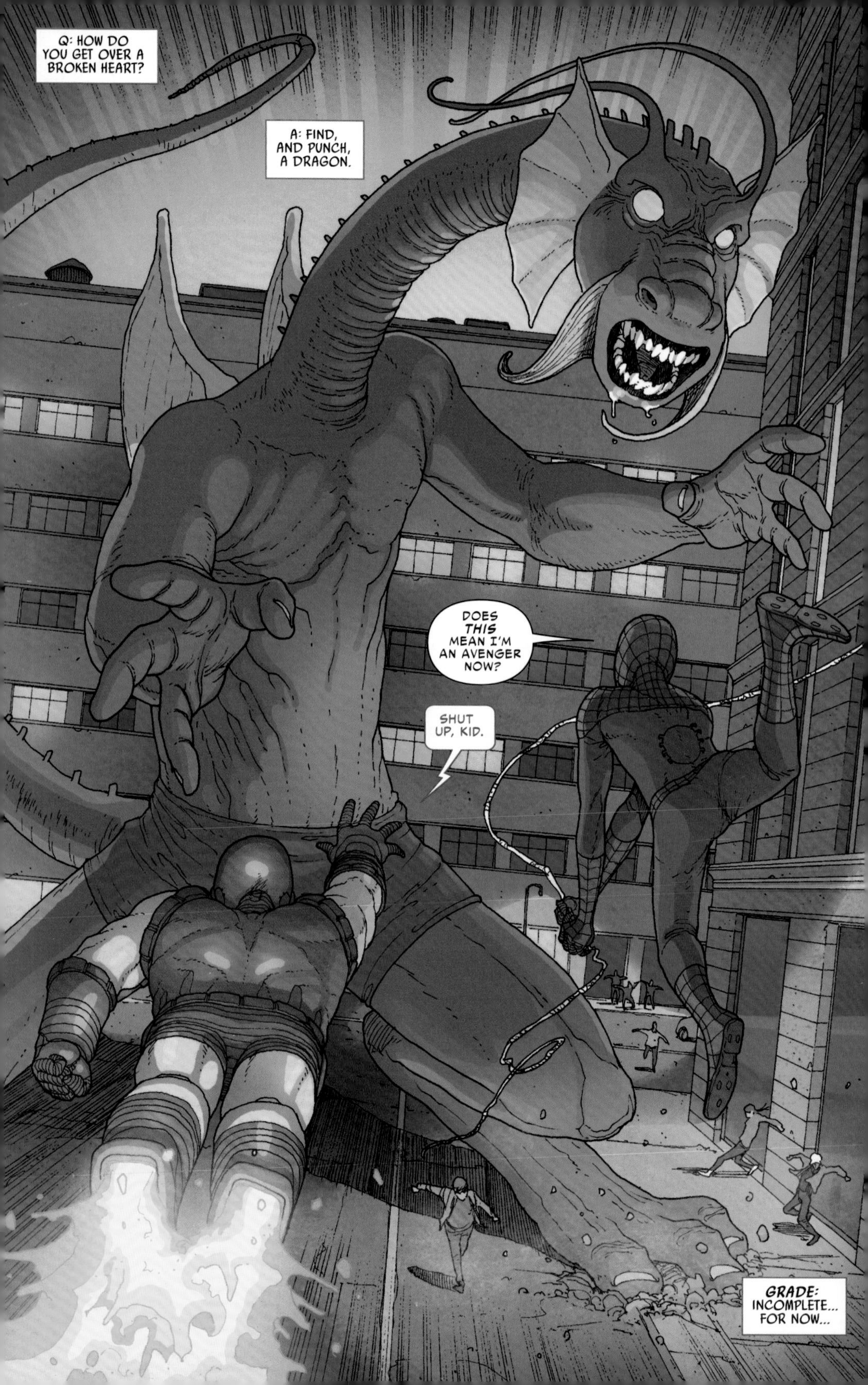
Q: HOW DO YOU GET OVER A BROKEN HEART?
A: FIND, AND PUNCH, A DRAGON.
DOES THIS MEAN I'M AN AVENGER NOW?
SHUT UP, KID.
GRADE: INCOMPLETE... FOR NOW...

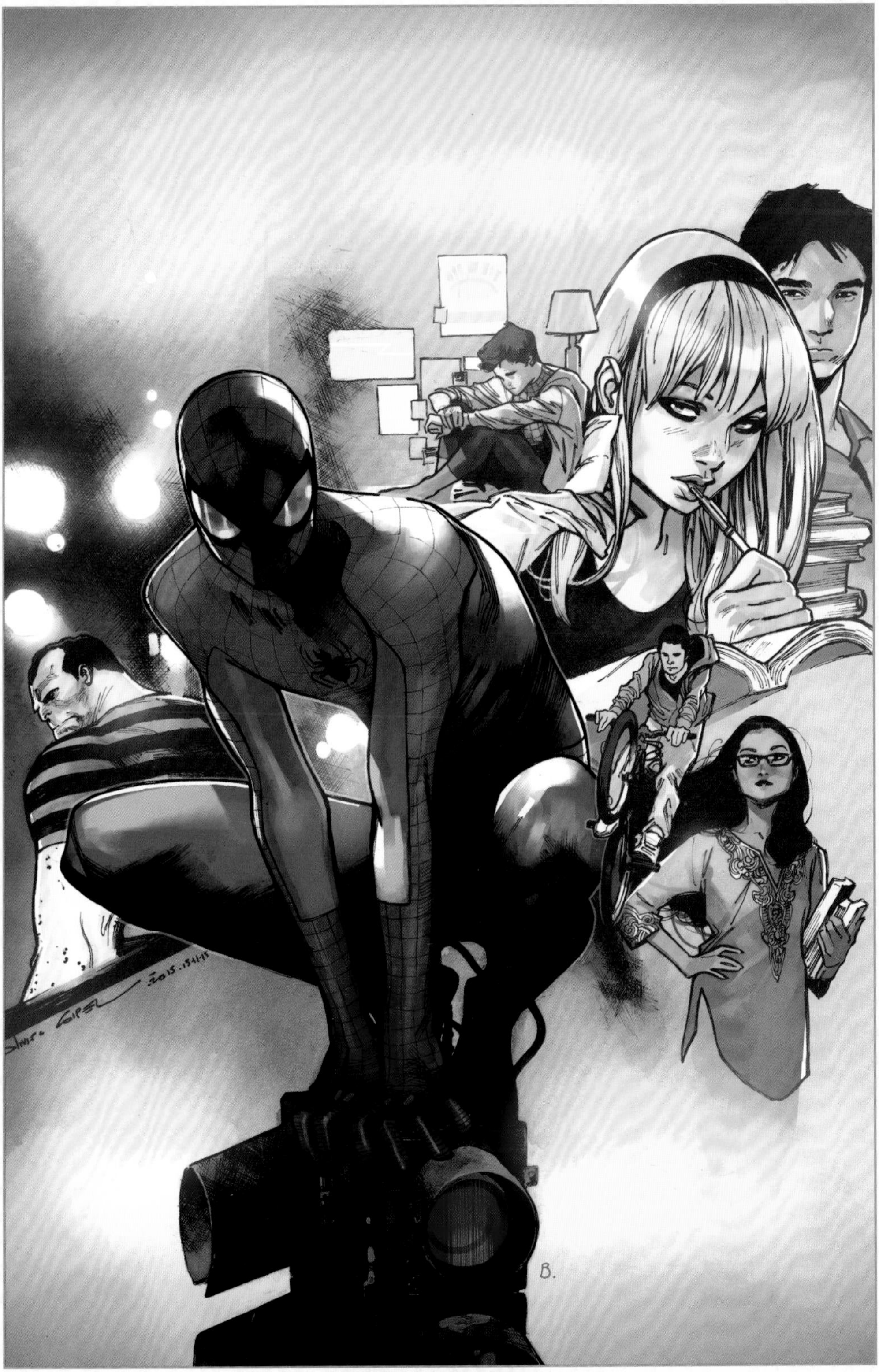

SPIDEY #2 VARIANT
BY OLIVIER COIPEL

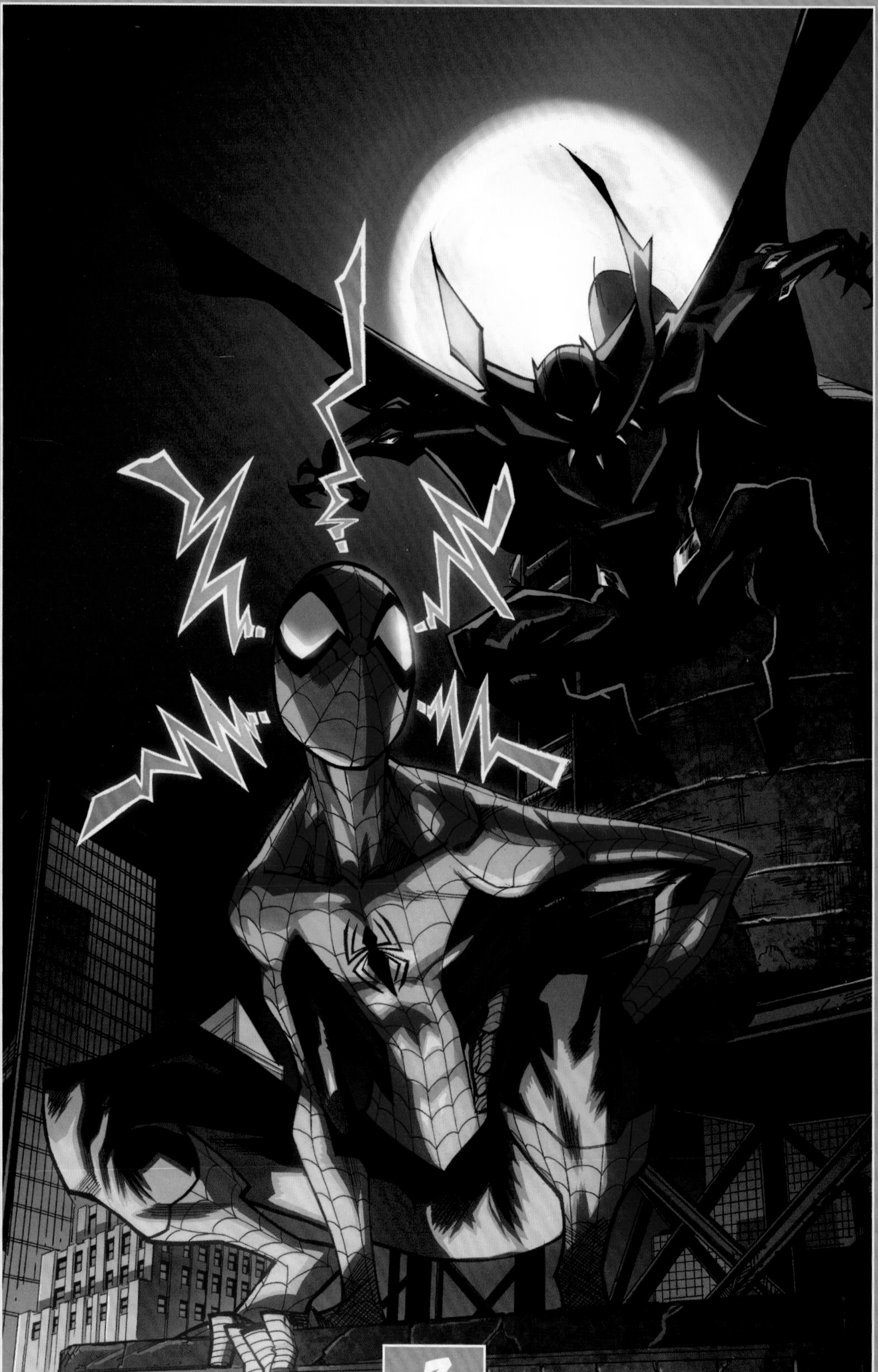

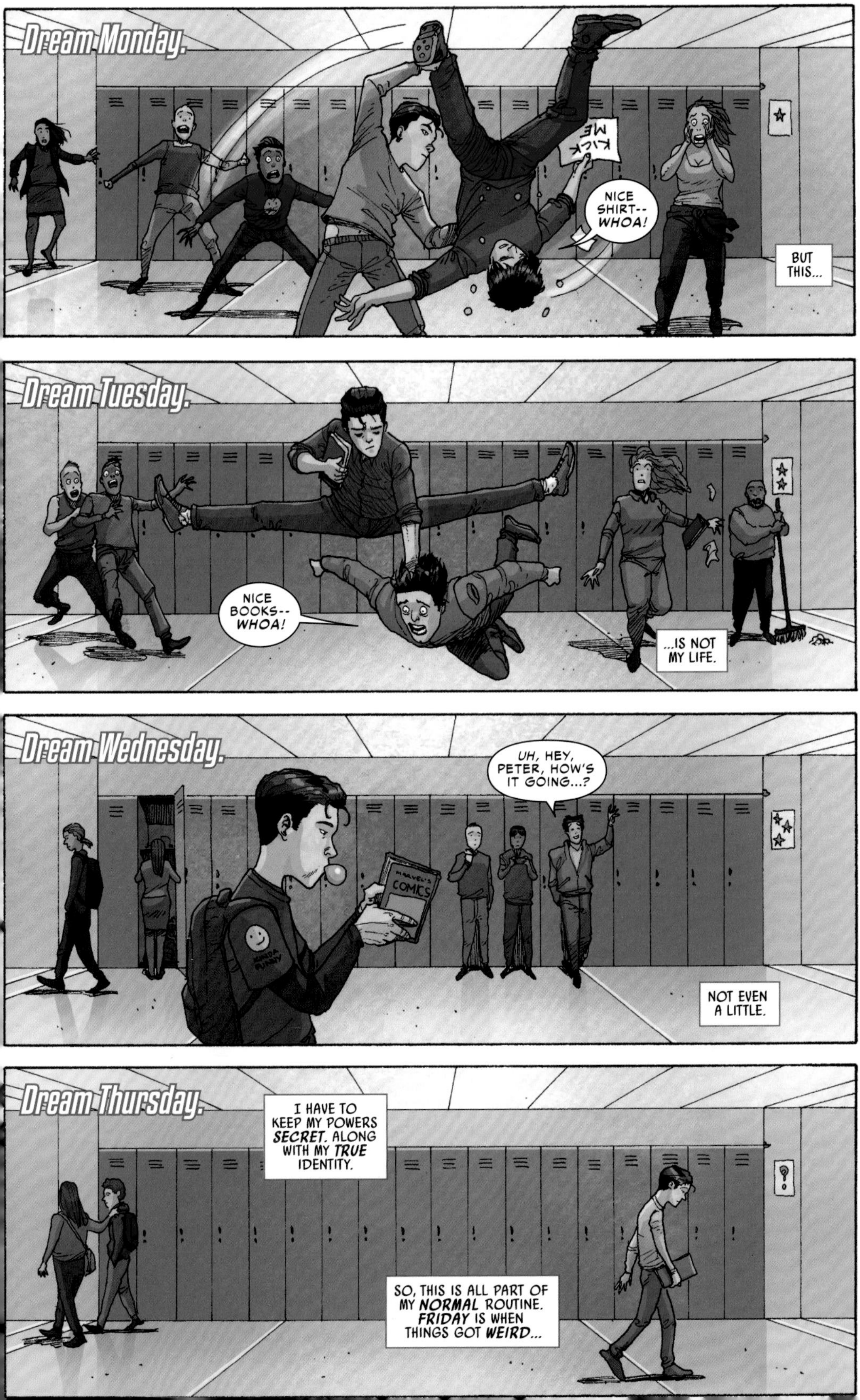
Dream Monday.
ME
KICK
NICE SHIRT--WHOA!
BUT THIS...
Dream Tuesday.
NICE BOOKS--WHOA!
...IS NOT MY LIFE.
Dream Wednesday.
UH, HEY, PETER, HOW'S IT GOING...?
COMICS
NOT EVEN A LITTLE.
Dream Thursday.
I HAVE TO KEEP MY POWERS SECRET. ALONG WITH MY TRUE IDENTITY.
SO, THIS IS ALL PART OF MY NORMAL ROUTINE. FRIDAY IS WHEN THINGS GOT WEIRD...

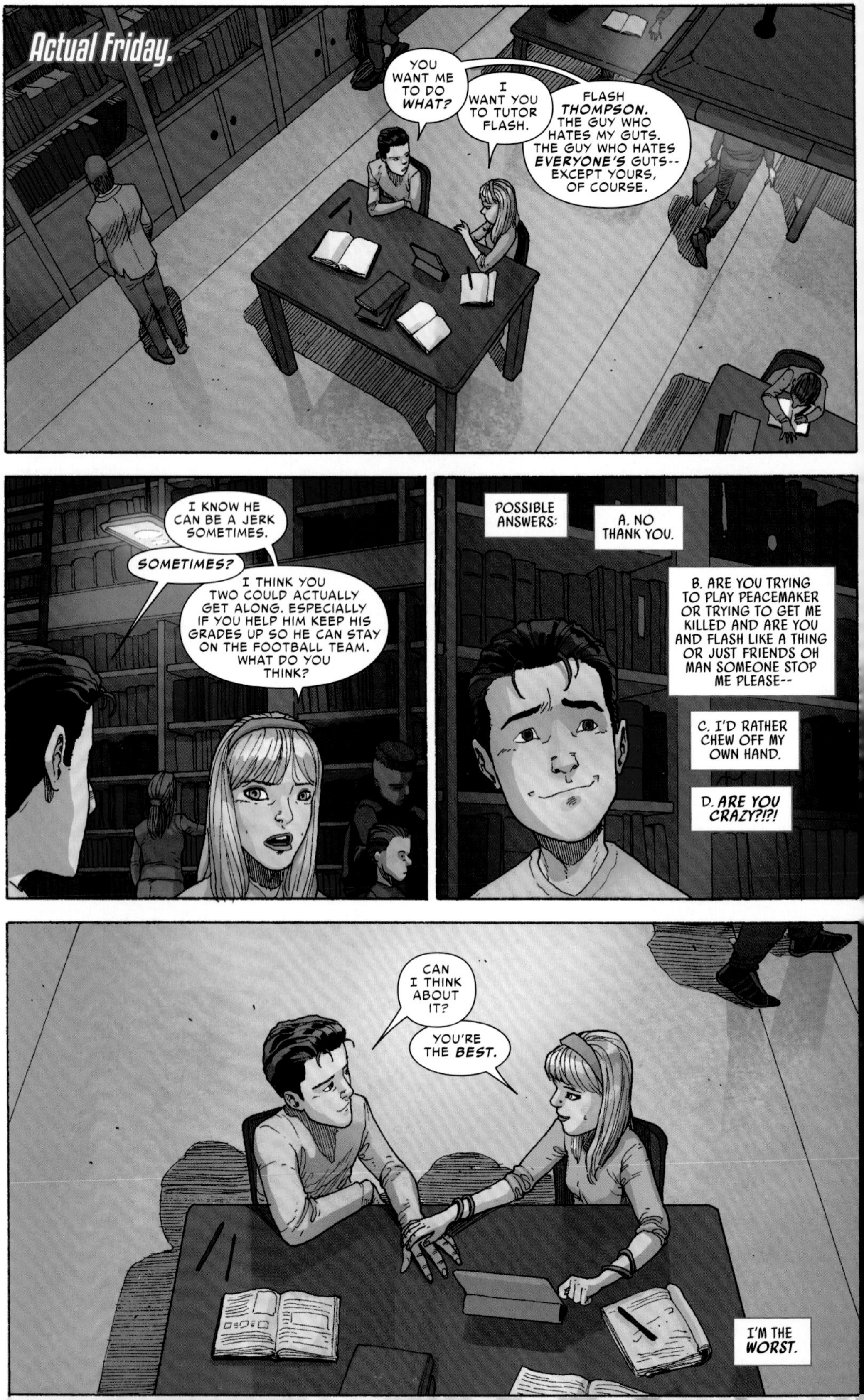
Actual Friday.
YOU WANT ME TO DO WHAT?
I WANT YOU TO TUTOR FLASH.
FLASH THOMPSON. THE GUY WHO HATES MY GUTS. THE GUY WHO HATES EVERYONE'S GUTS-- EXCEPT YOURS, OF COURSE.
I KNOW HE CAN BE A JERK SOMETIMES.
SOMETIMES?
I THINK YOU TWO COULD ACTUALLY GET ALONG. ESPECIALLY IF YOU HELP HIM KEEP HIS GRADES UP SO HE CAN STAY ON THE FOOTBALL TEAM. WHAT DO YOU THINK?
POSSIBLE ANSWERS:
A. NO THANK YOU.
B. ARE YOU TRYING TO PLAY PEACEMAKER OR TRYING TO GET ME KILLED AND ARE YOU AND FLASH LIKE A THING OR JUST FRIENDS OH MAN SOMEONE STOP ME PLEASE--
C. I'D RATHER CHEW OFF MY OWN HAND.
D. ARE YOU CRAZY?!?!
CAN I THINK ABOUT IT?
YOU'RE THE BEST.
I'M THE WORST.

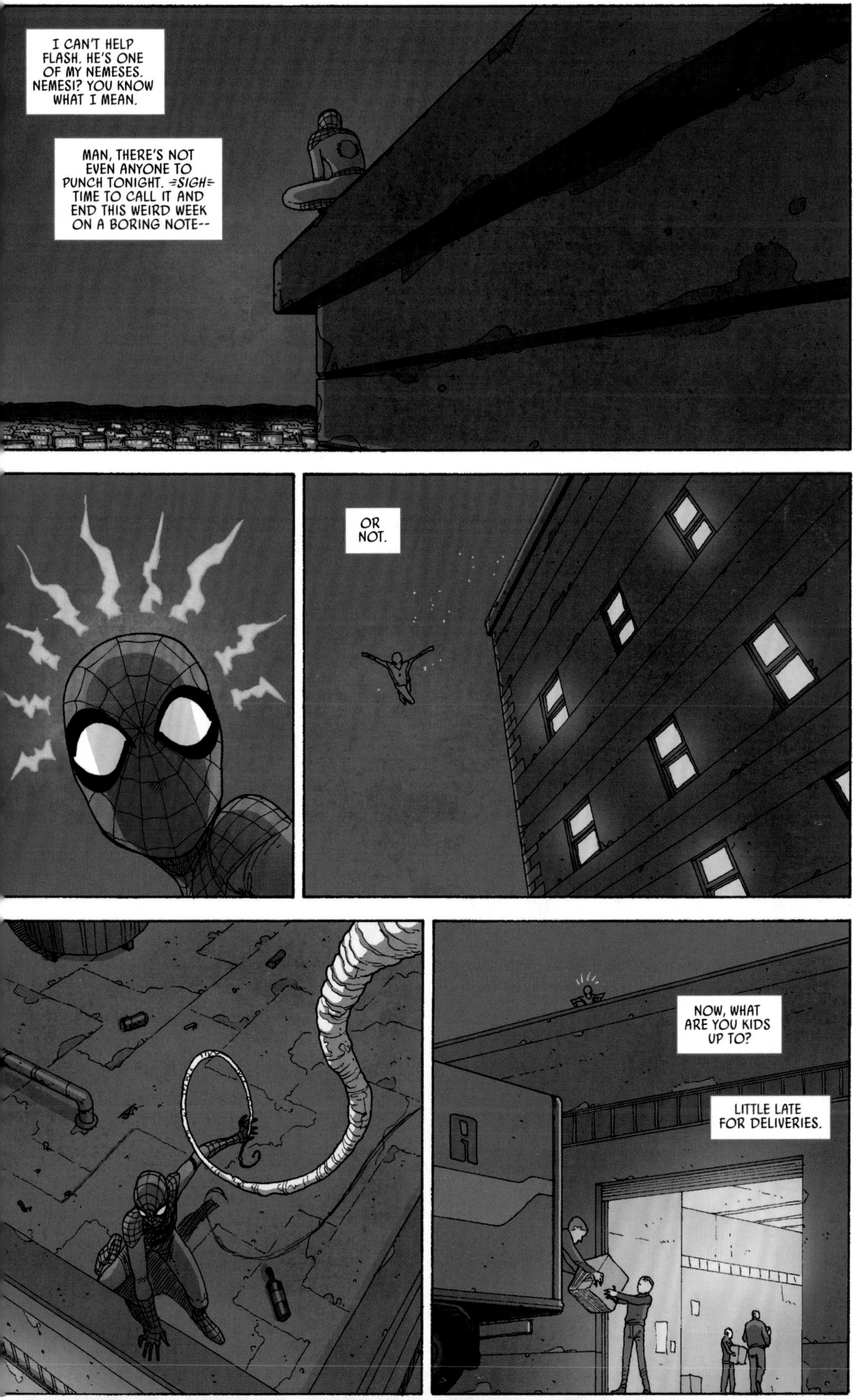
I CAN'T HELP FLASH. HE'S ONE OF MY NEMESES. NEMESI? YOU KNOW WHAT I MEAN.
MAN, THERE'S NOT EVEN ANYONE TO PUNCH TONIGHT. =SIGH= TIME TO CALL IT AND END THIS WEIRD WEEK ON A BORING NOTE--
OR NOT.
NOW, WHAT ARE YOU KIDS UP TO?
LITTLE LATE FOR DELIVERIES.

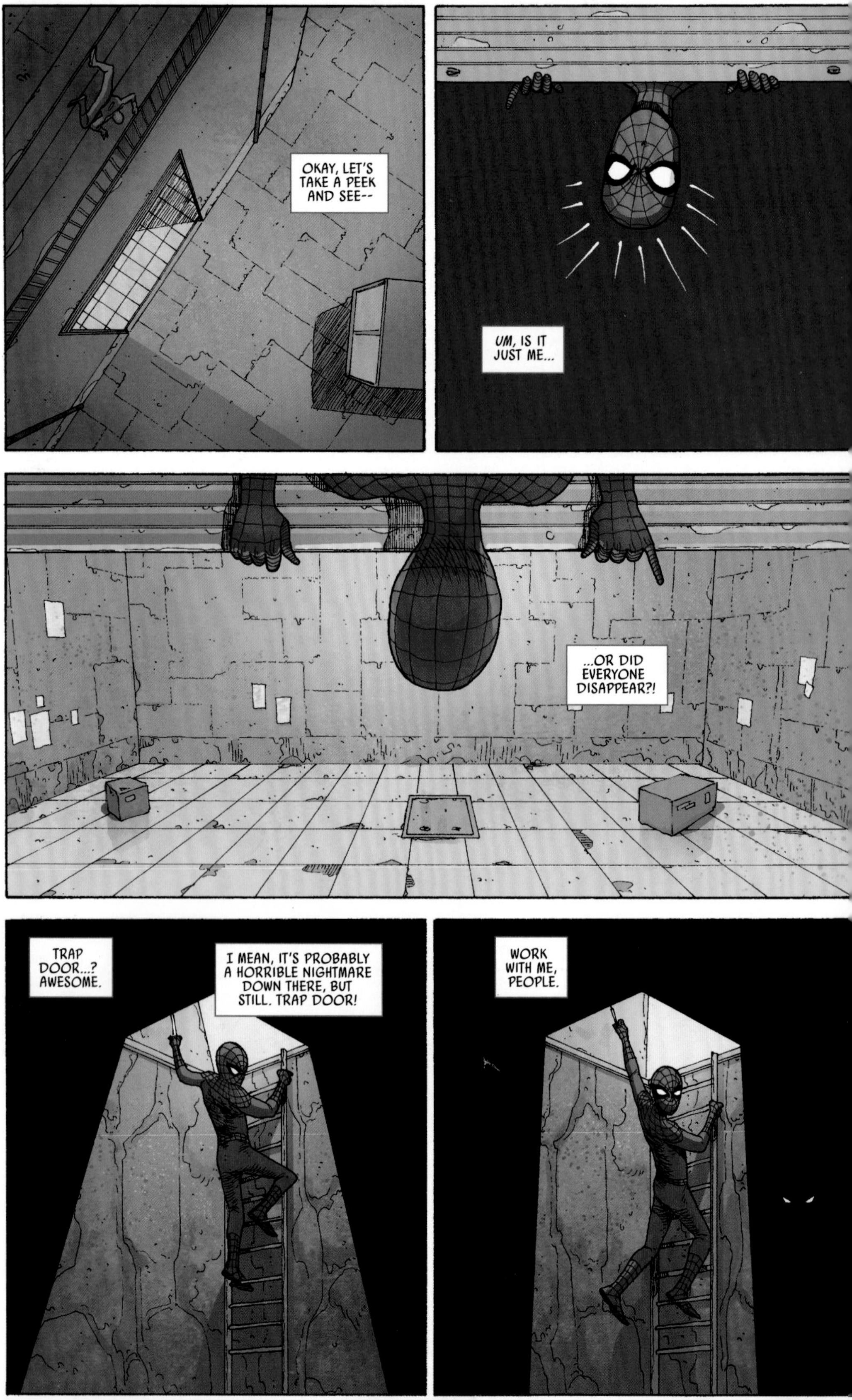
OKAY, LET'S TAKE A PEEK AND SEE--
UM, IS IT JUST ME...
...OR DID EVERYONE DISAPPEAR?!
TRAP DOOR...? AWESOME.
I MEAN, IT'S PROBABLY A HORRIBLE NIGHTMARE DOWN THERE, BUT STILL. TRAP DOOR!
WORK WITH ME, PEOPLE.

THIS IS ONE OF THE MANY TIMES IN MY SHORT, PERHAPS ABOUT-TO-END, CAREER THAT I WISH I COULD CALL FOR BACKUP.

'CAUSE DOWN THERE...

...ARE A LOT OF FACES TO PUNCH.

BETTER GET CRACKING. IT'S NOT LIKE THEY'RE GOING TO PUNCH THEMSELVES.

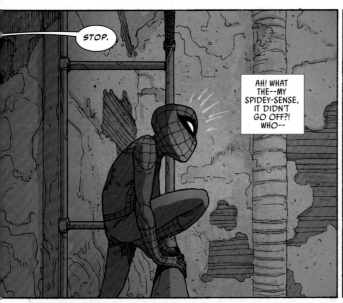

STOP.

AH! WHAT THE--MY SPIDEY-SENSE, IT DIDN'T GO OFF?! WHO--

OH. THAT EXPLAINS IT.

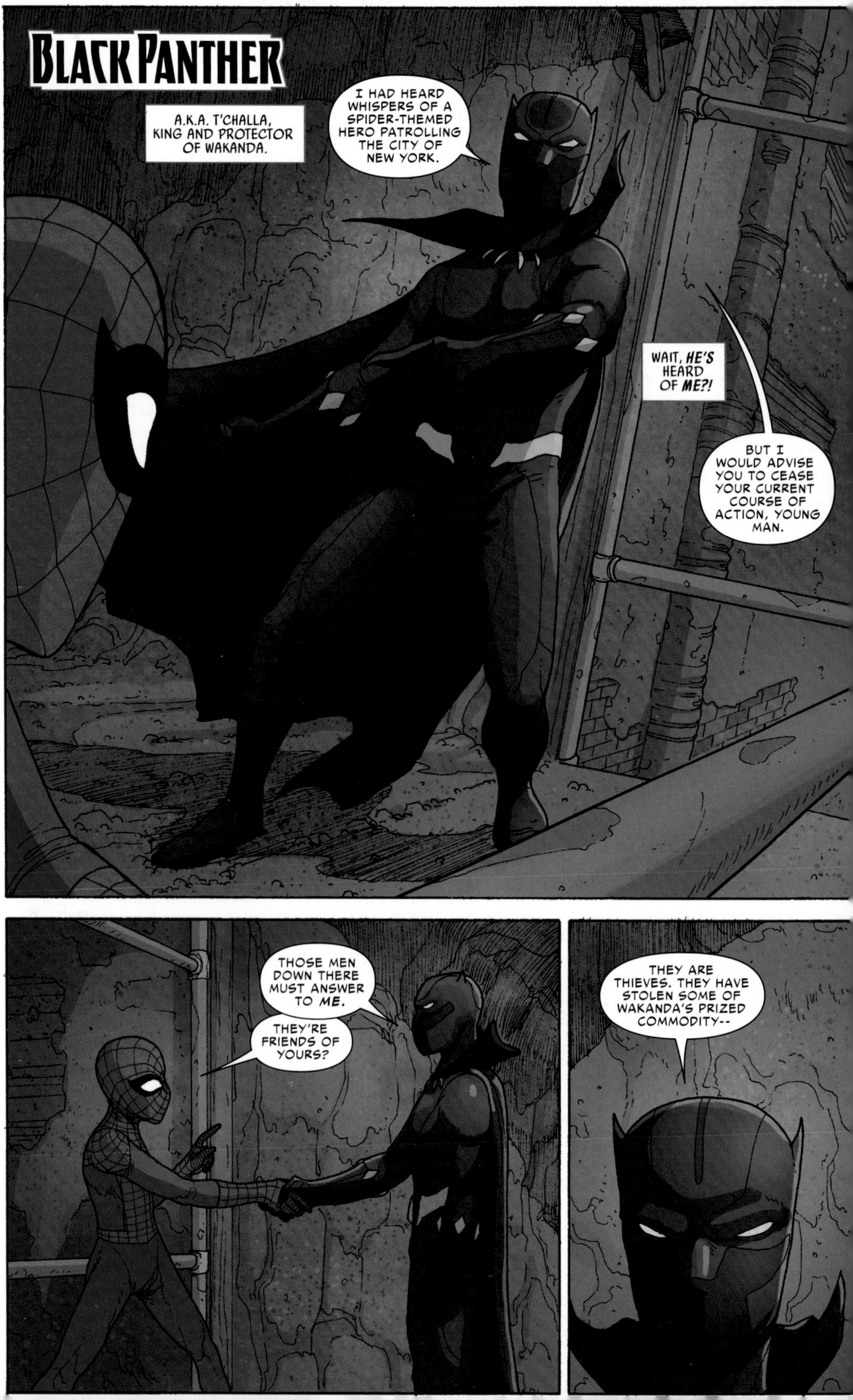
BLACK PANTHER
A.K.A. T'CHALLA, KING AND PROTECTOR OF WAKANDA.
I HAD HEARD WHISPERS OF A SPIDER-THEMED HERO PATROLLING THE CITY OF NEW YORK.
WAIT, HE'S HEARD OF ME?!
BUT I WOULD ADVISE YOU TO CEASE YOUR CURRENT COURSE OF ACTION, YOUNG MAN.
THOSE MEN DOWN THERE MUST ANSWER TO ME.
THEY'RE FRIENDS OF YOURS?
THEY ARE THIEVES. THEY HAVE STOLEN SOME OF WAKANDA'S PRIZED COMMODITY--

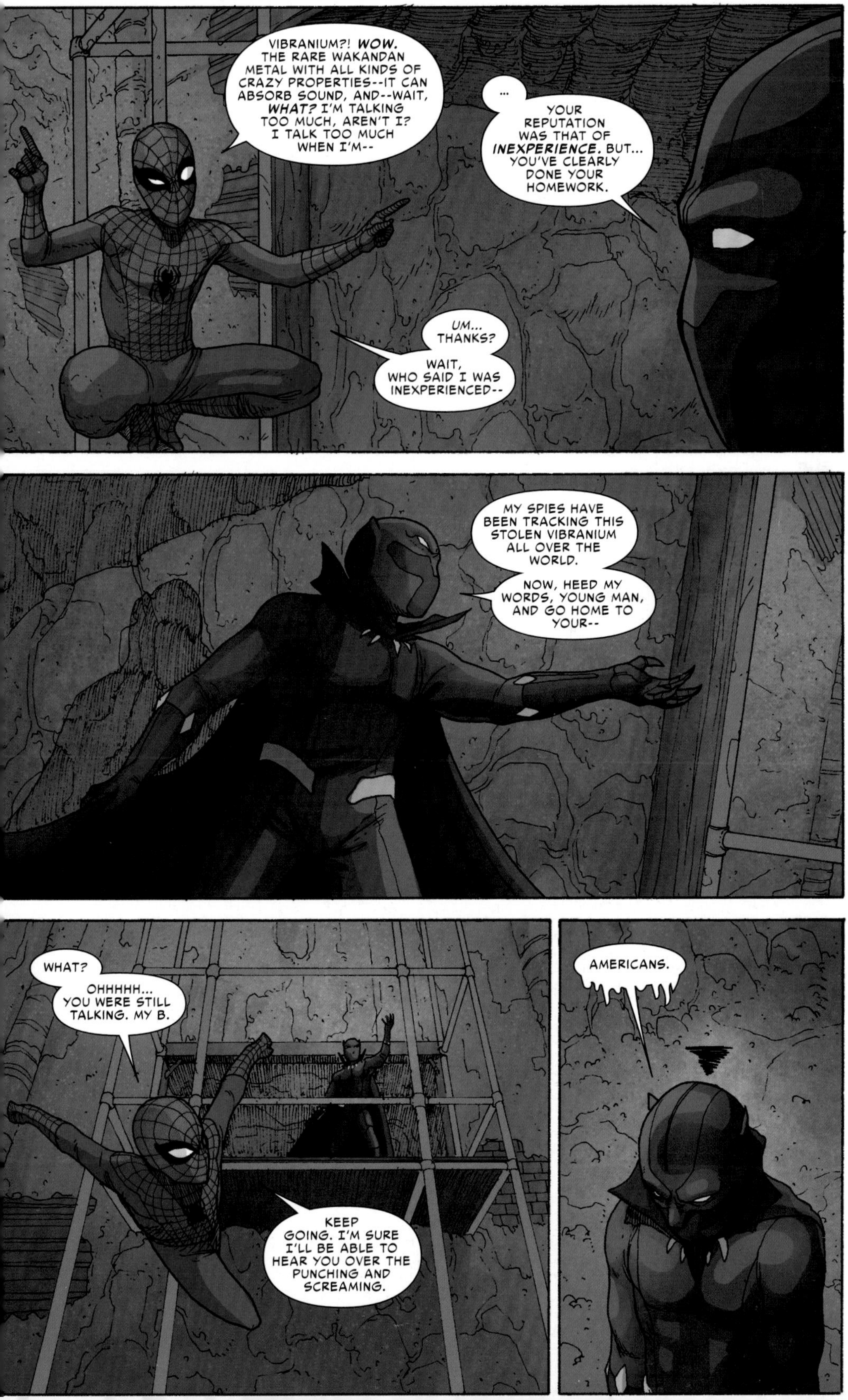
VIBRANIUM?! WOW. THE RARE WAKANDAN METAL WITH ALL KINDS OF CRAZY PROPERTIES--IT CAN ABSORB SOUND, AND--WAIT, WHAT? I'M TALKING TOO MUCH, AREN'T I? I TALK TOO MUCH WHEN I'M--
...
YOUR REPUTATION WAS THAT OF INEXPERIENCE. BUT... YOU'VE CLEARLY DONE YOUR HOMEWORK.
UM... THANKS?
WAIT, WHO SAID I WAS INEXPERIENCED--
MY SPIES HAVE BEEN TRACKING THIS STOLEN VIBRANIUM ALL OVER THE WORLD.
NOW, HEED MY WORDS, YOUNG MAN, AND GO HOME TO YOUR--
WHAT?
OHHHHH... YOU WERE STILL TALKING. MY B.
KEEP GOING. I'M SURE I'LL BE ABLE TO HEAR YOU OVER THE PUNCHING AND SCREAMING.
AMERICANS.

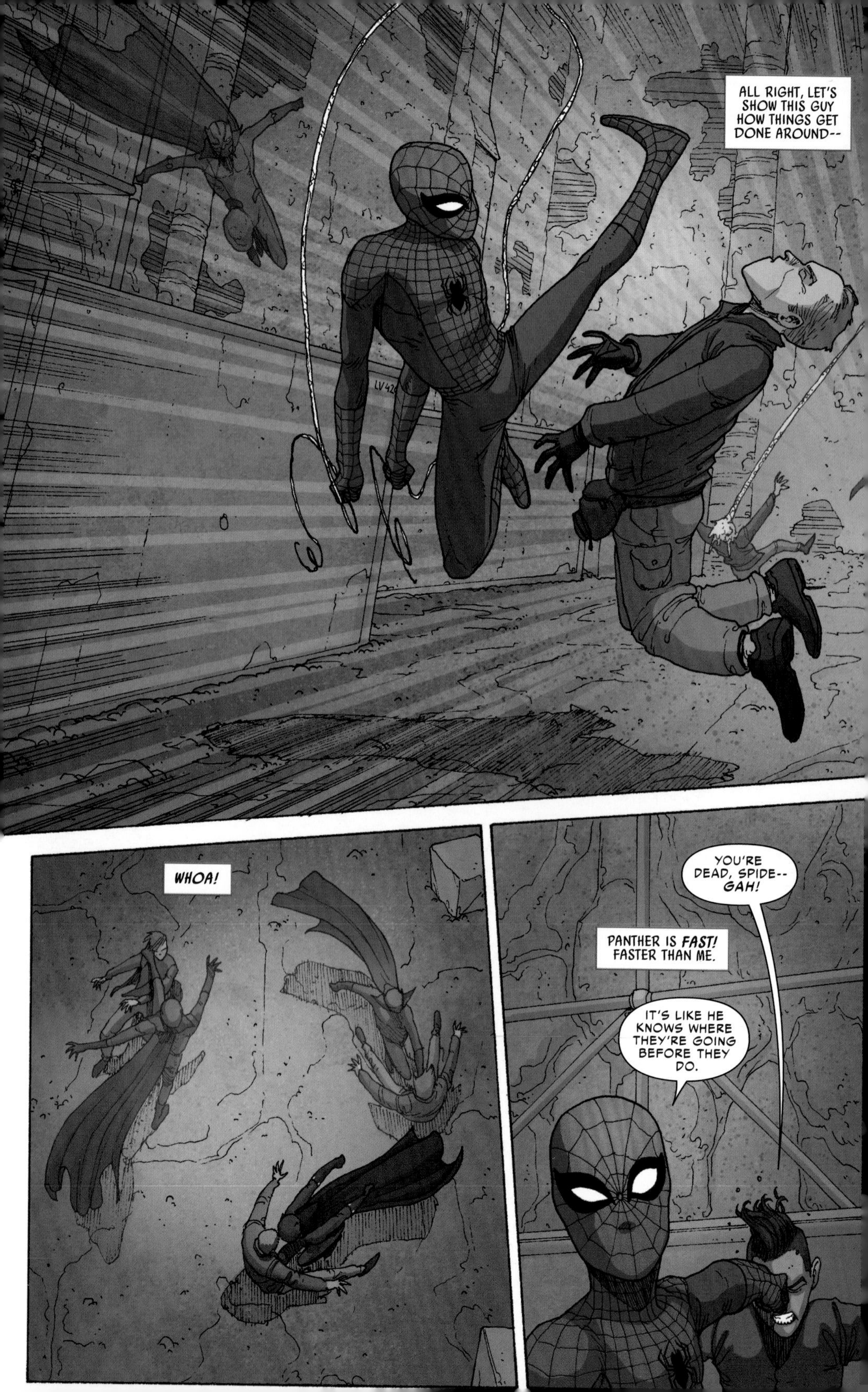
ALL RIGHT, LET'S SHOW THIS GUY HOW THINGS GET DONE AROUND--
LV 42
WHOA!
YOU'RE DEAD, SPIDE-- GAH!
PANTHER IS FAST! FASTER THAN ME.
IT'S LIKE HE KNOWS WHERE THEY'RE GOING BEFORE THEY DO.

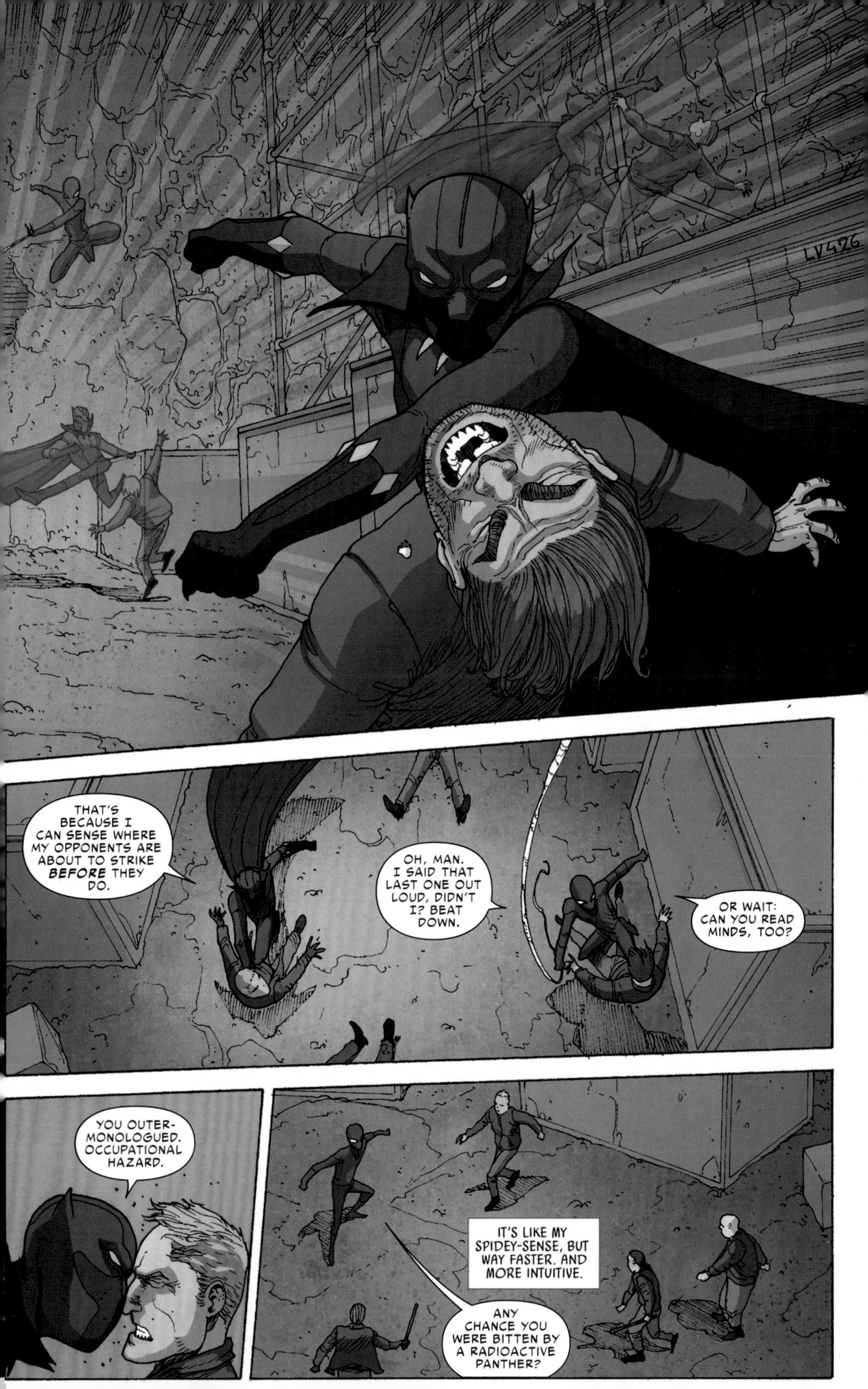
LV426
THAT'S BECAUSE I CAN SENSE WHERE MY OPPONENTS ARE ABOUT TO STRIKE *BEFORE* THEY DO.
OH, MAN. I SAID THAT LAST ONE OUT LOUD, DIDN'T I? BEAT DOWN.
OR WAIT: CAN YOU READ MINDS, TOO?
YOU OUTER-MONOLOGUED. OCCUPATIONAL HAZARD.
IT'S LIKE MY SPIDEY-SENSE, BUT WAY FASTER. AND MORE INTUITIVE.
ANY CHANCE YOU WERE BITTEN BY A RADIOACTIVE PANTHER?

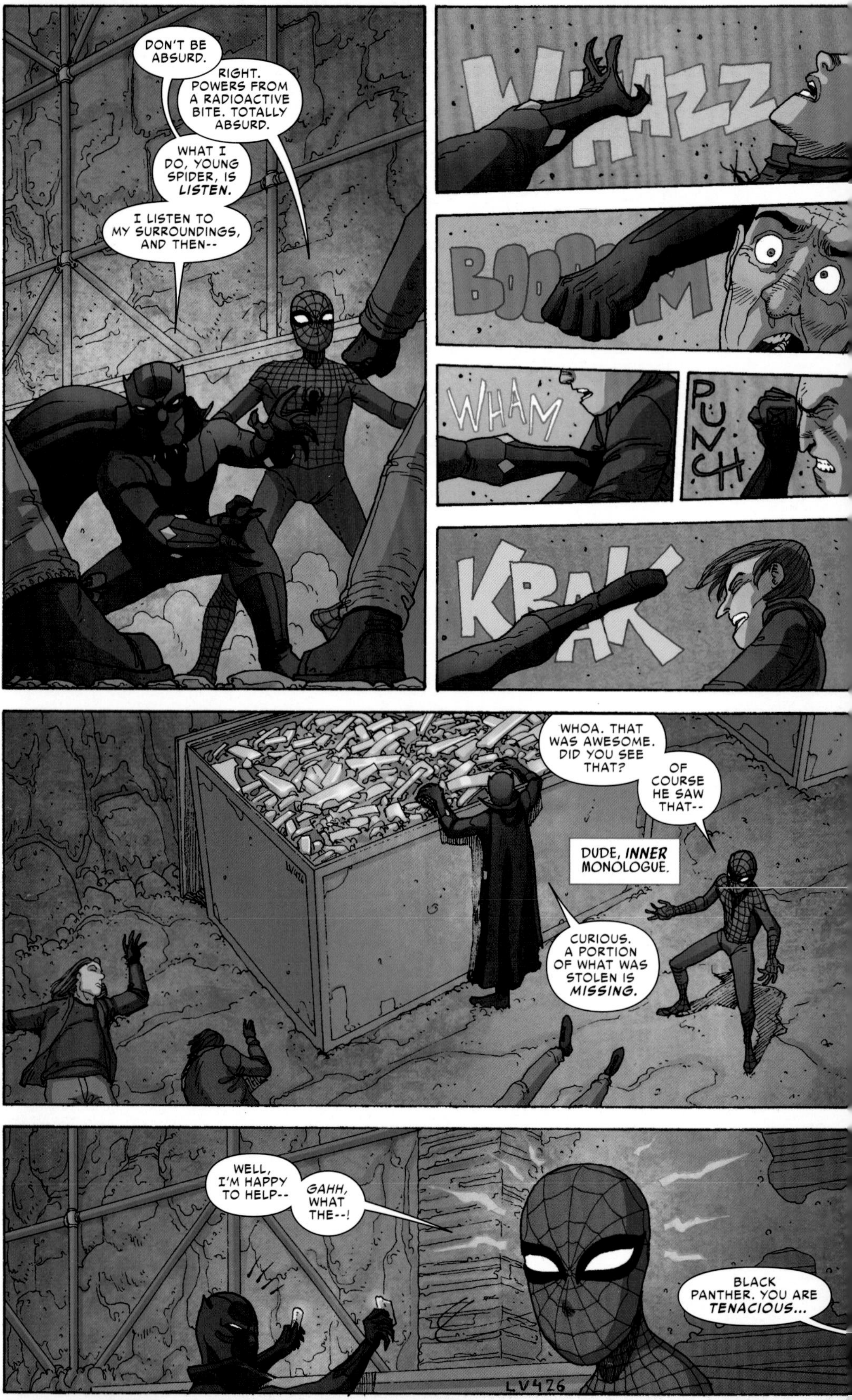
DON'T BE ABSURD.
RIGHT. POWERS FROM A RADIOACTIVE BITE. TOTALLY ABSURD.
WHAT I DO, YOUNG SPIDER, IS *LISTEN.*
I LISTEN TO MY SURROUNDINGS, AND THEN--
WHAZZ
BOOOOOM
WHAM
PUNCH
KRAK
WHOA. THAT WAS AWESOME. DID YOU SEE THAT?
OF COURSE HE SAW THAT--
DUDE, *INNER* MONOLOGUE.
CURIOUS. A PORTION OF WHAT WAS STOLEN IS *MISSING.*
LV426
WELL, I'M HAPPY TO HELP--
GAHH, WHAT THE--!
BLACK PANTHER. YOU ARE *TENACIOUS...*
LV426

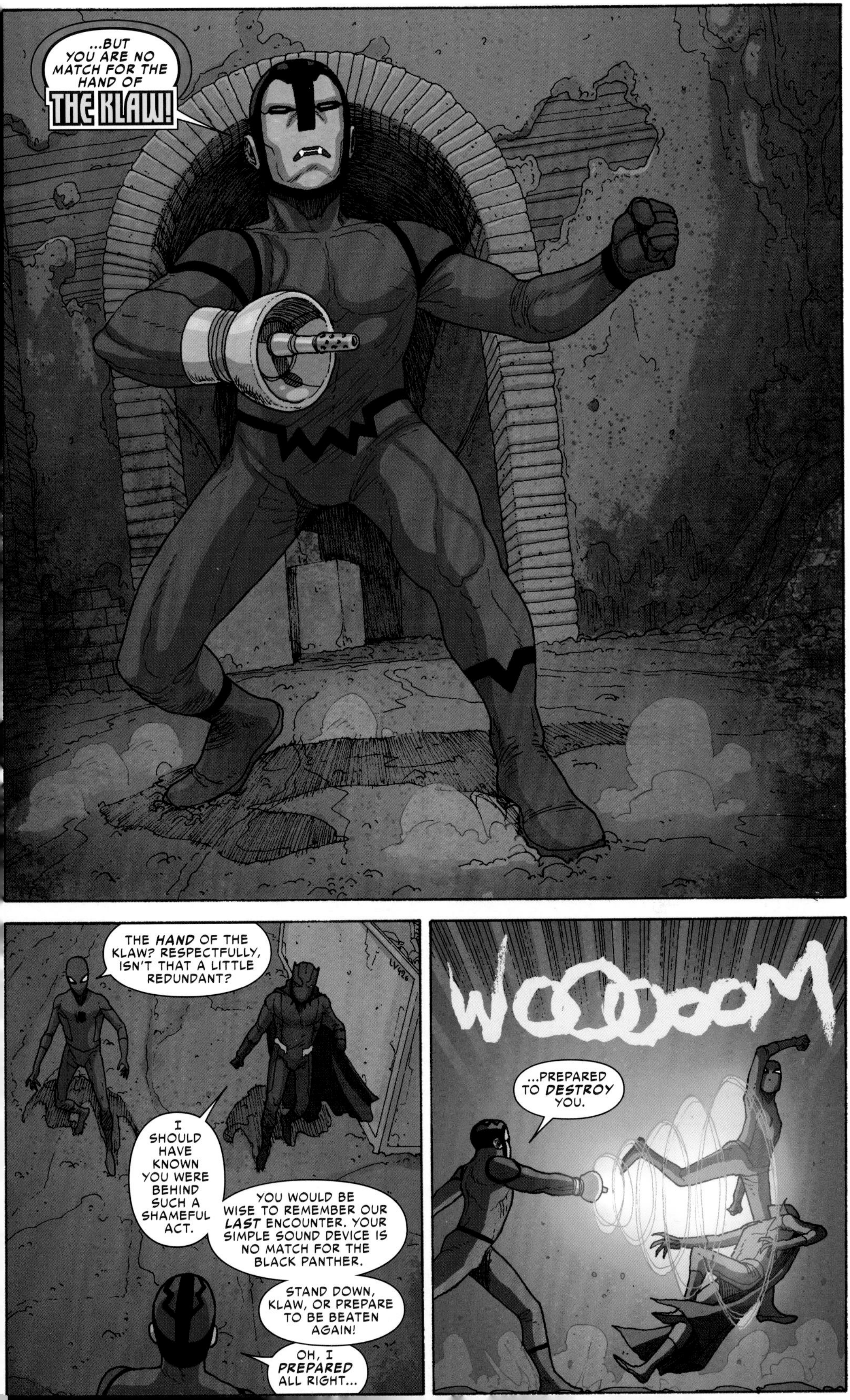
...BUT YOU ARE NO MATCH FOR THE HAND OF THE KLAW!
THE HAND OF THE KLAW? RESPECTFULLY, ISN'T THAT A LITTLE REDUNDANT?
I SHOULD HAVE KNOWN YOU WERE BEHIND SUCH A SHAMEFUL ACT.
YOU WOULD BE WISE TO REMEMBER OUR LAST ENCOUNTER. YOUR SIMPLE SOUND DEVICE IS NO MATCH FOR THE BLACK PANTHER.
STAND DOWN, KLAW, OR PREPARE TO BE BEATEN AGAIN!
OH, I PREPARED ALL RIGHT...
WOOOOOOM
...PREPARED TO DESTROY YOU.

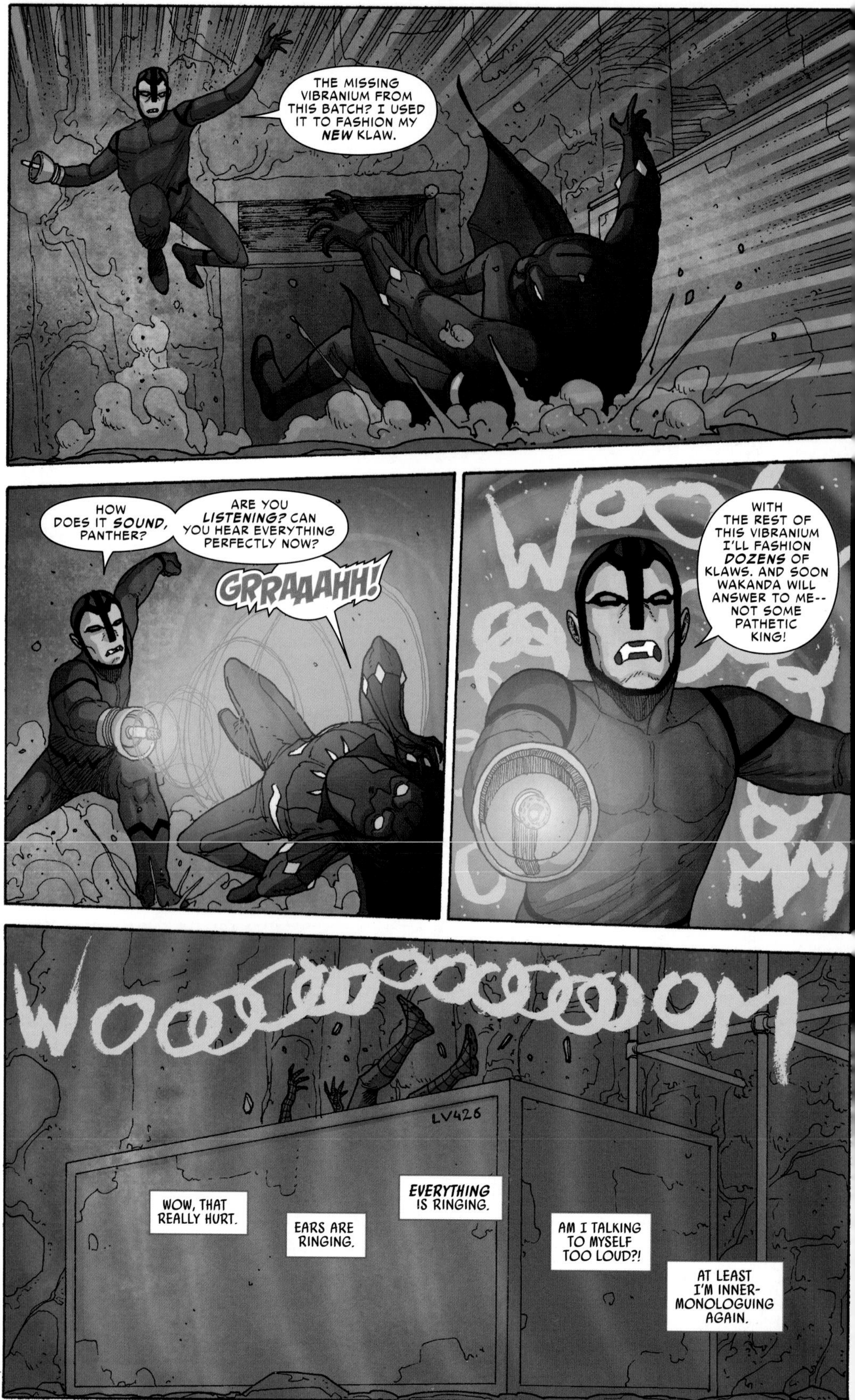
THE MISSING VIBRANIUM FROM THIS BATCH? I USED IT TO FASHION MY NEW KLAW.
HOW DOES IT SOUND, PANTHER?
ARE YOU LISTENING? CAN YOU HEAR EVERYTHING PERFECTLY NOW?
GRRAAAHH!
WITH THE REST OF THIS VIBRANIUM I'LL FASHION DOZENS OF KLAWS. AND SOON WAKANDA WILL ANSWER TO ME-- NOT SOME PATHETIC KING!
WOOOOOOOOOOOOM
LV426
WOW, THAT REALLY HURT.
EARS ARE RINGING.
EVERYTHING IS RINGING.
AM I TALKING TO MYSELF TOO LOUD?!
AT LEAST I'M INNER-MONOLOGUING AGAIN.

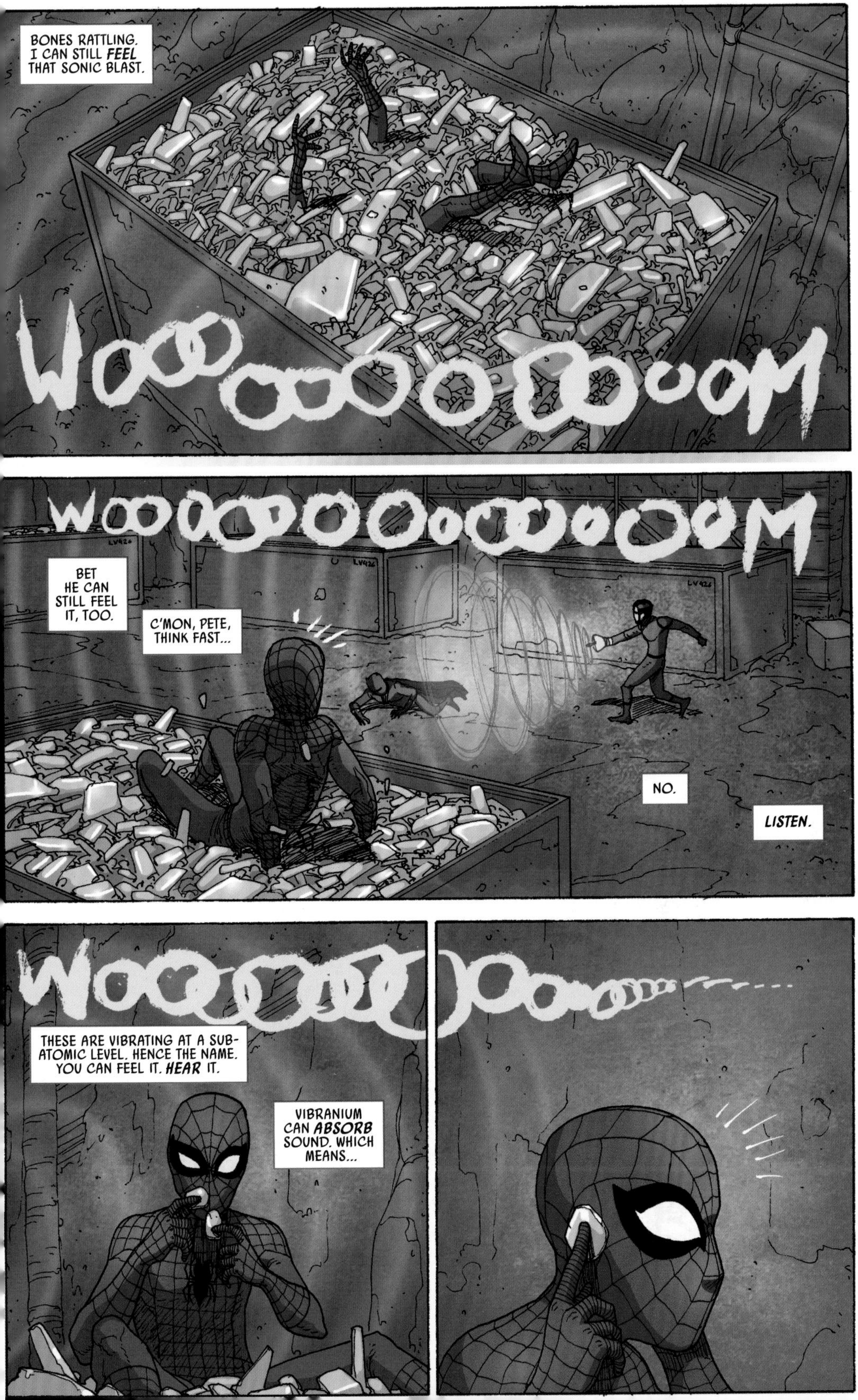
BONES RATTLING. I CAN STILL FEEL THAT SONIC BLAST.
WOOOOOOOOOOOM
WOOOOOOOOOOOOOOM
BET HE CAN STILL FEEL IT, TOO.
C'MON, PETE, THINK FAST...
NO.
LISTEN.
WOOOOOOOOOOOOO...
THESE ARE VIBRATING AT A SUB-ATOMIC LEVEL. HENCE THE NAME. YOU CAN FEEL IT. HEAR IT.
VIBRANIUM CAN ABSORB SOUND. WHICH MEANS...

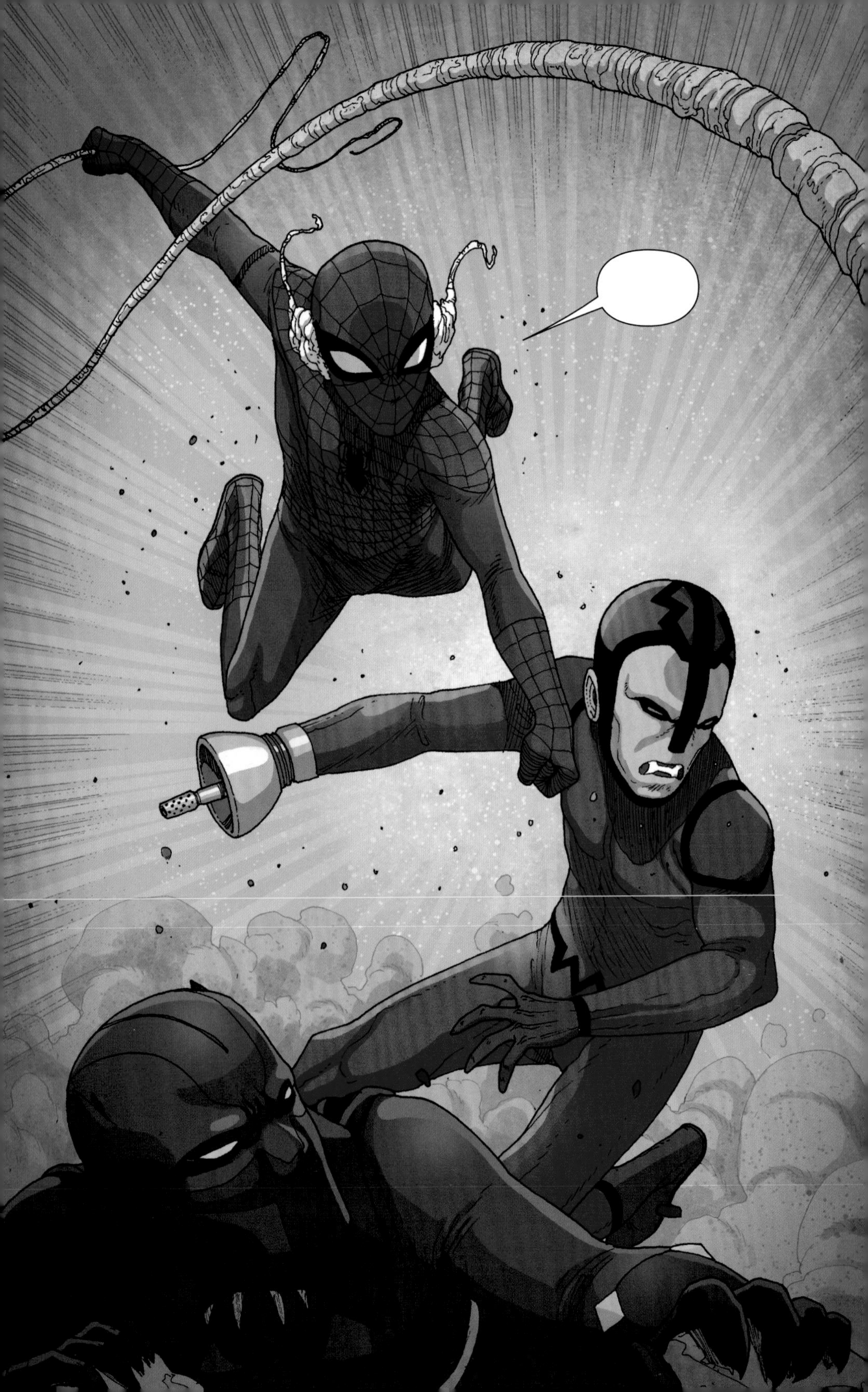

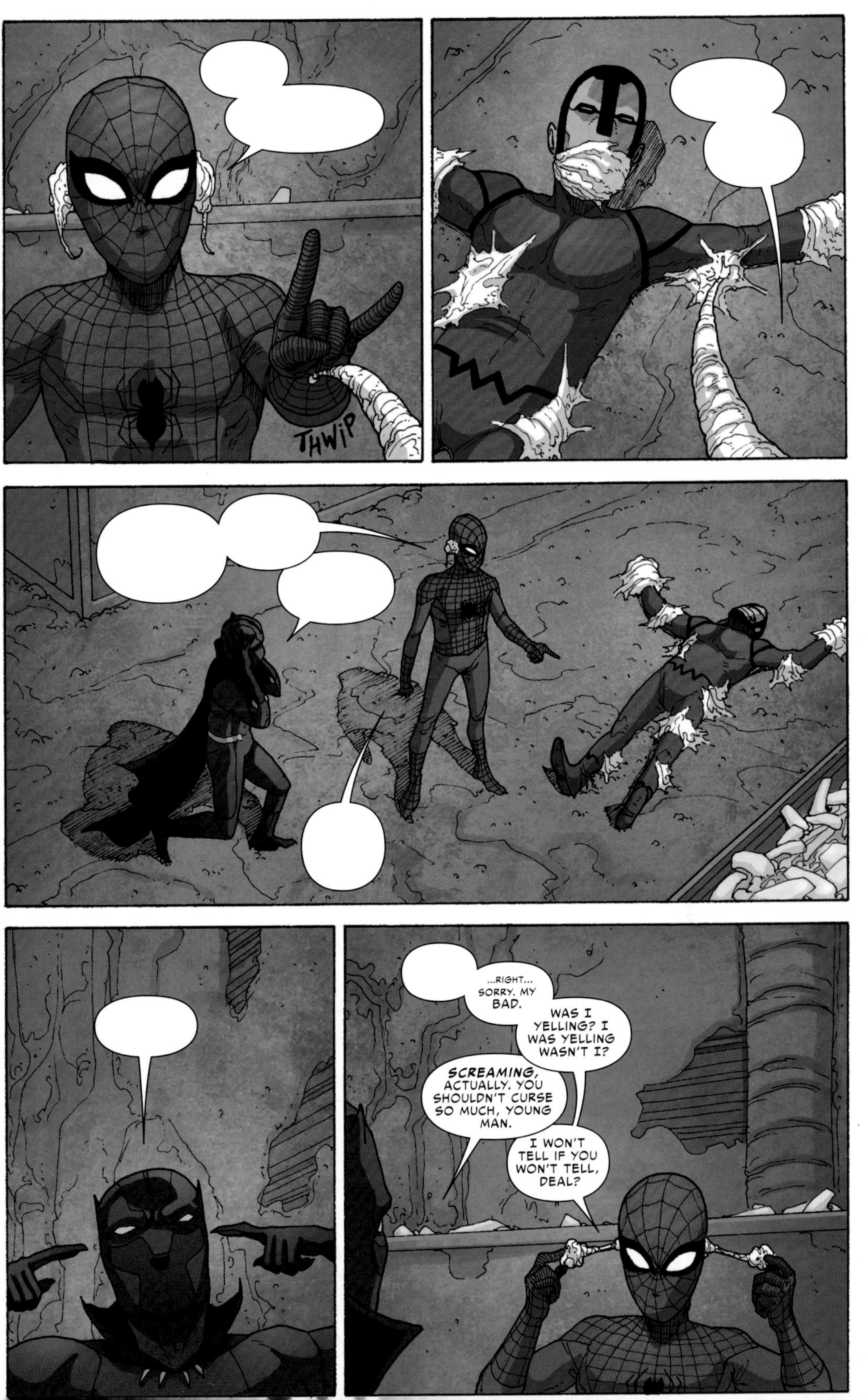
THWIP
...RIGHT... SORRY. MY BAD.
WAS I YELLING? I WAS YELLING WASN'T I?
SCREAMING, ACTUALLY. YOU SHOULDN'T CURSE SO MUCH, YOUNG MAN.
I WON'T TELL IF YOU WON'T TELL, DEAL?

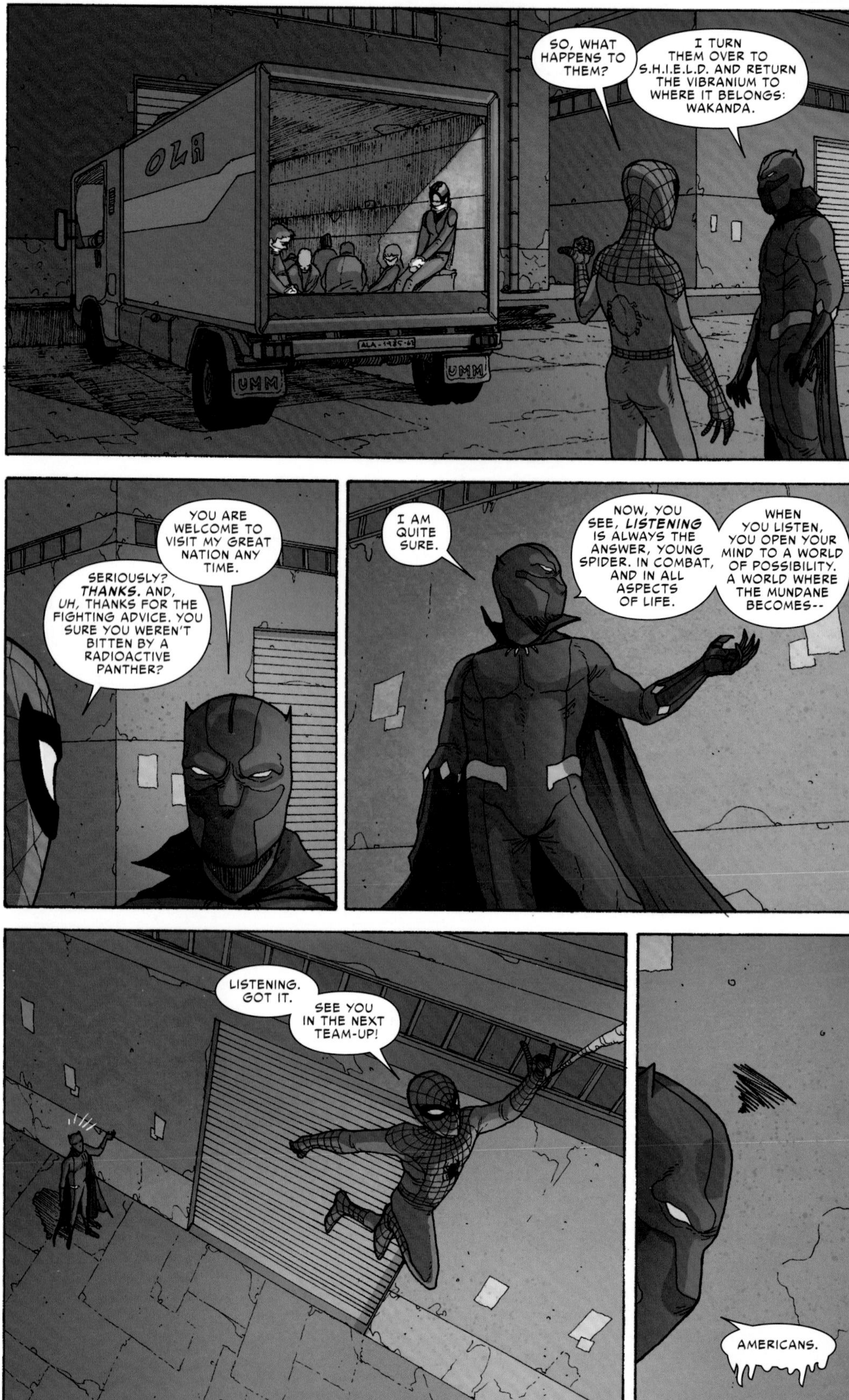
SO, WHAT HAPPENS TO THEM?
I TURN THEM OVER TO S.H.I.E.L.D. AND RETURN THE VIBRANIUM TO WHERE IT BELONGS: WAKANDA.
YOU ARE WELCOME TO VISIT MY GREAT NATION ANY TIME.
SERIOUSLY? **THANKS.** AND, *UH,* THANKS FOR THE FIGHTING ADVICE. YOU SURE YOU WEREN'T BITTEN BY A RADIOACTIVE PANTHER?
I AM QUITE SURE.
NOW, YOU SEE, ***LISTENING*** IS ALWAYS THE ANSWER, YOUNG SPIDER. IN COMBAT, AND IN ALL ASPECTS OF LIFE.
WHEN YOU LISTEN, YOU OPEN YOUR MIND TO A WORLD OF POSSIBILITY. A WORLD WHERE THE MUNDANE BECOMES--
LISTENING. GOT IT.
SEE YOU IN THE NEXT TEAM-UP!
AMERICANS.

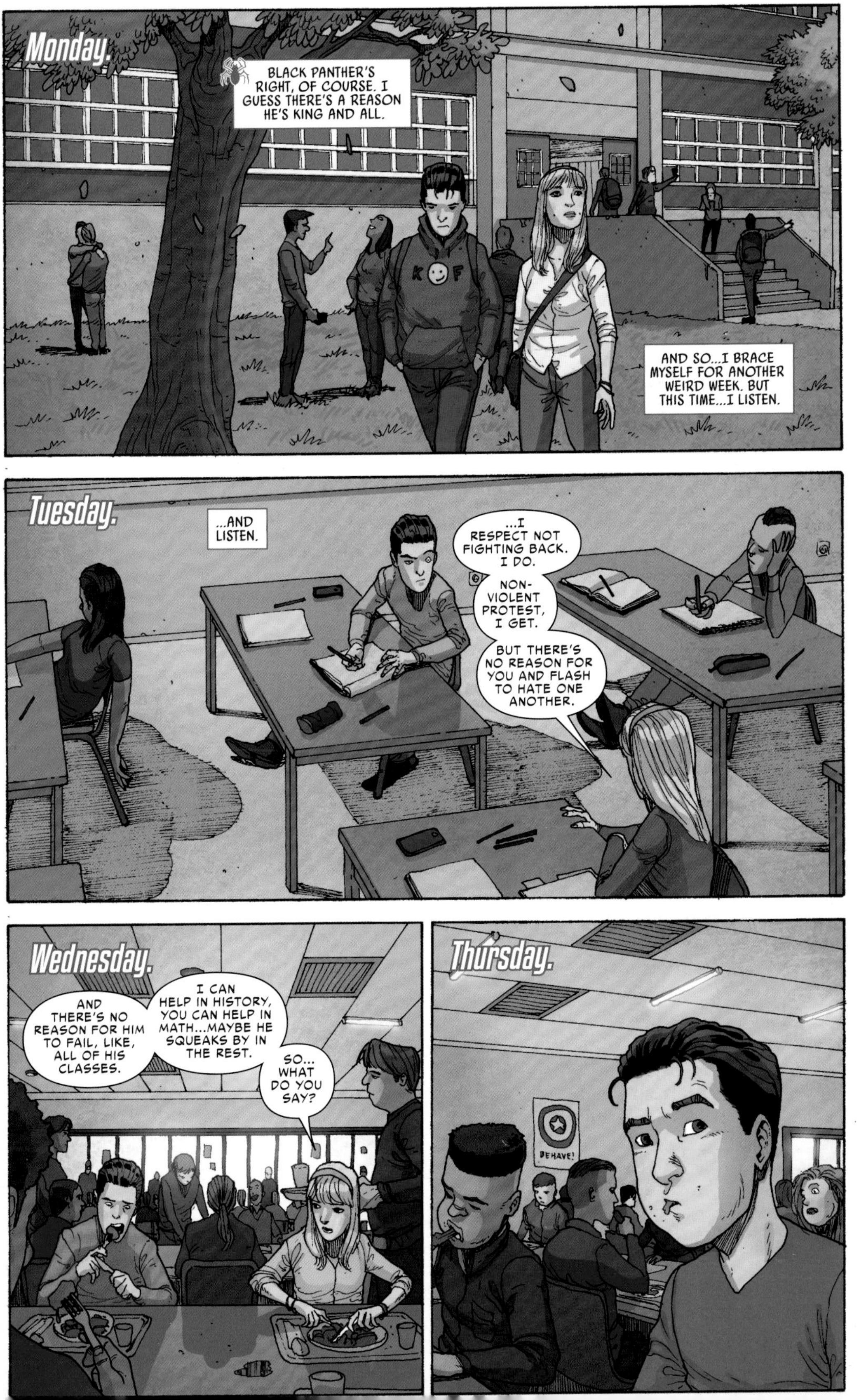
Monday.
BLACK PANTHER'S RIGHT, OF COURSE. I GUESS THERE'S A REASON HE'S KING AND ALL.
AND SO...I BRACE MYSELF FOR ANOTHER WEIRD WEEK. BUT THIS TIME...I LISTEN.
Tuesday.
...AND LISTEN.
...I RESPECT NOT FIGHTING BACK. I DO.
NON-VIOLENT PROTEST, I GET.
BUT THERE'S NO REASON FOR YOU AND FLASH TO HATE ONE ANOTHER.
Wednesday.
AND THERE'S NO REASON FOR HIM TO FAIL, LIKE, ALL OF HIS CLASSES.
I CAN HELP IN HISTORY, YOU CAN HELP IN MATH...MAYBE HE SQUEAKS BY IN THE REST.
SO... WHAT DO YOU SAY?
Thursday.
BEHAVE!

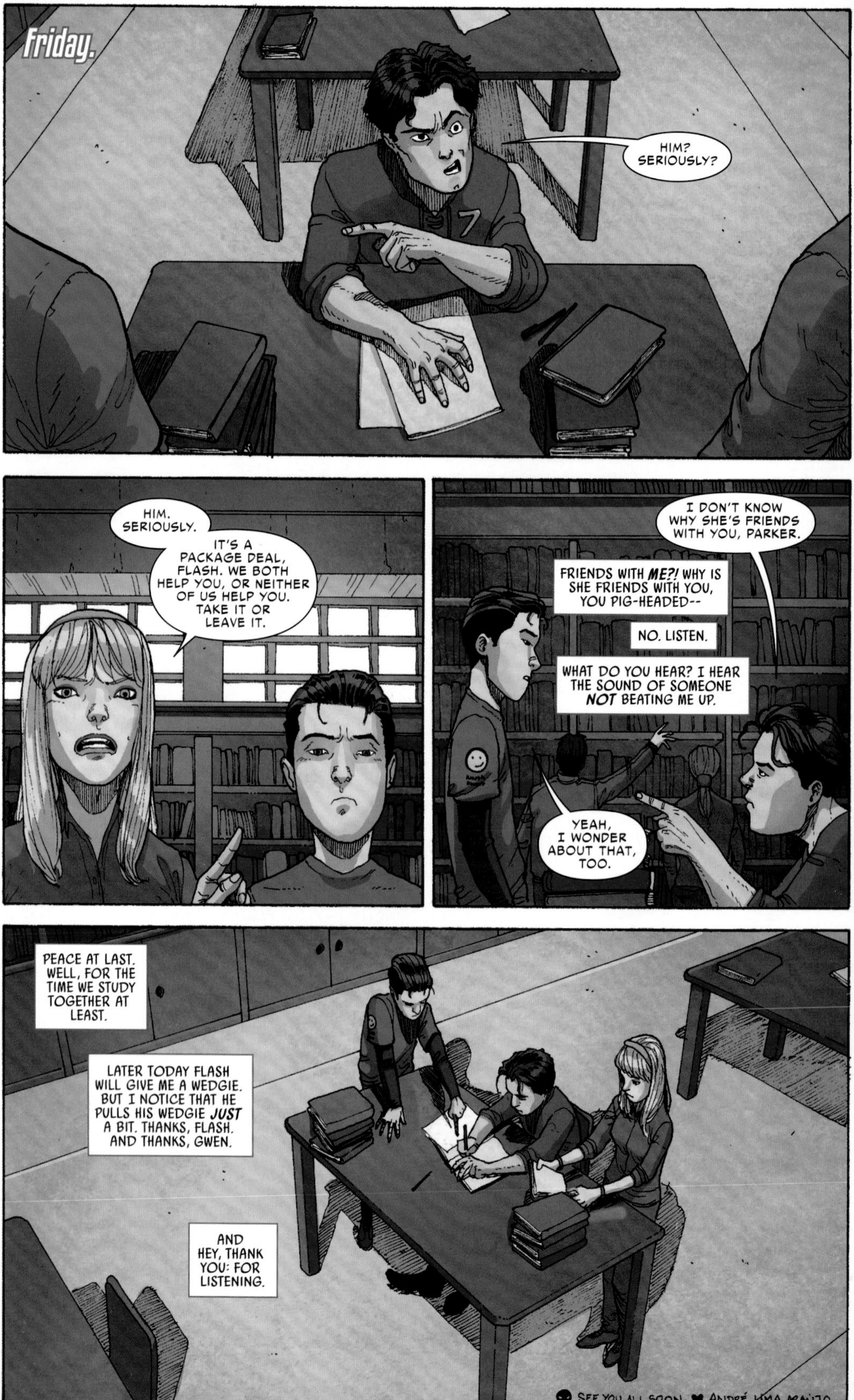
Friday.
HIM? SERIOUSLY?
HIM. SERIOUSLY.
IT'S A PACKAGE DEAL, FLASH. WE BOTH HELP YOU, OR NEITHER OF US HELP YOU. TAKE IT OR LEAVE IT.
I DON'T KNOW WHY SHE'S FRIENDS WITH YOU, PARKER.
FRIENDS WITH ME?! WHY IS SHE FRIENDS WITH YOU, YOU PIG-HEADED--
NO. LISTEN.
WHAT DO YOU HEAR? I HEAR THE SOUND OF SOMEONE NOT BEATING ME UP.
YEAH, I WONDER ABOUT THAT, TOO.
PEACE AT LAST. WELL, FOR THE TIME WE STUDY TOGETHER AT LEAST.
LATER TODAY FLASH WILL GIVE ME A WEDGIE. BUT I NOTICE THAT HE PULLS HIS WEDGIE JUST A BIT. THANKS, FLASH. AND THANKS, GWEN.
AND HEY, THANK YOU: FOR LISTENING.
SEE YOU ALL SOON. ANDRÉ LIMA ARAÚJO.

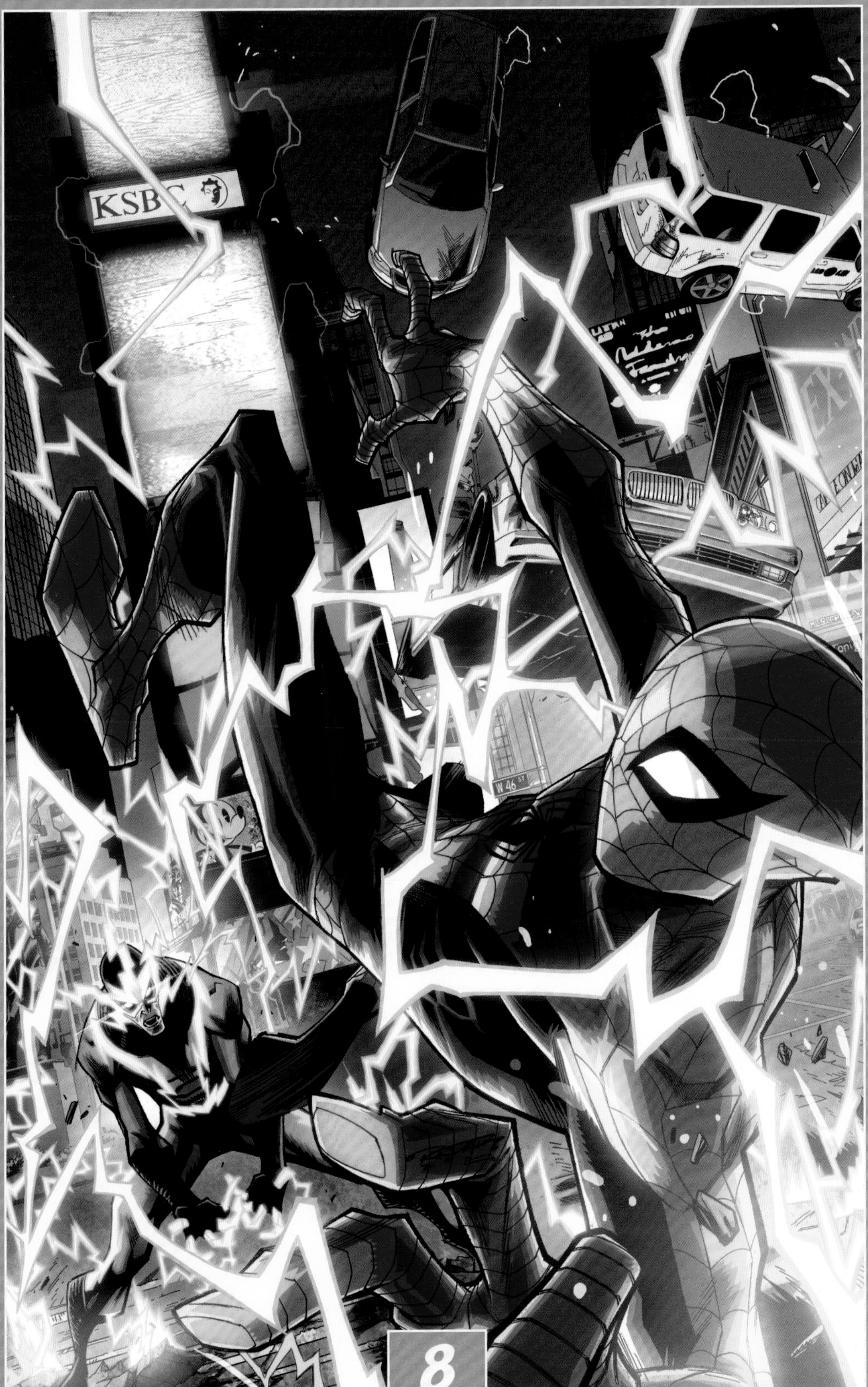
KSBC
W 46 ST

8

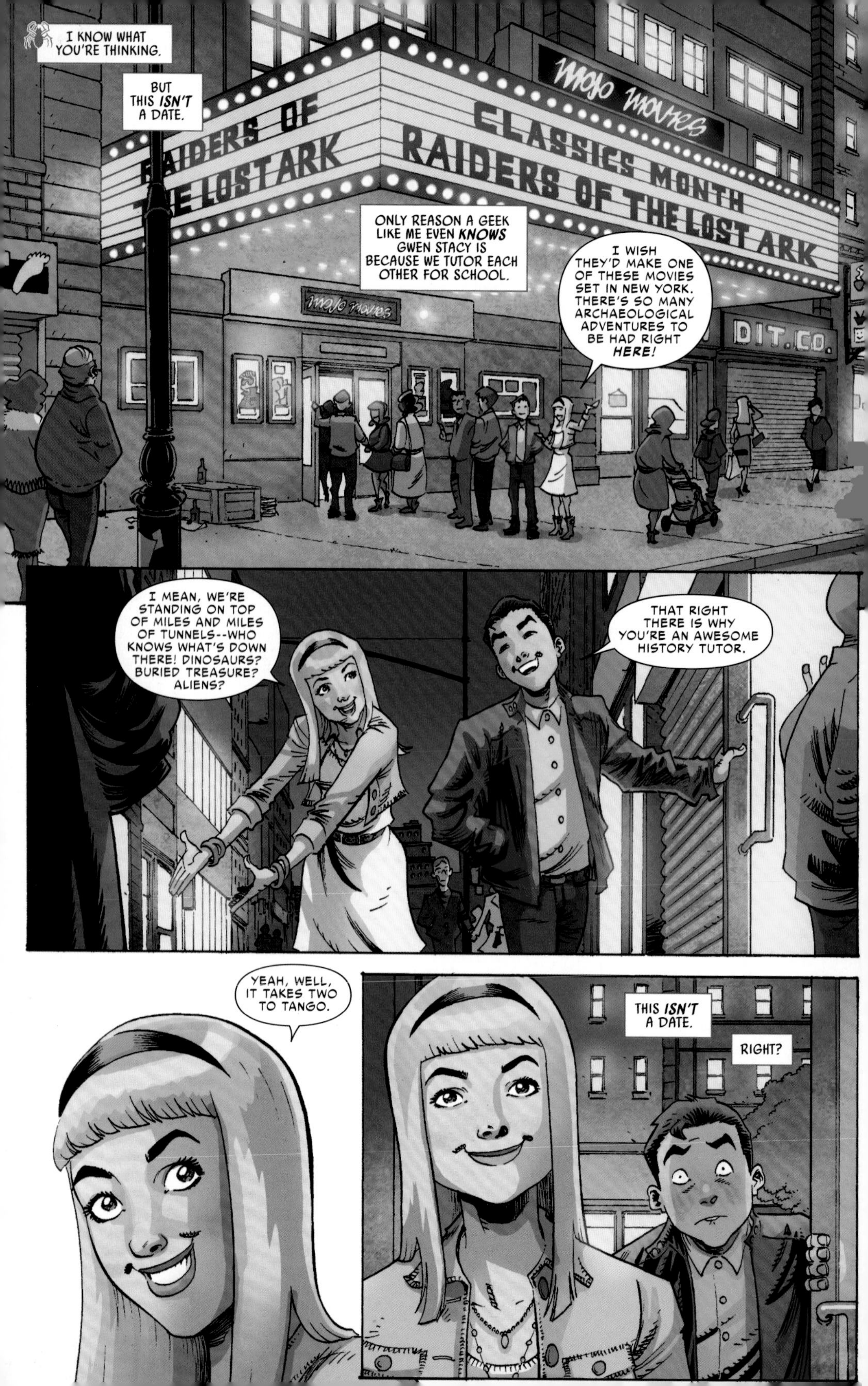

I KNOW WHAT YOU'RE THINKING.
BUT THIS *ISN'T* A DATE.
MOJO MOVIES
RAIDERS OF THE LOST ARK
CLASSICS MONTH
RAIDERS OF THE LOST ARK
ONLY REASON A GEEK LIKE ME EVEN *KNOWS* GWEN STACY IS BECAUSE WE TUTOR EACH OTHER FOR SCHOOL.
I WISH THEY'D MAKE ONE OF THESE MOVIES SET IN NEW YORK. THERE'S SO MANY ARCHAEOLOGICAL ADVENTURES TO BE HAD RIGHT *HERE!*
MOJO MOVIES
DIT.CO.
I MEAN, WE'RE STANDING ON TOP OF MILES AND MILES OF TUNNELS--WHO KNOWS WHAT'S DOWN THERE! DINOSAURS? BURIED TREASURE? ALIENS?
THAT RIGHT THERE IS WHY YOU'RE AN AWESOME HISTORY TUTOR.
YEAH, WELL, IT TAKES TWO TO TANGO.
THIS *ISN'T* A DATE.
RIGHT?

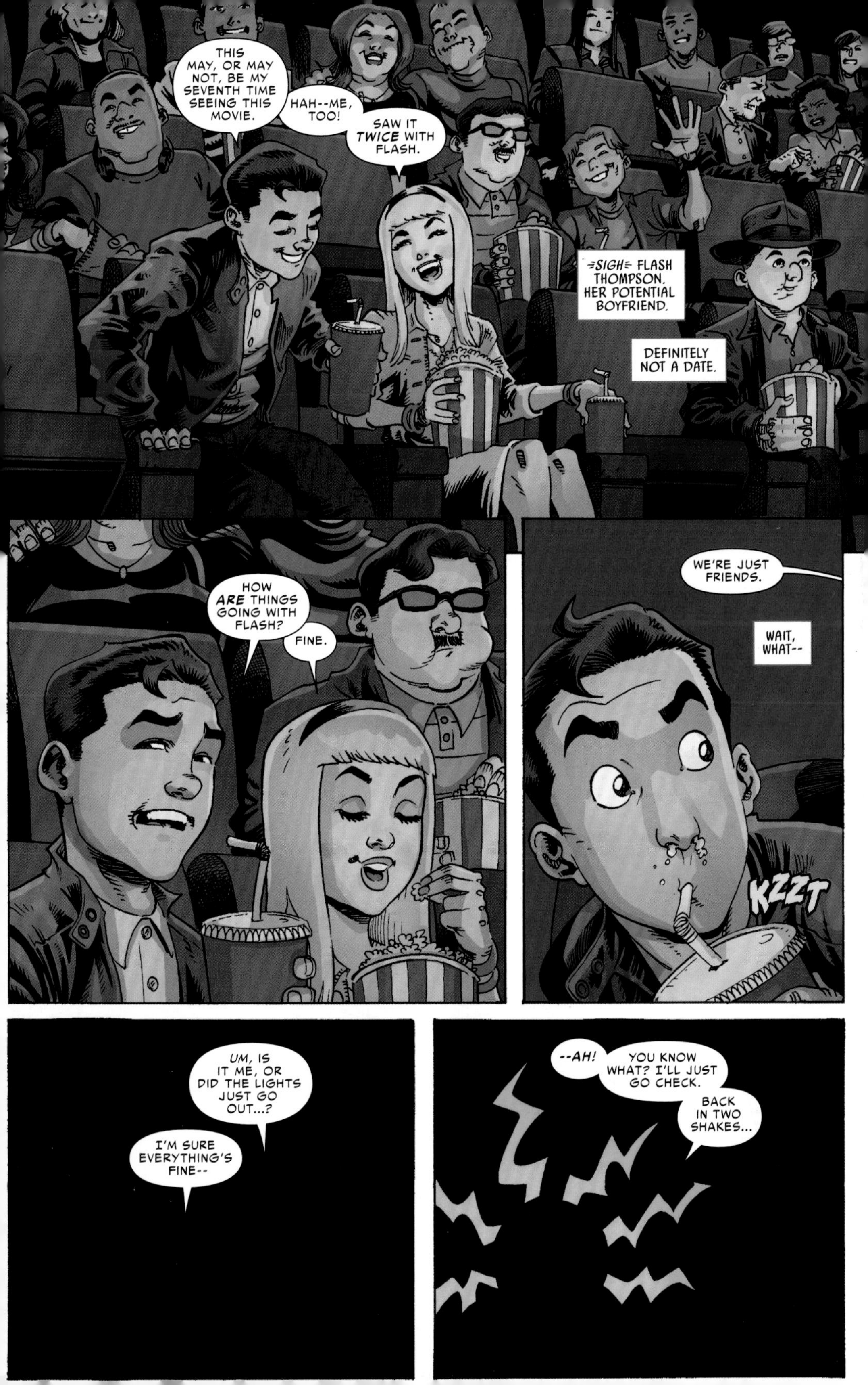
THIS MAY, OR MAY NOT, BE MY SEVENTH TIME SEEING THIS MOVIE.
HAH--ME, TOO!
SAW IT TWICE WITH FLASH.
=SIGH= FLASH THOMPSON. HER POTENTIAL BOYFRIEND.
DEFINITELY NOT A DATE.
HOW ARE THINGS GOING WITH FLASH?
FINE.
WE'RE JUST FRIENDS.
WAIT, WHAT--
KZZT
UM, IS IT ME, OR DID THE LIGHTS JUST GO OUT...?
I'M SURE EVERYTHING'S FINE--
--AH!
YOU KNOW WHAT? I'LL JUST GO CHECK.
BACK IN TWO SHAKES...

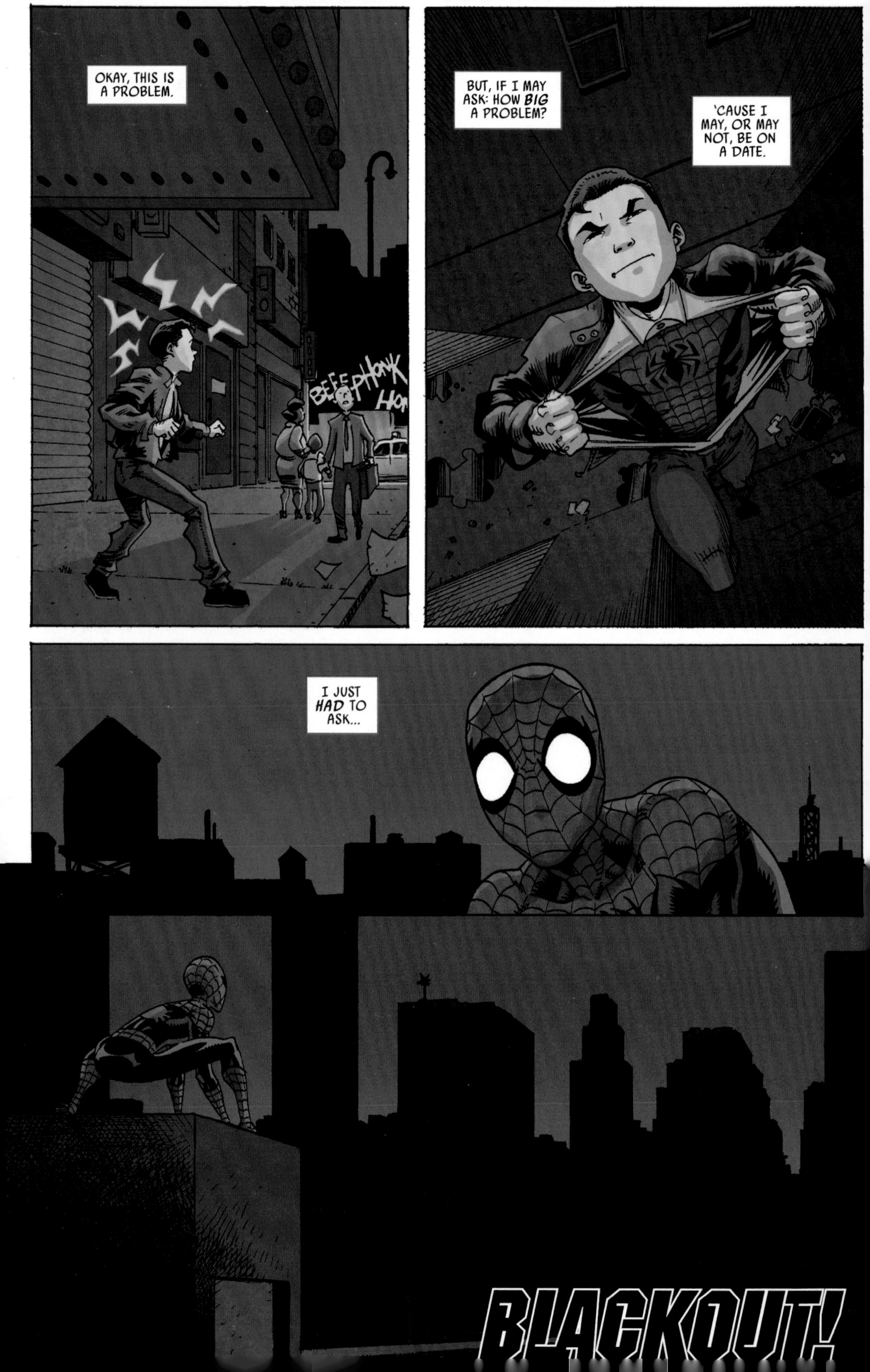
OKAY, THIS IS A PROBLEM.
BEEEP HONK HONK
BUT, IF I MAY ASK: HOW BIG A PROBLEM?
'CAUSE I MAY, OR MAY NOT, BE ON A DATE.
I JUST HAD TO ASK...
BLACKOUT!

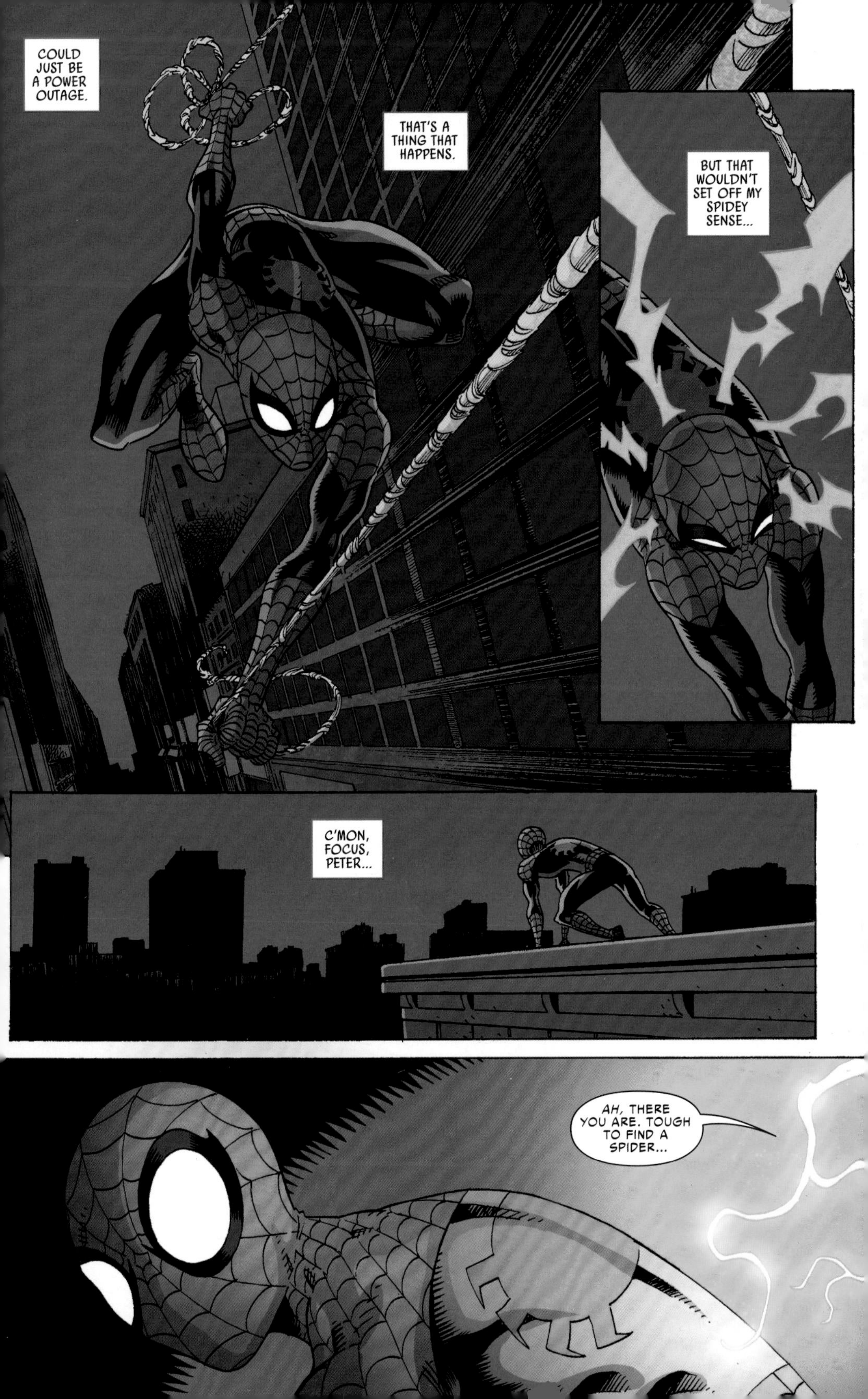
COULD JUST BE A POWER OUTAGE.
THAT'S A THING THAT HAPPENS.
BUT THAT WOULDN'T SET OFF MY SPIDEY SENSE...
C'MON, FOCUS, PETER...
AH, THERE YOU ARE. TOUGH TO FIND A SPIDER...

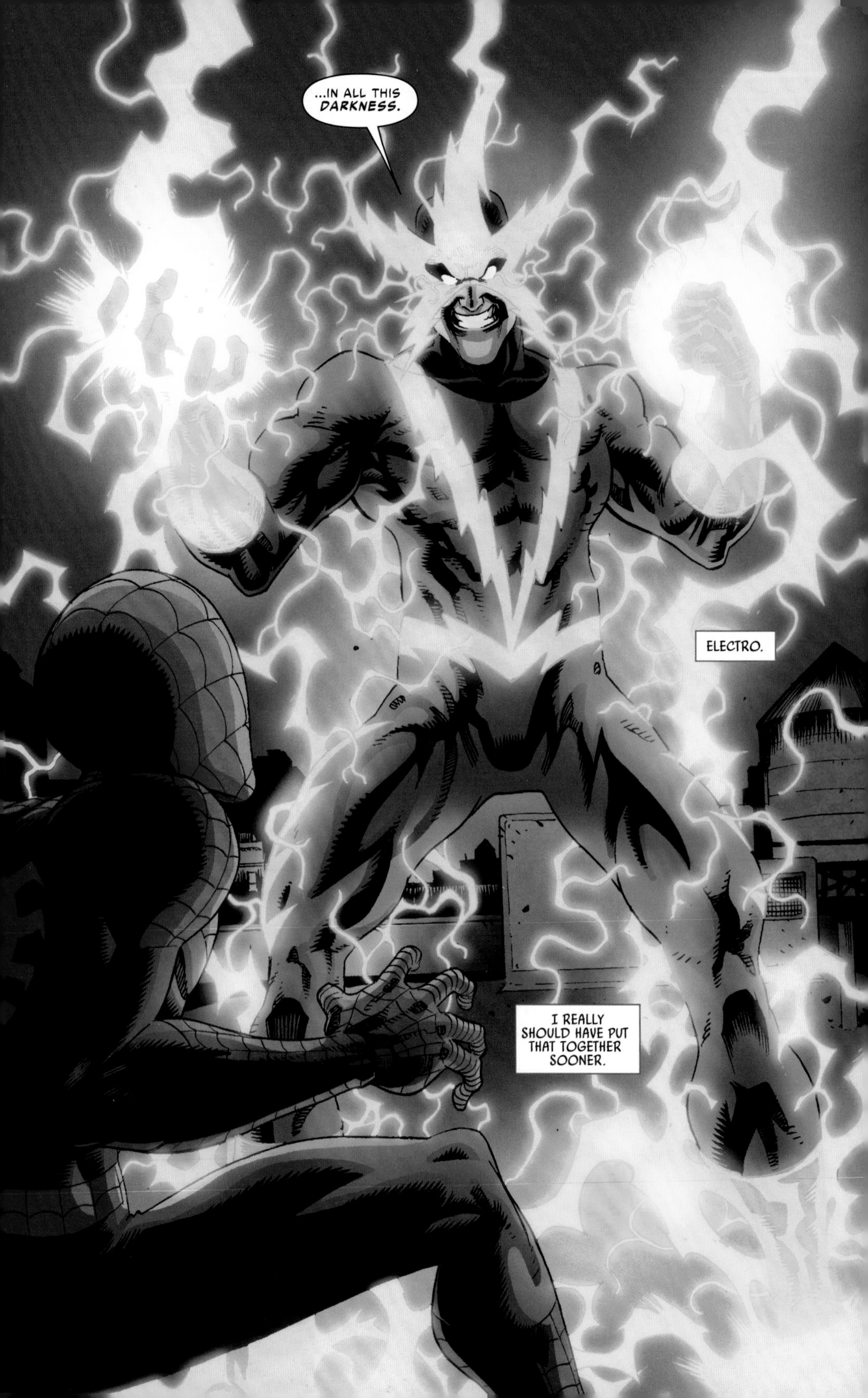
...IN ALL THIS DARKNESS.
ELECTRO.
I REALLY SHOULD HAVE PUT THAT TOGETHER SOONER.

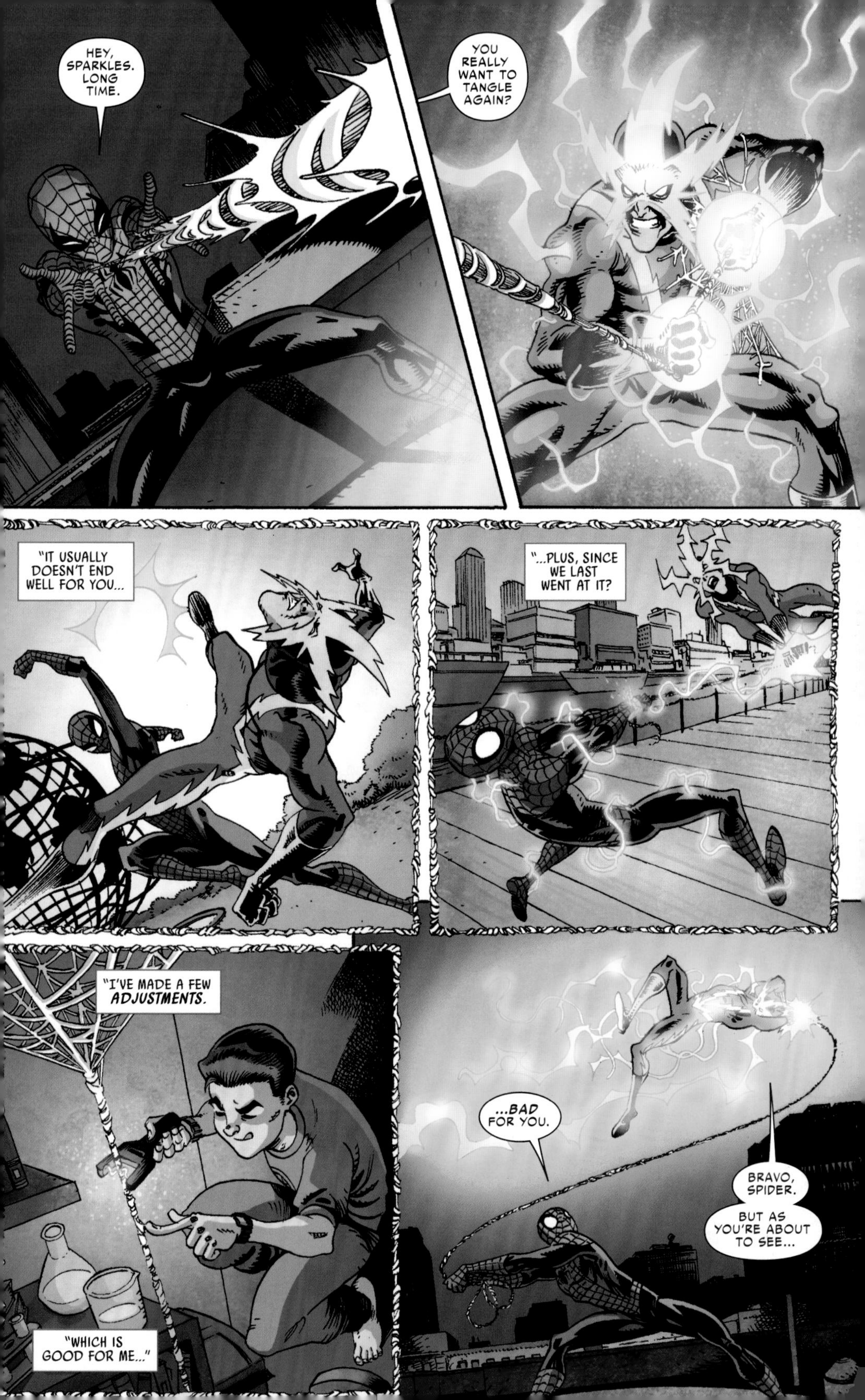
HEY, SPARKLES. LONG TIME.
YOU REALLY WANT TO TANGLE AGAIN?
"IT USUALLY DOESN'T END WELL FOR YOU...
"...PLUS, SINCE WE LAST WENT AT IT?
"I'VE MADE A FEW ADJUSTMENTS.
"WHICH IS GOOD FOR ME..."
...BAD FOR YOU.
BRAVO, SPIDER.
BUT AS YOU'RE ABOUT TO SEE...

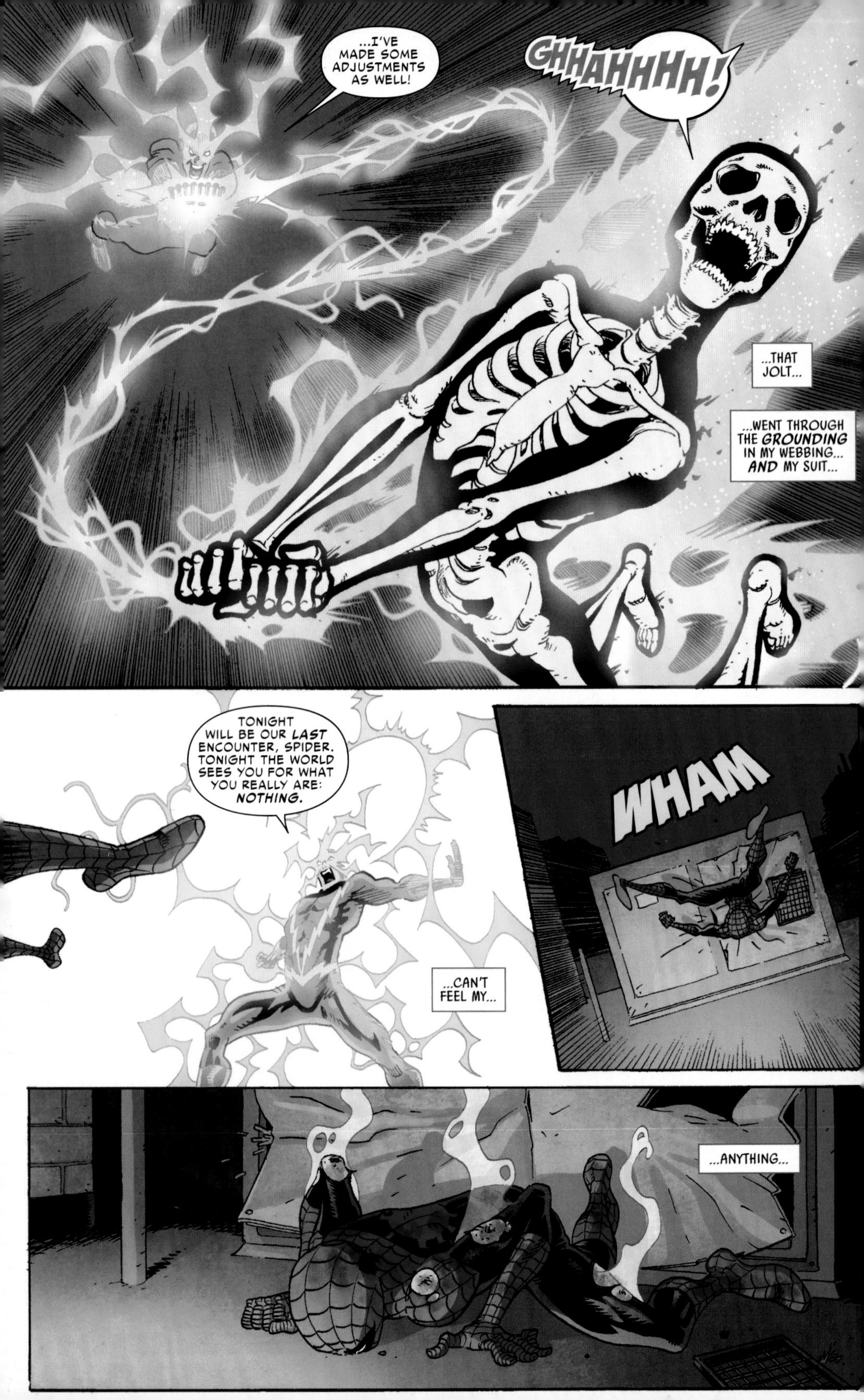
...I'VE MADE SOME ADJUSTMENTS AS WELL!
GHHAHHHH!
...THAT JOLT...
...WENT THROUGH THE *GROUNDING* IN MY WEBBING... ***AND*** MY SUIT...
TONIGHT WILL BE OUR *LAST* ENCOUNTER, SPIDER. TONIGHT THE WORLD SEES YOU FOR WHAT YOU REALLY ARE: ***NOTHING.***
...CAN'T FEEL MY...
WHAM
...ANYTHING...

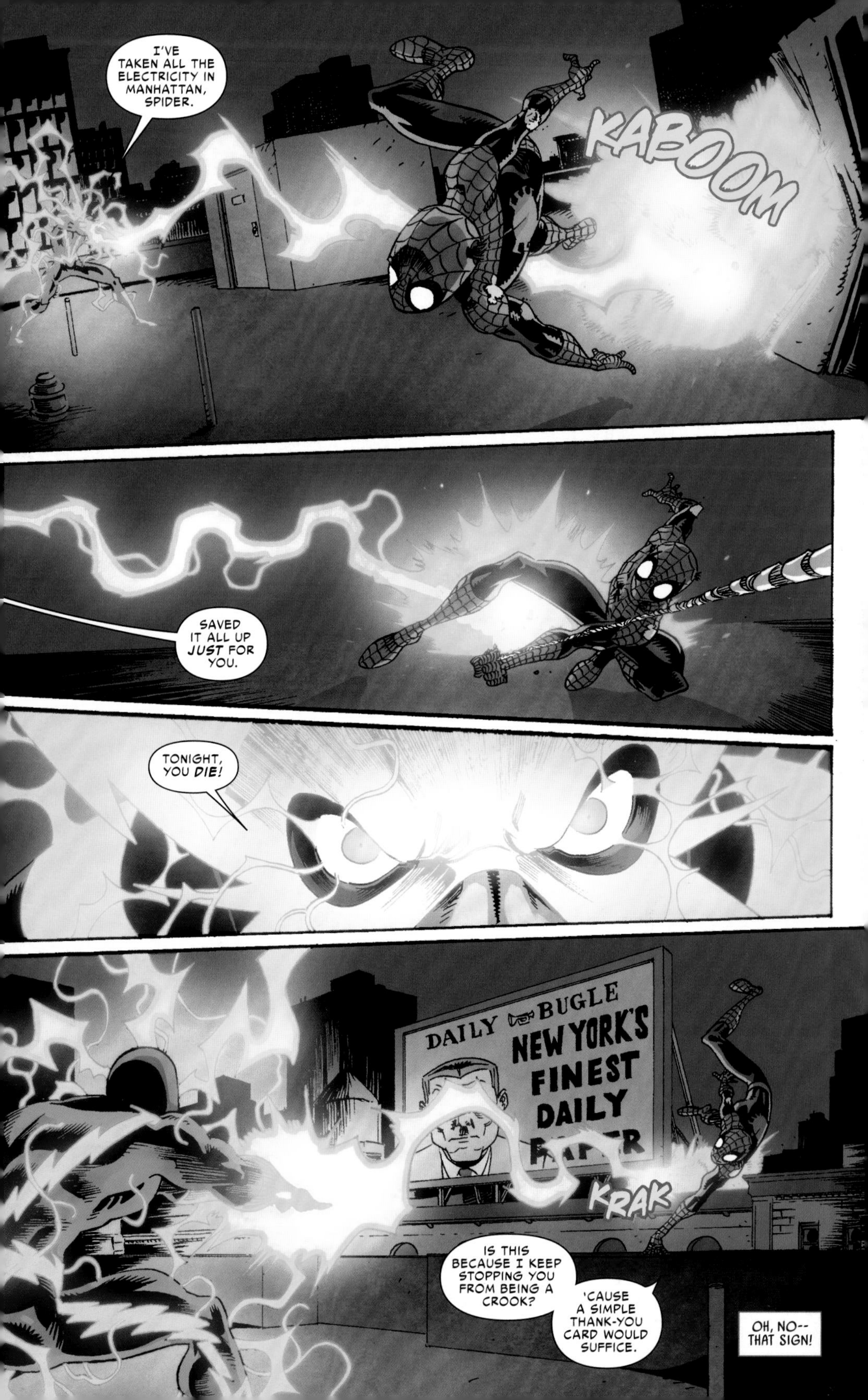

I'VE TAKEN ALL THE ELECTRICITY IN MANHATTAN, SPIDER.
KABOOM
SAVED IT ALL UP JUST FOR YOU.
TONIGHT, YOU DIE!
DAILY BUGLE
NEW YORK'S FINEST DAILY
KRAK
IS THIS BECAUSE I KEEP STOPPING YOU FROM BEING A CROOK?
'CAUSE A SIMPLE THANK-YOU CARD WOULD SUFFICE.
OH, NO-- THAT SIGN!

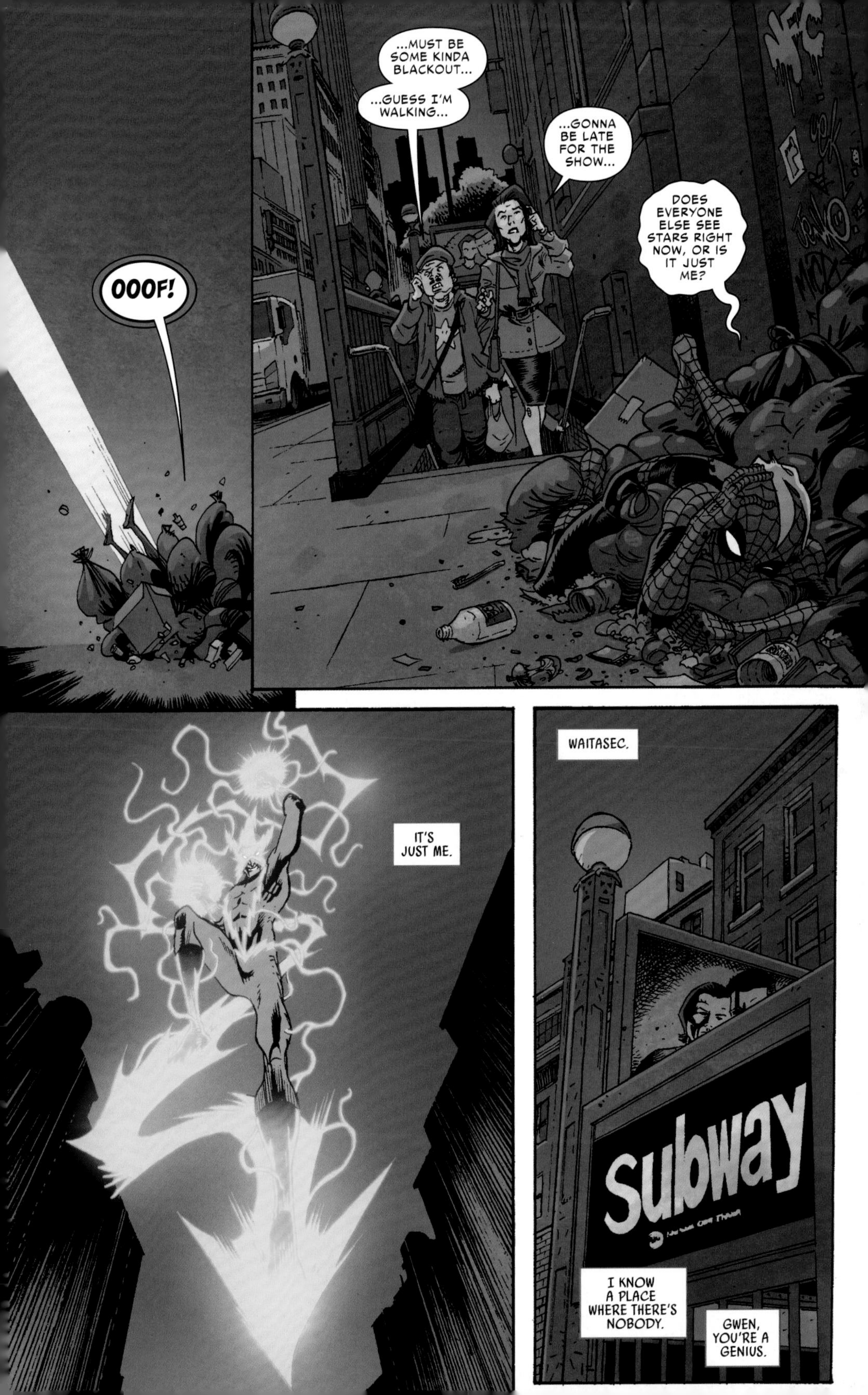
OOOF!
...MUST BE SOME KINDA BLACKOUT...
...GUESS I'M WALKING...
...GONNA BE LATE FOR THE SHOW...
DOES EVERYONE ELSE SEE STARS RIGHT NOW, OR IS IT JUST ME?
IT'S JUST ME.
WAITASEC.
Subway
I KNOW A PLACE WHERE THERE'S NOBODY.
GWEN, YOU'RE A GENIUS.

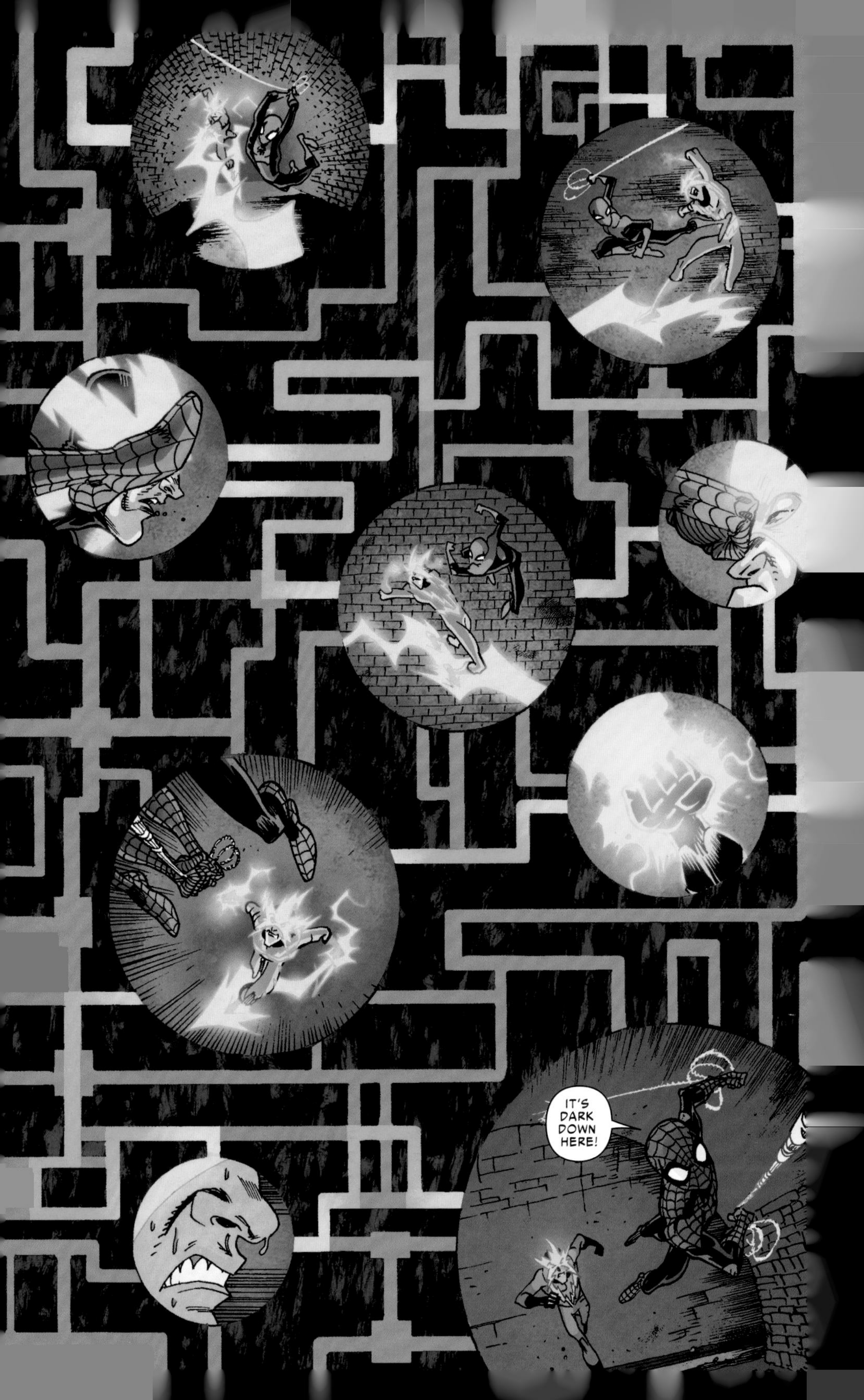
IT'S DARK DOWN HERE!

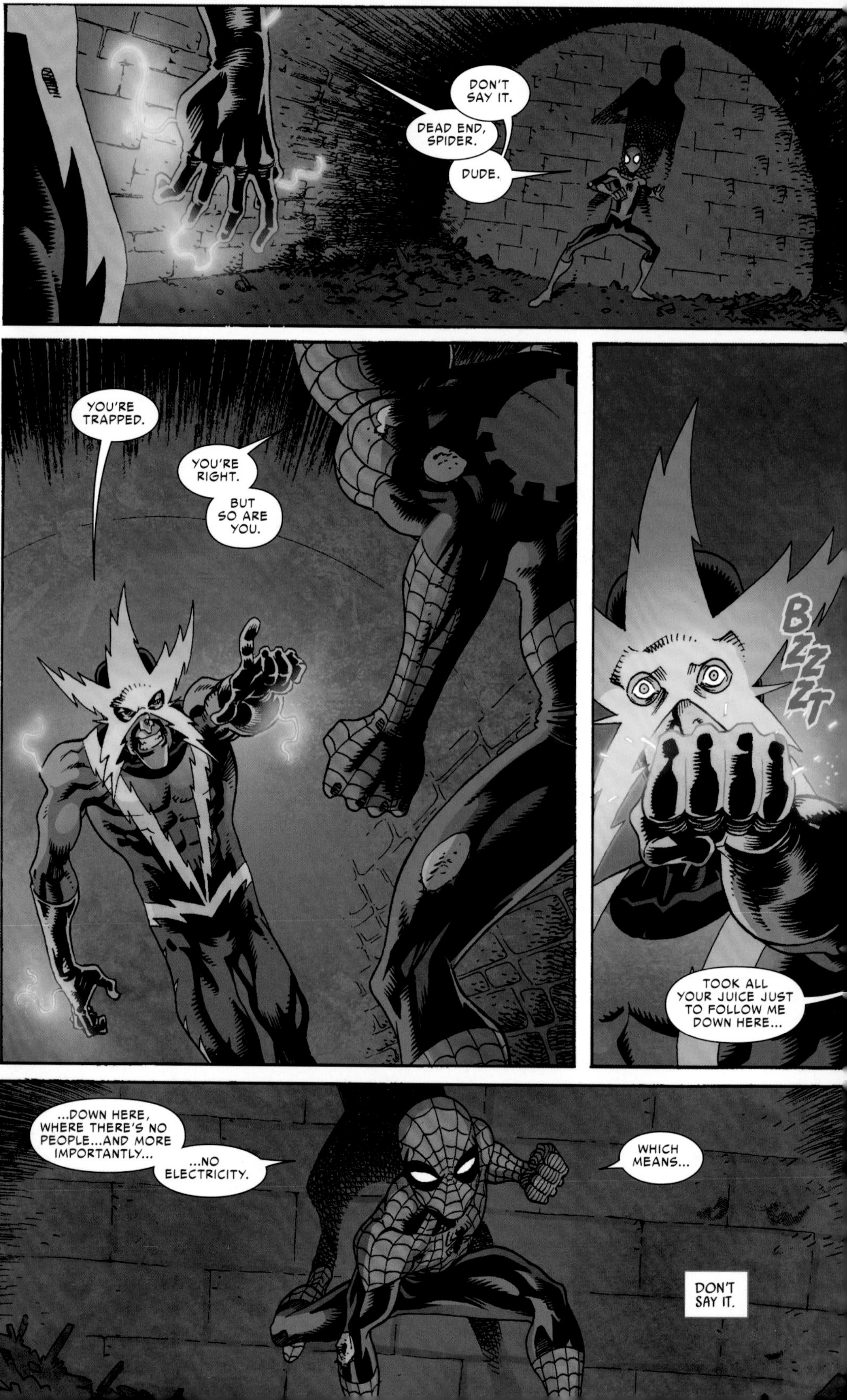
DON'T SAY IT.
DEAD END, SPIDER.
DUDE.
YOU'RE TRAPPED.
YOU'RE RIGHT.
BUT SO ARE YOU.
BZZZT
TOOK ALL YOUR JUICE JUST TO FOLLOW ME DOWN HERE...
...DOWN HERE, WHERE THERE'S NO PEOPLE...AND MORE IMPORTANTLY...
...NO ELECTRICITY.
WHICH MEANS...
DON'T SAY IT.

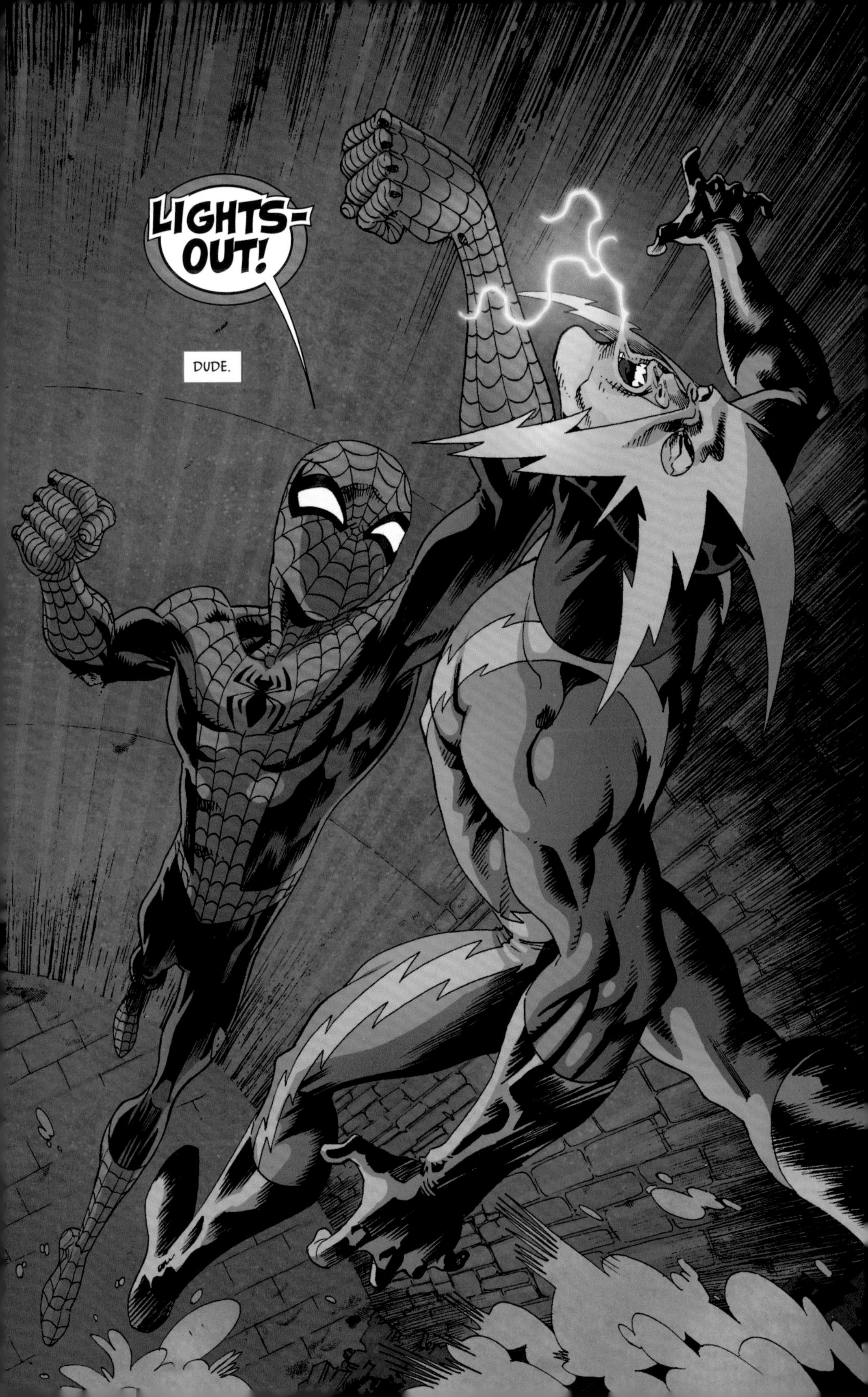
LIGHTS-OUT!
DUDE.

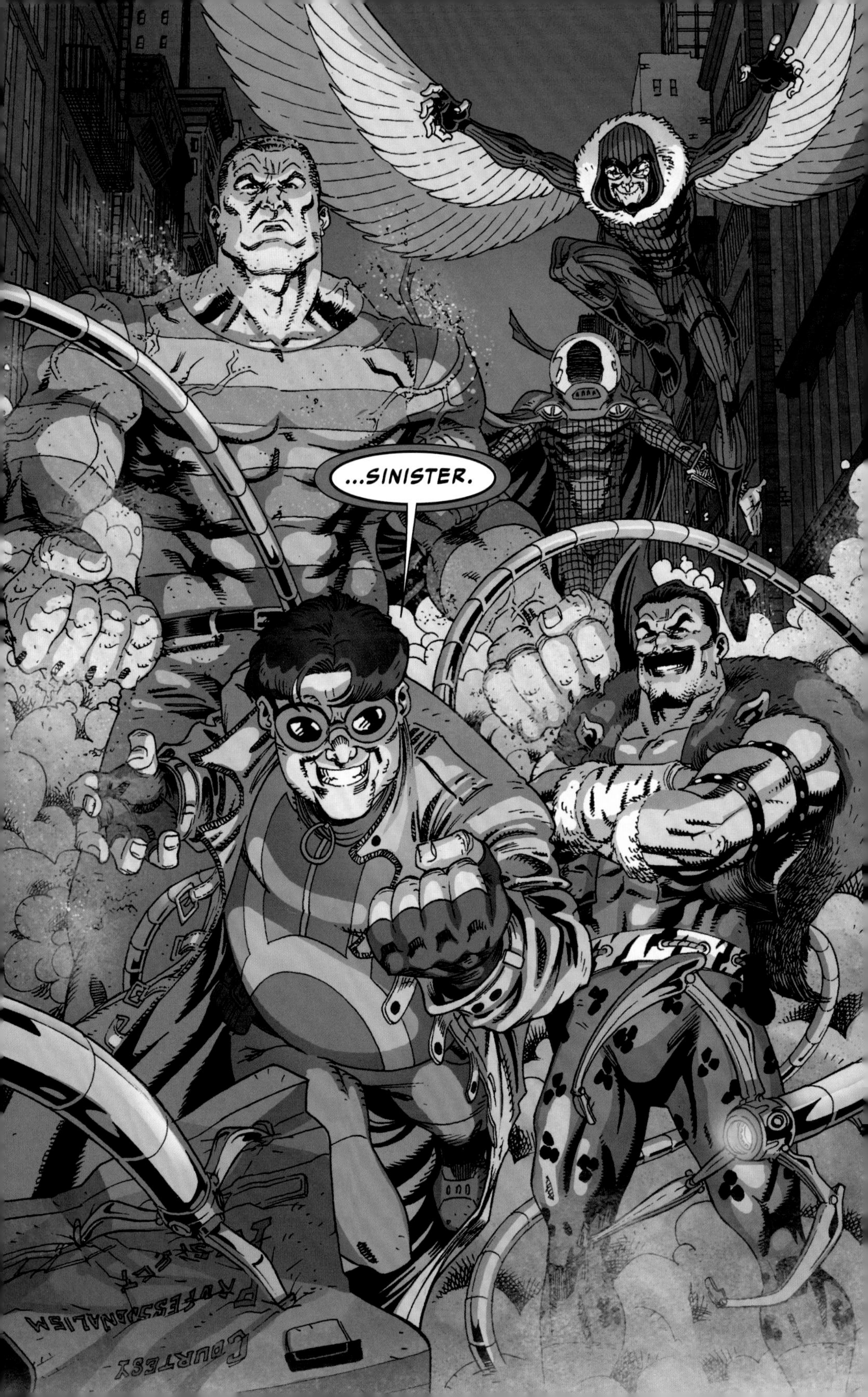
...SINISTER.
PROFESSIONALISM
COURTESY

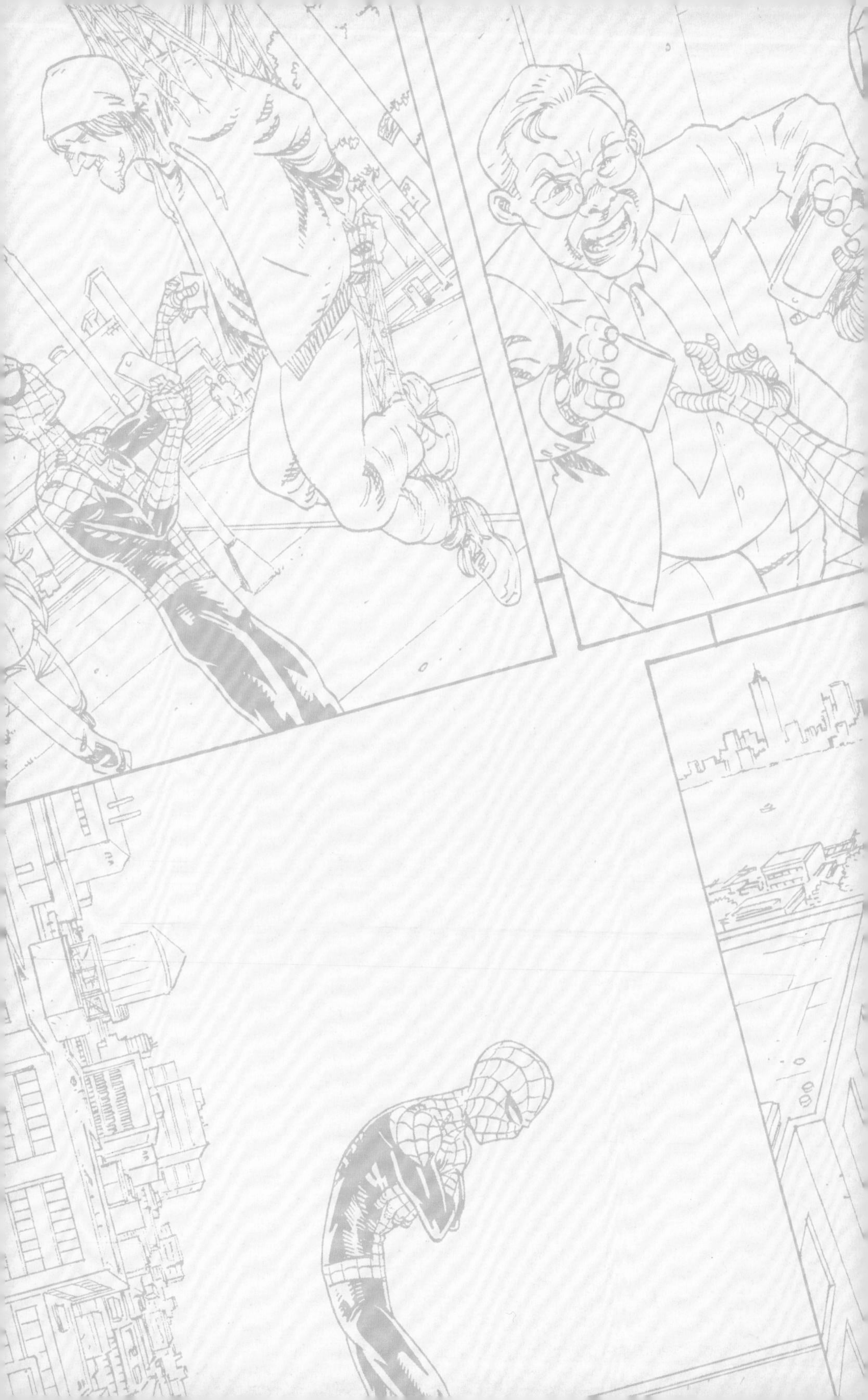

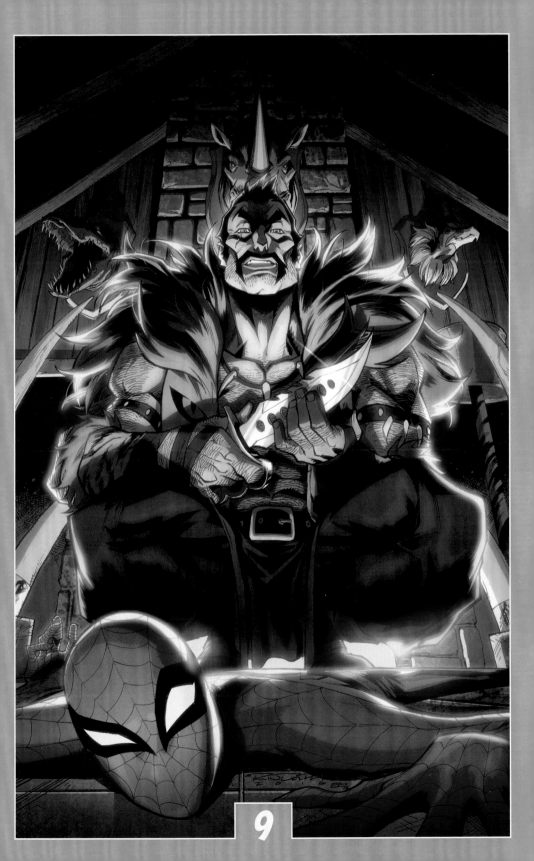

9

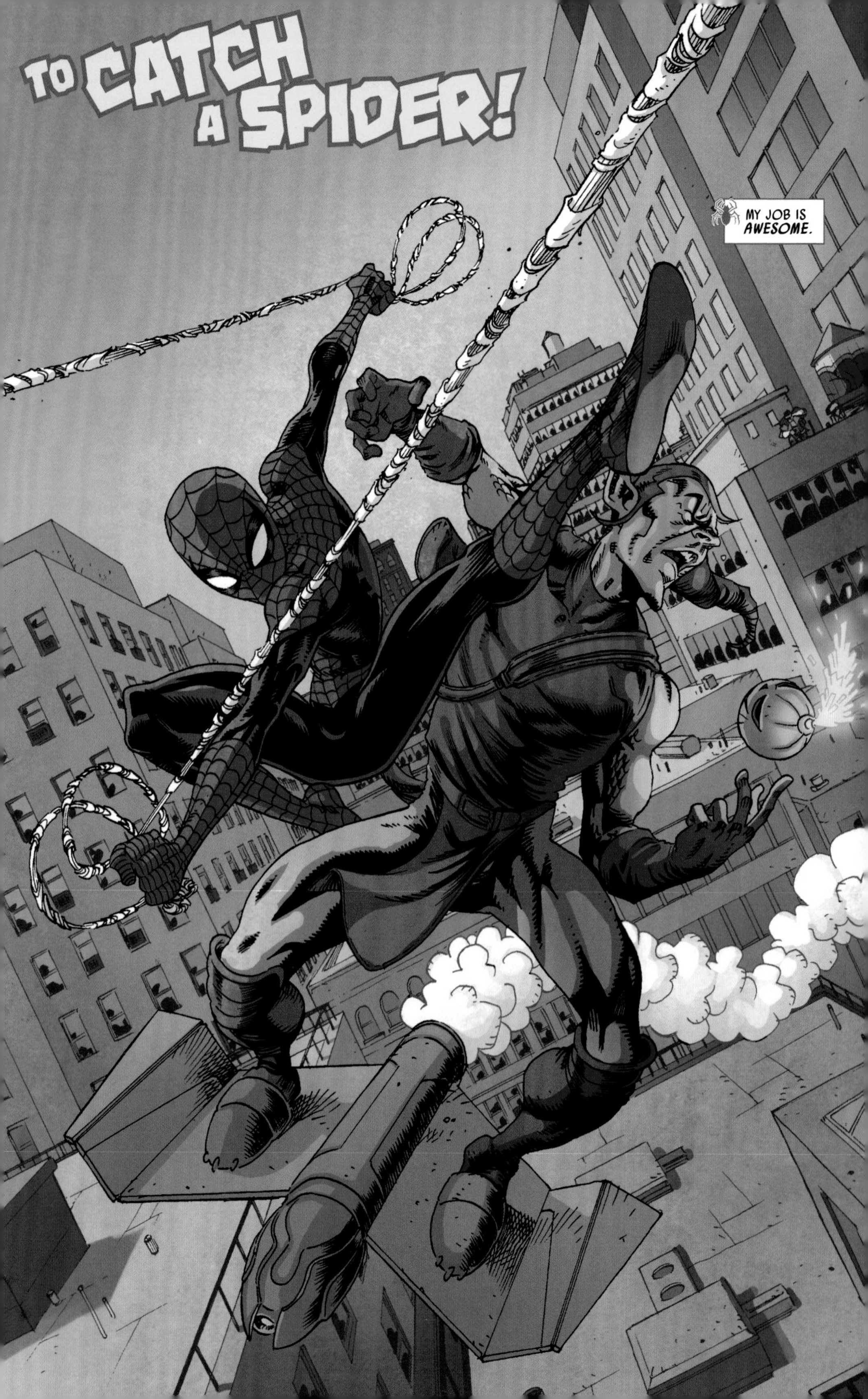
TO CATCH A SPIDER!
MY JOB IS AWESOME.

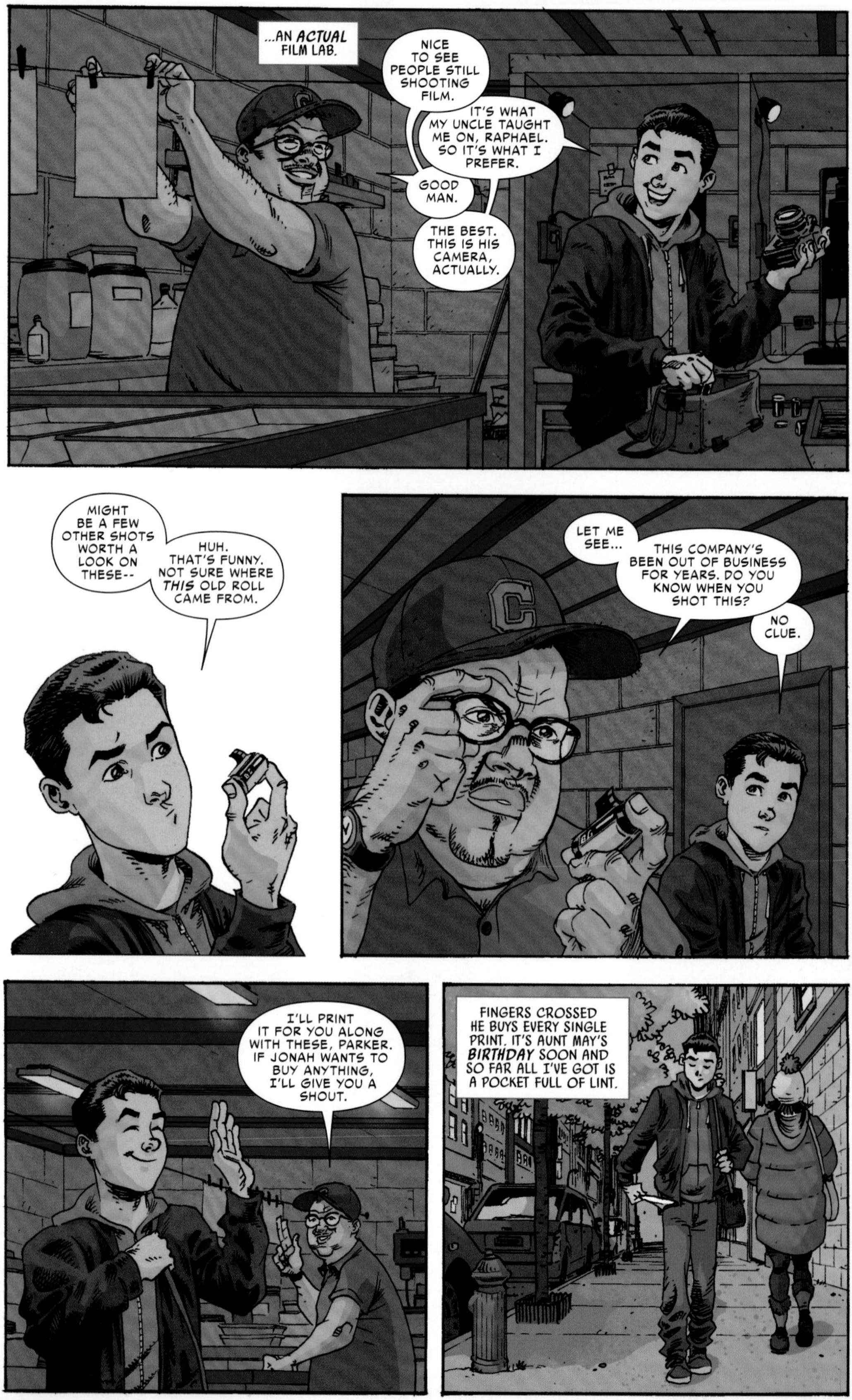
...AN ACTUAL FILM LAB.
NICE TO SEE PEOPLE STILL SHOOTING FILM.
IT'S WHAT MY UNCLE TAUGHT ME ON, RAPHAEL. SO IT'S WHAT I PREFER.
GOOD MAN.
THE BEST. THIS IS HIS CAMERA, ACTUALLY.
MIGHT BE A FEW OTHER SHOTS WORTH A LOOK ON THESE--
HUH. THAT'S FUNNY. NOT SURE WHERE THIS OLD ROLL CAME FROM.
LET ME SEE...
THIS COMPANY'S BEEN OUT OF BUSINESS FOR YEARS. DO YOU KNOW WHEN YOU SHOT THIS?
NO CLUE.
I'LL PRINT IT FOR YOU ALONG WITH THESE, PARKER. IF JONAH WANTS TO BUY ANYTHING, I'LL GIVE YOU A SHOUT.
FINGERS CROSSED HE BUYS EVERY SINGLE PRINT. IT'S AUNT MAY'S BIRTHDAY SOON AND SO FAR ALL I'VE GOT IS A POCKET FULL OF LINT.

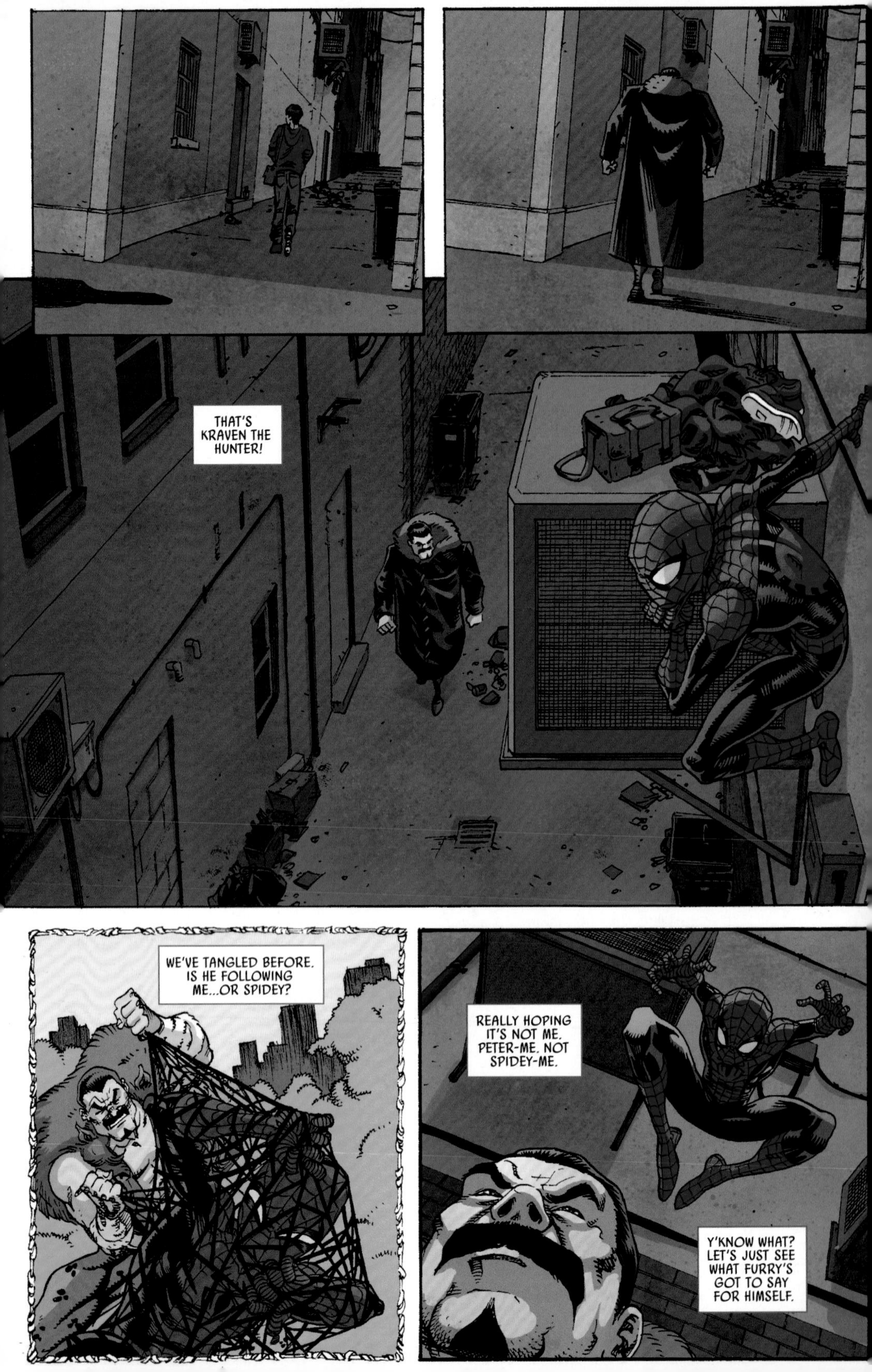
THAT'S KRAVEN THE HUNTER!
WE'VE TANGLED BEFORE. IS HE FOLLOWING ME...OR SPIDEY?
REALLY HOPING IT'S NOT ME. PETER-ME. NOT SPIDEY-ME.
Y'KNOW WHAT? LET'S JUST SEE WHAT FURRY'S GOT TO SAY FOR HIMSELF.

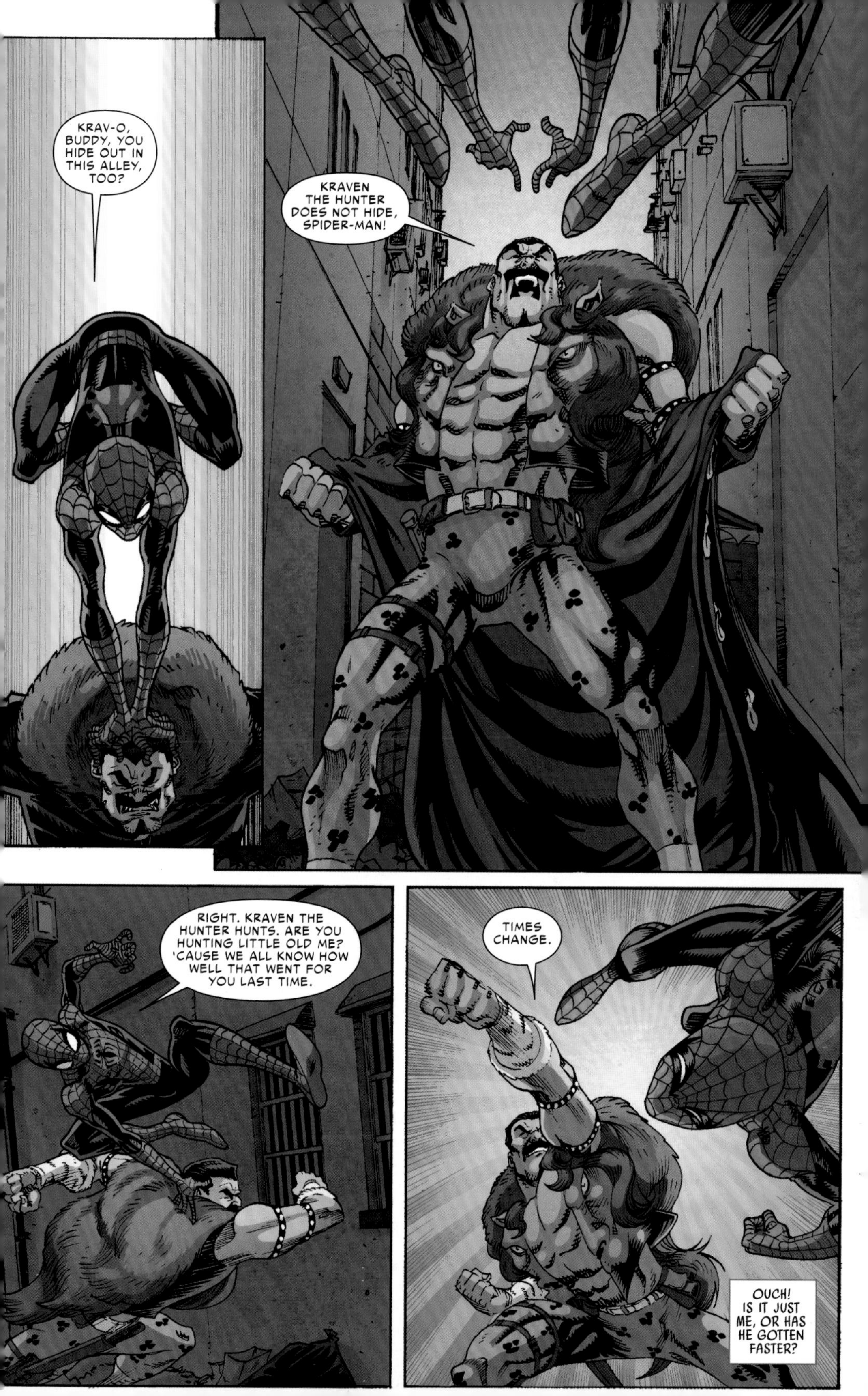
KRAV-O, BUDDY, YOU HIDE OUT IN THIS ALLEY, TOO?
KRAVEN THE HUNTER DOES NOT HIDE, SPIDER-MAN!
RIGHT. KRAVEN THE HUNTER HUNTS. ARE YOU HUNTING LITTLE OLD ME? 'CAUSE WE ALL KNOW HOW WELL THAT WENT FOR YOU LAST TIME.
TIMES CHANGE.
OUCH! IS IT JUST ME, OR HAS HE GOTTEN FASTER?

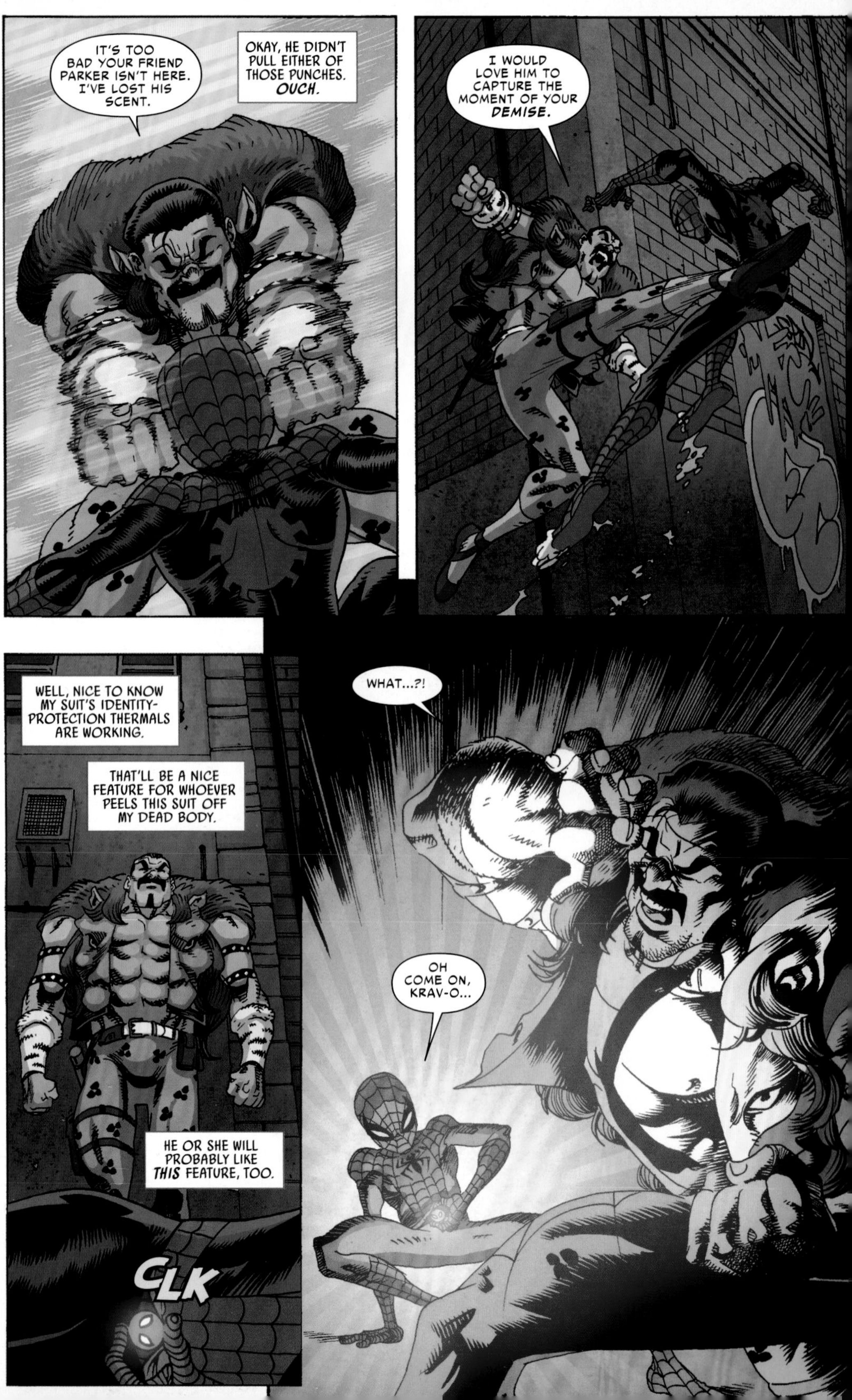
IT'S TOO BAD YOUR FRIEND PARKER ISN'T HERE. I'VE LOST HIS SCENT.
OKAY, HE DIDN'T PULL EITHER OF THOSE PUNCHES. OUCH.
I WOULD LOVE HIM TO CAPTURE THE MOMENT OF YOUR DEMISE.
WELL, NICE TO KNOW MY SUIT'S IDENTITY-PROTECTION THERMALS ARE WORKING.
THAT'LL BE A NICE FEATURE FOR WHOEVER PEELS THIS SUIT OFF MY DEAD BODY.
HE OR SHE WILL PROBABLY LIKE THIS FEATURE, TOO.
CLK
WHAT...?!
OH COME ON, KRAV-O...

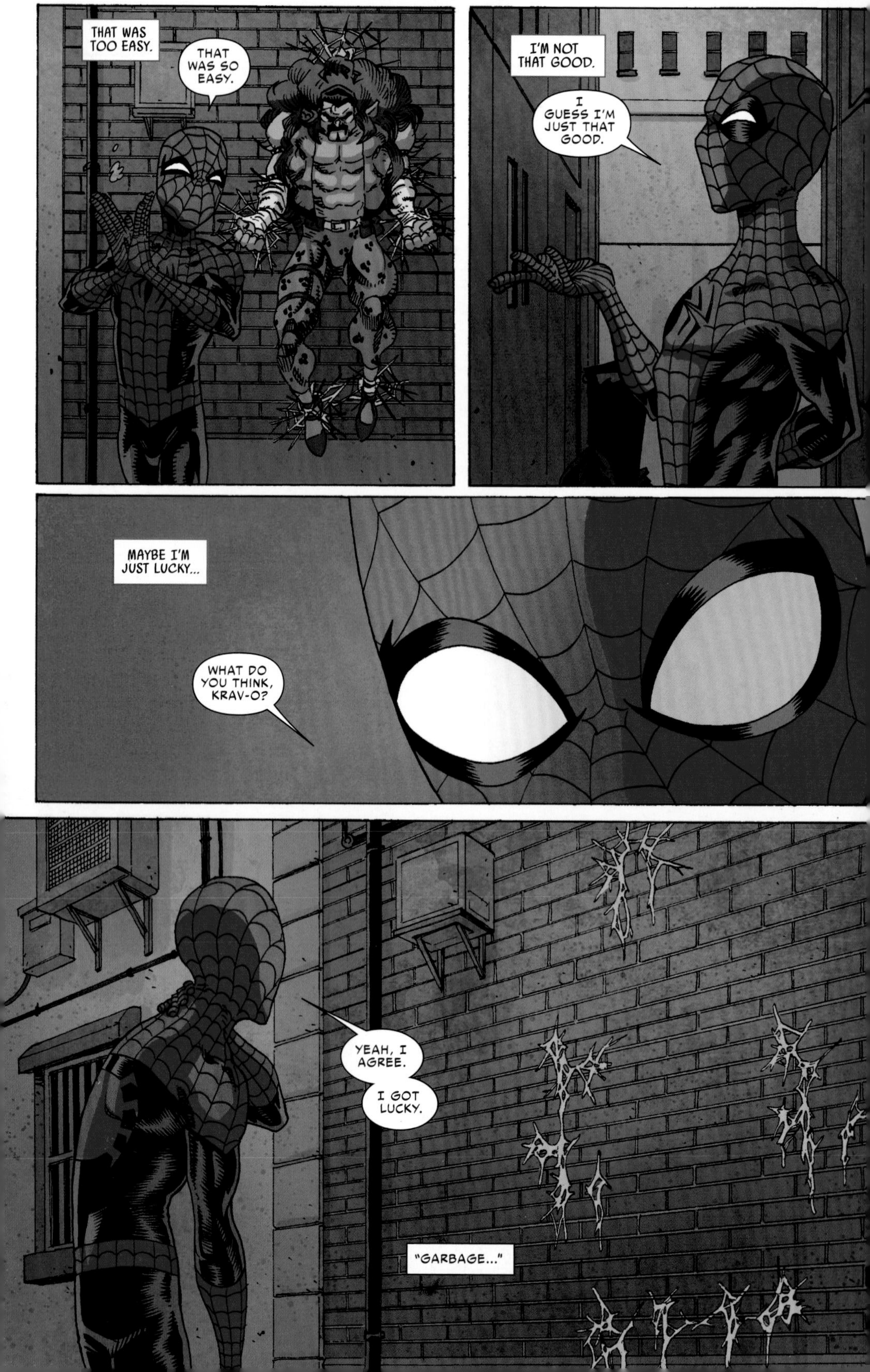
THAT WAS TOO EASY.
THAT WAS SO EASY.
I'M NOT THAT GOOD.
I GUESS I'M JUST THAT GOOD.
MAYBE I'M JUST LUCKY...
WHAT DO YOU THINK, KRAV-O?
YEAH, I AGREE.
I GOT LUCKY.
"GARBAGE..."

...GARBAGE. MORE GARBAGE.

WHERE'S THE KRAVEN FIGHT?

SIR?

SOME KIDS POSTED BLURRY PHOTOS ON THE INTERNETS. WHERE ARE THE PHOTOS FROM *THAT*, PARKER? KRAVEN TRIED TO RID THIS CITY OF THAT MENACE AND YOU MISSED IT?!

KRAVEN THOUGHT PETER BAILED...SO NO PHOTOS THIS TIME. NO PHOTOS, NO MONEY. NO MONEY, NO GIFT FOR AUNT MAY. AND ONCE AGAIN...

GUESS I BLEW IT, SIR.

GO CHECK IN WITH RAPHAEL, SEE IF HE FOUND ANYTHING ELSE ON YOUR FILM!

I'M NOT PAYING FOR ANY OF THIS GARBAGE!

J JONAH JAMESON
EDITOR IN CHIEF

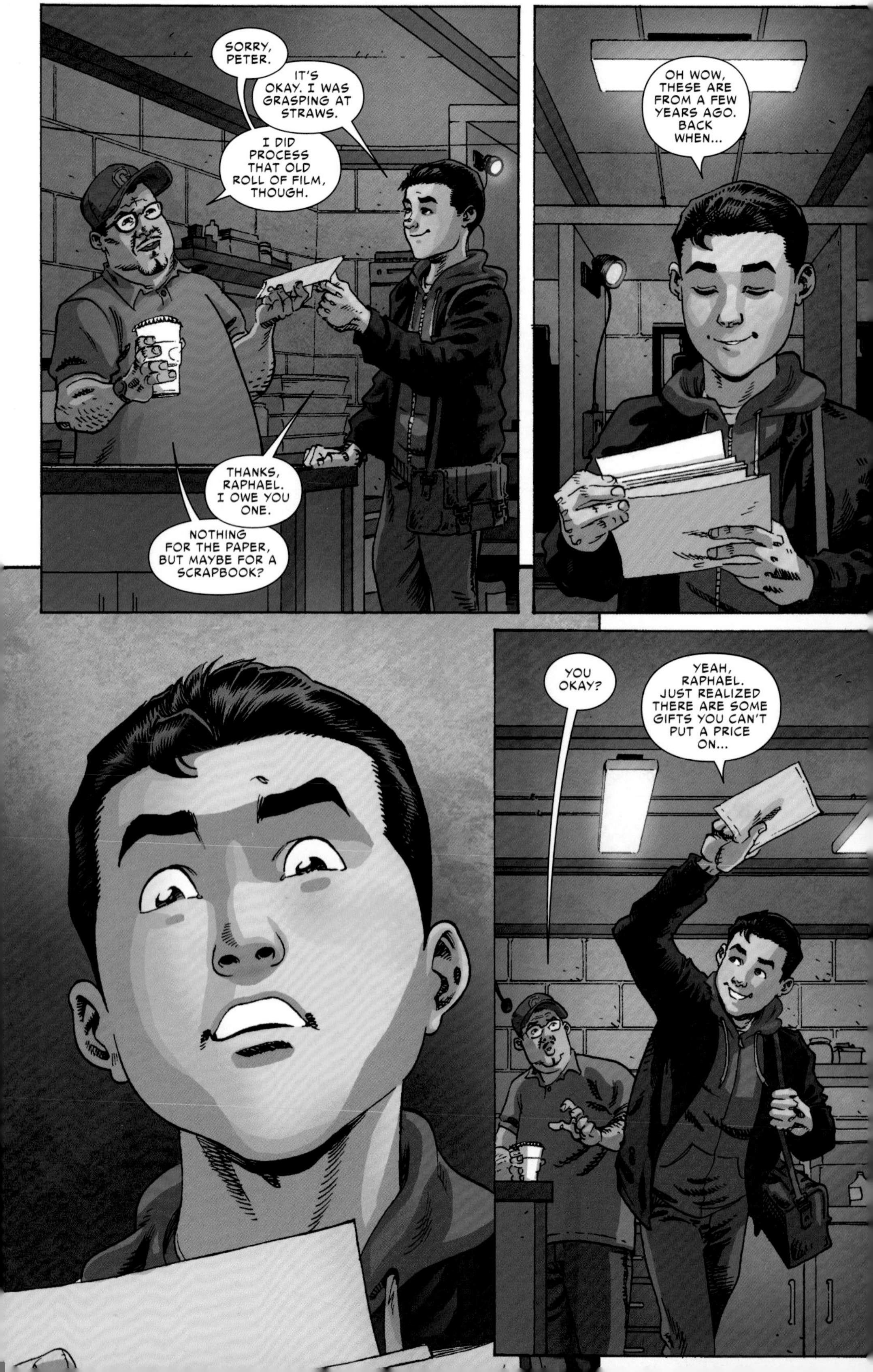

SORRY, PETER.
IT'S OKAY. I WAS GRASPING AT STRAWS.
I DID PROCESS THAT OLD ROLL OF FILM, THOUGH.
THANKS, RAPHAEL. I OWE YOU ONE.
NOTHING FOR THE PAPER, BUT MAYBE FOR A SCRAPBOOK?
OH WOW, THESE ARE FROM A FEW YEARS AGO. BACK WHEN...
YOU OKAY?
YEAH, RAPHAEL. JUST REALIZED THERE ARE SOME GIFTS YOU CAN'T PUT A PRICE ON...

...IT'S PERFECT.

HAPPY BIRTHDAY, AUNT MAY.

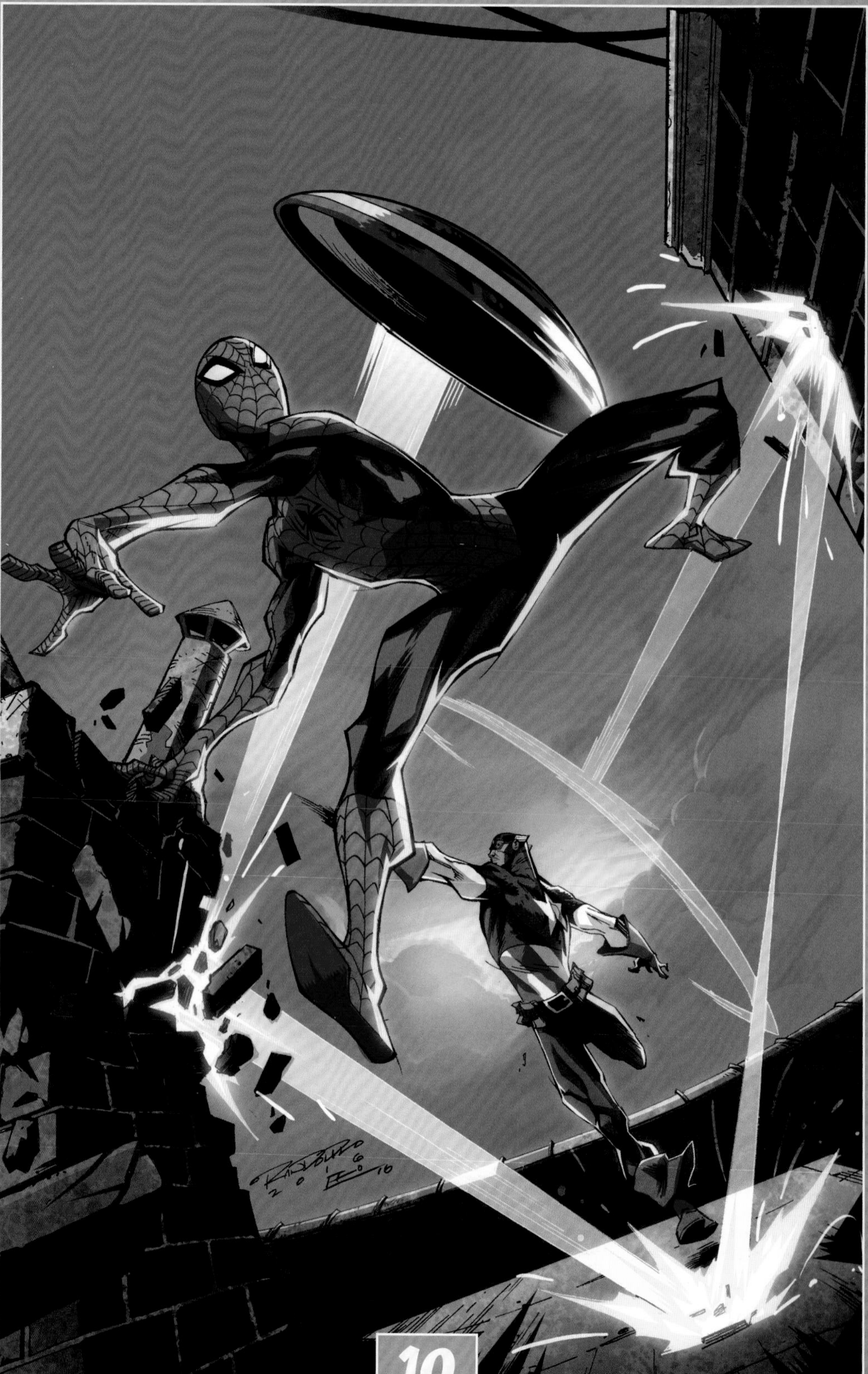

10

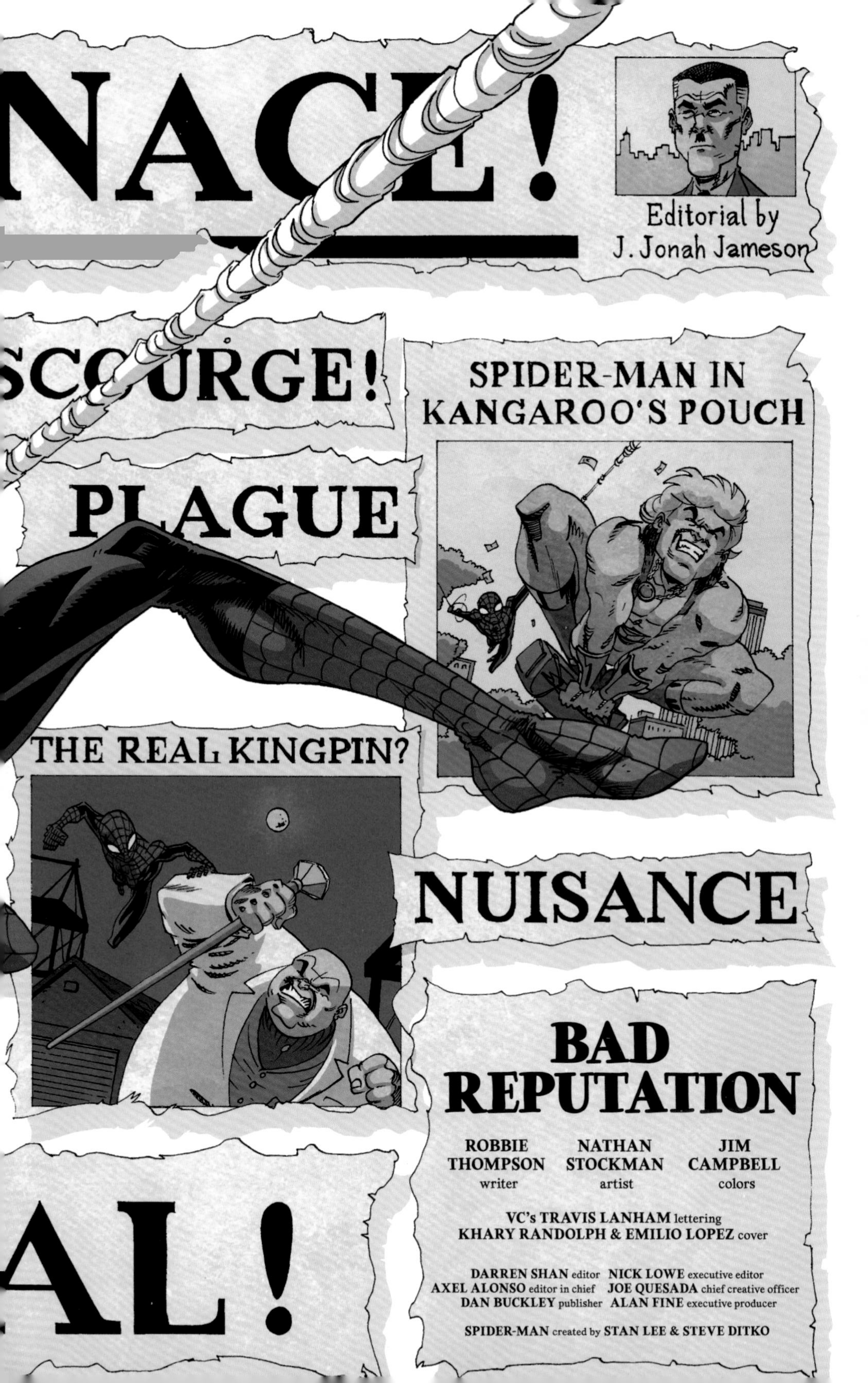
NACE!
Editorial by
J. Jonah Jameson
SCOURGE!
PLAGUE
SPIDER-MAN IN
KANGAROO'S POUCH
THE REAL KINGPIN?
NUISANCE
BAD
REPUTATION
ROBBIE THOMPSON writer
NATHAN STOCKMAN artist
JIM CAMPBELL colors
VC's TRAVIS LANHAM lettering
KHARY RANDOLPH & EMILIO LOPEZ cover
DARREN SHAN editor NICK LOWE executive editor
AXEL ALONSO editor in chief JOE QUESADA chief creative officer
DAN BUCKLEY publisher ALAN FINE executive producer
SPIDER-MAN created by STAN LEE & STEVE DITKO
AL!

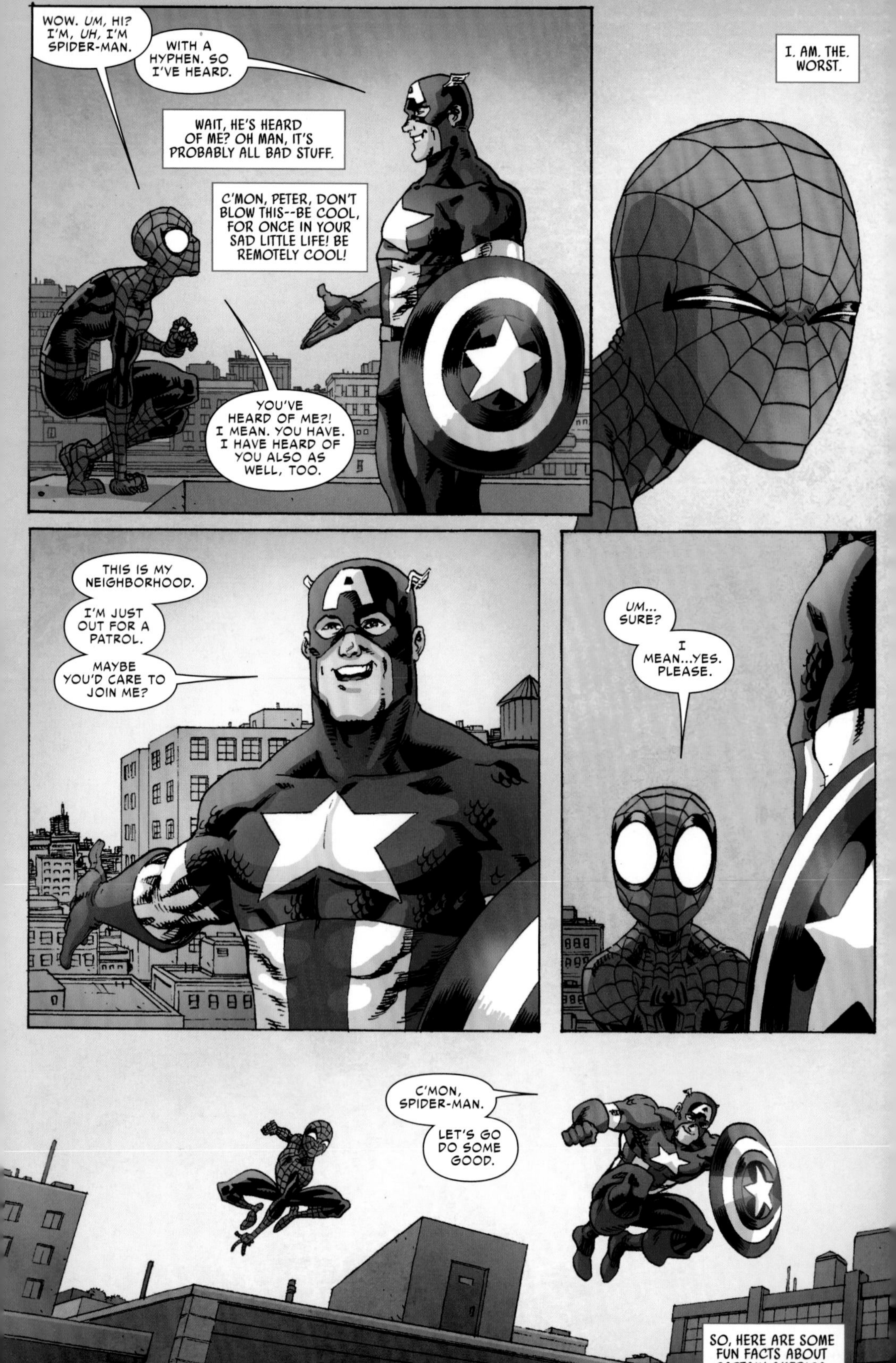
WOW. UM, HI? I'M, UH, I'M SPIDER-MAN.
WITH A HYPHEN. SO I'VE HEARD.
WAIT, HE'S HEARD OF ME? OH MAN, IT'S PROBABLY ALL BAD STUFF.
C'MON, PETER, DON'T BLOW THIS--BE COOL, FOR ONCE IN YOUR SAD LITTLE LIFE! BE REMOTELY COOL!
YOU'VE HEARD OF ME?! I MEAN. YOU HAVE. I HAVE HEARD OF YOU ALSO AS WELL, TOO.
I. AM. THE. WORST.
THIS IS MY NEIGHBORHOOD.
I'M JUST OUT FOR A PATROL.
MAYBE YOU'D CARE TO JOIN ME?
UM... SURE?
I MEAN...YES. PLEASE.
C'MON, SPIDER-MAN.
LET'S GO DO SOME GOOD.
SO, HERE ARE SOME FUN FACTS ABOUT CAPTAIN AMERICA.

HE IS A SUPER-SOLDIER.

PRODUCT OF GOVERNMENT EXPERIMENTS.

HE FOUGHT IN WORLD WAR II. PUNCHED HITLER IN THE NECK.

THEN GOT FROZEN FOR DECADES.

THAWED OUT IN MODERN TIMES.

HE'S POWERED BY A SUPER-SOLDIER SERUM.

BEFORE THAT? HE WAS A LITTLE GEEK...

...JUST LIKE *ME*.

UN-LIKE ME?

PEOPLE *LOVE* THIS GUY.

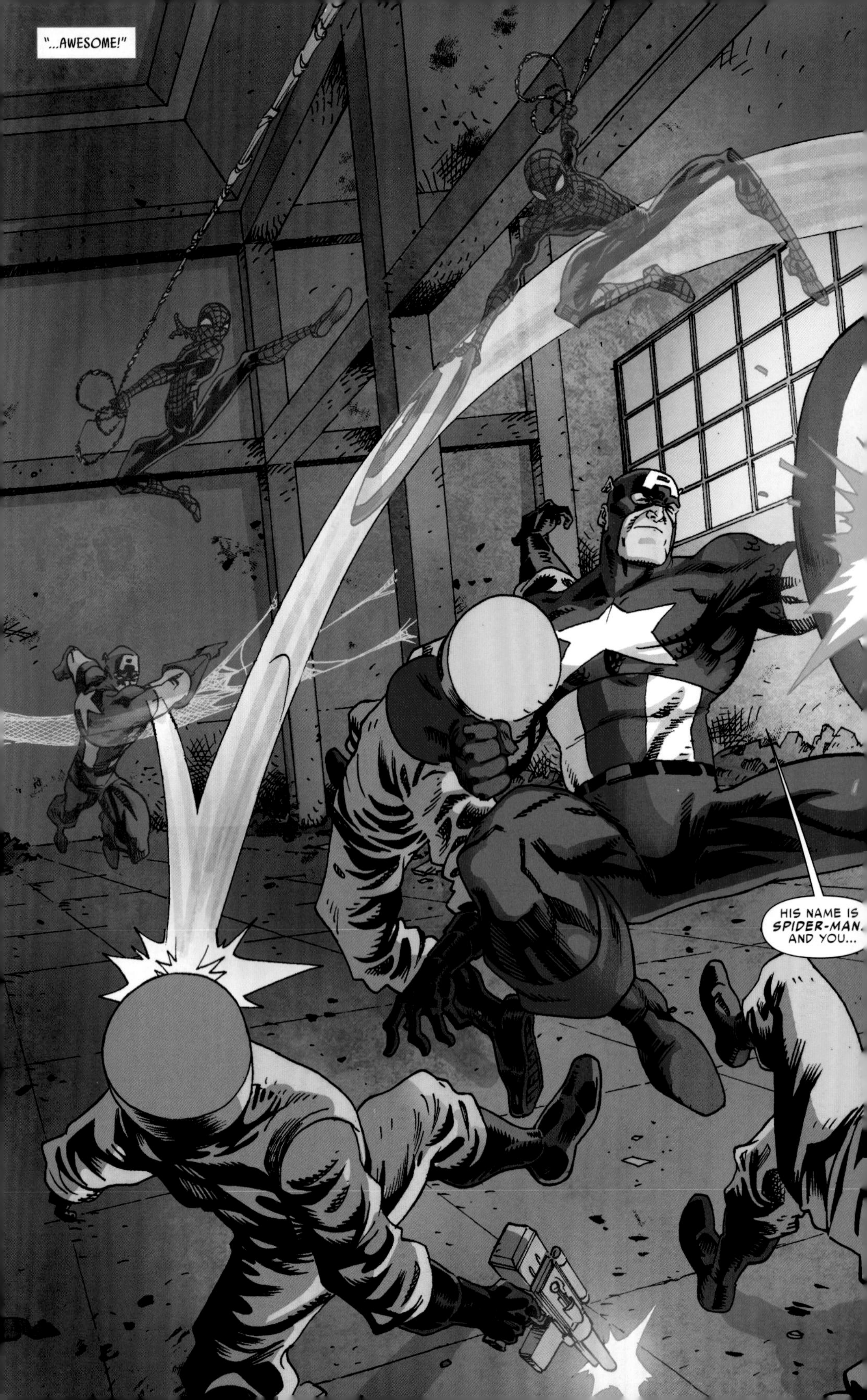
"...AWESOME!"
HIS NAME IS SPIDER-MAN. AND YOU...

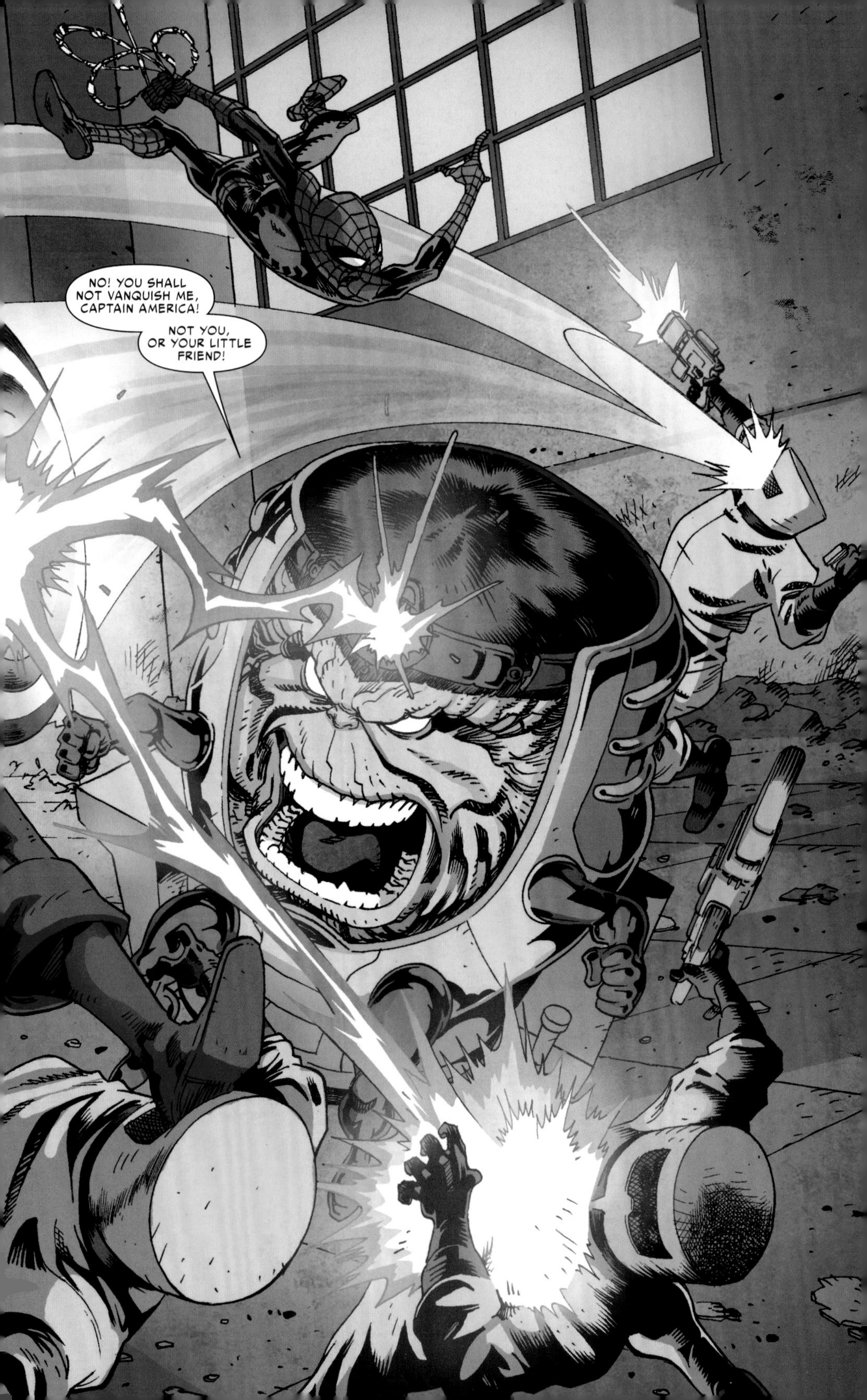
NO! YOU SHALL NOT VANQUISH ME, CAPTAIN AMERICA!
NOT YOU, OR YOUR LITTLE FRIEND!

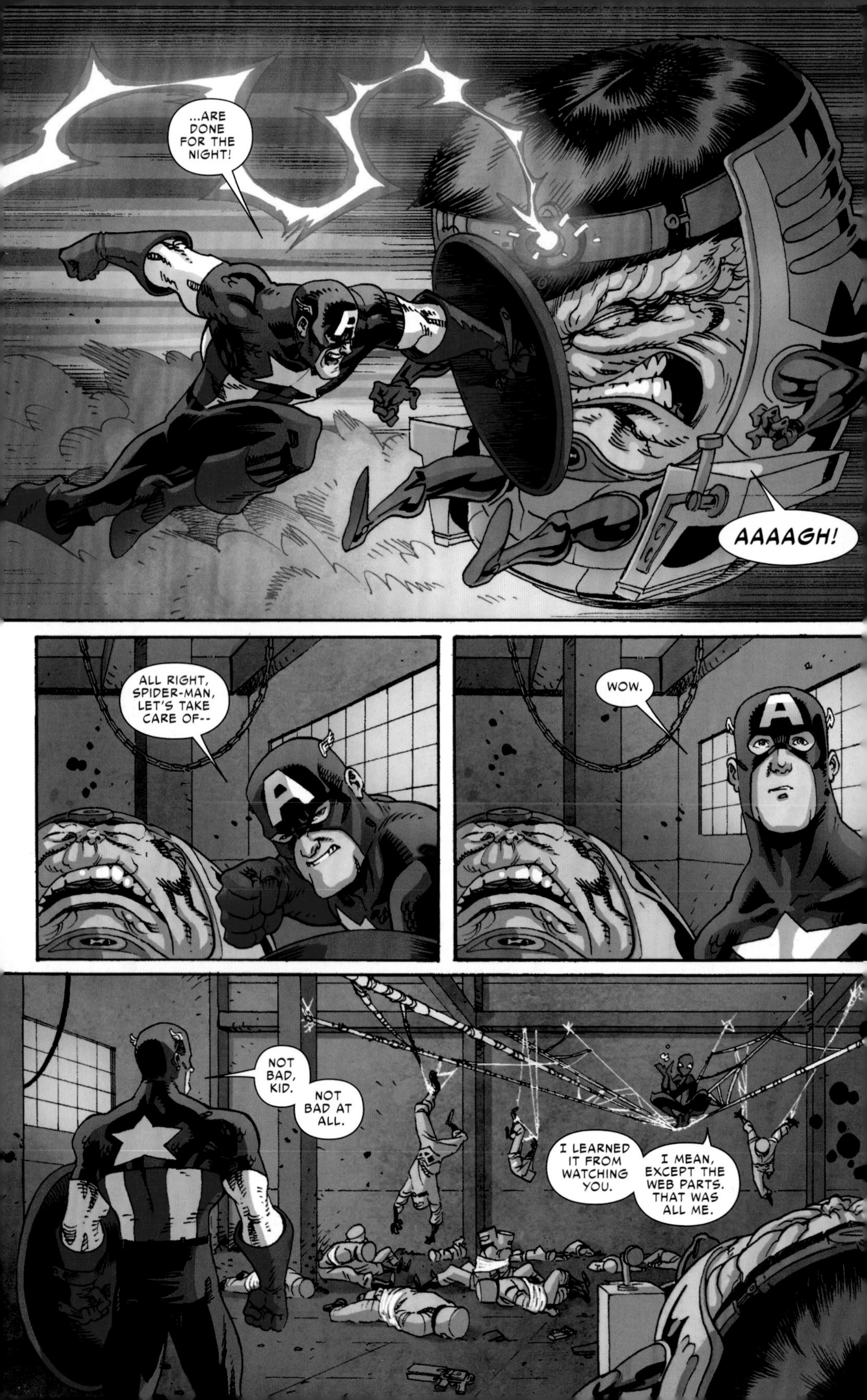
...ARE DONE FOR THE NIGHT!
AAAAGH!
ALL RIGHT, SPIDER-MAN, LET'S TAKE CARE OF--
WOW.
NOT BAD, KID.
NOT BAD AT ALL.
I LEARNED IT FROM WATCHING YOU.
I MEAN, EXCEPT THE WEB PARTS. THAT WAS ALL ME.

THE NEXT DAY...

?

DAILY 🎺 BUGLE

New York's Finest Daily Newspaper

SPIDER-MAN, AGENT OF A.I.M.?

Webbed menace seen training with A.I.M. soldiers

Editorial by J. Jonah Jameson

"I'M SORRY, MR. JAMESON, BUT--"

"I SAID NO CALLS OR MEETINGS, MS. BRANT! WHAT COULD POSSIBLY--"

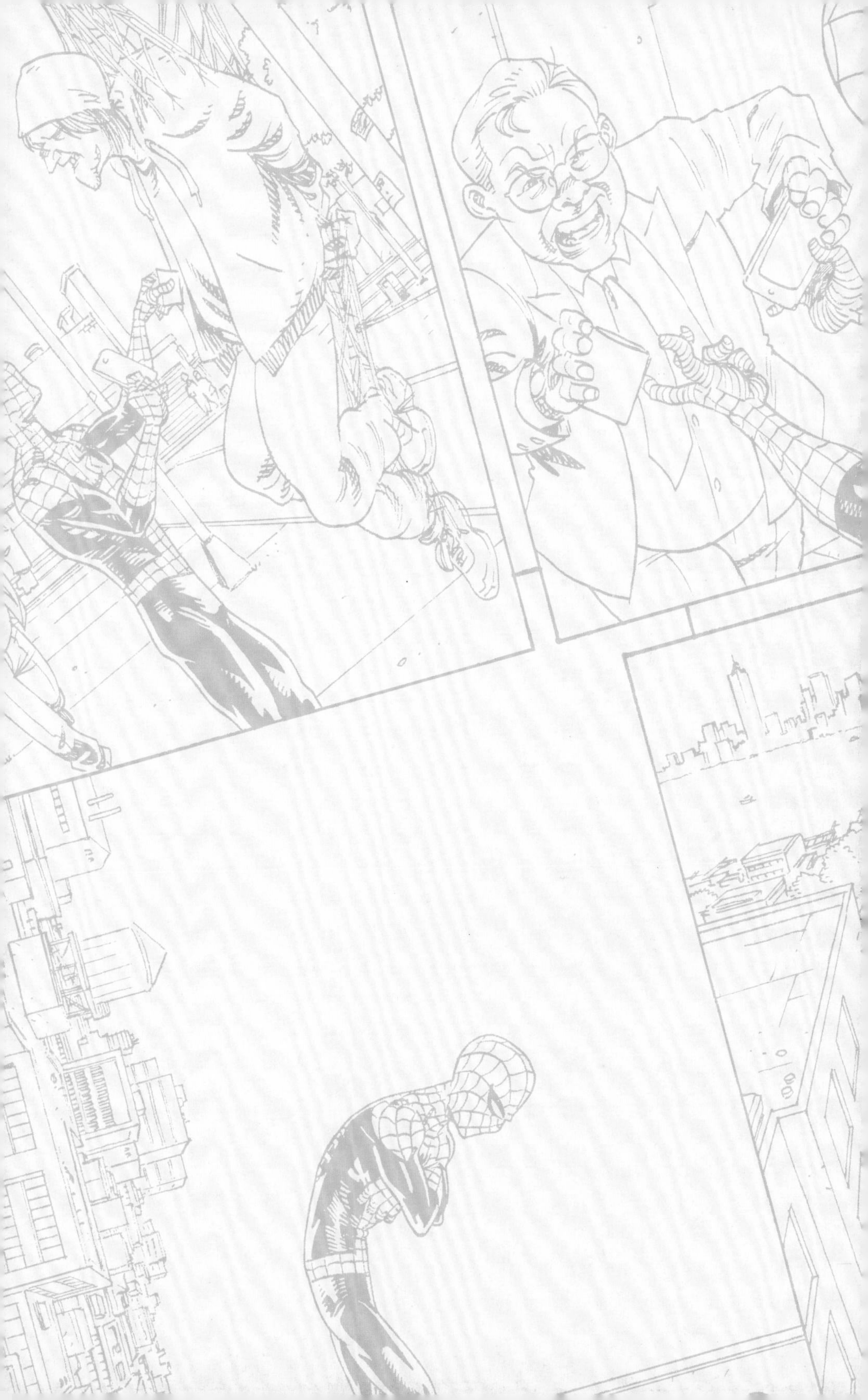

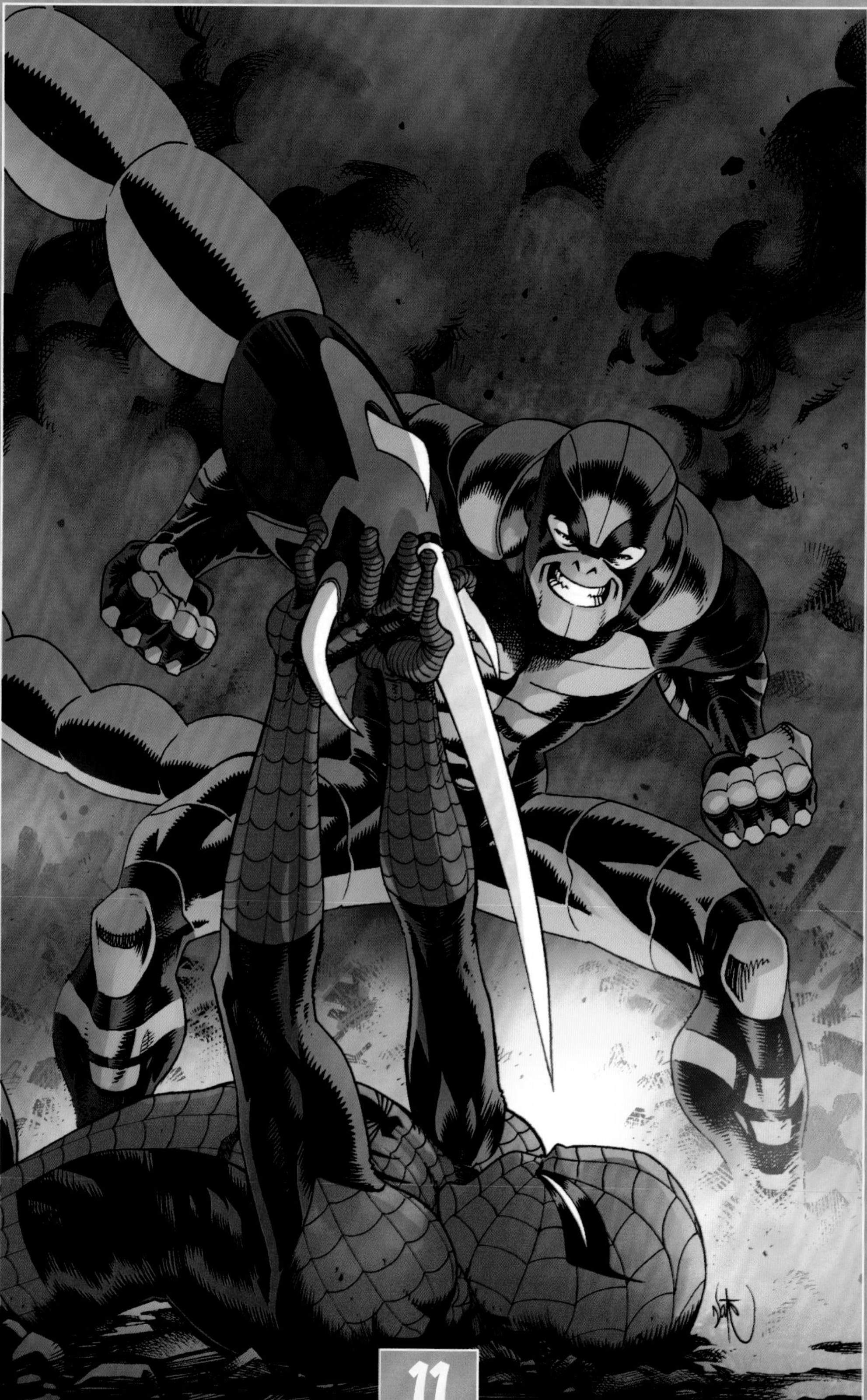

11

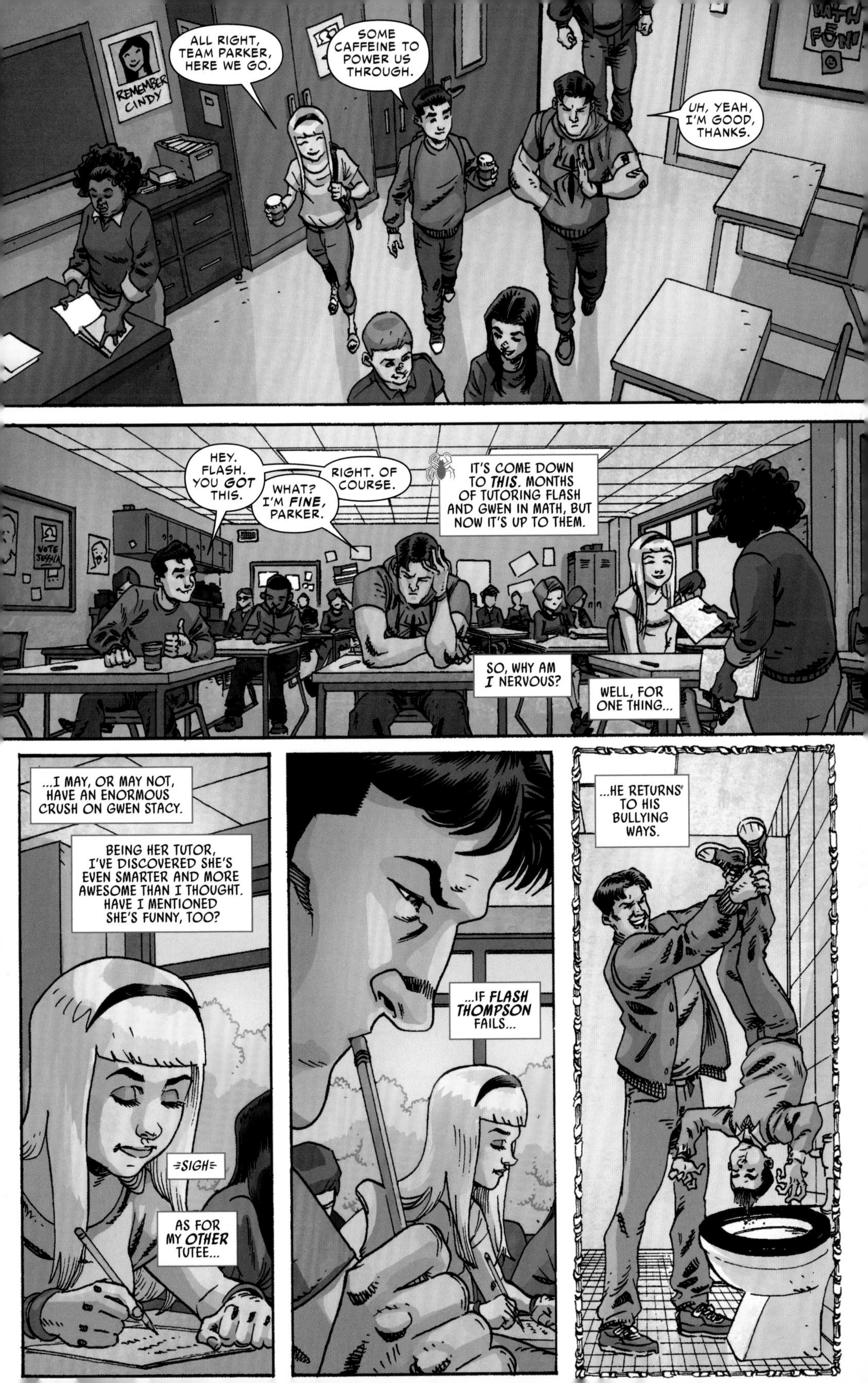

REMEMBER CINDY
ALL RIGHT, TEAM PARKER, HERE WE GO.
SOME CAFFEINE TO POWER US THROUGH.
UH, YEAH, I'M GOOD, THANKS.
HEY. FLASH. YOU *GOT* THIS.
WHAT? I'M *FINE,* PARKER.
RIGHT. OF COURSE.
IT'S COME DOWN TO *THIS.* MONTHS OF TUTORING FLASH AND GWEN IN MATH, BUT NOW IT'S UP TO THEM.
SO, WHY AM *I* NERVOUS?
WELL, FOR ONE THING...
...I MAY, OR MAY NOT, HAVE AN ENORMOUS CRUSH ON GWEN STACY.
BEING HER TUTOR, I'VE DISCOVERED SHE'S EVEN SMARTER AND MORE AWESOME THAN I THOUGHT. HAVE I MENTIONED SHE'S FUNNY, TOO?
SIGH
AS FOR MY *OTHER* TUTEE...
...IF *FLASH THOMPSON* FAILS...
...HE RETURNS TO HIS BULLYING WAYS.

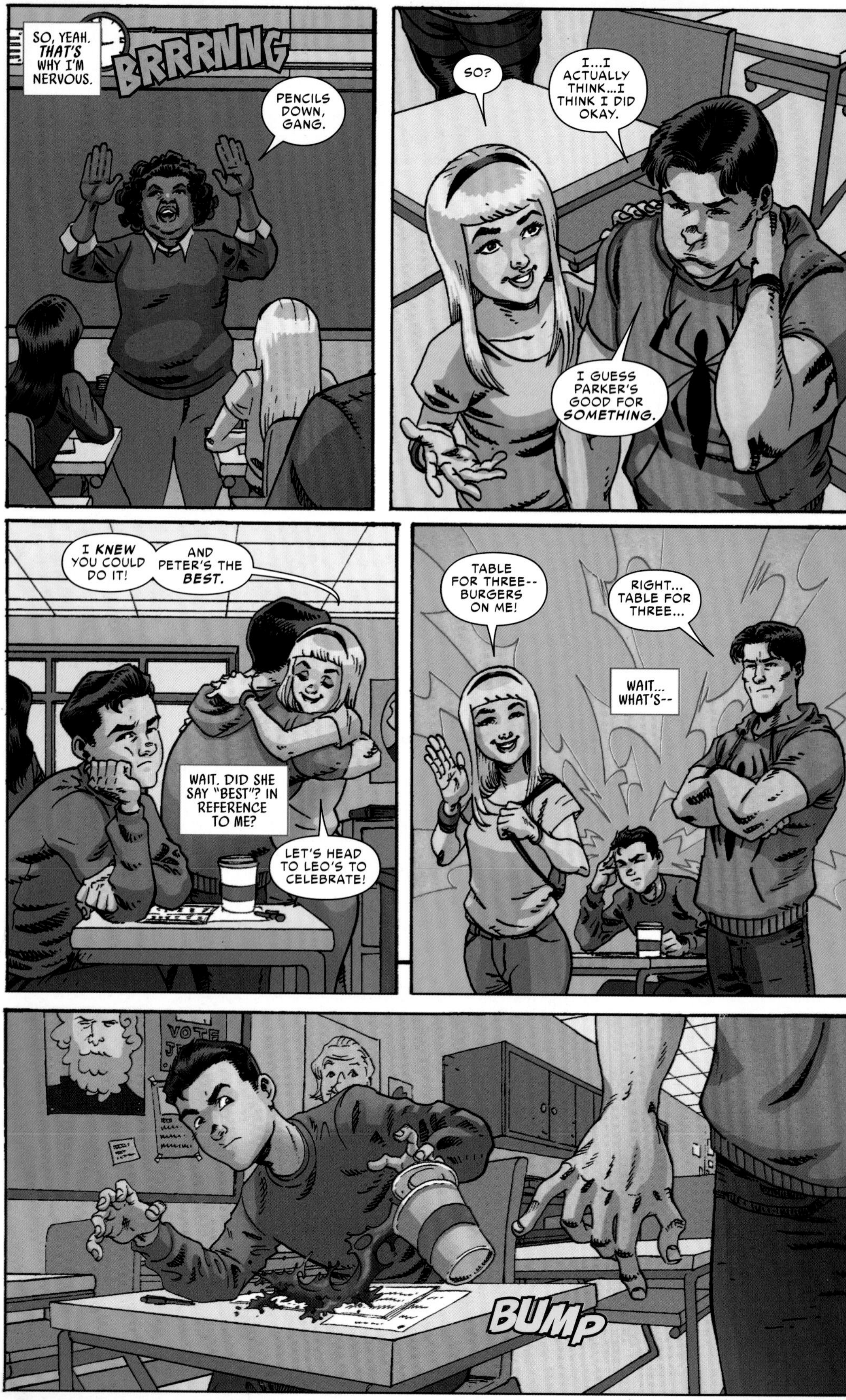

SO, YEAH. THAT'S WHY I'M NERVOUS.
BRRRNNG
PENCILS DOWN, GANG.
SO?
I...I ACTUALLY THINK...I THINK I DID OKAY.
I GUESS PARKER'S GOOD FOR SOMETHING.
I KNEW YOU COULD DO IT!
AND PETER'S THE BEST.
WAIT. DID SHE SAY "BEST"? IN REFERENCE TO ME?
LET'S HEAD TO LEO'S TO CELEBRATE!
TABLE FOR THREE-- BURGERS ON ME!
RIGHT... TABLE FOR THREE...
WAIT... WHAT'S--
BUMP

MISSING OUT

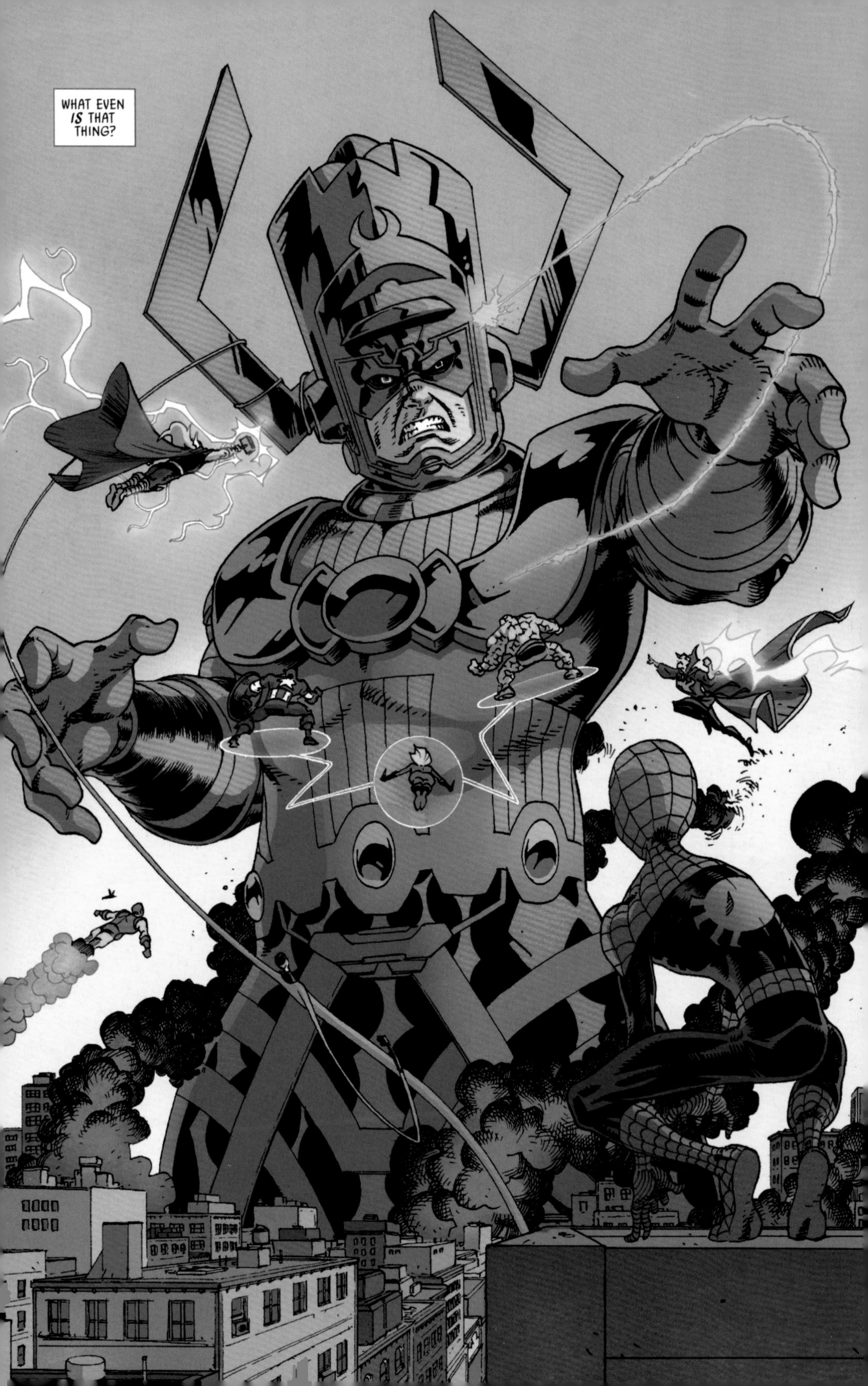
WHAT EVEN *IS* THAT THING?

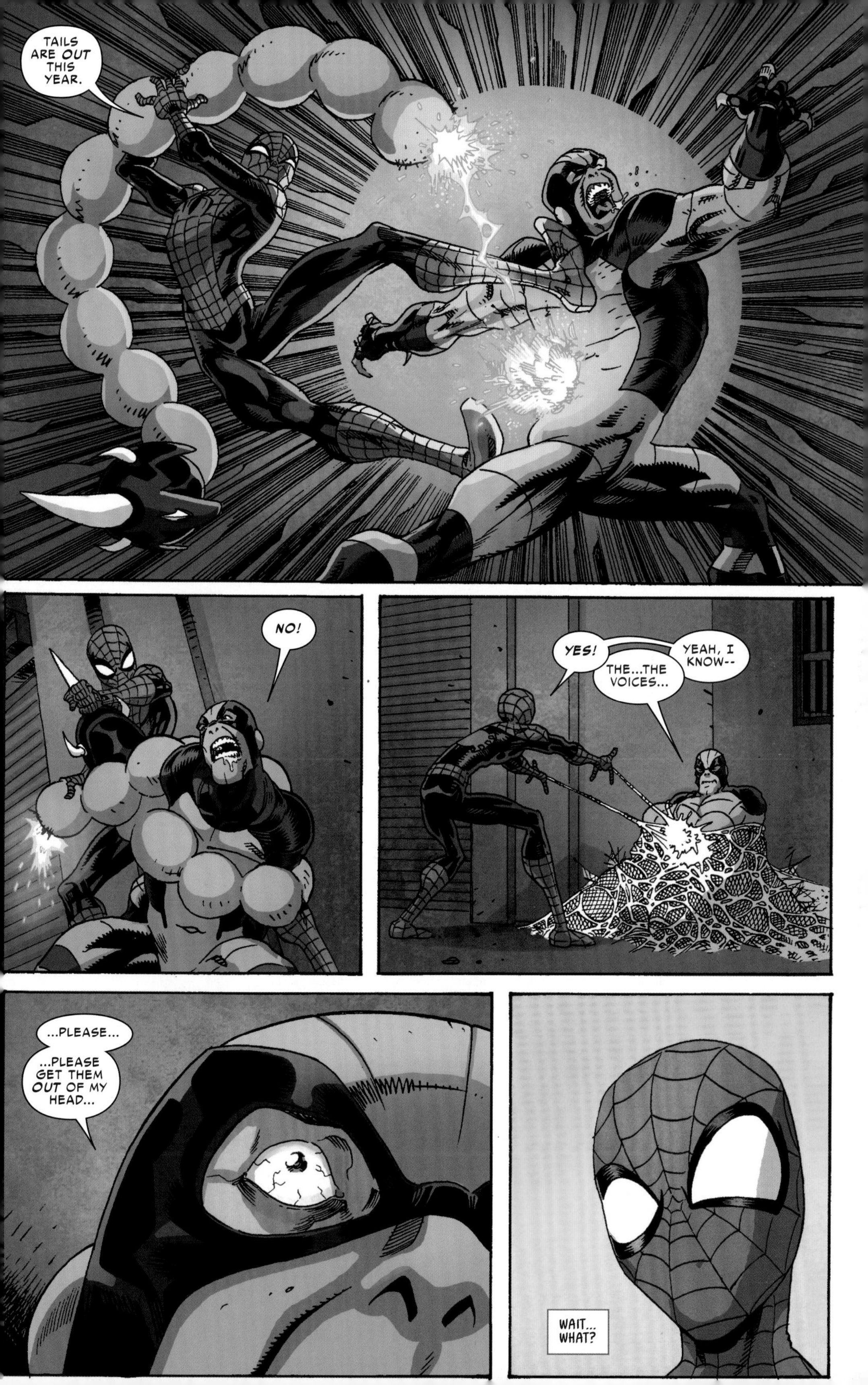
TAILS ARE OUT THIS YEAR.
NO!
YES!
THE...THE VOICES...
YEAH, I KNOW--
...PLEASE...
...PLEASE GET THEM OUT OF MY HEAD...
WAIT... WHAT?

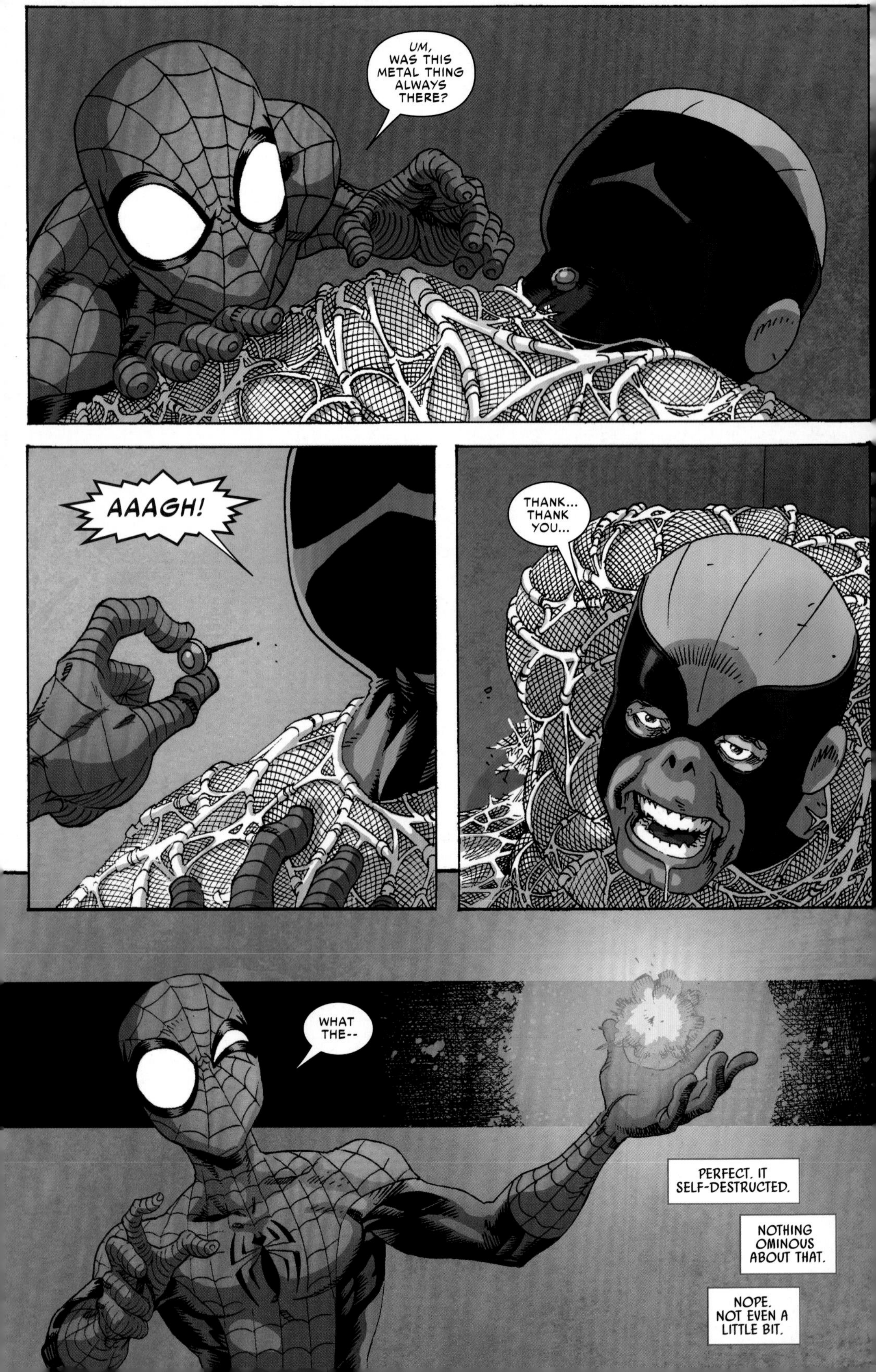
UM, WAS THIS METAL THING ALWAYS THERE?
AAAGH!
THANK... THANK YOU...
WHAT THE--
PERFECT. IT SELF-DESTRUCTED.
NOTHING OMINOUS ABOUT THAT.
NOPE. NOT EVEN A LITTLE BIT.

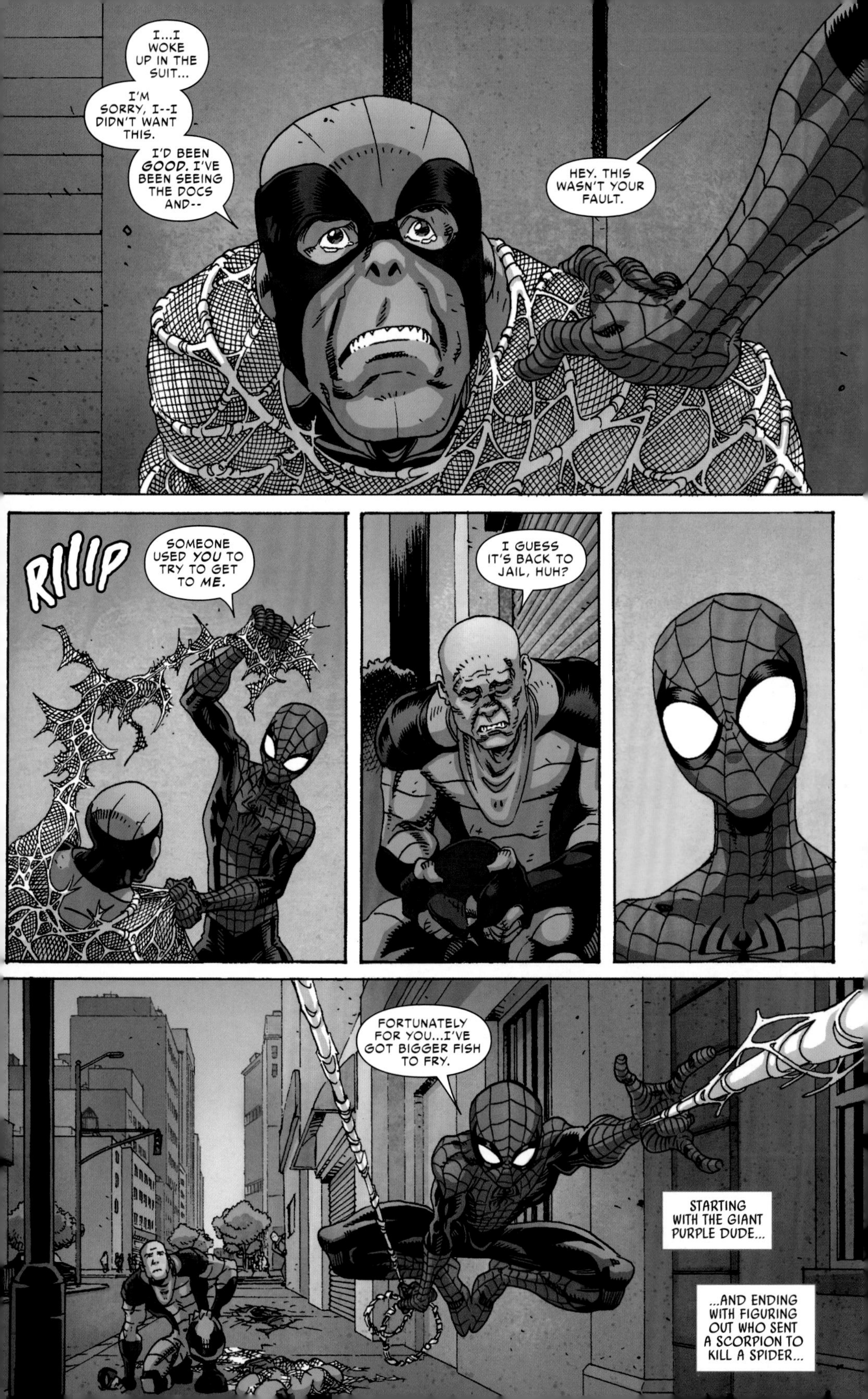

I...I WOKE UP IN THE SUIT...
I'M SORRY, I--I DIDN'T WANT THIS.
I'D BEEN GOOD. I'VE BEEN SEEING THE DOCS AND--
HEY. THIS WASN'T YOUR FAULT.
RIIIP
SOMEONE USED YOU TO TRY TO GET TO ME.
I GUESS IT'S BACK TO JAIL, HUH?
FORTUNATELY FOR YOU...I'VE GOT BIGGER FISH TO FRY.
STARTING WITH THE GIANT PURPLE DUDE...
...AND ENDING WITH FIGURING OUT WHO SENT A SCORPION TO KILL A SPIDER...

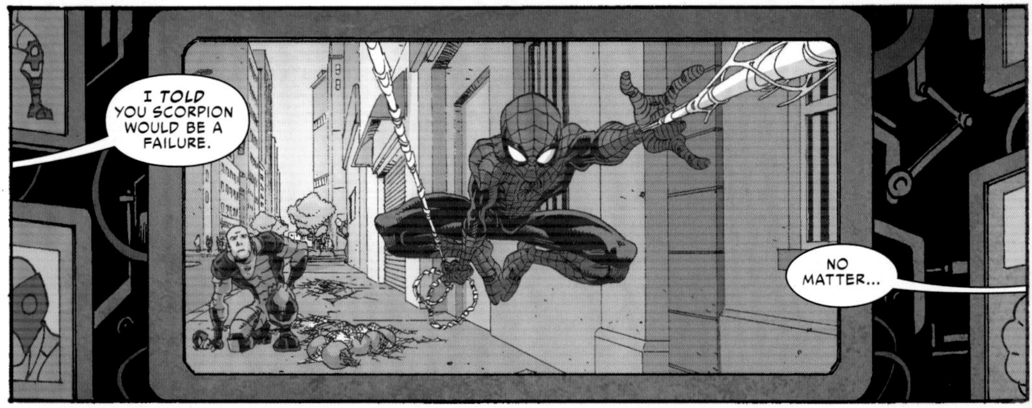
I TOLD YOU SCORPION WOULD BE A FAILURE.
NO MATTER...

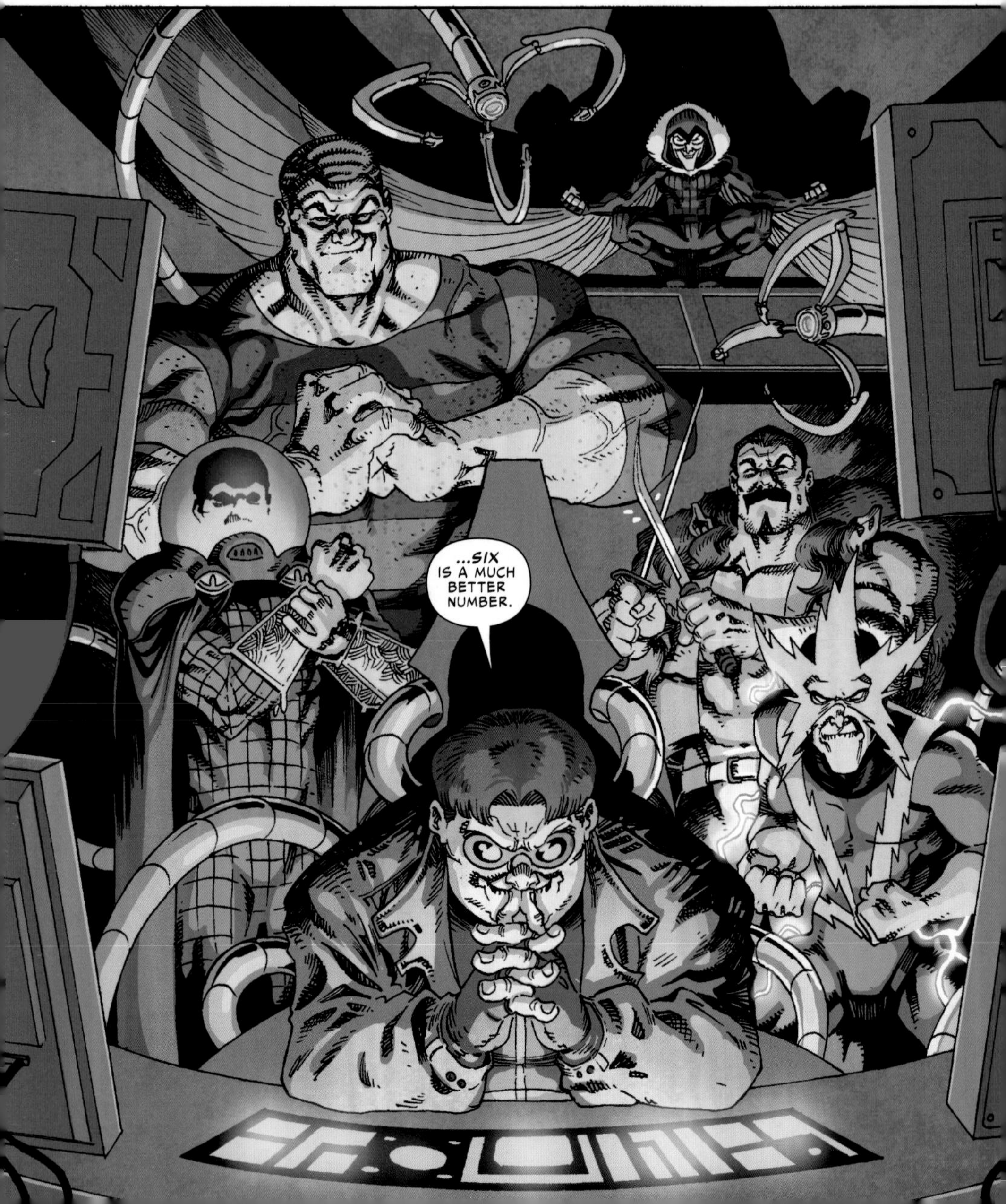
...SIX IS A MUCH BETTER NUMBER.

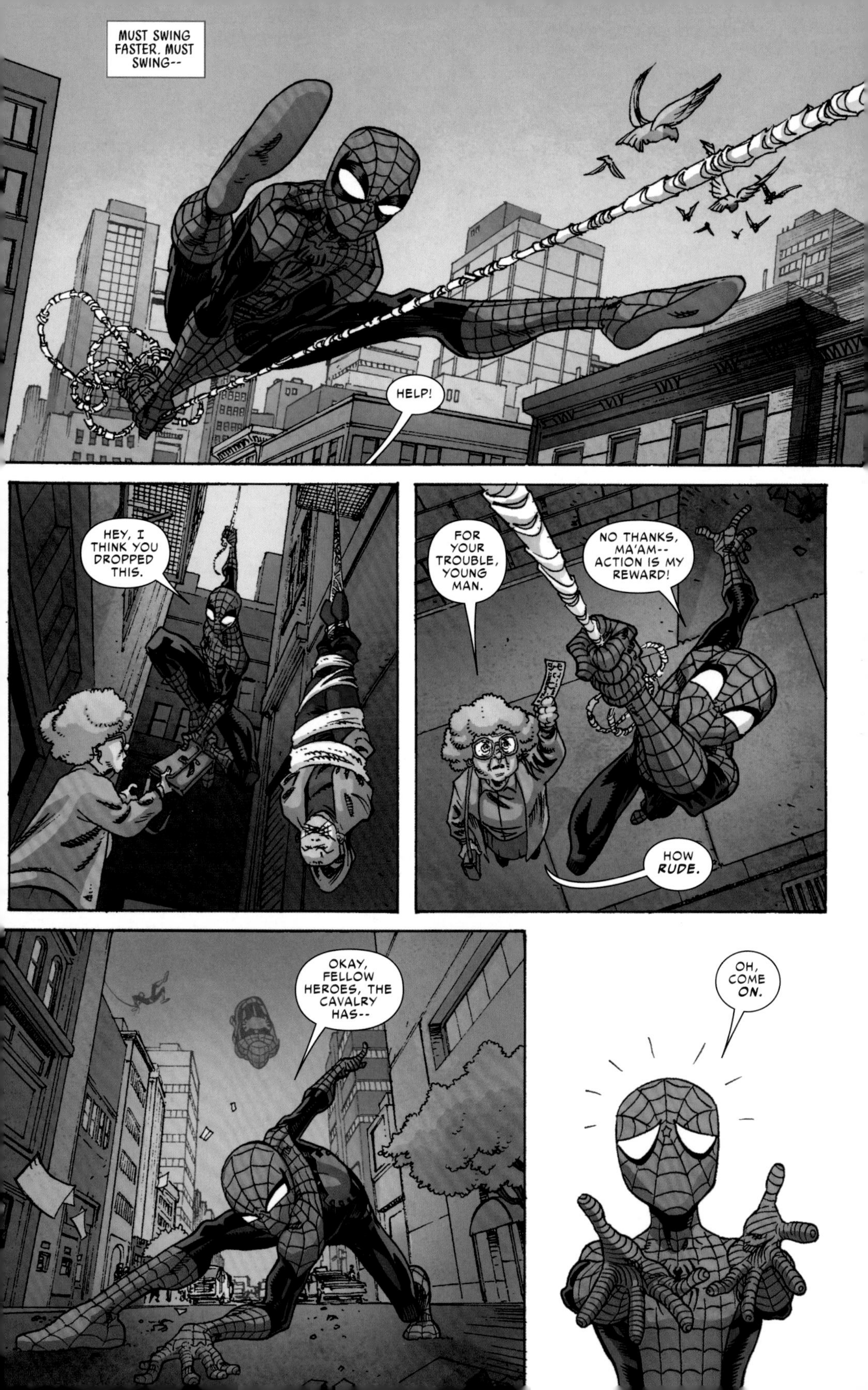
MUST SWING FASTER. MUST SWING--
HELP!
HEY, I THINK YOU DROPPED THIS.
FOR YOUR TROUBLE, YOUNG MAN.
NO THANKS, MA'AM-- ACTION IS MY REWARD!
HOW *RUDE.*
OKAY, FELLOW HEROES, THE CAVALRY HAS--
OH, COME *ON.*

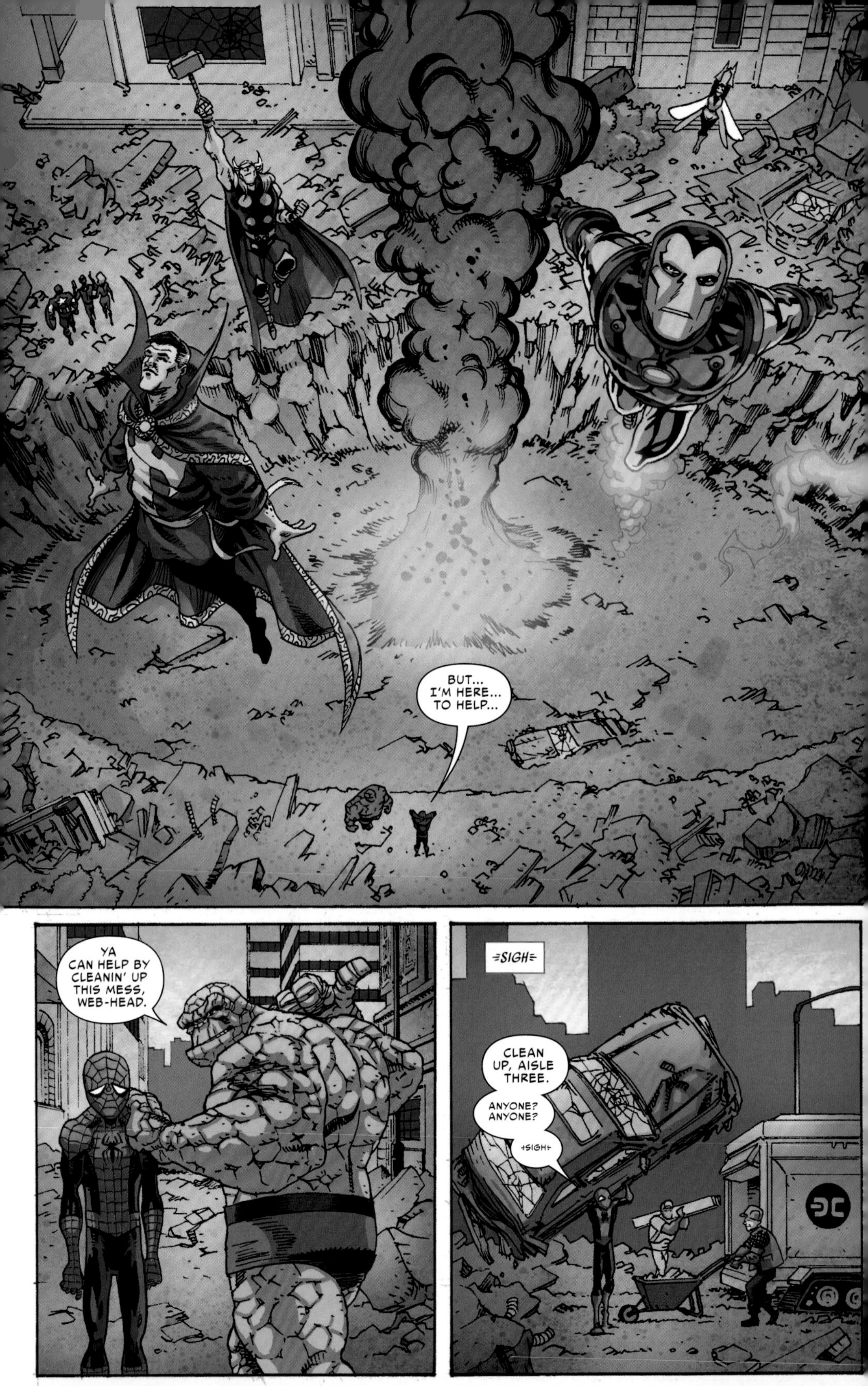
BUT... I'M HERE... TO HELP...
YA CAN HELP BY CLEANIN' UP THIS MESS, WEB-HEAD.
SIGH
CLEAN UP, AISLE THREE.
ANYONE? ANYONE?
SIGH

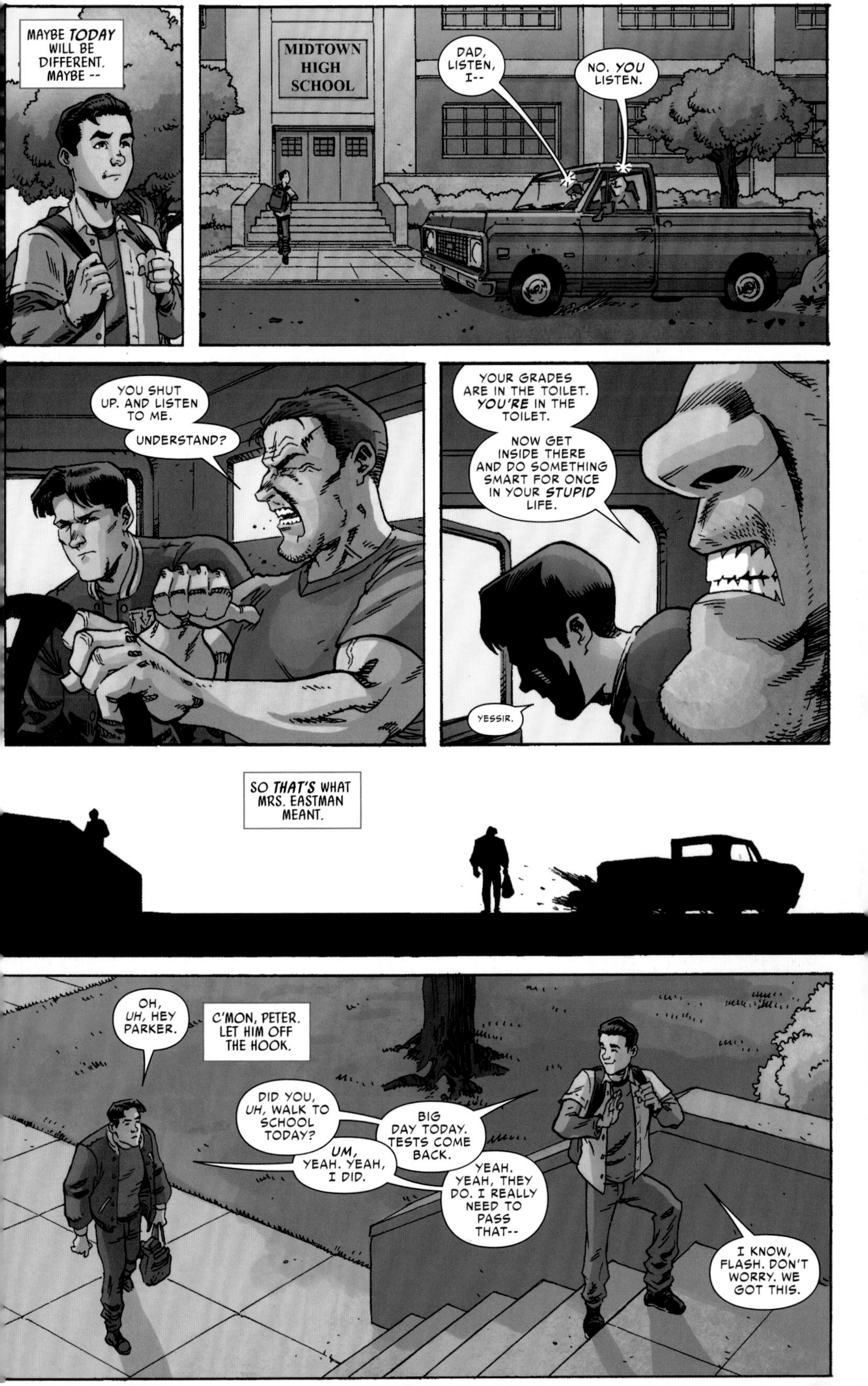
MAYBE TODAY WILL BE DIFFERENT. MAYBE --
MIDTOWN HIGH SCHOOL
DAD, LISTEN, I--
NO. YOU LISTEN.
YOU SHUT UP. AND LISTEN TO ME.
UNDERSTAND?
YOUR GRADES ARE IN THE TOILET. YOU'RE IN THE TOILET.
NOW GET INSIDE THERE AND DO SOMETHING SMART FOR ONCE IN YOUR STUPID LIFE.
YESSIR.
SO THAT'S WHAT MRS. EASTMAN MEANT.
OH, UH, HEY PARKER.
C'MON, PETER. LET HIM OFF THE HOOK.
DID YOU, UH, WALK TO SCHOOL TODAY?
UM, YEAH. YEAH, I DID.
BIG DAY TODAY. TESTS COME BACK.
YEAH. YEAH, THEY DO. I REALLY NEED TO PASS THAT--
I KNOW, FLASH. DON'T WORRY. WE GOT THIS.

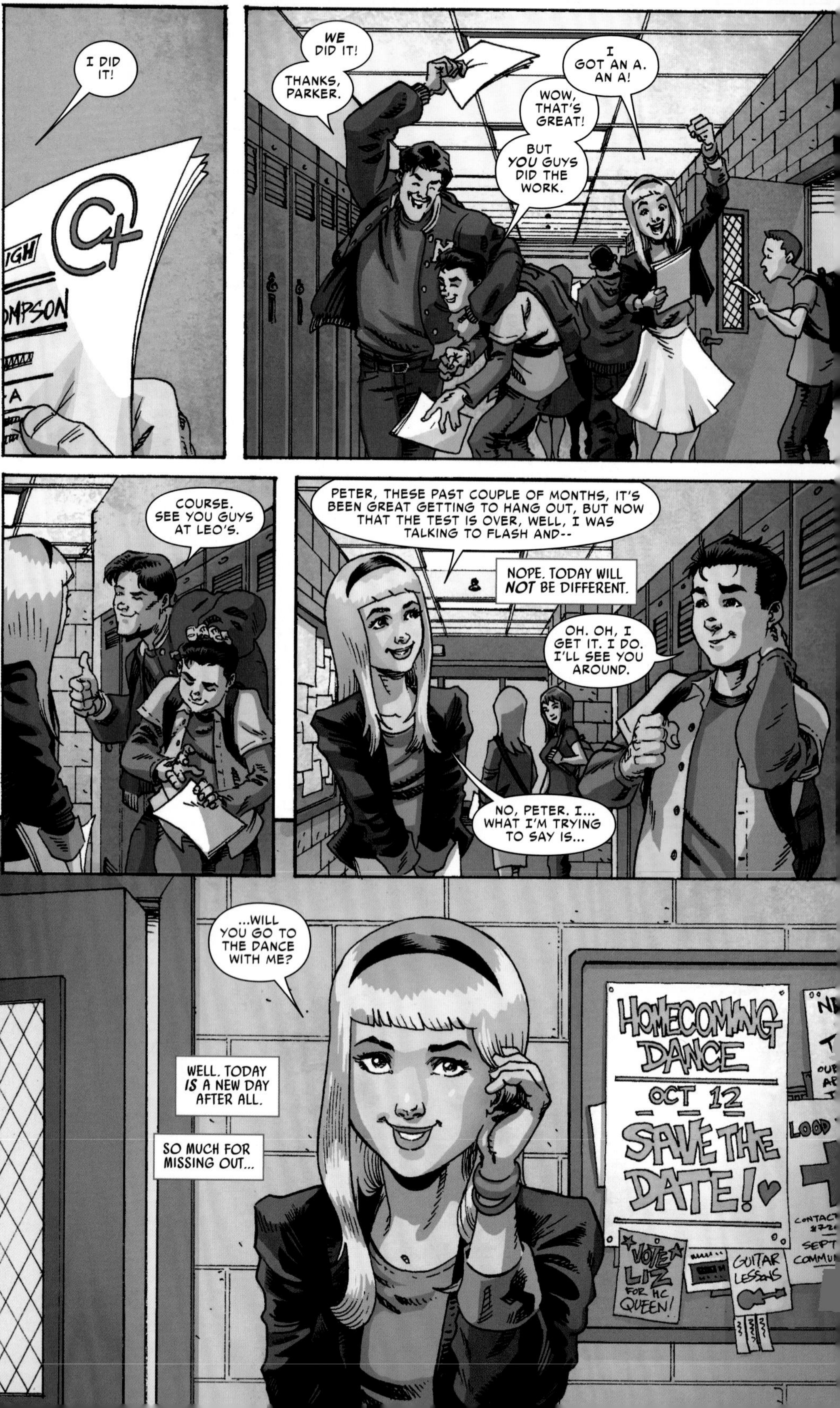

I DID IT!
IGH
C+
OMPSON
A
WE DID IT!
THANKS, PARKER.
I GOT AN A. AN A!
WOW, THAT'S GREAT!
BUT YOU GUYS DID THE WORK.
COURSE. SEE YOU GUYS AT LEO'S.
PETER, THESE PAST COUPLE OF MONTHS, IT'S BEEN GREAT GETTING TO HANG OUT, BUT NOW THAT THE TEST IS OVER, WELL, I WAS TALKING TO FLASH AND--
NOPE. TODAY WILL NOT BE DIFFERENT.
OH. OH, I GET IT. I DO. I'LL SEE YOU AROUND.
NO, PETER. I... WHAT I'M TRYING TO SAY IS...
...WILL YOU GO TO THE DANCE WITH ME?
WELL. TODAY IS A NEW DAY AFTER ALL.
SO MUCH FOR MISSING OUT...
HOMECOMING DANCE
OCT 12
SAVE THE DATE!
VOTE LIZ FOR H.C. QUEEN!
GUITAR LESSONS

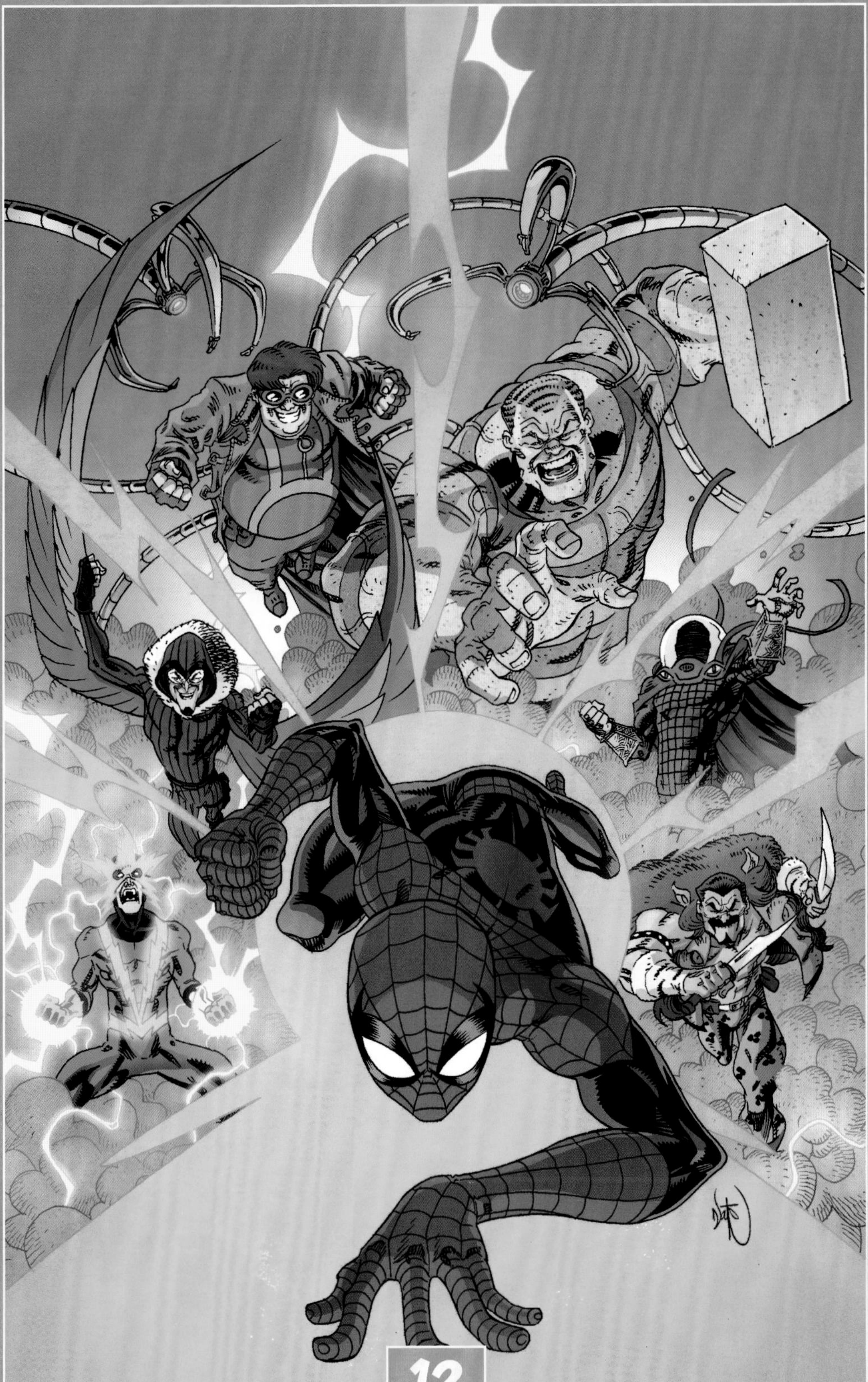

12

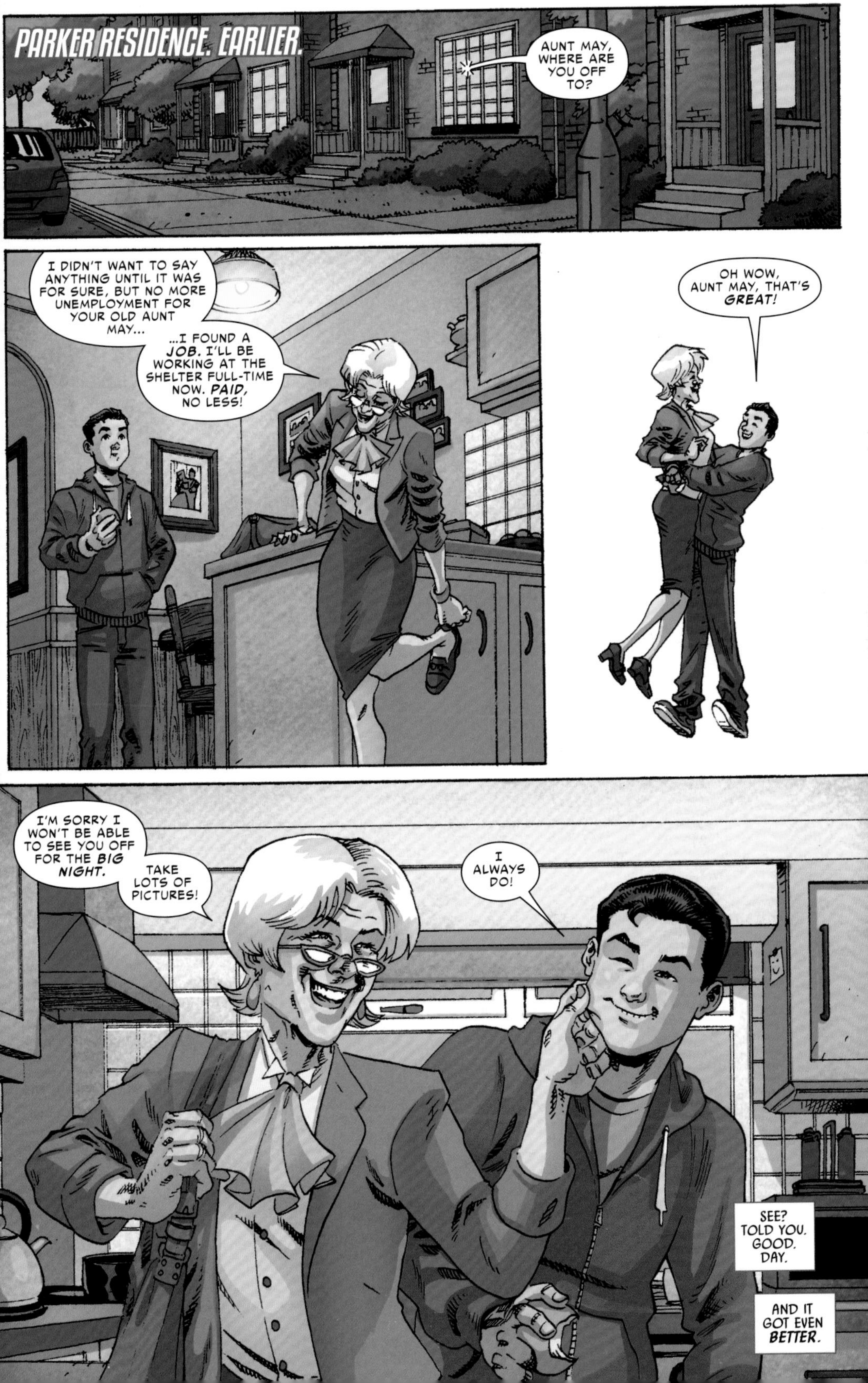
PARKER RESIDENCE. EARLIER.
AUNT MAY, WHERE ARE YOU OFF TO?
I DIDN'T WANT TO SAY ANYTHING UNTIL IT WAS FOR SURE, BUT NO MORE UNEMPLOYMENT FOR YOUR OLD AUNT MAY...
...I FOUND A JOB. I'LL BE WORKING AT THE SHELTER FULL-TIME NOW. PAID, NO LESS!
OH WOW, AUNT MAY, THAT'S GREAT!
I'M SORRY I WON'T BE ABLE TO SEE YOU OFF FOR THE BIG NIGHT.
TAKE LOTS OF PICTURES!
I ALWAYS DO!
SEE? TOLD YOU. GOOD. DAY.
AND IT GOT EVEN BETTER.

WELL, WHAT DO YOU KNOW, PARKER?

YOU *FINALLY* TOOK SOME PICTURES THAT WEREN'T *AWFUL.*

I'LL TAKE THESE TWO. THE REST ARE GARBAGE, AS USUAL.

UM, MR. JAMESON, IS...IS THERE ANY WAY I COULD GET PAID TODAY--

PAYDAY'S AT THE END OF THE WEEK. NO EXCEPTIONS.

NO... I KNOW. IT'S JUST... I--

SPIT IT OUT, PARKER!

DAILY-BUGLE

IT'S HOMECOMING AND I NEED MONEY FOR MY TUX AND FOR DINNER AND I KNOW THERE'S NO EXCEPTIONS BUT I HAD TO TRY AND I'M SORRY AND I'LL SEE MYSELF OUT.

JJONAH JAMESON
EDITOR IN CHIEF

PARKER! SHUT UP AND LISTEN.

SUITS & TUXEDOS

TUXEDO RENTAL FROM $99

CLOSED

SEE? AND THEN, AFTER ALL THIS...

...MY DAY WENT FROM GOOD...

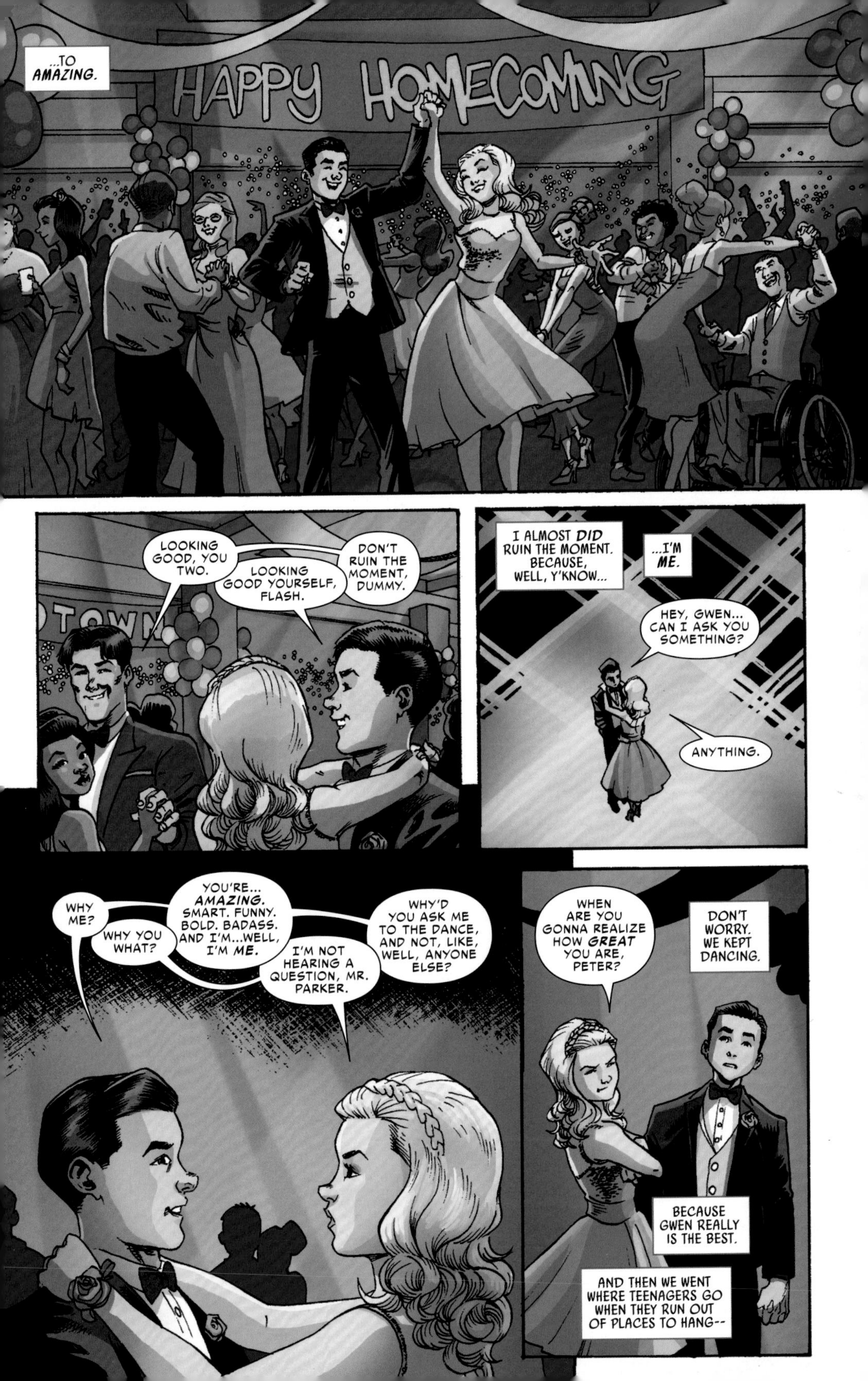
...TO AMAZING.
HAPPY HOMECOMING
LOOKING GOOD, YOU TWO.
DON'T RUIN THE MOMENT, DUMMY.
LOOKING GOOD YOURSELF, FLASH.
I ALMOST DID RUIN THE MOMENT. BECAUSE, WELL, Y'KNOW...
...I'M ME.
HEY, GWEN... CAN I ASK YOU SOMETHING?
ANYTHING.
WHY ME?
WHY YOU WHAT?
YOU'RE... AMAZING. SMART. FUNNY. BOLD. BADASS. AND I'M...WELL, I'M ME.
I'M NOT HEARING A QUESTION, MR. PARKER.
WHY'D YOU ASK ME TO THE DANCE, AND NOT, LIKE, WELL, ANYONE ELSE?
WHEN ARE YOU GONNA REALIZE HOW GREAT YOU ARE, PETER?
DON'T WORRY. WE KEPT DANCING.
BECAUSE GWEN REALLY IS THE BEST.
AND THEN WE WENT WHERE TEENAGERS GO WHEN THEY RUN OUT OF PLACES TO HANG--

--AN ALL-NIGHT DINER.

YOU TOOK THIS PHOTO?

YEAH. MR. JAMESON ACTUALLY LIKED THIS ONE FOR ONCE, TOO.

HUH. I'VE MET SPIDEY, Y'KNOW. HE LOOKS TALLER IN PERSON.

YEAH, I GET THAT A LOT--

--TOO, I ALSO GET THAT, A LOT, ALSO.

SPIDEY'S PRETTY GREAT, RIGHT? COOL COSTUME. SUPER-DUDE.

HE'S ALL RIGHT, I GUESS. HIS COSTUME COULD USE A LITTLE MORE *PIZZAZZ*.

REALLY? I THINK IT'S ICONI--

PLUS--

--HE'S NO PETER PARKER.

YUP. SHE SAID THAT.

AND IN THIS EPIC MOMENT?

MY SPIDER-SENSE WENT OFF. PERFECT TIMING.

AND THUS, MY *PERFECT* DAY CAME TO AN END. WELL, ALMOST...

UH, YEAH. I'M, UH, I'M SURE ME.

LISTEN, GWEN, IT'S PRETTY LATE, AND YOUR DAD'S A COP, SO--

YOU'RE RIGHT, YOU'RE RIGHT. WE SHOULD CALL IT A NIGHT.

THANKS FOR A PERFECT HOMECOMING, GWEN STACY.

AND THANK *YOU*, PETER PARKER...

...FOR THE PERFECT KISS.

WHA--

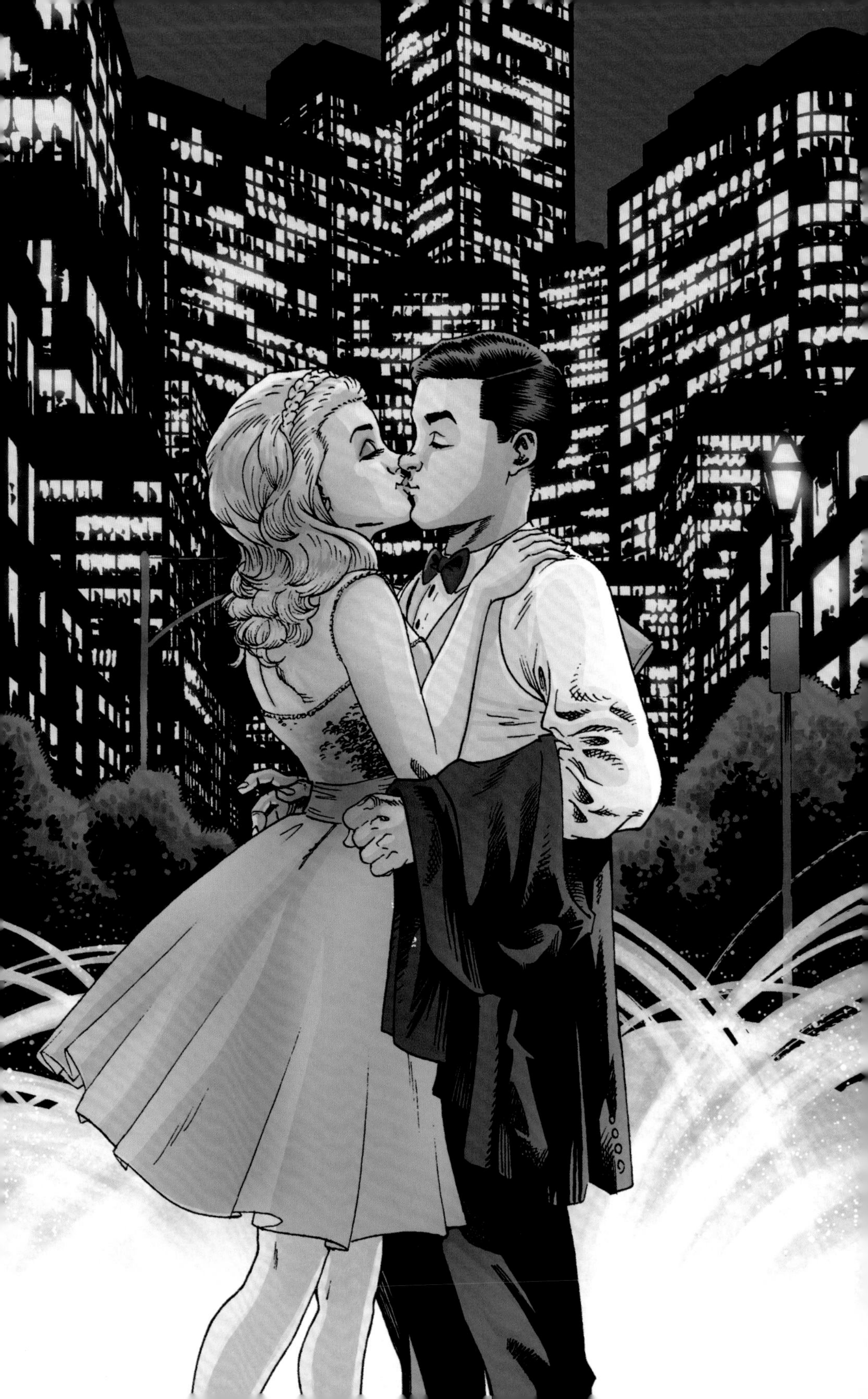

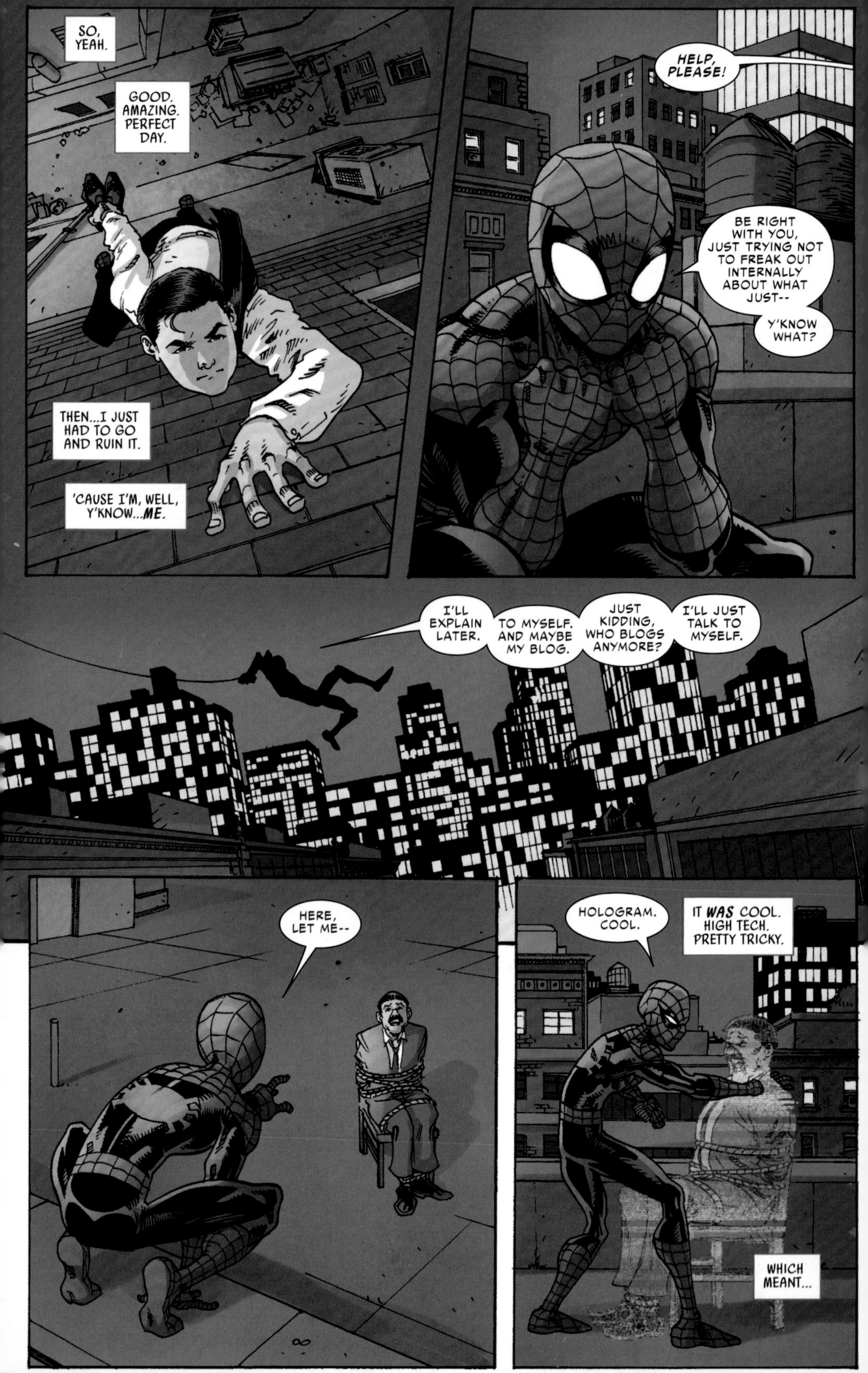
SO, YEAH.
GOOD. AMAZING. PERFECT DAY.
THEN...I JUST HAD TO GO AND RUIN IT.
'CAUSE I'M, WELL, Y'KNOW...*ME.*
HELP, PLEASE!
BE RIGHT WITH YOU, JUST TRYING NOT TO FREAK OUT INTERNALLY ABOUT WHAT JUST--
Y'KNOW WHAT?
I'LL EXPLAIN LATER.
TO MYSELF. AND MAYBE MY BLOG.
JUST KIDDING, WHO BLOGS ANYMORE?
I'LL JUST TALK TO MYSELF.
HERE, LET ME--
HOLOGRAM. COOL.
IT *WAS* COOL. HIGH TECH. PRETTY TRICKY.
WHICH MEANT...

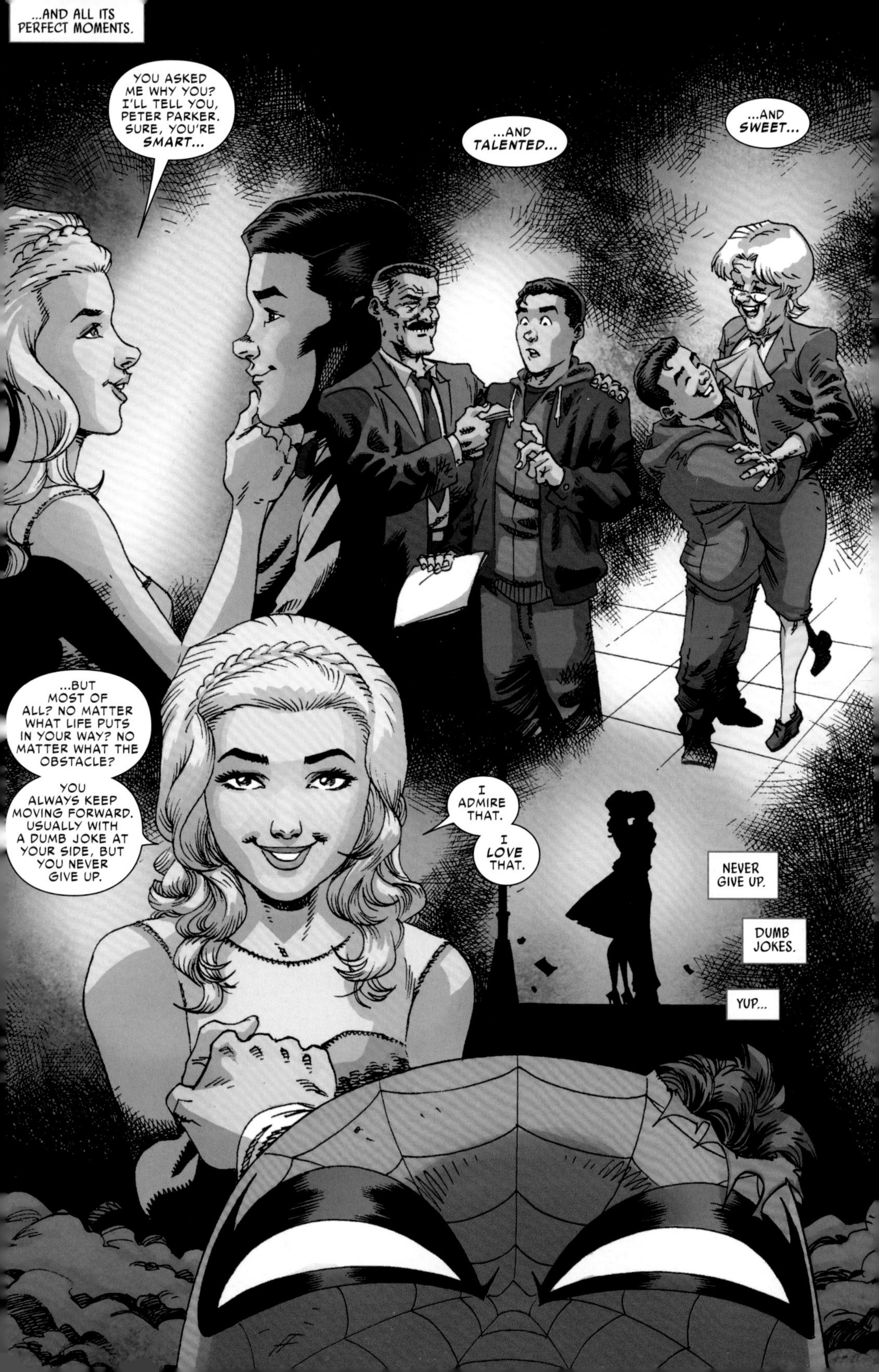
...AND ALL ITS PERFECT MOMENTS.
YOU ASKED ME WHY YOU? I'LL TELL YOU, PETER PARKER. SURE, YOU'RE SMART...
...AND TALENTED...
...AND SWEET...
...BUT MOST OF ALL? NO MATTER WHAT LIFE PUTS IN YOUR WAY? NO MATTER WHAT THE OBSTACLE?
YOU ALWAYS KEEP MOVING FORWARD. USUALLY WITH A DUMB JOKE AT YOUR SIDE, BUT YOU NEVER GIVE UP.
I ADMIRE THAT.
I LOVE THAT.
NEVER GIVE UP.
DUMB JOKES.
YUP...

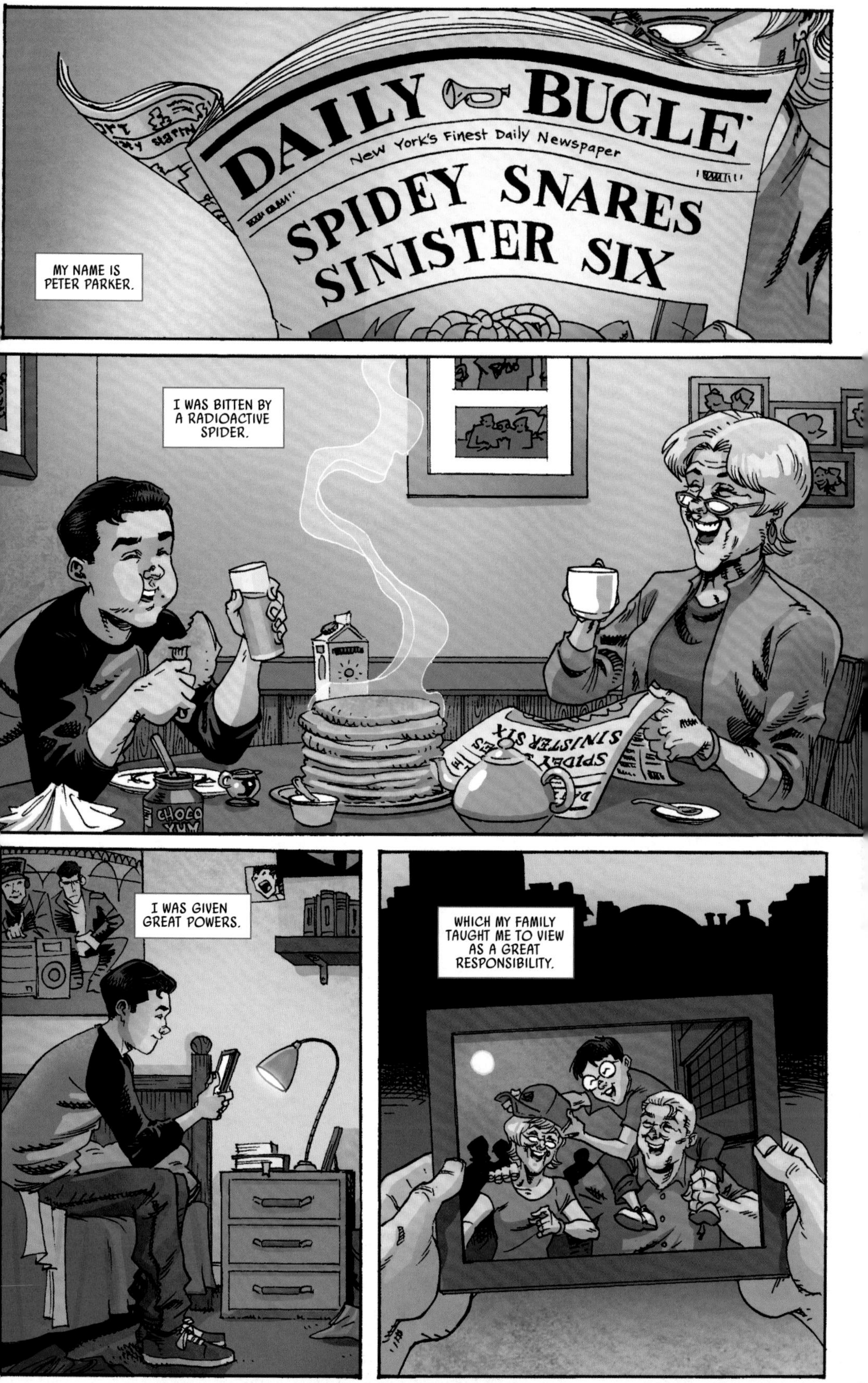
DAILY BUGLE
New York's Finest Daily Newspaper
SPIDEY SNARES SINISTER SIX
MY NAME IS PETER PARKER.
I WAS BITTEN BY A RADIOACTIVE SPIDER.
CHOCO YUM
I WAS GIVEN GREAT POWERS.
WHICH MY FAMILY TAUGHT ME TO VIEW AS A GREAT RESPONSIBILITY.

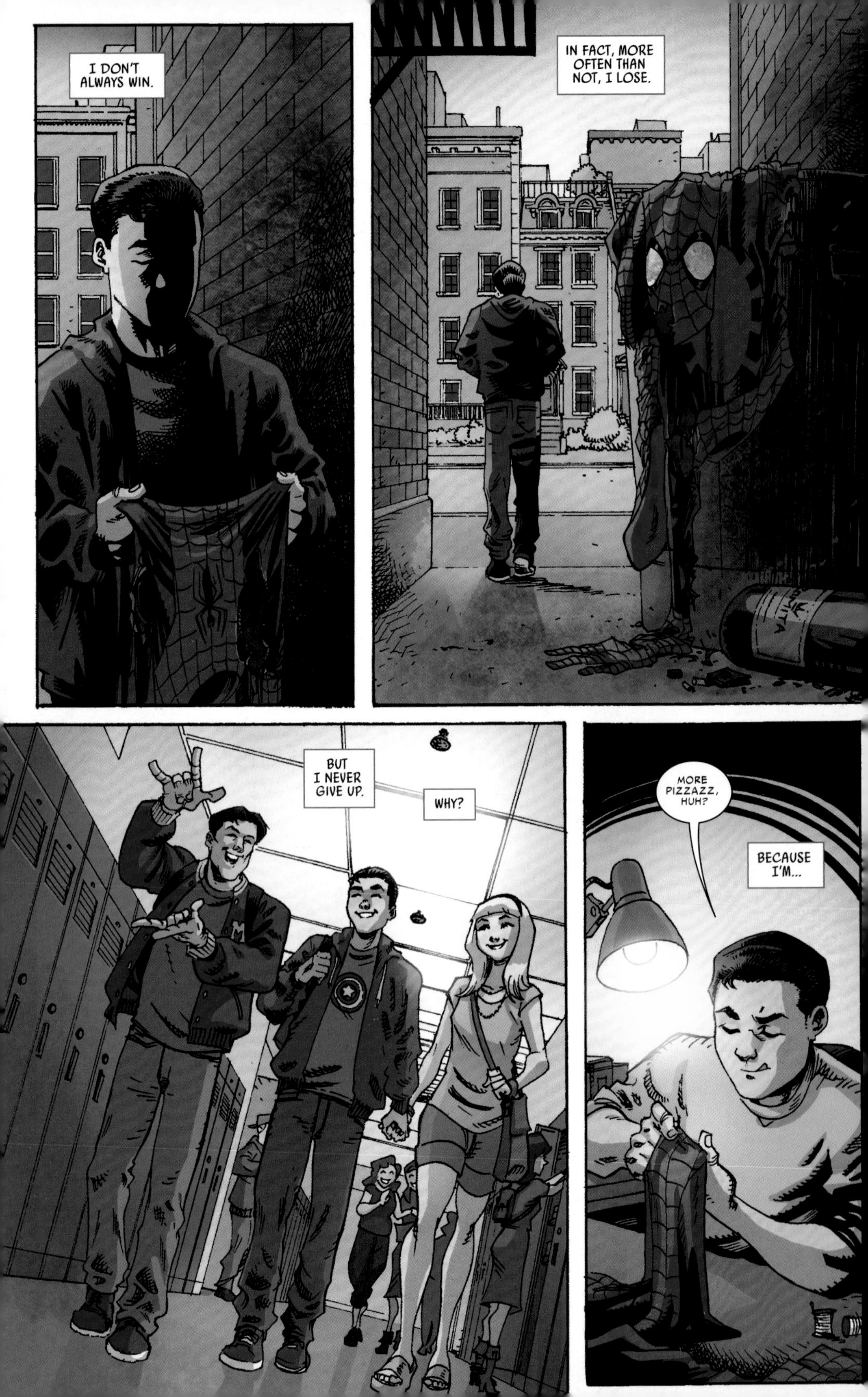
I DON'T ALWAYS WIN.
IN FACT, MORE OFTEN THAN NOT, I LOSE.
BUT I NEVER GIVE UP.
WHY?
MORE PIZZAZZ, HUH?
BECAUSE I'M...

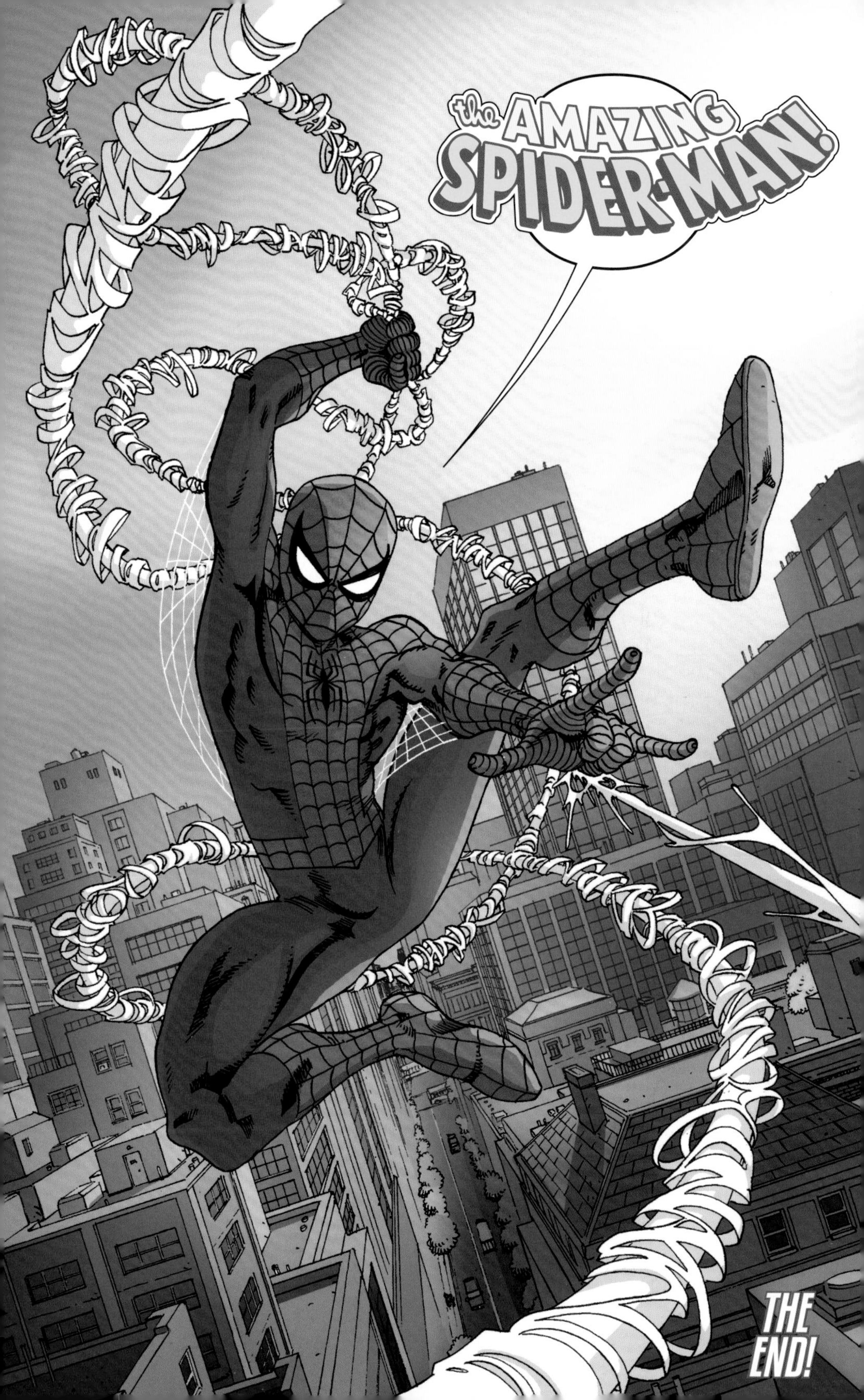
the AMAZING SPIDER-MAN!
THE END!

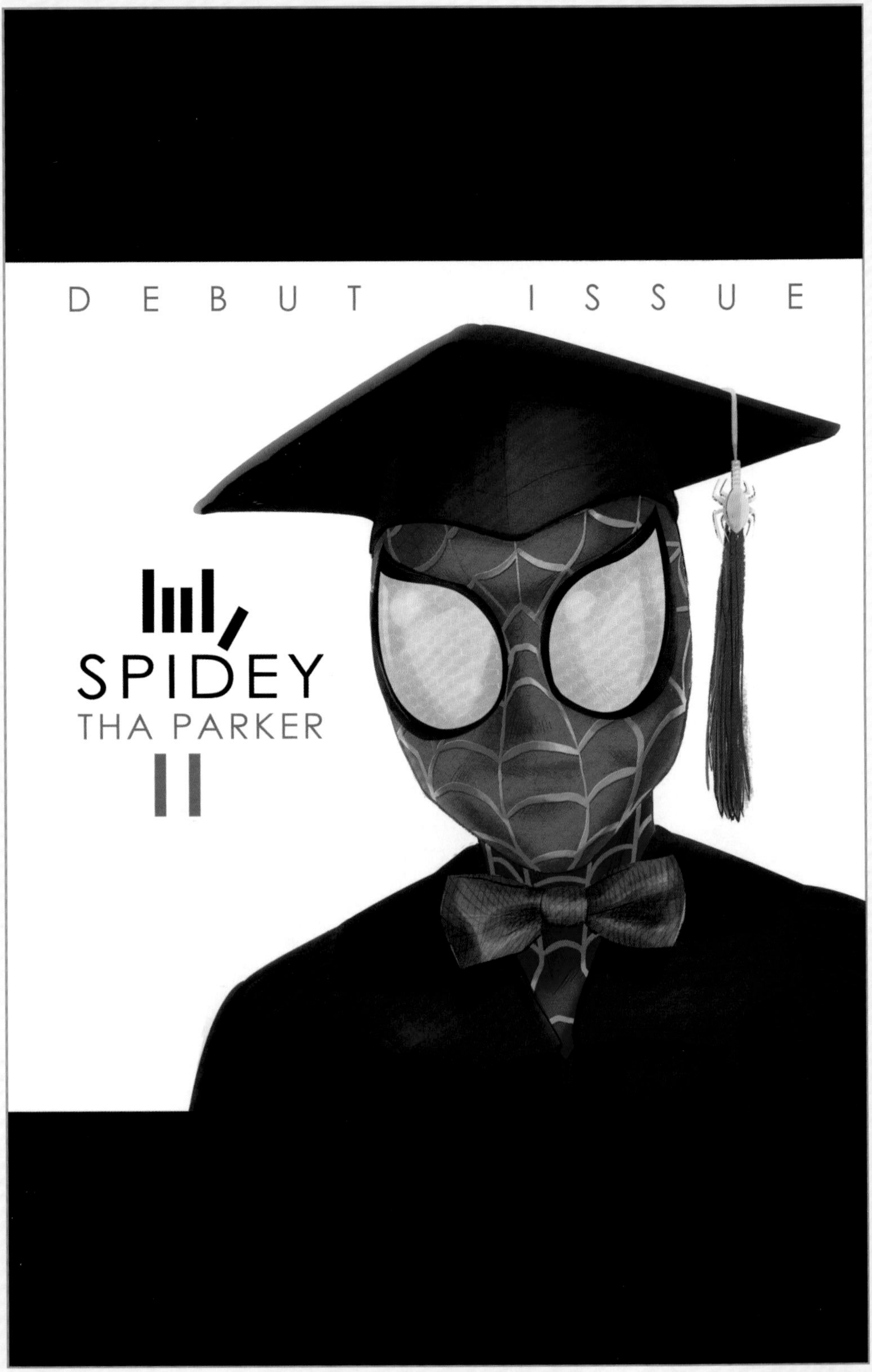
D E B U T I S S U E
SPIDEY
THA PARKER
II

SPIDEY #1 HIP-HOP VARIANT
BY JULIAN TOTINO TEDESCO

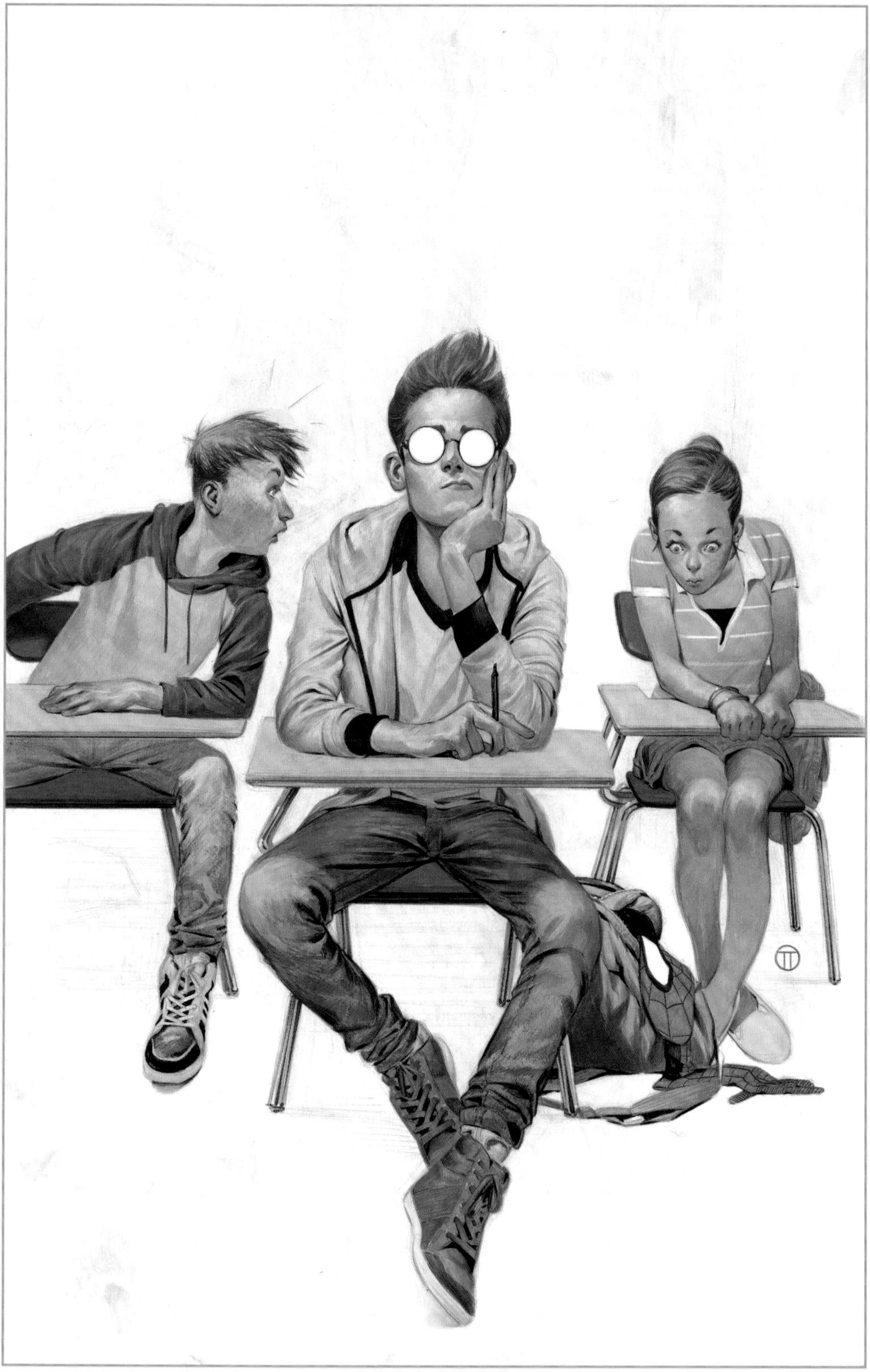

SPIDEY #3 VARIANT
BY JULIAN TOTINO TEDESCO

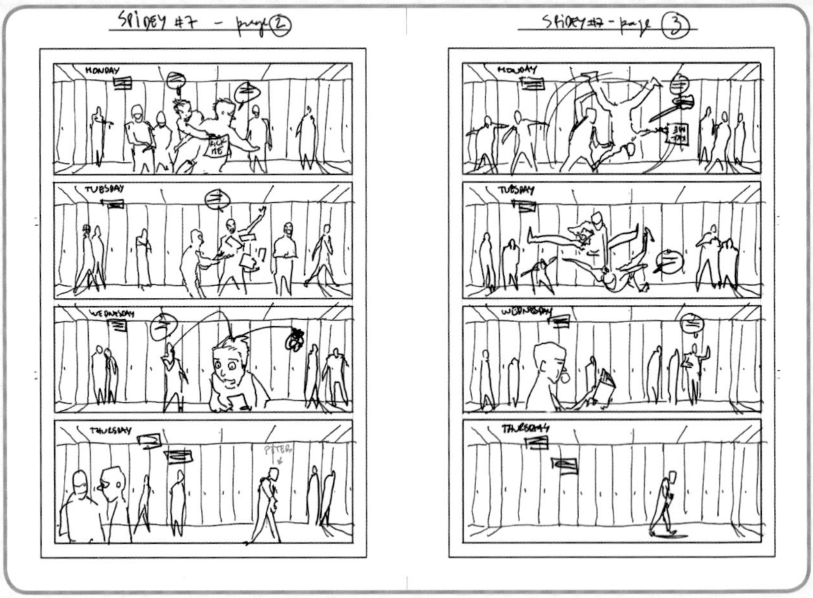
SPIDEY #7 - page 2
MONDAY
KICK ME
TUESDAY
WEDNESDAY
THURSDAY
PETER
SPIDEY #7 - page 3
MONDAY
KICK ME
TUESDAY
WEDNESDAY
THURSDAY

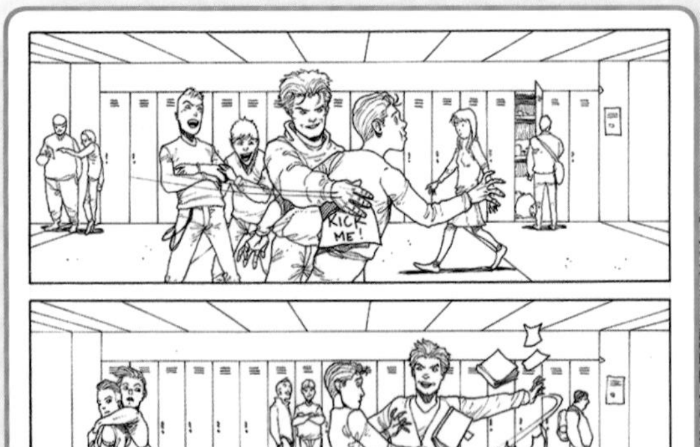
KICK ME!

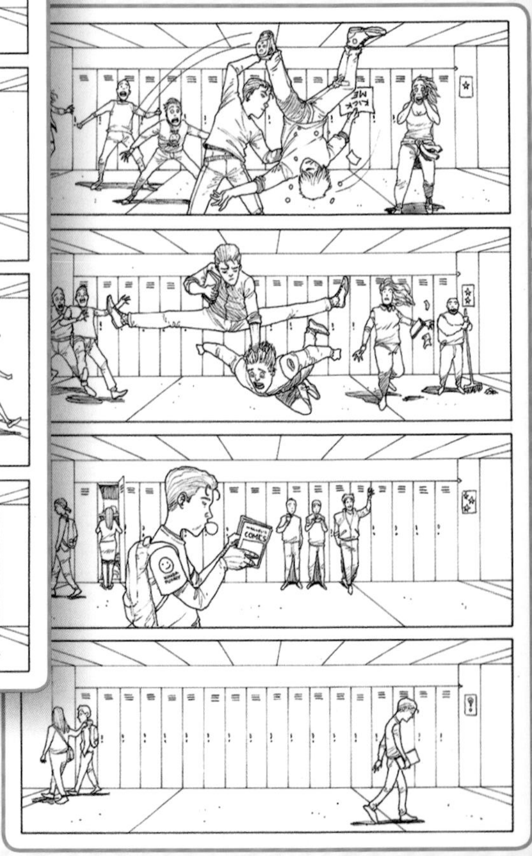
KICK ME
COMICS

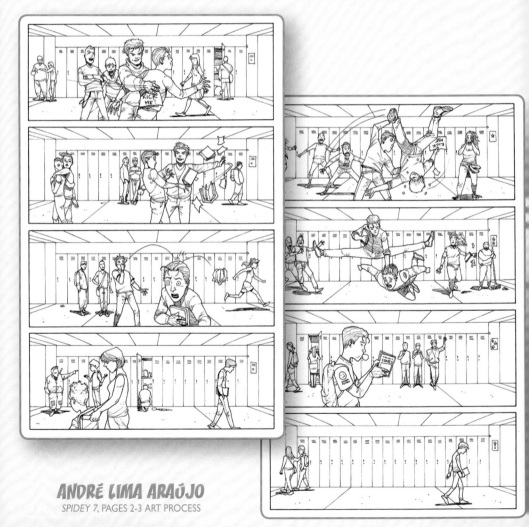

ANDRÉ LIMA ARAÚJO
SPIDEY 7, PAGES 2-3 ART PROCESS

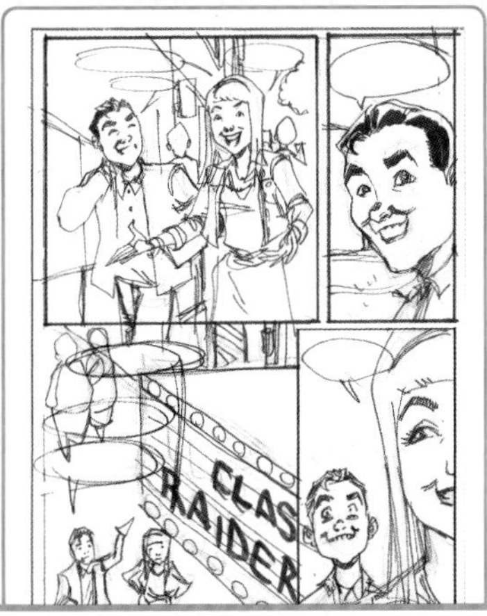
CLAS
RAIDER

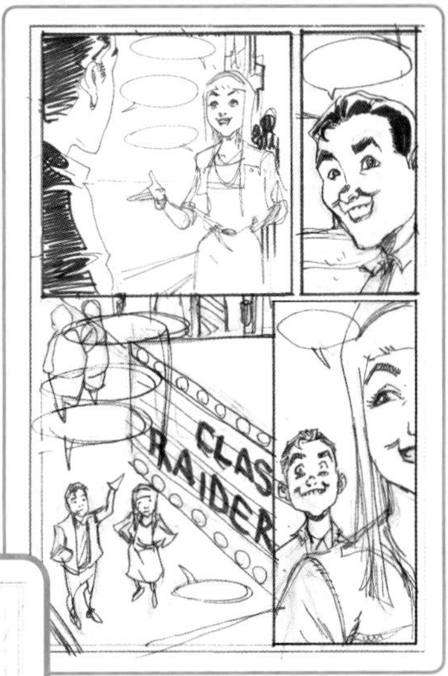
CLAS
RAIDER

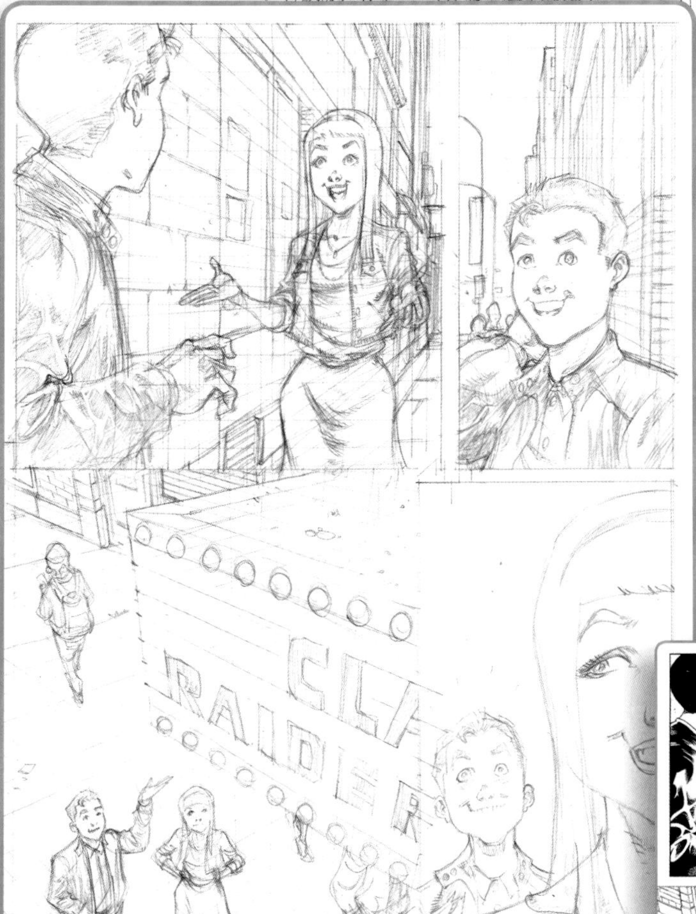
CLA
RAIDER

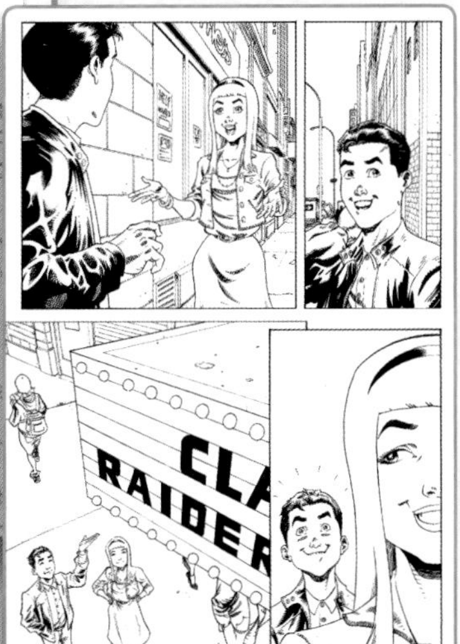
CLA
RAIDER

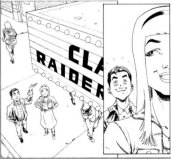

NATHAN STOCKMAN

SPIDEY 8, PAGE 18 ART PROCESS

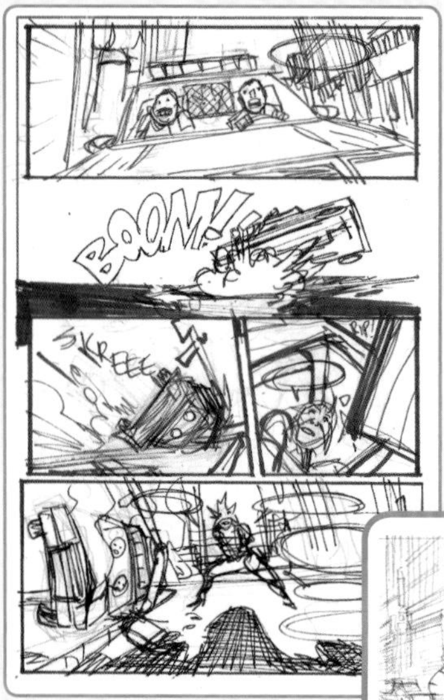
BOOM!

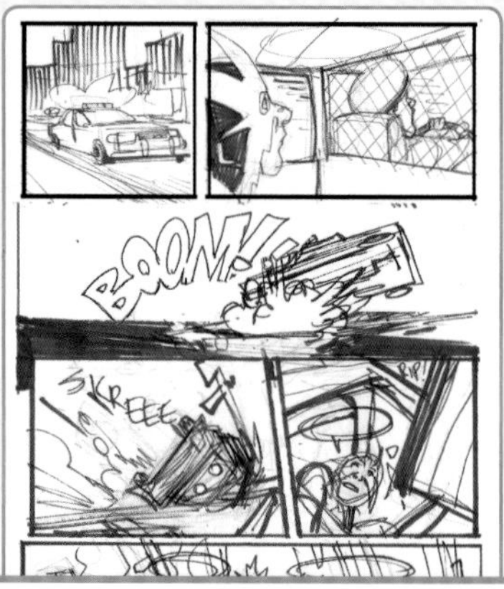
BOOM!

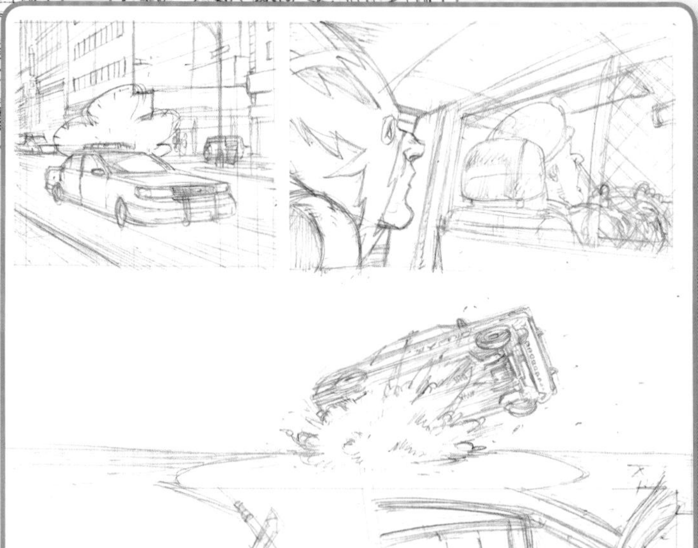

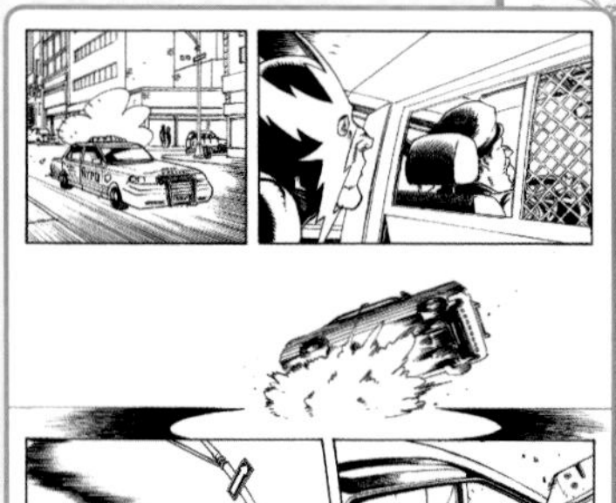

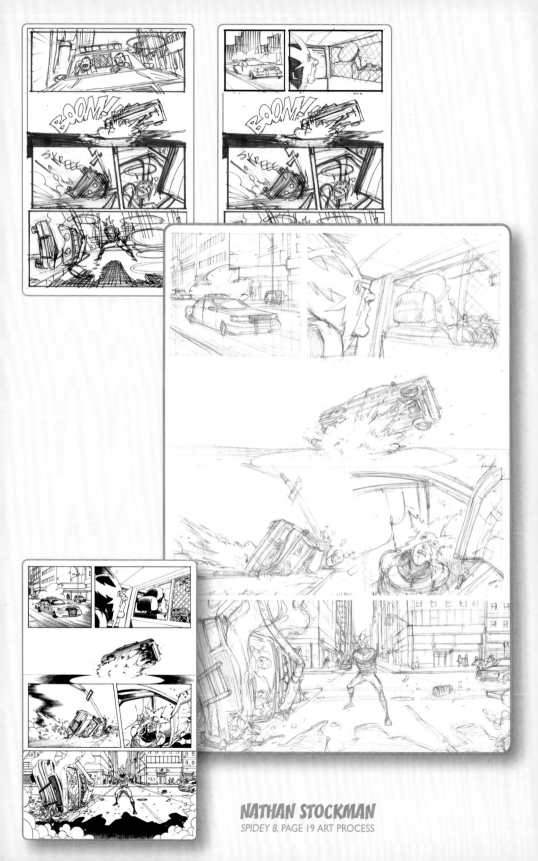

NATHAN STOCKMAN

SPIDEY 8, PAGE 19 ART PROCESS

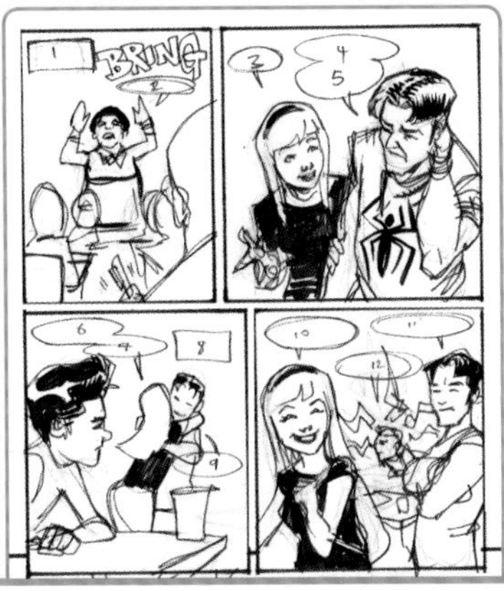
BRING
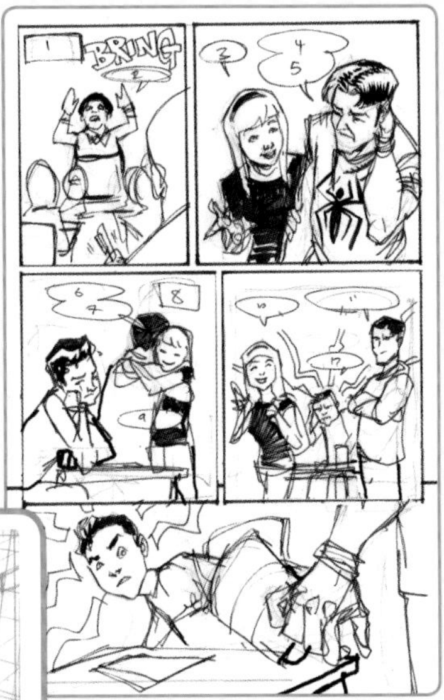
BRING
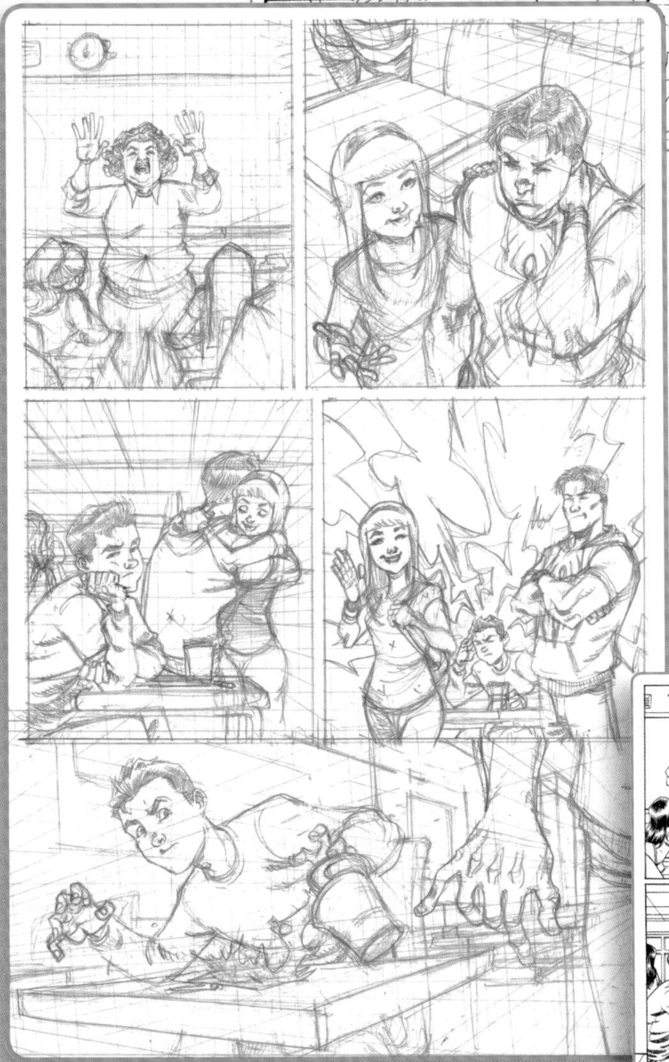
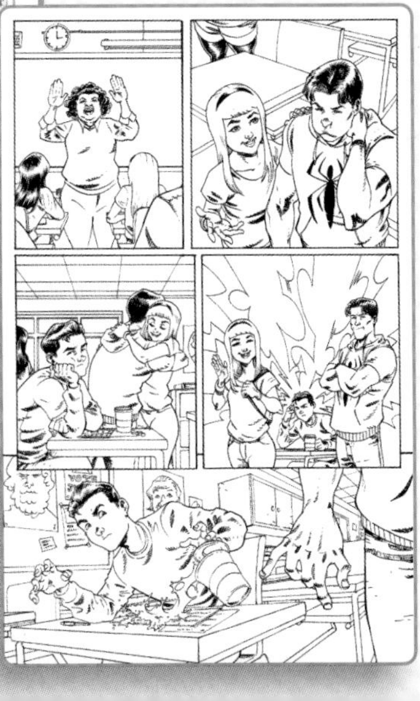

NATHAN STOCKMAN

SPIDEY 11, PAGE 2 ART PROCESS

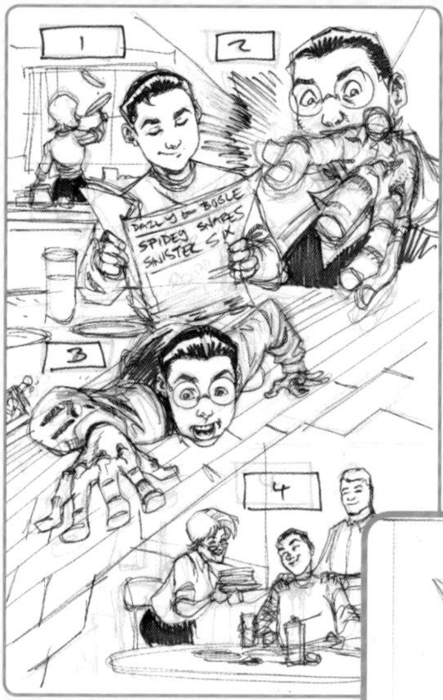
DAILY BUGLE
SPIDEY SNARES
SINISTER SIX

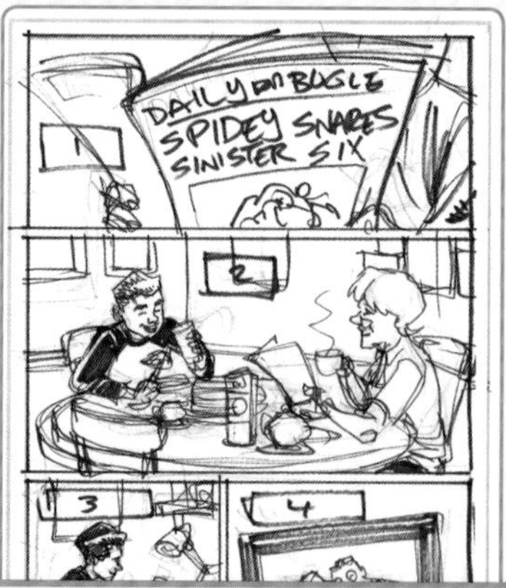
DAILY BUGLE
SPIDEY SNARES
SINISTER SIX

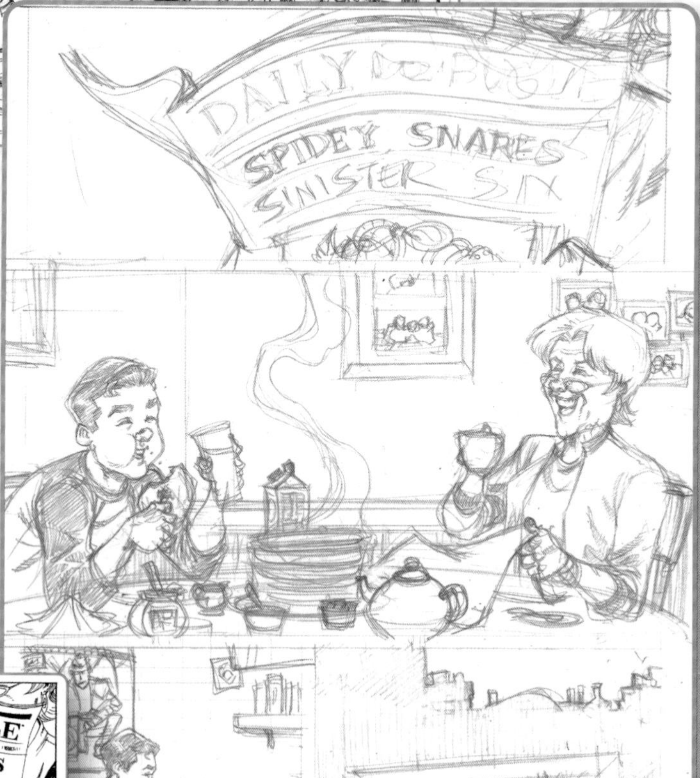
DAILY BUGLE
SPIDEY SNARES
SINISTER SIX

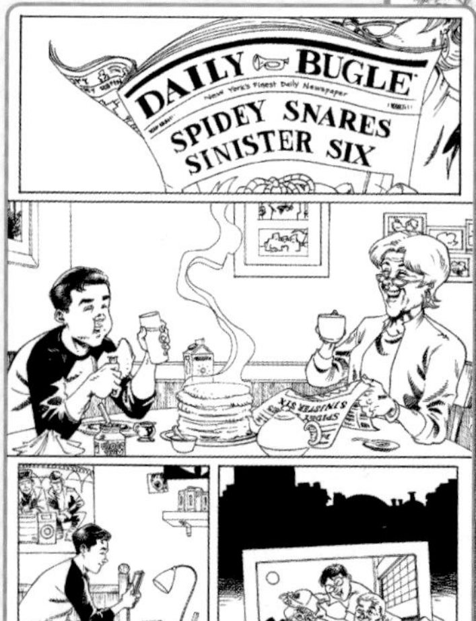
DAILY BUGLE
New York's Finest Daily Newspaper
SPIDEY SNARES
SINISTER SIX

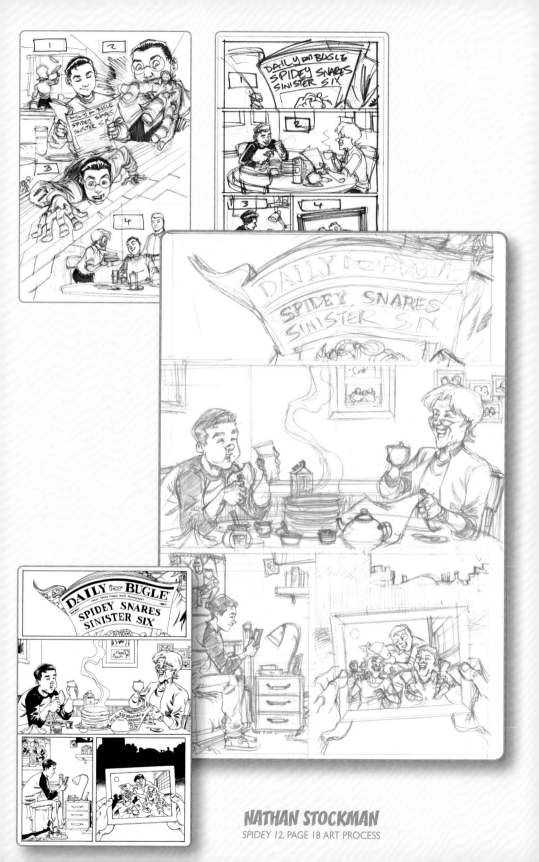

NATHAN STOCKMAN

SPIDEY 12, PAGE 18 ART PROCESS

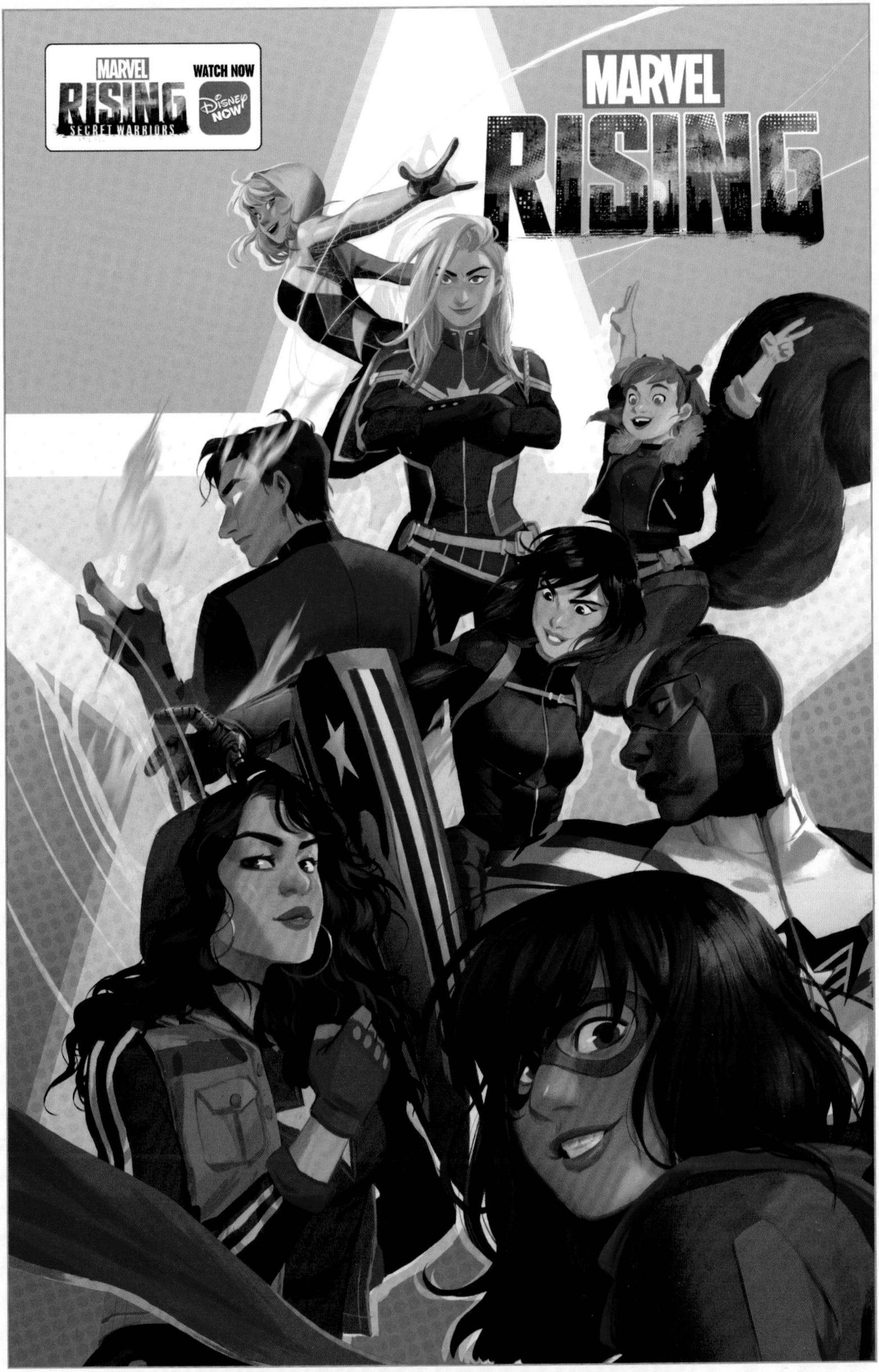
MARVEL
RISING
SECRET WARRIORS
WATCH NOW
DISNEY NOW
MARVEL
RISING

INTRODUCING MARVEL RISING!

MARVEL RISING

THE MARVEL UNIVERSE IS A RICH TREASURE CHEST OF CHARACTERS BORN ACROSS MARVEL'S INCREDIBLE 80-YEAR HISTORY. FROM CAPTAIN AMERICA TO CAPTAIN MARVEL, IRON MAN TO IRONHEART, THIS IS AN EVER-EXPANDING UNIVERSE FULL OF POWERFUL HEROES THAT ALSO REFLECTS THE WORLD WE LIVE IN.

YET DESPITE THAT EXPANSION, OUR STORIES REMAIN TIMELESS. THEY'VE BEEN SHARED ACROSS THE GLOBE AND ACROSS GENERATIONS, LINKING FANS WITH THE ENDURING IDEA THAT ORDINARY PEOPLE CAN DO EXTRAORDINARY THINGS. IT'S THAT SHARED EXPERIENCE OF THE MARVEL STORY THAT HAS ALLOWED US TO EXIST FOR THIS LONG. WHETHER YOUR FIRST MARVEL EXPERIENCE WAS THROUGH A COMIC BOOK, A BEDTIME STORY, A MOVIE OR A CARTOON, WE BELIEVE OUR STORIES STAY WITH AUDIENCES THROUGHOUT THEIR LIVES.

MARVEL RISING IS A CELEBRATION OF THIS TIMELESSNESS. AS OUR STORIES PASS FROM ONE GENERATION TO THE NEXT, SO DOES THE LOVE FOR OUR HEROES. FROM THE CLASSIC TO THE NEWLY IMAGINED, THE PASSION FOR ALL OF THEM IS THE SAME. IF YOU'VE BEEN READING COMICS OVER THE LAST FEW YEARS, YOU'LL KNOW CHARACTERS LIKE MS. MARVEL, SQUIRREL GIRL, AMERICA CHAVEZ, SPIDER-GWEN AND MORE HAVE ASSEMBLED A BEVY OF NEW FANS WHILE CAPTIVATING OUR PERENNIAL FANS. EACH OF THESE HEROES IS UNIQUE AND DISTINCT--JUST LIKE THE READERS THEY'VE BROUGHT IN--AND THEY REMIND US THAT NO MATTER WHAT YOU LOOK LIKE, YOU HAVE THE CAPABILITY TO BE POWERFUL, TOO. WE ARE TAKING THE HEROES FROM MARVEL RISING TO NEW HEIGHTS IN AN ANIMATED FEATURE LATER IN 2018, AS WELL AS A FULL PROGRAM OF CONTENT SWEEPING ACROSS THE COMPANY. BUT FIRST WE'RE GOING BACK TO OUR ROOTS AND TELLING A MARVEL RISING STORY IN COMICS: THE FIRST PLACE YOU MET THESE LOVABLE HEROES.

SO IN THE TRADITION OF EXPANDING THE MARVEL UNIVERSE, WE'RE EXCITED TO INTRODUCE MARVEL RISING--THE NEXT GENERATION OF MARVEL HEROES FOR THE NEXT GENERATION OF MARVEL FANS!

SANA AMANAT
VP, CONTENT & CHARACTER DEVELOPMENT

▶ **DOREEN GREEN** IS A SECOND-YEAR COMPUTER SCIENCE STUDENT – AND THE CRIMINAL-REDEEMING HERO THE **UNBEATABLE SQUIRREL GIRL!** THE NAME SAYS IT ALL: AN UNBEATABLE GIRL WITH THE POWERS OF AN UNBEATABLE SQUIRREL, TAIL INCLUDED. AND ON TOP OF HER STUDYING, NUT-EATING AND BUTT-KICKING ACTIVITIES, SHE'S JUST TAKEN ON THE JOB OF VOLUNTEER TEACHER FOR AN EXTRA-CURRICULAR HIGH-SCHOOL CODING CAMP! AND WHO SHOULD END UP IN HER CLASS BUT...

▶ **KAMALA KHAN**, A.K.A. JERSEY CITY HERO AND INHUMAN POLYMORPH **MS. MARVEL!** BUT BETWEEN SAVING THE WORLD WITH THE CHAMPIONS AND PROTECTING JERSEY CITY ON HER OWN, KAMALA'S GOT A LOT ON HER PLATE ALREADY. AND FIELD TRIP DAY MAY NOT BE THE BREAK SHE'S ANTICIPATING...

MARVEL RISING
PART 0

DEVIN GRAYSON
WRITER

MARCO FAILLA
ARTIST

RACHELLE ROSENBERG
COLOR ARTIST

VC's CLAYTON COWLES
LETTERER

HELEN CHEN
COVER

JAY BOWEN
DESIGN

HEATHER ANTOS AND **SARAH BRUNSTAD**
EDITORS

SANA AMANAT
CONSULTING EDITOR

C.B. CEBULSKI
EDITOR IN CHIEF

JOE QUESADA
CHIEF CREATIVE OFFICER

DAN BUCKLEY
PRESIDENT

ALAN FINE
EXECUTIVE PRODUCER

SPECIAL THANKS TO RYAN NORTH AND G. WILLOW WILSON

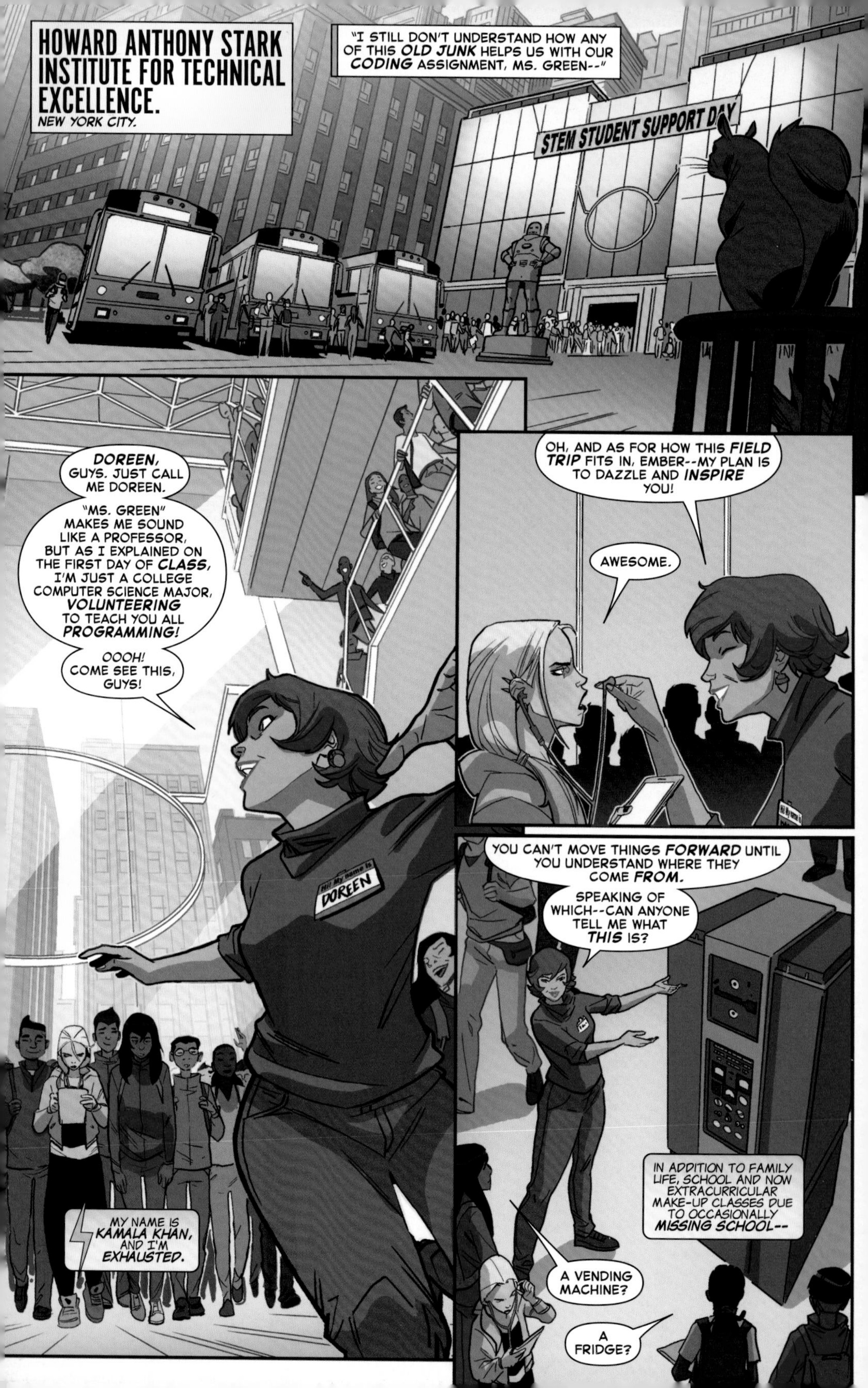
HOWARD ANTHONY STARK INSTITUTE FOR TECHNICAL EXCELLENCE.
NEW YORK CITY.
"I STILL DON'T UNDERSTAND HOW ANY OF THIS OLD JUNK HELPS US WITH OUR CODING ASSIGNMENT, MS. GREEN--"
STEM STUDENT SUPPORT DAY
DOREEN, GUYS. JUST CALL ME DOREEN.
"MS. GREEN" MAKES ME SOUND LIKE A PROFESSOR, BUT AS I EXPLAINED ON THE FIRST DAY OF CLASS, I'M JUST A COLLEGE COMPUTER SCIENCE MAJOR, VOLUNTEERING TO TEACH YOU ALL PROGRAMMING!
OOOH! COME SEE THIS, GUYS!
HI! MY NAME IS DOREEN
MY NAME IS KAMALA KHAN, AND I'M EXHAUSTED.
OH, AND AS FOR HOW THIS FIELD TRIP FITS IN, EMBER--MY PLAN IS TO DAZZLE AND INSPIRE YOU!
AWESOME.
YOU CAN'T MOVE THINGS FORWARD UNTIL YOU UNDERSTAND WHERE THEY COME FROM.
SPEAKING OF WHICH--CAN ANYONE TELL ME WHAT THIS IS?
IN ADDITION TO FAMILY LIFE, SCHOOL AND NOW EXTRACURRICULAR MAKE-UP CLASSES DUE TO OCCASIONALLY MISSING SCHOOL--
A VENDING MACHINE?
A FRIDGE?

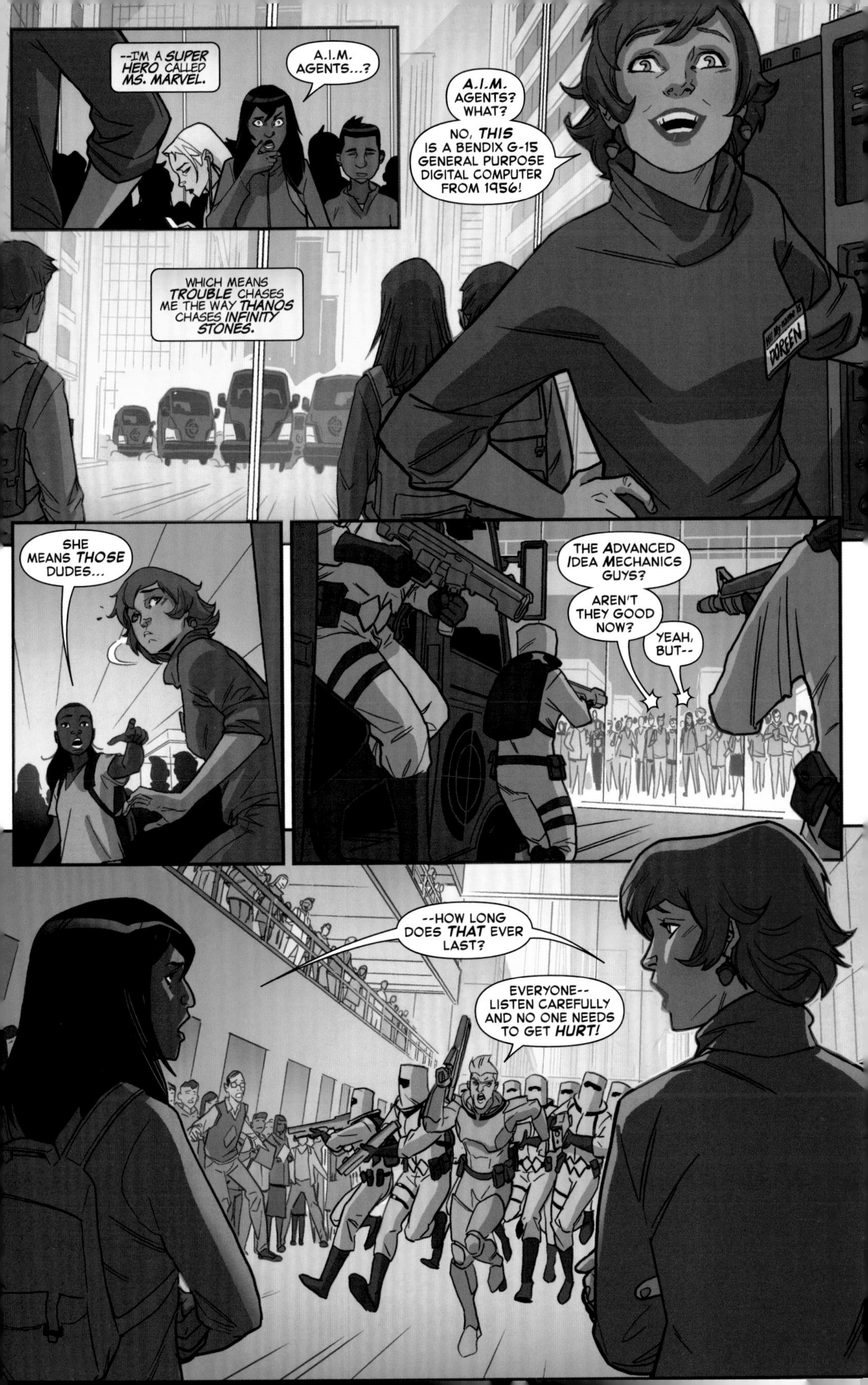
--I'M A SUPER HERO CALLED MS. MARVEL.
A.I.M. AGENTS...?
A.I.M. AGENTS? WHAT?
NO, THIS IS A BENDIX G-15 GENERAL PURPOSE DIGITAL COMPUTER FROM 1956!
WHICH MEANS TROUBLE CHASES ME THE WAY THANOS CHASES INFINITY STONES.
DOREEN
SHE MEANS THOSE DUDES...
THE ADVANCED IDEA MECHANICS GUYS?
AREN'T THEY GOOD NOW?
YEAH, BUT--
--HOW LONG DOES THAT EVER LAST?
EVERYONE-- LISTEN CAREFULLY AND NO ONE NEEDS TO GET HURT!

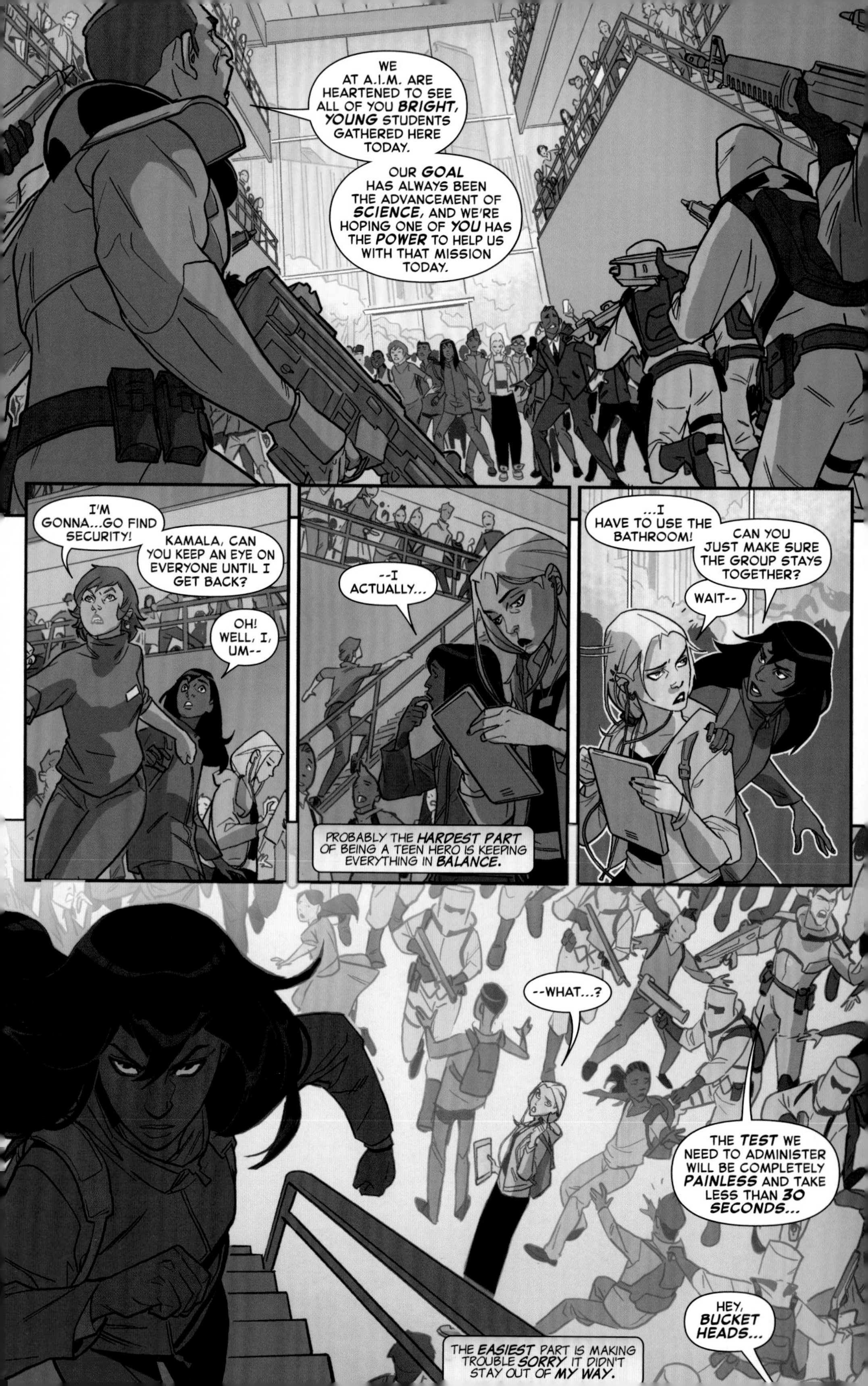
WE AT A.I.M. ARE HEARTENED TO SEE ALL OF YOU BRIGHT, YOUNG STUDENTS GATHERED HERE TODAY.
OUR GOAL HAS ALWAYS BEEN THE ADVANCEMENT OF SCIENCE, AND WE'RE HOPING ONE OF YOU HAS THE POWER TO HELP US WITH THAT MISSION TODAY.
I'M GONNA...GO FIND SECURITY!
KAMALA, CAN YOU KEEP AN EYE ON EVERYONE UNTIL I GET BACK?
OH! WELL, I, UM--
--I ACTUALLY...
PROBABLY THE HARDEST PART OF BEING A TEEN HERO IS KEEPING EVERYTHING IN BALANCE.
...I HAVE TO USE THE BATHROOM!
CAN YOU JUST MAKE SURE THE GROUP STAYS TOGETHER?
WAIT--
--WHAT...?
THE TEST WE NEED TO ADMINISTER WILL BE COMPLETELY PAINLESS AND TAKE LESS THAN 30 SECONDS...
HEY, BUCKET HEADS...
THE EASIEST PART IS MAKING TROUBLE SORRY IT DIDN'T STAY OUT OF MY WAY.

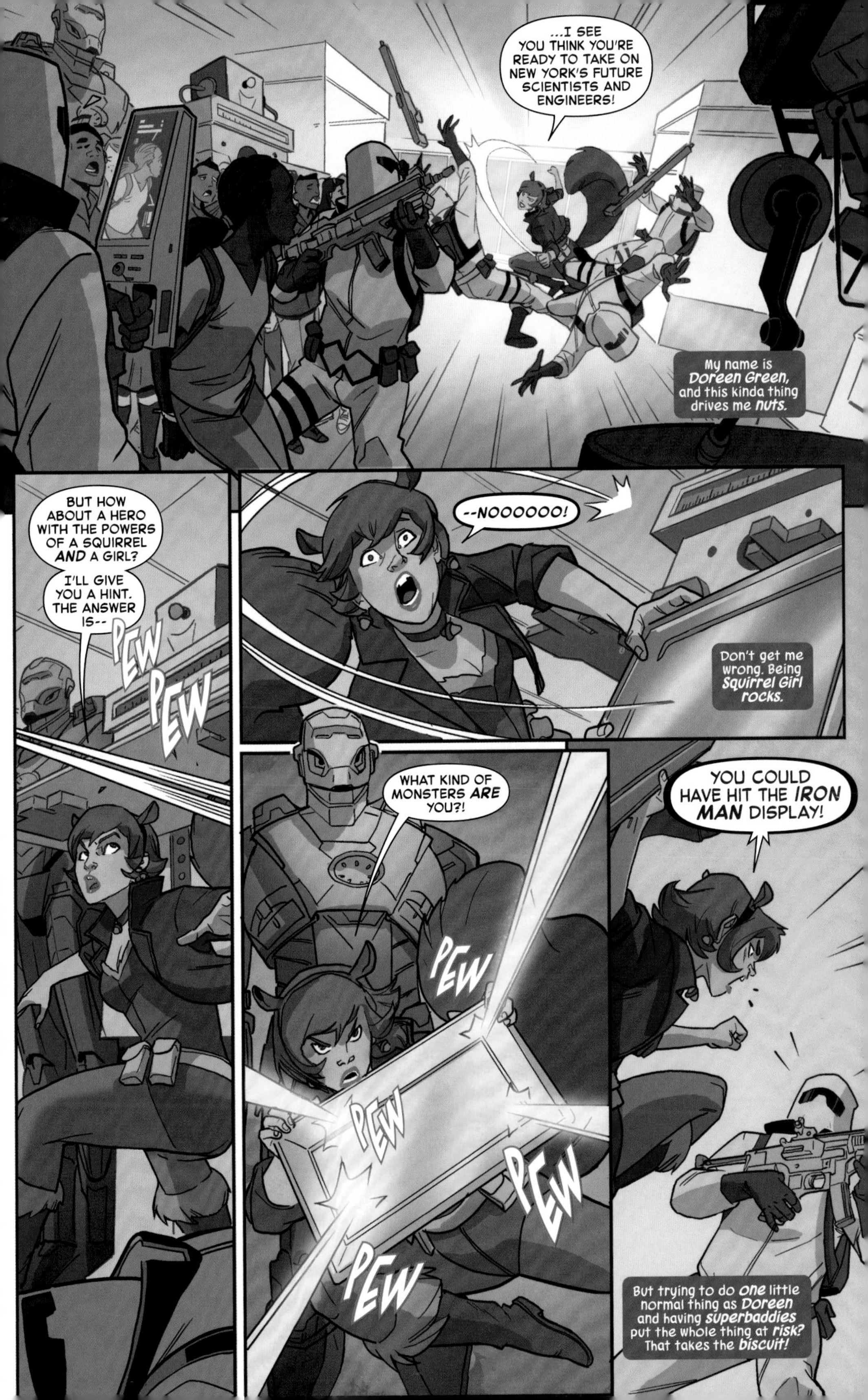
...I SEE YOU THINK YOU'RE READY TO TAKE ON NEW YORK'S FUTURE SCIENTISTS AND ENGINEERS!
My name is Doreen Green, and this kinda thing drives me nuts.
BUT HOW ABOUT A HERO WITH THE POWERS OF A SQUIRREL AND A GIRL?
I'LL GIVE YOU A HINT. THE ANSWER IS--
PEW PEW
--NOOOOOO!
Don't get me wrong. Being Squirrel Girl rocks.
WHAT KIND OF MONSTERS ARE YOU?!
PEW
PEW
PEW
PEW
YOU COULD HAVE HIT THE IRON MAN DISPLAY!
But trying to do one little normal thing as Doreen and having superbaddies put the whole thing at risk? That takes the biscuit!

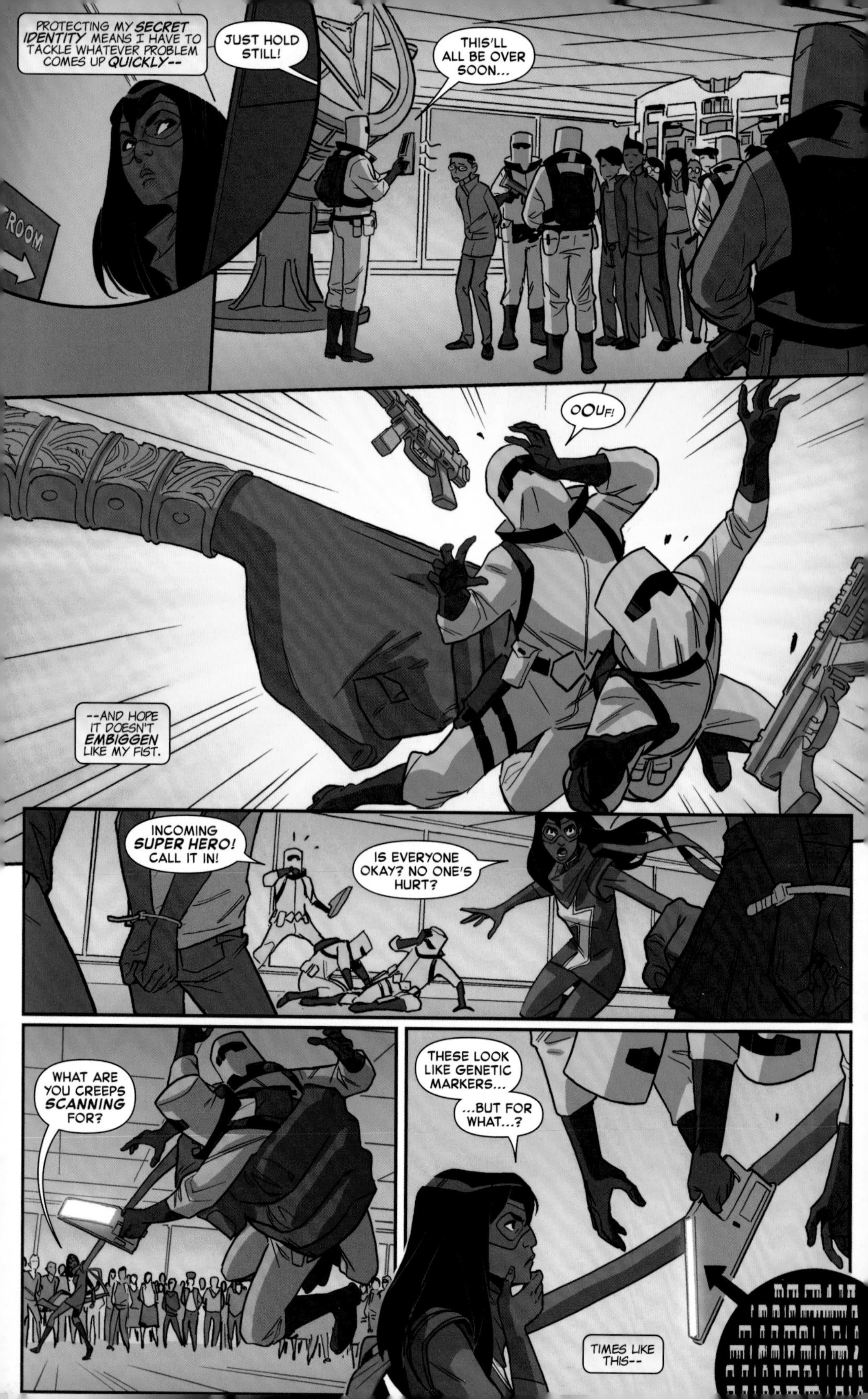
PROTECTING MY SECRET IDENTITY MEANS I HAVE TO TACKLE WHATEVER PROBLEM COMES UP QUICKLY--
JUST HOLD STILL!
THIS'LL ALL BE OVER SOON...
ROOM
OOUF!
--AND HOPE IT DOESN'T EMBIGGEN LIKE MY FIST.
INCOMING SUPER HERO! CALL IT IN!
IS EVERYONE OKAY? NO ONE'S HURT?
WHAT ARE YOU CREEPS SCANNING FOR?
THESE LOOK LIKE GENETIC MARKERS...
...BUT FOR WHAT...?
TIMES LIKE THIS--

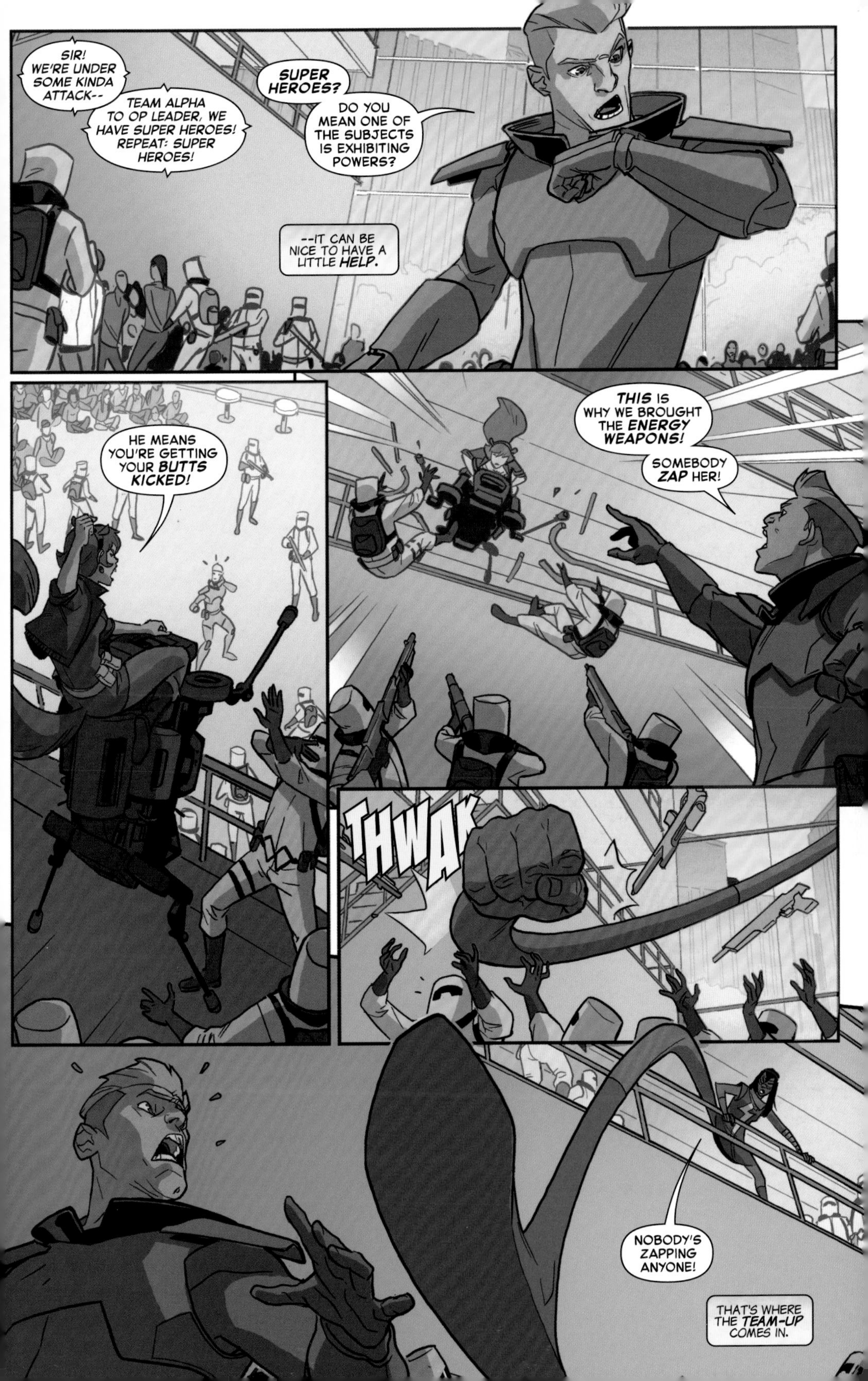
SIR! WE'RE UNDER SOME KINDA ATTACK--
TEAM ALPHA TO OP LEADER, WE HAVE SUPER HEROES! REPEAT: SUPER HEROES!
SUPER HEROES?
DO YOU MEAN ONE OF THE SUBJECTS IS EXHIBITING POWERS?
--IT CAN BE NICE TO HAVE A LITTLE HELP.
HE MEANS YOU'RE GETTING YOUR BUTTS KICKED!
THIS IS WHY WE BROUGHT THE ENERGY WEAPONS!
SOMEBODY ZAP HER!
THWAK
NOBODY'S ZAPPING ANYONE!
THAT'S WHERE THE TEAM-UP COMES IN.

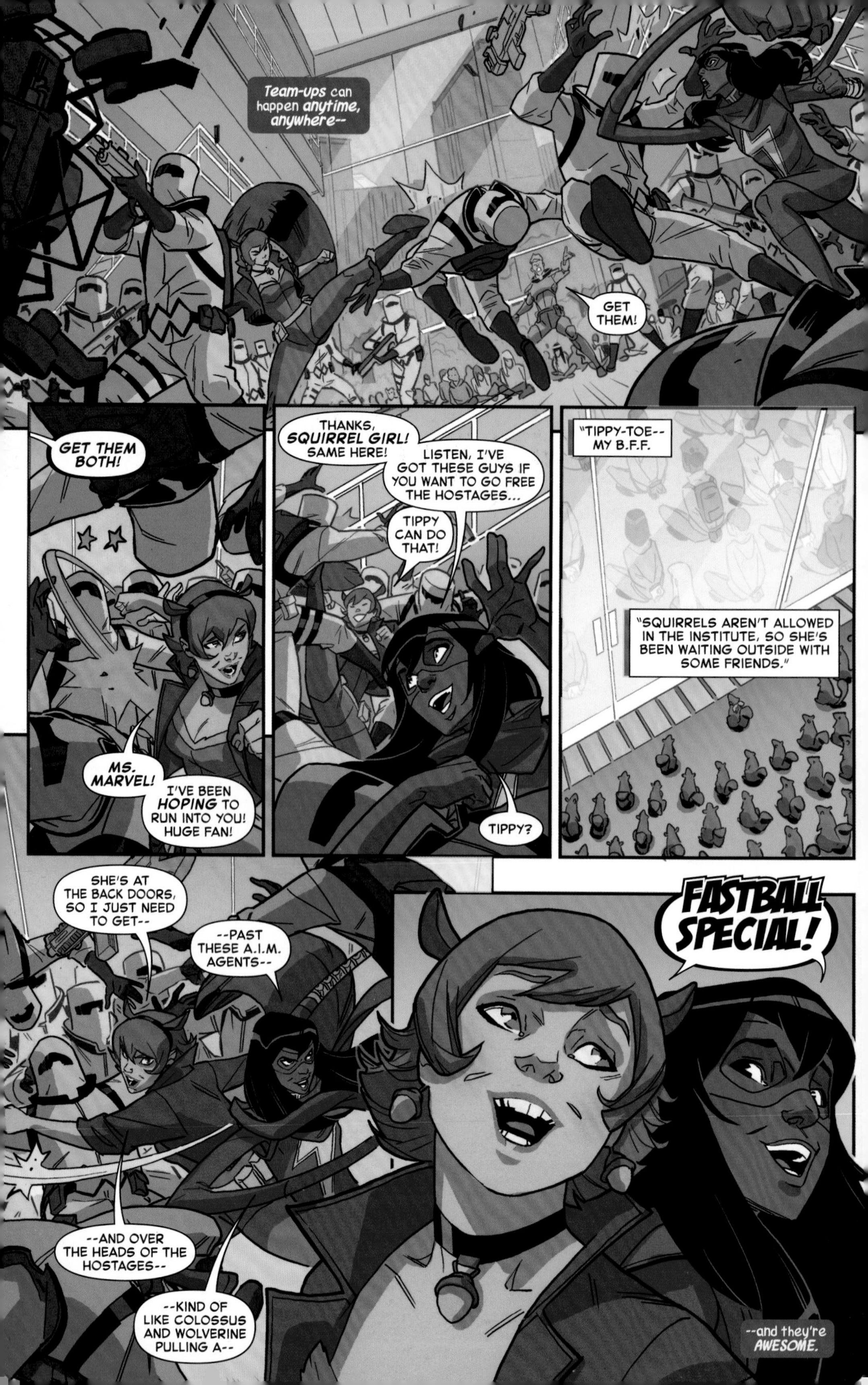

Team-ups can happen anytime, anywhere--
GET THEM!
GET THEM BOTH!
MS. MARVEL!
I'VE BEEN HOPING TO RUN INTO YOU! HUGE FAN!
THANKS, SQUIRREL GIRL! SAME HERE!
LISTEN, I'VE GOT THESE GUYS IF YOU WANT TO GO FREE THE HOSTAGES...
TIPPY CAN DO THAT!
TIPPY?
"TIPPY-TOE-- MY B.F.F.
"SQUIRRELS AREN'T ALLOWED IN THE INSTITUTE, SO SHE'S BEEN WAITING OUTSIDE WITH SOME FRIENDS."
SHE'S AT THE BACK DOORS, SO I JUST NEED TO GET--
--PAST THESE A.I.M. AGENTS--
--AND OVER THE HEADS OF THE HOSTAGES--
--KIND OF LIKE COLOSSUS AND WOLVERINE PULLING A--
FASTBALL SPECIAL!
--and they're AWESOME.

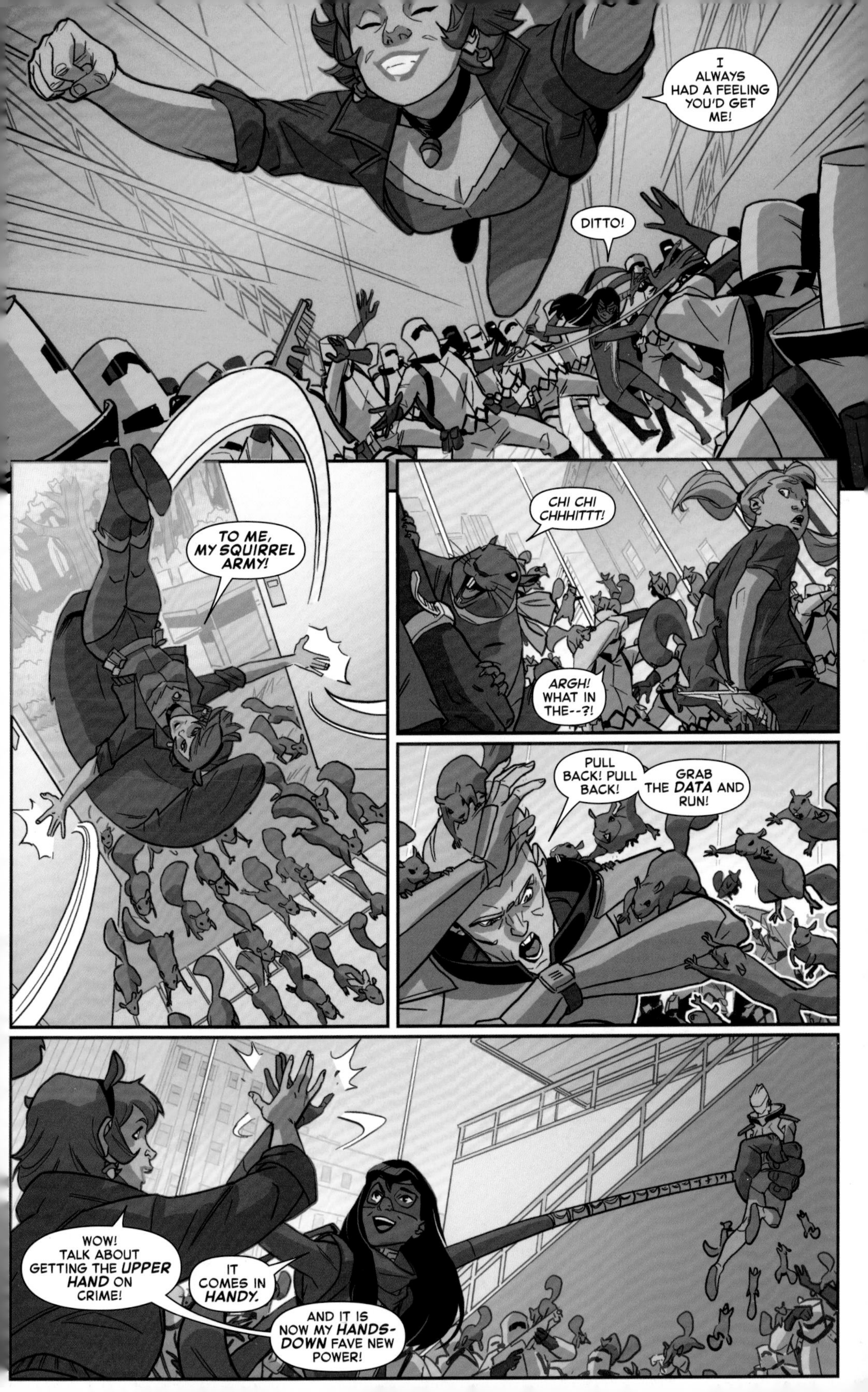
I ALWAYS HAD A FEELING YOU'D GET ME!
DITTO!
TO ME, MY SQUIRREL ARMY!
CHI CHI CHHHITTT!
ARGH! WHAT IN THE--?!
PULL BACK! PULL BACK!
GRAB THE DATA AND RUN!
WOW! TALK ABOUT GETTING THE UPPER HAND ON CRIME!
IT COMES IN HANDY.
AND IT IS NOW MY HANDS-DOWN FAVE NEW POWER!

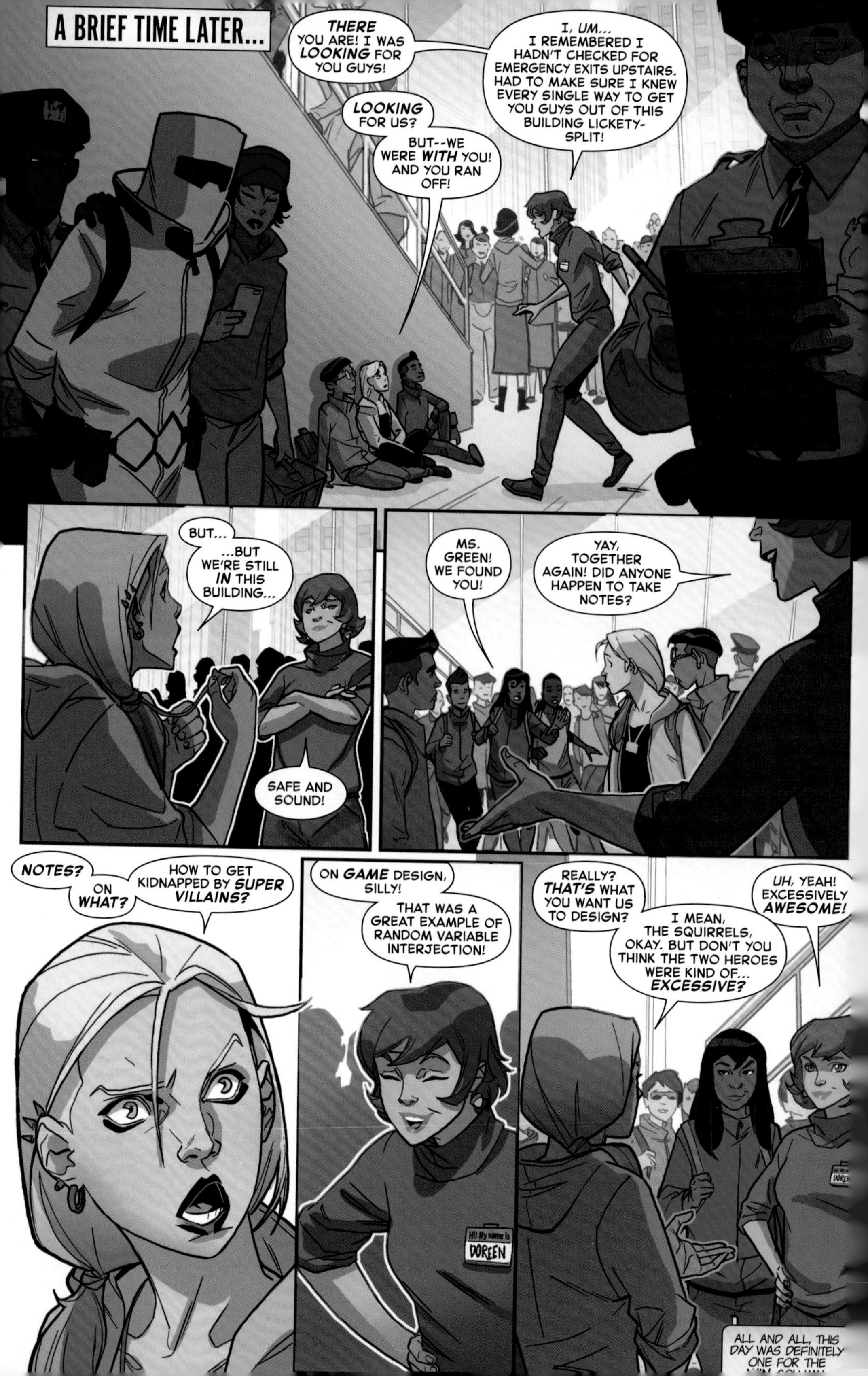
A BRIEF TIME LATER...
THERE YOU ARE! I WAS LOOKING FOR YOU GUYS!
LOOKING FOR US?
BUT--WE WERE WITH YOU! AND YOU RAN OFF!
I, UM... I REMEMBERED I HADN'T CHECKED FOR EMERGENCY EXITS UPSTAIRS. HAD TO MAKE SURE I KNEW EVERY SINGLE WAY TO GET YOU GUYS OUT OF THIS BUILDING LICKETY-SPLIT!
BUT...
...BUT WE'RE STILL IN THIS BUILDING...
SAFE AND SOUND!
MS. GREEN! WE FOUND YOU!
YAY, TOGETHER AGAIN! DID ANYONE HAPPEN TO TAKE NOTES?
NOTES?
ON WHAT?
HOW TO GET KIDNAPPED BY SUPER VILLAINS?
ON GAME DESIGN, SILLY!
THAT WAS A GREAT EXAMPLE OF RANDOM VARIABLE INTERJECTION!
HI! My name is
DOREEN
REALLY? THAT'S WHAT YOU WANT US TO DESIGN?
I MEAN, THE SQUIRRELS, OKAY. BUT DON'T YOU THINK THE TWO HEROES WERE KIND OF... EXCESSIVE?
UH, YEAH! EXCESSIVELY AWESOME!
ALL AND ALL, THIS DAY WAS DEFINITELY ONE FOR THE

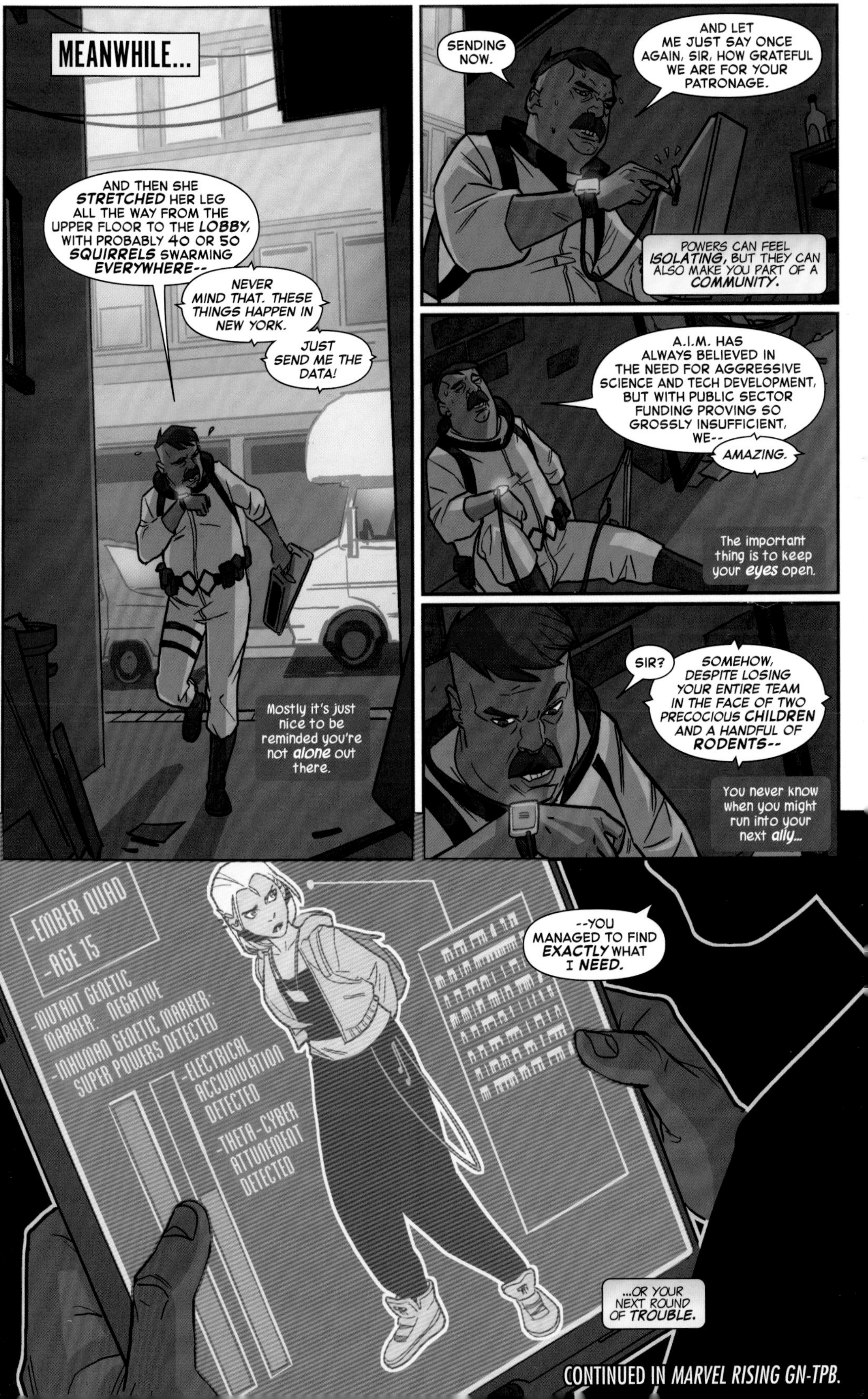
MEANWHILE...
AND THEN SHE STRETCHED HER LEG ALL THE WAY FROM THE UPPER FLOOR TO THE LOBBY, WITH PROBABLY 40 OR 50 SQUIRRELS SWARMING EVERYWHERE--
NEVER MIND THAT. THESE THINGS HAPPEN IN NEW YORK.
JUST SEND ME THE DATA!
Mostly it's just nice to be reminded you're not alone out there.
SENDING NOW.
AND LET ME JUST SAY ONCE AGAIN, SIR, HOW GRATEFUL WE ARE FOR YOUR PATRONAGE.
POWERS CAN FEEL ISOLATING, BUT THEY CAN ALSO MAKE YOU PART OF A COMMUNITY.
A.I.M. HAS ALWAYS BELIEVED IN THE NEED FOR AGGRESSIVE SCIENCE AND TECH DEVELOPMENT, BUT WITH PUBLIC SECTOR FUNDING PROVING SO GROSSLY INSUFFICIENT, WE--
AMAZING.
The important thing is to keep your eyes open.
SIR?
SOMEHOW, DESPITE LOSING YOUR ENTIRE TEAM IN THE FACE OF TWO PRECOCIOUS CHILDREN AND A HANDFUL OF RODENTS--
You never know when you might run into your next ally...
-EMBER QUAD
-AGE 15
-MUTANT GENETIC MARKER: NEGATIVE
-INHUMAN GENETIC MARKER: SUPER POWERS DETECTED
-ELECTRICAL ACCUMULATION DETECTED
-THETA-CYBER ATTUNEMENT DETECTED
--YOU MANAGED TO FIND EXACTLY WHAT I NEED.
...OR YOUR NEXT ROUND OF TROUBLE.
CONTINUED IN MARVEL RISING GN-TPB.

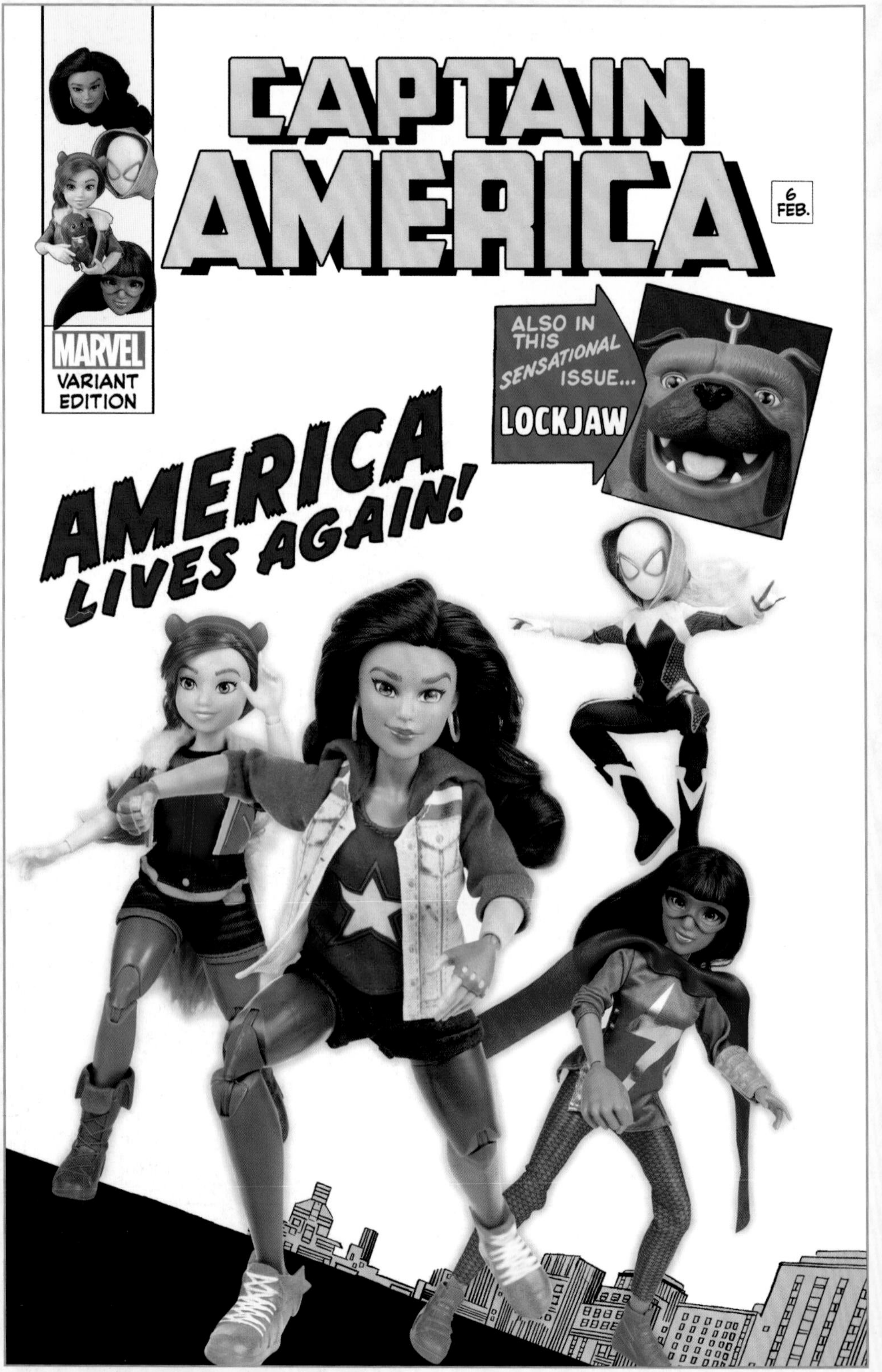
CAPTAIN AMERICA
6 FEB.
MARVEL VARIANT EDITION
ALSO IN THIS SENSATIONAL ISSUE...
LOCKJAW
AMERICA LIVES AGAIN!

CAPTAIN AMERICA #6 MARVEL RISING ACTION DOLL VARIANT

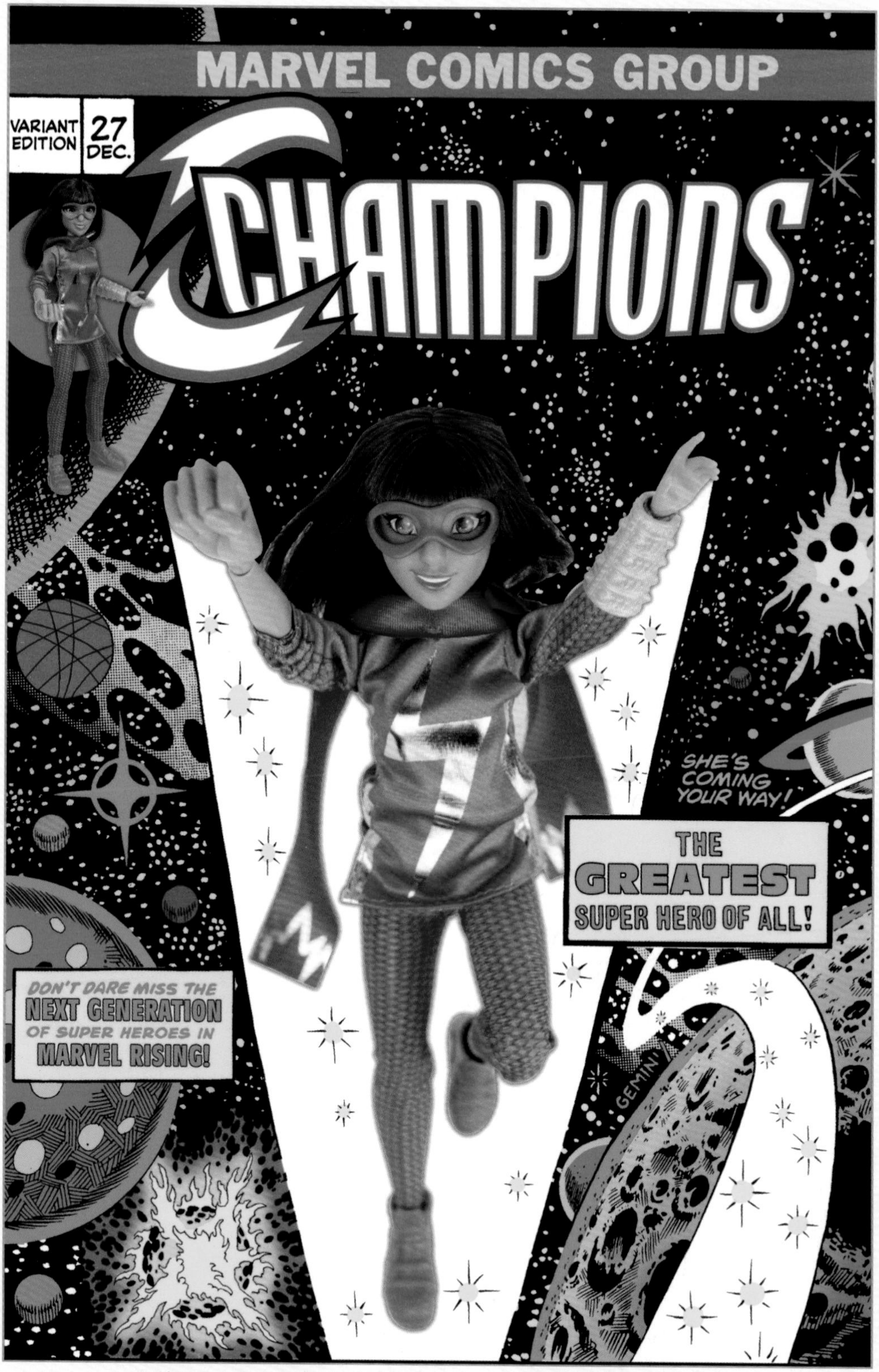
MARVEL COMICS GROUP
VARIANT EDITION
27 DEC.
CHAMPIONS
SHE'S COMING YOUR WAY!
THE GREATEST SUPER HERO OF ALL!
DON'T DARE MISS THE NEXT GENERATION OF SUPER HEROES IN MARVEL RISING!

CHAMPIONS #27 MARVEL RISING ACTION DOLL VARIANT

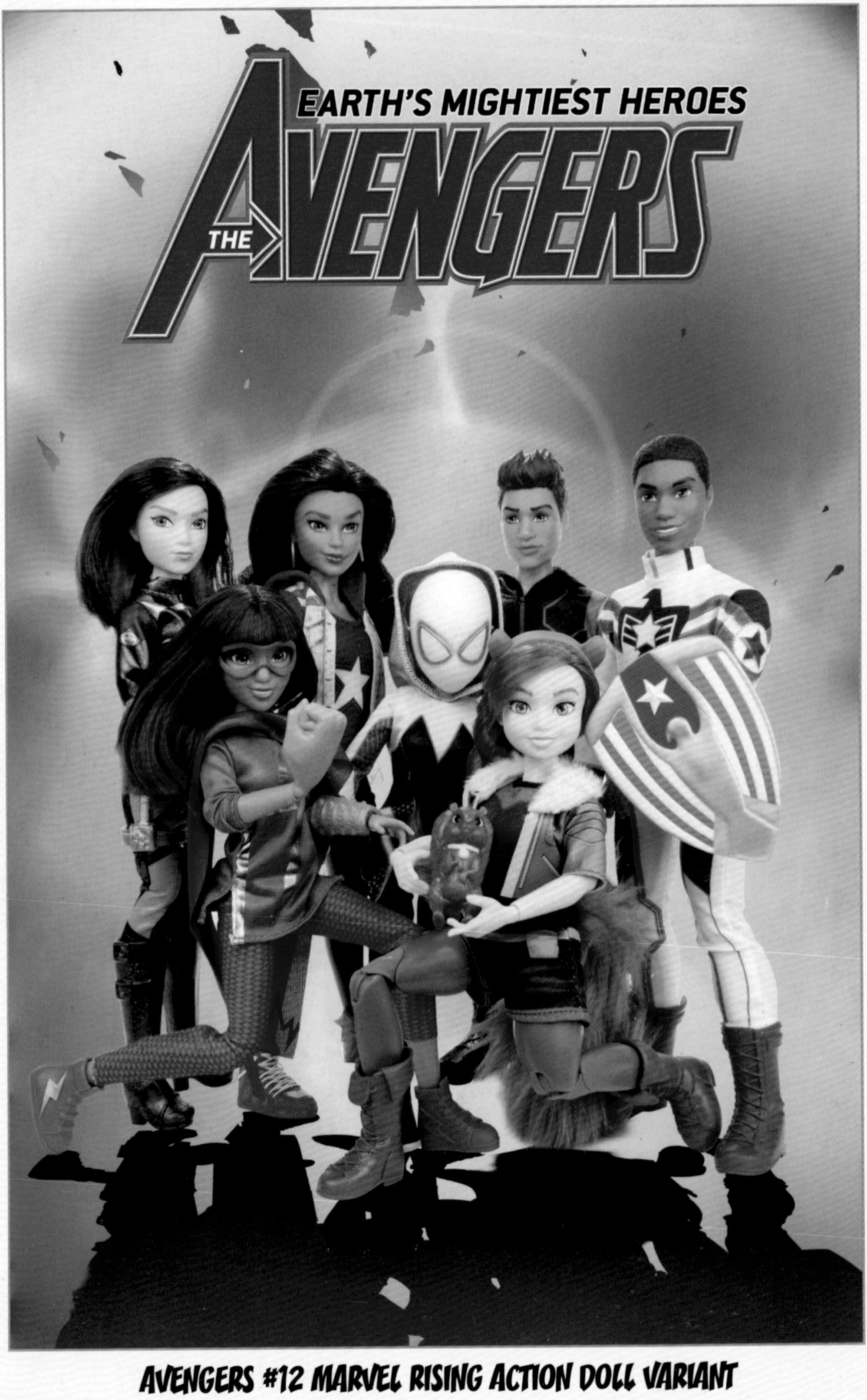
EARTH'S MIGHTIEST HEROES
THE AVENGERS

AVENGERS #12 MARVEL RISING ACTION DOLL VARIANT